THE One I Want

THE COMPLETE DUET

USA TODAY & WSJ BESTSELLING AUTHOR

SIOBHAN DAVIS

ISBN-13: 978-1-916651-00-5

Originally published © July 2023.

This print edition © February 2024.

Critique and research by Jennifer Gibson of The Critical Touch
Edited by Kelly Hartigan of XterraWeb
Proofread by Imogen Wells of Final Polish Proofreading
Cover design by Shannon Passmore of Shanoff Designs
Interior cover imagery © Depositphotos.com
Cover photography by Michelle Lancaster
Cover Model: Mick Maio
Formatted by Ciara Turley using Vellum

Note From the Author

This is a an angsty, emotional, new adult romance, recommended to readers eighteen and older. Contains some distressing scenes and sensitive subject matter. For a list of triggers, refer to my website.

SAY YOU'RE MINE - BOOK DESCRIPTION

I never intended to fall in love.

This girl had goals and guys were an unwelcome distraction.

Until I met Garrick, my sophomore year of college, and he blasted through the walls I kept around my heart, tearing them down.

He knew what he wanted, and he wanted *me*.

Falling hard and fast, I experienced the rollercoaster highs and lows of first love.

Until life threw us a curveball, and everything flipped overnight.

Now, I'm stuck in limbo. Falling apart as I try to be strong for my boyfriend.

But it seems fate has other plans.

THE ONE
I WANT
BOOK ONE
Say
YOU'RE
Mine
USA TODAY & WSJ BESTSELLING AUTHOR
SIOBHAN DAVIS

Say You're Mine

THE ONE I WANT BOOK ONE

USA TODAY & WSJ BESTSELLING AUTHOR

SIOBHAN DAVIS

Prologue

Stevie

“Hey,” I whisper as I enter the room for what I know is going to be the last time.

“Hey, beautiful.” His red-rimmed eyes shine with honest emotion, conveying so much without words. “Come sit with me.”

I walk quietly to the window and sit beside him, memorizing the stunning view I have always loved.

He takes my hand, giving it a gentle squeeze. “I’m so sorry, Stevie.”

“Me too.”

“I never meant to hurt you.”

“Nor I you.”

“I was selfish and cruel and reckless with your feelings, and I won’t ever forgive myself for it.”

“Forgive yourself,” I say without hesitation. “There’s been enough hurt, guilt, and blame.” I lean in and kiss his cheek with tears in my eyes. “I already forgive you.”

“You shouldn’t.”

"I love you and care deeply about you. That won't ever change. A part of my heart will always belong to you." Removing the jewelry he bought me, I place it on the coffee table, and it makes it final.

This is the last time we will ever see one another.

As much as this needs to happen, it's sad it has come to this.

"But you love him more." Pain underscores his words, and I hate I'm the cause of it.

My inclination is to refuse to answer or deflect, but we're not tiptoeing around one another anymore. "I do."

Agony flares in his eyes, and it hurts, but I'm not sorry I was truthful.

"I will always love you," he says as we stare at one another through blurry eyes. "It's because I love you I am letting you go. We need to let what we had stay in the past and move forward along different paths. We're very different people now."

"We are," I acknowledge with a nod. "And it's neither of our faults we have ended up here."

"I thought we would grow old and gray together," he says with a sad smile.

I'm not sure I did, but it's hard to remember exactly what I was feeling at the time. "Things happen for a reason. Some lucky woman is out there waiting for you to find her. I hope she doesn't have to wait too long."

He brings our conjoined hands to his mouth and brushes his lips across my knuckles. "I want you to be happy, and he's your happy place. I see it now."

He is, and I hope it's not too late to reclaim what we had.

"I won't ever forget you," I say over a sob. "I will always cherish the time we shared. Be happy." I swipe at the tears streaming down my face. "It's all I want for you. Don't ever stop fighting for that happiness because you deserve it."

I don't protest or pull away when he leans forward and kisses me softly and briefly on the lips.

It's the only goodbye we can handle.

I hug him for the last time, and then I get up and walk out the door and out of his life.

Chapter One

Stevie

"Watch out! Coming through!" I holler over the almost deafening noise of the music as I attempt to maneuver my way through the heaving crowd. Lifting the tray over my head, I shimmy sideways, slipping nimbly between a rowdy group of frat boys. Some dickhole squeezes my ass, and I shriek, almost dropping the tray of empty glasses as I fight my way back to the bar.

The End Zone—the sports bar where I work Thursday and Friday nights—is popular with my fellow Oregon students. Live music on the weekends is a big draw, and the boss is particular about the acts he books. While the manager is careful who gets in the door, and we have a strict alcohol policy, this is a regular spot for juniors and seniors who like to party it up on the weekends in downtown Eugene. Some of them are known to get more than a little disruptive when booze is involved.

Most of the college freshman and sophomores stick to the other sports bar or the tavern closest to campus because both establishments are known to pass a blind eye to fake IDs and clearly underage patrons.

It's one of the reasons I enjoy working here. The management never allows it to get too wild, and the crew is tight. We look out for one another. If I'd seen who groped me, I could tell Manford, and he'd kick the perv out. But an ass squeeze is the least of my worries tonight. Navigating the packed bar, and surviving without any breakages or spillages, is priority number one.

Pushing through the thirsty students swarming the bar, I maneuver to the end of the counter, to the area reserved for staff, and set my tray down with a relieved sigh. Glasses rattle as Camila instantly grabs it, making brief eye contact with me before she takes it straight to the dishwasher. Everyone is working at max speed tonight, and the manager called in extra staff when he realized we were going to be packed to capacity.

"Hey, Stevie. Is everything cool out there?" Manford—the head bartender on duty tonight— asks as he lands in front of me on the other side of the bar. "It's pretty insane tonight."

"It's a goddamned jungle, but I've seen it worse." Not often, but enough to know I'll get through it intact. Brushing damp tendrils of red hair back off my brow, I fan my face with my hands in an attempt to cool down. I'm glad I wear my long, thick auburn hair up in a messy bun for work. Despite the AC working full throttle, it's hotter than hell in the room, and we're all feeling it.

"The new guy has them eating out of the palm of his hand," Manford says, jerking his head toward the stage in the back as he reads my next order from the tablet in front of him. We went digital a few months back, and there's no denying it's very helpful on busy nights.

Casting a quick glance over my shoulder, I stare at the dark-haired guy on stage. I can barely see him through the throng of students standing and dancing around the high tables on that side of the bar. He is sitting on a stool, strumming a guitar, and belting out the lyrics to some classic pop and rock songs with his eyes closed.

"He's good," I agree, pouring myself a glass of ice water from the jug Manford keeps topped up for the servers. I have been subconsciously listening to him play as I work the tables. "His husky voice is very distinctive, and he definitely knows how to work a crowd."

"Doesn't hurt he's easy on the eyes." Camila smirks as she wipes the sticky counter down with a damp cloth.

"I wouldn't know. I haven't had a second to look, and you can hardly see him from here. I'll just have to take your word for it." I guzzle water as I wait for Manford to finish my order for table five.

"Go see for yourself." Manford smirks, thrusting a bottle of water and a glass filled with ice at me. "Take them to Garrick. He's overdue a refill, and he'll be taking a break shortly. Got to keep the new talent happy. Boss already confirmed he wants to book him for the regular Friday night slot."

If this is the kind of attention he attracts, can't say I blame the boss.

Taking the bottle and glass, I navigate my way around the perimeter of the room, heading toward the stage. A line of girls, two rows deep, crams the front of the stage, swaying and singing along as Garrick works the crowd like a pro. I roll my eyes at their obviousness as they jostle one another, vying for the best position in the hope he'll notice them first.

Donny is part of the security team tonight, and he looks like a grumpy sentinel standing guard at the side of the stage. With a curt bob of his head, he steps aside to allow me to pass.

Garrick brings the song to a close just as I walk up the five short steps to the platform. The girls at the front scream and shout vulgar proposals as he opens his eyes and grins at the adoring crowd. "Thank you. I'm gonna take a short break," he says, tilting his head to the side as I approach. His eyes flit between me and the audience. "But don't go anywhere. I'm not finished with you yet!" He flashes a blinding grin at the crowd, and I swear I hear audible swooning.

Swiveling around on his stool, he fixes me with the same dazzling smile, showcasing a set of perfectly straight, perfectly white teeth behind a wide mouth and lush full lips. Dark hair curtains his handsome face, and the tousled strands look like he was repeatedly running his fingers through it. A few errant tendrils are stuck to his brow, and there's a light sheen of sweat coating his skin. The lights are strong up here, and my shirt is already clinging to my spine. Sweeping his chin-length hair back off his face, he lifts his eyes to mine, and my heartbeat speeds up.

Camila wasn't wrong.

This guy is totally freaking hot. Like model or rock star hot.

He's also younger than I was expecting. If I had to guess, I'd say he's in his early twenties. High cheekbones, smooth olive-toned skin, a strong nose, and a chiseled jawline with an artful layer of stylish stubble complete the features of his gorgeous face. He has the most mesmerizing hazel eyes, framed by long, thick black lashes. His grin expands, revealing matching dimples, as we stare at one another, and I smother a sigh.

Of course, he has dimples.

As if he wasn't already gorgeous enough.

I realize I'm being rude and obvious in the extreme, so I shake myself out of it and break eye contact. Clearing my throat and the brain fog from my head, I hand him the bottle of water and the glass. "Manford thought you might be thirsty." I have to shout over the noisy bar to be heard.

Placing his guitar aside, he reaches for the drink. His fingers brush against mine in the exchange, and our eyes lock together again. "That was thoughtful of you both. Thank you."

My breath hitches in my throat, and butterflies swoop into my chest as he pins me with another glorious smile. Dimples and stunning smiles should be outlawed as a lethal combination capable of annihilating the female race. I'm pretty successful at deflecting interest from the opposite sex, but give me a set of dimples and a gorgeous smile, and I'm as ovary punched as the next girl.

Garrick climbs off the stool, unfurling to his full height. He towers over my five-feet-nine-inch frame, proving he's well over six feet tall. His torso is lean, but his shoulders are broad and there is clear definition in his chest, abs, and arms underneath his fitted white

T-shirt. Wrinkled jeans hug his long legs, and the dark denim hangs tantalizingly from his shapely hips. Worn tan boots encase large feet, and this guy truly is the full package.

It's just as well I've sworn off men and his effect will only be fleeting and temporary.

"Follow me," he says, snapping me out of my ogling. He's still grinning as he walks off, and I wonder if the guy ever stops smiling.

Confusion puckers my brow, but like a trained puppy, I trail him across the stage and through the small door at the back. It leads into a self-contained soundproofed area that was built specifically for the various entertainers who have graced the stage here. The main space, currently empty, holds a three-seater leather couch, a rectangular coffee table, a mini refrigerator, wall-mounted TV, and a table with snacks. Enclosed on the left is a small bathroom with a shower, and on the right is a private dressing area. It's compact but appropriate.

I close the door, instantly grateful for the silence as the noisy bar outside is muted. Standing by the wall, I watch Garrick dump the bottle of water into the glass of ice and knock it back. The way his throat works as he drinks is sexy as hell, as is the way his eyes remain locked on mine the entire time. He has barely taken his eyes off me since I arrived on the stage, and I wonder if he's always this attentive with everyone he meets. When he's finished, he places the glass down on the snack bar with his gaze still attached to mine in a way that is starting to make me uncomfortable.

"Can I get you anything else?" I ask, my eyes darting to the door. It's crazy busy and I need to get back. I also wouldn't mind putting some distance between the two of us. His presence is magnetic, and it concerns me that I've noticed.

Little beads of sweat cling to his brow before he swipes them away with the back of his hand. His disarming smile is firmly in place as he stalks toward me. "Just your company." He moves in closer, and his breath tickles my face when he speaks. "What's your name, and do you go to school here too?" Curiosity lights up his handsome face as his inquisitive gaze probes mine.

"Why do you want to know?" I step sideways to create some distance between us.

"I'm just making conversation."

There's a weird tension in the air. A crackling charge ripping across the space separating our bodies, and I don't like feeling some freaky connection between us. "Well, I'm working, and they need me outside, so I should go."

"It's too quiet in here, and I don't like hanging around by myself." His earnest eyes are shielding nothing, and I know it isn't a lie or a ruse to trap me into spending time with him. "Not when I'm pumped full of adrenaline. Normally, my friends would be here, but they all had shit to do tonight." His eyes soften. "You'd be doing me a big favor if you kept me company." He flops down on the couch, still maintaining eye contact with me. He pats the space beside him. "I only have a short break, and I promise I won't bite." He flashes me another ovary-clenching smile. "I'm betting you haven't taken a break all night. Rest your feet and take a breather."

A break does sound nice, and he's right. I wasn't able to take my usual ten minutes earlier because it was too busy. Suddenly, my feet feel heavy, and my legs ache like they might go out from under me.

Garrick hops up and grabs two chilled bottles of water from the mini refrigerator as I lower my tired butt onto the couch. Fridays are always nightmarish because I have classes until lunch, then I work my shift at Butterfly Flowers, and run back to the apartment I share off-campus with my friend Ellen to grab something to eat and a quick shower before showing up for my shift at the bar. I usually sleep in late on Saturday morning, too exhausted to get up early.

"You look like you need this as much as me," he says, handing me a water.

"Thanks, and I do. It's hot out there tonight."

"It's a veritable sauna," he agrees. "If it's like this every Friday night, I might start showing up in nothing but shorts."

"That would be one way of keeping your fans loyal," I tease as I uncap the bottle.

"I'm here for the music, not the girls." He flashes me a flirty look, that seems to contradict his statement, before gulping back his drink.

"Said no rock star ever," I deadpan, fighting a grin.

"I'm not a rock star nor do I have any desire to be."

"How come? You must know you're good, and isn't it what most musicians dream of?"

He shrugs before draining his second bottle of water and tossing the empty in the trash can. "Not me. Music is a hobby. It's a release. A way to indulge my creative side. It will never be anything more."

"It seems a shame to waste such natural talent, but I admire you for knowing what you want and sticking to your resolve."

"I still don't know your name." He twists around on the couch. His knee brushes against my jean-clad leg as he leans in closer, giving me his undivided attention.

It's unnerving, but I still can't force myself to get up and leave.

"And you didn't tell me if you go to UO too," he adds, looking at me like I'm the most fascinating person in the world.

"I'm Stevie, and yes, I go to school here. I'm studying floral management and just about to finish my sophomore year."

"Same here."

My eyes pop wide. I'm pretty sure there are no guys in any of my classes. Floral management is not really a guy thing.

He chuckles. "I meant I'm a sophomore. I'm majoring in family enterprise."

"Oh, cool. Does your family have a business?"

He nods as his tongue darts out wetting his lips. "My dad is CEO of Allen Lumber and Allen Wineries. I'll be joining the business when I graduate."

His tone is very matter-of-fact, and it doesn't seem like he's bragging. Wouldn't matter if he was. I'm hard to impress, and I can't think of any guy who has ever managed to do it. "I know Allen Wineries. The country club I used to work at back home buys their wine. So, you're from Seattle too?"

"Born and bred."

"What part?"

"Dad lives in North Bend, and Mom lives in Medina. I used to split my time between both homes." Air trickles out of his mouth as he drags one hand through his messy dark hair.

Something akin to desire pools low in my belly, but I ignore it.

"What about you? Where do you call home?" he asks.

"Ravenna. I live with my mom, and my nana is close by too."

"No dad?"

"I never knew him." I'm not about to get into it with a guy who is a virtual stranger even if he seems like an okay guy and the conversation is flowing easily.

"This feels a little like fate." His eyes sparkle with excitement.

"What does?"

"Us meeting like this."

I resist the urge to roll my eyes. "It's coincidence. Not fate. And it's not like there aren't a ton of people attending Oregon from Seattle."

"True, but I'm sticking to my convictions. You call it coincidence. I'm calling it fate." He attempts to dazzle me with that flirty smile again, and it almost works. Angling his body closer, he stares at my mouth like he wants to kiss me.

Which is crazy.

We only just met.

I can't deny I feel *something* between us, but I have zero intention of acting on whatever chemistry we share.

The spicy scent of his cologne calls out to me like a siren, and I scarcely resist the urge to lean into his neck and sniff him. He smells delicious because it's not enough that he's hot, has dimples and an amazing smile, is talented yet not stuck up his own ass, and seems like a genuinely nice guy. No, he has to smell incredibly tempting too.

It's just as well I'm a stickler for my self-imposed rules and a tough nut to crack.

Otherwise, this guy might smash through my shell and burrow his way underneath.

Garrick's eyes rise to meet mine, and it's so hard to concentrate on anything but him when he's fixing me with such a bewitching expression. His eyes are like magnets, drawing me closer, sucking me into his orbit, and making it almost impossible to break free of his spell. His warm breath fans across my face when he speaks, and I bite on the inside of my cheek to stop myself from groaning when his gorgeous scent swirls around me. "Do you have any plans tomorrow night, Stevie? Would you go out to dinner with me?"

A shudder works its way through me as his husky voice does funny things to my insides. I love how my name rolls seductively off his tongue, but I'm determined to remain immune to his charm. It takes considerable effort to sound unaffected when I reply. "I thought you were here for the music not the girls."

He chuckles. "I am, but I didn't expect to cross paths with you tonight." His eyes pierce mine, and I want to look away, but I can't.

Butterflies run amok in my stomach, and my chest heaves the longer he stares at me. Electricity crackles and snaps, and I am almost afraid to breathe. I bet Garrick has girls beating a path to his door without even trying.

"And just so we're clear, I'm not the kind of guy who goes around hooking up with different girls. That isn't who I am." The smile on his face and the look of appreciation in his eyes seem genuine, and if I was going to break my rules for anyone, it could be him.

But I can't.

"You seem like a nice guy, Garrick, and I appreciate the dinner invitation, but I have to decline." I move to get up, and he takes my hand, holding me in place.

"Please call me Gar. All my friends do. Tell me what I need to do to convince you to go out with me?" He cocks his head to one side, stabbing me with those stunning eyes that hold me hypnotized. His lips kick up at the corner. "I can be very convincing when I need to be."

"I don't doubt it," I murmur, shaking myself from my stupor and trying to retrieve my hand from his hold. His large palm dwarves my much smaller one as he holds my hand hostage. Calluses brush against my soft skin as warmth spreads from his hand into mine, radiating up my arm. His grip is firm, steady, and comforting, and it unnerves me. "Can I have my hand back now?"

"No."

"No?"

He lets loose an enormous smile while clutching my hand tighter. "Agree to go out with me, Stevie." His eyes drill into mine. "Please," he adds. "I promise I'll be the perfect gentleman, and if you don't want to continue dating, I'll back down."

"We would still see each other. You'll be playing here every Friday night."

"I promise things won't be awkward."

"You shouldn't make promises you can't guarantee you can keep."

"I have remained on good terms with my exes." He shrugs while his thumb rubs circles on the back of my hand. "This is all hypothetical anyway." His eyes twinkle with the weight of what he thinks he knows. "Just one date, Stevie. That's all I'm asking. It's not really that big of a deal."

Maybe not to him. Mention of ex-girlfriends suggests Garrick likes being in a relationship, and all it does is prove how incompatible we are. "You're wasting your time, Garrick. I don't date."

"It's Gar, and why not?"

"I don't have the time for distractions, and I really need to get back to the bar before Manford sends out a search party."

"What if I'm the best kind of distraction?" he asks, finally releasing my hand.

"You probably are, but I'm not changing my mind." Standing, I straighten a hand down the front of my tight-fitting black T-shirt. It's adorned with the bar logo on the front and my name on the back. All the staff have to wear them, but we can choose to pair it with whatever we like. I usually wear skinny jeans and black tennis shoes because I value comfort over sexiness any day of the week.

"Help a guy out here, Stevie." Rising to his feet, he stands in front of me, pinning me with puppy-dog eyes. "Just one dinner. That's all I'm asking. How distracting could that be?"

Tipping my head back, I peer up at him. I admire his persistence. But it won't alter my decision. "I have a feeling you could be the most distracting distraction of all."

"Just give me a chance."

I shake my head and take a few steps back. "There are tons of girls out there tonight who would love to go out to dinner with you. Ask one of them."

"I don't want to take any of them to dinner. I want to take you."

"We can't always get what we want." Stretching up on tiptoes, I press a soft kiss to his cheek, unable to resist a sly sniff of his intoxicating smell. "It was good to meet you, Garrick, and I'm flattered you asked me out, but it's not happening."

"We'll see," he shouts after me as I make my way toward the door. "I'm not the kind of guy who backs down at the first hurdle."

Chapter Two

Stevie

"Fuck off," I grumble, shoving my head under my pillow and ignoring the incessant vibration of my cell phone as it buzzes on top of my bedside table. It was just after four a.m. when I crawled into bed, and I have not had enough sleep. My cell continues to vibrate, and I spew a ton of expletives as I lift my head from under the pillow and reach for it. Whoever is calling is clearly determined, so I might as well face the music. I swipe to answer the call, squinting at the screen through blurry eyes. "This better be important," I mumble over a yawn as I haul my tired body up against the headboard and brush knotty hair out of my face.

"I'm sorry to wake you, sweetie," Mom says, and I instantly regret my snippy tone. "I just didn't know if I'd get a chance to call you again today. It's bedlam here."

Mom works Monday to Friday as the office manager for a Seattle architectural firm, and for the past few years, she has worked at Sand Point Country Club on alternate weekends as front desk manager of the restaurant. She only took on the second job to subsidize my college fund, and she refuses to quit until I have graduated.

I was lucky to receive one of a limited number of scholarships. It covers my tuition and books but not accommodations or food. I wanted to take out student loans, but Mom wouldn't hear of it. She doesn't want me saddled with huge debt coming out of college.

"Sokay, Mom. I just got in extra late last night, and you know what a grouch I am if I don't get enough sleep." I scrub at my heavy eyes, forcing them to open. My bedroom is pitch-black, thanks to the best blackout blinds money can buy.

Outside, car horns blare, thumping music pumps out through open windows, dogs bark, playful children laugh, and other sounds of normal Saturday morning activity ensure I won't be able to fall back asleep after this call.

Mom's tinkling laughter hits my ears. "You always loved your sleep. Even as a toddler, I often had to coax you out of your crib." More laughter trickles through the connection. "Can you believe I actually used to wake you if you slept too long? Until Mom discovered what I was doing and made me stop."

"You were doing your best," I remind her, my heart swelling with unconditional love for the woman who gave up all of her dreams for me.

"I tried, and look how amazing you are." Pride suffuses her tone, and warmth spreads across my chest. "Though I can't claim much credit. It's all on you. Being your mother is such a pleasure. You make it so easy."

I adore my mother, and we have a fantastic relationship. She was the only parent I had growing up. I'm super close to my nana too, but Mom was the one I lived with.

She was only twenty when she got pregnant. Basically, the same age I am now, and I don't know how she did it. The thought of being responsible for a tiny human terrifies me. I can only imagine how difficult it was for her. But she never complains or ever makes me feel like I ruined her life. She continues to put me first and make sacrifices for me, and I have never felt anything but loved and cherished. While I went through phases wishing I had a dad, I never felt his loss for more than fleeting moments in time because Mom was everything.

"It's entirely too early for mushy compliments, Mom, even if it's true." I'm smiling as the words leave my mouth, and my heart is full of love for my mother. "I won the mother lottery for sure."

"You make me proud, Stevie. Every single day. Never forget."

It would be impossible to. She is constantly boosting me up and very open with her emotions and her thoughts. "I don't think you called me to tell me I'm amazing. What's up?"

"I hate to ask this of you, honey, and I wouldn't if I had any other choice."

"What do you need?" Yanking the comforter off, I swing my legs out of bed.

"This is the first year of the new golf tournament, and it's been a massive success. Tomorrow is the final day, and it's going to be extremely busy. Unfortunately, a few of the servers have come down with a stomach bug, and I'm shorthanded."

"When do you need me to come in?" I stand and arch my stiff back as I stifle another yawn.

I worked at the restaurant in the country club for three years, on weekends, during high school to save money for college. Mom got me the job after she started working there. She could quit now. We saved up enough money, Nana insisted on making a contribution too, and I have a steady income from my two jobs here, so there is enough to cover the rest of my college costs. Especially if I keep accumulating credits and I can finish in one year instead of the standard two that are left. But Mom is stubbornly insistent, and she won't quit until I have my degree.

"Could you work a full day shift tomorrow?" she asks. "It will be at the premium rate, so it will be worth your while."

I still have two assignments to finish before classes end in a week. Exams start shortly after, but I'm well prepared so I can afford to forgo one weekend of study.

Even if I was behind, I would still agree.

Mom has sacrificed so much for me, and I would go out on a limb to do anything for her. "No problem. I'm gonna grab a shower and something to eat, and then I'll hit the road." It's a five-hour-plus car trip home, and I'd rather get into Ravenna tonight than get up early tomorrow and head straight to Sand Point. If Hadley is around, we could meet up for a drink. I haven't seen my childhood bestie in ages.

"You're an angel. Thanks, love."

"I'll see you tonight."

"Drive safe, and text me when you're leaving and when you get home."

"Aye, aye, Captain." I hang up with her laughter ringing in my ears.

I wander out into our main living space, in my panties and silk pajama top, still yawning and rubbing my eyes.

"Ahem." A pointed throat clearing claims my attention. My roomie is seated at the island unit enjoying coffee and breakfast with a good-looking guy with dark-blond hair and navy-blue eyes. Ellen's lips twitch as she rakes her gaze over my bare legs and the tangled bird's nest on top of my head. The strange guy sitting at the island unit beside her smiles behind his coffee cup.

"Shit, sorry. I didn't know you had company," I say, quickly backtracking. Mention of that word conjures up images of the hottie from the bar last night, but I punt the visual from my mind's eye, unwilling to go there.

"This is Will," Ellen says. "I did text you to say he was here."

"The bar was nuts last night, and I didn't get home until really late. I never thought to check my phone before I conked out." I wiggle my fingers in the air and smile. "Hi, Will."

"Hi, Stevie." He's fighting a smirk but purposely keeping his eyes fixed on my face, which I appreciate.

"I'm just gonna go put on more clothes," I say, making a hasty retreat out of the room. It's just my luck to meet Ellen's new boyfriend when I'm semi-naked.

Grabbing the robe off the back of my bathroom door, I wrap it firmly around my body and slip my feet into slides before I head back out to the kitchen.

We were incredibly lucky to get this place this year because student rentals are in high demand in Eugene. All freshmen have to room at one of the residence halls, which sucked butt last year. Except it's how I met Ellen. That was the only good thing to come out of it. We became instant friends, and it was a no-brainer to share a place off-campus this year. We both hated cramped dorm living and having to sneak guys into the building.

Our two-bedroom apartment is only a ten-minute walk from campus, and it's in one of the newer buildings, so it's modern and more spacious than a lot of student accommodations. We both have our own bedrooms with en suite bathrooms, and there is a large communal space, which is our kitchen, dining room, and living room.

"It's nice to meet you, Will," I say as I head toward the coffee pot. "I was beginning to think you were a figment of Ellen's overly active imagination," I quip.

"Nice to meet you too, Stevie. Ellen never shuts up talking about you."

"That's 'cause she's my boo."

Ellen smiles at me. "Ditto, babe."

I race over and give her a quick squeeze. A look of amusement washes over Will's face, and I'm not sure he knows what to make of us.

"What have you guys planned for today?" I ask while I fill a mug with rich coffee.

"A study date at the library," Ellen confirms before popping the last piece of waffle into her mouth.

"We're grabbing dinner at the taco place later. A couple of my friends are joining us," Will says. "You should come."

"Sounds fun, but I can't. I have to head home unexpectedly." I slide onto the stool across from the lovebirds.

Ellen frowns. "Is something wrong? Is Nana okay?"

"She's fine. Mom needs me to work at the country club tomorrow, so I thought I'd head home today and try to catch up with Hadley." I waggle my brows. "Meaning you have the place all to yourself tonight." My gaze flickers between Ellen and Will. "You're welcome."

"Girl, it's so good to see you!" Hadley squeals, throwing her arms around me and hugging me tight.

"I've missed you." I cling to her, squeezing her tightly, before breaking our embrace and looping my arm in hers. "You look amazing. Love the dress." My bestie has an eclectic sense of style I adore. She owns who she is and always looks stunning. Hads only ever wears dresses and boots. Never jeans, or sweats, or pants, or skirts. In the summer, when it's hot, she will exchange the boots for tennis shoes, sandals, or flip-flops, but that's her only concession. Tonight, she's wearing a patterned floaty dress, with a bird print, that skims the asphalt as we walk along the sidewalk, heading toward town.

"You look great too. A little pale from too much work, no doubt, but your makeup is on point, and I love your ripped jeans. They're very you."

We chat casually as we make the short walk into town, heading for our favorite diner. When we are settled in our usual booth at the back and the waitress has brought our drinks, we pick up our conversation. "How are things with Dave?" I ask, slurping my berry smoothie through a straw.

"Over." Hadley flicks her hair, and bouncy strands of long, messy corkscrew curls cascade over her shoulders and down her back.

Growing up, I hated my red hair and wished I had my friend's mess of brown curls. Now, I have embraced my glossy, thick auburn locks, and I'm proud to be a redhead. "Already?"

She shrugs, taking a sip from her soda. "You know me. I fall in and out of love and lust fast."

"Truth." I have lost count of the guys Hadley has gone out with. Most of them never last long.

"His dick was too small, and he suffered from premature ejaculation." She just voluntarily tosses it out there like she's commenting on something as mundane as the weather. "I felt sorry for the guy, but a girl has needs, and his inability to satisfy me in the bedroom killed the feelings I had for him."

"The poor guy."

"Enough about me. How about you? Anyone at UO catch your eye lately?"

I shake my head as images of Garrick resurface in my mind. I scowl for the umpteenth time today. It's like he has hijacked my brain all day, and I'm sick of thinking about him. Like, what is with that?

"Spill the beans, sister. I know that look." She props her elbows on the table, excitement skittering in her eyes as she stares at me. "Have you met someone?" Her tone notches up a few decibels, and she's grinning so wide she'll give herself lockjaw if she keeps it up.

"Keep your panties on. It's nothing to get excited about." I take another drink of my smoothie before I put her out of her misery. "The new singer at the bar asked me out last night."

"Oh. My. God." Hads is bouncing in her seat now like an excitable kangaroo. "This is awesome." Softly clapping her hands, she smiles with obvious glee.

"I turned him down."

She sighs as the smile fades from her lips. "Of course, you did." She shakes her head, looking at me like she'd love to throttle me—lovingly, of course. "How long are you going to keep this up?"

I shrug, holding back my reply when the waitress reappears. She slides our burgers and fries in front of us, offering a quick smile before she leaves. "You know the score. Guys are a distraction. I'm focused on my studies and my future career. I don't have time for boys."

"You are missing out on so much, Stevie. Before you know it, you'll be an old gray spinster with nothing but a houseful of smelly cats for company." She narrows her eyes before popping a fry in her mouth.

I dunk a few sweet potato fries in chili sauce. "I'm not missing out. It's not difficult to find a guy when I need a fuck, and that's the only kind of interaction I'm interested in right now with the opposite sex." Stuffing the fries in my mouth, I savor the taste and ignore the pitiful look on my bestie's face.

"You're not your mom, Stevie."

I chew my food, swallowing it before responding. "It's not about that."

"This is *me* you're talking to. Of course, it's about your mom." She reaches across the table, grabbing my hand. "Just cause your mom got pregnant and had to drop out of college does not mean the same thing will happen to you."

"I'm not an idiot, Hads, and do we really need to have this conversation again?" It's like Groundhog Day sometimes.

"Yes, we do." My stubborn bestie glares at me before biting into her burger.

I finish the food in my mouth, dabbing the sauce at the corner of my lips with a napkin before I speak. "It's not really about Mom getting pregnant so young and having to give up her dream career although I definitely don't want that to be me. It's more how she invests so much time and energy in every guy she meets only to be let down over and over again. I have mopped so many tears as she cried over some asshole who failed her. Why would I willingly put myself through that?"

Mom is an eternal optimist and a true romantic. No matter how many times she gets her heart broken, she keeps putting herself back out there, and she hasn't given up hope of finding "the one." I can't decide if she's incredibly brave or stupidly foolish.

"Not every guy is an asshole. There are good guys out there. And I invest energy into relationships, but you rarely have to dry my tears."

"You're abnormal. Sometimes I wonder if you're even human," I joke, wanting this conversation to be over.

"I worry you're missing out on the best years of your life, babe. College is a time to have fun. To date guys. Fuck guys. Have your heart broken. Break a few hearts yourself. You won't know when

Prince Charming lands in your lap if you haven't dated a few frogs first."

"It's not part of my life goals right now. There will be time for guys and relationships later."

Hads eyes me skeptically. "Tell me about this guy."

"Why?" I dunk more fries in the sauce, shoving them in my mouth and hoping that will end this line of interrogation.

"Humor me. Did you even like him?"

I chew slowly as I contemplate whether I should lie. But I can't do that to Hads. That's not how we roll. "Yeah, I did. There was chemistry, and he's hot. He even has dimples and a killer smile."

"And you turned him down? I think I should have you committed." She takes another chunk out of her burger as I finish my fries.

"He's a stranger."

"That's what dates are for. Duh." She rolls her eyes. "What harm would it do to go out on one date with the guy?"

"If I didn't know better, I'd say Garrick paid you to hassle me. You sound like his clone."

"It sounds like he's talking sense." She pulls out her cell. "What's his last name?"

I consider not giving it to her for like five seconds. "Allen," I reluctantly supply before diving into my burger.

Her fingers fly over the phone as I eat. "Woah. Holy fuck. He is smoking hot, and you're legit insane for rejecting him."

"You go out with him then."

"He didn't ask *me* out."

"This conversation is over."

"For now." Hads jabs her finger in my direction as she points at me. "But I'm not letting this go. Not this time. Someone needs to talk sense into you, and that someone is going to be me."

Chapter Three

Garrick

"Sup, dude?" I ask, lifting my head from the screen as Will walks into the living room of the house we share with Noah and Cohen. We all lived in the dorms on the same floor last year and became firm friends in no time. Noah is majoring in family enterprise too, and we share most of the same classes. "Did you stay at Ellen's place last night?"

"Yeah." Will drops down on the leather couch beside me. "I really like this girl."

"Good for you, dude." My fingers fly over the game controller as we talk.

"How did the gig go?" he asks, watching me kill a few rogue militants on the screen.

"It was good."

"It was more than good," Cohen says, jumping over the back of the second couch and landing spreadeagled across the cushions. "Manford said you killed it."

Noah wanders into the room, holding a large bowl and shoveling cereal into his mouth. Dude is addicted to the stuff, eating it at all times of the day and night. He has commandeered one entire cupboard for all his cereal boxes, and I think he single-handedly keeps Kellogg's in business.

I jerk my head in acknowledgment as Noah settles his butt on the arm of the couch Cohen is sprawled all over. My eyes meet Cohen's. "Your cousin is cool, man, and I appreciate him putting a word in for me with the boss." I return my eyes to the screen in time to witness my demise. "I appreciate you vouching for me too."

"Anytime, broski." Cohen gives me a two-finger salute before turning his attention to Will. "Are we still on for dinner?"

I finish the game and toss my controller down on the coffee table.

"Affirmative," Will replies. "But Stevie can't make it, so I'm not sure if you and Noah still want to come."

Sitting up straighter, I turn my head to look at my buddy. "Hold up there a sec. Who's Stevie?" Is it the same Stevie who has transfixed my mind and wrapped soft fingers around my heart? I haven't been able to stop thinking about the redheaded beauty since our paths crossed last night.

"Ellen's boo, bestie, and roomie."

"What's with the dinner invite?" I rest my ankle over my knee.

"We were planning a little matchmaking because Ellen says Stevie never dates and she needs a nudge in the right direction."

"Cohen doesn't date." I state the obvious as my friend smirks.

"I'm aware." Will shrugs before scrubbing a hand over his smooth jawline. "We were giving her different options."

"My invite must have gotten lost in the mail."

"Dude, you know I would've invited you if you weren't heading home tonight."

It's got to be the same Stevie, and there's no fucking way I'm letting Will set her up with Noah and especially not Cohen. Don't get me wrong. I love both guys like brothers, but if Stevie is being set up with anyone, it'll be me. I can't believe Will would even consider setting her up with Cohen anyway. Dude is a legend, and he's always got my back, but he's a dirty dawg, and he rotates through girls like they're a dying breed.

Cohen has no business putting his hands on a girl like Stevie.

I doubt she'd let him anywhere near her anyway.

She had no trouble standing her ground and declining my dinner invite last night, and I'm not a player.

"She wouldn't happen to be a tall, hot redhead with legs for miles and stunning green eyes?" I ask.

Will's brow puckers. "Yeah. That sounds like her. I met her this morning, and she's a sweetheart." He cocks his head to one side. "How do you know her?"

"She was working at the bar last night. I asked her out, but she turned me down."

Cohen bursts out laughing. "This is fucking priceless. Has the notorious Allen charm deserted you?"

I shove my middle finger up at him. "She confirmed she doesn't date, and I got a stubborn vibe from her."

"Let me guess." Will chuckles as he tucks his hands behind his head and leans back in the couch. "It only makes you more determined."

"Abso-fucking-lutely." I grin at my buddy. "You know I love a good challenge, but it's more than that. I might have only met her, but I really, really like her. She's sexy and sweet, and we just clicked. It was easy breezy."

"Until she rejected you." Cohen smirks.

I flip him the bird again. "That is only a minor obstacle, and she's the kind of girl worth making an effort for."

"If you say so." Cohen's stupid smirk is still firmly planted on his face, and a wave of irritation crests over me.

"I do, and I'm staking my claim now."

Will whistles under his breath, Noah almost chokes on a mouthful of cereal, and Cohen chuckles.

Calling dibs is the kind of douchey behavior Cohen is known for, not me, so I understand their reactions.

Noah hooks up occasionally, but he's not interested in dating. I think he's still hung up on his childhood sweetheart back home. She broke things off with him just before he left for Oregon, and I don't think he's gotten over her yet.

Will and I are into relationships, favoring dating over random one-night stands. I would not ordinarily make a claim on any girl 'cause it's a major dickhead move, but there is something about Stevie that makes me want to beat on my naked chest, throw her over my shoulder, and turn full Neanderthal. "We had insane chemistry, and I have never wanted to kiss a girl as badly as I wanted to kiss Stevie last night. I just want to see where this might go."

"Wow." Will grins. "Sounds intense."

"I think it could be."

"Your tie is crooked." Mom purses her lips as she strides across the large living room, making a beeline for me, when I materialize in the doorway.

"You look nice, Mom," I say as she approaches.

Ivy Allen-Golding-Smith doesn't look a day over thirty despite celebrating her forty-fourth birthday recently. Mom has her cosmetic surgeon on speed dial, and she spends an inordinate amount of time at the dermatologist's office and at the gym with her personal trainer, and it shows. Today, she is wearing an elegant, fitted navy lace dress with cream and gold high heels that accentuate her slim frame to perfection. Expensive pearls—gifted to her by Henry Golding during their short-lived marriage—adorn her neck, and she wears a matching bracelet on her wrist. Her dyed-blonde hair hangs in loose curls over her shoulder, and her makeup artist clearly paid a house visit.

She looks every inch the society belle she has molded herself to be.

Dad's current wife is the opposite of Mom. As if he purposely set out to find a woman who isn't anything like my mother. Dawn couldn't give a flying fuck what she looks like, and she's never seen the inside of a plastic surgeon's or a dermatologist's office. She favors jeans and yoga pants, and the only time I ever see her dressed up is when she attends an official business event with Dad. Dad married her three years after his divorce from Mom, when I was nine, and they have been happily married ever since.

I have a real laid-back relationship with my stepmom, and she's good people. She helps to balance the sometimes exhaustive high maintenance demands of my mother.

I love my mom, but she's hard work.

"Thanks, sweetheart." She fiddles with my tie as I arch my neck, look up at the ornate ceiling with the intricate molding detail, and try to resist rolling my eyes. Everything is about appearances with Mom. God forbid I show up to the country club with an askew tie. "Today is important. Your father is trusting you to represent the family, and you can't let him down."

Dad wouldn't give a shit about my crooked tie. As long as I show up, smile, shake a few hands, and say the right words, he'll be happy. Allen Wineries is sponsoring the inaugural golf tournament at Sand Point, and if it's a success, it will probably become a regular annual thing. Normally, Dad or my uncle would represent the company, but they are overseas meeting with clients, and they took their wives with them.

Dad asked me to fill in, instead of one of the management team, and I readily accepted. I need to start getting more involved in the business, and I'm proud to represent my family today. "Dad knows I won't," I supply as the doorbell chimes.

"Oh good. They're here early. We can have champagne on the terrace."

My eyes narrow to slits. "Who's here?"

She beams at me, the skin on her face remaining stationary with the motion. "Relax, darling." She squeezes my shoulder. "I just invited Cristelle and the governor." She brushes hair back from my face with an effort at a scowl. "I really wish you'd do something with your hair." If she had her way, it'd be much shorter and worn in a preppy style, and my wardrobe would consist solely of polo shirts, loafers, and dress suits and shoes.

"Is Pepper with them?" I ask although I suspect I already know the answer.

"Pepper will be accompanying us today too." Her smile widens, but I don't share her exuberance.

"Mom." My tone contains considerable warning. "Stop. Meddling."

"What?" She feigns surprise. Something that's hard to do when her brow barely lifts. "Pepper's a gorgeous girl. She's single. You're single, and you're both destined for amazing things. She's a great catch, Garrick. I don't know why you're resisting."

"I like Pepper," I admit. "She's a great *friend*." I enunciate the word in the hope it might finally get through to my meddlesome mother. "But friendly feelings are all we have for one another. You can't force something that isn't there, and you need to quit with all this matchmaking bullshit. I can find my own dates."

"Language, darling."

Air whistles out of my mouth in frustration. "Stop treating me like a little kid who can't make his own decisions. I'm a grown man, Mom, and you need to let me lead my life the way *I* choose."

"I'm only suggesting you keep an open mind. Feelings can develop over time, and the best relationships grow out of friendship." The sound of approaching footsteps echoes in the hallway behind me. Mom stops fussing over me and steps back. Her lips pull into a tight line. "Just look at your father. He's a ringing endorsement for friends to lovers."

"I don't know why you're still pissed at Dad. It was you who filed for divorce."

And you who had an affair, which broke up your marriage. I think it, but I don't articulate it. Everything that needed to be said on that topic was said years ago when the seedy truth came to light.

"You have repeatedly told me you weren't a good match," I continue. "You should be happy he's happy. I know that's all he wants for you." It's true. Dad doesn't have a bad bone in his body. He's content with Dawn, and he would love Mom to find someone she stays married to for more than a year or two. I think it's very generous of my father considering the hell he went through with Mom.

Sometimes, I wonder if she'll ever find true contentment and inner peace. She never seems happy even if that's the front she portrays. Deep down, I think she's riddled with insecurities and incapable of lasting happiness. It makes me sad. I remind myself of this at times when I'm close to losing my patience with her. She loves interfering in my life, believing she knows better than I do about what's best for me. Her meddling drives me insane even if I know she believes it's coming from the best place.

I'm not naïve. I know she would love me to get together with Pepper because her father is the governor, her mother is Mom's best friend, and there is talk of a future presidential run for Paul. Mom would love those kinds of bragging rights, but it's not happening. Pepper will never be anything more than a friend.

Chapter Four
Garrick

"Here. You look like you need this." Pepper hands me a bottle of beer as we make our way from the presentation room to the restaurant.

"Thanks. I have done as much schmoozing as I can handle today."

"It's exhausting at times though I mostly don't mind."

"You've grown up in political circles, so I imagine it's as natural as breathing for you," I remind her, holding the door open so she can walk through first. "Dad kept me sheltered from all the corporate bullshit that comes with the job until recently. He wanted me to have a normal upbringing."

"I envy you that, but I think you're being too hard on yourself. You're a natural. They were all putty in your hands," she says as we approach the woman at the front desk.

"Welcome, Mr. Allen and Miss Montgomery. We're so pleased you could join us today," the older woman says, smiling kindly. She's very striking with strawberry-blonde hair and warm green eyes.

"Thank you, Ms. Colson," I reply, discreetly skimming my gaze over her name tag. "We are delighted to celebrate the inaugural tournament and hope to sponsor the event going forward." It was a resounding success, and I already know Dad will want to strike a deal. No harm in putting it out there now.

Pepper tilts her head and grins. "Natural," she mouths, and my lips kick up at the corners.

"If you would follow me, I will show you to your table," Ms. Colson says.

Pepper loops her arm in mine as I escort her across the large room, both of us tipping our heads at guests as we pass.

When we reach our table, I pull out a chair for Pepper, and Ms. Colson smiles warmly at me.

"There is water on the table, but can I get you anything else?" she asks, circumspectly eyeing the beer in my hand and the wineglass Pepper is lifting to her lips. I turned twenty a few weeks ago, and Pepper isn't quite twenty-one yet, but my father is sponsoring this event, and our winery is supplying all the wine, so no one is going to call us out for underage drinking.

"We're fine for now, but thank you," I say as I claim the chair alongside my friend.

"I'll send my best waitress to your table as soon as your party is fully seated. Enjoy your lunch."

"This place is nice," Pepper says after Ms. Colson has left. "The views are stunning."

I glance out the window at the sumptuous grounds bordering the large lake. The water is calm today, and soft rays of buttery sunlight glint off the surface. Imposing mountains loom majestically in the background. "They are. It reminds me of my dad's house in North Bend. It's on a large private plot facing the lake, surrounded by mountains."

"It sounds like heaven."

"It is. I loved growing up there. I spent my youth hiking, cycling, fishing, and kayaking. When I have time, I go home over the weekend to take my brothers out on the lake." Dad and Dawn had twin boys seven years ago. I don't get to see much of John and Jacob since moving to Oregon, but I try to make it home a few weekends during the year, and I am there for most of summer break.

Gradually, Mom, her date, Winston, Pepper's parents, and another couple take their seats at our table, and conversation is lively while everyone peruses the menu. I'm grateful for Pepper's company at events like this. It stops the boredom from setting in too early.

"Good afternoon," someone with a somewhat familiar voice says, and I whip my head up, startled to find a stunning redhead standing at the side of our table. She's addressing Mom and not looking in my direction yet. "I'm Stevie, and I'll be your server today."

A slow grin spreads over my mouth, quickly transforming into a full-blown smile. Things just got infinitely less boring. "Well, hello again, Stevie. I wasn't expecting to bump into you so soon, but it's a most pleasant surprise."

Her eyes pop wide when she notices me. Air filters through her slightly parted lips, and her jaw slackens, for a few seconds, before she composes herself. Stevie clears her throat. "Mr. Allen. It's good to see you again." I hate the fake smile she plasters on her face, but I can't fault her professionalism.

She is even more stunning under the full glare of the late-spring sunshine pouring through the large window. Minimal makeup paints her pretty face, and her beautiful auburn hair is tied back in a high ponytail, highlighting her stunning features. Gorgeous green eyes framed by long lashes coexist with a cute nose, defined cheekbones, full lips, and delicate porcelain skin with the tiniest hint of freckles across the bridge of her nose. Her skin is flawless, and my fingers itch with a craving to touch her. To discover if her smooth skin feels like silk under my hands. The plain white blouse and black pencil skirt hug her womanly curves in all the right places, and she manages to make the drab uniform look enticing.

Her eyes connect with mine, and a spark of electricity charges the space between us.

Just like on Friday night.

I can't remember ever feeling such an immediate attraction to any woman before.

I'm sure I'm staring like a dog in heat, but I cannot help myself.

She is breathtaking, and I am enchanted.

I have got to convince her to go out with me.

Letting her go without exploring the connection between us would be sinful.

"How exactly do you two know each other?" my mother asks in a prickly tone I'm all too accustomed with.

No doubt, she has picked up on the vibe between us, and she's not happy.

If she could scowl, she would be doing so.

"Stevie attends UO," I explain, not taking my eyes from the woman who has instantly captivated me. "She's a sophomore like me. We met at the bar where I was playing Friday night. She was waitressing there too."

"What a hardworking young woman," the governor says, and I couldn't agree more.

I wonder if this is why Stevie said she didn't need the distraction. Is it more the case she doesn't have the time to date? I don't see how she can have much free time if she holds down two jobs and full-time studies.

Yet, I won't let that stop me.

Stubborn determination is practically my middle name.

"We need more young people setting such good examples," the governor adds. "Well done, young lady." Paul is a good man, and I know he means well, but it's coming off a bit patronizing.

"Thank you, sir." Stevie's cheeks pink a little, and I can tell she's uncomfortable.

"We should let Stevie do her job," Pepper says, sending a friendly smile in Stevie's direction. "The restaurant is full, and I'm sure she's busy."

Stevie shoots a grateful smile in Pepper's direction. "What would you all like?"

You to go out on a date with me.

I think it, but I don't articulate it. No sense in riling my mother up further.

But if Stevie thinks I'm giving up, she has another think coming.

I have never been more determined to win a girl over than I am in this moment.

Chapter Five

Stevie

"I think you have an admirer." Mom lets loose a grin as she subtly jerks her head in the direction of the Allen table while I enter more orders into the system.

"Mom," I hiss, glancing up briefly. "Stop looking. He'll notice."

"Garrick Allen has not taken his eyes off you. I've watched him staring at you from across the room all afternoon. He looks smitten."

"I'm sure his mother loves that." I know who everyone is at that table because Mom and the club manager updated me so I would take extra care of the VIPs of VIPs.

The room is swarming with important people, but it's vital we keep the Allen family happy so they'll agree to sponsor the event annually. It's the only reason I didn't beg to be reassigned after I realized Garrick was here. Most of the experienced servers are out sick, and I didn't trust any of the others not to fuck it up. I loved working here. They were always good to me, and they treat Mom well, so I'm sucking it up and doing my duty.

"Ivy has dined here a few times in the past year," Mom says, lowering her voice so no one can hear. "She's a snooty bitch. She always finds something to complain about, and she's extremely rude.

It's no wonder Hugh Allen divorced her. He's such a nice man. I don't know how he married her in the first place."

"Is Garrick their only child?" I ask despite my better judgment.

Mom nods. "Hugh has twin sons with his current wife. They're such a lovely family. I spoke with Garrick earlier, and I can tell he takes after his father. He has lovely manners and good taste if you have caught his eye!" She winks at me, and I roll my eyes. "He's very handsome too."

"Mom, just stop. I already got the same pitch off Hads last night."

Her eyes widen. "I knew there was more to this. Spill the beans, missy."

"Mom, I'm working."

"Fine, but you're not leaving until I get all the tea!"

The rest of my shift is busy, and I try to attend to my duties without thinking about Garrick Allen, but it's challenging when I feel his eyes trailing me around the room and he avails of every opportunity to engage me in conversation when I'm at his table. Much to his mother's clear annoyance. I was tempted to flirt back, purely to wind her up, but that would be counterproductive.

I need to discourage Garrick, not egg him on.

I feel sorry for his pretty date because it's obvious he's distracted and fixated on me.

True to form, his mother complains her steak is overcooked. I make a speedy retreat from the kitchen after returning her plate as the chef explodes with anger and a slew of obscenities. I wouldn't be surprised if he spit on her freshly cooked steak before I handed it to her.

I breathe a sigh of relief when they finish their meal and make their way outside, but my relief is short-lived.

I'm clearing their table when I sense his presence behind me. My spine stiffens as I straighten up.

"I was hoping we could talk for a minute," Garrick says.

Planting a smile on my face, I spin around to face him. "I am working, and fraternizing with the clientele is frowned upon." I made that last part up, but it sounds plausible.

He chuckles. "You're determined to make me work for this."

"I don't know what you mean."

He flashes me one of his brilliant smiles, and those tempting dimples come out to play. Goddamn it. He doesn't play fair. I have been trying to ignore how freaking gorgeous he looks in his designer suit, and how delicious he smells, all afternoon. My limits are being severely tested with him all up in my personal space.

"It's okay, Stevie. I love a good challenge."

My mouth hangs open for a split second before I pull myself together. "I'm not a challenge or a game, Mr. Allen."

He takes a step closer, and I suck in a strangled gasp as his purely male scent hits the back of my nose. It's unfair for any man to look and smell this good. "I know you're not. You're so much more." His eyes seem more brown than green today, and they have stunning little amber flecks. "Go out with me, Stevie. Please." His eyes drill into mine.

"No, and you need to stop asking."

"I'll beg if I have to. I'll get down on one knee, right now, if that's what it'll take." He moves to lower himself, and I grab his arm.

"Don't you dare. All humiliating me will do is earn you a permanent spot on the top of my shit list."

"You're right." He straightens up, pinning me with the full extent of his hypnotic smile. "I should reserve the knee bend for more important occasions."

My eyes almost bug out of my head. He cannot mean what he's insinuating. "I think you might be crazy. Have you ever had your brain examined, because I think it's malfunctioning."

"There is nothing wrong with my brain or any other part of my anatomy." His eyes sparkle with mirth as his lips twitch.

"You're awfully cocky for someone I keep rejecting."

"Deep down, I know you want to say yes."

"There is that Allen arrogance again."

"You say arrogance. I say confidence." He leans in close to my ear. "I am going to uncover every single objection you have and smash them into smithereens."

"Good luck with that plan, buddy, 'cause you're gonna need it."

"Do you think I could leave now?" I ask Mom a couple of hours later as I collect my tips and remove the apron from around my waist. "I would like to get a head start before it gets dark." That's no lie, but I have ulterior motives. Like not wanting to elaborate on what Garrick said to me earlier or explain what went down on Friday night. Mom is already gushing over him, and I'm not in the mood.

Why won't he just leave me alone?

Mom glances around the room as staff members continue the cleanup. "We can manage it from here. I'd prefer you set out now rather than traveling so far in the dark." She pulls me into her arms and kisses the top of my head. "I know you're also avoiding, but it's okay. I'll grill you on the phone on Wednesday."

A groan slips from my mouth as I shuck out of her embrace, muttering about interfering mothers under my breath. Mom laughs. "He's a nice young man. You could do a lot worse."

"Bye, Mom!" I wave goodbye to the remaining staff as I make my way into the locker room to get changed.

Walking out the rear staff entrance with my bag slung over my shoulder, I wish I had brought my coat as a gust of wind rushes over me and a shiver whips through me. Despite the sun earlier today, it's been colder than usual for the end of April this past week. We should be welcoming warmer weather soon, and I'm looking forward to it.

Rounding the corner of the clubhouse, I slam to a halt at the sight awaiting me. "You have got to be shitting me," I grumble under my breath as I watch Garrick climb out of his car. Narrowing my eyes in his direction, I stride toward my silver Honda CR-V. It was a present from Mom and Nana for my sixteenth birthday. It's ten years old now, but I get it serviced regularly, and until I moved to Oregon, I didn't clock up many miles. She's in good condition and should last at least until I graduate.

"You really don't take no for an answer, do you?" I say as I unlock my car with the key fob and stop in front of the stubborn guy leaning against the side of a newish-looking Range Rover parked right beside my vehicle. "How did you know this was my car?"

Garrick's dimples make an appearance when he smiles. "I have my ways."

"And that's not stalkerish at all," I drawl, playing up the sarcasm.

He holds up his hands. "I'm just a lonely guy trying to get a pretty girl to say yes to a date."

I can't hold back my laughter. "You are ridiculous, and I'd hazard a guess rarely lonely." A guy who looks as good as Garrick is not short of female company. "I'm sure your lovely date from earlier would be upset to hear such statements."

"Pepper is a family friend, and it wasn't a date."

"I'm betting your mom wishes it was."

"You caught that, huh?" Reaching out, he tucks a stray strand of hair that has come loose from my ponytail behind my ear. His fingers brush against my cold cheek in the process, igniting a heady warmth under my skin. "Definitely not just a pretty face. I can add observant and intuitive to my list."

"You have a list?"

He nods, smiling as he maintains eye contact with me. "It's a long list and growing longer by the minute."

"You are so full of shit."

He chuckles. "Every interaction with you only heightens my interest, Stevie. You're funny, hardworking, intelligent, charismatic, and stunningly beautiful. If you want me to go away, stop being so captivating."

My pulse races, and my heart speeds up. It's a little OTT but still one of the sweetest things anyone has ever said to me. Not that I'm admitting to it or letting this go any further. "We should stop interacting then, Garrick," I say, turning around and opening my driver's door.

"Even the way you say my name enchants me."

I glance over my shoulder as he plants one hand against his chest and taps it.

"It gets me in here." His lips pull into a wild smile. "And other unmentionable places."

A laugh bursts from my mouth before I can stop it. "You have a certain charm. I'll give you that," I admit, and his face lights up. I am momentarily stunned, but I snap out of it quick, realizing what I've just said. "But it makes no difference. I told you already. I don't date." Climbing into my car, I get comfortable behind the wheel.

Garrick steps right up in between me and the open car door. He crouches down, and his face is so close I have an unhindered view of the stunning amber flecks in his eyes. "Make an exception for me."

"I can't. I'm sorry."

"I'm not giving up."

Air whooshes out of my mouth even as a shot of excitement races through my veins. "You should." Butterflies go crazy in my chest as I lock eyes with him. His gaze drifts to my lips for a couple seconds, and lust pools low in my belly. I gulp over the sudden dryness in my mouth.

What is this guy doing to me?

I do not have these reactions to men.

Garrick has me all flustered, and there's a teeny part of me questioning whether I shouldn't just go out with him.

Averting my eyes, I glance down at my lap as I struggle to regain my usual composure. When I feel in control, I lift my head and look at him. Garrick has straightened to his full height, and he's leaning his arm against the top of my open door, patiently waiting for me to reject him again.

"You seem like a nice guy, Garrick. If the timing was different, maybe I would agree. But it's not. I can't go out with you, and you need to accept my decision."

His smile fades as he slowly nods, taking a step back. "Okay."

"Okay?" I blurt, unconvinced he would give up that easy. Then again, why would he chase someone who keeps rejecting him? A guy like Garrick has no problem scoring dates. He's hardly going to pursue someone who keeps shooting him down. A pang of disappointment slaps me in the face, which is ridiculous.

I want him to give up.

This is a good thing.

I should be happy he's backing off.

So why aren't I?

"You know how I feel. Should you change your mind, let me know." He taps the top of my car. "Drive safe, Stevie."

Chapter Six

Stevie

The enticing smell of coffee lures me from my bedroom on Monday morning. Delicious scents of caramel and nuts reels me into the kitchen, and that can only mean one thing — Ellen grabbed takeout from Bumble Bees.

Have I mentioned how much I love my college bestie?

I float into the kitchen with a massive smile on my face, and it blossoms into a full-blown cheesy grin when I discover Ellen and her boyfriend in a charged embrace. My roomie is in love, for real this time, and I love seeing her so happy. Will has Ellen caged against the counter, and the look on his face is downright feral.

"Don't mind me," I say, moving seamlessly around them. "I'm just here for the coffee."

Reaching for the paper holder containing four takeout coffees, I remove the cup with a large S on top. "If this is a caramel macchiato, I will love you forever and ever, babe," I say, grinning at my bestie.

"Now that's what I'm talking about," someone with a rich, deep, decidedly male voice says from behind me.

All the fine hairs on the back of my neck lift as warmth hits my spine. I already know who I'm going to find before I turn around—the hot, charming guy occupying prime real estate in my head and holding a recurring role in my stubborn dreams these past few nights.

There is no ignoring the swarm of butterflies that swoops into my chest as I spin around and face him. Fuck, why does he have to be so irresistible? "What are you doing here?" I blurt, trying my best not to drool as my gaze skims quickly over Garrick.

His chin-length hair is hanging in tousled strands around his chiseled jawline, and a thin layer of dark hair adorns his chin and cheeks. Those mesmerizing hazel eyes simmer with pleasure and amusement as he fixes them on my face. Plush lips I am *not* daydreaming about tasting part as a trickle of air seeps from his mouth.

Ripped dark-rinse slim-fitting jeans mold to his long legs. A black designer hoodie with a splash pattern on the front emphasizes his broad shoulders, defined arms, and toned chest and abs. A worn pair of black and white Nike Dunks covers his large feet, and some kind of Garmin sports watch is strapped around his wrist.

It's clear the guy has money, but he doesn't appear to flaunt it. His look is casual and effortless, and he exudes confidence. Garrick owns who he is, and that's the most attractive thing about him.

I hate I'm finding more reasons to like him, but it's the truth.

No matter how much I want to evict him from my thoughts and my dreams, he has hijacked my mind and ensnared me.

"Garrick and Will grabbed coffees on their way over," Ellen pipes up, looking slightly sheepish as she stares at me with pleading eyes. "Isn't that super nice of them?"

"It is," I acknowledge, lifting the cup under my nose. They obviously checked what we liked, and that kind of thoughtfulness speaks volumes.

If Garrick is trying to impress me, great coffee is a good start. I eyeball him with sincerity. "Thank you."

"You're welcome."

Closing my eyes, I softly moan as the delicious aromas of one of my favorite coffees tickles my nostrils, making my mouth water in anticipation. I lick my lips before raising the cup to my mouth and taking the first reverent sip.

When my eyes pop open, Garrick is staring at me with dilated pupils, and his lips are slightly parted as he drags a hand through his messy, dark hair. He loudly clears his throat and arches a brow. "Good?"

"Yep." I attempt to ignore the erratic beating of my heart and the fluttering feeling in my chest as I meet his heated gaze. "In general, the coffee is shit in Oregon compared to Seattle. But Bumble Bees has my heart—and a decent amount of my weekly paycheck," I add, laughing a little.

"Next to my family, great coffee is the thing I miss most when at college." Garrick smiles, and it lights up his entire face. "Though you're right. Bumble Bees is good. I won't drink coffee from any other local place."

"Don't get me started on the shit they try to pass off as coffee on campus." A shudder works its way through me. "I almost threw up the first day when I tasted it."

"It's nasty, for sure."

Before he can dazzle me with another panty-melting smile, I take a second sip of my coffee and tilt my head to the side. "You didn't answer me. How come you're here?" I'm guessing Garrick and Will are friends, but that doesn't explain Garrick's motives for showing up at my house with coffee.

"Will and I share a house with two other buddies a few blocks from here. He mentioned he was driving Ellen to campus today, so I thought I'd bum a ride and see if you wanted to come with us?"

Ellen and I usually take turns driving Monday through Wednesday, because our schedules align, but that doesn't mean I'm comfortable riding with Garrick and Will.

"Thanks, but I'm fine to drive myself."

The smile doesn't fade from his face as he says, "Parking is tight on campus, and it's cleaner for the environment to only have one car on the road."

"Garrick raises valid points," Ellen agrees, and I whip my head around, glaring at my treacherous best friend.

All sense of pretense is gone now as she grins at me. "I already checked, and the guys will be leaving the same time as us. We're on their route home, so it's a no-brainer."

"We should hit the road unless we want to drive around for ages trying to locate a parking spot," Will says, distributing the other coffees. "Let's make a move."

"I thought you were giving up?" I say in a low voice as I sit in the back seat of Will's SUV, alongside Garrick, heading in the direction of UO.

I drink my coffee as he turns to face me, his knee brushing against mine with the motion. Sincerity oozes from his face as he holds my eyes captive. "I told you I'd back down, and I meant it." His tongue darts out, licking his lower lip.

That shouldn't be hot, but it is.

"I never want to make you uncomfortable or disrespect your wishes. You've made yourself clear on the dating front." His lips twitch. "That doesn't mean we can't be friends." A full smile blooms across his mouth. "Our best friends are dating. We're going to be seeing more of one another, so we might as well make the best of it."

I stare at him through narrowed eyes, and he chuckles. "Friends? You just want to be friends now?"

He shakes his head, sending strands of dark hair skating across his strong brow. "You know what I want, but I'll settle for friends if that is all that's on offer."

"It is!" I confirm, ignoring the devil whispering naughty thoughts in my ear.

"Okay." His smile is so wide it threatens to split his face in two.

"That *is* all that's on offer!" I rub at a tense spot between my brows, hating how flustered I feel in his presence. It is most unlike me, and I don't like it.

"I know."

"I hope you do, because if this is some kind of ruse to convince me to date you, it won't work. I don't break my rules. I haven't had a boyfriend since junior year of high school, and even then, the only reason I caved was due to peer pressure. I'm way more assertive now, and I don't let anyone pressure me into doing something I don't want to do."

"Understood." He flashes me a perfect smile, and I'm torn between wanting to scream at him and kiss him.

Purely to wipe the smug grin from his mouth.

That's all.

"I mean it," I warn, scooting over to the door to put as much space between us as possible.

"I'll be the perfect gentleman, and I promise I won't hit on you again." Leaning back against his door, he pins me with a searing-hot look that burns through my flimsy defenses, igniting every part of me. Resolve and confidence are written all over his face, and I feel like the only person in the room not getting the joke.

"What?"

He feigns innocence as his brows tip up, but that infuriating smile is still firmly planted on his tempting lips. "Nothing, *bestie*."

I'm waging an internal war with the excitement and adrenaline coursing through my veins. "It won't work. Whatever you're planning. You should give up now."

He lifts his coffee to his mouth. "I don't have a clue what you mean."

I legit growl under my breath.

He chuckles, still grinning at me, and I realize it's his superpower the same time I understand I'm far from immune to the effects.

Waggling his brows, he points at my half-empty paper cup. "Drink up before it gets cold."

"I'm divorcing you," I grumble at Ellen as we make our way through the packed cafeteria toward the table at the back. "I'm serious. You're supposed to be on my side, not helping Garrick with whatever his nefarious plan is."

"Of course, I'm on your side." She giggles before looping her arm in mine. "You can thank me by making me maid of honor at your wedding."

My mouth hangs open in shock for a few seconds. "You did not just go there."

"Girl, the sparks were flying in the kitchen and the car. You cannot deny you two have chemistry," she says, weaving a path around a group of obnoxious frat boys blocking our way.

A few guys whistle as we pass, their gazes roaming appreciatively over us, but we don't acknowledge them. "It doesn't matter. I don't have time to date Garrick."

"That's bullshit, and you know it. I'm as busy as you, and Will has a crazy schedule too, but we're managing. That's what you do when you like someone and *You. Like. Him.*" She levels me with a knowing look, pulling us to a stop a few feet away from the table where Garrick, Will, and a couple of other guys wait. "I saw the way you were looking at one another. Garrick is hot, he's crazy about you, and Will says he's the best guy he knows. What harm would it do to go out on one date with him?"

"It has the potential to get messy. What if I took a chance on him and it didn't work out? That would make things extremely awkward for you and Will."

She vigorously shakes her head. "Nope. You're not going to use that as an excuse. It has nothing to do with Will and me. Our relationship won't be affected whether you date Garrick or not." She sighs. "Look, I don't want to be an interfering old hag, so I'm not going to pressure you. I just think you could be missing out on something great, and I want you to be happy."

"I am happy, Ellen. I don't need a guy to be fulfilled."

"That's not what I'm saying, and you know it." She tugs me forward. "Just promise me you'll keep an open mind. That's all I'm asking."

"That's asking a lot."

She stops again, stabbing me with a serious expression. "No matter how much we want to map out every path on our life journey, there are always unknown turns and unforeseen dips in the road." She squeezes my arm. "You gotta roll with it, babe. You never know where this path might lead, and you won't find out unless you take that leap."

Chapter Seven
Garrick

"Incoming." Will sports a lovesick goofy grin as he nudges me in the ribs, tipping his head in the direction of the two pretty ladies coming our way. He quickly removes his backpack from the chair beside him so it's free for his girlfriend. It's the busiest time to grab lunch in the cafeteria, and the place is teeming with students and buzzing with the sounds of raucous conversation and boisterous laughter.

"They're both hot," Noah proclaims, in between monstrous bites of his burger, as we watch Stevie and Ellen make their way toward our table. They stop for a bit, locked in what appears to be an intense conversation, and I wonder what that's all about.

On the other side of our table, Cohen is deep in conversation with two of his football buddies. The jocks' table is behind us, and Cohen usually sits with them. Today, he has graced us with his presence because he's curious to meet the girls.

Cohen is facing away, with his back to us, so he hasn't noticed their approach. I already warned him to be on his best behavior, and I'll kick his ass if he steps out of line. The odds are already stacked against me, and I don't want him perving over Stevie or Ellen and giving them the wrong impression of me and Will.

"Hey." Ellen smiles, waggling her fingers at me and Noah before claiming the seat beside her boyfriend.

Will leans in, planting a kiss on her mouth, and she visibly melts.

Dude is totally smitten.

"Hey, Stevie." I attempt to reassure her with a smile as she stands awkwardly at the edge of the table, looking like she wishes she was any place but here. "I kept this seat for you," I add, patting the empty space beside me. "Sit. I promise I won't bite."

Unless you ask. Then all bets are off.

I keep those thoughts firmly trapped in my head because they're premature. I'm focused on developing a friendship with Stevie in the hope she'll lower the shield she protects so fiercely and let herself act on the obvious chemistry we share. I know I'm not alone in feeling this, but I promised I wouldn't keep pushing, and I'm a man of my word.

Irrespective of how badly I want her, I will let her set the pace.

The ball is firmly in her court.

"Unless you're into that kinda thing, and then I'm sure my buddy would be more than happy to oblige," Cohen says, swirling around in his seat to join our conversation.

I drill him with a heated glare. A not-too-subtle reminder that he needs to tone down his assholish ways. It's like he just can't help himself when he's around a pretty girl. I'm still watching when he looks over at Stevie, so I spot the instant spark of recognition the same time Stevie sucks in a small startled gasp. My eyes flick to hers as she finally sits beside me, setting a brown paper bag down on the table and dumping her book bag on the ground at her feet.

Nibbling on the corner of her mouth, she glances swiftly between me and Cohen, and it clicks with me instantly. A sour taste pools in my mouth, and knots form in my gut.

"You two know one another?" Will asks what I'm afraid to, now he's no longer sucking face with Ellen.

Cohen's lips twitch as his gaze roams leisurely over Stevie, and I don't like it one little bit. "If you mean know in the biblical sense, then—"

"Watch your mouth." I cut across him, working hard to keep my ass in the seat when I long to reach across the table and ram my fist in his face. "Show some respect."

Cohen loses the smirk, but his jaw tightens in clear aggravation as he levels Stevie with a neutral look. "Apologies, Stevie. I meant no disrespect."

"None taken," she says, recovering her composure fast. Her slender fingers open the paper bag, and she removes a wrap, a bottle of water, and an apple. She must have bought it from the deli on campus, and it's surprising we didn't bump into one another there.

"He can't help himself," Noah supplies, balling up the wrapper from his burger and depositing it on the tray along with the rest of the remnants of his lunch. "His default setting is stuck on asshole."

"Hey!" Cohen tries to defend himself. "I'm not that bad."

"I'm sure we don't want to get into all that here." Will slides his arm around Ellen's shoulders, attempting to defuse the situation.

"We're cool, Stevie, right?" Cohen leans back in his chair and smiles at her.

"I have no beef with you." Her smile is tight, but I detect no animosity. Just the same awkwardness the rest of us are feeling with the obvious elephant in the room.

"Awesome." Cohen offers her a tame smile before diving into his meatball sub.

A pregnant pause ensues, and it's cringing.

Clearing my throat, I slide one of the smoothies in front of me across the small gap to Stevie. "I got you this. Ellen said you like them."

"That was extremely thoughtful. Thank you, but you don't need to keep buying me things. Unless you're like this with all your friends?"

Cohen almost chokes on his sandwich. Is it bad, for a fleeting second, I wished he did? I don't want to start shit with my buddy, especially for something that happened before I met Stevie, but knowing he's probably hooked up with her sticks in my gut.

"Gar is a generous guy," Noah says before adding, "I'm Noah, by the way."

"Nice to meet you," Stevie says. "How do you guys all know one another?"

"Cohen and Noah are the roomies I mentioned," I confirm. On the other side of me, Ellen and Will are whispering, which is rude, but whatever. I'm kind of over this lunch already.

"And Gar and I are both family enterprise majors," Noah confirms. "You're a sophomore too, right?"

Stevie nods as she picks at her wrap.

"What's your major?"

I am uncharacteristically quiet as I finish my sandwich, lost in my thoughts, but I'm listening to the conversation around me.

"Floral management." She confirms what I already know in between drinking sips of the smoothie.

"That's an interesting choice," Cohen says. "What made you pick that?"

I fight the urge to snarl at him, which is unfair because he's not hitting on her and he's trying to be sociable, which is a big concession for a guy like Cohen. I'm pissed at whatever has transpired between them in the past, but I'm not asshole enough to blast either of them for it. I know Cohen isn't any competition. If he'd been interested in pursuing her, he'd have done it already, so I wish I could snap out of this funk.

"My nana runs a garden center back home in Ravenna. Her parents set the business up in the nineteen twenties, and she took it over when they retired. I've been helping her out since I was a little girl, and I always find it peaceful surrounded by nature and plants and flowers." She shrugs, sending waves of glossy red hair cascading over her shoulders, and my fingers twitch with a craving to touch the silky strands. "I guess it's in my DNA."

The awkwardness dissipates as the conversation picks up at the table, but I'm quieter than usual as I listen to everyone talking, too lost in my head to properly engage. Breathing a sigh of relief when lunch ends twenty minutes later, I gather all the trash from the table onto my tray and walk off to throw it away. I need some space to shake myself out of my bad mood.

So what if Cohen hooked up with the girl I'm crushing on?

It was in the past.

Everyone's got a past. I know that. So why does this hurt? Why does it matter so much?

The normal me would be able to let it go, but Stevie has me twisted into knots, and I'm not acting like myself.

When I return, everyone is ready to go. "We'll meet you out by the car at six," Will says to Ellen before planting another kiss on her swollen lips. My buddy is infatuated in a way he hasn't been before. From what I have seen, it appears mutual, which is good, because Will is a decent guy, and he doesn't deserve to be jerked around if Ellen doesn't share his feelings.

"Thank you for the smoothie and for saving me a chair, Garrick," Stevie says as she slings her bag over one shoulder.

"No problem, and it's Gar. All my friends call me Gar," I remind her, desperately wanting her friendship, because if it's the only way I can get close to her, I'll take it.

She tilts her chin up, and a soft smile ghosts over her mouth. "I like your full name. If you don't mind, I'd much rather call you Garrick."

Now I know it's not because she's keeping me at arm's length, I love that she calls me that. "I don't mind."

"Cool." Threading her arm through Ellen's, she waves at all of us before walking off.

"Gar." Cohen steps beside me as we head off in the other direction, toward the rear exit.

"I don't want any details," I say, shoving my free hand in the pocket of my jeans. "But were you with her?"

There's a brief pause before he confirms it. "Yeah, it was a couple of months into freshman year and—"

"I'm not trying to be an asshole, but that's as much as I need to know."

"Stevie is great, but I'm not going to hit on your girl. I know I'm a jerk at times, but I'd never go there."

"I get it, and it's fine." I push out through the door, joining other students leaving the cafeteria. "And for the record, she's not my girl."

"Yet." Noah slaps me on the back. "It's only a matter of time before Cohen and I'll be flying solo while you two are all wifed up."

Chapter Eight

Stevie

"Are you in a rush, or could we go inside to talk in private?" I ask Garrick the second Will kills the engine curbside at our apartment building.

Garrick slowly turns his head, his brownish-green eyes scrutinizing my expression for a few beats. I see no hint of gold in his irises today, and I miss it. He truly has the most arresting eyes. It's no wonder I'm having trouble concentrating when he fixes his peepers on me.

"Sure." He nods, and I release the breath I was holding as I climb out of the back seat of the SUV. Garrick was quiet at lunch, and quiet on the ride home, and I suspect I'm the reason for it.

I about died when Cohen turned around at the table and I realized who he was. I know I don't owe Garrick any explanation, but I don't want things to be strained between us. Especially when he's been so sweet and thoughtful today. I wonder if he feels differently about me now he knows I engage in random hookups.

That thought shouldn't send panic racing through my veins like it does.

But if he's going to turn all judgmental, then it will help my cause. I won't apologize for who I am or how I live my life. And I'm certainly not apologizing for something that happened before we knew one another. Especially when we're not dating. I know he likes me, and I get it probably pisses him off I've hooked up with his friend. Honestly, if the tables were turned, I would feel the same. Which is why we need to have a conversation.

Will and Ellen have their arms wrapped around one another in the elevator as we make our way up to the fifth floor. Ellen shoots concerned glances our way as we stand silently side by side, the tension accelerating with every passing second, and I'm glad when we reach our floor and the doors ping open.

Will and Ellen make a beeline for the couch after we close the door to our apartment, stopping to grab snacks and drinks on the way. I busy myself making coffee while Garrick hovers in the background, doing a good impression of a brooding rock star. "Cream or sugar?" I ask after I've poured coffee into two mugs. "We have a sugar substitute too, if you prefer?"

He shakes his head. "I'll take it black."

"It's not Bumble Bees, but it's decent," I say, handing him a mug.

"Thanks." His appreciative smile is sincere, and I don't think Garrick is the type of guy to stay grumpy for long. At least I hope he's not.

After stirring some sweetener in my coffee, I dump the spoon in the sink and jerk my head for him to follow me. His footsteps are quiet as he trails me down the hallway and into my bedroom. I close the door behind us, purely for privacy. Ellen is a nosy bitch, and she loves getting all up in my business. I wouldn't put it past her to try to eavesdrop even though she knows I'll tell her everything later.

Gesturing for Garrick to take the seat at my desk, I plonk my butt down on the end of my bed and just go for it. No point in pussyfooting around the subject. "We need to discuss Cohen. I didn't want to say anything at lunch, because it wasn't the time or place, but I'd hate for things to be awkward between us."

"It's cool," he says, wrapping his large hands around his mug. "You don't need to say anything."

"I know, but I'd prefer to clear the air all the same."

He takes a healthy mouthful of his coffee as his eyes invite me to continue.

"I met Cohen at the first frat party I attended, about a month into freshman year. I was with a few of my classmates. Ellen wasn't there." I don't want him thinking my roomie knew and was keeping it from him. It's important to Ellen that she gets along with Will's friends. "I overindulged, and I was fairly tipsy. Not to be disrespectful to your friend, but he's not my usual type."

Truthfully, I usually run a mile from jocks.

I know they aren't all promiscuous idiots, but enough of them are for me to avoid taking one to my bed.

"Not to be rude, Stevie, but I don't want to hear all the details."

"I would never kiss and tell," I calmly reply.

"Cohen wouldn't either. I know he's no saint, but he doesn't dish the dirt. He hasn't told me the specifics, and I would never ask."

It says a lot about the kind of man Garrick is that he'll defend his friend even when he's clearly angry with him. "It was a onetime drunken hookup. I barely remember it, to be honest, and I'm sure it's the same for him. It didn't mean anything." I square my shoulders and look him in the eye. "But he's not the first guy I've hooked up with, and he most likely won't be the last. I might not have time for a relationship, but I've still got needs. When I need sex, I go and get it. It's no different than when a guy does it, but if you think differently of me now or—"

"I'm not judging you, Stevie, and I don't think differently of you."

"Yet, you're upset."

Putting his mug down, he claws a hand through his hair and leans forward with his elbows on his knees. "I am upset, and honestly, it surprises me. This isn't my usual MO. I'd be a dick to hold something in your past against you. I know that, but I can't shake this feeling. I've been mulling over that more than anything. But I'm not upset with you or Cohen for hooking up before either of you knew me. I'm not an asshole. It is what it is. It's just..." He trails off, his eyes lowering to the hardwood floor.

"It's just what?" I ask in a gentle tone, coaxing him to let it out.

Lifting his head, he drills me with a confident look I'm more used to seeing on his face. "I'm jealous."

I thought it might be jealousy except this seems nuts when we've only known each other a few days. "Does it strike you as odd how potent our reactions are to one another?"

His lips curl at the corners, and I'm glad to see it even if I slipped up by admitting the truth. "It's not usual for me, if that's what you're asking. It's—"

"Do not say fate!"

His smile expands. "Wouldn't dream of it."

"Ugh." Tilting my head back, I stare at the ceiling wondering what the hell I'm doing.

Like, legit, what the fuck am I doing?

"It's good to know you're not totally in denial," he says, reclaiming my attention. A full grin slips over his mouth, and his dimples come out to play.

Yep, just kill me now!

"You know it—"

"Changes nothing."

I flip him the bird, and he chuckles, picking up his mug again.

A comfortable silence descends for a few seconds while we both drink our coffee and contemplate whatever the hell is going on between us.

He breaks it first.

"Can I ask you something?"

Although wary, I nod.

"Why are you so against relationships?"

Air expels from my mouth. This is a pretty heavy convo for such a new friendship, but I'm not going to hide from him or lie. I move up to the top of the bed and rest my back against the headboard with my mug in my hands. "Come join me." The words have barely left my mouth, and he's striding across my bedroom, eating up the space quickly with his long legs.

Garrick gets comfortable beside me, and I angle my head so we're face-to-face. "I'm the first to admit I'm a bit of a control freak," I say.

He fights a smirk, and I level him with a dark look. "I've only known you five minutes, and I can already tell you like things orderly." His gaze skates around my tidy bedroom. "Case in point. I don't think I've ever seen a student's room so neat, tidy, and regimentally organized." He brushes hair out of his face, smiling in amusement while he peers at me. "If you ever end up in my room, I'll have to blindfold you so you don't see the mess."

"Oh no. That's it." I shake my head. "We can't be friends."

He chuckles. "Maybe you'll be a good influence on me."

"But will you be a good influence on me? That's the million-dollar question."

"What if I want to be a *bad* influence?" Heat flares behind his retinas as he pins me with a suggestive look that has me discreetly squeezing my thighs together. I playfully push his chest. He's solid and warm beneath my touch, and it's almost impossible to resist the urge to crawl into his lap and siphon some of that body heat.

"Stop with the innuendo." It takes massive self-control to withdraw my hand from his chest. "We're just friends, remember?"

"Of course." The grin is firmly planted on his face, but it's good to see it. I only realized I missed it when he was quiet and sullen this afternoon. "And you were going to tell me why you're allergic to dating."

A laugh spills from my lips. "I guess that's one way of putting it."

He finishes his coffee and puts the empty mug down. Moving closer, he reaches out, softly threading his fingers through my hair. "Sorry, I know we're trying to have a serious conversation, but I can't hold back any longer. You have the most beautiful hair, and I've been dying to touch it."

I'm in a daze as I stare at his lush mouth while he rakes his fingers in my hair.

"I wondered if it would feel soft as silk, and now I know."

Our eyes meet, and attraction smolders in the small gap between us. It would be easy to bridge the distance and press my mouth to his. I know he wouldn't turn me away, but I can't get distracted by his full lips, those naughty dimples, or the warmth and vitality brimming in his eyes.

I do not do this.

And I need to get a grip.

Scooting over to the edge of the bed, I drink the dregs of my now lukewarm coffee and give myself a silent pep talk. Anything to avoid surrendering to the feelings simmering under the surface of my skin.

"Is it fear?"

My eyes meet his.

Concern glimmers in his eyes. "Did someone hurt you?"

I place my empty mug on my bedside table and lie down on my side facing him. "No one hurt me, but I suppose fear plays a small part."

Garrick mirrors my position except he tucks a hand under his head as he waits for me to elaborate.

"My mom got pregnant at twenty, just before the start of her sophomore year at UO. She wanted to be a doctor until she met a handsome sailor one night in Seattle, and they had a wild night together." A shudder works its way through me. I peer directly into Garrick's eyes, loving how he clings attentively to everything I say. "Those were her words, not mine, and yes, it's gross, and I'd rather she hadn't overshared, but it's good to know I was the product of fun if I wasn't borne out of love."

"I'm sure your mother loves you. I imagine it'd be impossible not to."

And there he goes again. If I didn't know better, I'd swear I conjured Garrick out of my vivid imagination—a mashup of every book boyfriend I've ever swooned over.

"My mom is great." I pluck at the comforter as I smile. "You met her actually. She works the front desk at the Sand Point restaurant."

"Ms. Colson." He bobs his head. "I don't know why I didn't spot the resemblance. You look alike."

"I have her eyes, and we share the same stubborn streak though it manifests in different ways." I run my fingers back and forth across the comforter as we speak. "Mom is an eternal optimist and the biggest romantic. She had to sacrifice her dreams when she became pregnant with me. I know she doesn't regret it, but it's hard not to feel guilty sometimes. Especially when I have to endure watching her falling for the wrong guy, over and over, and I can't help wondering if things would be different if she wasn't a single mom."

"That's not your burden to bear." Reaching out, he touches his pinky against mine.

"I know and I don't carry it. Sometimes, I shoulder it, but mostly, it feels like a lesson to be learned."

He hooks his finger around mine, and my heart pounds against my rib cage. "In what way?"

"Mom was always chasing boys and yearning for love, and ultimately, she sacrificed her career because she wasn't focused on the right things. It feels wrong to call it a mistake, as if I'm acknowledging I am a mistake, which I know I'm not, but I don't want to follow the same path. I want to make something of myself. I have career goals and a plan for the next ten years of my life."

"And if you let any boy distract you, your life might veer off track?" he surmises, threading his fingers fully in mine.

"Exactly. I'm not saying I don't believe in love or that I don't want to get married and have kids one day, because I do, but that's not even remotely in the cards now."

"How old are you, Stevie?"

"I'll be twenty in June."

"You are so mature and way more determined and self-aware than most girls your age, and I don't mean that to be insulting to you or other girls."

A laugh bursts from my lips. "I know. I sound ancient. Ellen and my friend Hadley are always telling me that."

"There is nothing wrong with being goal-orientated or knowing what you want from life and going after it. I have goals too, but I live by the motto you should work hard and play hard. When do you get to play, Stevie? When do you have fun?"

The insinuation I don't have fun rubs me the wrong way, and I yank my hand back, sliding it between my knees. "I find *that* insulting." Fire burns in my eyes. "I know how to have fun, and I have plenty of it. I'm not some boring bitch who is all work and no play."

I sometimes hang out with the crew at The End Zone on Friday nights after our shifts end. It usually involves copious Patron shots and drunk dancing until the early hours after the bar is officially closed. I always go out Saturday nights, either to a party or a movie or I head home to hang out with Hadley. I've had wild one-night stands. I have cliff jumped and skinny-dipped, and I'm game to try anything once. I could say all that, and a lot more, but I don't have to explain myself to a guy who is virtually a stranger.

"I'm sorry. I didn't mean to offend you or imply anything. I'm just trying to get to know you. To understand your motivations and what you're passionate about. You know I think you're fascinating. I already told you and I'd never lie."

I pull myself back up until I'm sitting against the headboard. It feels too intimate lying side by side, and I need to mark clear boundaries between us if we are to become friends. Tucking my hair behind my ears, I attempt to leash the sudden rush of anger his baseless assessment has induced. "I know I'm not your typical college student, but that doesn't mean I'm some nerdy bore."

"I didn't think you were. I see how hard you work, and you're clearly very driven. I just wanted to know if you make time to relax." He sits up and raises his palms. "I swear that's all I meant."

"I've shared stuff with you today I don't readily talk to others about," I truthfully admit. "It shocks me that I opened up so easily to you, and now I'm wondering if I should have."

"Please don't say that. I'm honored you felt you could talk to me about it."

"You seem to own who you are, and I admire and respect you for that. All I'm asking is for you to give me the same courtesy."

"I admire and respect you a hell of a lot, Stevie."

"Even if I have casual sex instead of committed relationships? 'Cause it seems to me we both have very opposing views in this regard."

He exhales heavily. "God, I'm making a mess of everything." Dragging his hands through his hair, he shakes his head. "Now you think I'm a judgy asshole, and I'm not. I swear I'm not. I'm just an idiot who seems to have forgotten how to speak to a woman he likes."

The edge slices off my anger. I might not know him well, but I think I'm a pretty decent judge of character, and Garrick *is* a good guy. I haven't exactly been making it easy for him either.

"It's fine. I probably overreacted. I get defensive when people get on my case, and my friends and my mom are always nagging me. I think I was the only seventeen-year-old in the whole of Seattle who had their mom begging them to go out and party instead of staying home to study."

He chuckles, and it helps to break up the tense atmosphere. "Your mom really did that?"

I nod. "All the damn time. She was always worrying I was wasting my youth." I roll my eyes. "One time, she locked me out of the house and threw a bag out the window at me. This was after having called my best friend Hadley to come take me to a party one of our classmates was throwing. She refused to let me back in until I'd gone for a minimum of an hour and kissed at least one boy. And I needed to provide photographic proof."

Laughter rumbles through his chest, emitting as a loud booming sound as he cracks up. "I knew there was a reason I liked your mom. She's awesome."

"She really is."

"So, did you do it?" His smile is back in place, and I'm hypnotized all over again.

"Do what?" I blurt, the picture of confusion as brain fog sweeps through my head.

He rubs his chest, attempting to smother his laughter this time. "Kiss a boy and provide photographic proof?"

"Hell yeah." Now it's my turn to smirk. I can't keep the grin off my face when I say, "I kissed three and had the pics to prove it."

Booming laughter erupts from his mouth, and I love how his whole persona lights up when he laughs.

Garrick truly is a beautiful man, and I must be insane to deny him. But my self-imposed rules are there to keep me on track, and I can't lose sight of that. "There is one really important thing you should know about me," I say.

Dimples wink at me as he holds his smile. "Let me guess. You never back down from a challenge?"

"Never back down and always raise the stakes. If you test me, I'll test you right back." I flick his nose. "And that's the only warning you're getting."

Chapter Nine

Garrick

"We should put a date in the calendar for our camping trip," Hudson says as we talk Wednesday night on the phone. It's the first day of May, and there are officially only four weeks until school is out, so we are making plans for summer break like we did last year.

"I'll need to talk to Dad and Dawn, check my work schedule, and find out if Mom has planned anything on the weekends, so I'll get back to you."

Swiveling on my chair, I drum my fingers on top of the desk in my bedroom. Books are scattered around me, and my laptop is open on my final assignment of the year. It's due next Monday, and I'm trying to finish it before my gigs over the weekend. The guys are coming on Saturday, and it'll probably turn into a session. Our last blowout before we knuckle down to study and take exams.

Glancing around the messy room, I smile as I imagine the horror on Stevie's face if she was here. She'd probably have a coronary. I've never paid much attention to the organized chaos that surrounds me until a gorgeous redhead showed up in my life, turning it upside down. Shit, I really need to clean up my act before I completely blow my chances with her.

"Is Ivy still trying to set you up with Pepper?" Hudson asks, yanking me from my inner monologue. To say my best friend is not a fan of my mother is an understatement. He can't stand her and hates how she tries to manipulate me.

I shrug even though he can't see me. "It's like talking to a brick wall, but Pepper is cool. She gets it, and it could be worse."

A few beats of silence pass before he clears his throat, refocusing the conversation on our trip. "I'm available any time except for the last two weeks in July," my childhood buddy from North Bend confirms. "That's when I'm going on a post-divorce trip with Dad."

"Is he still depressed?"

"His wife was having an affair with her personal trainer, who happens to be fifteen years younger, and she walked out on her marriage for him. I'm pretty sure it's going to take Dad more than a few months to get over it."

"I was too young when my parents divorced to notice whether either of them was depressed, but I'm sure everyone who experiences it goes through it. Your dad will pull through." I know Hudson has been worried about him, and he's still not talking to his mom, so he's focusing all his energies on his dad.

"I'm just glad I got him to agree to a vacation. He's been pulling crazy hours at the hospital, and I know he's throwing himself into work to avoid dealing."

"Can't blame the man."

"I still can't believe my mother has done this."

"Yeah, it sucks. I can relate." When I was fourteen, I discovered my mother's second husband was the man she'd been having an affair with while still married to my dad. I didn't speak to her for over a year that time, only relenting when Dad encouraged me to let go of the past like he had.

"I remember how angry you were, and I feel the same way. I'm so pissed at my mom and worried about Dad."

"This could end up being a good thing for your dad though. Look how happy mine is now. Sometimes, things happen for a reason."

We end the call, promising to catch up before the weekend and agree on a date for our trip. I have only just turned the page on my leadership development book when Dad calls. "Hey, Dad. What's up?"

"Just calling to check in. How's school, and are you all set for your exams?"

I lean back in my chair, stifling a yawn. "It's good. More than good."

"Tell me more." I can hear the smile in his tone.

"I met a girl."

He chuckles, and I know what he's thinking.

"Stevie is special. Things feel different with her. Good different."

"I can't wait to meet her."

"I just have to convince her to go out with me first."

Laughter filters down the line. "She's making you work for it. Good for Stevie. I already like her."

"You're going to love her, and I have faith in my ability to win her over."

"I have no doubt you will. You love big, and you don't give up when you want something. I admire those traits in you."

"Thanks, Dad. How are Dawn and my troublesome brothers?"

"Dawn is good. The twins are still troublesome, but someone's got to keep me on my toes!"

"Tell them I miss them and we'll hang out over the summer."

"They miss you too, and that's why I called. I didn't put you on the roster for the first week. Figure you need some R & R after your exams."

"Thanks, Dad." I have learned about balance from the man who raised me. Dad works hard, but he always makes plenty of time to destress. His family and his health come before the business, and I don't think there are many CEOs who could make the same claim.

"If you like, you can join us in Cyprus. We'll be there for the month of June."

Dawn's great-grandparents were from Cyprus, and when Dad took her to Paphos, in the early years of their marriage, they loved it so much they bought a vacation home there. It helps that it's in a five-star golf resort with an award-winning course and a bunch of amenities on site. You can even see the clubhouse, driving range, and the first tee from the upper level of our house. Dad is like a little kid on Christmas morning whenever we vacation there.

"Thanks for the offer. It's tempting. But I'll pass. I want to hang out at home and do a bit of hiking."

"The place is open all of July, so feel free to avail of it. I can take you off the schedule for a week or ten days."

My heart swells with love for my old man. "I'll keep it in mind." Perhaps Stevie might be up for a Cypriot vacay.

"One last thing, I've split your schedule between the winery and the lumberyard this year. Alternate weeks. You need to gain a firmer understanding of both businesses."

I have worked with Dad at the lumber company every summer since I was fourteen. It's like a home away from home. The winery was a fledgling business back then, only in operation a few years, but its growth has been nothing short of miraculous, and it now accounts for twenty percent of the Allen Company overall annual gross income. So, it makes sense I need to get more involved.

"I look forward to it."

"Good man." Pride suffuses his tone. "You can stay at the cabin there on those weeks if you don't want to drive in and out every day."

I chuckle. "Dad, it's only a forty-minute drive to Woodinville. It's not like I'd be driving to Oregon every day."

"I stay over sometimes, and it's nice not to have a commute occasionally. I'm just saying it's an option."

"I hear you, and I've got to go. This assignment won't write itself."

I'm up early the next morning for a run, but I ditch my usual route through Hendricks Park in favor of a shorter route around the area where we live because I've got an early morning tutorial.

When I round the next bend, a smile spreads across my lips as I spot the distinctive redhead walking a few yards in front of me. Stevie is pounding the sidewalks, moving at an energetic pace, her long legs striding easily as her arms swing at her sides. Wearing a sleeveless running top and tiny little running shorts, she is a vision for my tired eyes. Damn, her ass looks good in those shorts, and my dick wholeheartedly approves.

I jog faster to catch up to her, noticing the ink on her neck for the first time as her ponytail swishes side to side. Slowing my pace, I walk the last few steps toward her so she hears me and isn't surprised. But I didn't realize she's got AirPods in.

Stevie jumps and emits a startled scream when I appear alongside her. Stumbling, she almost trips over her feet, and I hold her elbow to steady her.

Tugging the pods from her ears, she rubs a hand across her chest. It takes considerable effort not to lower my eyes. I've noticed she's got a killer rack, and her chest is heaving from exertion, so not peeking is monumentally difficult. But I don't ever want to objectify her or make her think what we have is purely physical. My attraction to her is way deeper than how she looks or the electrifying chemistry we share.

Everything about Stevie Colson enchants me.

"Fucking hell, Garrick. You almost gave me a coronary." She thumps my upper arm. "You can't go creeping up on people like that."

"I wasn't creeping. I stopped running so you'd hear me walking up. I didn't realize you were listening to music."

"I'm listening to a podcast actually." Her eyes skim over my training top and shorts as we walk at a brisk pace. Her tongue pokes out between her lips, and her eyes widen when she notices my hair is tied back in a man bun. I fucking hate that term. The only time I rock this look is when I'm exercising and I need to keep my hair out of my eyes so I don't trip and crack my skull or drop a weight on my foot.

"Which one?" I inquire.

"It's a true crime podcast. I listen to a bunch of different ones. If I'm not listening to music when I run, I am usually listening to this."

"Sounds interesting."

Her eyes narrow in suspicion. "How are you here? This feels semi-stalkerish."

I laugh. "If I'm going to do something, I go all in. If I was stalking you, you wouldn't know it. I'd be all about the stealth."

She rolls her eyes. "I'm not sure I believe you."

"It's the truth. I usually run at the park, but I need to be on campus early today, so I decided to run locally."

"So, it's just a coincidence we bumped into one another then?" Her expression conveys her continued wariness.

"You call it coincidence. I call it—"

She blocks her ears with her hands and starts singing, "La, la, la."

Warmth spreads across my chest as I chuckle. She's too fucking cute. I wait until she stops singing and lowers her hands. "Fate, but we're not labeling shit, so pretend I said nothing." After our heart-to-heart on Monday night, we agreed to not put any labels on anything and to just hang out.

"You're incorrigible."

"You get what you see." I gesture toward myself, pleased when her eyes drink me in like a cold refreshing drink on a hot Texas day.

"I didn't know you had ink," I say, purposely changing the subject. "What is it?"

She slams to a halt and turns around. "See for yourself." Lifting her ponytail, she bends her head so I can see the small design.

The artwork is sublime, and whoever tattooed it is clearly talented and master level. Encased in a black circle is a triple spiral symbol in a rotational pattern. Gold and silver are entwined with the black to create a stunning visual. "It's beautiful." I sweep my fingers over it. "Is it a Celtic symbol?"

"Yes." Her one-word reply comes out in a throaty whisper.

"What does it mean?" I ask, removing my hand and freeing her ponytail from between her fingers.

She turns to face me. "It's called a triskelion or triskele, and it's a complex ancient Celtic symbol that can mean many things like life, death, rebirth. Father, mother, child. Past, present, future. Power, intellect, love. My dad was of Irish ancestry. That was something he divulged to Mom that night."

I want to ask her about him. To understand why he's not in her life. But it's a bit too heavy for six thirty a.m., so I dampen my natural curiosity.

"I wanted to get a tattoo of something that would represent my father," she continues, "so I had a piece of him with me but also something that had deeper meaning for me. It's an emblem of resilience and determination in the Celtic culture, and I knew this was what I wanted when I found it."

"It's perfect for you, and it's a stunning tattoo. Why hide it where no one can see?" I hadn't seen it at The End Zone or the country club, and she was wearing her hair in a ponytail on both occasions. But her hair is thick, and the ink is small, so it's well hidden from prying eyes. I am guessing that's probably the point.

"This is just for me."

God, this girl. The more I learn about her, the more I like her.

Stevie moves to start walking again, but I place my hand on her lower arm to stop her. Delicious tremors dance across my skin from where we're touching and it's like I've been tasered.

No one has *ever* affected me like this.

"I need to show you something." I whip off my shirt and point at the tattoo over my left pec. Her eyes are out on stalks as she checks out my bare chest. I run, work out at the campus gym, and I'm an outdoors person, hiking and biking when I get the time. I know I'm in good shape, and I like that she seems to approve.

Her hand hovers over my chest, and her eyes lift to mine. "Can I touch it?"

"Of course." My lips tip upward. "I probably should've asked before I touched yours."

"It's fine," she says, and I try not to flinch as her soft fingertips coast over my tattoo. Warmth seeps underneath my skin at her touch, and I try to think of gross things when I feel my dick twitching in my pants. I'm only wearing light running shorts, and they do nothing to disguise a boner.

"This is Celtic too," she surmises, inspecting the design up close. Her face is right by my chest, and heat rolls off her body, washing over me in heady waves.

My dick stirs, and panic sets in. I need to keep things friendly between us. Sporting a semi from the slightest touch is not cool, and I silently plead with my body to get with the program. Thankfully, Stevie is too engrossed in my ink to notice how badly I'm struggling to maintain control.

"What does it mean?" Tilting her chin up, she stares at me with her gorgeous, big emerald-colored eyes, and I could easily drown in the way she's looking at me.

Fuck. I really have it bad.

"It's a Trinity knot," I explain, my voice gruffer than usual. "It's one of the earliest symbols of Christianity. Not that I'm religious. I chose it because it symbolizes father and son."

Her eyes attentively hold mine, and it's hard to breathe, but at least it's distracting the snake in my pants.

"Technically, it symbolizes Father, Son, and the Holy Ghost," I continue. "I'm close to my dad, and I wanted to get something that represented him and our relationship. There's Irish ancestry in my family on my dad's side." Something else we have in common. "So, this seemed appropriate, and it called out to me. If I'm going to permanently mark my skin, I want it to mean something, and I need to be comfortable looking at it for the rest of my life."

"I totally get it. It was the same for me though I have to look in the mirror to see mine."

Does it make me a pussy that I feel like crying when she removes her hand and takes a step back?

"I constantly find myself touching it," she admits. "At times when I need comfort, or often, I'll just absently touch it. It gives me a sense of..."

"Inner peace."

She bobs her head. "Yeah. That's it."

Silently, I pull my top back on, and we set off walking at a more leisurely pace.

"The Trinity knot is in the Book of Kells in Dublin. Someday, I want to go to Ireland and visit it."

Her eyes spark to life and she's almost giddy as she looks up at me. "Oh my god, yes! Me too. The Triskelion is found at the entrance to Newgrange, which is this ancient stone passage tomb, in Ireland. It's on my mug list to go there."

My lips twitch. "Mug list?"

She giggles. "It's my version of a bucket list."

"I like it," I say as we round the next corner, and her apartment building materializes in the near distance. "And you know what this means?" I let a wide grin loose on my face.

She groans, thumping me in the arm. "Do not say fate or kismet or anything else cheesy, or I'm liable to thump you somewhere a lot less pleasant."

Chapter Ten
Stevie

"I don't know how I let you talk me into this," I shout in Ellen's ear as she bounces around on her stool at our table close to the stage. A large speaker is right in front of us. Add that to the noise of an enthusiastic crowd, and it's almost impossible to speak. At least without shouting directly in someone's ear.

"It's one last blowout before our heads are stuffed in books and we're drowning in study and exams. The gang is all here. You couldn't have sat this one out." Nudging me in the side, she grins like a loon as she directs her attention to where Garrick is performing on stage.

It's Saturday night, and he must be exhausted because he also played a set at The End Zone last night. I was on shift. My last one until next semester because I'm finishing up early to concentrate on my upcoming exams, and then I'm heading back to Seattle for summer break.

Last night was even busier than his opening night, if that's possible, and it was pretty hellish. I was dead on my feet by the time I flopped into my bed at three a.m. I barely got a second to myself all night, and the only break I managed to grab was a ten-minute breather with Garrick during his interval.

We've settled into an easy friendship despite the frisson of electricity that threatens to zap us every time we're together. I'm sure it will die down in time. Right now, I like hanging out with him, and I'm not inspecting that further.

Garrick asked me to come out tonight, and I initially said no. This sports bar is on the other side of town and notorious for underage drinking and bar fights. I tend to avoid it. Besides, I had planned on studying until Ellen badgered me into coming out. It was that or listen to her relentless list of reasons why I should go on a repetitive loop all afternoon.

Seemed counterproductive, so here I am.

Squeezed into a tight-fitting black lace crop top that makes the girls appear bigger and ripped black skinny jeans with high heeled boots, I know I look good. My hair hangs down my back in soft waves, and my makeup is on point. I'm in a great mood, on a buzz and enjoying myself, though that could be the three beers I've had or the stream of heated looks leveled my way from the gorgeous man on the stage.

When his eyes aren't closed, lost in a song, Garrick has been keeping me in his sights. He has barely taken his eyes off me, and the girls shoving and pushing one another at the front of the stage, competing for his attention, are starting to notice. The next time he looks over here, I make a slicing motion across my neck in a "cut it out" maneuver.

Sitting up there, with the lights shining down on him, a guitar on his lap, and a mic at his lips, he looks like he was born to be a rocker. The sleeves of the tight black shirt he's wearing are rolled up, showcasing delicious arm porn, and a hint of smooth skin peeks out from the unbuttoned opening at his neck. A few leather bands wrap around one wrist, and a thick silver chain rests low on his collarbone. I'm fascinated by the veins in his arms and the way his muscles flex and roll as he plucks the guitar strings. Watching his long slim fingers expertly work the guitar sends a tremor of heat shooting through my nether regions.

Not that I'm imagining those fingers working their magic on me.

I'm not imagining that at all.

Friends don't have those kinds of thoughts about friends.

And that's all we are.

F.R.I.E.N.D.S.

I hate that I keep needing to remind myself.

Garrick's messy hair hangs around his gorgeous face like tangled dark sheets. Navy denims and scuffed black boots complete the look. It's understated, and I doubt it took him long to get ready, but he's one tempting package, that's for sure.

He belongs up there.

It's a shame to waste such talent, but I would never tell any person how to live their life. Garrick is close to his family, and he's proud of their business. Sparks glow in his eyes when he talks about them, in the same way it does when he talks about music. It's clear he's not being forced into the family business. He has chosen it, and I sense it's a source of pride for him. There is nothing wrong with that. Even if I look up at the god on the stage and wonder how he can turn his back on something that could be a major deal for him.

Garrick announces a break, and Will and Cohen head to the bar to grab more beers before we join him in his dressing room backstage.

Noah barges into the room without knocking. "Oh, shit," he exclaims as the rest of us pile into the small space. "I didn't know you had company." Rubbing the back of his neck, Noah glances at me with a slightly apologetic expression.

I swallow over a lump in my throat at the scene in front of me. A stunning girl, with long sheets of straight golden-blonde hair, is pressed against Garrick, smiling up at him like he put the stars in the sky. She's teeny and petite, and if it wasn't for the skyscraper heels on her feet, she would barely reach his chest. Dainty hands rest on his bare lower arms where they hang at his sides. Her delicate curves are draped in a black bandage-style minidress, and she looks every inch a rock star's princess.

The chicken I ate at dinner threatens to make a reappearance, so I turn around, mumbling about needing the bathroom, and hightail it out of there.

I berate myself the entire way across the crowded bar for acting so recklessly. I should have gritted my teeth, forced a fake smile, and stood my ground. Now, I look like I care more than a friend should.

I am an idiot, I grumble to myself, ducking away from a clearly drunken guy who stumbles toward me and racing into the safety of the bathroom. It's busy, but there is one stall free at the end. Girls are huddled against the sinks on my left, fighting for mirror space, as I pass by them. A girl with a crop top and minuscule matching skirt eyeballs me through the mirror, scowling as she gives me a once-over. "Bitch," she says before I dive into the stall and shut the door.

That is all I need. Garrick's groupies targeting me in a place known for fights.

I knew I should not have come out tonight.

Whatever buzz I was feeling is long gone.

But I won't go home and look like even more of a loser. To save face, I've got to get back out there.

This isn't an issue. It's a good thing if he's planning to hook up with that girl. It helps solidify the friendship line between us.

"Stevie!" Ellen shouts to be heard over the noise in the bathroom. "Where are you, babe?"

"In here," I say as I open the door.

Ellen pushes me inside, and I sit on the closed toilet seat as she locks the door behind her. "Talk to me." Leaning against the wall, she crosses her arms over her chest. "What's going on?"

"I'm an idiot."

"You're not an idiot."

"I am. Ugh." I bury my face in my hands for a few seconds before looking up at her. "I have told Garrick I don't want to date him, that I just want to be friends, so that scene shouldn't have upset me."

"But it did."

I nod. "Like I said." I poke myself in the chest. "Idiot."

"You like him, and that scares you."

"I don't *want* to like him."

She crouches down in front of me. "You can't help how you're feeling. Even if you try to control it, try to push it away, it's not going to change how he makes you feel."

"I have made a fool of myself."

"You haven't, and I don't think it's what it looked like either. It seemed pretty one-sided to me, and Garrick was upset when you took off."

"I don't know why. We're only friends. He's free to date or hook up with who he likes."

"True, but he seems to only have eyes for you." She stands. "Do you want to leave?"

I consider it for a few seconds.

"I'll go with you. We can call an Uber."

I climb to my feet and hug my bestie. "I love you, and I'm not tearing you away from your man. Nor am I leaving." I release her and straighten my spine. "I had a moment, but it's over now. I'm good, and I need to save face. Running away is something a coward would do. We're staying."

"That's my girl."

Garrick is back on stage when we return, and I spend the second part of his set avoiding eye contact with him, unsure what I'll see and unable to face it. My bravery only stretches so far.

"Hey." Cohen moves his stool in closer to mine. "You okay?"

"Fine." My smile is as fake as my lashes.

"You sure? You looked upset back there."

"I wasn't upset," I lie. "I just needed to use the restroom."

"Okay." He sips his beer as he turns to face me. Our knees brush in the exchange, and there is no shiver coasting over my body like when Garrick touches me. "This is why I don't do relationships. Too much shit. Casual hookups are much less hassle." His slightly glassy blue eyes bore into mine before dropping to my chest.

"My face is up here, buddy," I say through gritted teeth.

"And what a pretty face it is." A suggestive smirk materializes on his mouth as his eyes rake over my features.

"Whatever you're doing, don't."

Out of the corner of my eye, I spot Will frowning and Ellen watching with concern.

"I'm just trying to have a conversation." He waves his hands around, almost dropping his bottle of beer. "You know, clear the air and all that jazz."

"There is no air to clear. We're cool."

"I like you," he proclaims, his words slurring a little.

I don't dignify that with a response, staring straight ahead and sipping from my beer in the hope he'll get the hint.

He doesn't.

Leaning in closer, he pins me with a flirtatious look. "I've been known to return for repeats when it's prime pussy. So how about it?"

His leering grin is like acid crawling up my throat. How could I have slept with this jerk? And how are Will, Noah, and Garrick friends with him? They are all decent guys, and Cohen isn't.

"You're disgusting. Get away from me. I wouldn't touch you again if you were the last man standing." I'm tempted to say more, but I don't want to start an argument either.

"Sure, you wouldn't." His sleazy smirk expands. "You were all over me like a rash, bouncing up and down on my dick like you were riding a bucking bronco." One hand drops under the table. "Fuck, I'm hard just thinking about it."

"You make me sick." How can he claim to be Garrick's friend and then proposition me?

"Quit lying. You loved every second of it. I hate sluts who enjoy a good dicking and then pretend like they're above it. News flash, doll.

You were so into it you came all over my dick after creaming all over my fingers and my mouth. It's too late to pretend you're a stuck-up prissy bitch." He presses his revolting lips super close to my ear. "I remember every second of our night together, and you fucking loved it."

"You're a pig, and I'm glad I have no recollection of that night." I don't care if he's one of Garrick's best friends. I won't put up with this misogynistic bullshit. "I was clearly too drunk to make a sound decision, because, trust me, if I'd been sober, I never would have lowered my standards and ended up in bed with you."

The smirk slips off his mouth, replaced by a cold nasty expression. "Bitch, you're lucky I lowered *my* standards and gave you a turn on my cock. If I'd been sober, I wouldn't have given you a second glance." He rakes derisory eyes over my body, and I feel ill that I let this asshole anywhere near me. It's a lesson in never getting so drunk my judgment is impaired. I hate he has carnal knowledge of me, but at least my brain wiped all memory of that night in what was clearly a protective mechanism.

I am disgusted with myself. I wish I had a time machine so I could return to that night and turn the jackass down.

"Hey, Stevie. I'm doing a bar run, and I need an extra pair of hands." Noah plants himself in between me and the douche, so Cohen has no choice but to back off.

"I'll have another beer." Cohen levels a glare at his friend as a muscle pops in his jaw.

"You're cut off." Noah returns the glare and then some.

"Fuck off, Dad." Cohen slides off the stool, swaying a little. "I'll get my own beer." He takes off, and three seconds later, a girl with jet-black hair and bright red lips is tucked under his arm like she'd love to live there.

Poor bitch.

"I'll help." I stand, keeping close to Noah's side as we navigate our way to the bar.

"I know you probably think the worst of Cohen, and I don't

blame you, but he's not a bad guy when he's sober. He's a perfect example of someone who shouldn't drink. He turns into a raging asshole with alcohol in his veins."

"That isn't an excuse, and I honestly don't know how you can defend him or how any of you can be friends with him."

Noah claws a hand through his hair, looking contemplative. "Maybe we make too many allowances for him. Maybe we should hold him more accountable." Hooking his arm around my waist, he steers me away from a group of unruly frat boys. "I hate this place. I'm glad this is Gar's last night playing here." He automatically releases his protective hold on me when we are clear of the idiots.

"I'm not fond of it either," I agree as we stand in line behind two girls waiting to be served at the bar.

"Every time I've been here, there's been a fight," he adds. "Make sure you stick with one of us at all times."

"I can handle myself, but I appreciate the gesture."

After we get our drinks, we return to our table a few minutes after Garrick has finished his set. I'm tempted to slink off home to avoid an awkward conversation, but that would be a shitty thing to do. So, I hang around, biting the edge of one nail as I sink another beer and chat with Noah. Ellen and Will are making out like high schoolers on a first date and Cohen has, thankfully, made himself scarce. If I never had to see that asshole again, I'd die happy.

When Garrick emerges from the side door, he's immediately deluged as a gaggle of girls swarms around him, shoving and pushing one another as they try to get close to him. Noah guffaws and shakes his head. "Can you imagine what it'd be like if he was a bona fide rock star? He'd have to carry a stick to beat them away."

Although music is pumping out of speakers now, it's not as loud as earlier, and it's a bit easier to speak without shouting. My dry throat thanks whomever lowered the volume. "For sure. He's magnetic when he's on a stage. Far too good for small-town bars. It's a shame he won't pursue it."

"Music is a hobby for him. I don't think Gar will ever stop playing, but he truly doesn't want the big stage. We've talked a lot about it, and he's very sure about what he wants from life." Noah clinks his bottle against mine. "Like someone else I hear."

Garrick chooses that moment to appear at our table, saving me from having to respond. "Hey." His greeting is for the table, but his eyes lock instantly on mine.

I hold his stare for a few beats, flashing him a soft smile as I attempt to forget my earlier embarrassment. "You were amazing up there, and the crowd loved you."

"Thanks. That means a lot." A tinge of concern lingers at the back of his eyes as he returns my smile.

He accepts congratulations from the others as he swipes a bottle of water and a beer from the table. Noah switches stools, leaving the one beside me free for his friend. Garrick sits and pulls deeply from the water.

Watching his throat bob as he drinks shouldn't be sexy, but it is.

Nerves fire at me from all angles, so I drink my beer faster than is wise.

Garrick drains his water, picks up the beer, and spins on his stool so our legs are touching. It's like dipping my limbs into flames as scorching heat sears me through my clothes. Lowering his head, he leans in closer, peering deep into my eyes. "Can we talk?"

"I'm sorry for making it awkward earlier," I blurt. "I was just being silly. Ignore me."

He eyeballs me for a few seconds. "You were jealous."

I open my mouth to dispute his allegation, but I can't. "I was," I whisper, rubbing at my temples. "I didn't like it."

He peers deep into my eyes, like he's trying to drill a hole in my skull and extract my innermost thoughts. "Will you be mad if I tell you I do?"

"Depends on why."

"It means you care, and I like that."

Or I'm certifiable. I think it, but I don't say it.

He opens his mouth to add more but clearly thinks better of it, drinking a mouthful of beer instead.

"I have no claim on you, Garrick. I have no reason to be jealous. You are free to date or hook up with whoever you like."

Setting his bottle down, he licks his lips, and it takes serious self-control not to follow the motion with my eyes, but I succeed, and I'll consider that a win.

"I'm not interested in Carrie. She's an ex," he explains. "I dated her for three months at the start of freshman year. We parted ways amicably, and she's been dating a basketball player for the past year. He's here with her tonight, but she stopped by to say hi. We were just catching up. It wasn't anything more, and I'm sorry if it upset you."

Relief washes over me. "You don't need to explain yourself to me, but I'm thankful you did. Sorry for being an idiot."

"No need to apologize. I just want to ensure we're okay."

"All is good." This time, my smile is sincere, and I silently berate myself for being such a dumbass.

His thumb brushes against the corner of my mouth, shooting tingles across my skin. "You had a drop of beer there." Lifting his thumb to his mouth, he sucks on it while piercing me with a heated look. His eyes are a smoldering warm brown tonight, and they are glued to mine like he physically can't pull away. I can't either, and I wonder who I'm kidding with our friendship pact.

He continues sucking his thumb, and it's seriously turning me on.

Holy fuck. I squeeze my thighs so tight I might have given myself muscle strain.

"What was Cohen saying to you?" he asks a minute later, breaking whatever spell we were under. His hand wraps around his beer again, and I loosen my thighs and breathe a little easier.

"Are you sure you want to know?" I don't want to start an argument within his friend group, but he should be aware exactly how much of a dick Cohen is.

"I wouldn't ask if I didn't want to know. I could tell he was making you uncomfortable. If he was rude to you, I'm gonna kick his ass all over the bar."

"I'll tell you, but I think we should park this conversation until tomorrow when we're all sober." I'm not going to lie to Garrick. He deserves to know his friend was propositioning me and how nasty he turned when I didn't entertain it. However, I don't think it's wise to have this conversation when we've all been drinking. I don't want it to turn into World War Three in a place that is notorious for mass-scale fights. The last thing I want is Garrick getting hurt. I'd have less concerns about Cohen. Perhaps a few punches to the head are just what that asshole needs.

Garrick scrutinizes my face. "I know he's a friend, but I won't tolerate him disrespecting you for a single second. If it's something I need to know, I want to know it now."

Before I can reply, I'm almost pushed off my stool as a girl with long, wavy blonde hair shoves past me, flinging her arms around Garrick and smacking a hard kiss against his lips.

Chapter Eleven

Stevie

Garrick grabs the girl by the arms, yanking her lips off his, and forcibly creates distance between their bodies. "What the hell, Simone?"

"Baby, I have missed you so much." She attempts to get close to him again, but Garrick keeps her at arm's length as his eyes meet mine.

I'm two seconds from leaving. I need additional drama like a hole in the head, and I've had a gutful tonight. My temples throb in a combination of stress, frustration, and the aftermath of drinking too many beers.

"Don't leave." Garrick stares at me as he astutely reads my intention. "Let me handle this, and then I'll explain."

"What the fuck, Gar?" Simone spews, glancing over her shoulder at me with a poisonous expression. "Why the hell are you even with her?" An ugly sneer crawls over her face as her gaze skims me from head to toe. She snorts out a laugh, and all it does is highlight her unattractiveness. "She's a fucking *ginger*. You cannot seriously have ghosted me for this ugly bitch?"

Keeping my tone level and my expression neutral, I respond

before Garrick gets a chance. "If you think I give two shits about a single word that comes out of your nasty mouth, think again. Envy really isn't a good look on you."

"Shut your stupid ugly face!"

"That's enough!" Garrick snaps. He stands, looking like he wants to throttle Simone. It won't take any convincing for me to help him. He jerks his head at someone or something over my shoulder before leveling her with a cool glare. "Stevie is a friend, and I'm not letting you insult her out of petty jealousy. As for ghosting you, that's a fucking lie. I told you I didn't want to see you again. I couldn't have made myself any clearer. But let's set the record straight for good."

One of the bouncers appears, and Garrick hands the girl off to him. "One sec, Rex."

The beefy dude nods, struggling to hold on to a wriggling Simone while she screeches her outrage at the top of her lungs.

Garrick folds his arms as he eyeballs her, a frown creasing his brow when he notices the people around us pointing, whispering, and taking out their phones. "You are drawing attention, and unless you want to be broadcast all over social media, I suggest you stop fighting Rex, stay quiet, and listen carefully."

"Gar, come on." Simone sniffles as silent tears stream down her cheeks, and she deflates in the bouncer's grasp. The girl is a hot mess. "I love you!" she wails. "Why are you doing this to me? You can't seriously be picking her over me?"

"I'm not interested in you, Simone," Garrick calmly explains, purposely keeping his voice low. "We went out one time, and I tried to let you down gently. But now I'm spelling it out. I don't want to date you. I don't even want to speak to you. We aren't compatible, and we have no future. You need to quit messaging me, quit stalking me on campus, and quit hanging around me at gigs. This is your final warning. Next time, I'll ask the management to permanently ban you. For now, you can cool your heels outside." Garrick nods at the bouncer, and he starts ushering the blonde away.

"Fuck you, Gar! No one rejects me for a ginger!" She's still screaming abuse when the bouncer throws her over his shoulder and pushes his way through the crowd.

"Never a dull moment," Will deadpans.

I had almost forgotten we had an audience.

"Your crazy radar must have been on the blink when you took that raving lunatic out," Noah adds.

"You're telling me." Garrick sighs, looking contrite as he slides back on his stool. "I'm sorry about that, Stevie. She was way out of line."

"Does drama follow you everywhere?" I work hard to lighten my mood when the truth is I'm done.

"Not usually. I swear."

I shrug, finishing the last of my beer. "None of my business anyway."

Garrick ensnares my gaze as he explains. "I went out with her once, a few weeks ago, before I met you. I knew instantly it was a major mistake. She's in one of my study groups, and she seemed normal. But she freaked me out, talking about weddings and babies and how she's had the biggest crush on me since last year and she knew if she was patient I would finally notice her."

"She's a legit creeper," Will supplies as Ellen snuggles into his side while shooting concerned looks in my direction.

"I was polite but firm when I told her I didn't want to date her," Garrick continues. "I don't lead girls on. But she's not backing down. She seems to think it's some kind of challenge."

"You should report her for harassment to the university," Noah says. "That should get her off your back for good."

"I didn't want to get her into trouble with UO, but it looks like she's leaving me with no choice."

"I would definitely report that crazy bitch before she turns nasty on you or whomever you date next," I say.

"The only woman I'm interested in dating is you," Garrick replies, breaking our self-imposed rules already.

"I'm not an option!" I don't mean to snap, but my patience reservoir is running on empty now. "And redheads are clearly not your type."

"That's not—"

I cut across Garrick before he can finish his sentence. "You should date Carrie again," I suggest, finishing my drink and standing. "She might have a boyfriend, but she's obviously still hooked on you." Grabbing my bag, I clutch it to my chest as I cast a glance at Ellen. "I'm so over this night," I say. "Are you coming home or staying at Will's?"

"We'll come with you," Will says, helping Ellen to her feet.

"Stevie, please. Don't go. Let's talk and I'll make sure you get home safely." Garrick reaches for me, but I step back, avoiding his hand.

"I'm capable of making my own way home, and you should stay. Find some other blonde to date, and leave me out of your woman drama."

I wait to emerge from my bedroom the following morning until after I hear Will leaving. I slept fitfully, and I'm grumpy. A dull ache slices across my brow, and my tongue is partially glued to the roof of my furry mouth. Ugh. I am *never* drinking again.

"Hey." Ellen thrusts a paper cup at me when I emerge in the kitchen. "I was about to knock on your door and see if you were alive. Garrick just picked up Will. They're planning to work through their hangovers at the gym. He stopped off at Bumble Bees on the way and grabbed us all coffee. There are pastries too," she adds, pointing at the box on the counter.

"He makes it so hard to stick to my resolve," I murmur while popping the lid on my coffee and inhaling the delicious aroma.

"He's a good guy." Ellen rests her elbows on the counter as I hop up onto a stool. "But after all that drama last night, maybe you're right to relegate him to the friend zone."

"Yeah, I have zero desire to become a target for his crazed fans and lovesick exes." I lick the froth off the top of my cinnamon caramel cappuccino as I remove a poppyseed pastry from the box, realizing Ellen must've given Garrick a list of my Bumble Bees favorites.

"However." Ellen draws out the word as she watches me rip a piece of pastry and pop it in my mouth. "What happened last night wasn't really his fault."

"Except for questionable judgment in relation to some of the girls he has dated," I supply in between mouthfuls of the luscious pastry.

"True, but he dumped the crazy after one date, and it's not on him if his ex has lingering feelings. You probably didn't notice before you hightailed it, but he wasn't encouraging her. Carrie was the one all over him."

"You sound like you're back on Team Garrick."

She jabs her finger in my direction before swiping a vanilla Danish from the box. "Girl, I'm always Team Stevie. Just trying to put things into perspective."

I'm still mulling over her words later as I set out on foot to meet Garrick at the coffee shop closest to the campus gym. He'd texted me while I was nursing my hangover and attempting to study, asking if we could talk. I figure some fresh air would do me no harm, and I don't like how I left things last night with him. I was probably a little harsh, and he's been nothing but nice to me all week. I at least owe him an opportunity to defend himself.

Garrick is sitting in the corner by the wall when I arrive, his eyes peeled on the door. His legendary smile is toned down today but still welcoming. I hurry across the semi-busy room toward him. He stands and pulls out a chair for me. "Hey, thanks for coming."

"I'm glad you reached out to me," I say, sitting down as he reclaims the seat across the table.

A waitress arrives at our table. She refills Garrick's coffee as she asks me what I'd like. "I hear you're partial to caramel macchiatos, and we do a great one," the older woman says as she shares a conspiratorial look with Garrick.

"Don't tempt me," I groan. "This guy already hand-delivered my favorite cappuccino and pastry earlier. My blood sugars will be through the roof if I ingest any more sweet stuff."

She pats Garrick on the shoulder. "This one's a keeper."

Yeah, I'm not touching that.

I smile up at her. "I'll have an unsweetened chai latte if you have it."

"Coming right up, sweet cheeks."

"Another fan?" I ask when she's out of earshot, quirking a brow.

Scrubbing his hands down his face, he sighs heavily. "I'm not making a great impression, am I?"

"Women seem to gravitate to you like moths to a flame, and that's really not my scene."

He leans forward, straining toward me across the table. "I swear I'm not into the whole rock star groupie thing. I'm only up there to play my guitar and sing my favorite songs. I'm not interested in any of the other bullshit."

"I believe you, but I loathe drama and tend to run a mile from it. You seem to attract it wherever you go."

"I don't purposely invite it."

"I know it comes with the territory," I admit, sweeping my hair over my shoulders. "You don't have a choice, but I do."

"I'm really sorry, Stevie. You got caught in the crossfire last night, and it wasn't fair."

"It wasn't, and if that's the way it always is, I won't ever be hanging out with you at gigs. I won't be a target."

"I won't let it happen again, and though it'll be difficult, I'll stop watching you when I'm on stage."

"Yeah, that doesn't help. I was on the receiving end of some hostile looks in the bathroom from girls who noticed your attention was on me."

"Can I be honest with you?" he asks as the bubbly waitress returns with my latte.

I wait for her retreat before answering. "I always want honesty—no matter how much it might hurt."

"I'm trying to respect your wishes and be your friend even though we both know I want more. But you're sending out mixed signals. Last night, you were pissed, and it's not really what I'd expect from someone who says she's only my friend."

"I'm a little conflicted, but you're right. It's not fair to give you mental whiplash. It won't happen again, I promise."

He looks a little crestfallen as he nods, and I feel like a bit of a bitch. "Can I ask *you* something?" I inquire as I taste my drink.

"I always want honesty too, and you can ask me anything at any time."

"Why are you so into relationships? Most guys I meet are more interested in working their way through the entire female student body than dating and getting attached to any girl. You and Will aren't like that, and I'm curious." I know not all college students are interested in partying and playing the field, but based on my limited experience of college life, Will and Garrick are more the anomaly than the norm.

Leaning back in his chair, he shrugs. "I've never given it much thought. I'm just not into the whole hookup scene. Girls throwing themselves at me, purely for bragging rights, breaks me out in a cold sweat. I was too young to remember much about my parents' relationship, but I've grown up watching my dad with my stepmom, and I think deep down I've always tried to replicate what they have. They're happy. Unlike my mom who recycles boytoys and husbands on a regular basis. That's not what I want for my life. I want intimacy and someone I can connect to on multiple levels. I want something real, not temporary gratification."

"Wow. That's hardcore for someone so young."

He shrugs again, and his mouth kicks up at the corners. "I told you I know what I want, and I always go after it." His goldish-brown eyes convey everything he's not saying as he stares at me with steely determination before dropping his gaze briefly to my mouth.

"We've both been influenced by our parents' experiences." I swirl a spoon in my latte as I contemplate it. "I'm determined to not be like my mom when it comes to relationships, and you want a relationship like the one your dad has with your stepmom. Those goals are not in sync."

"I don't see it like that at all." He rests his hands on top of the table as he holds my gaze. His long, slender fingers gently tap out a silent beat. His grin returns full force along with those damned dimples. I swear he knows what they do to me, and he does it on purpose to fuck with my head. "If you really think about it, it all boils down to the same thing. We both want something meaningful and long-lasting."

"That doesn't mean it wouldn't be distracting."

"The right guy won't be a distraction. He'll be a support. This might sound a little cheesy," he adds, shooting me a goofy grin. "But he'll want you to soar to dizzy heights and do what he can to help you reach them."

Pushing my empty mug to one side, I concede he's good at this. Perhaps he should be a lawyer. He almost has me believing it. I wet my lips and just put it out there. "And you think that's you?"

He doesn't hesitate to reply, exuding the confidence I now associate with him. "I think that guy could be me, yeah." Stretching across the table, he removes a stray strand of red hair from my face, tucking it tenderly behind my ear. Sincerity oozes from his pores when he says, "We're a lot more compatible than incompatible. You just need to open yourself up to the possibility we could be so damn good together."

Chapter Twelve
Garrick

A bell chimes as I step through the door of the floral shop in Eugene. Butterfly Flowers is one of several florists in the area, but the only one the woman I seek works at. Stevie is behind the counter, chatting with an older coworker as they wrap up an order. Her head lifts at the sound of approaching footfalls, an automatic smile already painted on her lips. It could be my imagination, but I swear her eyes light up and her grin expands when she sees it's me.

"Garrick, hey. What are you doing here?"

Her coworker's eyes are out on stalks as she blatantly checks me out. The blue-haired woman wears quirky glasses with purple frames, and a flirtatious smile toys on her thin lips. Both women are wearing branded T-shirts and jeans behind their aprons.

"I'm in the market for flowers, and I've heard there's a discount for friends of the staff," I joke, not giving a flying fuck about any discount. I just needed to see Stevie. Now classes are out, and we have some time off before exams start, I've had no excuse to see her this week. Though it's only Wednesday and we had coffee on Sunday, I'm suffering huge withdrawal symptoms.

I have it bad.

"You have been misinformed." Stevie's smile looks forced as she straightens her spine.

"Oh, I don't know about that." Her colleague licks her lips as she continues giving me a thorough once-over. "I'm thinking a hottie discount is in order."

"A *hottie* discount?!" Stevie splutters, her eyes popping wide as she stares at the pint-sized woman like she's sprouted an extra head. "Please tell me my ears are deceiving me and you did *not* just say that." Pink colors her cheeks.

"Said it. Meant it." The blue-haired pixie nudges Stevie with her hip, pushing her to the right a little, and then she grabs my hand and pulls it toward her. "Such manly hands. Firm and strong and powerful."

A chuckle filters from my mouth.

Her fingers explore the back of my hand before moving to my palm. The fine lines at the sides of her eyes crinkle as she grins at me. "These hands are solid and steady, and they create magic. I bet you know how to put them to good use too. Am I right, or am I right?"

"Oh my god, Sharon." Stevie slaps a hand to her brow. "You are legit insane. I feel like I should call Tim this minute and tell him he needs to take you in for a psych eval."

Ignoring Stevie, she clings to my hand and pins me with a naughty look. "If this idiot won't go out with you, I will."

Stevie rolls her eyes. "You're married."

"Tim will understand," she fires back, showing no signs of letting my hand go.

"You're acting like a creepy stalker. Let his hand go."

Amusement bubbles in my chest as I watch them face off. This is priceless, and I love it. I also love that she told Sharon about me. It's got to be a good sign she is talking about me, right?

"I'll release his hand when you agree to a date with him." Tearing her gaze from mine, Sharon flashes Stevie a mischievous smile.

"There is only one legit insane person around here, and it's not me! If anyone's getting committed, it's you!"

"I like you, Sharon. You talk a lot of sense."

"That's what they all say. Among other things." She winks at me, and I roar laughing.

"I deserve a bonus for all this additional stress. Employers are not supposed to harass their staff," Stevie says, fighting a smile as she finishes taping the bouquet they were working on when I walked in and interrupted them mid-flow.

"Pfft." Sharon lets my hand go, albeit reluctantly. "It's not harassment. It's life advice, missy." She prods Stevie in the chest. "Advice you'd do well to listen to before this fine specimen of a man is snapped up by some other lucky woman."

"You're incorrigible, and quit it. You'll give Garrick a big head."

I kid you not, but Sharon, matriarch and employer, leans across the counter and ogles my crotch. "No sign of any big head yet, but the evening is young."

"Oh my fucking god." Stevie buries her head in her hands but not before I see the laugh dying to break free. "I just can't with you." Her face is flushed when she lowers her hands and pins her boss with a stern look. "Go out back and work on the accounts before I permanently quit."

"You wouldn't dare." Sharon squeezes her arm. "Give the poor guy a break, and go on a date with him. If I was younger and Tim-free, I'd be scaling that mountain and conquering the peak in record time." Tossing one last flirty wink over her shoulder as she walks off, she sashays her curvy hips and wiggles her ass before disappearing into the room at the back.

I bend over, clutching my stomach, as I convulse in fits of laughter. Stevie joins me, and we're both cracking up and wiping the dampness from our eyes. "Damn, she's a hoot. I only came in to buy flowers!"

"Sharon is insane in the best possible way," Stevie says when she's composed herself. "There is never a dull moment around here."

"I get that. She's a cool boss."

"She is, and she's been very flexible with my hours, which I appreciate. Today's my last shift till school is back, and I'm going to miss her." Stevie leans in closer, pressing her delectable mouth to my ear. "Don't ever admit I said that though. I like to keep her on her toes."

"Your secret is safe with me."

We trade a mutual grin, and there's a definite shift in the air the longer we stare at one another. "You look very pretty with your hair like that," I say, shoving my hands in the pockets of my jeans before I do something reckless like grab her to me and plant one on her. Her hair is wrangled in a messy bun on top of her head, and wispy strands frame her stunning face, only serving to showcase her exquisite features. She has barely a lick of makeup on, and she's flawless.

"I'm sure I look a hot mess, and you're clearly biased, but thank you." Propping one hip against the counter, she clears her throat. "Did you actually come to buy flowers, or was there another reason you dropped by?"

"I came to buy flowers."

She straightens up, losing the easy demeanor, and I can guess why.

"For my mother and my stepmom," I add.

"Oh." Her shoulders relax, and I do too.

"Is there a special occasion?"

"Nope." I shrug. "I just felt like sending them flowers. I tend to do it a couple times a year, just to remind them how much they mean to me." I might have ulterior motives this time, but it's no lie. My father buys Dawn lilies and chocolates every Friday on his way home from work. They aren't expensive or extravagant, by any means, but the way Dawn's face lights up you'd think they were. Even after all these years, and copious bouquets and chocolates, she still cherishes the gesture.

Stevie stares at me as if she's seen a ghost. Shaking herself out of it, she drags her lower lip between her teeth before releasing it. "You are so bad for my heart, Garrick," she whispers, like the words might hurt her. "Stop being so sweet."

"I only ever want to be good for you," I admit, hoping she hears the sincerity in my tone. "Now, what would you recommend?" I inquire, changing the trajectory of the conversation on purpose.

I leave the store twenty minutes later with a gorgeous, big, colorful bouquet. I placed a delivery order for Dawn's flowers but refused delivery for the second bunch, making up an excuse Stevie seemed to buy. Placing the bouquet down carefully on the back seat of my SUV, I drive around town, listening to music and fastidiously watching the clock until I know Stevie's shift ends. Then I circle back to the shop, park at the curb, and wait for the enchantress to show her beautiful face.

When she walks outside, zipping up her raincoat, her feet falter as she spots me exiting my car. "Need a ride?" I ask, already knowing she does. Light rain falls as I stride toward her. Judging by the stormy gray clouds in the sky, it won't be long before it turns heavy. "I know your car is in for service, and I thought I could drop you home."

Tipping her head back, she stares at the darkening sky and the tinkling rain tumbling from above. I expect her to fight me, and I'm pleasantly surprised when she doesn't. "Thanks, Garrick. A ride home would be great."

I open the passenger door for her, closing it softly after she climbs inside. Running around the hood, I jump behind the wheel just before the rain turns heavy and a deluge falls from the heavens.

"Perfect timing." Stevie rubs her hands together as I crank up the heating.

"I've been known to have my moments." A trademark grin crosses over my face as I power up the engine.

"I love your car. Nana has an older Range Rover, and I drive it sometimes. They're solid."

"They are," I say as I maneuver out onto the road. "Dad got me this last year when I moved to UO. I protested, because these babies aren't cheap, but he insisted. He knew I'd be driving back and forth a lot, and he wanted me to be safe."

"Your dad sounds awesome."

"My dad is as awesome as your mom." Delicate floral notes stretch across the console, tickling my senses, and I can't deny how much I love Stevie sitting in my car beside me. She looks comfortable and like she belongs there. I intend to ensure she knows it one day too.

Taking the next turn, I risk posing the question lingering on my tongue. "Are you hungry? Want to grab something to eat?"

She shakes her head just as her tummy emits a loud rumble.

The grin that skates across my mouth is so wide it threatens to rip my face apart. "I think your body has spoken," I say, taking the next right and heading in the direction of the taco place that is popular with UO students. "How about some tacos? I don't know about you, but I could murder a few."

She runs her hands through her hair, glancing out the window, before she concedes. "Tacos sound good. I had a small salad at lunch, and I'm starving."

Ten minutes later, we are huddled at a table in the back near the window. It's not too busy today because classes are finished and most students are studying at home or the library, trying to cram last-minute knowledge into overtired brains.

"Was this your plan all along?" Stevie asks, eyeing me over the rim of her glass after we've placed our order.

"I'm sure I don't know what you mean." My lips purse as I smother a grin.

"Are you trying to tell me this wasn't intentional?" Cocking her head to one side, she peers deep into my eyes.

I could stare at her beautiful face all day and all night and never grow tired of it.

"Not really." I take a sip of my soda before continuing. "I'll admit I came to the store because I wanted to see you, and I knew you didn't have your car today, so I was hoping to drive you home, but I didn't plan this. Would have if I thought you'd go for it."

"Guess you got your date after all."

Leaning across the table toward her, I ensure her eyes are locked on mine when I speak. "If this was a date, you'd know it and we sure as fuck would not be here."

"Where would we be?" she blurts, looking like she regrets the words the instant they leave her mouth.

"At that nice steakhouse or the new sushi place. If we were in Seattle, I'd take you to the winery."

"What's wrong with here?" Her gaze trips around the long narrow room.

"Nothing. I love this place, and the tacos are to die for, but it's only a diner. If I'm lucky enough to score a date with you, I'll be taking you to a nicer place. You deserve to be treated like a queen."

"Fuck me," she moans before resting her brow on the table.

With pleasure. The snake in my pants reacts immediately to her words, and I silently talk the beast down. I would give my left nut to fuck Stevie but only when it means something to both of us. I have zero desire to be friends with benefits or a one-night stand. With someone as special as Stevie, I want both of us to be all in.

The waitress arrives with our food, and Stevie sits back up, eyeing me curiously. I wait her out as the server sets plates in front of us, taking long pulls of my soda as I silently plead with the universe to help me out.

I have just picked up my silverware when she speaks. Warmth floods her tone and fills her eyes as she holds my gaze. "You make me want to break all my own rules, Garrick."

"You say that like it's a bad thing."

"It's a dangerous thing."

Reaching across the table, I tentatively place my hand on top of hers. "It doesn't have to be. It could be the greatest thing of all."

Chapter Thirteen

Garrick

Pulling up outside the apartment building Stevie lives at, I pray she invites me in because I'm not ready to say goodbye to her yet.

I'm aware I'm acting like a lovesick teen, but I don't care—guilty as charged.

I am certifiably crazy about this girl, and I don't care who knows it.

The conversation flowed easily at the taco place, and it's like I've always known her. It just seems so natural with us, and it's rare to find that kind of connection. I get the sense Stevie is feeling this too, and though she's still fighting the attraction, there are holes in her protective shield. I plan to poke them until they grow bigger and eventually become nonexistent.

"Thank you for the ride and dinner."

"You can't thank me for dinner." I wanted to get the check, but she insisted on paying half. I didn't argue even if the old-world manners instilled deep inside me protested. Stevie likes her independence, and I like that about her. I'm not about to be *that guy*. The one who claims hurt male pride because his date insists on paying her share of the meal.

Stevie lifts her head with confidence. "Of course, I can. It's not about who paid. Thank you for taking me there."

"You're welcome."

"And Sharon said to say thanks for the business. She was thrilled."

A smirk dances on my lips. "I appreciated the hottie discount." I was given a fifteen-percent markdown, which was kind of Sharon.

Stevie rolls her eyes. "You're never going to let that one go."

"Damn straight."

"I'm considering proposing it as an official discount." A grin runs across her face. "Some permanent eye candy at the store would be nice."

I fake a scowl as I unbuckle my seat belt. "Sharon will never go for it. It was a onetime thing because she likes me."

"Doesn't mean I can't try."

"If you need permanent eye candy, I can make myself available." I lean back in my seat and shoot her a flirty smile.

"Nice try, Casanova, but no. I'd never get any work done if you were always around."

I'm taking that as a win. Before I can celebrate, her hand curls around the door handle as she prepares to make her escape, and instant panic sets in. "Do you want to hang out some more?" I blurt, hoping I don't sound as desperate as I feel.

This girl has me acting like an inexperienced first-timer with zero game.

"Sorry, no can do. I need to glue my eyeballs to my retail floristry operations management book, or I won't be prepared for that exam. What about a rain check Saturday night? I think Will and Ellen are planning takeout and a movie at our place. We could gate-crash."

"I'm down with that plan."

"Great." Her enthusiastic smile does weird things to my insides.

"Thanks again, Garrick. I'll catch you later." She slides out of the car before I can get her door.

Hopping out my side, I open the back door and grab the bouquet. Stevie is halfway to the building when I call out after her, running to catch up. Turning around, she frowns, looking confused as I thrust the flowers at her. "These are for you."

"What?" she splutters, looking between me and the bouquet with a crease between her brows. "I thought these were for your mom?"

"I might have told a little white lie. I hope you can forgive me." I don't bother telling her my mother would scoff if I showed up with anything that wasn't the most expensive roses, gardenias, or orchids. There is nothing wrong with this bouquet. It's exquisite, and Stevie is talented, but Mom is as snobbish with flowers as she is with most other things in her life.

Dawn will love her delivery like I know she'll love Stevie when she meets her.

"These are for *me*?" Stevie stares at them in a bit of a daze, like she can't believe they're for her.

"Hasn't anyone ever bought you flowers?"

"I'm surrounded by flowers, thanks to my nana," she admits, her fingers tracing reverently over the bouquet that is still in my hand. "But no one has ever bought me flowers before."

"I'm glad to be the first," I truthfully say, gently pushing them at her. I hope it's the start of many firsts we have together. Stevie doesn't know what it's like to be in a committed relationship, and I look forward to educating her. To spoiling her as she deserves.

Cradling the flowers against her chest, she buries her nose in the scented petals and inhales deeply. "You're chipping away at my resolve," she softly admits, looking up at me with a tender sheen in her eyes.

"There is no ulterior motive." My fingers wind through the wispy strands of hair cupping her face. "I wanted to buy you flowers, so I did. I expect nothing in return."

"Thank you so much, Garrick. I love them, and it was really thoughtful."

"You're welcome." Though I hate to walk away, I want to prove to her I won't be a distraction from her life goals. "Good luck with your studying." I press a light kiss to her cheek, relishing the feel of her soft, satiny skin against my lips. "I'll see you on Saturday."

The air in the kitchen plummets a couple of degrees the instant Cohen steps foot inside it on Saturday morning. Will and I have been giving him the cold shoulder since Stevie informed me of the vile things he said to her last Saturday night. Noah is tiptoeing around all of us, hating the tension and trying not to pick sides. He was angry when he heard the truth, but he's trying to play mediator in the hope we can reconcile.

I'm not sure that's possible.

Since all this has gone down, I am reconsidering everything I thought I knew about my friend. Blaming alcohol is no excuse, and I realize we have been making excuses for Cohen from the moment we met him. His behavior is not acceptable, and it's time we stopped sweeping it under the rug. Stopped enabling him.

"How long do you plan to keep this up?" he asks, sounding bored as he pours coffee into a mug while eyeballing me.

"This isn't a game, Cohen."

"I'm well aware." He points at the colorful bruising surrounding his left eye.

"You deserved that," I calmly reply, drinking my coffee and schooling my features into a neutral line.

"You deserved more than a black eye," Will says, entering the kitchen with a yawn.

"You're both overreacting, and you know it. We always said we'd never let any chick come between us, yet here we are." Folding his arms, he slouches against the counter and drills me with a sharp look.

I finish my coffee and stand. "We are here because you are way out of line. With Stevie and with other women. You have no respect, and we've been letting you get away with it for far too long. I can't speak for the others, but I won't stand by and tolerate it anymore."

"I'm with Garrick." Will edges around the island unit and heads for the refrigerator.

"Of course, you are. As long as you're sticking it to Stevie's friend, at least."

"Watch your fucking mouth." Will glares at him. "This is the exact kind of shit we're talking about."

"You're such hypocrites!" His voice elevates a few notches. "All of a sudden, I'm no longer good enough for the mighty Garrick Allen and his sidekick?" He scoffs at us, letting out a laugh, as he pushes off the counter. "At least have the balls to admit this is nothing to do with how I treat women and everything to do with the fact *I* nailed the girl who keeps rejecting *you*."

His nasty smirk and crude words rub me the wrong way and I clench my hands into fists at my side. "Ever had a light bulb moment, Cohen? 'Cause I had a big fucking bright one when you hit on the girl I like after you promised me you wouldn't. The way you spoke to Stevie was disgusting, and while this *is* about her for me, it's about way more. You treat women like shit, and we were wrong to laugh it off. I'm ashamed I called you my friend when you were behaving like the biggest fucking asshole."

"Tell me what you really think," Cohen snarls, and the mean contempt on his face makes me question how I ever liked the guy. I fucking hate he had sex with Stevie because no guy has ever been more undeserving of a woman.

"Guys, please." Noah stalks into the kitchen with a towel wrapped around his waist and water dripping down his chest. "Do we have to do this again?"

"No, we don't." Snatching my keys and wallet from the table, I bend down and grab my bag from the floor. "I'll be making myself scarce for the day and for the rest of the time we have left," I add making a beeline for the front door.

I'm still all riled up hours later as I stand outside the door to Ellen and Stevie's apartment, waiting to be let in.

When the door swings open, Stevie stands before me like a fiery goddess in a simple black dress with short sleeves and a knee-length hemline. It molds to her tempting rack, clings to her trim waist, and curves around her slim hips. Her beautiful hair hangs in glossy soft waves over her shoulders and down her back, and she has her usual light makeup on. She steals the breath from my lungs as she smiles at me, her stunning green eyes vibrant and full of life as she drinks me in. I'm just wearing jeans and Nikes with a plain white tee under my open black shirt, but her appreciation is obvious, and it helps to dispel the lingering threads of my bad mood.

"Hey, you," she says, in a soft throaty voice that sends a shot of lust straight to my dick.

I have a feeling tonight is gonna be an extreme test of willpower, and I already gave my libido a stern talking to on the walk over here.

"Hey, yourself," I say, finally finding my voice. I dart in and kiss her cheek. "You look beautiful."

A flattering blush blooms across her skin, and it's clear Stevie isn't accustomed to praise from the opposite sex. Another thing I intend to remedy. "Thank you. You look pretty good yourself."

I hand her the bag I'm carrying. "I brought some drinks and snacks."

"Great, thanks." Taking the bag, she steps aside. "Where are my manners? Come in."

"I bumped into Will and Ellen at the library earlier," I say as we walk into the kitchen. "Are they here yet?"

Stevie sets the bag down on the counter and shakes her head. "There's been a change of plan. They went out to eat, and I have a baked ziti in the oven for us. I hope you like it?" She removes the bottle of white wine from the bag along with the goodies for the movie.

"Love it," I reply, sliding onto a stool. "Dawn makes it every week, and it's my brothers' favorite pasta dish."

"That's funny," she says, going to the refrigerator. She places the wine I brought on the interior wine shelf and removes a couple of beers. "I used to make it weekly for my mom and my nana." She hands me a cold beer, and our fingers brush in the exchange, sending a tingling sensation shooting over my hand and up my arm.

"Thanks." I lift the bottle to my lips as she opens the oven door to check on dinner. Tempting aromas hit the back of my nose, and my stomach rumbles appreciatively. "It smells incredible."

"It should be ready shortly," she says, closing the oven door and walking to the counter where a chopping board and ingredients are laid out. "I'm just making a salad and some garlic bread to go with it. Will that be all right?"

"Anything you cook will be amazing. This is a first for me," I admit with a wink.

Her brows climb to her hairline. "Are you saying none of your girlfriends cooked you a meal?"

"Nope, not a single one. The only woman who has ever cooked for me is Dawn."

"Wow."

"Most girls I have dated were clueless in the kitchen."

"My mom is a disaster." Stevie pops the top of her beer, taking sips as she finishes the salad. "She only has to glance at the kitchen, and the fire alarm goes off." Her light laughter is music to my ears, and I'm obsessed with watching her hands as she prepares the rest of our meal.

"Is that how you learned to cook?"

"My nana taught me. She tried to teach Mom when she was a little girl, but that was an utter failure. It was either I learned or we starved." She laughs again and my cock jumps behind my zipper.

"You sound super close to your nana." She has mentioned her before, and it's clear to see the admiration on her face and hear it in her tone.

"I am." Sliding the salad in the fridge, she removes a bowl with butter. "My nana was as much my mom as my mom growing up. It's why I never felt like I missed out with my dad." She continues talking as she moves around the kitchen. "Mom and Nana ensured they were there for me for everything. Nana had breast cancer a few years ago, and it was so scary. The thought of ever losing her terrifies me."

"Is she okay now?" I ask.

She bobs her head as she slices bread. "Thankfully, yes. She's in remission, and her health is good."

We continue chatting about everything and anything as she places the garlic bread in the oven and sets the small table in the corner. We quickly finish our beers, and she grabs the now chilled wine from the fridge, inspecting the label.

"It's one of our best bottles," I explain. "Ellen said you preferred white to red and that pinot gris or sauvignon blanc were your favorites."

"They are, but I tend to drink New Zealand wines if I want a sauvignon." She walks toward a cupboard and removes two wine-glasses. "I thought most Seattle wineries produced chardonnay or riesling?"

"They account for eighty percent of white wine production in Washington, but other variations are becoming popular. We produce a wide variety, but Dad is focusing heavily on new-world wines because he believes they will become just as popular. Our sauvignon is more like a full-bodied French wine than a crisp Marlborough, but I think you'll like it."

"It smells delicious," she says while pouring wine into both our glasses. "And you clearly know your stuff."

"Thanks," I say, accepting the glass. "I wish I did, but the truth is, I know very little about the winery side of the business. Something I hope to rectify this summer."

"You're going to be in Seattle over summer break?"

I nod, savoring the citrusy apple-scented flavor of the cold white wine as it fills my mouth and glides down my throat. "I have worked at the lumberyard every summer for years. This year, I'll be alternating my weeks between the yard and the winery. What about you? What are your plans?"

"I'm heading back to Ravenna. I help Nana out with the business every summer."

"We have that in common too." I can't help mentioning it as I like to reinforce our similarities in the hope it'll shatter her belief our interests aren't aligned.

"I guess we do," she says with a shrug, and I wonder if I might possibly be getting through to her.

Dinner is sumptuous, and I have second helpings and clear my plate. After, we top off our wine and head into the living room to watch a movie. There is still no sign of Ellen and Will.

Not that I'm complaining.

I'm enjoying having Stevie all to myself.

We have the lights turned off so the only illumination in the room is from the TV screen. I couldn't tell you what movie we agreed on or what we're watching because I'm highly attuned to the woman sitting close to my side, and I can't focus on anything but her.

Tension slithers into the air, but it's the good kind. Sparks crackle around us, and I'm conscious of every little puff of air that slips out of her mouth and how her tongue darts out, tracing a line back and forth across her full lips. I track the way her chest heaves up and down, how her fingers dig into the side of her thigh, and every movement of her long shapely legs as she crosses and uncrosses them.

I'm wound tight, afraid to move a muscle in case I lose hold of my tenuous control, grab the back of her neck, and pull her mouth to mine like I'm dying to do. When I can't take it any longer, I turn my head and blatantly stare at her as I inch a little closer on the couch. Our thighs brush, and she sucks in a subtle gasp, letting me know I'm not in this alone.

Warmth seeps through my clothes and skin, embedding deep. My cock stirs, eager for action, and there is no talking myself down this time. Deliberately, I hook my pinky in hers, willing her to turn and meet my obsessive gaze.

I know she knows I'm looking at her.

Her pulse jumps in her neck, and I can almost hear her heart thumping wildly against her rib cage. Blood rushes all over my body, and my heart pounds in my chest as butterflies swoop into my stomach, turning somersaults and cartwheels as I unwind her tense fingers and link them with mine.

Slowly, she turns toward me, and time seems to stand still. I stop breathing. My pulse thrums in my ears, and my heart beats out of control as our gazes lock and hold tight. Liquid heat radiates from her eyes as they drift to my mouth. I wet my lips and stare at her mouth, dying to taste her and understanding there will be no going back if I do. My cock is rock hard, straining against my jeans and leaking precum behind my boxers.

I am painfully attracted to Stevie, and not kissing her, not touching her, is the worst form of torture.

But I gave her my word, and I'm already testing it.

I can't be the one to push us over the edge.

She has to give me a sign or meet me halfway.

We continue staring at one another as the movie plays in the background and electricity hums in the air. She gulps, twisting her body ever so slightly as our eyes connect again. My heart is beating so fast I fear it'll beat right out of my chest. Her lips part, her chest rises, and I spot the moment she makes her decision.

Stevie grabs my shirt, ready to pull me toward her, when the front door swings open, slamming noisily against the wall as Will and Ellen crash into the apartment and ruin the moment.

Chapter Fourteen
Stevie

I stare at my best friend and her boyfriend in a kind of slow-motion daze. I'm still clutching a handful of Garrick's shirt as we turn and watch our friends stumble their way around the kitchen, frantically tearing at their clothes as they kiss passionately against the counter, the island unit, and up against the wall. It's hot and a fleeting pang of jealousy stabs me in the chest. Will grabs her leg as he plasters the full length of his body against hers, hooking her leg up and around his waist while grinding his hips against hers. Ellen lets out a gravelly moan, yanking clumps of his hair as he buries his face in her chest and his hand slips under her skirt.

That snaps me out of my shock, and I let go of Garrick, briefly sharing a look with him before I loudly clear my throat. "Ahem, guys. You have an audience. As much as I love porn, I'm not down for a live performance in the kitchen."

"Oh, shit," Ellen mumbles, slurring her words. Her head pivots in the direction of my voice. She squints through blurry eyes. "Um, sorry. We might be a teeny bit drunk." She giggles, looking deliriously happy and more than a little tipsy. Will chuckles as he lifts his head from her chest. "And horny," she adds, sending him a scorching hot look we all feel. "So fucking horny."

Will molds his lips to hers, thrusting his pelvis against her as he dry fucks her into the wall, and I squirm on the couch, uncomfortably turned on and about ten shades of awkward. Garrick is staring at them with a mix of amusement, horror, and something akin to...envy? "Get a room," he drawls a few beats later in a decadently deep voice that sends shivers all over my body. "For the love of god, please get a room."

Will removes his lips from Ellen's mouth and his hand from under her skirt, lifting her effortlessly, and her legs automatically circle his waist. "Oops. Our bad," he says with a grin, looking in no way apologetic. Ellen's arms go around his neck, and she digs her fingers in his hair while whispering something in his ear. From the way his pupils dilate and his hands squeeze her ass I'd say, it was something dirty.

Good for Ellen.

At least one of us is getting some.

You could be too, the devil on my shoulder taunts, and I know it's the truth. I was literally seconds away from throwing caution to the wind and mauling Garrick.

I should probably thank my bestie for the timely interruption.

Will sprints down the hallway toward the bedrooms, and I breathe a sigh of relief when the door to Ellen's room slams shut.

However, it's only temporary relief.

The banging starts almost immediately.

A rhythmic *thump, thump, thump* as the headboard slaps repeatedly against the wall.

It does nothing to quell the awkwardness or the simmering tension in this room. It's like throwing gasoline on a small flame. Heat blooms in my cheeks, and the throbbing between my legs is now a crescendo of potent need.

I sense Garrick looking at me, and I know if I look at him this inferno will explode. I'm confused, horny, and scared, and it feels like

I'm coming out of my skin. I hop up, avoiding eye contact with him, as I force a laugh out of my lips. At any other time, we'd probably both be cracking up at the scene we just witnessed, but we're too highly strung. Too amped up on the fiery desire crackling and burning in the space between us. "I don't know about you, but I need a drink. Or some noise-canceling headphones," I mutter under my breath as I stalk toward the refrigerator.

More alcohol is not the solution, but I desperately need something to occupy my hands and my mouth before I pounce on the gorgeous guy sitting on my couch, no doubt staring at me like I'm crazy.

The thumping of the headboard continues, accompanied by a chorus of moans and groans, and I could happily murder my bestie right now. How come I never realized the walls were paper-thin before?

"Hey." Garrick wraps his fingers around my wrist just as I reach the refrigerator, and I jump about ten feet in the air, not noticing he'd walked up behind me. His low chuckle washes over me like an aphrodisiac, and I'm seconds away from throwing my self-imposed rules out the window. "I have a better idea."

"What could be better than alcohol?" The giggle that bursts from my mouth is borderline hysterical, and inside, I'm cringing.

Garrick's hands land lightly on my hips, and he turns me around, tipping my chin up with one long finger until our eyes meet. "Let's dance."

I stare at him in utter confusion, sure I must have heard him wrong.

His fingers thread through mine as he smiles. "You need a distraction, and drink isn't it. I know you have plans to study tomorrow, so more alcohol probably isn't a good idea." Heat flares behind his eyes, and I know what else he isn't saying. I know if I drink more my inhibitions will fly out the window and we'll be making out before I've drawn a breath.

My heart swells with the realization he's saving me from myself.

Garrick is putting aside his own needs to prioritize mine, and that only makes me like him more. It's time I accept this thing between us is inevitable. I am on this train, whether I wanted to be there or not, and there's no getting off.

I don't want to.

Deep down, I know I want this.

Garrick is right.

I'm afraid.

Afraid of losing my heart and getting it broken.

Terrified he'll become my entire world and nothing else will matter.

"Stevie, breathe." He squeezes my hand. "It's okay."

"I'm terrified, Garrick."

With his free hand, he traces his fingers down my cheek in an infinitely tender gesture that warms my heart and cranks my arousal a level higher. "I know you are, but there is no pressure, and nothing is going to happen tonight. We're going to put music on. Loud. Really loud," he adds when Ellen screams Will's name from the top of her lungs.

Laughter bursts from my lips. "I am going to fucking kill her for this."

Garrick chuckles. "We both know it's funny, and it's great to see our friends so in love. I'm happy for them."

I step a little closer and our chests brush. "Me too. You're such a good guy, Garrick Allen."

"I try my best." He waggles his brows and grins, clasping my hand tighter as he pulls me into the living room. I cling to his hand as he hooks his iPhone up to our sound system, and loud rock music blares from the speakers, drowning out the sounds of our best friends banging their brains out.

The music instantly unlocks some of the tension in my stiff limbs, and we rock it out, throwing wild moves and crazy shapes, laughing and shouting the lyrics as we dance around the living room like we're connected to the electrical supply. Elation is the only emotion I'm feeling as we work up a sweat, and I haven't had this much fun in ages. I can be myself around Garrick, and he appears to be the same. He's goofing around, causing me to emit deep belly laughs, and nothing has ever felt more natural or more real.

Unexpectedly, the music changes, and my eyes pop wide as Karen Carpenter's distinctive voice belts out around the room. "You listen to The Carpenters?"

"You know who they are?" he asks, sounding incredulous as he walks toward the sound system.

"Don't turn it off!" I blurt. "They're my nana's favorite band. I grew up listening to them and Abba on repeat."

Garrick lowers the music a little, and we stare at one another from a few feet apart. "My stepmom would love your nana. She loves all the music from that era. It was Dawn who introduced me to them. She's the reason I have a playlist on my phone." He looks a little sheepish, and now I'm intrigued.

"I sense a story."

He rubs the back of his neck and grins. "I was taking my first crush to winter formal, the year I was a freshman, and I couldn't dance."

I find that so hard to believe because Garrick is a fantastic dancer, and it seems innate, like his musical ability.

"I asked my mom to teach me, but her suggestion was to arrange formal dance lessons with a private instructor. It was a shit show, and I canceled after the first lesson. Then Dawn stepped in. She taught me to dance to the backdrop of The Carpenters." A tinge of pink stains his cheeks, and it's adorably cute. "At Christmas, I usually end up dancing with her around the kitchen. It's kind of tradition now."

I think that's the moment I give myself full permission to fall.

I can't deny it any longer, and I don't want to.

Closing the gap, I walk toward him and hold out my hand. The opening notes to "Close to You" start up, and it's like a sign from the heavens. "You never cease to amaze me, Garrick. That is one of the sweetest things I've ever heard. If it's okay to start a new tradition with me, I would love to dance with you to my favorite Carpenters song."

"It would be my honor." He takes my hand and gently reels me into his body.

My arms encircle his neck as his hands gravitate to my lower back. He applies soft pressure, pulling me in flush against his body as we sway in time to the music. Heat seeps from his body into mine, and I'm acutely aware of his solidity and masculinity as we move in perfect tandem. My heart is so full when he softly twirls me in his arms before drawing me back in close. His attention is solely focused on me, and his smoldering golden-colored eyes bore into mine, pinning me in place as I melt in his embrace, feeling cherished and adored in a way I have never felt before with any man.

Butterflies run amok in my chest when he starts singing, peering deep into my eyes as he serenades me, and I fall even deeper.

More Carpenters songs flood the room as the playlist goes on, and we continue dancing. Garrick swirls me around as he sings. He never misses a lyric, and he never moves his attention from me.

I'm enraptured, and it's one of the most romantic moments of my life.

I never want it to end.

And I never want to stop feeling the things he makes me feel.

Chapter Fifteen
Stevie

"Oh my god, that is so romantic," Mom swoons over the phone the following night when I recount the details of my magical night with Garrick. He was a perfect gentleman, and despite the explosive chemistry we share, the night ended without any making out. We danced, sang, and exchanged longing looks and lingering innocent touches—over clothes—and yet it was still the most intimate night of my life.

"Your nana is gonna love him!" Mom's blatant excitement breaks me out of my head.

Everyone is gonna love him.

It's impossible not to.

"You should bring him to her birthday party next weekend!"

Her gleeful shriek has me momentarily covering my ears. "Mom, calm down, seriously. You are getting too carried away."

"My little girl is finally in love." Her delight filters down the line. "You don't know how much I have prayed for this moment. I'm so happy for you!"

"Woah. Hold your horses, crazy woman. I did *not* say that."

"You don't need to. I hear it in your voice."

"Mom, I say this with the greatest respect, but you're insane. And delusional. I told you I like him and I think I'm ready to give this thing between us a shot. No one said anything about the l-word, and you need to dispel that notion right now. Unless you want to freak me out and have me end it before it's even begun."

"It's okay to be scared, honey. Feeling vulnerable is part of being in love. You can't open yourself fully to another person without it."

"Mom, we haven't even kissed, and you are totally overreacting. Right now, I really like him, and even admitting that is a big deal for me. Nothing will happen until after my exams anyway. I already told him I couldn't get distracted before then, so he knows the score."

"You can't place limitations on love, sweetheart. The heart wants what it wants, and practicalities just don't come into it."

Maybe that's true if you're Monica Colson.

But I am not my mom, and whatever happens with Garrick will happen on my terms and my timeline.

I won't be rushed into anything by anyone.

The next week, in the run up to exams, is hectic, but Garrick and I manage to find time to hang out every day. We either cohabit the library companionably or study at my place. I avoid his place like the plague. I have no desire to bump into that asshole Cohen. I saw him in the cafeteria on Tuesday, sporting a fading black eye, and Will confirmed Garrick gave it to him because he was talking shit about me. Perhaps I shouldn't silently applaud such behavior. Nana always says violence is not the answer, but I won't criticize any guy who uses his fists to defend me when provoked.

On days where we need to be on campus, Garrick picks me up in his Range Rover with a coffee from Bumble Bees. We ride there to the backdrop of The Carpenters, Abba, the Bee Gees, The Beach Boys, The Monkees, The Rolling Stones, The Doors, and a host of other popular bands from the sixties and seventies.

The ride home is usually accompanied by contemporary sounds as Garrick educates me on indie rock and pop. We talk about everything and anything, and I wake up every day excited to see him.

We eat together most evenings, grabbing dinner on campus or at one of the local diners or I cook something at home. Ellen and Will join us occasionally. Garrick seems to enjoy my cooking, and I like making food for him.

It's all very domesticated, and I'm shocked at how much I don't dislike it. Nothing is official, but we already feel like a couple except there's been no touching or kissing. We share plenty of sultry looks, and I know he's as eager as I am to move things to the next level, but abstaining only heightens the anticipation.

I almost cracked last night when he showed up with flowers and a bottle of wine. The fact it was Friday didn't go unnoticed by me. Is Garrick emulating his father? I can't even be mad he stole the idea because I'm overjoyed at his thoughtfulness and giddy at the prospect of weekly flower and wine deliveries.

I nearly caved and planted one on him.

I think he was the same a few hours ago when I handed him a Tupperware container of homemade cupcakes and cookies. Garrick does so much for me, and I wanted to do something nice for him too, so I got up at the crack of dawn to bake. I hated having to kick him out at lunchtime, but I had laundry to do, and I needed to pack a bag before making the trip home for Nana's birthday.

Something that is now appearing less and less likely. I turn the engine on my CR-V again, and it splutters and chokes before dying. "No!" I groan, resting my head on the steering wheel and cursing the shit timing. I had my car serviced recently, so this should not be happening. Glancing at my watch again, I already know I'm cutting it close. I could take public transportation, but it's over six hours on the train and almost seven on the bus, and that's before I make it to the station and wait for the next available train or bus. Then I'd have to grab an Uber from Seattle to Ravenna, and I'd be lucky to make the tail end of Nana's party.

Briefly, I consider calling Ellen, but she's out in Sutherlin, meeting Will's family for the first time. She could be here in an hour if I could reach her—but I'm not sure if she has cell phone coverage while hiking the North Umpqua Trail. I know she'd come if I asked, but I don't want to ruin my bestie's day.

That only leaves one other option. One other person. As I take out my cell to call Garrick, I console myself knowing he'll be delighted to spend all this time with me, steadfastly refusing to acknowledge how much I'll enjoy spending the time with him too.

GARRICK

"It's no problem, Stevie. I don't have any major plans for the rest of the day." That's no lie. I was just going to hang out in my room. Now, she's saving me from an evening of avoiding Cohen.

"Are you sure? I wouldn't ask if it wasn't important. I have never missed Nana's birthday."

"Honestly, it's fine. Let me grab a shower, and I'll be over as quick as I can."

"Thank you, Garrick. I really, really appreciate this."

"See you in a few," I say before hanging up.

"That didn't take long," Cohen says, creeping up behind me.

I didn't realize he was here. Will is hiking with Ellen and his folks, and I left Noah at the gym as he has a boxing lesson. Ignoring Cohen, because I'm not in the mood to argue with him, I grab a glass out of the overhead cupboard and reach for the tap.

"You're so fucking pussy-whipped already it's pathetic," he continues, trying to get a rise out of me as I fill my glass with water. He pops the top on the bottle of beer in his hand.

Grinding my teeth to the molars, I work hard to compose myself before I turn around to face my ex-friend and soon-to-be ex-roommate—if I have my way. "I don't give a shit what you think." I drill him with a dispassionate expression while I drink greedily from my glass.

"She giving up the goods yet, or are your balls still bluer then blue?" He smirks before taking a mouthful of his beer.

"Fuck off," I snap, losing my cool. "My relationship is none of your business." I drain my water and stow the empty glass in the dishwasher.

"Unless I make it my business." He folds his arms across his bare chest and smirks.

I jab my finger in his chest, and it takes considerable self-control not to punch him in his smug face. "Stay the hell away from Stevie, and stay the hell away from me."

I'm still fuming as I stand under the steaming-hot shower a few minutes later, wondering how I was ever friends with that douche. Cohen has shown his true colors these past few weeks, and alcohol can no longer be used as an excuse. Even Noah is fed up with his childish moods and nasty digs. I don't think it'll take much more for Will and I to convince Noah that Cohen needs to transfer to the frat house with his jock buddies for junior year. Neither of us wants to live with him any longer.

Will and I have discussed possibly getting a place with the girls. I told him it's premature on my side, but I'm open to it. Stevie and I are both returning to Seattle for summer break, and I'm hoping it'll be the turning point in our relationship. She told me last week she's onboard, but she wants to wait until our exams are finished before making anything official, and I'm fine with that. I was prepared to wait as long as it took to convince her to go out with me, so I'm thrilled we both seem to be on the same page now.

Not touching her is slowly driving me insane. The more time I spend with her, the more I long to hold her in my arms, lay claim to her lips, and worship her body like the temple it is. But I can be patient for a little bit longer.

Stevie is worth it.

All it takes is visualizing her gorgeous face in my mind's eye, and I'm hard as a rock. Wrapping my fingers around my aching dick, I close my eyes and imagine Stevie is in the shower with me. I jerk off fast as the fantasy plays out in my head, and it's not long before I'm coming hard, spraying jets of cum all over the tile wall.

At least that should tide me over for the long journey ahead. While I relish the idea of spending hours in close confines with the woman occupying a starring role in my dreams, it's also the sweetest torture. Being near to her and not getting to touch her is killing me softly.

"This is really sweet of you, Garrick, and I owe you big time," Stevie says, buckling her seat belt as I kick-start the engine.

"I'll add it to my Stevie list, and we can work out a reward later," I tease, pulling out onto the road and peeling away from her apartment building.

"You and your list." She rolls her eyes, but she's smiling as she looks across the console at me. "Will I ever get to see this infamous list?"

"It's a mental checklist, but I can type it out if you like." Taking my eyes off the road for a split second, I flash her a flirty grin.

"I'm not sure which would be best—seeing the list or just imagining what's on it."

"Depends on how vivid your imagination is." I level her with a dirty look in case she missed the innuendo.

"I have a pretty vivid imagination." She coolly stares me down with a hint of mischief glinting in her eyes. "I'll see your dirty and raise you depraved."

I bark out laughing, wishing I could pull over and impale her on my throbbing cock. "Damn, Stevie." I adjust myself behind the zipper of my jeans. "You can't say shit like that to me when I'm driving. I'm liable to drive us into a ditch."

"Sorry." Her lips curve up, and she looks completely unapologetic as she shucks off her coat and tosses it in the back seat.

My eyes are out on stalks as I rake my gaze over her pretty sage dress. It's draped across one shoulder, ruched at her slim waist, and fitted over her hips, ending just below her knee. One side has a slit, revealing an expanse of creamy skin, and my eyes trail the length of her shapely legs, admiring the sparkly silver sandals on her pretty feet. Her toenails are painted a glittery blue color matching the polish on her fingernails. "You look beautiful," I say over the lump wedged in my throat. "Your dress is gorgeous."

Her cheeks flush with my compliment, like I've noticed they always do. "Thank you."

"So, ugh." I clear my throat. "Tell me about the party. Is this a special occasion birthday?"

She shakes her head, sending waves of auburn hair cascading over her shoulders. I think I have an unnatural obsession with her hair. The few times she's let me run my fingers through it has only enhanced my addiction. My favorite shower fantasy is imagining my hand fisting her hair as I yank her head back and ram into her gorgeous body from behind.

And now I'm leaking precum like a horny teen.

This drive just got infinitely longer.

"What are you thinking about?" she asks, craning forward a little in her seat. "Your face is all flushed."

"Trust me, you don't want to know."

Her mouth forms an O shape, and now I'm thinking about driving my cock between those tempting lips, and it's a miracle I haven't blown my load already.

So much for the one I rubbed out in the shower providing relief.

My balls are fit to burst.

"Tell me about the party," I say, desperate to talk about non-sexy shit to regain my control. "Is it a special birthday?"

"Every birthday Nana celebrates is a special occasion to me. She is sixty-seven today. Our birthdays are exactly two weeks apart," she explains.

Ellen already mentioned it was Stevie's twentieth birthday in a couple weeks. Apparently, her friend Hadley is organizing a night out in Seattle, and she personally asked Ellen to invite me. I'll be there, but only if Stevie invites me. So far, she hasn't mentioned it, and I'm not pushing.

"That's cool."

"It is." Stevie kicks off her sandals, throwing her bare feet up on the dash. "For a period when I was little, I used to insist we have a joint birthday party, and Mom and Nana always humored me."

"That's cute."

"Not sure my friends appreciated hanging out with a bunch of oldies, but I always got a kick out of it."

"Will there be many at the party?" I inquire, taking the exit for the I-5. It's straight on the highway all the way to Seattle. It's a boring drive, but I don't mind. If I'm alone, I welcome the time to listen to music and think about stuff. With Stevie, it means I can put the car in cruise control, and we can talk the entire ride.

"Nah. Just a few of my nana's friends and neighbors, my mom, and Hads." She worries her lower lip between her teeth before turning her head to mine. "You're welcome to come in."

I was hoping to be invited, but I didn't want to presume anything. I also don't want her to feel obligated to invite me. "I don't want to intrude."

"You wouldn't be, and the least I can do is feed you before you set out on the return journey."

"I'm going to stay at my mom's tonight." Like Stevie, my exams don't start until Tuesday, so I can afford to lose a few study hours. I'm as prepared as I can be anyway. There isn't much more I can cram in my brain with the time I have left.

"That makes sense," she agrees, bobbing her head. "Medina is what? A twenty-minute drive from Ravenna?"

"Yep, so don't worry about me."

Lowering her feet to the floor, she sits up a little straighter before turning on her side. "Look, I'm just going to put this out there. There is no chance my mom or my nana are going to let you leave when they know you drove me home. You have zero possibility of escaping this party."

I smile as I settle back in my seat, removing my foot from the accelerator when I switch on cruise control mode. "Why exactly is that?"

She bites down on her lip before sighing. "Mom is all excited because I told her about you. She's adding two plus two and getting fifty."

My smile expands into full-blown grin territory. "I already told you I liked your mom, and now I like her even more."

"Heads-up, Monica is going to flap and fuss over you like you wouldn't believe. My nana won't be so obvious. She'll quietly observe to see what you're made of. They can both be pretty intense in completely different ways."

"I can handle it, but don't feel forced to invite me." I'm probably underdressed in my white T-shirt, jeans, and boots, but I doubt Stevie's friends or family will mind too much. It's not like I'm rocking up to one of my mother's friend's houses dressed casually. Mom would have a coronary if she saw what I'm wearing and knew I was attending a party dressed like this.

"I don't," Stevie says, yanking me out of my head.

"I will be there if you want me there, but otherwise, I'll head on to Medina."

A pregnant pause ensues for a few tense moments. "I'd like you there," she admits in a soft tone. "But you don't have to come if it's not your scene."

"I wouldn't want to be anywhere else," I truthfully reply, reaching out to touch her hand. "In case you haven't noticed, I'm finding it hard to be anywhere but by your side."

The most glorious smile lights up her face, and I want to spend a lifetime looking at it.

Some might call me crazy. Hell, most would, but I feel it in my bones.

Stevie is *the one.*

I refuse to let anyone sway me from the truth—I have found my forever.

Chapter Sixteen

Stevie

"You should be writing love songs for a living, Garrick. You have a beautiful way with words." It's the truth. With any other guy, what he just said might sound cheesy, but Garrick is too genuine for it to come across as anything but sincere. "And a beautiful voice to match."

"I'd rather reserve all the words for you."

See what I mean? This guy has already wormed his way into my life and into my heart, and I'm in real danger of giving the whole damn thing away.

"Are you like this with all your girlfriends?" I ask before I can stop to question the wisdom of it. "Not that I mean I'm your girlfriend or anything. I'm just curious."

He drills a hole in my head as he drives with one arm, coasting at a consistent speed in the slow lane of the I-5, like he wishes he could extract the thoughts from my mind.

"I don't want to talk about my exes, and they all fade into nonexistence when compared to you. I have never felt this strongly about any girl before, and that's the truth."

"Have you ever been in love?" I blurt, and I don't know why I'm asking questions that have the power to hurt, but it's like I've lost all control of my mouth.

He wets his lips before clearing his throat and eyeballing me again. "I thought I was one time, but it wasn't the real deal. It was infatuation and nothing more."

I'm tempted to probe further, but I'm also keen to avoid getting too heavy for fear I'll scare myself into regressing.

"Have you?" he asks even though he already knows the answer.

"Nope."

"Not even with your one and only high-school boyfriend?"

I vehemently shake my head. "I told you that relationship was me caving to peer pressure. All my friends had boyfriends, and I went and got myself one to fit in. He was a nice guy but way more into me than I was into him. When he told me he loved me, I broke things off, and it was such a relief."

"Wow, okay, I'll add that reminder to my list."

I can't tell if he's teasing or sincere. "I was a kid then. It's different now."

Garrick pushes his dark hair behind his ears, looking deep in thought as he stares out the windshield. A couple beats later, he turns to face me, keeping one eye on the road and one on me. "I know you said you didn't want to put any labels on us or move things to a new level, not until after our exams, but do you think you'll want to be my girlfriend?"

Ugh. So much for not wanting things to turn heavy. "Do we really have to do this now?" Hurt splays across his face, and I feel like an evil bitch. Taking his free hand in mine, I lace my fingers through his. "I like you a lot, Garrick." My chest heaves as I stare into his eyes. They look more green than brown today. He is so gorgeous, and sometimes it's so hard to not touch him. "I think the answer to that question is yes, but I haven't processed it all yet. I have an all-consuming personality, and if I start thinking about it now, it'll distract me. I know that probably sounds stupid to you, but I swear I'm not stringing you along. I'm being honest. Just let me get through my exams this week, and then we can talk."

"I'm sorry for pressuring you. I shouldn't have said anything." He squeezes my hand, and warmth spreads across my skin. I love holding his hand, and I love being in his arms. He makes me feel safe and loved. For a new-to-me emotion, I'm embracing it wholeheartedly and not letting guilt do a number on me.

I know when I give in to Garrick I will give him my all.

I just need to ensure I'm fully ready for it.

The last thing I want to do is hurt him and hurt myself in the process.

"You aren't pressuring me, and don't apologize. You've been letting me set the pace and taking the scraps I throw you. If anyone should be apologizing, it's me. I know I'm not like other girls. I know it's most likely really frustrating for you, but when I decide to do something, I give it my all. I never jump lightly into anything, especially where it pertains to my heart." I pull my legs up under me and clutch his hand tighter.

Garrick's gaze alternates between me and the road. "Those are all reasons why I like you, Stevie. I like that you're cautious. I'm just impatient to get to the next part because I haven't ever felt like this about anyone before."

"I haven't felt like this before either. It's totally new. I'm not used to being so vulnerable. It scares me as much as it excites me."

"You can trust me. I won't ever do anything to deliberately hurt you. That's not who I am."

"I know, Garrick. You have shown me that already. That doesn't mean I won't get hurt though. Or that you won't."

"No one knows that or can make any guarantees when they enter into any kind of relationship with another person. You risk getting hurt every time you open yourself up to others." Raising our conjoined hands to his mouth, he brushes his lips against my knuckles. "But that is life, and that is love. You risk far more by not putting yourself out there. You risk never knowing the pure elation of loving another person so completely you'd take a bullet for them. You risk never knowing true happiness and contentment."

"How are you so wise?" I ask as he lowers our hands.

"I'm not wise, nor am I experienced. Not when it comes to love. But I know what I've learned from my parents. My mother never truly opens herself up, and that's why all her marriages fail."

I suspect her rotten personality is the reason for marital failure, but I keep those thoughts to myself. After all, I've only met the woman once. I don't think my first impression is wrong, but she did give birth to Garrick, one of the most amazing people I know, so she can't be all bad.

"My father is vulnerable with Dawn, and watching how they support one another through the bad shit is even more inspirational than seeing them happy and glowing in the good times."

"I watch my mother risking herself for love all the time and getting burned," I quietly admit, rubbing circles on the back of his hand with my thumb. "I see her being vulnerable, and it backfires every time." I lift my eyes to him. "I am cynical and skeptical. I know that, but for the right person, I am willing to try." Gulping back nerves, I force the remaining words out of my throat. "I think you're the right person, but I want to be sure before we make that step. I owe it to both of us to have fully thought it through. I'm eighty percent there."

Garrick presses a kiss to my brow. "That's good enough for now."

"Are you sure you're okay to do this?" I ask one final time before we get out of Garrick's car. He parked his Range Rover beside Nana's older version in front of the house, alongside a row of other cars. I spot Hadley's in the mix, so even if she hadn't already texted me to say she'd arrived, I'd know she was here.

He chuckles as he tweaks my nose. "Relax, Stevie. It's fine."

"Okay, but don't say I didn't warn you," I singsong, curling my hand around the door handle.

"Wait!" he exclaims, and I pause mid door opening. "Let me get that."

Before I can protest, Garrick jumps out, races around to my side and opens the door.

I peer at him in amusement.

"I'm making it an official rule," he says, taking my hand and helping me down. "You don't get in or out of this car unless I'm opening the door for you."

On instinct, I reach up and kiss his cheek, lingering a few seconds longer than necessary. His spicy scent is delicious, and I have a sudden urge to lick him like a popsicle. "And they say chivalry is dead." I beam up at him, and gosh, he really is fucking hot.

I deserve a medal for not pouncing on him yet. "For the record, I have no issue agreeing to your rule. It's sweet." I pat his chest. And yes, I am using the opportunity to salivate over the hard muscles flexing under my palm.

"Good." Without warning, he hauls me into his arms, and I don't protest, falling easily against him and resting my head on his chest. He dots kisses into my hair, and I silently swoon as I grip his waist and savor the moment.

A girl could get used to this.

"Let me write this card super quick." Easing out of our embrace, he places the birthday card he insisted on buying at the store on Main Street down on the hood. Pulling a pen out of his jeans pocket, he writes a message in neat penmanship before sealing the card in the envelope.

I grab the cake box and bag with Nana's gift from the back seat as Garrick opens the trunk. He reappears with two bottles of sparkling wine carrying the Allen Wineries label. "Do you just happen to have wine in your trunk, or did you bring them on purpose?" I ask.

"I brought them for your nana. Even if I wasn't invited in, I planned to gift them to her for her birthday. You're only sixty-seven one time," he adds with a grin.

I could kiss him for his generosity and his thoughtfulness. He makes it so hard to stay away from him.

Light pokes out between the curtains in the open living room window, and the sounds of lively conversation and background music filter out into the nighttime air. Just as I'm opening my mouth to reply, the front door swings open, and I figure the welcoming committee has run out of patience.

Honestly, I'm surprised Mom didn't rush out the door the second Garrick's car pulled up.

"Darling." Mom runs toward me, flinging her arms around my neck as I stand awkwardly with a cake box in one hand and a gift bag in the other. "I'm so glad you're here. Nana would've been devastated if you hadn't made it."

"I'm just lucky Garrick was available to drive me," I say, kissing Mom on the cheek.

"Thank you so much for bringing our girl home," Mom says, giving Garrick a quick hug.

"It was no problem, Ms. Colson. Getting to spend time with Stevie is never a chore."

Mom positively beams at him as she loops her arm through his and swoons. "Please call me Monica, and I know what you mean. My daughter is a delight."

Oh my freaking god. I just know she's going to embarrass the hell out of me tonight. I must be insane to even consider bringing him inside, but it's too late now. This shit show is already in motion.

I'm all but forgotten as she drags Garrick through the door. "Did Stevie ever tell you about the time..."

I'm glad I don't hear the rest because I'd rather not know which humiliating childhood story she's telling him first. I shuffle in through the door, closing it behind me before heading toward the kitchen where I deposit the cake I baked this morning.

Then I walk into the main living room, at the front of the house, where everyone is congregated. Nana's neighbors and friends descend on me en masse, enveloping me in a cloud of floral perfume, sticky kisses, and motherly hugs. Over their heads, I spot Garrick being interrogated by my mom, her best friend Julie, Hadley, and Nana. He looks relaxed and not in need of rescue.

Yet.

Mom is busy pouring the sparkling wine into flutes while she keeps one ear on the conversation. She gives me a none too subtle thumbs-up, and I don't hold back on the eye roll. Playing it cool does not exist in Mom's vocab.

Nana's friends bombard me with questions about UO, my jobs at the bar and floral shop, my summer plans, and mostly about the handsome stranger I brought with me. Me bringing a guy around is a novelty, and no one is letting me leave without telling them everything about Garrick.

When Mom hands me a glass of wine, I knock half of it back in one go, wondering how I can extricate myself without seeming rude.

Nana comes charging to the rescue, squeezing her way in between her friends to claim me in a bear hug. "Little Poppy. Come show your nana some loving."

Bending down, I wrap my arms around her, burying myself in the familiarity of her hug.

"I've missed you, sweetheart."

"I've missed you too. Happy birthday!" Although I call Nana once a week, it's been six weeks since I last saw her. We break our embrace, but she grasps my hands in her smaller ones as she looks me over, ensuring I'm in one piece. "It's almost summer break. You can glut yourself on me soon," I say, laughing.

"I'm looking forward to it," she says as I hand her the gift bag. "Silly girl. What have I told you about buying me things?"

"It's your birthday. If I can't spoil you on your birthday, when can I?"

"You spoil me with your presence, and that is all I need." She's starting to sound a lot like Garrick.

"You look stunning, Nana. I love the dress. Is it new?" Her wine-colored velvet dress has little gold birds dotted all over it, cute cap sleeves, ruched detail at the bust, and it flows softly from the waist over her small, slender frame. Sparkly gold shoes with a low heel adorn her tiny feet. Her long gray hair is pulled into an elegant chignon, and I spot my mother's handiwork. I always say Mom could have been a hairdresser. She has never formally trained, but she cuts a lot of the neighbors' kids' hair, like she used to do mine as a child, and she's a magician with up styles.

My nana is the epitome of a glamorous granny. Mostly, she wears work pants, shirts, sweaters, and heavy-duty boots, but she loves an opportunity to dress up for an occasion.

"It was your mother's birthday gift. We went shopping on Monday," she explains.

"I wish I could have been there."

"Next time, dear. We're long overdue a good shopping trip." Threading her arm in mine, she steers me over toward one of the purple velvet couches. Garrick is now wedged on the other couch, nestled snugly in between Mom on one side and Hadley on the other. They look like they're firing questions at him, and he's starting to look a little uncomfortable.

Ha! I'm almost proud of my mother and my bestie for rattling my man.

My man.

Look at me tossing that out without hesitation. I've got to admit it has a nice ring to it.

"You look smitten," Nana says, pulling me down beside her on the couch. She looks over at Garrick with a contemplative expression on her face.

"I fear I am," I truthfully reply, watching as she settles the bag on her lap.

"'Nothing in life is to be feared. It is only to be understood,'" she replies, carefully unpacking the cross-stitch materials in the bag.

"Who said that?"

"Marie Curie. A very smart woman. First woman to win the Nobel Prize. First person to win a Nobel Prize twice, and first person to win a Nobel Prize in two scientific fields."

Nana is the most amazing woman. She always has an appropriate inspirational quote for every situation and conversation. How she remembers all of them astounds me. I struggle to remember the contents of the chapter I studied this morning on planting design and maintenance, and there's Nana with a whole encyclopedia of knowledge stowed away in her head. She is truly remarkable, and she will always remain the most inspirational woman to me.

"I'll try to heed her advice."

"This is too much." Nana shakes her head as she surveys the supplies covering her lap.

"No, it's not. I love you. It's your birthday, and I can never repay you for everything you've done for me."

She kisses my forehead. "You give me so much joy, Stevie. That's all the repayment I ever need."

"I'm looking forward to coming back to work. I learned a few new things from Sharon I thought we could try."

A slight grimace slides across her face, but it's gone fast. Still, I know Nana. "What was that look for?"

"It's nothing we need to talk about now."

"Nana." I fix her with my fiercest expression. "Tell me now."

"I don't want you to worry, but we had a bit of an incident this week. The roof caved in on the barn, destroying most of the shop and supplies."

Nana's floral business is not your typical floral business. She used to buy flowers from the market and sell them from the barn her grandparents set up as a floral shop years ago. This property is on fifty acres of land, and most of it was going to waste until Nana established a flower farm fifteen years ago to grow her own flowers. It was a way to ensure a variety of flowers and to keep the prices down. She hired a guy to help her develop the farm, and he recommended these specialist greenhouses that mean we can grow cut flowers all year round. It was quite cutting edge at the time, but most flower farmers use this method now.

The barn was remodeled at the same time. A large area contains shelving where buckets of various flowers are stocked daily. Customers can pick the exact flowers they want for their bouquet or purchase one of the ready-mades. A variety of accessories are for sale, and at the back of the room is a small seating area where customers can avail of snacks, baked goods, and coffee, all supplied by local businesses. One of Nana's friends manages it. It's proven to be a great draw for locals who sometimes only come here for coffee but end up walking out with flowers.

"Oh no. Will the insurance cover the costs?"

"Unfortunately not. The last safety inspection we had noted a weakness in the left side of the roof. Because I failed to act on it in a timely manner, the insurance company is refusing to pay out."

"Why didn't you get it fixed?" I cry, horrified at what this might mean for the business. That kind of damage will cost thousands to fix. Another horrifying thought flits through my mind. "You couldn't afford it, could you?"

She pats my hand, her gaze flicking to Garrick intermittently as we talk. "I don't want you to worry. I'll figure out a way to resolve it. We'll have to manually repair most of the damage to the shop ourselves, so prepare to get your hands very dirty."

"You shouldn't have given me that money for college," I protest, mentally calculating how much I have in my savings account. "I have money I can give you. It's not going to make a dent, but it's a start."

"Absolutely not." She clasps my face in her hands. "Listen to me, Stevie, and listen to me good. This is my problem to fix, and fix it I will. I gave you that money because I wanted to contribute to your future, and that still stands. I will not take a penny of your money, and don't insult me by attempting to offer me anything but your labor." Air expels from her lips as her features soften. "This is why I didn't want to have this conversation tonight. And we're not discussing it anymore. I don't want you to worry, honey." She kisses both my cheeks as she pulls me to my feet. "This is a party, and I'll have no glum faces." Tucking her arm in mine, she leads me toward Garrick. "Now, let's go rescue this young man of yours."

Chapter Seventeen

Garrick

"What about anal?" Hadley asks, popping a square of cheese in her mouth and fixing me with a cool expression like she hasn't just put that out there. "Into it or not?"

I stare at her like she just sprouted horns from her head.

She could be the devil.

It sure seems like she's only here to torment me.

"Kidding." She smirks before slurping her vodka cranberry through a straw. "Kind of." She giggles. "You should see your face right now."

"I'm not used to being drilled on my kinks while sitting beside my future girlfriend's mother."

Man, I wish I didn't have to drive.

I could use a beer or ten.

Stevie wasn't joking when she warned me. These women are nuts. The shit they've been asking me must be heard to be believed.

"Don't worry, Garrick," Monica says, turning around and patting my hand. "I only have half an ear on your conversation, and I'm not easily shocked." Monica and her friend spent fifteen minutes peppering me with questions while Stevie was surrounded by a fawning group of elderly women who clearly adores her.

"I'll keep that in mind," I say, reaching for the bottle of wine. I hold it up in front of Stevie's mom. "Would you like a top off?"

"That would be wonderful." Monica grabs Julie's glass, holding both wineglasses out to me. "And you were right about this vintage. It's delicious. I will be recommending this year to the restaurant manager at Sand Point when I'm on shift."

"I'll be starting work at the winery the week after my exams finish. Let me organize to send you a sample of this and some of our new-world wines, and you can sweet-talk the management into bumping up their order." I fill both glasses up to the halfway mark.

"Sounds like a plan." She winks. "Throw in a couple of bottles for yours truly, and we have a deal."

"Put in a good word with your daughter, and I'll keep you permanently supplied," I fire back with a grin.

Her smile is wide as she hands a wineglass to her friend. "I'm only finding more reasons to like you, Garrick, and I was already sold. Any guy who puts that big of a smile on my daughter's face is worthy of my seal of approval."

We all look over at Stevie as if it was planned. She's sitting on the other couch, deep in conversation with her nana.

"She is positively glowing," Hadley agrees, smiling before narrowing her eyes at me. "You better not have knocked her up."

Fucking hell.

I'm unsure what to make of Stevie's childhood best friend. I don't know if she's being outrageous to put on a show, if she has no filter and is just always like this, or she's testing me to see if I'm good enough for her best friend. Maybe it's a combination of those things. I'd like to point out sex would have to be involved to knock Stevie up and, given how we haven't so much as kissed yet, it's impossible, but I won't be rude, and what has or hasn't happened between Stevie and me is private.

Monica almost chokes on her wine. "Sheesh, Hadley. Anyone

would think you don't know your best friend. Stevie will probably make poor Garrick triple bag it before he gets anywhere near her lady parts."

I'm not easily embarrassed, but I'd quite happily sink into the ground and disappear if it was an option.

"Oh dear," someone with a soft lilting voice says. "Have they been terrorizing you?"

I look up at Stevie and her nana, thrilled at the timely intervention.

I scramble to my feet in record time as if my ass is on fire. The women behind me snicker, clearly enjoying my obvious discomfort. I'm most definitely of the view this was a test, and I only hope I passed. I clear my throat. "It's been interesting, ma'am." Stepping aside, I gesture toward the couch. "Take my seat."

"Nonsense, and I told you to call me Betsy," she says, waggling her finger in her daughter's face.

Stevie's nana said hello earlier but otherwise was a silent observer while her daughter and Stevie's best friend proceeded with their Spanish Inquisition.

"Scoot, missy," she tells Monica. "You've tormented this young man enough for one night." Her gaze flits to Hadley. "You too, little Miss Mischief."

"Moi?" Hadley stands, looking the picture of innocence. "I'm sure I don't know what you're talking about."

"Please tell me you didn't grill him on his sexual preferences or start a debate over biodiversity or the overexploitation of natural resources," Stevie says, pursing her lips and eyeballing her friend.

"We were just getting to the end of the kink portion of the interrogation though it's worth noting Garrick avoided answering the anal question."

My cheeks heat in an uncharacteristic blush. I can't believe she said that in front of Stevie's nana. I don't think it's for show either. I get the sense these kinds of conversations occur naturally when Hadley is around.

"Anal is overrated," Betsy says, scoffing and waving her hands around. "Unlike DP. Now that's an entirely different conversation."

I have a feeling my face is as red as a tomato and the sweat beads forming on my brow are visible.

Stevie is trying hard not to laugh. "I did try to warn you," she says, resting her hand on my forearm.

"Your warning was lacking in detail," I murmur in her ear as Monica, Julie, and Hadley walk away to mingle with the other guests. Thank fuck for small mercies.

"You survived," she says, letting a giggle free. "I promise they're not always quite that intense, but Hadley is unnaturally invested in my sex life, and I can't promise she won't get inappropriate again."

Betsy pats the space beside her on the couch. "Come sit by me, Garrick, and don't mind little Hadley. That one missed out on the sixties, and she's determined to make up for it by living her best free-love high-spirited hippy life."

"Hadley is very passionate about sexual freedom and equality, the environment, books, and ridding the world of injustice," Stevie explains, sitting on the arm of the couch, right by my side. "I'll get her to tone it down next time you meet."

"Now I know what to expect, it's cool. These are not the kinds of conversations I'm used to having at parties." I chuckle. "I would love my mother to meet Hadley. The look on her face would be more than worth the lecture I'd receive after."

"That can be arranged." Stevie smirks. "Though it's probably not advisable if I want to get in her good graces. Something tells me I'll have my work cut out for me with your mom."

I thread my fingers through hers. "She'll come around when she sees how much I care about you."

"My Little Poppy hasn't told me much about you, so I want to know everything," Nana says. "Start from the beginning. How did you two meet?"

"So, are you scarred for life after that ordeal?" Stevie asks an hour later when we step outside.

"It wasn't so much bad as unexpected, and I think I'll be fine." I squeeze her hand and grin down at her. "After hours of intense therapy."

She throws back her head and laughs, and I'm glad to see it because she has seemed a little tense. "I'm sorry. I probably should've warned you more thoroughly, but I was dying to see how you'd hold up."

We linger by my car. "Did I pass the test, or should I be worried?" I ask, raising our interlinked hands to my lips and brushing my mouth against her soft skin.

A gentle shudder ripples over her body, and I silently fist pump the air.

"You passed with flying colors. I knew everyone would love you, and I was right."

"Your mom's a hoot. Your nana is adorable, and well, the jury is still out on Hadley, but if she's your oldest friend, I know she's a good one." I pull her in close to my chest, resting my hands lightly on her hips. "You wouldn't be friends with anyone who wasn't good to their core."

"Hads *is* good people. She's just...an acquired taste. Like absinthe, brussels sprouts, and liver." A grimace crawls over her face, and I laugh.

"Will I ruin everything if I mention I love brussels sprouts?"

"Yes. Absolutely," she says, making no effort to extract herself from my embrace. She beams up at me. "Though I'll probably cope as long as you don't try to kiss me after eating those hideous things."

My eyes lower to her lips on autopilot, and my dick suddenly realizes how strategically we're aligned, springing to life. It's becoming problematic around Stevie. I am so turned on by her. Sometimes she just has to look at me, and I sprout a boner.

My tongue darts out, licking my lips as I note how her pupils dilate, and she strains toward me. Her gaze is fixated on my mouth, and tension bleeds into the small space between our bodies. Abstaining is the ultimate test, and I'm not sure I'm going to pass. "I want to kiss you so badly right now," I admit, desire seeping into my gruff tone.

"Me too," she whispers, tentatively lifting one hand to my face. "You're so gorgeous, Garrick, and I really like you." Her soft fingers brush against the light stubble on my cheeks. "But I'm afraid if we kiss now, we'll never stop, and making out in your car in front of my nana's house is not how I picture our first time."

Pulling her to me, I press a kiss to the top of her head and briefly close my eyes. "Nor me. I think I should go."

"Yes," she agrees, albeit reluctantly.

Clasping her face in my hands, I tilt it up to look at me. "Before I go, I just want to ask if everything is okay. You seemed a little preoccupied back there."

"You caught that, huh?"

I nod, and she sighs. "Nana told me some bad news. The roof of her barn collapsed, destroying her shop and ruining thousands of dollars' worth of supplies. The insurance won't pay out, and she doesn't have the money for repairs and replacements. I'm worried about her business."

"That's not good."

"No, it isn't." She sighs again, and I hear the pain behind the exhale.

"Is it far from here? Can you show me?"

"It's only a ten-minute walk, and yes, if you like. I wouldn't mind seeing the damage for myself."

Stevie retrieves her overnight bag from my car and darts back into the house to change her shoes. She reappears a few minutes later wearing boots and a cardigan. After grabbing my hoodie from the car, we set out on foot, hand in hand, and Stevie points out things as we walk past row upon row of greenhouses.

I draw to a stop when we reach a large field of poppies, blowing gently in the dark nighttime breeze. "Does this have anything to do with Betsy calling you Little Poppy?" I ask, pulling Stevie in front of me as I turn us to face the field. My hands skim around her waist as I hold her flush against my chest and rest my chin on her shoulder with my face pressed against the side of hers.

She places her hands on top of mine, and I hold her a little tighter, feeling like I never want to let her go. She fits perfectly against me, like she was made especially for me.

"Yes. This poppy field has been here for eons. As a little girl, I used to love running into it and rolling around. When friends came over, we'd play hide and seek in there, and I was always picking the poppies and decorating my bedroom with them. Nana gave me the name, and it stuck." Her back rumbles against my chest as she laughs. "Hads spent a year calling me Opium Poppy after a local farmer was caught growing a poppy field and manufacturing opium from it for sale. She tried to convince Nana to permanently change my nickname, but she was having none of it." Amusement and nostalgia underscore her tone. "Those were fun times."

"It seems like you had a great childhood."

"I did. Mom and I lived here for the first few years of my life before she bought the house we currently live in. Even after we moved, I still spent time here most every day. This is as much my home as our house is."

"What about your grandpa? You never mention him."

"He ran off with Nana's best friend when Mom was five, and he didn't come back. They never divorced, and she was notified twelve years ago when he died. We don't talk about him, and I never think of him. Hard to think of someone you never knew."

"I know I have only just met her, but your nana is an amazing woman. How anyone could desert her, and their own flesh and blood, makes no sense to me."

"Same here." She shivers, and I quickly shuck out of my hoodie, ignoring her complaining as I put it on her.

"Come on. It's getting colder." We pick up our pace, and it

doesn't take long to spot the barn. Even in the dark, and from this distance, I can see the devastation wrought on the large structure.

"Fuck. It's way worse than I imagined." Unhappiness laces her tone as we approach the damaged barn. A giant-sized gaping hole in the roof is admitting the elements, and when we open the door, it's clear everything inside will have to be gutted and replaced.

Bits of the roof and weather-strewn debris cover the interior floor. Chairs, buckets, garden accessories, and other supplies are scattered around the place. Puddles of water, from recent rainfall, are dotted all over the ground ensuring there is no recovering anything inside. A large plastic sheet hangs down from one side of the hole in the roof, and it's obvious whoever tried to tack it up didn't do a good enough job.

It's a mess, and Stevie is right to be concerned.

"This is so bad," she says in a low voice, clinging to my hand.

"Yeah, it's not good."

"I don't know how we fix this, but I'm going to find a way." Steely determination resonates in her previously dejected tone as an idea forms in my mind. "Nana is not losing her family business." She looks up at me with a face steeped in determination. "Not if I have anything to say about it."

Chapter Eighteen

Stevie

I push through the crowded cafeteria with my heart pounding in my chest, my eyes darting everywhere, searching for the man I came to find. Ignoring the curious stares of the students I pass, I pick up speed when I spot Garrick in the corner of the large room, leaning against the wall as he talks with a short stocky guy with a mass of jet-black hair. Behind him, seated at a table, are Will, Noah, Ellen, and two other guys I don't know.

Butterflies careen around my chest, and my heart is so full it feels like it might burst. Tears prick my eyes as I race toward him, wondering how I could have ever considered rejecting this man.

Garrick Allen is a god among men, and I am so fucking lucky I caught and held his attention.

A smile ghosts over his mouth when he spots me approaching, and I lose all self-consciousness and self-control as I full-on run toward him, uncaring what anyone thinks. His brows climb to his hairline when I throw myself at him, snaking my arms around his neck and yanking his head down to mine as I smash my lips to his.

Garrick doesn't disappoint, winding his strong arms around my back and holding me close as I kiss him. Our surroundings disappear, and it's only the two of us in our own little bubble. Angling my head, I trace my tongue along the seam of his lips, demanding entry. His lips willingly part to welcome me, and we both groan as my tongue slides into his mouth and tangles with his. Garrick takes control. Tightening his hold on me and deepening our kiss, he meets every stroke of my tongue with a caress of his own, and his full velvety-soft lips worship my mouth in a way that exceeds my every fantasy.

Butterflies are running riot in my chest and blood is pumping through my veins as liquid lust combusts in my lower belly, and an almost painful ache throbs between my legs. Garrick keeps me close, kissing me passionately like he never thought he'd get to do it. His hard length presses into my stomach, and knowing he wants me as much as I want him thrills me. My fingers thread through his gorgeous hair as we kiss, and I pour everything I'm feeling into every sweep of my tongue and every brush of my lips.

Kissing Garrick is everything I dreamed of and more.

I never want to stop, but reality comes crashing back when a chorus of whoops, hollers, and calls of "get a room" break the bubble we're in, and I'm instantly aware that I'm devouring his mouth in full view of a packed cafeteria.

I don't really care. The moment called for this, but I'm not about to give them more of a show.

Garrick must reach the same conclusion at the same time I do because we both pull back in sync, keeping a hold of one another as we break our kiss. He rests his brow against mine. "Fuck, Stevie." His warm breath fans over my face like magical mist, and I kiss him again, because now I know what he tastes like, I don't think I can stop. "If we were anywhere but this cafeteria," he growls over my lips, leaving the rest of the statement unsaid because we both understand what he means.

"I know." My voice comes out all raspy and seductive. Clasping his face in my hands, I force him to look at me. Our eyes meet, and mine fill with fresh tears. "Thank you." A single tear trickles out of the corner of my eye and runs down my face. "First my car, and now this." Garrick called in a favor with a friend, and by the time we returned to Eugene on Sunday, my CR-V was back in full working order.

This guy has stomped all over the shields I usually keep around my heart and laid siege to it—in the best possible way.

"It's not a big deal," he says, softly wiping the dampness from my cheek.

"Don't downplay it. It's a huge deal, and you know it. Nana told me about the visit from your dad. How you're going to repair the barn free of charge. That you would do this for us." I slap a hand over my chest, and I'm close to breaking down. No one has ever done anything so amazing, and I'm all up in my feels. "I can't ever repay you for your kindness."

"I'm sure I can think of a few ways." He flashes me a flirty smile, and I laugh. It helps to break up the heavy emotion of the moment.

"I'm sure you can, and you can bet I'll raise the stakes."

"I look forward to it, beautiful." He kisses the tip of my nose, and I swoon in his arms.

I'm in so much trouble with this guy.

"All joking aside, Garrick, what you have done is nothing short of miraculous. I just." I pause, all choked up, unable to articulate my thoughts or say what I want to say. "I can't thank you and your dad enough, but I'm going to try."

"We're glad to help." He moves us farther into the corner away from prying ears. He plays with my hair as we lean against the wall, so close there is barely any space between our bodies. "And it wasn't completely selfless. At least this way, we get to spend more time together."

I arch a brow.

"I'll be part of the crew working on the barn next week," he confirms.

"I thought you were taking a week off to chill out and catch up with Hudson?"

"Plans change." He shrugs, and his selflessness blows my mind.

In this moment, I don't feel worthy of Garrick Allen. "Hudson has agreed to help too. Between everyone, we'll get the barn fixed up and have Nana back in business in no time."

You are so getting laid.

I think it, but I don't say it. Not yet. It's only Wednesday, and exams aren't over until Friday. We're hitting The End Zone to celebrate, but Saturday night, he is all mine, and I'm going to commit to him. It's no longer a choice. I am all in now and dying to dive in with both hands. Wild horses couldn't separate me from this amazing man.

I want to be Garrick's, and I want him to be mine, and I'm done denying both of us what we so desperately need.

By the time Saturday night rolls around, I'm a bundle of nervous excitable energy as I dash around the kitchen putting the finishing touches to the special dinner I cooked for Garrick in between packing. Ellen left for home this morning with Will in toe. I'm heading home tomorrow, and I need to take most of my shit with me because the apartment has been sublet over the summer. Thankfully, we secured a lease for our junior year, and it's good to know we'll be coming back here, but it's a pain we can't leave everything behind.

Still, I count our blessings. Places like this are in high demand, and we're lucky we get to keep it for another year.

I am so glad exams are behind me, and now I have the whole summer to look forward to. A summer with Garrick. I'm itching for him to get here so I can confirm what I suspect he already knows—I'm ready to officially be his girlfriend.

I have just covered the dinner to keep it warm when the doorbell chimes. The biggest, goofiest grin spreads across my face as I sprint to the door and fling it open. We move as one, our arms and lips meeting as I pull him to me, and he claims my mouth in a fervent kiss I feel all the way to my toes. Since our first very public kiss in the cafeteria on Wednesday, we've been kissing any chance we get and struggling to keep it PG-13. But with exams and studying, there was no time to indulge in anything else.

Now the obstacles are gone, I look forward to taking our relationship to the next level tonight.

"Something smells good," Garrick purrs against my neck after we end our kiss. "And I'm not just talking about dinner."

"You smell delicious yourself," I admit, burying my nose in the gap between his neck and his shoulder and inhaling the purely masculine smell emanating from his pores. His scent is a mix of citrusy shower gel and spicy cologne, and I can't get enough.

"Invite me in, little minx, before we give the neighbors a show." He drags his nose up and down my neck as a door opens and closes behind him.

"Stop being so fucking hot, and I won't lose my head," I say, grabbing him by the shirt and yanking him into my apartment.

He backs me up with his body until my spine hits the counter. Placing the box of chocolates in his hand down beside us, he leans in and kisses me sweetly. One, two, three times, and I virtually melt into a puddle of goo at his feet. "I missed you."

"We didn't part until the early hours of the morning," I remind him.

Garrick showed up last night to collect me for our night out with our crew, with flowers and a bottle of wine, and it's a miracle we managed to make it to The End Zone because I basically attacked him with my lips and my hands, and it took mammoth self-control not to trap him in my bedroom and have my wicked way with him.

"So?" His brows crawl up his face. "That was hours ago. In case you've forgotten the memo, I miss you every second I'm not with you."

I place my hands on his trim waist. "I'm so into you, Garrick Allen."

"I'm glad to hear it," he says before stealing another kiss. "Because I'm so hooked on you, Stevie Colson."

We grin at each other like lovesick fools, and the pure elation charging through my veins is like nothing I've experienced before. I have fallen headfirst into this whirlwind with Garrick, and there isn't a single molecule of my body that regrets it.

"We need to eat before dinner is ruined." I trace my fingers through the stubble on his chin and cheeks. "But I promised you an official answer today, and I don't want to wait a second longer." I cup his handsome face. "I'm all in, Garrick. I want to be your girlfriend. Nothing would make me happier."

His answering kiss is deep, decadent, and hypnotic, and I'm barely capable of standing when we finally break apart, both of us panting and flushed with matching cheesy grins.

"Told you I'd convince you to go out with me," he says, shooting me a smug look.

"You did, and you were right." My arms glide around his neck, and I stretch up on tiptoes to kiss him. "Thank you for not giving up on me," I add when I end the kiss.

"That wasn't ever going to happen, beautiful. I had no intention of giving up."

The adoring look on his face as he messes with my hair does wonderful things to my insides. I think about how easy it's going to be to love this man, and while the thought still holds a modicum of fear, I'm ready to fall deep. Nothing has ever felt so right.

"You were always going to be mine, Stevie, and now you are." His lips glide over my mouth in a soft featherlight kiss, sending delicious tremors rippling across my skin. "Thank you for giving me a chance, and I promise you're not going to regret it. I'm going to be the best boyfriend because failing you is not an option. I'm in this for the long haul, and I'm going to worship the ground you walk on because you deserve everything and more."

When he hauls me into a hug, cradling my head against his strong chest, I close my eyes and absorb his words, letting them sink skin-deep as I relish the feel and smell of him. He's so solid and warm and all man. Nothing feels insurmountable if I have Garrick by my side. I don't have to lose my independence or any of my goals just because

I'm in a relationship. I know Garrick won't ever let that happen. I can be a better version of myself with him in my life, and I'm excited for this summer and all the possibilities it offers.

Garrick is mine. I know I won't stop pinching myself to believe it's real for a while, but I'm determined to fully embrace our relationship because making him happy is now one of my goals.

And once I set my heart and mind to something, there is no going back.

Chapter Nineteen

Garrick

"That was delicious," I say, rubbing a hand across my full stomach as I push my empty plate away. Stevie went all out with filet steak, shrimp, a homemade garlic sauce, and gratin potatoes, and she even made me brussels sprouts—cooked to perfection, soft and mushy, just how I like them. For dessert, she made a berry meringue roulade, and if I eat another bite, I'm likely to keel over and die.

"I'm glad you enjoyed it." She reaches across the table to take my hand. "I wanted to cook something special to thank you for everything."

"Getting to be with you is all the thanks I need."

"How did I get so lucky to meet you?" She squeezes my hand and smiles.

"It was fate." I laugh when she predictably rolls her eyes. "You won't convince me otherwise."

"Believe what you like, but you'll never convince me. Fate is how lazy people explain inaction or an abstract notion clung to by stubborn people who refuse to believe in coincidence." She grins and then releases my hand. Her chair scrapes across the tile floor as she abruptly stands and begins gathering up the dinnerware.

"And the cynic is in the house, ladies and gentlemen," I tease, climbing to my feet and snatching the plates from her hands. "You cooked. I'm on cleanup duty. That's always how it worked in my house." Well, my dad's house. Dawn maintains no son of hers will grow up spoiled, and we all had daily and weekly chores. My brothers constantly complain, as I did when I was younger, but Dawn is right, and I'm glad she was insistent. At least I can cook and clean and fend for myself. If I'd grown up solely with Mom, I'd be a spoiled little prick, waited on by staff for my every whim.

"You have good manners." She darts in to kiss my cheek. "And I'm never one to look a gift horse in the mouth."

After stacking the dirty dishes in the sink, I return to the table to top off her wineglass. I lean in to snatch a quick kiss, but she's quick to shove me away. "Not a chance in hell until you've rinsed that brussels sprout taste from your mouth."

I chuckle as I swat her ass. "It's not like I carry my toothbrush with me wherever I go."

"You can borrow mine," she says, "or just rinse your mouth with mouthwash."

"If that's what it'll take to steal more kisses, so be it." I whistle under my breath as I head off in the direction of the bathroom.

"Oh, and Garrick?!"

I spin around on my heels to face her.

"I'm not cynical. I'm pragmatic, and I'd much rather believe in unplanned coincidental events than supernatural predetermined nonsense that can't ever be proven."

When I return a few minutes later with minty-fresh breath, I find my girl spreadeagled on the couch, trawling through movies on Netflix. Leaning down, I claim her lips in a brief tender kiss. "Better?" I murmur before brushing my lips against hers again.

"Much." She reaches up to kiss me, but I pull back and straighten up with a smirk.

"I'm on cleanup duty, remember."

"Leave it," she coaxes, pinning me with a seductive smile. "Making out is a far better use of your time."

"I don't doubt it, but I never shirk my responsibility."

She pouts, and I laugh as I make my way into the kitchen and clean the place in noteworthy time.

When I return, Stevie is sitting upright on the couch and sipping her wine.

"Thank you," she says, when I flop down beside her, setting her wineglass on the coffee table and crawling toward me. "You really didn't have to do that, but I appreciate it. The more Garrick layers I uncover, the more impressed I am." She climbs onto my lap, straddling my hips.

"It's only fair." I glide my palms up her thighs. "We're both tired after finals, and you've been slaving away over a hot stove all day. I wanted you to relax."

"I am relaxed," she purrs, looping her arms around my neck as she grinds down on me. "I think it's time you relaxed too." An impish grin crests along her mouth as she bends down and puts her face all up in mine. "I have a few ideas in mind."

"I like where this is going," I grit out as my fingers breach the hem of her dress and creep up underneath it.

"I'm so horny for you," she whispers, kissing one corner of my mouth. "All week, I've been getting myself off daydreaming about your hands on me."

"Only my hands?" I quip as she plants another teasing kiss to the other side of my mouth.

There is zero hesitation in her response. "Your tongue and your cock too." Her thumb traces a path along my bottom lip, and I'm like steel in my pants as she slowly rotates her hips and pivots against me.

My fingers move up toward the Holy Land, the tips grazing the edge of her lace panties, and she sucks in a needy gasp. "I've been fantasizing about you too," I admit, holding her gaze as I trail my fingers back and forth against her lace-covered crotch. A shiver works its way through her as she holds her hips up a little, granting me better access. "Kiss me," I demand, and she groans into my mouth as I push her panties aside and run my finger up and down her slit.

Her lips plunder mine as I continue teasing her with one finger, slowly dragging it back and forth against her wet folds, until I can't hold back any longer. Driving my finger inside her, I almost come in my boxers when I feel her warm walls gripping my digit and holding it tight.

Our kissing intensifies, and she's whimpering against my lips as I add another finger and pump them in and out of her pussy. She feels like heaven on my fingers, but it's not enough. I need more. I need to feel her arousal on my tongue. Breaking our kiss, I nip at her jawline and her earlobe before whispering, "I need to taste you. Can I?"

"God, yes. Please," she rasps, grinding on top of me before smashing her lips to mine and devouring me with the same potent desire I feel churning in my veins.

My dick is begging for release, dying to plunge inside her and make her fully mine, but I want to get on my knees for her first. This is about Stevie's needs, not mine, so I reposition her on the couch and slide to the floor, parting her thighs and licking my lips. Keeping my eyes on her, I reach under her dress, hook my thumbs in the side of her panties, and carefully drag them down her legs. I remove her heels, one at a time, and discard her panties.

Her chest heaves, and her breath huffs out in exaggerated spurts as I glide my palms slowly up her legs. Starting with her perfectly formed feet, moving over her shapely legs, along the curve of her knee, and up along her satiny-smooth thighs.

"You're killing me here," she pants over a moan as I lean in and press a kiss to the side of one thigh.

"Good things come to those who wait," I tease, fighting a chuckle when she flips me the bird. "That's what I constantly told myself these past few weeks as I waited for us to be on the same page."

Something close to adoration paints her face as she stares at me. "You're about to get your reward."

"I would have waited forever for you, Stevie. I hope you know that," I truthfully admit as I push her dress up to her waist and expose her most intimate parts to me.

"I know." Her voice is a throaty whisper that cranks my desire to a new level.

Her thighs tremble as I push them farther apart so I can see all of her. "Show me your pussy," I instruct. "Give me my reward. I want to see every bit of you."

She gulps audibly as she lowers her hands to her cunt and pulls her folds back with shaking fingers, showcasing her glistening clit and the tempting wetness of her soft pink flesh.

"You're perfect, Stevie," I say, leaning in for a closer inspection. Her arousal tickles my nostrils, and my dick is throbbing in anticipation. "Such a pretty pink pussy. So beautiful and all mine." I lave my tongue up and down her slit, lapping up her juices and licking her fingers where they open her up to me. She tastes divine, like the sweetest nectar, and I sense a new addiction forming. "Touch your tits," I say before diving in with my tongue and my fingers, working her soaking cunt as she gropes her tits through her dress. I shove my tongue inside her warm tight channel while I rub her swollen bundle of nerves with two fingers. Then I alternate, pushing three fingers inside her as I suck on her clit, moaning against her quivering flesh as she rocks her hips, writhing above me, with her eyes closed and one hand on her boob.

"Look at me, baby," I command a few minutes later when I feel she's close. "I want you to watch me eating you out as you come all over my face."

"Fuck, Garrick," she mumbles, arching her back and grinding her cunt on my face as she loses herself to lust.

"Eyes on me, Stevie," I demand, curling my fingers inside her and hitting the perfect spot.

"Oh, god, Garrick. That feels so good. Don't stop. I'm so close."

"I know, beautiful. Keep your eyes on me, and fall apart on my fingers and my tongue." I wait until her eyes are fixed on mine to press down inside her at the same time I gently bite her clit, and she crests the peak. Screaming my name repeatedly, Stevie rocks against my face, writhing and moaning, her thighs spasming and her pussy quaking as she comes and comes on my tongue.

I milk every drop of her desire, even after she's gone quiet and stopped moving, unable to tear myself away from her magical cunt. Sounds cheesy as shit, but it's the fucking truth. I am utterly addicted to this woman. She has cast a spell on me, and it's one I never want to emerge from.

"Garrick." Her fingers roam through my hair, exploring and tugging, and it sends fresh tremors of need crawling all over my body. "That was the best thing anyone has ever done to me. Holy fuck."

Reluctantly, I pull my face away, feeling her arousal coating my lips and dripping onto my chin. I crawl up her body, holding onto the back of the couch as I lower myself down over her and claim her lips, letting her taste herself on me. Driving my tongue into her mouth, I explore and devour as my cock aches painfully behind the zipper of my jeans.

"Your turn," she says, palming my dick through the denim and piercing me with a searing-hot look.

"I won't say no." I'm physically incapable of turning her down, such is my need. My dick is so hard it could hammer nails. Pushing off the couch, I strip out of my jeans, boxers, and socks in record time, and then I yank my T-shirt off over my head, standing before her completely naked.

Her eyes are bugging out of her head, she's licking her lips, and her pupils are blown with the depth of her arousal. Not gonna lie. It does wonders for my ego.

"You're so beautiful, Garrick," she says, sliding to the edge of the couch. Her dress falls down around her upper thighs, and the sight of her fully clothed while I'm butt naked makes what we're about to do even dirtier.

"Spread your legs and lean back," I say, stroking my erection as I stare at her gorgeous mouth. I'm already salivating at the prospect of those plump lips wrapped around my cock. Stevie gets into position, and I stand between her thighs as I lean forward and rest my hands on the back of the couch, my dick straining and leaking precum as it bobs in the vicinity of her face. She scoots down a little until the angle is right, and then she circles her soft fingers around my dick and guides it to her mouth.

She licks the tip, groaning as she sucks down the beads of precum at my crown. Closing my eyes, I curse under my breath as she takes her time caressing my hard length. Nibbling, sucking, and lightly grazing her teeth along my shaft, she moans in appreciation while worshiping my dick like it's the best thing she's ever put in her mouth.

My hips jerk of their own accord, desperate to slam into her and craving release. Stevie reads my cues, hollowing her cheeks and sucking me down as far as she can go. When my cock hits the back of her throat, a guttural moan rips from my lips, and I fist her hair in one hand and take control.

Our eyes meet, remaining locked on one another as we work in tandem to drive me to blissful oblivion. I thrust my hips and pump in and out of her mouth as she widens her lips, stretching her jaw as far as it will go, sucking and licking like a fucking queen. Tears spill from her eyes and saliva leaks from her lips as I quicken my pace and tighten my hold on her hair.

Stevie stays with me the whole time, and I'm watching her carefully for signs she's uncomfortable, but I see none. The heat in her eyes and clear joy on her face tell me to keep going, so I do. Until my balls pull up, a familiar tingle snakes up my spine, and I know I'm close. "I'm going to come." I loosen my grip on her hair a little, peering deep into her emerald eyes. "You want me to pull out?"

She shakes her head over a mouthful of my dick, and the visual sends me steamrolling toward my climax. I detonate in her mouth, shooting jets of hot cum down her throat as I shout out my release, calling her name in worship as I empty everything inside her. Stevie doesn't let up until I've stopped thrusting and my cries have died out. My dick slides from her mouth with a loud pop, and I collapse in a sated heap, holding her as I maneuver onto my back, lying lengthways on the couch, with Stevie on top of me.

Her bare pussy rubs against my softening shaft, instantly hardening it again.

"Was that—"

"Fucking incredible," I confirm before she's even finished her sentence. I kiss her deeply, rolling my tongue inside her mouth as I hold her head firmly between my palms. "You're amazing." I dust kisses all over her face. "So fucking amazing."

"Want to take this into the bedroom?" she suggests, waggling her brows while gyrating her hips and rubbing her pussy against my fresh erection.

Keeping her in an embrace, I sit us up and lay her legs sideways across my thighs as my feet plant on the hardwood floor. Nuzzling my nose into her neck, I inhale her sweet scent while my arms tighten around her waist. "More than anything," I finally reply, looking her straight in the eyes. "But that's exactly why I think we shouldn't."

Her eyes pop wide as she stares at me. I tuck her gorgeous hair behind one ear. "I don't want to be a casual fuck."

"You aren't, Garrick." Gently, she places her small hand on my bare chest. "You never could be."

I can't believe I'm going to say this, but it feels like the right thing to do. "I need you to be sure, Stevie. It wasn't that long ago you were adamant relationships weren't for you. I couldn't handle being a fling. Not when I'm so invested in you."

"I'm invested in you too, and I'm sure, Garrick. I swear. I told you when I go for something I give it my all. I didn't say that lightly. I'm fully on board."

I kiss her soft cheek. "I'm glad to hear it, but I still think we should wait."

Hurt flickers behind her eyes, and it guts me. I don't want her thinking it's a rejection when it's not. I'm just trying to do the right thing for both of us. "Listen up, beautiful." I hold her closer. "You mean everything to me. I want to fuck you so bad my balls are throwing a pity party right now. But I want our first time to be special. It's a moment that will stay with us for the rest of our lives. I want it to be memorable so it always brings a smile to our faces and tears to our eyes. I have no doubt if I took you back to your bedroom now it would be amazing, but I want more than that for us. I want to make it magical. I want it to be romantic and somewhere that means something to us and preferably surrounded by candles, not packing boxes." I try to bring some humor to the moment to lighten it.

"Is that the truth?" Her eyes probe mine.

"Absolutely. I would never lie to you."

"I don't like it, or agree, but only a bitch would say no to wanting it more romantic. You've patiently waited for me, so I guess I can summon patience from somewhere to wait for you."

I chuckle at the grumpy look on her face. "It won't be forever. Trust me when I say I can't wait long, but just think about how amazing it's going to be when we've waited and planned it for the perfect moment." I rub my thumb along her swollen lips, basking in the beauty of the woman sitting on my lap. Stevie has never looked more gorgeous than she does now with tangled hair, flushed skin, and a resigned pout on her delectable mouth. "A wise woman once told me anticipation makes it all the sweeter, and I'm sticking by that."

Chapter Twenty

Stevie

"Why the grumpy face?" Nana asks as we unpack the boxes of supplies that have just been delivered.

"I thought having Garrick here this week would mean lots of time together, but I've barely seen him."

On Monday, we joined Garrick and his crew, along with friends and neighbors, to clear out the barn, tossing everything into industrial dumpsters because nothing was salvageable. It was painstaking back-breaking work, and I collapsed in a heap that night, covered in sweat and grime and aching all over.

Garrick has been traveling to Ravenna with a team of workers from the lumberyard every day, and they leave promptly at six. We barely manage to grab lunch and a quick kiss in the middle of the day.

Nana chuckles. "You sure have changed your tune."

"You know me." I shrug as I cut through packing tape on one of the boxes and extract some cute vases and exterior wall hangings. "Once I set my mind to something, I give it my everything."

Last week, I set up a donation page online to raise funds to restock the shop, and everyone rallied around. We ended up tripling the donation target, and I'm glad because it's taken the pressure off

Nana. There is enough to replace all the damaged items and to pay the staff this week even though most of them haven't been needed after Monday.

Garrick and the Allen Lumber crew have been working alone Tuesday, Wednesday, and Thursday to repair the roof and reinforce the structure so the barn is more robust and less likely to suffer damage in the future. Garrick promised to show up with double the crew tomorrow to finish the interiors before lunchtime on Saturday so we can get ready for the celebrations planned for later that night.

It was my idea to throw a barn party to thank everyone for riding to the rescue. Hadley canceled the bar booking she made for my birthday night out in Seattle, inviting my friends to come here instead, so it'll be a double celebration.

As soon as Garrick found out, he roped a few friends he knows, who are in a country music band, to play at the party. Hadley called a friend from college, who is a national line-dancing champion, and she's going to put us through our paces on the night. Nana's friends and a few local restaurants are providing the food. Mom got Sand Point to provide some complimentary booze, and I know Garrick will show up with boxes of wine.

The dress code is country and western, and I went shopping with Hads last night for a new outfit. I bought a navy, brown, and orange paisley print dress with elbow-length sleeves and a full swishy skirt that ends just above my knees. It came with a gorgeous crochet-style belt and a navy straw cowboy-style hat, and I bought my first pair of cowboy boots to wear with it. I love it, and I can't wait for Garrick to see me in it.

"Earth to Little Poppy." Nana snaps her fingers in my face, a look of amusement glittering in her eyes. "You're miles away."

"Sorry, I was just thinking about the party, and I guess I zoned out."

"Happiness looks good on you, sweetheart," she says, removing some garden decorations from a box and arranging them on the long table in front of us. We tidied up the barn she uses as a stockroom, to make way for the new supplies, over the past couple of days, and we've been unpacking daily deliveries in between making up bouquets for prepaid orders. Hadley and I have been driving around town delivering them most evenings.

"I have never felt like this about any boy before. Is it normal to obsessively think about him all the time?"

Nana chuckles. "I'd be worried if you weren't obsessively thinking about him." She fans her face with one hand. "Have you seen those muscles in his arms and the way they flex and roll in his back as he's working? Sheesh." She fans her face with both hands now. "If I was forty years younger, I'd be challenging you for him!"

I burst out laughing. "Nana, stop. At least I now know why you're always taking water and iced lemonade to the workers."

"I've got to get my kicks where I can." She swipes sweat off her brow as she winks at me. "All that young naked flesh on display is giving this old woman the thrill of a lifetime."

"We aim to please." Garrick's deep voice floods the space as he strides into the barn, grinning like all his Sundays have come at once. He's bare chested, like most of the workers, because it's been unseasonably hot these past few days, and they're not working under ideal conditions. A wrinkled T-shirt is stuffed in the back pocket of his dirty jeans as he ambles toward me.

"If that was the case, you'd be working buck-ass naked," Nana replies, staring my boyfriend straight in the eye without as much as a blush.

"Nana!" I shriek as Garrick busts out laughing. "Good god. Between you and Hads, you'll send me into an early grave."

Garrick slides his arm around my waist, pulling me into his sweat-slickened chest. "Don't worry, beautiful. The only eyes feasting on my naked body are yours."

I trail my fingers over the Trinity knot ink on his chest. "I wish. We've barely had time to talk this week, let alone anything else." I'm still so fucking hot for my boyfriend and dying to bounce on his cock.

He kisses me sweetly, uncaring Nana is watching, though he does keep it PG because we have an audience. "I'm planning to rectify that right this second. I drove today and was hoping you'd want to grab dinner?"

"Sounds great," Hadley pipes up, sauntering into the barn after finishing her flower deliveries. "Hudson and I will join you. It can be a double date."

Hads has decided Garrick's best friend from North Bend is her next victim. I have tried talking her out of it, but my free-spirited bestie is as stubborn as a mule, and she's set her sights on him, so there's no persuading her otherwise.

An hour later, the four of us are seated at a cozy table in the back of a local Italian restaurant, nibbling on bread sticks and sipping ice-cold Limonata. Nana let the guys shower and change at her place while Hads and I went back to my house to freshen up. Mom wasn't home yet from work, but I left her a note telling her I was out on a date. I whipped her up a chicken salad and left it in the refrigerator. I'll grab a tiramisu to take home to her before we leave.

Hads chattered excitedly about Hudson as we got dressed. I didn't bother warning her to behave, because she wouldn't listen, and anyway, I never want to clip her wings. What you see is what you get with my bestie, and if Hudson doesn't like her direct approach, I'm sure he'll let her down gently. Garrick says he's a good guy, and I trust him. I'm glad we got this opportunity tonight. There hasn't been much time to get to know Garrick's childhood friend thus far, and I'm hoping to change that now.

Garrick slides his arm along the back of my chair as he scoots in closer to my side. I look up at him, grinning like a loon as he bends down and pecks my lips. "You look beautiful," he says, toying with the spaghetti straps on my white summer dress. "Like a ray of sunshine." His fingers wind in my hair as he stares at me like I put the sun in the sky. I've noticed he always seems to be touching my hair, and I love it. Every time he puts his fingers on any part of me, I tingle all over.

"You two are so stinking cute I could puke," Hadley says, beaming at me. I know she's thrilled I've found a guy worth risking a relationship for.

"I agree." Hudson's deep voice reverberates in the busy restaurant. "You make a good couple." Hudson has dark hair, worn longish and loose around his face, like Garrick. But that's where the resemblance ends. His pale silvery-blue eyes are the opposite of Garrick's warm hazel ones, and he's a few inches shorter in height. Though they are both muscular, he's stockier than Garrick's lean build. I can see why Hadley has her panties in a bunch. He's a good-looking guy with a smoldering presence that's hard to ignore.

"I know." Garrick's smug tone is laced with pride as he wraps his arm around my shoulders and pulls me in close to his body. "Life doesn't get much better than this."

My heart thumps wildly against my chest wall as he peers deep into my eyes, conveying so much with that one look. Falling this deeply and this quickly is scary, but when his protective arms are around me, I feel like I could scale mountains and nothing seems insurmountable.

Including my own entrenched fears.

"When they get married, I'll be maid of honor to your best man," Hadley tells Hudson, instantly claiming my attention.

My jaw slackens, and I silently pray for her to drop this line of questioning. Garrick and I have only started dating, for fuck's sake, and mentioning the m-word is like waving a red flag in front of a bull. My palms are sweaty as I grip the edge of my chair, wondering what is going to come out of her mouth next.

Life is never dull when Hadley is around, that's for sure.

"We'll probably end up banging then, so we should do a trial run." She pops an olive in her mouth, drilling him with a pointed look. "See if we're sexually compatible."

I breathe a sigh of relief, relaxing against my amused boyfriend as

I wait to see how Hudson responds. To give him credit, he barely looks ruffled. I'm guessing Garrick forewarned him. "I'm down to fuck." He shrugs and rubs his neatly trimmed beard. "Just tell me the time and place, and I'm there."

"Awesome. No time like the present." Hads slaps a fifty down on the table and eyeballs me. "Get our food to go, and drop it by my place on your way home." Tugging on Hudson's arm, she stands. "Come on, mountain man. This pussy waits for no penis."

Garrick's chest rumbles with laughter as we watch them exit the restaurant in a hurry.

"Did that really just happen?" I turn to look at him as the waitress brings our pasta dishes. I quickly explain the situation, and she removes Hudson's and Hadley's plates to box them up.

"How did you and Hadley end up best friends when you're polar opposites in so many ways?" Garrick asks, removing his arm from around my shoulders.

"I think that's why it works." I twirl creamy spaghetti around my fork. "She encourages me to break free of my rules, and I rein her in when she gets too crazy. We balance each other out." I stifle a moan as I chew my food, the flavors bursting on my tongue, and it's a close second to sex.

Which reminds me.

Glancing at Garrick, I admire his side profile, wondering if the guy ever looks bad. I run my fingers through the scruff on his cheeks, loving how I can touch him at will now. "Right now, I'm envious of my bestie because she's getting cock while I'm over here with my weeping pussy and a constant throbbing ache between my legs."

Garrick almost chokes on his meat cannelloni, and I smirk as I hand him a napkin quickly followed by a glass of water.

"I take it back," he says, tweaking my nose when he's composed himself. "You two are more alike than I realized." He tucks a piece of hair behind my ear. "It's as hard for me, you know. Literally." Discreetly, he pulls my hand under the table and slides it across to his crotch. He places my palm atop the obvious bulge in his jeans. "All week, I've been walking around in pain. The second I see you, my dick springs up. If you walk past the barn and your scent tickles my nostrils, I'm hard. When your laughter wafts through the air, I'm leaking precum and angling my body so the crew doesn't see I've got a boner." He leans in, pressing his mouth to my ear, as he returns my hand to my lap. "I'm dying to fuck you, my sunshine, and I have a plan."

"You could have led with that," I tease, snuggling into his side, more interested in touching my boyfriend than eating. We're picking up some curious glances from other patrons, but I couldn't care less.

"Do you think you could get away early next Saturday and come stay with me at the winery?" he asks. "The cabin is cozy and romantic and very private. It's surrounded by woodland, and the river transects our property, so we can go swimming or kayaking or hiking on Sunday. I think you'll love it there, and it's perfect for what I have in mind for Saturday night." He pins me with a suggestive look that has me visibly squirming on my seat and squeezing my thighs together.

"That's a whole week away," I grumble, resting my chin on his shoulder.

He chuckles, leaning in to kiss me as our food goes cold. "I promise I'll make it worth the wait."

I cup his handsome face. "I already know that." I peer deep into his eyes. "I know I'm bitching and whining, but it actually means a lot to me that you've put thought into this." All week, I've been thinking about what he said back in Oregon. He wants to make this different from every other time I've had sex because what we share is like nothing I've experienced before. He wants to ensure we give our relationship the respect it deserves and that we are starting out on the best footing.

As sexually frustrated as I am, I can't fault him.

It only intensifies my feelings for him.

We're new as a couple, but already, he cares so much. He has proven how willing he is to put my needs first. In this, I bow to the fact he knows more about what I need than I do. And I already trust him with my heart, so it makes sense I should trust him with my body too.

"I don't want to scare you, Stevie, but I already know you're my forever." His fingers sweep over my cheeks while I internally battle euphoria and panic. "The memories we're making now will stay with us for a lifetime." His lips brush against mine. "I only ever want to give you the most magical memories, and it starts from the very beginning."

Chapter Twenty-One

Stevie

The barn is bustling with activity, and my heart is swollen behind my rib cage. All the food and drink are laid out on two long rectangular tables, buffet style, so everyone can help themselves. Everywhere I look, people are enjoying themselves and having a great time. Laughing, talking, dancing, singing, eating, and drinking is happening in abundance, and I'm drunk on all the feel-good endorphins flooding my system. I was a little stressed out earlier. Worrying we wouldn't be able to pull this off in time, but it came together better than I expected.

Garrick and I are taking a well-earned breather, sipping beers from our position at the side of the dancing area as we watch everyone having a good time. I'm pressed against his side, and his arm is around my shoulders, and I've never felt more content. Seeing everyone I love in one place is amazing. But the cherry on top is noticing how relaxed Nana is now. It's like the weight of the world has been lifted from her shoulders. My eyes seek her out, finding her and Mom nestled in the center of the jiving crowd on the new hardwood floor. They are laughing as they loop arms and dance, and it brings tears to my eyes to see them so happy.

It's been a stressful few weeks for our family, and I'm glad we were able to put it behind us. It's a shame Garrick's dad and stepmom are on vacation. It would've been lovely to have them here. I'd like to meet them, and I know Nana wants to thank the man in person.

Shared tears of joy were shed this afternoon when Garrick's crew finished the barn remodeling and we saw the wonders they had worked inside. Overhead, sturdy beams prop up the solid new roof. Rows of new lighting have been installed, illuminating the large space. New shelving units and matching tables jut against either side of the front of the structure, ready to house flowers, displays, and accessories.

The coffee area at the back has been completely transformed. An L-shaped counter runs the length of the back with a host of brand-spanking-new kitchen appliances fitted against the rear wall, ensuring it's a complete kitchen so Nana can offer more than just snacks, if she chooses. Comfy chairs, tables, and couches occupy the long space on the left while two new customer bathrooms are tucked into the space on the far right.

Glistening wide hardwood planks cover the entire floor space. They are currently being put to the test by boisterous partygoers as they dance to popular country songs played by the talented band recruited by Garrick.

"Come on," my boyfriend says, setting both our beer bottles down on the table behind us. "I want to dance to this song." I let him steer me into the middle of the dance floor, looking around in amazement at the incredible transformation. The barn looks virtually unrecognizable now, and I still can't wrap my head around it.

The Allen crew went above and beyond, and what they managed to achieve in a week is nothing short of miraculous. They had help from local tradesmen, who gave their time for free and provided parts at cost. Nana is well regarded in the town, and the way the community came out to support her only proves it.

My heart is so full tonight, and the fact it's my twentieth birthday accounts for none of it. It's all thanks to the man, twirling me around the dance floor, smiling at me like I'm a precious jewel. Garrick looks superhot in a plaid blue, red, and white shirt, open over a tight-fitting white tee. Dark jeans hang temptingly from his toned hips. Scuffed boots and a cowboy hat complete his ensemble, and I'm ready to climb him like a jungle gym.

Yanking his body into mine, I stretch on tiptoes and shout in his ear. "I feel like you should get lucky tonight. How else can I repay you for everything you've done?"

"Nice try, sunshine," he says, wrapping his strong arms around my back and dipping me down low.

For some inexplicable reason, he's started calling me his sunshine in recent days. In the past, I have always gagged at couples who have pet names for one another, but I can't deny how much I love Garrick's term of endearment. Cheesy as it is, I'm lapping it up like it's manna from heaven.

"We're not caving to wild monkey lust." He straightens us up as his words and the resolve behind them burst the erotic fantasy bubble playing out in my head. "Anticipation. Remember?"

He cups my face in his large palms, and his mouth descends on mine before I can protest or attempt to convince him to throw away his plan.

I lose all semblance of thought, like I do every time he kisses me. My hands find purchase on his hard, warm chest, and I swoon as he devours my mouth in a very public display of affection. Garrick's kisses consume me to the point where nothing else exists. I get lost in him and the powerful sensations he entices from my body until the only things I'm conscious of are his lips gliding against my lips, his tongue tangling with mine, the heat rolling off his body as he presses flush against me, and the possessive way he firmly holds my face as he makes love to my mouth.

Keeping his lips locked on mine, he lowers his hands to my hips and sways us in tune to the music. My arms encircle his neck, and a sigh of contentment eases through our joined lips. The band is playing a slower song now, and I grind my body against his, reveling in the feel of his hard-on against my stomach as we kiss and dance and basically dry-hump in the middle of a crowd of neighbors, friends, family, and coworkers.

Hadley must be proud.

When the song ends, whoops, hollers, and catcalls ring out, finally breaking us out of our little sexed-up bubble. Garrick's chest rumbles with laughter as he breaks our kiss, holding me tight to his chest. "I think we might have been making a scene," he mumbles against my ear, half laughing.

"I'm thinking I don't really care," I truthfully reply, but my words are muffled against his chest.

The song ends, and the band calls him to the makeshift stage. He drags me with him, but I don't complain. I'd challenge anyone to physically separate us right now.

Mom, Nana, Hadley, Hudson, Ellen, Will, and Noah are crowded beside the side of the stage, grinning and screaming encouragement.

My eyes flick to Garrick as he grips my hand in one hand and accepts a guitar in the other. "What are you up to?" I ponder when he turns to face me.

"You'll see." His eyes radiate mischief as he rests the guitar against the stool propped in front of the mic and lifts me onto an adjoining stool. "Just hold still, and let me do my thing." He kisses me, and it's no chaste meeting of lips, and the crowd goes nuts again. Mom and Hads are jumping up and down while Ellen has her phone out and pointed at my face.

Garrick sits on his stool with his guitar on his lap. After adjusting the mic, he introduces himself. "Now, I know we're all here tonight to help Betsy celebrate the relaunch of her business, but it's a double celebration. Tonight is also my girlfriend Stevie's birthday, and I want to sing a song for her."

A chorus of oohs and aahs rings out around the room before a reverent hush descends.

"This song reminds me of you, babe," he says, moving his fingers into position on the strings. "Of us. Happy birthday, my sunshine." Tears well in my eyes with the way he's looking at me, and how considerate the gesture is. Everything else fades away in this moment and Garrick is all I see. "This is 'You Make it Easy'."

He starts singing, ignoring the audience as he stares into my face, pouring his heart and soul into the lyrics. It's exquisite, and I'm enchanted. I haven't heard this song before, but the words are beautiful, especially when sung in such a heartfelt way. Garrick's distinctive husky voice wraps around me, and I'm reminded how talented he is.

When he gets to the guitar riff portion of the song, my chest is heaving, and I'm struggling to hold my feelings inside. A tear slips out when he sings about sunshine and being his better half, like God made me for him, and I can't control my emotions anymore.

This guy is unreal.

I didn't think men like him existed outside of books.

He's almost too perfect.

Certainly, when compared with my imperfections and fears about relationships.

I wonder if someone like me could ever permanently hold on to someone like him.

As soon as that thought lands in my brain, I mentally swat it away, unwilling to let any of my insecurities ruin this beautiful moment. Swiping at the tears spilling from my eyes, I smile and gaze adoringly at him as he finishes the song.

Garrick gets rid of the guitar, scoops me up into his arms, and kisses me passionately as the crowd roars their approval around us.

"Garrick," I choke out when he finally puts me down and releases my swollen lips. "That was so romantic and one of the most beautiful things anyone has ever done for me."

He brushes the dampness on my cheeks as his arms tighten around my back. "I plan to serenade you every day for the rest of my life, sunshine."

Now I understand the meaning behind the word, I practically

melt into a puddle of goo. Garrick undoes me in the best possible way. "I love the song, but I don't think I've made it all that easy for you." My fingers trail up his solid arms as I lean back and stare up at him.

If ever there was a pinch-me moment, it's now.

I cannot believe I landed a guy like Garrick. I must have done something right in this life to deserve him because he's like the manifestation of my every dream and then some.

"That's not how I see it." He rests his brow against mine. "You make me into the man I want to be. A man worthy of you, and it's as easy as breathing being with you. You feel like the other half of my soul, Stevie." He slaps a hand over his chest. "I've never felt so whole, so complete, so content."

"Stop it," I say, half laughing, half crying. "You're too perfect, and I'm the one who isn't worthy."

"How about this," he says, moving his mouth to my ear so I can hear him over the noise of the crowd. "We are worthy of each other, and we won't ever stop to question it."

"I like that," I say, clutching his waist as I sense movement behind me.

Garrick turns us as one, pulling my back against his chest as he circles his arms around me from behind. Mom and Nana lift a small table with a large birthday cake onto the stage.

Garrick has spoken plenty about moments and memories, and I know this one is one I will cherish forever. Enveloped in the arms of the guy I'm falling in love with while my mother and my nana join my friends and our neighbors in singing happy birthday to me.

As I blow out the candles, I make a wish.

Wishing to always remember how loved I am in this moment and to never be without this feeling.

Chapter Twenty-Two

Stevie

"You were right. It's beautiful here, and I love it," I truthfully admit after Garrick has given me a tour of the vineyards and winery in Woodinville. It's their flagship operation and the most successful one under the Allen Wineries brand. The setting is idyllic, nestled on acres of mature lush land. The sleek wood and glass modern building at the front of the property houses the tasting room, a restaurant, and a massive shop. A small function room is tucked into the back with floor-to-ceiling windows offering breathtaking views over the exquisite grounds. Garrick explained it is rented out by wine clubs and book clubs and for small parties and weddings.

The building faces the high ornate wrought iron entrance gates and the road at the front, but it's walled in on both sides, ensuring security and privacy. The entire rear of the structure surveys the sweeping landscaped gardens abundant with neatly trimmed shrubs and colorful flower beds. In the distance, bracketed by dense woodland that appears to run the perimeter of the estate, are several large barn-like structures where the wine production takes place, and beyond that, barely visible from here, are rows upon rows of vineyards. Sweet floral notes waft on the warm evening breeze, comingled with earthier tones, tickling my nostrils, and tempting my palate.

"I'll give you a tour of the vineyards tomorrow," Garrick says, threading his fingers in mine after we drop my weekend bag off at the cabin. The three-bedroom wooden cabin manages to be luxurious and homey at the same time. Visions of drinking wine in front of the open fireplace, naked after making love on the rug, was the first thought to accost my mind when I stepped foot inside. From the way Garrick looked at me, I suspect he knew exactly where my mind had gone. Nerves fired at me as he showed me around the place I'm staying the next couple of nights, which is another first for me.

"And I thought we might go hiking and take a picnic," he adds, yanking me out of my inner monologue. "The weather forecast is good."

"That sounds great. I'm happy to do whatever." This is Garrick's territory, and I trust him to show me the best time. Hopefully, there will be many more weekends in Woodinville before summer ends.

This place automatically feels like home, and I could easily get used to hanging around here more often. It's serene with no outside world interferences, and I felt instantly relaxed the second I arrived. It's like a little corner of heaven in Seattle and our own private getaway.

Garrick points out places on the grounds as we stroll from the cabin back to the commercial side of the property. He's as animated as when he is on stage, and I can tell his enthusiasm is coming from a genuine place. He truly loves it here, and he's passionate about his family business. It's one of his most endearing qualities, and I'm happy to sit back and let him do all the talking.

It's still light out, though nightfall is encroaching, and a gentle scented breeze swirls around my bare shoulders as we take our time meandering the grounds of the winery. My white cardigan and Garrick's sweater are draped over his free arm as we walk. Garrick's palm is solid and comforting against mine, and I'm blooming with happiness as I listen to his husky voice and his obvious pride.

Our feet crunch on the stones underfoot as Garrick leads me around the main building heading toward a cute outside area. I'm glad I wore white tennis shoes with my dress. I had a sense wearing heels on the grounds of a winery might be challenging. I'm also glad I opted for pretty over sexy with my choice of dress.

Tonight's a special night. The night we're going to have sex for the first time, and I agonized over what to wear. In the end, I ignored Hadley and chose this pale green and peach patterned ankle-length summer dress over the tight black minidress she was suggesting. If we'd been having dinner at a trendy spot in the city, it would have been perfect, but it wasn't right for this setting. I'm glad I listened to my gut, and I feel on top of the world in this dress. It has delicate straps and gentle ruching at the bust, and then it skims over my hips and waist in floaty chiffon that sways along my legs as I walk.

I left my hair down, because Garrick loves it like that, but Hadley used the curling iron on my tresses, and it hangs in soft glossy curls down my back. The heart-shaped locket Garrick gave me for my birthday rests delicately in the curve between my collarbone and my chest.

"We're lucky this area wasn't booked tonight," Garrick says, ushering me toward the most beautiful outside area.

A wide, tall wooden gazebo covers the space, protecting it from the elements. Enclosed by tall hedges and shrubs, it offers complete privacy in a very romantic setting. Stunning purple and pink flowering plants creep like ivy along all the posts and wooden frames. Tinkling spotlights are interwoven between the flowers, casting dancing reflections across the myriad of glass-topped tables. Little candles and vases with colorful flowers adorn each of the twelve tables, centered around a small stone water feature.

"It's stunning." I stare in awe as Garrick leads me to the only table set for dinner. He pulls out a wicker chair with comfortable cushions, waiting for me to sit before pushing my chair in. He's such a gentleman. Tipping my head back, I pucker my lips, and he doesn't disappoint, kissing me tenderly and sweetly from above.

"Not as stunning as you," he replies when we break our kiss. Garrick moves around the table to the silver wine cooler and removes a bottle of sparkling wine. "You're so gorgeous I won't be able to take my eyes off you tonight," he adds, filling two wineglasses with the bubbly liquid.

"You don't look so bad yourself." He's wearing black pants with a white shirt rolled to the elbows and open at the top so the edge of his tattoo peeks out. An expensive silver watch is strapped to his wrist, and his hair has been tamed with hair gel and tucked behind his ears. "You scrub up well, Allen," I tease as a server appears carrying a tray.

Garrick reaches across the table, linking our hands as the woman sets a bread basket down with olives and oils and a bottle of sparkling water.

We chat amicably as our meal is served, and any anxiety I was feeling on the drive here has long since gone. At least for now.

After a sumptuous meal of sage and butter ravioli, hake and ratatouille, and the most devilish chocolate fondant, we grab a bottle of wine from the store and set out hand in hand for the walk to the cabin. Nightfall has descended, but the stone path is lit by spotlights embedded on either side guiding our way.

Nerves prick at me when we arrive at the cabin, and a swarm of butterflies is stumbling around my chest like they're drunk or high.

"Don't be nervous, sunshine." Garrick places his hands on my shoulders and smiles. "I'm going to take care of you, and you don't have to do anything if you've changed your mind."

"I haven't." I rest my hands on his trim waist as a lump rises in my throat. "I want this with you, but it's different than what I'm used to." Anticipation has been building all week, which I love, but it also means I've been thinking more than I usually do, and it's left time for insecurities to rise to the surface.

Garrick palms one side of my face. "It's why I wanted to do it like this." He drops feather-soft kisses on my lips until I melt against him and relax. He reels me into his chest, and his smile is laced with adoration, before tucking me under his chin. "You make me feel so much, Stevie," he whispers against my hair. "I'm scared too because I don't want to mess this up with you. I want it to be perfect. Memorable."

I dance my fingers along his spine before tilting my face up to his. "I already know it will be. I adore you, Garrick." My heart is beating so hard, and I know that's not the totality of what I'm feeling for this man. "I trust you, and I trust in us. Nothing that feels this good can be wrong. I can't ever remember feeling this happy. My heart permanently feels like it's going to burst."

"You're already my everything, Stevie," he whispers against my face.

All the words we haven't said linger in the tiny gap between us, but we silently acknowledge tonight is for a certain first and the other first can wait.

As I stare into his eyes, I know I'm committed to giving this man all my unclaimed firsts. With that acknowledgment comes confidence, and my nerves flitter away. Placing my hand on his chest, right in the spot where his heart is beating as frantically as mine, I say, "Make love to me, Garrick. Make me fully yours."

I sip wine on the couch while Garrick readies the bedroom, my eyes skimming over the myriad of family photos lining the mantelpiece and the walls. Tucking my bare feet underneath me, I savor the warmth of the homey room as I drink it all in. Every item seems carefully chosen, and I spot tons of ornaments and decorations from foreign travel. The Allens are clearly well traveled, and I wonder if that is something Garrick and I will get to do one day.

"It's ready," my man says, and I whip my head around. Garrick pads soundlessly across the floor in bare feet, smiling as he approaches. He stretches out his arm. "Come, my sunshine."

Setting my wineglass down on the end table, I take his hand and let him pull me to my feet. Garrick instantly wrangles me into a bear hug. "Any cold feet?" he inquires, peering deep into my eyes as we embrace.

"My feet are toasty warm." I press a kiss to his chest through his shirt as I look up at him. "I want this, Garrick. There are no hesitations or doubts."

He heaves a sigh of relief. "Good." Taking my hand, he places it on the bulge straining against the zipper of his pants. "I might have died from blue balls if you'd changed your mind."

I stretch up and nip at his jawline as I give his cock a gentle squeeze. "We can't be having that."

"I'm crazy about you," he says before diving in and claiming my lips in a passionate kiss I feel all the way to my toes.

"I'm crazy about you too," I readily admit when he breaks our liplock and threads his fingers in mine.

Chapter Twenty-Three

Stevie

We don't talk as he leads me upstairs to his bedroom, making me close my eyes when we reach the landing. Butterflies swoop into my chest, and excited adrenaline courses through my veins as he positions me how he wants me and says, "Open your eyes."

"Oh my god, Garrick." Tears prick my eyes as I look from the bedroom to him and back again.

Scented candles line the floor on all sides and occupy empty space on the shelves and bedside tables. Soft light flickers against the wooden walls and vaulted ceiling, and notes of jasmine, orange, lavender, vanilla, and sweet floral smells waft around the room, drawing me inside. Red rose petals form a path from the door to the giant king bed dressed in luxurious white bedding. More rose petals cover the bed, and it almost seems a shame to disturb it. A free-standing silver bucket holds a bottle of expensive champagne, and Garrick produces two flutes from somewhere behind him. Sensual music plays in the background, adding to the overall romantic ambience.

It's stunning and set against the backdrop of the hauntingly beautiful forest visible through the wide unrestricted windows; there is no place that could be more perfect for what we're about to do.

"This is..." My voice cracks with emotion as I turn around and fling my arms around him. "Utterly amazing. So romantic and perfect, and I'm going to cherish this night forever."

"No pressure then," he says over a chuckle, leaning down to kiss me slowly and seductively.

"Thank you, Garrick. This is incredible, and I've never felt more special in my life."

"Nothing but the best for my girl." He laces our fingers and pulls me farther into the room.

We drink champagne, sharing the bubbly, amber-colored liquid between our mouths as we dance around the room, careful not to knock over any of the candles. It seems Garrick has crafted the perfect soundtrack for our first time, and every song that plays heightens my emotions and cranks my arousal to new levels. Some songs I recognize; others Garrick has to educate me about. It's an eclectic mix of new and old, romantic and sexual, and by the time we've finished our drinks, I'm high on champagne and Garrick and more than ready to take our relationship to the next level.

"Turn around," he whispers as "Good for You" by Selena Gomez begins to play.

Garrick sweeps my hair over one shoulder before starting to unzip my dress at the back. He dusts kisses along my spine as he lowers the zipper, sending a river of delicious tremors cascading across my skin. Lowering one strap at a time, he pushes the dress down my arms until it pools at my feet, leaving me in only a flimsy pink lace thong. "You are so beautiful," he whispers, his fingers slowly investigating every inch of my skin and leaving simmering flesh in every spot he touches.

Leaning my head back against his shoulder, I moan as his hands mold to the bare cheeks of my ass. Thrusting his pants-covered erection against me, he confirms he's as turned on as me, and I'm quickly losing my sanity to mind-blowing desire. My breath oozes out in exaggerated spurts when his fingers traipse over the curve of my hips, skate across the band of my thong, and move upward with purpose. I arch my head back more, leaning fully against him, as he rocks his hips, pressing his hard-on firmly against my back. "Your skin is like satin under my fingers," he murmurs against my ear, and I feel his hot gaze skimming over my bare breasts.

"You're perfect," he rasps when he reaches my breasts. His fingers flick over the hard peaks of my nipples before he fully clasps my boobs in his hands, squeezing and caressing with tender care. "These are perfect." Closing my eyes, I rotate my hips, feeling warmth flood my thong as his hands go on the prowl again. When his fingers dip under the lace, he cups me down there, and my legs almost go out from under me. His amused chuckle raises all the fine hairs on the back of my neck as his breath fans across my sensitive skin. "You want me, baby?" he whispers, sliding two digits into my slippery cunt.

"So bad," I whimper, already enthusiastically riding his hand.

"Get on the bed, get rid of the thong, and spread your legs for me," he instructs, and I don't hesitate to oblige. Garrick relocates some of the candles, ensuring they are safely out of the way, while I get into position.

"Fuck, look at you." He stands at the end of the bed, raking his gaze over every overheated inch of me.

"Please, babe," I purr, writhing on the bed as I pin him with my sexiest look. "Fuck me now. I can't wait a second longer."

He chuckles as he slowly removes his clothes, drinking me in with his heated stare. "You are exquisite, Stevie. So fucking perfect," he says, crawling onto the bed naked.

"I can say the same for you." I lick my lips as I ogle his straining cock, imagining how incredible it will feel inside me. Garrick is thick and long, and I can already tell he's going to fill me to the max. "Come up here." I wiggle my fingers. "I need to touch you, taste you."

Garrick slides his body purposefully against mine as he moves up and over me, straddling my face with his powerful thighs. A satisfied moan leaks from his lips when I wrap my hand around him, enjoying the feel of his velvety-soft skin as I stroke him languidly. His hips thrust forward, and his thighs clench as I explore his shaft, enjoying seeing him come apart at my touch. A soft hiss flees his mouth when I cup and fondle his balls, replaced with a shout of agreement when I take his hard length into my mouth.

Giving Garrick head is top of my list of favorite things to do. I freaking love seeing my man so lost to the ecstasy I'm giving him. Veins throb in his neck as he tilts his head back, groaning, cussing, and thrusting his pelvis, while I suck and love on his erection with enthusiasm. His natural earthy scent mixes with the minty, citrusy essence of his shower gel, making for a potent combination as I draw him deeper into my mouth. He tastes divine, and I can't get enough of him as I hollow my cheeks and suck him greedily while fondling his balls and running a finger along his taint.

He pulls out unexpectedly with a loud pop a few minutes later, leaning down to slam his lips against mine. "I fucking love how you suck my dick, but I want to come inside you."

"I need you," I whimper, grabbing fistfuls of his gorgeous hair as I nibble on his lips.

"And you shall have me." His eyes shimmer with lust and mischief. "After I've made you come all over my face and heard you scream my name."

Garrick shoves my legs up against my chest, spreading me wide, before he dives in with his tongue, lips, and fingers. I come in record time, leaking cum all over his face as I scream his name from the top of my lungs, just like he wanted.

He wastes no time after that, and it's almost like a race to get a condom on.

Holding himself still on top of me, with his tip notched at my entrance, he's ready to turn my world upside down. "You're so beautiful to me, always, but never more so than now." Bending down, he kisses me softly a few times, and my pussy clenches and unclenches as I feel his crown press a little inside. A strangled moan rips from my mouth when he eases his head back. His lips tilt at the corners as he stares directly into my eyes, balanced on top of me by his elbows. "Do you still want this?" he asks, and I love how he's making sure I'm fully comfortable even if he can tell by how my body is responding to him.

"I do." I stretch up and peck his lips. "Make love to me, Garrick. No more holding back."

Maintaining eye contact, he eases inside me, inch by slow inch. Feeling the man I'm falling in love with fill me so carefully and completely is the most alluring and sensual moment of my life. We stare at one another as we connect in the most intimate of ways, both of us barely breathing by the time he buries himself to the hilt. My pussy hugs him greedily, and the feel of him throbbing inside me is indescribable.

"Jesus, Stevie," he whispers. "You feel incredible."

Words hover in the gap between us, but I'm too scared to let them loose. I'm overwhelmed and coming undone underneath this beautiful man. Emotion floods my eyes, and I spot the same reflection in his heated gaze.

"It's okay." He sweeps his fingers along my cheek. "I've got you, sunshine. Always."

Garrick moves then, and no words are spoken for some time. I wrap my legs around his waist as he pivots his hips, driving in and out of me in breath-stealing slow strokes that unravel me. We kiss as we rock against one another, our hands exploring every bit of flesh as we discover one another. My hands roam over his back, reveling in the defined muscles and solidity of his form. My fingers dig into his ass cheeks as I try to drive him deeper inside me, desperate for more even when he's giving me everything. He sucks on my neck, his tongue tracing the path of my collarbone, and his expert fingers pluck and tweak my nipples and grope my breasts.

Garrick pushes my legs back more and picks up his pace, pumping his hard cock inside me as he slams in and out. A line of sweat drips down his back, matching the one tiptoeing down my spine. Our kissing grows more frantic as we both chase our highs. My back lifts off the bed when his lips latch on to my nipple and his teeth graze the sensitive tip.

Flipping me over, he fucks me from behind while urgent fingers rub my clit. The moans escaping my mouth don't even sound like me as I lose all inhibition, surrendering to the blissful sensations he's coaxing from my body.

"Tell me when you're close, baby," he pants, doing a hip-gyrating maneuver that has him hitting my G-spot, causing me to cry out as stars burst behind my eyes and my orgasm creeps up on me.

"I'm close," I cry, ramming back against him, needing him deeper, deeper, deeper.

Garrick flips me around onto my back again, thrusting inside me in one powerful lunge I feel deep in my core. "Need to see you come on my cock," he rasps, grabbing my legs and placing them over his shoulders.

At this angle, he buries himself even deeper, and I'm whimpering and moaning every time he pulls out and slams back in hard, hitting the perfect spot over and over. I'm cresting the mountain, getting closer and closer, and the anticipation is almost killing me, such is my need to come. His eyes bore into mine as he drives hard and fast inside me. My breasts jiggle, and my body is jostled along the bed as he fucks me into oblivion.

"Garrick," I scream as intense pressure builds to a crescendo in my core. "I'm going to come."

His fingers move to my clit, and he ruts into me with renewed feverish thrusts. Sweat beads cling to his brow and his chest, and the veins on his neck strain as he roars out his release the second he pinches my sensitive bundle of nerves, and I detonate all over his big cock. I'm crying and screaming as the most intense orgasm rockets through me, barely conscious of the grunts coming from Garrick as he shouts my name, falling apart on top of me as his release powers through him.

We collapse on the bed in a heap of sweaty tangled limbs, and he instantly reaches for me, curling into my body as he holds me tight against him. After a couple minutes, he gets up to dispose of the condom before climbing back under the sheets with me. No words are spoken as we cling to one another, waiting for our bodies and our hearts to fully recalibrate.

Garrick dots kisses into my hair as we embrace, and my heart is a mushy pile of goo behind my rib cage. I have never felt so close to another person as I feel in this moment with him. I press kisses to his sweaty chest as I hold him close, never wanting to let him go.

"Are you okay?" he asks a few beats later, tilting my chin up with one finger.

"I'm perfect." I smile at him as I inspect his gorgeous face with my fingers. "That was amazing, Garrick, and I already want to do it all over again."

His answering smile renders my entire body to Jell-O. I'm putty in this man's hands. He could ask me for anything right now, and I'd give it to him. "You're amazing, and that was the most incredible experience of my life." His lips claim mine in the tenderest kiss that also manages to be possessive. "You're mine now, sunshine." His arms envelop me in a bear hug. "Mine to protect, love, and shower adoration on." His dick twitches against my crotch, and fresh need coils low in my belly. "I'm nowhere near finished with you." He squeezes my ass, sliding one leg between my thighs and pulling my pussy in flush with his erection. "I hope you have stamina because you're going to need it."

Chapter Twenty-Four
Garrick

The weeks fly by, and I wish I could slow them down. I spend my working days alternating between the lumberyard in North Bend and the Woodinville winery, and my nights all belong to Stevie. We are inseparable, spending every spare minute together, and I am so crazy in love with this girl. Date nights are usually dinner or a movie, and they always end with me buried balls deep inside the woman of my dreams because we're ravenous for one another, and I can't go a day without touching her.

It's challenging at her place even if Monica is laid back and she's given me permission to stay there. We are loud in the bedroom, and I hate having to hold back. Stevie does too. So, the weeks where I'm at the winery, Stevie usually stays at the cabin with me. It's only a thirty-minute drive from Ravenna, so it's doable. North Bend is a little farther, and I don't like how the burden is always on Stevie to make the trip, so the weeks where I'm working at the lumberyard, we usually just spend weekend nights together.

Stevie has come to dinner at Dad and Dawn's numerous times, and as I predicted, they love her. My twin brothers have kiddie crushes on her, and they drive her insane when she drops by, begging her to play video games or watch them play basketball. She's a good sport and readily gives them her time.

Betsy invited my family to dinner at her place after Dad and Dawn returned from Cyprus, and she wouldn't take no for an answer. Stevie's nana put on a lavish spread, and she was profuse in her gratitude. Weekly flower deliveries are now the norm, and Nana personally drops in every Monday with them. Stevie usually accompanies her, sometimes with her mother in tow, and they stay for coffee and cake or occasionally dinner. Dawn and Monica became instant friends, and I couldn't be happier our families have gelled.

Well, at least part of my family has.

My mother is another matter entirely.

"You should go." Stevie circles her arms around me from behind, snapping me out of the depressive thoughts starting to swirl through my head. "I can't hog you forever, and we've just had the most amazing vacation where I had you all to myself."

I gave Stevie plane tickets to Cyprus as the second part of her birthday present the morning after we had sex for the first time. She refused them at first, like I knew she would. But I talked her around.

Although she has a passport, Stevie had never been out of the US, and I loved getting to share that first experience with her. Briefly, I toyed with the idea of inviting Ellen and Will, and Hudson and Hadley, to join us for a few days, but I'm utterly selfish when it comes to my girlfriend, and I didn't want anyone encroaching on our alone time.

"I wish we could've stayed there forever," I admit, turning around in her arms. I kiss her lips, wishing I didn't have to leave. Getting to live every second of the last ten days with her was sheer bliss. If I had my way, we'd be moving in together when we return to UO in three weeks, but that's an argument to be rehashed a different day.

"I know. It's so idyllic there. Every day, I woke feeling like I was living a fairy tale." Her arms wind around my neck. "Thank you so much for taking me. It was incredible."

"Please stop thanking me. All I did was book a flight." I wanted to pay for everything, but Stevie wouldn't hear of it, insisting on paying for our meals and excursions because I'd provided the airfares and the accommodations. I love that she's independent, but I know money is tight, and I hate she was using money saved for her next semester of college to fund our vacation.

We had the worst argument about money before we even stepped on the plane. At one point, I thought she'd back out of the trip altogether, so I had to concede. Biting my tongue when we were in Paphos was hard too, but I knew not to go there again.

I loathe that money is a contentious issue between us. I have more than enough, so why can't I just pay? We'll be returning to campus soon where Stevie will resume her two jobs, and we'll barely have time to see one another. If she had let me pay for things all summer, she would have saved enough to only have to work one job around her studies, and we'd have more time together. I don't see how it was selfish of me to suggest it, but she went crazy, leveling that accusation when I put it to her like that, and I eventually had to drop it.

"Well, I'm grateful," she says, easing out of my embrace to return to her unpacking. "And I was brought up to never take anything for granted, so you'll have to get used to me thanking you until the end of time."

Monica pops her head through the bedroom door. "Are you staying for dinner, Garrick? We can order in. I won't subject you to my cooking. I'd probably poison you, and my only daughter would hate me for eternity."

"That's not an exaggeration." Stevie grins at her mother over her shoulder.

"Thanks for the offer, but I'm heading to Medina to see my mother." I rub at the tightness in my chest. "Under duress," I mumble under my breath, and Stevie's head whips around to mine.

"Another time then." Monica smiles before leaving us alone.

"I don't want you falling out with your mother over me," Stevie repeats, linking her pinky in mine. "She hasn't seen you for weeks, and it's not too much for her to ask."

"She needs to stop being such a bitch to you." I clutch her hand, bringing it to my lips to kiss her knuckles. "I have made so many excuses for her over the years, but this is the final straw," I admit, releasing her hand.

"Babe." Stevie steps in front of me, moving her hands up my body to rest on my chest. She peers at me through pleading eyes. "Don't go to war with your mother because of me. I'm begging you. She will hate me forever if she thinks I'm the reason you're pulling away from her. The best way to alter her opinion is through perseverance and patience."

"She won't even meet you," I grumble, hating how horrible my mother has been to my girlfriend. "If she did, she'd see everything I do." I grip her hips, hauling her in flush against me. "Maybe you should come tonight. Just show up on my arm and force her to interact. She won't make a show in front of the snooty rich crowd or the press."

"That's a terrible idea," Stevie says, "and besides, I have nothing to wear to a charity ball and no way of getting gala ready in time."

"I swear that's why she sprung this on me at the last minute." She knew Stevie wouldn't be able to attend without notice, so she waited until I was getting on a plane to demand my presence tonight. "It's not like she gives a shit about Autism Awareness. It's all about schmoozing with the right people, trapping Winston into marriage, and shoving me at Pepper any chance she gets."

I'm lucky my girlfriend isn't the jealous type. Mom has tricked me into attending two other events over the summer, knowing full and well that Pepper would be there with her father, and she was as subtle as a brick with her matchmaking, ensuring Pepper and I were seated together and deflecting anyone else from approaching us so we spent the night talking alone.

I told Stevie all about it, and I'm grateful she's cool with the situation.

I'm not sure I'd be so understanding if it was the other way around.

I'm an insufferable jealous prick when it comes to my girl, and I won't apologize for it.

When you find the one, you hold on tight with everything you've got.

Stevie tilts her head to one side, sympathy splaying across her pretty face. "I know it'll be a nightmare, but she's your mother, and it's only one night." She pats my chest. "You'll survive."

"You look miserable," Pepper says, walking up to me with a crystal tumbler in each hand.

Around us, the gala is in full-on party mode now the boring dinner and speeches part of the night is over. I'm hoping I can make an escape shortly. I showed up, smiled, and made nice with people. Mother cannot throw shade at me for ditching early when I played my part. Especially when I'm still on Cypriot time, and it's basically the middle of the night according to my body clock. It's a miracle I'm not curled in a ball sleeping in a corner someplace. Not that Mom would give me a free pass. I'm seriously getting tired of her excessive demands and questioning why I always bow to her whims.

"Please tell me one of those is for me," I plead, tugging on the collar of my pressed white shirt. I hate wearing a tuxedo, and I'm on a countdown until I can get this damned suit off.

"Of course." Pepper hands me a tumbler of whisky with ice. "It's Laphroaig 18. They don't have any Macallan."

"Bloody heathens."

"Don't be ungrateful. This is a rare bottle. They discontinued making the eighteen in 2015. I had to promise the bartender a date to get us these."

I swirl the nectar in my glass and raise it to my nose, inhaling the woodsy scent with a hint of fruity citrus and sharp pepper hidden underneath. I've learned a lot about wine this summer, and my nose is better trained now to sniff out the essence of any alcohol. The Laphroaig reminds me of the cabin. Currently my most favorite place on this earth. "You should always prostitute yourself for good scotch," I tease, clinking my glass against hers.

"Asshole." She nudges me in the side with a smile on her face. "I bet you wouldn't say that to Stevie."

"Hell no. Although the punishment might be worth it if she tried." I let loose a grin as Pepper drops her head and fixates on her drink. I take my first sip, letting the full, rich, sweet flavor roll around my tongue. A sharper smoky taste hits the back of my mouth as it glides easily down my throat.

We might be known for our wood and our wines, but Dad is somewhat of a whisky connoisseur, and I've tasted more than my fair share in recent years.

"I thought she might be with you tonight," Pepper adds, lifting her head and nodding at an older couple who walks past us.

"Mom sprang it on me at the last minute, but even if she didn't, you know Stevie wouldn't get an invite."

"She's still being difficult?"

I bob my head, swallowing hard over the lump in my throat. "My happiness clearly doesn't mean much to her. She knows she's hurting me by continually refusing to acknowledge Stevie's place in my life, and denying her invitations, yet she keeps doing it."

"I'm sorry, Garrick. That sucks." Sympathy is etched upon her pretty face. "Ivy is such a snob at times."

"Ivy *is* a snob, period." I take another mouthful of the whisky hoping it will disguise the sudden sour taste in my mouth.

"What are—"

"There you are!"

Speak of the devil.

Mom rushes up to us, cutting across whatever Pepper was about to say. "I've been looking for both of you. The photographer is waiting because we want to get some group shots."

"Of course." Pepper drains her drink, urging me to do the same with her eyes.

I knock my scotch back, dreading this next part. I don't know how socialites, influencers, and celebrities do it. I hate getting photographed at events as much as I hate wearing this monkey suit.

"You look stunning, dear." Mom sweeps her eyes up and down Pepper's fitted red dress. With her jet-black hair and her gorgeous face, she really does stand out in the crowd. "Gucci? Am I right?"

"Yes. Daddy's assistant organized it as I was far too busy this week to go shopping." Pepper smiles at me. "Unlike some who were lazing around under a hot Cypriot sun."

I'm tempted to tell her it wasn't even close to lazy. Stevie and I fucked like rabbits nonstop the entire vacation. Our sex life is off-the-charts hot, and I'm a very lucky man. The only rooms we didn't christen were Dad and Dawn's room and the twins' bedrooms. We even fucked in the pool, out on the loungers, and on the balcony in the dead of night when we were sure no one was around.

As much as I'd love to see Mom's face if I said all that, I won't disrespect Stevie by discussing our private business. It wouldn't help our cause either. Mom would only feel justified labeling her a gold-digging whore. "It's a tough life for sure," I say, smirking.

"Doesn't Pepper look gorgeous?" Mom says, pinning me with a sharp look as she puts me on the spot.

"Pepper always looks lovely," I say, not wanting to embarrass my friend by saying nothing. The truth is, I barely notice what Pepper wears although I know she is always impeccably dressed. You can't grow up the way she did, or mix in the circles she does, and not look the part. "Red is definitely your color, and the dress really suits you."

Her face lights up at my compliment. "Thanks, Garrick."

"You two look striking together. Think of how pretty your babies would be!"

Pepper grimaces, looking awkward in the extreme, and I grind my teeth to the molars, wondering if I'd get away with gluing my mother's mouth shut.

When neither of us dignifies her remark with a comment, Mom loops her arm through Pepper's and smiles at her with deliberate fondness. I've seen that look on her face before, and I can't decide if Mom genuinely likes Pepper or it's all an act. It's getting harder and harder to tell these days. Mom ushers Pepper forward and glances over her shoulder. "Garrick. Get a move on. We can't keep the governor waiting."

Pepper's parents are already in the room cordoned off for official press photographs, standing in front of the large Autism Awareness logo affixed to one wall. Freestanding heavy-duty lighting is arranged around the area, and a group of about ten photographers is lined up in front, like vultures, waiting for the money shot.

Mom steps into the frame alongside Cristelle Montgomery while Pepper gravitates to her father's free side. I move over beside Mom, and she attempts a scowl. "What are you doing?" she hisses, grabbing my arm. "Go stand beside Pepper!"

"What difference does it make where I stand?"

"Don't start with me, Garrick. I ask so little of you, and I've hardly seen you all summer thanks to that—"

I glare at her. "Say one nasty thing about my girlfriend, and I'll walk. I swear."

"Just go stand beside Pepper," she says, shaking her head as she looks behind me at someone.

"I'm not being photographed beside a woman who isn't my girlfriend," I reply, working hard to keep my tone calm.

"The jealous type, is she?" Mom sneers, and I clench my fists at my sides.

"Stevie isn't jealous at all. She trusts me. She knows I only have eyes for her."

Mom waves her hands in the air. "So, what's the problem then? It's only a picture, Garrick. It's not like I'm asking you to take her to bed."

"Sorry I'm late, dear." Winston shuffles in between me and Mom, planting a beefy arm around her shoulders. Noxious cigar fumes waft from his fleshy mouth, and his beer gut is straining over the waistband of his too tight dress pants.

Winston heads up a global TV network, and I know he's mega rich and successful, but the guy is loud, obnoxious, hugely self-centered, and clearly only with Mom because she looks good on his arm. He's at least ten years older than her usual prey, and with his thinning gray hair and weather-beaten face, he could pass for her dad.

Mom is angling for an engagement, and I'm praying daily that it never happens. She might be top of my shit list right now, but I'd hate to see her tied to such an egotistical jerk. I have liked all of Mom's ex-husbands. They were decent guys and kind to me, for the short period they were in our lives, but this idiot breaks the mold. I have nothing in common with him, and he clearly has no time for me either, so I'd rather she didn't saddle me with him for a stepfather.

"Garrick!" Mom snaps, giving me a push in Pepper's direction. "Stop acting like a toddler, and go and stand beside Pepper."

There is no point fighting any longer, so I walk over beside my friend with steam practically billowing out of my ears. Pepper's brow is puckered as I line up beside her. She leans in, and I lower my head to hear her. "Is everything okay?" she whispers, looking into my eyes with evident concern.

"My mother is getting on my very last nerve," I whisper back.

Pepper reaches across my body to squeeze my hand. "She'll come around."

I've been telling myself that for weeks, but the truth is, I don't think she will.

I know, when it comes down to it, I'm going to have to decide between my girlfriend and my mother. Right now, as I watch my mother suction herself to Winston and primp and preen for the cameras, I despise her for forcing me to make a choice. Especially when it won't end up in her favor.

Chapter Twenty-Five

Stevie

"So." Hadley draws out the word as she drives Nana's Range Rover away from the greenhouse, loaded up with deliveries.

"So, what?" I ask, stifling a yawn. I'm still on Cypriot time, and my body clock is all messed up. I stayed awake all day yesterday, not that it helped much when I was overtired and couldn't sleep last night. At least I got all my unpacking and laundry done.

Nana told me to take today off, but I've been gone for almost two weeks, and I don't like slacking. The decision was made for me when Nana's main delivery guy called in sick today, and I was needed to fill in for him. It's not like driving to and from the shop, and making house calls, is any real chore. Although, I was thrilled when my bestie showed up ten minutes ago and offered to help. I'm struggling to keep my eyes open, and it's safer if Hads drives.

"It's as I figured. You don't know." Her mouth pulls into a grimace.

"Know what?" My brow puckers in confusion as she slows down, pulling over at the curb and killing the engine. "Why are we stopping?"

"I need to show you something." She plucks her cell from the cubbyhole in the console. "Have you spoken with Garrick today?"

I shake my head as worry pricks at my nerves. "I missed a call from him at lunch, but I haven't had time to call him back yet." I sit up straighter, drilling my bestie with a sharp look. "Is this something to do with him?"

She nods, and sympathy splays across her face as she hands me her cell. An image of Garrick and Pepper fills the screen, and acid crawls up my throat. From the caption, it's evident the photo was taken at the charity event last night. It's a close-up of their faces as they lean into one another in an intimate pose that looks like they're having an intense private moment or getting ready to kiss. Bile coats my mouth as I gulp over the messy ball of emotion clogging my throat. "He wouldn't cheat on me," I croak, finally forcing words out my mouth as I stare at the picture in a kind of dazed horror. Stabbing pain pierces me through the heart, and I'm struggling to breathe.

Hadley smooths a hand up and down my back in a soothing gesture. "I don't think he would," she agrees. "But this looks pretty damning."

"It does." I rub at the tightness spreading across my chest as tears prick my eyes. I thrust her cell back at her, unable to look at it anymore. "Has he been playing me for a fool? Have I turned into my mom?"

"I don't think you can jump to conclusions, but if he has, he deserves a fucking Oscar for his performance. The guy is nuts about you, Stevie. Hudson told me he's never seen Garrick like this with any girl before. I spoke to him earlier, and he swears this is innocent. That Garrick doesn't have feelings for Pepper."

"He would say that if he wanted to cover for his best friend."

"True." Hads sighs as she leans back in her seat. "But unless Hudson is delivering an Oscar-worthy performance too, I believe him."

Hadley and Hudson have been hanging out a lot this summer. Fucking a lot. Unusual for her, they are not exclusively dating, and she seems to be working hard to keep it casual. It takes one to know one, so I see what she's doing. I suspect she's afraid of developing real feelings, so she's keeping distance between them. Hadley is in complete denial. I think she likes him a lot.

But I get it.

Hudson is returning to Brown in a couple of weeks while she attends UW. There is an end date in sight as they have agreed to end their fling then. I get not wanting to do the long-distance thing, especially when they have two more years of college left.

"How does Garrick know her?"

"Her mom is best friends with Garrick's mom. They have known one another for years. I have tried to be cool about Pepper because Garrick genuinely seems to only consider her a friend, but it's been challenging when I know his stuck-up bitch of a mom wants him with her. She tries to force them together any chance she gets."

"What's she like?" Hadley's corkscrew curls tumble around her shoulders as she turns sideways to look at me.

"I only met her one time, briefly, at Sand Point. She seemed decent, friendly, and she didn't eye me like I was a threat, but I don't know her. It could have been an act."

"Or it's not, and this is all completely innocent." Hadley drums her fingers on the steering wheel. "You won't know until you speak to Garrick, and there is no point second-guessing." Her pretty eyes bore into mine. "You need to look him straight in the eye and ask him if something is going on with Pepper."

"I know." I exhale heavily as the tightness in my chest almost becomes unbearable. Tears prick my eyes again at the thought of losing Garrick. I don't know how I'll survive it. Not when he's become so embedded in my life. "This is what I was afraid of," I admit, resting my head against the window. "Becoming too invested in a guy and him letting me down."

"Don't do that, babe." Hads grabs my hand, squeezing it in a comforting gesture. "Don't assume the worst, and don't put those guards back up. Not unless it's justified. Then I'll help you stack them into place."

We make our deliveries in relative silence after that, and I'm grateful when Hads drops the topic and puts music on. She knows I need to retreat into my head and think this through.

Pulling out my phone, I discover a ton of missed calls from Garrick in the last hour, so he has clearly seen the evidence and knows how bad it looks. I don't return his calls, deciding to go home, get showered and changed, and head out to North Bend to see him.

Except I don't need to. Because he's already beat me to it. When Hads pulls Nana's car alongside the house an hour later, Garrick is pacing back and forth in front of the door, repeatedly dragging his hands through his hair, looking panicked and agitated and concerned.

Good. I'm glad I'm not the only one upset.

"Do you want me to stay?" Hadley asks as she parks and powers off the engine.

I shake my head. "Thanks, but I've got to do this alone. I'll call you later."

"Just hear him out." She hauls me into a hug. "I stand by my assertion he's a good guy and he's head over heels for you."

"I hope you're right." I force a weak smile as we break apart.

"If I'm not, I'll help you dispose of the body." She waggles her brows and grins wickedly.

That raises a genuine smile on my face. "Love you, babe."

"Right back at ya, beautiful." She hugs me one final time as Garrick watches our interaction through the window. He's not approaching the car, and I don't know if that's because of a guilty conscience or his fear of Hadley. He constantly denies it, but I think my bestie scares him. Hadley is intense and fiercely protective of me, and he knows it.

"Call me," she reiterates as she opens her door and climbs out.

My heart is tripping over itself as I slide out my side, and an anxious fluttering feeling has taken up residence in my chest. Hadley narrows her eyes at Garrick as he moves in my direction, stalling for a moment to drill him with a pointed look. His Adam's apple bobs in his throat as he keeps his gaze firmly locked on mine, but I know he feels the tense charge in the air and the weight of Hadley's stare.

"It is not what it looked like," he says, striding to my side. His usual deep voice contains an undercurrent of panic as he reaches for my hand.

I yank it back, shoving both hands into the pockets of my jeans. Lifting my chin, I channel my inner Nana as I stare at him. Pain radiates from his eyes, and a crestfallen look washes over his face. "I swear there is nothing going on with Pepper. She's only a friend. Nothing more. Please believe me, Stevie." His voice cracks a little. "I would never cheat on you. I deplore cheaters. It's personal for me after what my mom did to my dad."

He confided in me on vacation how his mom had been having an affair before she filed for divorce from his dad. I didn't need additional reasons to loathe that woman, but I got them. She's such a selfish bitch. I remember the hurt when he talked about it, and his words go some way toward reassuring me. "Take a walk with me?" I suggest.

"Of course. I just want an opportunity to explain."

"I will give you that," I confirm, striding forward in the direction of the poppy field. "But before you say anything, I need you to understand how much this has hurt me." I look up at him, shielding nothing. Pain eviscerates me on the inside, and it's hard not to collapse into tears. Except I'm made of sterner stuff, and I refuse to break down over any man. "Do you have any idea how humiliating it is to see my boyfriend in a compromising position with another woman and for it to be splashed all over newspapers and on social media? I've had calls and texts in the last hour from tons of people commiserating with me because they believe you have cheated on me with the governor's daughter. I look like a fool." I don't mention the cruel text I received from Cohen as that will only sidetrack us, but I don't plan on hiding it from him either.

"Nothing happened, Stevie. Please say you believe me." Agony is supplanted across his handsome features, and he looks genuine, but am I just a sucker who has taken everything he's given me at face value when I'm being played all along?

"Who is Pepper to you, Garrick? I need you to be completely honest with me. Is something going on with her, or has it in the past?"

"She's just a friend, Stevie. I don't have feelings for her." His eyes penetrate mine, flickering with a host of emotions. "We have never touched, or kissed, or had sex, or had anything but a friendship. That is the whole truth."

"I want to believe you, but this has me questioning everything that has happened between us."

"Don't say that!" he exclaims, reaching for my arm as I turn left into the field. Bittersweet, smoky, nutty scents accost my nostrils as I plow through the poppies, confused and hurt and disappointed and feeling a host of other things.

"I won't lie to you, Garrick," I say, turning around and spinning to a stop. My fingers trail the tops of the flowers, skimming over the soft red petals as they swish and sway against my thighs. "I always promised you honesty, and this has shaken me. I'm wondering if I've been played all along."

"I promised not to lie to you either, Stevie." He firmly clasps my face in his hands, forcing me to look directly into his eyes. "Nothing happened with Pepper. Not last night or ever. She's a friend. That's it."

"Does she know that?" I hiss, letting hurt imbue my words. "Because she's looking at you in that picture like you hung the stars in the sky just for her."

"The photographer twisted it to make it look like that! She doesn't have those feelings for me either. She could tell I was upset, and she was just inquiring if I was okay. We were lined up with my mom and Winston and her parents in the shot. Ivy was giving me shit because I wouldn't stand beside Pepper."

His earnest eyes plead with me for understanding that is in limited supply right now. My thoughts are consumed with the way their faces were super close and the intensity in their eyes as they stared at one another. I think it will be imprinted on my brain for eternity. Although I am humiliated, I care less about what others think. I'm more concerned with the way they were looking at one another.

It fucking hurts to see my boyfriend looking at another woman like that.

"I didn't want to get in a photo beside any woman who wasn't you, but you know how my mother gets, and I just relented to get it over and done with. I had no idea they would twist it or that they would cut out the others and plaster us all over the internet." He cradles my face in his hands, and tears well in his eyes as he stares at me. "Please, sunshine. Please believe me. Don't let this come between us." Steely determination glints in his eyes, and that's the only warning I get before he presses his mouth to mine in a hard possessive kiss.

I don't return the kiss. I'm still too hurt and too confused.

He pulls back, looking wretched. "Stevie, I'm so sorry. The last thing I ever want to do is hurt you. I should have refused my mother and gone home." He loosens his hold on my face, brushing his fingers across my cheek. "You're the most important person in my life, and I'm done letting her come between us. I'm giving my mother an ultimatum. Either she accepts you and stops trying to push me at Pepper or I'm done with her."

"I don't want you to do that," I softly reply. "She'll only hate me even more."

"I don't care. I've let her dictate my life too much, and it stops now. I can't lose you. I won't lose you." He reels me into his arms, and this time, I don't protest. His arms wind around my back as he holds me close against his body. Arching my head back, I peer into a gorgeous face I love so much. Garrick's eyes are more green than brown today, but they are clear and determined as he stares at me. Electricity surges in the air around us, a reminder of the potent connection we share.

"I have wanted to tell you this for a long time, Stevie, but I held back out of fear over how you would react. But I'm done repressing my emotions."

Gentle fingers dig into my lower back as he leans in, gliding his lips gently against mine. Emotion shines in his eyes when he eases back a little, never losing eye contact. Dimples wink at me as he smiles through his tears. "I love you, Stevie. I love you so freaking much, and I'm not letting anyone, not Pepper, not my mother, or anyone else, tear us apart. You are it for me. You're my one and only, and I'll get down on one knee right now if that's what you need for me to prove it to you."

Chapter Twenty-Six

Garrick

Stevie stares at me in shock, her mouth opening and closing like a fish out of water. It's a fitting analogy because it looks like she's drowning in my words. I'm not sorry I spoke my truths. I only wish I'd spoken them earlier. Maybe then she wouldn't be analyzing everything and rethinking our entire relationship.

I'm in full-on panic mode.

I cannot lose her.

She means the world to me.

I was sick to my stomach when I saw that picture and further sickened when it started popping up all over the net. I don't get the exaggerated interest. So what if the governor's daughter is apparently dating the heir to the Allen Empire? Who the fuck cares? It's not like my family is that big of a deal.

"Are you serious?" she blurts, eventually finding her voice.

"About loving you or wanting to marry you?" I splay my hand flat against her lower back, and it's killing me to show restraint. I want nothing more than to lay her down in this field, strip us of our clothes, and bury myself so deep inside her I eradicate every single doubt written across her beautiful face.

"Both, I guess."

"I am speaking nothing but the truth, sunshine." I trace my finger along her plump lower lip. "I have loved you for a long time. I was afraid to tell you in case it scared you away, but I regret it now because I see the doubts in your eyes, and maybe they would not be there if you knew the intensity of my feelings for you."

Tears glisten in her eyes as she slides her hands up my chest. "You swear you're telling me the truth? You swear you don't have feelings for her because a picture speaks a thousand words, Garrick, and I don't like how you are looking at one another in it."

"I know how bad it looks, but I am not lying to you, Stevie. If I wanted to be with Pepper, I'd be with her. If I wanted to have an easy life and not clash with my mother, I'd be with Pepper. But I'm not with her because I don't want to be with her." I tug her flush against my body, needing to be as close as possible so she sees, hears, and feels my truths. "I want to be with *you*. I don't love her. I love you." I punctuate the words, praying they embed deep. "I love you so fucking much, Stevie."

"I love you too," she whispers as a tear runs free down her face.

Relief courses through me at her admission. I envelop her in a mammoth hug, dotting kisses into her hair as I repeat how much I love her over and over again. A fine layer of stress lifts from my shoulders, but I'm not out of the woods yet. I know how deep-seated Stevie's fears are about men and relationships, and this has, undoubtedly, set us back. But I won't ever stop fighting for us because she's my woman and I'm her man, and that is the only truth that matters.

"You're my forever, Stevie. I've never been surer of anything. If I had my way, we'd get married right now."

Her head jerks to mine, fresh shock seeping from her pores. "You cannot be seriously saying you know you want to marry me when you're only twenty, Garrick. That is the definition of insanity."

"I know what is in my heart, and it won't ever change. I know, categorically, that I want to marry you. My age or the passing of time has nothing to do with it. I knew I wanted to marry you yesterday.

Like I know I want to today, and I'll know tomorrow and every day after that."

She wrestles out of my arms, stepping back and clawing her hands through her hair in jerky motions. "Woah, you need to slow down. This is way too intense."

"Is it?" I bridge the gap between us, gently unfurling stiff fingers from her hair. "You need to know if I'm being truthful, and that's as truthful as it gets. I won't apologize for finally admitting the totality of what's in my heart. It's fine that you're not on the same page yet. I will wait for you to get there."

She chews on the edge of her lip. "This is a lot to take in in one day. My emotions have veered from one extreme to the other."

"I get that." I clasp her hands in mine, squeezing gently. "But it doesn't change how I feel. I want it all with you now, Stevie, but I'll settle for moving in together."

Her brows pinch together as she scowls at me. "You really want to do this again?"

I shrug. "Might as well get it all out on the table. You know how I feel, so I'm hoping it means you'll consider our living arrangements more seriously when we return to Eugene." I tuck her hair behind her ears. "I want to wake up beside you every day and go to sleep at night with you curled around my body."

My eyes probe hers for any sign she's relaxing her stance on the subject, but she's giving nothing away. We had this conversation before, and it turned into a steaming argument. "We're not going to see a huge amount of each other between college and work commitments. At least this way, it'll make it easier to spend time together." My fingers caress her soft cheeks. "If you need proof of my love and my intentions toward you, it doesn't get any clearer than this. Share my life with me, Stevie. Move in with me, baby." I press a kiss to her brow. "Please."

Strained silence ensues as we stare at one another, and I can almost see the wheels turning in her head. Pain stabs me all over when she breaks free of my embrace and shakes her head. "This is too much, Garrick. You're moving too fast, and I can't think straight."

Pain drives my next angry words. "What do you want from me then, Stevie?" My voice elevates a few notches. "One minute, you're accusing me of lying to you and hiding secret feelings for Pepper, yet when I lay it all on the line...when I lay *my heart* on the line and tell you I want a future with you, you shut me down! I don't know how to make it any clearer. I want a future with you that involves marriage and kids and growing old together. I have never been surer about anything in my life. It's a future I want to grasp now with both hands, starting with moving in together." I throw my hands in the air. "I really don't get what the issue is? If this isn't what you want from me, then what is?"

"I don't know," she whispers with tears streaming down her face. She swipes angrily at them before jutting her chin up. "I need space. Time to digest all this and work out how I feel."

The last thing I want to do is give her space to talk herself out of a relationship with me. My anger instantly subsides, replaced with abject fear. "You're killing me, sunshine." I hear the dejection in my voice, but I won't shield it from her. "I don't know what else I can do. I just want to be with you. That's it."

"And I want to be with you." She steps up to me, carefully circling her arms around my neck. "I do love you, Garrick." She presses a feather-soft kiss to my lips. A sheen of tears clings to her lashes as she stares at me. "I don't mean to confuse you, but I'm confused too. Just give me a few days to mull everything over. I promise I will give your proposal about moving in together serious consideration."

"I need to tell Noah tomorrow if we're in or out." The lease on our old place is available, and Noah has asked Will and me if we want to live with him again. Cohen is, thankfully, moving into the frat house for junior year. Noah is the only one who has been in contact with him over the summer. Will and I have cut him out of our lives, and I haven't lost any sleep over it. "He has to give the landlord an answer, and he doesn't want to agree unless he knows Will and I are in."

"Okay. I will let you know tomorrow."

Stevie turned me down. Citing distractions and independence and how I need to back off because I'm scaring her with my intensity. Not going to lie. It hurt. A lot. I know she loves me. She shows me in many ways, but I feel like she's erected some of those shields again, and she's more cautious with her heart. She's trying to apply the brakes when I want to go full throttle.

When I'm with her, everything is amazing, but when we're apart, doubts creep in because I know she's purposely creating distance between us. And that can't be good.

Ellen chose to live with Stevie instead of Will. I knew she wouldn't abandon her bestie even if Will's girlfriend was open to moving in with him. So, Noah, Will, and I are back living together again, and the girls are in their apartment a few blocks away.

It's as I predicted. We are struggling to find time to see one another between work and college, and I'm terrified she's slipping away from me. It's only October, a couple months into classes, but the course load is savage this year, and I'm already drowning under numerous assignments.

I'm getting ready for my gig at The End Zone Friday night when my cell vibrates with an incoming call. Pain lodges at the base of my throat when I see who the caller is. My mother hasn't attempted to reach out to me since we had our fateful argument at the end of July. I gave her my ultimatum, like I promised Stevie I would do, and my mother reacted as expected.

I stare at my cell for a few seconds, wondering if I should pick up or not. If she's offering an olive branch, maybe I need to hear what she has to say. So, I press accept before the ringing stops.

"Garrick."

"Mother."

She sniffles. "I hate this."

"You brought it on yourself."

"I know."

Surprise shuttles through me, but I don't react.

She clears her throat. "I know now I was in the wrong. You are old enough to make your own decisions, and I need to respect that."

If I was sitting, I'd probably fall off my chair. Ivy Allen-Golding-Smith rarely apologizes, and I feel like I need to record this moment for posterity.

She coughs again. "In my defense, I have only ever had your best interests at heart, but I went about it the wrong way. For that, I am sorry, and I hope you can forgive me."

"That depends," I say, propping one hip against the wall as I tap out a quick text to Stevie letting her know I'll be five minutes late picking her up.

"On what?"

"On whether you're willing to accept my choice and accept my girlfriend."

A pregnant pause ensues for a few beats. "I didn't give Stevie a chance, and I understand your anger and frustration. I'm willing to make amends now. If you'll let me."

Relief flows through my veins and the corded knots in my shoulders relax a little. "I would like that. Stevie would too."

Stevie hates how fractured my relationship is with my mom, but she acknowledges I had no choice, and I know she's pleased I defended her. Yet, she can't help feeling guilty. What she doesn't understand is, I don't have the same kind of relationship with my mother that she has with hers. I never have. It would be sad not to have my mother in my life, but I'd get over it. I have Dad and Dawn, and Dawn supports me fully on this. Dad doesn't like rocking the boat, and he's been encouraging me to try a mediation approach, but I knew this was my best shot at getting through to my mother, and it appears to have worked.

"Wonderful. Thank you, darling. I have missed you so much. Perhaps we could have lunch on Sunday? Just the two of us?"

"I'd like that."

"And I'd like to invite you and Stevie to dinner here with Winston and I on Thanksgiving."

I alternate special occasions between my parents, and it's Mom's turn to share Thanksgiving with me this year while I'll be with Dad for Christmas. "I will ask her."

"Make sure to do it soon so I can instruct the caterers."

"I'll ask her tonight, and speaking of, I need to go." I grab Stevie's flowers and wine and my jacket off the back of the chair in my bedroom. "I have a gig, and Stevie won't want to be late for work."

"I won't keep you, darling. Be here at one on Sunday, and you can update me then."

"This is a good thing," Stevie says, reaching across the console to squeeze my hand as I drive us to the bar where we're both working tonight. "I'm so glad she has come around, for your sake. I hate coming between you and your mother."

"It was never your fault." I lift our conjoined hands and kiss her fingers.

"I know, but I was still the reason."

"What do you think about Thanksgiving?"

"I'll talk to Nana and Mom, but I think they'll be fine if I'm not there this year. Nana usually invites a few friends and neighbors, so they won't miss me too much."

"That's highly debatable, but I won't say no if it means you get to spend Thanksgiving with me."

"Your mom has extended an olive branch, and I'm not going to turn it down."

"Thank you for being so gracious about this. I know she hasn't made it easy." I park the car outside the bar and lean over to kiss her.

She clings to my chest, angling her head and kissing me deeply. "I'm happy for you, Garrick," she says, smiling at me when we break apart.

"I love you." I peck her lips as Manford appears in the corner of my eye.

"I love you too," she replies, rolling her eyes as Manford makes kissy faces at us through the window.

"You're an idiot," I say to the bartender when I hop out and race around the hood to open Stevie's door. As much as he likes to wind me up, I like the dude. Thankfully, he's nothing like his cousin Cohen.

I wanted to knock the fuck out of my ex-friend when Stevie showed me the nasty text he sent her the day that photo of Pepper and me aired, but my girlfriend talked me off the ledge, convincing me ignoring him is the best way of handling him. And so far, she's been right.

"I want an invite to the wedding." Manford waves his finger between us. "I was the one who played matchmaker after all." He puffs out his chest and grins, not sensing the glimmer of tension crackling between me and my girlfriend at the mention of a wedding. I haven't gone there again as it's a very touchy subject.

Stevie is skittish.

I understand why, and I know I'm abnormal.

It's unusual to know you want to get married this young.

But when you have found the girl of your dreams, why wait is my motto. I'm only holding back because I don't want to scare Stevie off.

I convinced her to go out with me, so I know I'll eventually convince her to marry me.

I just need to channel patience for a while.

Chapter Twenty-Seven
Stevie

"Whore!" The word is hissed in my ear the second I exit the cafeteria after eating lunch with Garrick. He went out the rear door with Will and Ellen, so I'm alone for this encounter with Simone.

A heavy sigh escapes my lips. I'm not in the mood for this shit today. I'm quickly running out of patience with this girl, but I'm also conscious she seems to have a mental health issue, so I try to tread carefully whenever she accosts me. Something that is occurring more regularly in recent weeks, and I'll have to take serious action soon if she doesn't stop.

Garrick made a report to the dean at the end of last semester after the shit that went down at the bar and the vile things she said to me. I reported her at the start of this semester when it became clear she had switched her harassment from him to me. I blocked her number and her email after she sent me several abusive messages. Manford spoke to the boss at the bar, and Simone is permanently banned from The End Zone, and Sharon banned her from Butterfly Flowers, but I still see her around campus. I can't quite call it stalking, but it's enough to piss me off despite trying not to let her rile me up.

"Simone. I'm not doing this with you again," I say as she steps in front of me, blocking my path. "You need to get over this, and I highly suggest you sign up for therapy." I attempt to move around her, but she mirrors my position, thwarting my attempt to break free. "Move out of my way, Simone." I'm already cutting it close for my shift at the flower shop, but Sharon will be cool if I'm a little late.

"You're drugging him," she snaps, spittle flying from her mouth. "It's the only reason that makes sense. He should have kicked you to the curb by now. You have nothing on me," she adds, raking her gaze over me in a derisory fashion I'm well used to by now. "Nothing."

I'm tempted to tell her to take a look in the mirror because the girl looks like shit. The only reason I don't snark back is because her outward appearance hints at the state of her troubled inner mind, and I don't want to set her off or have her harm herself because of my actions. I never let her words affect me. They coast over my head every time. I feel sorry for her more than anything else. But she's a fucking nuisance, and Garrick and I are both short on patience now. I know the college spoke to her, but I don't know what else may or may not have happened.

Whatever the intervention was, it's clearly not working, and something else will have to be done.

I am not putting up with this harassment for much longer.

I make one last attempt to get through to her. "You need help, Simone. Garrick isn't interested in you. Whether I am his girlfriend or not doesn't change that fact." I deliberately use a soft voice and talk to her like I'd talk to a child. "You are wasting your college experience on a guy who will never return your interest. You need to forget about him and concentrate on yourself."

"I don't take advice from gingers," she screams, and the wild look in her eyes has me stepping sideways. But I'm not fast enough. "How dare you patronize me!" she yells, throwing herself at me and taking us both down.

My body slams into the asphalt as I land heavily on the ground with the crazy bitch on top of me. My bones rattle, and pain splices through my head as my skull meets the hard ground. Stars whizz before my eyes. I cry out when stinging pain radiates across my scalp as the bitch yanks on my hair, roaring in my face and yelling obscenities.

"Fuck, Stevie. Are you okay?" a man with a somewhat familiar voice asks as Simone's weight is suddenly gone from on top of me.

My eyes are blurry, and a metallic taste lands on my tongue as it darts out, dabbing over a small cut on my lip.

A strong arm goes around my back when I'm gently lifted into a sitting position. "Are you hurt?"

I attempt to take stock of my injuries as the guy converses with a few other voices. I'm vaguely aware of Simone screeching in the background.

"I'm going to call Garrick," he says as I raise trembling hands to my face and brush hair away from my eyes.

Gradually, my sight and my hearing return to normal as the adrenaline coursing through my veins calms down. My back aches, and pain throbs in my skull, but I don't think I'm seriously injured.

"Garrick is on his way," my savior says, and I blink profusely as I stare into Cohen's concerned face.

"You," I croak, immediately clearing my throat. "Get away from me," I add, suddenly aware his arm is still around my back and he's keeping me propped up. A small crowd has formed around us, and I spy two campus policemen approaching. Two of Cohen's jock buddies are restraining a thrashing Simone as she cries, shouts, and writhes like someone on the verge of a nervous breakdown.

I should hate her for what she just did, but pity is my predominant emotion as I look at her. I'm super pissed as well, but hopefully, this is the end of the harassment and I can breathe easier around campus. The girl needs psychiatric help, and perhaps now she'll get it.

An earnest expression materializes on Cohen's face. "I'm not leaving you alone until Garrick gets here." Remorse floods his features. "I owe you an apology, Stevie. Several, actually."

"You do, but that's the least of my worries right now." I attempt to get up, but my sore limbs protest.

"Let me help. Please." Cohen seems sincere, but I don't want him touching me. However, my overriding need to get up off the ground before some asshole records the scene supersedes my distaste, so I nod and let him help me to stand. Cohen guides me over to a bench just as campus police arrive. Cohen sits beside me as I give a quick verbal statement. He corroborates my story because he and his buddies witnessed the unprovoked attack.

Pounding footsteps approach, and then Garrick is there, crouching down in front of me, inspecting my face with worried eyes. "Jesus, Stevie. How badly are you hurt?" His eyes flicker to my cut lip and the way I'm hunched over with my arms crossed around my middle. "I am going to ensure the book is thrown at that crazy bitch, and don't even consider not pressing charges," he says through gritted teeth.

Cohen obviously fully updated Garrick on his call. "I'm okay." I take his hand, needing him to ground me right now. "I'm more shocked than anything."

"I about died when I got Cohen's call." He presses a tender kiss to my brow. "I was so scared, sunshine."

"I'm fine, babe." I cup one side of his face. "Stop worrying. I'm a little sore, but it's nothing some pain pills, time, and a few hot baths won't cure."

"She needs to be medically assessed by a paramedic," one of the policemen says to Garrick.

"And we'll need you to make a formal statement," the other one adds, glancing over his shoulder at where Simone is being strapped to a gurney and carried to one of two ambulances now parked on the grass. I hadn't even heard them arriving.

"Can it wait?" Garrick asks, perching his butt on the arm of the bench and gently sliding his arm around my shoulders. "She really needs to rest."

"That's fine." The taller of the two policemen hands Garrick his card. "Call me in a couple days, and we'll arrange a time."

They leave as a female paramedic arrives to inspect me. I ask Garrick to call Sharon and explain the situation before I go with the paramedic to the second ambulance. I sit up on the floor at the open back of the vehicle with a blanket wrapped around my shoulders while the nice lady asks me a bunch of questions and conducts a few quick checks.

Garrick and Cohen stand off to one side, talking in hushed tones. Though it looks like they are having an intense conversation, Garrick's eyes never wander from mine.

When I'm done, he's by my side in a nanosecond, gently cradling me against his body as we listen to the instructions from the paramedic. "You have a mild concussion, Stevie, and you need to take it easy for a few days and rest at home. If you experience any nausea or vomiting, you feel repeatedly dizzy or light-headed, or you have any issues concentrating or remembering things in the next few days, go straight to the emergency room. For now, take these painkillers and go home to bed."

Over the course of the next week, Garrick fusses over me like you wouldn't believe. He moves in—temporarily—to take care of me, but I don't protest. I have a permanent headache, and my body is sore all over, so it's nice having him here. He won't let me lift a finger, and he insists I skip all my shifts this week, making me promise I won't return to either job or classes until I'm feeling well enough. I've built up a lot of credits, so I can afford to miss a few classes. I know I have the time to catch up.

Mom and Nana drive down on Sunday to check on me, and a girl could get used to being mollycoddled.

After we patch things up with Cohen, he apologizes profusely to me and the guys, finally admitting something we all know—he's got an alcohol problem. He is attending an outpatient program, around classes and training, and he's moved out of the frat house and into a single dorm. He's quit partying and is focusing instead on his studies, football, and his recovery. He seems sincere, and we are giving him the benefit of the doubt. I don't think Garrick will ever have the same relationship with him, but at least it's amicable now, and we don't have to dodge him around campus.

Simone is gone for good. It turns out she was doing this to three other guys and their girlfriends. The college was already taking steps to kick her out when her parents showed up and took her home. The last we heard, she is receiving psychiatric care, and I hope it helps.

I didn't suffer anything more than aches, pains, and bruises, and I can't find it in me to hold a grudge against her. Garrick isn't as charitable, and he wasn't pleased I dropped the assault charge. He is entitled to his feelings, and I understand it. I'd feel the same way if he was the one who'd been hurt, but I prefer to put it behind us and move forward.

Things are finally back on track with us after a few rocky weeks, and life has settled down.

Before I know it, Thanksgiving has arrived. Which means today I'm finally getting to meet his mother officially.

I'd be lying if I said I wasn't a complete basket case.

A lot hinges on today, and I want it to be perfect.

I already know the odds are stacked against me.

Despite the assurances she has given her son, I expect Ivy is only doing this to humor Garrick. I very much doubt she has changed her opinion of me or given up on her plans to marry her son to the governor's daughter. But I owe it to Garrick to give her the benefit of the doubt, so I'm attending Thanksgiving dinner with an open mind.

"Are you sure this dress is good enough?" I ask for the umpteenth time as we exit my house.

"You look gorgeous." Garrick's slow perusal as he drags his eyes the length of my body brings a blush to my cheeks.

He has been staying over at my apartment a lot lately—I refuse to sleep at his place because his bedroom is a mess, and it gives me anxiety anytime I set foot inside it—and the sex is insanely good. He's learned how to turn me on with one sultry look, and I walk around in a state of near-constant need.

Regular sex on tap is definitely a perk of being in a committed relationship. I never realized sex could be like this. Sleeping with someone I love is intense and intimate, and I feel it on a transcendental level. I never feel closer to Garrick than when he's buried deep inside me, looking straight into my eyes, as he summons pleasure from my body like a skilled magician. Postcoital snuggling is heavenly too, and I love going to sleep wrapped up in his warm embrace.

He hasn't mentioned marriage or moving in lately, and I appreciate he is respecting my wishes and toning things down.

It's not that I don't love him.

I really truly do.

He makes me incredibly happy.

I love having someone to support me. Someone who will listen when I've had a shit day or someone to share exciting news with.

Garrick was there to hold my hand when I sent off my DNA test to that ancestry place, and he was there to console me when the results showed no paternal connections.

Having talked to my boyfriend about it, I've decided to make a concerted effort to find my father. Garrick knows the background story now. How Mom had no contact details for my dad and how uncooperative the Navy was when she reached out to them. All she knew was his first name and the date his ship was docked in Seattle. The Navy agreed to forward some letters she wrote, but we have no proof if he ever received them. Or maybe he did, and he chose not to contact her. To this day, we don't know.

It's not that I need him in my life, but I need to understand if he even knows about me. I don't want this unresolved question to hang over me my entire life, so I'm taking proactive steps to find answers I need.

I haven't told Mom yet. I know she wouldn't stop me from trying to locate him, but I'm not sure how it will make her feel. Dragging this history up again might upset her, so I decided not to say anything unless the results showed a connection.

Garrick gave me the strength to pursue this, and I probably wouldn't have done it without his support and encouragement.

I could not ask for a better boyfriend.

He is so devoted—showing up regularly with my favorite coffee and pastries from Bumble Bees, always making time to grab lunch or a coffee on campus during the day, and escorting me to and from work when his schedule permits it. Every Friday, he shows up to drive me to work at the bar, and he always has wine and flowers for me.

He constantly showers me with love and affection, and I try to do the same. Getting up early on weekends to bake him his favorite cookies and cupcakes. Battling the annoying groupies every Saturday night to support him at his gigs. Cooking him meals, giving him massages, and running him baths when his old back injury flares up and he's in pain, and sucking his dick like a motherfucking pro. Garrick loves my blowjobs, and it's our mutual favorite way to let off steam.

I know I'm lucky to have found him. That we're lucky to have found one another. I appreciate him so much, and my life is much happier having him in it.

But the intensity of my feelings for him, and his for me, still scares me. This is all new, and I don't want to rush into anything. I don't see the need. We are still young, and we have our whole lives ahead of us.

Right now, I'm enjoying spending time with him, being in love, and managing to focus on my relationship while not sacrificing my goals. I'm not sorry to be proven wrong about distractions or that Garrick has opened my eyes to possibilities. I'm content, and I don't need anything else. Except for him to be content going at this pace and not to push for more before we're both ready.

"Earth to my sunshine." He tips my face up, fixing me with a crooked grin. "Where'd you go, babe?"

"Sorry. I just zoned out."

"Please don't worry." He laces his fingers in mine as he leads me toward the passenger side of his Range Rover. "I promise it'll be fine. I will be by your side the entire time, and I'll keep Mom in check if she gets out of line. Winston too, if he acts his usual asshole self."

"I just want to make a good impression, and first ones count." I glance down at myself. "Are you sure this is fancy enough?"

I'm guessing his mom's house is some big posh mansion, and from what Mom's told me, she is always dressed to the nines, so I put extra effort into today. I don't want to let Garrick down. But I don't have the money for expensive dresses or jewelry or matching bags and shoes. I splurged on a designer dress I found on sale in a department store in Seattle. It's a patterned A-line black silk dress with gorgeous purple, green, and white flowers all over it. It has long sleeves and a deep vee at the front. While it showcases cleavage, it's classy. It stops just under my knee, and my legs look long and slim in my skyscraper black heels. Nana loaned me her emerald necklace, and Mom loaned me her black Gucci purse. Hadley helped me with my hair and makeup, and I feel great. However, I still worry my efforts will fall short of Ivy Allen-Golding-Smith's exacting standards.

"Baby, you're perfect. You couldn't be any more beautiful if you tried. She will love you. She just hasn't had a chance to get to know you yet."

I wish it were as simple as that.

Garrick's naivety when it comes to his mother is a weakness but one I can't fault him for. He's a good son. A good boyfriend. And today I'm going to do my absolute best to turn his mother around.

For him.

Chapter Twenty-Eight

Stevie

My eyes are bugging out of my head as we drive through high wooden gates and along a winding gravel driveway, bordered by mature trees and colorful shrubs on both sides, heading toward the extravagant property looming in the near distance. A shocked gasp escapes my lips when we round the bend and the house comes into full view.

I was partly right in my assumption, but calling this palatial home a 'posh mansion' is doing it a disservice. Positioned at the bottom of the driveway, surrounded by tall trees and landscaped lawns on either side, is a vast, highly impressive modern two-story building, comprising various outhouses and side structures, and constructed mainly of glass and gray stone. Different size vaulted roofs highlight a myriad of solar panels, and it's clear no expense has been spared on this property.

It's like something you'd see in a celebrity magazine, and my nerves are presently jumping through the roof.

"Breathe, babe," Garrick murmurs, helping me out of the car.

"This place is something else." My eyes are out on stalks as I try to drink it all in.

He shrugs, taking the flowers from my hand. "It's just a house." Only someone who has grown up surrounded by this kind of wealth could be so flippant. I like that Garrick isn't flashy, but it's possible a little reality check is needed now and then.

I hug the cake carrier to my chest as we walk up the steps toward the entrance door. Before we've had time to knock, the door swings open, and a stately gentleman with salt-and-pepper hair bows his head and steps to one side. "Mr. Allen. Do come in. Your mother is expecting you in the rear living room."

Garrick grasps my free hand firmly in his as we enter the hallway of his mom's home, stalling until the man in uniform has closed the front door and urged us to follow him. Butterflies float anxiously in my belly as I realize I am completely out of my depth.

Garrick should have prepared me better.

This kind of wealth is obscene, and this house is nothing like his dad's and Dawn's homey place in North Bend. Don't get me wrong, that's a massive house and very impressive too but in a much more subtle manner. It's a true family home with dogs running around, toys, games, and sports equipment underfoot, and it's lived in. I feel comfortable there, whereas I'm immediately uncomfortable amid all this opulence.

It's not at all what I was expecting either. I thought his mother would go for an old-worldly charm with wood paneling, ornate papered walls, patterned rugs and carpets, and antique mahogany furniture. Instead, the house feels light and airy as we follow the butler on pristine gray-and-white-marble tiled floors, passing by light-colored walls adorned with modern art, and tall tables housing glass lamps and vibrant vases filled with white roses.

I can't deny how stunning this house is, but it feels more like a model home than somewhere you'd actually live.

As we bisect other hallways, bypassing rooms exquisitely decorated with contemporary furniture and glossy hardwood floors, I feel like I might be sick. I don't belong in a place like this, and I instantly feel underdressed and out of my comfort zone.

Today is going to be ten million times worse than I imagined.

Sensing my inner panic, Garrick rubs soothing circles on the back of my hand with his thumb, but it does nothing to quiet the mounting alarm invading every nook and cranny of my being.

That sensation multiplies when the butler leads us into a long wide room where several people wait for us.

So much for it just being his mother and her boyfriend Winston.

The governor, his wife, Cristelle, Pepper, and an unfamiliar man all turn around to greet us with matching tight smiles. The three women are wearing expensive over-the-top ballgowns, and I feel like I've shown up in my nightgown.

Anger radiates off Garrick in potent waves as he tightens his hold on my hand and glances at me. His eyes plead for understanding behind his fury, and I'm glad he's surprised. If he had been a part of this ambush, I would turn around right now and walk out of his life.

Garrick leans in to kiss my cheek, brushing his lips against my ear. "I swear I didn't know she'd invited them."

I squeeze his hand in reply as I swallow back nerves and plaster a fake smile on my face. It will just be like at Sand Point during any of those times I had to wait on pompous rich pricks and their bitchy wives and girlfriends. I can fake it with the best of them, and I'll hold it together until we can make our escape.

"Darling. Don't whisper. It's rude." Ivy strides toward Garrick wearing an elaborate blue ballgown that sweeps the floor as she walks, not even looking in my direction.

Garrick is like a pot ready to boil over. I can almost see the steam billowing from his ears. Judging by the looks exchanged between the governor and his wife, it's evident they spot it too.

The way I see it, we have two choices. Leave now and make it clear we don't appreciate being ambushed. Or suck it up for a few hours, bite our tongues, and play this stupid charade until we can leave at the earliest opportunity.

As much as I loathe his mother, and I really do, she would not take kindly to being shunned by her son in front of her VIP guests.

Garrick has only just repaired his relationship with his mother after it broke down over me. There are plenty of other reasons for him to cut ties with the interfering bitch, and I would prefer that over something that potentially has the power to come between us in the future. So that only leaves option number two.

Sucking it up and pretending.

Staying here, in the face of a setup, requires enormous lady balls, and I intend to prove to Ivy bitchface that I have them. It also sends a message to Pepper that I'm not threatened by her.

So, I'm going nowhere.

Even if I'd rather bathe in hot oil than sit through Thanksgiving dinner with these obnoxious people.

Digging my nails into Garrick's hand to reclaim his attention, I subtly shake my head just as he prepares to give his mother hell. His brow puckers momentarily as he stares at me, and his Adam's apple bobs pointedly in his throat. Quickly recovering his composure, he smooths out his expression and bends down for his mother to kiss him on both cheeks.

"It's so wonderful to see you," Ivy gushes before her mouth pulls into a narrow line. "Did you forget your tie?" She snaps her fingers over her head, and a young man, dressed in a similar uniform to the butler, races across the room from his stationary position at the wall.

"Mom, don't start," Garrick says as Ivy eyeballs the poor server and demands his tie. The man raises fumbling fingers to the black tie around his neck as Garrick's jaw pulls tight.

There is nothing wrong with what Garrick is wearing. He has on a light-blue dress shirt, open at the top, and pressed black slacks with matching dress shoes. He looks handsome and smart though he's underdressed compared to Winston, the governor, and the unidentified man shuffling awkwardly on his feet behind Pepper, who are all dressed in custom suits with ties.

"Leave it," Garrick snaps at the poor server before whipping his head around to his mom. "Drop it," he says under his breath. "Or I'm leaving."

Ivy looks momentarily annoyed before she plants a false smile on her face to match the false laughter that falls from her lips. She casts a quick glance in my direction for the first time. "It's clear neither of you got the dress code memo, but never mind." Her disdainful eyes are like claws raking down my body. "It's your presence that matters," she adds as Garrick moves in closer, wrapping his arm protectively around my shoulders.

"These are for you," Garrick says in a clipped tone, thrusting the bouquet at his mother.

"Oh, how lovely." Taking the pink, white, and purple floral arrangement from her son's hands, she barely glances at them before handing them off to the server.

"They are from Stevie," Garrick adds, tightening his hold on me. "From her nana's greenhouse. Stevie picked and arranged the bouquet especially for you."

"Garrick said gardenias were your favorite," I say in my most serene tone. "I hope you like them."

"I prefer roses." She offers me a tight smile that is completely insincere, and I just know it's going to set the tone for the day.

"Oh, I adore roses too." I smile prettily like she hasn't just offended me. "I'll remember that for next time." I let my smile grow bigger, enjoying the way her eyes narrow suspiciously on me.

Ha! As if there will be another time. The only way this bitch will ever get flowers from me again is if I'm putting them on her grave.

"This is for you too." I pass the cake carrier to her, keeping the smile supplanted on my face. "I got up early this morning to bake a Black Forest gâteau."

A visible shudder works its way through her. "Well, with all those calories, I certainly won't be eating it."

"Black Forest cake is my favorite," Winston says, stepping forward to meet us while Pepper and her family huddle next to the floor-to-ceiling window, talking in hushed tones while they drink champagne and pretend this entire situation is not all kinds of awkward.

"Did you know I'm of German descent?" he asks, taking the carrier from Ivy's hands, prying the lid off and licking his lips as he stares at my creation.

"Of course," I lie, knowing this will wind Ivy up. "I chose this particular cake after Garrick mentioned it." It's pure coincidence, but he doesn't need to know that. The only things Garrick has mentioned to me about the man his mother hopes will be hubby number four are unflattering in the extreme.

"A woman after my own heart." Winston guffaws before waggling his bushy brows and looking at me with uncomfortable appreciation. Ivy barely hides her glare, and I feel a smug sense of satisfaction. Perhaps I shouldn't have encouraged her beau, but fuck that bitch. She's already been super rude, and I know she'll be even ruder to me before the day is out.

Ivy doesn't disguise her disgust when Winston swipes a digit through the top of the cake, groaning as he licks cherry, chocolate, and cream from his meaty finger. I bite on the inside of my cheek and keep a fake smile plastered on my face as I internally scream. That fucking selfish twat has ruined the cake I spent hours making. I even made the morello cherry jam myself earlier in the week, and now that fat prick has put his grubby finger in it as if he's five years old and he can't contain himself.

"This tastes incredible. I look forward to eating it later." Winston pats his portly tummy before handing the cake to the sever and fixing me with a leering smile. "I do love a woman who is creative with her hands."

Rage rolls off Garrick in waves at Winston's blatant innuendo, and I'm ready for World War Three to kick off when Pepper rides to the rescue.

"Garrick, you're looking well, and it's so good to see you again, Stevie," she says, materializing at my side and redirecting Garrick's attention from Winston. She darts in to kiss me on the cheek, acting as if we're the best of friends. "I got you a glass." She hands me a flute filled to the brim with champagne, and I have a sudden urge to knock it back. Alcohol would help me get through this ordeal, but getting drunk would not be smart. Who knows what's liable to pop out of my mouth uninhibited?

Pepper pulls me and Garrick away from his mother and Winston, leading us over to the window and introducing us to her date, Randall Clemmings VI. She actually introduces him like that. The poor fucker looks suitably embarrassed, gulping back his champagne and looking nervously out the window. Apparently, he works for her father, and Pepper got to know him over the summer when she was interning. They have just started dating. Pepper dropped that information dump in the first few minutes of conversation, and I'm sensing it was intentional.

I'm just not sure whose benefit it was for—mine or Garrick's.

Garrick keeps his arm around my waist as we chat, while the older couples congregate at the bar behind us, perched on tall stools. My eye is drawn outside to the lavish pool area, gorgeous grounds, and the dock at the back leading to the lake. A large boat is stationed behind the property, and I'm guessing it belongs to Winston or Ivy.

After a tedious hour of forced conversation with Pepper and her date—and restrained drinking on my part—we are ushered to a grand dining room and escorted to our assigned seating at the opulently decorated table. A large crystal chandelier hangs overhead, matching the lit crystal candelabras up and down the center of the table. Plain gold-colored vases hold bunches of white roses, complementing the white and gold table linen.

I'm already terrified of spilling something and being chastised.

"Darling, you're seated beside Pepper," Ivy tells Garrick when he moves to claim the seat beside me.

Of course, he is.

This woman has no shame.

A card with Randall's name is propped on the table in front of Garrick, and I wonder if Pepper was told to bring a date purely so they could foist him on me.

I'm hurt and fuming on Garrick's behalf. He accepted his mother's olive branch in true faith, but she had no intention of making any effort with me. I am not sure exactly what her agenda is today, but it's definitely not welcoming me to the family.

Garrick drills an angry look at his mother. "I'm sitting beside my girlfriend, or we're leaving."

Ivy emits a high-keeled laugh. Everything about that woman is fake from her plastic face to her plastic tits, her pretend posh accent, her nauseating compliments-slash-ass-licking to the governor, and her obvious false humor. "There's no need to get your panties in a bunch, darling." She flashes us a syrupy-sweet smile laced with hidden venom. "I don't know where your newfound dramatics have come from, but it's rather unbecoming. I did not raise you to conduct yourself in this manner."

She barely raised him from what I've been told. Dawn and his dad had a strong influence on Garrick growing up, and he spent most of his time in North Bend even if the divorce granted them joint custody of their only son. Ivy was often busy with society events, whichever husband she was married to at the time, or abroad on overseas trips, so he grew up largely with his father, and it shows. It's lucky for Garrick his father and stepmother were the main influence in his life. I shudder to think of how conceited he might be if his mother had had more of a role in his life.

"I don't see how speaking the truth amounts to drama, and what is wrong with my boyfriend wanting to sit beside me?" I ask before swigging from my champagne.

Across the table, Randall sits down beside Pepper in the seat that was meant for Garrick. Her mother is on her other side. Ivy and the governor have taken up position on either end of the table, and Winston slides into the seat beside me, much to my distaste.

"I don't expect you to understand how things work in high society, dear," Ivy says, her patronizing tone laced with sarcasm. "But it's traditional to sit apart from one's spouse or date at formal events."

"We're not royalty," Garrick hisses, glaring at his mother. "This is supposed to be a family Thanksgiving dinner. One I fully expected to attend with my girlfriend by my side."

Ivy sucks in her cheeks before her features smooth out. She claps her hands, choosing to ignore her son's statement. "Let's eat!"

Chapter Twenty-Nine

Stevie

I hold on to Garrick's hand under the table during the meal, and I'm on a countdown to when we can leave. Pepper makes polite conversation with me from across the table while Garrick and Randall talk sports, music, and wine. She asks me about college and my jobs, and she seems nice and genuinely interested, but I don't know if it's all a front. I ask her about her poli-sci major and her plans for the future, and she's animated and bubbly when discussing following her father into politics.

Ivy's heated glare sits firmly on my shoulders, and after a while, and probably too much champagne, I decide to challenge her on it. "Do I have something on my face?" I ask, sitting up straight in my chair and angling my body so I'm looking Garrick's mother straight in the eye. "Or perhaps you're staring at me nonstop because you'd like to know where I get my hair done?" I smooth my hand over my long glossy locks. "If you're considering a hair color change, I can highly recommend red. It's certainly classier and less common than blonde." I keep a sweet smile affixed to my face the entire time I'm insulting her, purposely focusing on her bottled-blonde shade. "Though mine is natural and almost impossible to replicate with a dye."

"I have never had any desire to color my hair red," she drawls, lifting her wineglass and stabbing me with a sharp look. "Even less so now." She guzzles her wine while I count that a win.

Then she pointedly steers the conversation at the table to politics, purely to end the discussion I'm having with Pepper and most likely to embarrass me. As soon as the conversation turns political, I'm out of my comfort zone and forced to remain quiet because I can't contribute anything. Ivy wastes no opportunity to take a potshot at me, chipping away at my bravery, and I wonder how much more of this I can withstand.

Garrick growls at his mother, constantly intervening to shut her up. Until the next time, and we do it all over again.

It's exhausting, and I'm slowly losing the will to live.

The array of silverware on the table confuses me along with the convoluted menu consisting of amuse-bouche, soup, scallops, crab claws, and caviar to start and lobster as the main event with a host of different accompaniments. Ivy laughs when I pick up the wrong utensil and laughs again when Garrick subtly points out the silverware to use.

You just can't win with that bitch.

"We regularly have dinner at Dad and Dawn's," Garrick says, angrily forking some gratin potatoes on his plate in between shooting contemptuous looks at his mother. "They don't feel the need for all of these silly trappings. This is supposed to be a family dinner. We're not at some stuffy social event, and I don't see why there is a need for all this pomp and ceremony or your attempts to belittle my girlfriend. I'm running on limited patience, Mother, and I'd advise you to choose your words carefully. Unless your plan is to permanently drive a stake through the heart of our relationship? In which case, carry on and see what happens."

"Again with the dramatics," Ivy murmurs, looking like she wishes she could smother me in my sleep. "Everyone, eat." She waves her hands around. "The food is getting cold."

Her go-to MO seems to be ignoring shit she doesn't like and pretending it wasn't said. She truly is a piece of work.

Garrick spends the rest of dinner defending me, glowering at his mother, and whispering we can leave at regular intervals. I want to go, but I've come this far. I can make it until the end of dinner. Then I'm getting out of here, and I'm never coming back.

I pick at my food, appetite slaughtered thanks to the tension and stiltedness in the room. I miss good old-fashioned turkey, green beans, and mashed potatoes, and I wish I had turned down this invite and gone to my nana's. Memories of previous Thanksgiving dinners, surrounded by good company, traditional food, delicious wine, tons of laughter, and nonstop music surges to the forefront of my mind, adding to my misery.

Discussion among the women turns to haute couture while we're awaiting dessert, and I'm still out of my depth. "Your dress is pretty, Stevie," Ivy says, and I'm instantly on high alert. "Even I might be tempted to wear last season if I found something that complimented my hair so well. It must be challenging finding vibrant clothes that don't clash with the red."

"I don't have that problem, and Garrick loves my hair," I retort, struggling to keep the sickly-sweet smile on face as I drain my wine.

I ditched restraint the second I sat at this table. Right now, alcohol is getting me through this ordeal, and I couldn't give a flying fuck what might come out of my mouth. I am beyond caring. There is no way of salvaging anything with Garrick's mother, and I'm not going to sit here and take her bullshit. "He's always finding ways to touch it." I bite my lip and wear my most suggestive expression as I blatantly eye fuck my boyfriend. "Especially in the bedroom. Isn't that right, babe?"

"Abso-fucking-lutely." Garrick doesn't let me down, gently fisting a hand in my hair, tipping my head back, and bringing his lips to mine. Ivy lets out a shriek of outrage as we kiss in front of everyone at the table, and I giggle against Garrick's lips. When we have pushed it enough, we break apart, and I rest my head on his shoulder as he plays with strands of my hair. "Your hair is stunning, like every part of you," he loyally supplies.

I hate he must choose between me and his mother, but she's the one who forced this, not me.

"That's enough." Ivy slams her clenched fist down on the table. "I won't have any more disrespectful behavior at the dinner table."

"Perhaps you should excuse yourself then," I say, unable to help myself.

Surprised shock splays across Cristelle's face while Ivy stares at me with barely concealed hatred. Garrick laughs and makes a point of lacing his fingers through mine on top of the table. The governor quietly sips his wine while Randall stares abjectly into space, looking like he wishes he could be zapped out of here—I can relate—and Pepper wears a worried frown as she looks at Garrick.

Winston chuckles. "You really need to remove that stick up your ass, Ivy." He waves his wineglass in her direction, spilling ruby-red liquid all over the white tablecloth. "Leave the girl alone." Winston tilts his head to look at me, planting his large hand down on my thigh under the table.

I jump, instantly removing it before Garrick or Ivy notices.

"I like your dress," Winston adds, slurring his words and hiccupping.

He's been knocking the wine and champagne back like it's going out of fashion. Not that I'm one to talk. Although alcohol has loosened my tongue, I think I'm too angry to get drunk. Even though he's a bit of a letch, I would still take pervy Winston over evil-bitch Ivy any day. And honestly? If I was dating that witch, I'd be permanently drunk.

"Especially the front." Winston's eyes latch on to my cleavage, and it's not the first time.

I take back what I just said.

They're both as bad as one another and deserve to be miserable together.

"Keep your eyes on Stevie's face," Garrick barks, leaning across me to glower at Winston. "Or I'll fucking make you."

"Garrick!" Ivy feigns shock, placing her hand over her mouth. "Apologize right now."

Garrick throws his napkin down. "I'll apologize when he apologizes for leering at my girlfriend all through dinner." He stands just as the servers come into the room with dessert. "And after you apologize for your rude treatment of Stevie."

"This is supposed to a be a celebration," the governor says, projecting his voice around the room as he intervenes for the first time. "Everyone, just sit down and let bygones be bygones."

Fucking typical politician. I wonder would he be so dismissive if it was his daughter subjected to Ivy's verbal abuse?

Tugging on Garrick's leg, I implore him to sit with my eyes. "It's nearly over," I mouth as the servers set dessert down in the middle of the table. "We'll eat dessert, then make excuses and leave."

Reluctantly, Garrick reclaims his seat. "I'm so sorry, Stevie," he whispers in my ear. "We should never have come."

"We'll discuss it later," I whisper back, noticing the fresh frown crawling over his face.

"Where is Stevie's cake?" Garrick asks.

The servers are busy distributing crème brûlée and baked Alaska, but there is no sign of the cake I baked.

"In the trash," Ivy says, fighting a smug smile. "You can blame Winston for infecting it with his germs."

The cake was still edible. Just scrape off the top layer, cut it into slices, and it would have been fine. There was no need to toss the entire thing. It was pure maliciousness, and I've reached my breaking point. Swallowing painfully over the lump in the back of my throat, I force tears to retreat from the backs of my eyes. I will not let this bitch get to me, any more than she has, and I'm not staying here a second longer.

"I'm done," I say, standing and throwing my napkin on the table.

"Be a dear and fill me up before you leave." Ivy holds out her wineglass. "At least that should make you feel at home." An evil grin spreads over her mouth. "Maybe we should have had you serving us through dinner and show my son, once and for all, that you don't fit in his world."

Snatching the red wine bottle up, I walk quickly along the table, heading toward the bitch. She's so arrogant she actually believes I'm going to top off her glass.

What a dumb cunt.

Her strangled shriek as I empty the bottle of wine all over her hair, face, and expensive in-season ballgown is music to my ears. Winston's loud laughter bounces off the walls of the otherwise eerily quiet dining room.

I think I've managed to shock everyone else into silence.

Chapter Thirty

Stevie

The silence is shattered when Ivy emits a rage-fueled roar and lunges for me.

"Shit!" Garrick yanks me back before his mother reaches me, prying the wine bottle from my tight fingers.

"You stupid classless whore!" Ivy screams, wiping wine from her eyes before she lunges at me again. She wobbles on her heels and reaches out to clutch the edge of the table before she falls. I watched her push food around her plate while drinking glass after glass of wine and champagne, and it's quite possible she's very drunk.

"Enough!" Garrick bellows, stepping in front of me and partially shielding me with his body. "You deserve that and more." He jabs his finger in his mother's direction. "Just remember I gave you a chance to prove you could be a normal human. A normal mother. But you couldn't even attempt to try for my sake. You orchestrated this to humiliate Stevie, and I'll never forgive you for it. Never."

The governor and his wife stand on either side of Ivy, trying to keep a straight face, while Winston is slouched in his chair, eyeing proceedings with drunken amusement. I briefly wonder if their relationship will survive this dinner. Randall and Pepper are standing in the corner by the wall, attempting to smother their laughter.

At least I provided the entertainment.

Let's call it my legacy.

"She's not right for you!" Ivy screeches, sounding like a banshee as she plucks strands of wet hair off her face. "She's beneath you, and she's only after you for your money! Everyone can see it but you. She's a gold-digging harlot, and I'm not going to sit back and let her trick or trap you into marriage! This dinner was for you! It was about opening your eyes to the truth."

"The truth?!" Garrick yells, and I cling to his arm, offering silent support. "The truth is, you're a snob who cares more about appearances and social progression than her own son. If you took the time to get to know Stevie, you would realize how wrong you are, but you made your mind up from day one. You want the truth, Mother?" He leans toward her, shielding nothing from his face as he says, "I love Stevie!" He moves me under his arm, tucking me into his side. "I. Love. Her," he shouts. "She's the only one for me. Someday, soon if I have my way, Stevie will be my wife."

Ivy rears back in horror.

"That's right, Mother. I'm going to *ask her* to marry me, and there is nothing you can say that will change it."

I turn my head to the corner, watching as tears gather in Pepper's eyes. Shock is mixed with pain and longing on her face, and she's doing nothing to disguise it. Randall and I exchange a look, both understanding it. No one else has noticed, but it's plain to see. I can't say I'm hugely surprised.

Garrick clasps my hand in his. "You are dead to me," he tells his mother as I watch Pepper flee the room. "I am done making excuses for the shitty human you are. You need to take a long hard look at yourself, Mother, before you end up alone." He looks down at me, pain and resolve stretched across his strained face. "Come on, we're leaving."

We don't speak as we exit the room, leaving devastation in our wake. Garrick strides forward with purpose, like he can't wait to put distance between us and this disaster. Up ahead, I spot Pepper slipping into the bathroom. "I need to use the toilet," I tell Garrick when we reach the front door. "You go ahead." I stretch up and kiss his cheek. "Get the car started, and I'll be out in a few minutes."

"Stevie." He takes my hands in his. "I am so incredibly sorry about all this. I am ashamed and appalled at the way she has treated you. We should never have stayed. I should have made that decision the second we arrived when I saw the Montgomerys were here."

"I made the choice to stay, Garrick. You were willing to leave, and you did your best to defend me. This isn't your fault, and you need to stop apologizing for that woman. I'm done trying to seek her approval. She's your mother. What you do from here is your decision, but I will not be making any more effort, and I won't be having any contact with her ever again. I will not put myself through another nightmare like this one."

"I would not expect you to," he agrees, clasping my face in his hands and pressing a kiss to my brow. "I love you." He pecks my lips. "Go to the bathroom, and hurry. I need to get out of here before I'm tempted to murder my own mother."

The door to the bathroom is unlocked, and I slip inside, quietly closing it behind me. Resting against the solid wood door, I wait for the woman in the voluminous red dress to turn around and face me.

I could have left without confronting her, but I need to know.

Pepper is leaning against the counter, face forward, with both hands propped on the marble, her gaze fixed straight ahead as she stares into the mirror.

Tension bleeds into the air as she slowly turns to face me with tearstained cheeks and red-rimmed eyes.

I wet my lips and clear my throat. "How long have you loved him?"

"Forever," she whispers.

"Does he know?" I don't think Garrick does, but I have to ask. I need to know if he's just in denial.

She shakes her head. "He's clueless. I've ensured it."

"Why?"

"He doesn't see me like that. Not yet."

"Ah." I push off the door, knotting my hands in front of me. "You are biding your time. Waiting for the right moment to make your move."

"That was the plan, yes." She straightens her shoulders and brushes the moisture from under her eyes. "But I waited too long. You're different than the other girls he has dated. None of them were a threat. None of them were worthy of him, and I mistakenly believed you weren't either. But I was wrong."

"His mother would disagree."

"Ivy is a bitch and a snob, and what she did to you today was despicable."

"Yet you said nothing. All of you just sat there and let her treat me like that. You may not have gone out of your way to hurt me, Pepper, but you wanted me exposed. You were hoping to benefit by letting Ivy do the dirty work. If Garrick was free of me, you could finally make a move."

Her chest rises, and she audibly gulps as she stares at me. "You are right," she admits. "It was wrong of us to sit there in silence. Mom would never undermine her best friend in front of an audience, and Daddy values Ivy's connections too much to go to bat for someone he doesn't know. Randall is a stranger, and he couldn't speak out for fear of upsetting Daddy."

"But you could have. Yet you did nothing."

"I am sorry for not intervening, Stevie. I should have called her out on her treatment of you." Remorse undercuts her tone and flashes on her face, but I have no clue if it's genuine. These people are skilled manipulators, and she grew up in a world where it's acceptable to trample over everyone and everything to achieve the end goal. I doubt Pepper gives a flying fuck about me. All she cares about is Garrick.

"What do you think Garrick would do if he knew you purposely chose to remain silent for personal gain?"

"He may not know the real reason why, but he's disappointed in me. As his friend, he would expect me to take your side."

Yes, my boyfriend would. Hopefully, now he'll see her true colors and want to end this charade of a "friendship."

"I'm shocked Garrick stayed," Pepper continues, "but that was you, wasn't it? You didn't want to back down."

"I'm not a quitter, and I never wanted him to fall out with his mother because of me. I thought I could handle it for his sake, but I was mistaken. We should have left the instant we arrived when I saw it was another matchmaking attempt." I unknot my hands and stand tall. "Tell me, was Randall part of it? Did she tell you to bring him here for me?"

"Absolutely not. If she even attempted that with me, I would have told her to fuck off. I don't blame you for thinking the worst of me, Stevie, but I would never purposely hurt you. That isn't who I am."

"So why bring him then?" I cock my head to one side. "It's obvious you're not into him."

She winces, having the decency to look ashamed as she wraps her arms around her middle. "I knew you'd be here with Garrick, and I wanted to bring a date. I couldn't sit through another dinner watching the man I love with someone who isn't me. Randall had been asking me out all summer, and I repeatedly said no. I decided to give him a chance. To see if I could move on, but I was delusional. Garrick is all I see."

At least she's being honest. I respect her for that. I hold Pepper's gaze as I make her a promise. "I won't step aside and let you steal my man."

"I wouldn't ask you too, and I never will. As much as it pains me, it's clear Garrick loves you and you love him. You make him happy. That's all I want for him. You're the one he wants forever, and I'll just have to find a way to make peace with it."

"You expect me to believe you'll just walk away?" Skepticism bleeds into my tone.

"No. You're too smart for that." We size each other up. "In different circumstances, I think we could be friends. It would be far easier for me if I hated you, but I don't. I couldn't hate any woman who brought the high and mighty Ivy Allen-Golding-Smith to her proverbial knees." Condescension rings clear through her tone before she laughs. "The look on her face when she lunged at you." More laughter bursts from her mouth. "It was priceless. I will never forget it. That woman has had that coming for a long time."

I shrug, needing to wrap this up before Garrick sends out a search party. Besides, I'm done wasting breath on that awful woman. "I don't want you around him," I say in a nonthreatening manner. I want her to understand my position and her place going forward, but I'm not going to sink to Ivy's despicable levels to make my point. "It's not fair to me, and it's not fair to him when he believes you only wish to be friends. Surely, it would be easier for you not to be around him either?"

Pain ghosts over her face as she clutches her arms more tightly around her waist. "It would," she quietly admits after a few beats. "I don't think it will be a problem anyway. If Garrick is determined to cut ties with Ivy, and I believe he is, there'll be limited opportunities for us to meet." She loosens her arms, letting them drop to her side. "I know I have no right to ask anything of you, but I'd rather Garrick didn't know how I feel about him."

"We agreed to honesty in our relationship, and I don't like keeping secrets from him." Even if this one would work to my advantage. I don't particularly want Garrick to know Pepper loves him. But it's complicated now I have this knowledge. If he finds out some other way and he discovers I knew and didn't tell him, would he understand the reasons why?

"It's not your secret to share," she says, offering me an excuse on a silver platter.

"Why don't you want him to know?" I narrow my eyes in suspicion.

"What good would it do any of us? He doesn't love me. He loves you. He wants to marry you." Her voice chokes, and she briefly averts her eyes. "We will occasionally run into one another, and I'd rather it isn't awkward," she continues, lifting her head and piercing me with an earnest look. "Isn't it better to let our friendship peter out than dragging all this into the open? It will only hurt more that way."

"Okay." I nod. "I agree. I won't tell him."

"Thank you."

"I'm not doing it for you."

"I know."

We look at one another for a few seconds more before I turn and unlock the door.

"Stevie," she calls out as I swing the door open. I turn one final time to look at her. "Take care of him and love him good. He deserves to be happy."

Chapter Thirty-One

Garrick

"What time are you meeting Stevie at?" Will asks in between stuffing clothes haphazardly in his bag while I lounge on his bed, throwing a tennis ball up and down in the air. Classes ended today for the holidays, and we're all heading home for Christmas this weekend.

"We're meeting at Bumble Bees in an hour."

"Do you have any idea what the gift is?"

I shake my head, tossing the ball in the corner, and sit up. "All she said was she wanted to give me my Christmas gift early and we had to do it before we went back to Seattle."

"Intriguing." Will zips up his bag and flops down beside me. "How are things between you now?"

"Better but still strained. She has retreated a little since that disastrous dinner. Not that I blame her. It was awful. I should have left immediately. I made a mistake not forcing the issue. Stevie says she doesn't blame me, that it was her call to stay, but deep down, I suspect she is aggravated I didn't make the decision to leave when we got there and saw Pepper and her family."

"You can't change history, and you chose her over Ivy. You've cut your mother out of your life. That speaks volumes."

"Sometimes, it's hard to tell with Stevie. She's not like other girls, and she has big hang-ups about relationships." I gulp over the messy ball of emotion at the back of my throat. "I don't want to lose her."

"You won't. She knows how much you care, and she's always your priority."

"But am I hers?" I murmur, admitting something I've been terrified to confront.

"She's nuts about you, Gar. It's just a rough patch. You'll bounce back. Every couple goes through highs and lows. You two will last the distance. Just like Ellen and me."

"I want to believe that, but sometimes, I think she remembers how uncomplicated her life was before she met me. There were no annoying groupies, crazy exes, or bitchy mothers to deal with."

Air whooshes out of my mouth as I lean back against his headboard. "Stevie is so focused on her goals, and I'm really not sure where I land on her priority list." I angle my head to look at my buddy. "We had a fight on Monday because I brought up next year. She'll have built up enough credits to graduate in May. I asked her to consider holding off, to come back for senior year with me, and she accused me of being selfish."

"What did you say?"

"That I *was* selfish because I didn't want to be separated from her and I didn't want to lose her. She contended I wouldn't even if we have to do the long-distance thing. That it wouldn't be for long, and we could still see one another on weekends."

"That doesn't sound unreasonable."

"It's not." I cross my feet at the ankles. "But I don't want to be without her. It's more than just a wish. It's a physical need. I physically cannot be away from her for any length of time. She clearly doesn't feel the same way, and this relationship is starting to feel more and more one-sided."

"Have you told her that?"

"Yeah. She was hurt. Told me I was being unfair. That it would be hard for her to be away from me too, but we needed to maintain our independence within the relationship."

"And you haven't seen her since then?" Will arches a brow.

"Nope. We've been texting, but between exams and work, we haven't found time to meet up all week."

"It seems to me that Stevie needs more independence than most girls but the same level of reassurance. Just give her that, and trust things to work out. You two are meant to be, and it'll all be fine."

I wish I shared his optimism.

"Hey, you." Stevie hops up when I arrive at our table in Bumble Bees, flinging her arms around me and squeezing me tight. "Missed you."

"I missed you too." Wrapping my arms around her, I lift her off her feet and kiss her lips.

"I ordered you a black coffee and a chocolate chip muffin," she says when I put her down, smiling as Marie approaches with a tray.

"Thanks, babe." I kiss her cheek before she reclaims her seat, and I drop into mine.

Marie leaves our coffee and muffins and wanders off to attend to other patrons. "Can we clear the air?" Stevie asks, sipping her caramel macchiato and moaning as it tickles her taste buds.

My dick stirs at the sound and the look of abject pleasure on her face. "What else is left to say?" I shrug, taking a drink of my coffee. "We have a difference of opinion, and it's not like I'm going to force you into staying if you don't want to."

"It isn't about not wanting to stay, Garrick." Her hand slides across the table, and her fingers hook around mine. "If I had a choice, of course, I'd stay with you. But I set out on this path before I knew you. It makes no sense to hang around UO for another year when I can easily graduate in May. And this isn't just about me. Another college year means more money for food and accommodations, and it's one more year Mom will continue working her weekend job. I can't ask that of her. She has already given me so much."

When she puts it like that, I feel like a selfish prick. That thought hadn't crossed my mind. "I understand. I don't like it, but I understand."

"It's not even a full year, and we'll see each other on weekends and during the holidays."

"Maybe you could get a full-time job in Oregon?" I suggest, lifting her hand and kissing the tips of her fingers.

Her face twists into a grimace. "That's not an option."

"Why?"

"I have set ideas for my future career. I don't want to open a floral shop. I want to provide a professional service to corporate clients and provide a themed service for weddings. I won't be catering to the public or spending my days making bouquets."

My eyes pop wide in surprise. Of course, we've talked about our futures. I know her ambition is to run her own business after she has worked for others for a few years, to build up experience, but I didn't realize she had such set ideas. "What about your nana's place? Won't you be expected to take over?"

"Nana would never force me into anything. Mom will inherit the business, and either she'll take over the management of it, with some input from me, or she'll hire a suitably qualified person to run it. At some point in the future, I may change my mind. I might want to run it full-time, but for now, my goal is to start something of my own." She takes back her hand, straightening up and shrugging. "Who knows? Maybe, at some point, I can amalgamate the two businesses and run them together."

"So, how does this tie in with not being able to stay in Oregon?"

"The kind of business I want to run is quite niche. There's this start-up company in Seattle similar to the business model I have in mind. They are making a name for themselves, so I sent them my résumé." A massive grin spreads across her mouth. "And they have offered me a job!"

"You didn't even tell me you were applying for jobs." Hurt mixes with pride in my voice.

Her face falls. "I was going to tell you, but every time we talk about the future and me not being here for senior year, you get pissy. I wasn't going to say anything unless I got the job."

That she feels she can't tell me these things hurts even worse. "I thought we were a team. That I meant something to you."

"Garrick, of course, you mean something to me. I love you." She gets up and moves her chair over beside mine, snuggling into me as she tips her chin up. "I am serious about you. About us. But I've been honest with you from the start. I told you I have set goals and our relationship, while very important to me, can't take away from what I want to achieve."

"I love how ambitious you are, and I want you to succeed. But it seems like I'm relegated to the bottom of your list of priorities, and I'm scared I'm losing you." I'm aware I sound like a petulant child, but I can't help how I feel.

"I promise you're not, and I don't want to lose you either." Her fingers sweep through the stubble on my face. "We have to accept we need to give each other space to grow into the people we're going to be, time to develop our careers, and time to map out a plan for the future. We can still be together while pursuing independent paths."

She ducks down under the table, grabbing her purse and extracting an envelope. "I think this might help." Her eyes light up as she hands it to me.

"What is it?"

She nudges me in the ribs. "Open it and see."

I remove a square piece of paper from the envelope first, admiring the circular looped drawing. "Is this Celtic?"

She bobs her head, looking a little nervous as she explains. "It's a Celtic shield knot also called a dara knot. The Celts used the symbol in battle, but they also gave it to people they cared about the most. It's a promise to protect and look out for the person you love for all eternity. It's named after the Irish word for an oak tree, and it's said to mimic the roots of an oak tree. It's supposed to encourage and support people through challenging times. I think it's perfect to represent who we are to one another. Our love is as strong as the roots of a tree, and though they may branch out along different paths, we will forever remain interconnected."

She pulls out the other paper from the envelope and hands it to me. "That's an appointment for this afternoon at Mystical Tattoo. I thought we could both get this inked so we have a constant reminder of our love, no matter how many miles or how much time might separate us in the future." Her eyes glisten with emotion and a hint of vulnerability. "You know how I feel about tattoos. Anything I ink on my skin will become a permanent part of me." She taps the inside of her wrist. "I'm going to get mine here. I want this one visible, in a place where I can touch it when I need to feel close to you, and somewhere others will see it and know how much you mean to me."

My lips crash down on hers as potent emotion replaces the blood flowing through my veins.

As gestures go, this is perfect. Stevie couldn't have suggested anything better. As we kiss, my heart swells with love for this woman, and I hope this blatant display of her commitment will settle that inherent restless fear of losing her that resides inside me.

Chapter Thirty-Two

Garrick

"Oh god, yes, baby. Right there." Stevie moans and writhes underneath me as I bury myself deep inside her before slowly withdrawing and thrusting back in. My gaze skims over the new ink on her wrist, visible through the clear Tegaderm bandage, while her hands are flung out to either side, and pride wells inside me. I opted to get my tattoo in the same place on my left wrist, and every time I look at it, it brings a huge smile to my face.

"You are so good at this," my girlfriend pants, wrapping her legs more tightly around my waist as I fuck her on the rug in front of the roaring fire at the cabin. We're spending Christmas with my folks in North Bend tomorrow. Monica and Betsy are joining us too. Tonight, I wanted my beautiful sunshine all to myself, so we snuck away to the winery earlier to enjoy some alone time.

Things have been perfect these past few days, and I'm happy our relationship is back on track. Not even my mother's pitiful weepy message has dampened my good mood.

Ivy made her bed, and she can lie in it.

"I love you," Stevie rasps, pulling my face down to hers for a passionate kiss as I drive in and out of her.

"Love you too." I nibble a trail from her lips to her jawline and along the elegant slope of her neck, dotting kisses along her collarbone and lower. Locking my lips around one nipple, I suck hard on the taut peak, basking in the noises she makes as I lavish attention on both tits.

"I'm close," she pants, lightly dragging her nails up and down my back.

"Stay with me," I grunt, picking up speed and ramming in and out of her with feverish need. I straighten up into a kneeling position and hold her legs around my waist as I pound into her. She looks like a fucking goddess underneath me with her gorgeous red hair fanned out around her, a pretty blush covering her chest, and her magnificent tits bouncing and jiggling as I fuck her into the floor.

My balls tighten, and delicious tingles build at the base of my spine. Rubbing her clit, just the way she likes it, I pivot my hips, hitting deep inside her, and we fall off the ledge together.

Sex with Stevie is out of this world, and I want to continue doing it forever.

We collapse in a heap of tangled limbs and sweaty skin, clinging to one another and softly kissing, as we come down from our high. After snuggling for a while, I wrap her in a soft blanket and head to the bathroom to get rid of the condom. Then I grab a chilled bottle of wine, two glasses, two spoons, and a tub of ice cream and return to my woman.

Stevie is propped against the base of the couch, swaddled in the pink and gray blanket as she stares into the crackling flames dancing around the hearth. "Penny for them?" I ask, handing her the ice cream and spoons before easing down beside her. Setting the bottle and glasses on the ground, I proceed to pour the wine while she pries the lid off her favorite black cherry chocolate chip ice cream. I always ensure the cabin refrigerator is stocked up with the stuff. I buy it from a local parlor in Woodinville. It's one of their most popular cartons, and they regularly sell out, so I like to pick up a few when they're back in stock.

Stevie turns on her side, handing a spoon to me. "I was just thinking about how this was my fantasy the first time I came here."

I hand her a wineglass and take a sip of my own drink before digging my spoon into the yummy, creamy goodness. "Eating ice cream naked in front of the fire?"

"Not that part," she says before licking her spoon and moaning.

My cock stiffens because those sounds she makes are my own personal aphrodisiac. "Which part then?"

"The sex part. The second I saw this rug and the open fireplace, I had a vision of us drinking wine and making love in front of a roaring fire, and now we've done it."

I lean in and kiss her chocolaty lips. "I want to fulfill all your fantasies."

"You do, handsome. You're the best boyfriend." She snuggles into my side, dropping kisses along my arm and my shoulder. "I mean it, babe." She looks up at me through a layer of long, thick, gorgeous lashes, looking sweet as sin and good enough to eat. "You look after me so well, and you make me feel loved and protected."

"Loving you is as easy as breathing."

"I'm happy we're all spending Christmas together."

"Me too. I want to prove you can join my family for the holidays and it will be normal and wonderful, not like that Thanksgiving nightmare." I leave Stevie to finish the ice cream while I savor the crisp sauvignon blanc.

"I already know tomorrow will be nothing like that disaster. It's going to be great."

"You better believe it." I tweak her nose before handing her the bag with the small gift-wrapped box. "I want to give you your gift now while we're alone."

Discarding the half-empty ice cream tub, she sits up straighter, placing the bag on her lap. The blanket falls from her shoulders, pooling at her waist. Strands of messy auburn hair tumble over her shoulders, brushing the tops of her perfect round tits. Her nipples are hard, and my dick is flying at full mast now, pointing at her like a loaded weapon.

I'm already salivating at the prospect of round two.

But I want her to open her gift first.

Stevie is quiet as she removes the package from the bag. Trembling fingers tear at the pretty purple wrapping. Her head jerks up, and panicked eyes meet mine when she reveals the small square jeweler's box.

"It's not what you're thinking. Breathe, baby. Please." My fingers caress her face and neck in a soothing motion.

Her chest rises and falls as she opens the box. Wide, dazed eyes stare at the custom piece of jewelry.

"It's a promise ring," I explain because she's gone deathly pale. I sit cross-legged in front of her, watching all manner of emotions flit over her face as she stares at the ring.

A layered red topaz stone occupies center stage, surrounded by small diamond edging, arranged to look like petals, resting on a rose gold band. I couldn't be more thrilled at how it turned out. "It's a poppy ring," I blurt, staring to panic when she still hasn't said anything. "I had it made especially for you. I wanted to give you a ring that was uniquely you and something that represented my commitment to us." I tap a gentle finger across my plastic-wrapped wrist. "In the same way you gave me a gift of your commitment."

"It's beautiful, Garrick," she whispers, looking up at me with glassy eyes. "But this is too much and far too expensive."

"You are worth it." I wind my fingers in her hair. "Put it on. It should fit. I measured your finger one night while you were sleeping. I wanted to ensure I got the right size."

"That was sneaky," she says, carefully removing the ring from the box.

"Here. Let me." Taking it from her, I slide it onto the ring finger of her left hand. "There. Perfect." I almost choke on emotion as I force the words out. I can't describe the joy I feel seeing my ring on her finger. If I had my way, it'd be an engagement ring, but

I knew Stevie would balk if I proposed to her. I'll have to build up to that.

She holds out her hand, admiring it. "It's stunning." Biting on her lip, she stares at it like she's almost scared of it.

"If you don't like it, we can return it and pick something together."

"I love it, Garrick. I really do. I couldn't have picked anything more perfect."

"But?"

Air expels from her mouth in a rush. "I'm happy to wear your promise ring, Garrick, as long as we're on the same page about marriage, and I'm fearful we're not." She scoots in closer to me, her features softening with love as she peers deep into my eyes. "I want to marry you someday, but that's a long way away for me. I'm not even twenty-one yet."

"I know, and it's cool."

"Is it?" Her troubled eyes probe mine. "I don't want to hurt your feelings, but sometimes, it feels like we're on a high-speed train, and you're up there in the driver's cabin, screaming at him to go faster and faster, impatient to get to the destination, while I'm begging him to slow down so I can enjoy the scenery and savor every place we pass."

"Is it wrong I love you so much I want to marry you sooner than later?"

"It's not wrong to feel how you feel."

"But you don't feel it in the same way I do."

"I'm not saying that."

"Then what are you saying?" My tone is harsher than I intended, but hurt is mushrooming inside me. I wanted to give her something that was as thoughtful as the gift she gave me, but I seem to have completely misjudged the situation. "I'll take it back," I snap, reaching for her finger.

"Garrick, please." Tears well in her eyes, and her voice cracks. She whips her hand away. "I don't want you to take it back. I love it, but I want to ensure you're not reading too much into this. I'm not ready to get married, Garrick, and sometimes, it feels like you're smothering me."

I can scarcely breathe over the lump in my throat or the tight pain spreading across my chest. "I just want to love you." I scramble to my feet. "Why do you make that so hard?"

Chapter Thirty-Three

Stevie

"Talk to me," Nana says, resting her wrinkled palm on top of mine as we sit on the wooden bench outside. Classic Carpenters hits trickle out of the open glass double doors behind us as Garrick dances with Dawn. The twins are in the game room, playing their new Xboxes while Mom and Hugh sit at the kitchen table, chatting and drinking wine, as Garrick swirls his stepmom around the tile floor.

It's super sweet and a timely reminder of how good a guy my boyfriend is. The heightened emotion, mixed with obvious tension between Garrick and me threatened to break me apart. So, I fled to the safety of the patio, bundled in my coat, staring out at the blanket of trees curtaining the rear of Garrick's family home in North Bend, lamenting my insensitivity and wondering if there are critical cells missing from my brain.

"I hurt his feelings," I croak, "and I ruined Christmas for both of us, and I hate myself for it."

"Shush now, Little Poppy. Nothing was ruined. We had a lovely dinner, with lots of laughter and delicious wine, and the night is far from over."

"Why am I like this, Nana?" I turn to face her. "What is wrong with me?"

"There is nothing wrong with you, honey." Her eyes drift to the gorgeous ring nestled on the ring finger of my right hand.

Garrick's frosty gaze this morning when he noticed I'd changed it to my other hand could have cut glass. When I explained how everyone would jump to conclusions if I wore it on my left hand, he merely nodded and left the room.

"Is it something to do with this ring?" she asks, always uncannily observant.

"Yes." I fill her in briefly, careful to keep my voice low in case any of our conversation carries inside. "I should have waited to say anything, but we made promises to one another to always be truthful, and honestly, the intensity of his feelings for me, and the certainty he possesses about our relationship, really scares the shit out of me at times."

"You can't help how you feel any more than Garrick can." She cups my face. "You are mature beyond your years, Stevie, in so many ways."

"Except when it comes to love." I beat her to the punchline.

Nana's soft smile and loving gaze ghost over me. "I'm proud of you for knowing what you want and always prioritizing it. You should never beat yourself up over speaking your mind and sharing your truths. It is better to openly communicate instead of keeping things locked up inside. Perhaps compromise and a little sensitivity in relation to the timing of conversations might be something to work on."

"You're right. I should not have expressed those thoughts last night. He tried to do something romantic for me, and I trampled all over it with my words, and I hurt him. Maybe I'm too blunt. I need to stop and think before I open my mouth. I love Garrick. I truly do, but he wants to drive a thousand miles an hour and I can't keep up."

"You're both still so young, and you have your whole lives ahead of you. Now is the time to have fun and not worry about the consequences." She tucks a wayward piece of my hair behind my ear. "You're both intense in different ways."

"Is that a good or a bad thing?"

"It is neither good nor bad. It is what it is." Her papery lips kiss my brow. "We can't predict what is around the corner, and I personally believe one shouldn't spend too long trying to. Live in the moment is my motto. And what is meant to be is what will transpire."

"Am I interrupting?" Garrick asks, standing awkwardly behind us with his hands shoved deep in the pockets of his black pants.

"Never, sweetheart." Nana rises stiffly to her feet, and Garrick offers her his hand. She grips on to him with an affectionate smile. "There are so few gentlemen left in this world, Garrick, but you are one of life's rare treasures."

The look on his face conveys how much those words mean to him, and I couldn't love Nana any more than I do in this moment. Her words were not solely for him either, and I see what she's doing.

Nana slips quietly into the house, leaving us alone to stew in the strain.

I'm the one who did this, so it's up to me to mend it. I stand and turn around, wrapping my arms around my waist as I stare at my forlorn-looking boyfriend. "I'm so sorry, Garrick. I didn't mean to hurt you, and I hate that I did. Your gift was thoughtful and beautiful, and I was insensitive. My timing sucked."

He moves closer. "I'm sorry too. I promised I wouldn't pressure you and I keep fucking up."

"I love you so much," I whisper with tears in my eyes, closing the gap between us and leaning against him. "But I worry we want different things."

His arms encircle my waist as he hugs me close. "We want the same things, just at different times and in different ways." He rests his chin on top of my head. "I never want you to feel like you need to apologize for speaking your mind. I always want to know what you're thinking even if what you're thinking might hurt me. It's better than being lied to."

"I didn't mean to ruin Christmas."

"What are you talking about?" He tilts my chin up with one finger. My heart does a little dance when his golden-brown eyes latch on to mine. Those rich amber flecks sparkle as his eyes crinkle with a smile. Beautiful dimples I dream about come out to play, and I melt against him, hating all the cross words and silence between us today.

"You didn't ruin anything," he continues. "I have always said everything is right in my world as long as you are by my side, and that was true today. We might have been distant and upset with one another, but we still spent the day together. You are mine, and I am yours. That hasn't changed." He smooths his hand down my hair. "Our love will endure the challenges, and we'll come out stronger on the other side."

"There he is, my lyrical poet." Stretching up, I press my mouth to his. Our lips linger, gliding gently together in tender kisses that transmit all the unspoken words behind the potent emotion charging the air.

Garrick kisses me softly and lovingly, and my heart equally rejoices and melts.

I don't know what the future holds for us, but in this moment, he is all that I want and all that I need.

"I'm starting a new tradition," he purrs in my ear before pulling back, treating me to another glimpse of those dashing dimples. "Dance with me, sunshine?" he asks, extending his hand.

"I would love to." I place my hand firmly in his, smiling and full of his love as he leads me into the kitchen where he proceeds to spin me around the floor to The Carpenters with our families whoops and hollers ringing in our ears.

We return to campus in January, after a lazy Christmas break, with a greater understanding of where we stand as a couple. We love one another, and we're committed to making it work. I just hope that's enough.

The months race by in a whirlwind of classes, study, work, and nights spent huddled under the sheets in my bedroom, enjoying one another in a way that never ends in an argument. On Saturdays, the crew and I show up to Garrick's gig to support him, and I do my best to ignore the women who throw themselves at my boyfriend any chance they get. I know he has no interest in them, and I trust him, but it's annoying they act like such hobags when they know he has a steady girlfriend.

Sunday nights are date night, and we grab dinner out, or catch a movie, or I cook at home, and we make love for hours.

Thankfully, his friendship with Pepper is virtually nonexistent now, so that's one less complication to worry about.

Garrick is still giving his mother the cold shoulder, and he shows no sign of changing his tune. Especially after I played him the nasty drunken messages she left on my phone recently. Garrick refuses to speak to her, so he got his dad to talk to Ivy. Hugh made it clear her harassment had to stop. He was highly embarrassed telling us the things she accused me of. Dawn made a point of pulling me aside afterward to confirm how much she and Hugh adore me and love the relationship I have with their son. They have stated repeatedly they know our love is real and I'm not the gold digger Ivy is trying to paint me to be.

Is it wrong to want to make a voodoo doll in my boyfriend's mother's likeness so I can stick pins in her eyes any time she pisses me off? Because I have seriously considered it. I even went as far as googling how I could get a custom doll made and fell down a tempting rabbit hole of witchcraft and spells.

Spring break comes and goes. We forgo a Cabo trip with Will and Ellen, and Noah and his new girlfriend, to return to our cabin in

Seattle. Our days are spent hiking, biking, kayaking, and walking the grounds of the winery. Nights are spent with family, or enjoying a romantic meal at the outdoor restaurant, or cooking together.

It's a nice sojourn before we return to UO for our last few months together at college.

In April, I surprise Garrick with a night away in a five-star hotel in Seattle for his twenty-first birthday and a couples boudoir photography shoot. The night after, we attend a party at the winery, organized by his dad, for family and close friends. It is a great weekend, and we are storing plenty of entries in the memory bank.

However, as the weeks close in, and exam stress piles on, we are arguing more and more, and I'm feeling the strain.

Chapter Thirty-Four

Stevie

Ellen and I grab the opportunity for a girl's spa day, one Sunday in May, a few weeks before exams start. The guys have gone to Sutherlin to hike the North Umpqua Trail. It's an organized event to raise money for a local kid with leukemia. Will's family knows the little girl, so he is keen to support the fundraiser, and he roped the guys in.

"Will is going to move in with me for senior year," Ellen explains as we're seated side by side in matching leather recliners getting pedicures.

"I'm glad you got the lease again and you're able to stay there over the summer. At least you won't have to pack up all your shit this time."

"I'm going to miss you like crazy. You better not forget your college bestie when you're a hotshot floral corporate exec hightailing it with flashy bigwigs in suits."

I crack up laughing. "What the heck is a floral corporate exec? And you do know I'll be stuck in the office, behind a computer, most of the time, learning the management side of running the business?"

"Bish." She waves her hands in the air. "You'll be running the show single-handedly in no time."

"Thanks for the faith, but the closer it gets, the more terrified I am. A lot is hinging on this job. If I don't like it, it will throw all my plans into disarray."

One of the workers approaches, holding up a bottle of prosecco, and we both raise our glasses for a top off. We only come to this salon for the complimentary bubbly.

"I'm sure it'll work out, but if it doesn't, you have a degree, smarts, confidence, and other options. You also have a man who would walk through fire for you." She pats my hand. "You'll be fine."

"That's if I still have the man," I mumble under my breath, half hoping she hears me, half hoping she doesn't.

Ellen sits up straighter, and the girl painting her toenails shoots her an evil side-eye. "Why would you even say something like that?"

"Sometimes, my relationship feels like such hard work."

"*All* relationships are hard work."

"You and Will don't argue half as much as Garrick and I do."

"That's only because we do it behind closed doors."

I turn my head to the side and stare at her. "I love him, and I'm really going to miss him. I know I can handle the long distance. I'll throw myself into work, and I'm used to being by myself."

"But Garrick isn't."

"Exactly." I chew on the corner of my lip, staring up at the ceiling, counting the water stains on the off-white plasterboard. They really should hire a painter. Shaking myself out of my errant thoughts, I look back at my friend. "Garrick is used to being in a relationship and doing things with his girlfriend. Will is moving in with you, and Noah is all loved up. I don't see Garrick hanging out with Cohen much, so what'll he do? He's going to get lonely, and all his little groupies will love I'm not there."

"You'll be here on weekends, or he'll be with you in Seattle. The groupies don't matter, and Garrick would never cheat. You need to have a little faith, boo."

Garrick plans to cancel his regular Saturday night gig, and our mutual boss has agreed he can switch from Friday nights to Thursday nights at The End Zone, so he'll be free on weekends to meet up with me. "Deep down, I know that."

"So, what are you saying?"

I sigh heavily. "I don't really know." Pain lances me through the heart. "Just that I don't know how this will play out or"—I draw a brave breath—"whether we're meant to be forever."

Ellen blinks profusely as she stares at me. She roughly clears her throat. "No one can say that with any guarantee, babe. Not even married couples. I think you're overanalyzing and reading too much into things."

"What would you say if Will proposed to you tonight?"

A dreamy expression appears on her face. "I'd say yes."

I knew she would. I drill her with a look. "If Garrick asked me, I'd say no."

"Of course, you would. You have big career plans, and you always said you didn't want to get married until you were thirty."

"But shouldn't I say yes? If he's the one, it shouldn't matter."

Ellen sits upright and glares at the beautician, daring her to say anything. "Babe, listen to me." She reaches over and grabs my hand. "You have yourself all worked up over this, and I blame Garrick. He has always come on way too heavy with the marriage stuff."

"He can't help it. It's how he rolls."

"Yes, but you don't, and compromise is the name of the game. I think that gets lost in translation sometimes. If he wasn't going on about marriage all the time, you wouldn't give it a second thought, and half of these doubts would disappear."

"True."

"The way I see it, you have two choices. Try the long-distance thing and hope your love is strong enough to survive. For the record, I believe it is. Or break up with him now. If it's meant to be, you'll find your way back to one another when the timing is right."

"I don't want to break up with him," I rush to admit, rubbing at the pain in my chest. "The thought makes me equally ill and tearful."

"Then you have your answer. Forget about proposals and weddings. It's simply a case of the wrong time. But it doesn't mean you're with the wrong person."

"Boo, Garrick is here," Ellen says, poking her head through my bedroom door.

"Tell him I'll be right there," I say, stuffing the last of my toiletries in my weekend bag. "Do I look okay?" I ask before she leaves, running a hand over the front of my tight, short green and gold minidress. I have teamed it with a pair of knee-high leather boots, and my hair is in a half-up, half-down style that is very sixties. I went heavy on my eye makeup and pale on the lips.

"You look beautiful, like always." She darts in and kisses me on the cheek. "Garrick is going to eye fuck the shizz out of you when he sees how sexy you look."

"Is it too much for Nana's birthday?"

"Are you kidding?" She cracks up. "Nana will love it." Ellen hops from foot to foot, emitting a tiny squeal that is kinda weird.

I narrow my eyes at her. "What is wrong with you?"

"Nothing is wrong." She's practically bouncing off the walls now. "I'm just excited for you."

"Okay." I draw out the word. "Weirdo."

"What's taking so long?" Garrick asks, materializing in my room. "Wow." His gaze roams appreciatively over me. "Baby, you look sexy as fuck."

I give a little curtsy. "I aim to please."

Garrick grabs me to him, smacking a loud kiss on my lips as he squeezes my ass. "You're gorgeous, and I'm a lucky man."

"You're about to be a very lucky woman!" Ellen squeals, and I don't miss how Garrick shoots daggers at her.

"What's going on?" I ask, my gaze bouncing between them.

"Your bestie has no poker face." Garrick leans around me to grab my bag. "Come on. I've got a surprise for you."

The surprise is a new car. Some kind of flashy BMW SUV. I'm so stunned I can't even form words. Ellen and Will are opening doors and oohing and aahing over it while Garrick stands in front of me, looking increasingly alarmed.

"You bought me a car?" I splutter, shock rendering my voice barely louder than a whisper.

"Yes." He takes cautious steps toward me. "If you don't like the color or the make or model, we can get you something else."

"Why?" I stare at him as shock turns to anger. "Why did you buy me a car?"

"Because your car is on its last legs, babe, and I want you to have something safe for all the driving we'll be doing on weekends."

"I know my car has become unreliable, but it still drives fine." It's been in the garage a lot recently for one thing after another. "My plan was to save up to buy a car this summer."

"Well, now you won't have to." He smiles as he hands me the keys. "Take a look inside. Sit behind the wheel. See what it feels like."

"No." I throw the keys back at him, rubbing at a tense spot between my brows. "I can't let you buy me an expensive car, Garrick."

"Why the hell not?"

"Because it's too much! We've not even been dating a year!" I throw my hands in the air.

"Who gives a fuck how long we've been dating?" he shouts, my anger sparking his. "You're going to be my wife one day, and I want to know you're safe. Why does everything have to be such a big fucking deal with you? Most girls would be knocking me to the ground and dry humping me by now. But not you. You have to give me shit for doing something nice. What the hell is your problem?"

I shove my finger in his chest. "My problem is, I can buy my own fucking car! I don't need you bankrolling my future, Garrick!

You know I like to be independent. Why is this such a surprise to you?"

"Maybe because I thought we'd moved beyond all this bullshit over my money, but I can see I was wrong."

Ellen and Will are nowhere to be seen, and I guess they must have slipped back inside the building when we started arguing. They're probably afraid it's contagious.

I work hard to calm down. I know he means well, and I'm coming across as ungrateful. But he just doesn't get it, and it's damn frustrating at times. "Garrick, I love you, and I love how generous you are."

"Obviously not enough, or you'd accept the fucking car," he hisses.

"Being independent is important to me. I've been raised by women who instilled that repeatedly in me." I thump a fist over my chest. "It's deeply ingrained in here. I know you only want to help, but you've got to let me do things my way. I want to support myself."

"Is that the whole truth, or is this to do with my mother?"

"It's mostly the truth, but I won't lie and say what your mother thinks of me has no bearing. If I accept this car, she'll feel vindicated in calling me a gold digger."

"Fuck what she thinks, sunshine." His anger fades as he steps up to me. "I just want you to be safe. Protected. Cared for."

"I know." I rest my head on his chest, clinging to him with pain in my heart.

"I don't want to undermine you. I'm trying here, Stevie. I'm really trying, but everything I do seems to be the wrong thing. I don't know what else to do."

"This isn't about you. It's my hang-up. I'll try to work on it, but you can't keep forcing the issue."

He sighs heavily. "It's getting late. We should make a move. Why don't you drive the car to Ravenna and see how it feels?" He holds up his palms. "No pressure or expectations. If you don't want it, I'll return it."

"Of course, I'll want it if I drive it! That's not the point." I step back and rub my temples. Who the fuck wouldn't want such a gorgeous car? She's a beauty, and if I'd bought it with my own money, I'd be champing at the bit to drive it. But I didn't pay a penny for it, and therein lies my problem. "How about I drive my CR-V home? You can park the BMW in my spot while I'm gone, and I promise I'll think about it?"

"You're not saying no?"

"I'm saying I'll think about it. It's not a yes or a no."

He considers that for a moment. "Okay. Let's go."

I let Garrick drive to keep the peace. I'm lost in thought most of the journey, wondering if I'm cut out for relationships. I don't seem very good at it. When things are great, they are incredible, and I'm deliriously happy. But when shit goes down, it makes me feel like a worthless piece of crap.

Garrick is a good guy, and I'm beginning to think he deserves someone better than me. Someone who appreciates everything he brings to the table. Not someone with deep-seated fears and multiple hang-ups who can't accept the intensity of his love or the many extravagant ways he likes to show it.

"I'll return it," he says when we're close to the exit for Ravenna. "I thought it'd make you happy. Instead, you're miserable."

"I told you I'd think about it, and I will."

"I already know what your decision will be, and so do you." He uses the blinker and takes the left exit. "Do you not see a future with me? Is this what it's really about?"

I sit up straighter. "This is about you buying me a fifty-thousand-dollar car."

"Ninety," he says, tearing around the bend too fast for my liking. "It was ninety thousand dollars."

My jaw slackens. I'm definitely getting him to return it now. I'd be a basket case driving around in a car that's worth so much.

"Slow down!" I shout as he almost hits the rail at the side of the road.

"Fuck!" His face turns ghostly white as the car hurdles down the last stretch of the exit toward the busy road.

"You're going too fast!" I scream, starting to worry. "Slow down!"

"I can't!" he yells, repeatedly pressing his foot down on the brake. "The brakes aren't working!"

"Oh my god." Terror, unlike anything I've ever felt before, powers through me as we race downhill toward the intersection.

"Get in the brace position," Garrick shouts, turning the hazard lights on. Setting his palms down on the horn, he attempts to alert the traffic on the main road to our predicament.

Facing forward, with my head pressed firmly against the headrest, I pray like I have never prayed before. I'm shaking and trembling all over, and it feels surreal as my life flashes in front of my face. The busy road approaches, and nausea travels up my throat. We are powerless to do anything but brace ourselves and pray.

"Stevie!" Garrick yells, panic and fear lacing his tone. "I love you. No matter what happens, you are the best thing that ever happened to me."

I'm sobbing and screaming as we careen onto the main road, and my bones rattle as the first impact is felt when a vehicle viciously slams into us. Screeching metal, squealing tires, and the shattering of glass accost my eardrums as we spin round and round, hitting off other vehicles as we spiral out of control. White spots fly across my retinas, and I'm lightheaded and nauseated as I'm jostled violently behind my seat belt when the car flips upside down and spins. "Garrick!" I cry out in between screaming. "I love you!" My head slams brutally against the side of my CR-V, and the last thing I think before I black out is I should have accepted the car.

Chapter Thirty-Five

Stevie

An irritating persistent beeping noise rouses me from sleep. Hushed whispering tickles my eardrums as I slowly come to. Blinking my eyes open, I wince as the glare of the overhead light ignites a pounding in my head.

"Sweetie. It's okay. I'm here. Nana is too." Mom's soft voice is laced with concern as my eyes shutter, and a moan filters from my dry lips.

My tongue feels superglued to the roof of my mouth, and my throat aches as I swallow thickly. I attempt to move onto my side, but my limbs are lethargic, and they refuse to cooperate. Forcing my eyes to open again, I wince a second time as glaring light pummels my skull.

"I'm turning the main light off." Nana pads to the wall to flick the switch, plunging the room into semi-darkness. The only illumination now is from the recessed lighting by the door and trickles of sneaky daylight filtering in through the window blind.

Slowly, I take in my surroundings. My horror grows as I note the pale gray walls, my position on an elevated hospital bed, the dresser and table off to one side housing copious vases with vibrant flowers, boxes of sweets and chocolates, and cards, and a machine beeping someplace behind me.

Instant panic consumes me as the events of the car accident resurface in my mind, and it's like being punched in the gut. Air wheezes out of my mouth in strangled puffs as a surge of adrenaline courses through my veins. "Garrick," I croak as tears instantly form in my eyes. "Where's Garrick?" I frantically scan the small private room, but it's only me, Mom, and Nana in here.

Nana and Mom exchange a pained look, and terror has a vise grip on my heart. The beeping from the machine accelerates as I struggle to breathe. "Mom!" I rasp over a scraping throat. "Where is he?" I move onto my side, ignoring the heaviness cloaking my bones as I attempt to pry the covers from my body. Tubes run from my hand to a drip propped alongside my bed. "Where is my boyfriend?!" I scream, my gaze bouncing from Mom to Nana. "Tell me!" I try to get up as Mom stands, crouching over me with tears in her eyes.

The door to the room bursts open, and two female nurses rush in.

"Shush, honey," the older lady with the short gray hair says. "You need to calm down, Stevie."

"Nana." I turn pleading blurry eyes on my grandmother while the nurses add a different pouch to the drip. "Please."

She leans down, brushing delicate fingers against my cheek. "He's alive, Little Poppy. He's alive."

Temporary relief floods my veins until I see the doleful expression they share. The hand around my heart squeezes, constricting my oxygen supply until I can barely breathe. I force the question out of my mouth. "How...bad...is...he?" I can hear the hysteria peppering my stammering words as I try to force myself into an upright position.

The younger nurse gently pushes me back down, her mouth moving in speech, but I don't hear the words. All I can see are the tears clouding Mom's vision and the pain in Nana's eyes.

"Tell me!" I screech in a louder voice, barely feeling the pain the motion produces in my throat. Finding strength, I shove at the nurses and thrash around in the bed. "Take me to him!" I beg, fighting the nurses as they attempt to thwart my efforts to get up.

Nana leans down, putting her wrinkled face in mine. Her eyes are awash with compassion as she says, "Garrick is in a coma, sweetheart."

Her words hit me like a sledgehammer. A painful lump wedges in my throat, and an all-consuming pressure sits on my chest. "No!" I croak, sobbing as reality slams into me. "No!" I protest, slapping at the hands trying to restrain me as I lose it. "It's all my fault!" My eyes dart manically between Mom and Nana. "I should be in a coma, not him!" I can barely see through the tears falling relentlessly from my eyes. "I should have accepted the car, and I should have worn his ring on my main ring finger." I glance down at my right hand, and panic erupts from my chest. "My ring!" I shout in a hoarse voice. "Where's my ring! I need to find it!" I thrash around again, howling as pain rips through me of the physical and emotional kind.

"Sweetheart, it's okay, it's okay." Mom reaches out, trying to console me. "I have your ring and your locket. They were with the things recovered from the car. Relax."

"Here, Little Poppy." Nana slides the ring on my left hand as my sobs reach epic levels of hysteria.

"Garrick!" I slur, fighting to keep my eyes open as whatever sedative the nurses administered starts entering my blood stream.

"Shush, honey." Nana and Mom are both crying as the older nurse urges me to calm down before I exacerbate my injuries.

"It's my fault." Agony attacks my heart, battering it until it feels like there's nothing left of the organ. "It's my fault," I mumble just before the world goes dark and quiet again.

When I wake the next time, Mom is alone sitting by my bed with a book open on her lap. The room is much darker, and the only sound is the steady beep, beep from the medical machine.

"Honey." Mom sets her book down and pulls her chair in closer to my bed. "How are you feeling?"

"Garrick," I whisper over the clawing pain of my throat. Tears instantly well in my eyes as I look down and spot the poppy ring on my left ring finger. "How..." I can't get any more words past the ragged lump in my throat and the suffocating pain in my chest. It feels like I'm dying.

My sobs and the repetitive beeping of the machine are the only sounds in the room as I slowly self-destruct.

Sorrow is etched across Mom's face as she clasps my hand in her warm one. Moisture pools in her tired eyes, and dark circles cling to the skin underneath. "Garrick is a fighter, and I know he's fighting to come back to you. He has the best doctors working on his case, and he has youth on his side. We have to cling to hope and keep the faith."

"What if he doesn't ever wake up?" I wail.

"Don't think like that. It's early, and there is still hope. A coma is the brain's way of repairing itself after significant trauma. His brain and body are taking the time they need to heal, and when he's ready, he'll wake up."

I wish I had Mom's optimism. I know she fully believes if she says it enough she'll manifest it. But I'm a more pragmatic being, and I need more than hope and faith to cling to.

I will never forgive myself for this, and if he doesn't wake up, I don't want to live.

"It's my fault," I choke out as tears cascade down my cheeks. "This is all on me, and I hate myself."

"It was an accident, honey. A tragic accident. You have to stop hating yourself for something that wasn't your fault."

I shake my head, crying out when pain splinters my skull.

"Shush, sweetheart." Mom carefully brushes hair back from my brow. "You need to remain calm, Stevie, and you can't make any sudden movements. You have a concussion, a broken arm, and two broken ribs."

"I need to see him."

"Only family is permitted in ICU for now, but Hugh is working on getting you in to visit him." She kisses my cheek. "Hugh and

Dawn have stopped by every day to see you, and Hugh even arranged for you to be transferred to this private room."

"How long have I been out?" I ask as Mom lifts a pink plastic cup with a lid and straw from my bedside table.

"It's been two days since the accident," she confirms, pressing a button on the bed to elevate it until I'm in a more upright position. "The nurses say it's important for you to drink plenty of water, or I can get you some ice chips if your throat is too sore." She places the straw to my lips. "Just small sips for now."

I take a few sips as Mom holds the cup and straw to my mouth. When she sets it back on the bedside table, I turn my head to stare at her. Dried tear tracks tighten the skin on my face. "How bad are Garrick's injuries?"

She rests her hand on mine while peering deep into my eyes. "He broke one arm, both legs, and three ribs, but the damage to his spine and his head trauma are the most concerning injuries. He seems to have borne the brunt of the initial impact." Tears pool in her eyes. "You are so lucky you weren't more seriously injured." She swipes at the tears coursing down her cheeks. "The terror I felt when I got that phone call will stay with me for the rest of my life. Nana and I were so worried. Scared of what we'd find when we got here. We prayed nonstop the entire ride to the hospital, begging God to let you be okay."

"Was anyone else hurt?" I brave asking.

"One male driver has whiplash and a concussion, and a couple of other people were taken to the hospital to be checked out, but they only have minor injuries. You two suffered the most severe damage."

A pregnant pause ensues as I let that intel settle in my tormented brain. "Where am I?" I ask, realizing I don't know which hospital I'm in.

"You're at UW Medical Center – Montlake, and you are both in the best hands."

"Garrick bought me a car, and I refused it." A sob erupts from my lips as more tears spring to my eyes.

"I know, honey. Ellen explained. But that doesn't mean this is your fault. It was an accident. You can't blame yourself."

"Ellen was here?"

"She came immediately when she heard the news, and she stayed here all day yesterday. Hadley too. I made them leave last night. I knew you wouldn't want either of them missing their exams, and before you panic, I have spoken with UO, and they'll let you take your exams over the summer break, whenever you feel ready, so you don't need to worry about that."

Right now, that's the least of my worries. "Garrick wouldn't be in a coma if I'd said yes to the car. Even if I'd just agreed to drive it without making a commitment, like he suggested, this wouldn't have happened." Anguished sobs rip through the air as I cry. "Why did I have to be so stubborn? Why couldn't I have just accepted it? Why am I so selfish and stupid?" Pain spears me all over, and I'm choking on air as I struggle to breathe. "I want to die!" I howl. "I want to trade my life for his because he doesn't deserve this, but I do!"

"No, honey. Don't say that. Neither of you deserve what happened." Mom perches on the side of my bed, wrapping me in a gentle embrace, holding me tenderly against her chest as I cry and cry, soaking her blouse and making my eyes sting. Her tears mingle with mine for a few minutes before she pulls herself together. "Honey, please, you need to calm down. The best thing you can do for Garrick is to get better so you can be there for him. He wouldn't want you blaming yourself. You didn't know the brakes would fail. It's not your fault. It was a terrible, terrible accident."

The door opens and closes, and Mom briefly glances over her shoulder, getting rid of whomever it is with a look of silent communication. "Garrick will need you to be strong for the both of you," she adds, softly stroking my hair. "And you need to prioritize your recovery."

"How long do I have to be here?" I ask when I finally stop crying, looking up at her through bloodshot throbbing eyes. My head is killing me, and I ache all over. It seems there is no part of me that isn't sore. My gaze treks over the multitude of bruises covering my arms, and I'm glad I'm suffering. I deserve every bit of pain I'm feeling and more.

"They want to keep you under observation for another few days, but you should be able to go home by the weekend." She dots kisses into my hair. "You're going to need a lot of rest, but we'll make sure you get to visit Garrick every day."

"Where is Nana?"

"I sent her home to get some sleep. She was exhausted." Mom kisses my head one final time before releasing me. "You should try to sleep more too. Your body needs it to heal."

The following morning, I'm taken in a wheelchair to the ICU to visit my boyfriend. Only two to three visitors are allowed in at one time. Garrick's parents are with him now, and I figure they want privacy, so I wait with the nurse and Mom in the private waiting room until Dawn and Hugh leave Garrick's room.

They join us in the waiting area a few minutes later. "Sweetheart, it's good to see you awake." Hugh leans down and hugs me.

"I'm so sorry," I cry, hating how tears instantly swim in my eyes. It's like my tear ducts got injured in the accident as well. "This is all my fault." Choking sobs cleave from my mouth as pain tears across my chest, adding to my heartbreak.

When I'm conscious, I exist with a constant constricting pain in my chest. My heart is a shredded mass of tissue, broken beyond repair.

"I'm glad we are on the same page about something," a snooty unfortunately familiar female says as the door flies open behind me, admitting another visitor.

"That's uncalled for and untrue, Ivy," Hugh says, straightening up as Mom places her hand on my arm and stands stoically by my side.

"It was a tragic accident," Dawn agrees, softly squeezing my hand.

"Garrick would want us rallying around Stevie, not blaming her for this," Hugh adds, and I wonder if he knows about the BMW. I doubt he does. I know Garrick's dad is a good man, but surely even he would struggle to accept I'm blameless if he knew the truth.

"Everything turned to shit for my son the moment he met that gold-digging slut," Ivy hisses, her words infused with the usual poison she reserves for me.

Mom spins around with fire in her eyes. "Would you like to say that to my face?"

"Garrick loves Stevie, and your hurtful accusation is the last thing anyone needs right now." Dawn levels Ivy with a cool glare.

"You agreed not to come until twelve," Hugh says, sliding his arm around Dawn's waist.

"You knew Stevie was coming to see Garrick, and you planned this on purpose," Dawn adds in a clipped tone. "You should be ashamed of yourself, Ivy. Look at the poor girl. Stevie is as devastated as we are. Bickering about blame is pointless when our son is in there fighting for his life." Her voice cracks, and she bursts out crying.

Hugh is barely holding it together, and silent tears crawl down my face and drip over my chin.

Mom squeezes my hand, and when I look up at her, she is crying too.

"Don't lecture me about how I feel," Ivy snaps. She's the only one in the room with dry eyes. "Garrick is my only flesh and blood. He's my everything, and all that little bitch has done is try to take him away from me." Ivy shoves Dawn out of the way and thrusts her cosmetically altered face all up in mine. "You better hope and pray my son recovers because I will make your life a misery if he doesn't."

Chapter Thirty-Six
Stevie

"Don't mind her, Stevie." Dawn crouches down in front of me, gently wiping the tears from my face. Ivy departed after making her threat and it's good riddance. "She's a miserable bitch who takes her unhappiness out on everyone around her."

"She's upset and not able to express it," Hugh says.

I can see where Garrick gets this side of his personality from now. I don't think Hugh Allen has said a bad word about anyone at any time in his life. He always tries to see the best in everyone. It's probably how that poisonous bitch managed to get him to marry her.

Dawn straightens up, leveling her husband with a stern look. "You need to stop making excuses for that woman, and I'm done biting my tongue. She's a horrible, selfish, uncaring bitch, and I hate that we're saddled with her."

Internally, I'm fist pumping the air and high-fiving Garrick's stepmom.

"I don't want her upsetting Stevie," Mom says.

"We'll work out a roster of visiting times," Hugh confirms. "We're both listed as family spokespersons, so I'll talk to the nursing staff, and I'll talk to my ex-wife." He pats my shoulder. "I'll ensure she stays away from Stevie."

"Make sure she doesn't try to have her banned," Dawn adds.

"I will ensure the nursing staff knows Stevie is on the priority list and no one is to remove her visitation rights without consultation with me. If she tries anything, I'll deal with it."

"Thank you, Hugh," Mom says.

"I'm sorry," I whisper, "I don't mean to cause extra trouble."

"You're not, sweetie." Dawn's smile is sad. "This isn't on you."

Yeah. Pretty sure it is.

But I don't argue the point.

I just want to see him.

"Can I go in now?"

"Of course." Hugh gently pats my shoulder.

"You should prepare yourself, Stevie." Dawn bends down in front of me again. "He doesn't look much like himself."

I nod even though I'm in no way prepared.

Pain has a stranglehold on my throat and my heart as the nurse wheels me out of the waiting room and down the hallway toward Garrick's ICU room. I sanitize my hands and put on a medical mask at the door. "Do you want me to come in with you, honey?" Mom asks. A veil of concern shrouds her face.

"No," I whisper. "I need to do this alone."

"I'll be right out here if you change your mind."

My heart plummets to my toes, and acid churns in my gut as the nurse wheels me into Garrick's room.

I desperately need to see him, but at the same time, I don't want to.

It's going to make this real.

And I don't know if I'm strong enough to handle this horrific new reality.

It seems there is no limit to my cowardice.

Every time I think about my boyfriend being in a coma, I break down in floods of tears.

Garrick is always so full of life, and I don't think I can bear to see him any other way.

Especially when I know I'm responsible for his condition.

Tears are already forming in my eyes. This is going to hurt so bad.

I don't look up at him as the nurse positions me alongside his bed, fixing the freestanding drip beside my wheelchair before she discreetly slips out of the room. It's eerily silent in the room except for the annoying beeping of monitoring devices and a sucking mechanical sound emitting from the machine that's helping him to breathe.

Tears roll down my face, plopping onto my clasped hands on my lap. I draw in big lungsful of air as I try to pluck up the courage to look at Garrick.

I'm petrified.

Shaking and trembling all over.

Scared to be confronted with the evidence of every mistake I have ever made when it comes to this man.

It feels like my heart is disintegrating behind my rib cage.

I don't know if I'll ever be able to look at myself in a mirror again, knowing I did this to him.

Finding strength from somewhere, I lift my head and look up at him. More tears spill from my eyes as I stare in horror at my love. His arms are visible under the short sleeves of his hospital gown, and a cast covers one while the other is heavily bandaged. Both legs are encased in plaster and slightly elevated within some metal contraption.

I'm shaking all over and sobbing as I reluctantly drag my gaze up his body to his face. My hand goes over my mouth of its own volition when I stare at Garrick's almost unrecognizable features.

The head of the bed is elevated, and his neck is in some kind of brace. Garrick's cheeks are puffy, one eye is red and swollen, and his entire face is bloated underneath a multitude of cuts, abrasions, and bruises. His hair—his beautiful, gorgeous hair—is all gone, shorn tight to his scalp and completely shaved on one side of his head. A large incision runs from just in front of his ear, curving along his skull and ending at the top center of his forehead. Steel stiches hold the sealed skin in place, and a cluster of rectangular white bandages cover the back of his head. Small tubes run from his nose and mouth into larger tubes hooked up to a ventilator.

My sobs ring out in the room, audible over the beeping of the machines and the mechanical clacking sound of the machine as it helps him to breathe. Pain eviscerates me on all sides, and I clutch an arm around my middle, whimpering and sobbing as I stare at my comatose boyfriend.

Nothing could have prepared me for this.

This is truly awful.

Way worse than I imagined.

I want to die.

I want to trade places with him and be the one hooked up to machines and tubes with half my body in a plaster cast. "I'm so sorry, Garrick," I sob. "This is all my fault, and I am so, so sorry. I wish I could go back and do everything differently," I cry, tentatively reaching out to touch his hand. His flesh is warm, but it offers little comfort. Curling my hand underneath his, I am careful not to displace the tubing that links to a drip. "I love you, and I need you to wake up, baby. Please wake up. Please be okay." I cling to his hand, dusting soft kisses over his skin as I pray and beg and plead.

"Come on, honey," Mom says sometime later, materializing at my side with the nurse. I hadn't even heard them coming into the room. "You need to rest."

Sympathy splays across the young nurse's face as she hands me a box of tissues. I wipe my nose and rub at my eyes as tears continue to leak my sorrow. Placing one last kiss on his hand, I raise bleary eyes to his face. "I love you, Garrick. Please don't give up. Keep fighting. I'll be back. Every day. I'm not going anywhere. I won't ever leave you."

Silent tears stream down my face as I'm wheeled out of the room. Ivy bitchface is out in the hallway, waiting to see her son, but we purposely avoid looking at one another. Tracing the ink on my wrist with my fingers the entire way back to my room, I hope the matching Celtic shield knot on Garrick's skin lives up to the symbolism. That it protects him and imbues him with power, strength, and endurance because he's going to need every bit of help he can get.

The next few days pass by in a numbed daze. It seems I've broken my tear ducts, and now I can't produce a single tear. My vocal cords won't cooperate either. I'm like a living corpse. A shell of a person who has lost the will to survive. Seeing Garrick like that has irreparably broken me. I'm drowning in guilt and self-loathing, and I pray every night, begging God to take my life force and funnel it to Garrick. To sacrifice me so the best man I know can live.

Mom and Nana sit by my bed all day—taking it in turns at nights—and they chat away, trying to engage me in conversation, but I just lie there, staring into space, running everything through my sore head, wishing I had a time machine so I could go back and change the events of that day.

Hadley shows up every evening after her exams, and she does her best to cheer me up as well, but it's useless. She burst into tears when she visited Garrick, and I know she's been in contact with Hudson. Poor Hudson. He wants to be here, but he's on the East Coast, taking his finals this week at Brown. I've been texting with him every day, and I know he's purposely checking in on me because it's what Garrick would expect of him.

I know everyone is worried about me, and I want to stop moping so it lessens their concern, but I can't summon the strength to fake it. Mom, Nana, and Hads play my favorite music, bring my favorite foods, and stream my favorite movies and shows to raise my spirits, but it's a futile exercise.

The only thing that would lift my spirits is Garrick waking up, and he's showing no signs of it.

Dawn and Hugh have been keeping us updated, much to Ivy's

disgust. If she had her way, I'd have been kicked out of the hospital by now and banned from visiting her son's bedside. Hugh has promised me he won't let her do that, and I'm so grateful for his support and graciousness.

I hate seeing Garrick in such a condition, but it would be so much worse if I couldn't see him at all.

I have been visiting him as much as I can in between sleeping and trying to heal.

Hudson's father, Harvey Edwards, is one of the country's most skilled neurosurgeon's and he is the primary neurosurgeon assigned to Garrick. It's fortunate he works here, and this hospital is an acute care hospital and home to one of the largest and most experienced neurology and neurosurgery teams in the US.

Harvey has consulted with esteemed colleagues, and they are discussing every aspect of Garrick's case. The more time passes without him coming out of the coma, the less likely it is he will, or so we've been told. Nerves have been severed in his spinal cord, and Harvey has warned us it's likely he'll suffer some form of paralysis. He underwent brain surgery to relieve pressure on his brain, and while the surgery was a success, they can't say what the aftereffects of his brain trauma might be either.

Hugh relayed that shocking news this morning, and after initially being inconsolable, I've decided to worry about one thing at a time. Right now, Garrick waking up is the priority, and it's what I'm focusing on.

As long as he is alive.

What happens after that can be dealt with one step at a time. So, for now, I'm trying to put those other fears into a box to worry about at a later point.

When Saturday rolls around, my doctor arrives to confirm I'm being discharged at noon. While Mom handles the paperwork, I get dressed and pack up my things. The nurse helps me with my arm sling, and then I make the solo journey on foot to Garrick's room to see him. I'm still weak, and my ribs throb like a bitch, so it takes far longer to get to the ICU, but I need to start reclaiming some independence.

A set routine is in place where I visit him for an hour in the morning and an hour in the afternoon after Ivy is gone, and I usually spend a couple hours at night sitting with Hugh by Garrick's bedside. We talk to him and among ourselves, trying to remain upbeat, but it's challenging.

Hugh regales me with stories from Garrick's childhood, and it's bittersweet learning of all his boyish escapades. Sometimes, we're too heartsore to talk, so we play Garrick's favorite songs. I asked Dawn and Mom to bring in some photos, and I pinned them and some of his get well cards to the walls because you're not allowed plants or flowers in the ICU, and I wanted to do something to make it look less clinical and more homey.

Dawn visits every day, but she can't stay for too long as someone has to be home for the twins. They are still at school, and they have a ton of after-school activities. Dawn and Hugh are keen not to disrupt their schedules, believing normalcy is important. John and Jacob are only eight and this has been super hard on them. They adore their big brother, and seeing him like this reduced them to tears, so the decision was taken not to have them visit every day. It's too much for them to handle.

I'm seated by Garrick's bed, holding his hand and staring at his face, willing him to wake up, like I always do, when there's a knock at the door. I glance over my shoulder as Ellen and Will step into the room. They haven't been able to visit all week because of exams, but Ellen has been calling and texting when she can.

"Hey, babe," Ellen rushes to my side, leaning down to hug me gently. "How are you holding up?"

I offer her a feeble smile and a weak shrug. Behind her, I watch the devastation wreaked on Will's face as he sees his friend for the first time since the accident. Tears prick his eyes, and he scrubs a hand back and forth across his mouth as he stares at Garrick. Will is leaning against the wall, like he needs it to prop him up, struggling to hold back tears.

"Oh god," Ellen whispers, tears instantly pouring down her face as she stares horror-struck at Garrick.

The shock of seeing him like this never subsides. Every time I visit, I have to suck in brave breaths before opening the door. It doesn't get any easier seeing him lying there, so still and quiet, his broken body supported by braces and casts, all the color gone from his cheeks. Not getting to look into his gorgeous golden-greenish-brown eyes is torture as is not feeling his fingers curling around mine when I hold his hand.

Tears stab the backs of my eyes as I watch my best friend cry and her boyfriend fight a multitude of emotions. But my tears don't fall. I feel weirdly numb even though I'm awash with powerful emotions that keep me awake at night.

"It doesn't look like him at all," Ellen wails, dropping into the chair beside me and clinging to my arm.

I stare at Garrick, seeing everything she sees, agreeing with it, but unable to voice those thoughts.

"This is awful, so awful." She clings to me harder. "I'm so sorry for your pain, babe. I can't even begin to imagine what you are going through."

"What *she's* going through?" Will barks. He stalks over to the bed. "What about what Garrick is going through?!" He jabs his finger in my face as he pins angry eyes on me. "Do you even care?"

"Of course, she cares!" Ellen retorts when I'm incapable of a response. "Why the hell would you say that?"

"Doesn't much look like it from where I'm standing."

I stare at him in a daze, wanting to defend myself, but how can I? We all know I'm responsible for this, and Will has every right to his rage.

"Cat got your tongue, Stevie? Or are you doing what you do best? Retreating into your selfish shell and pushing everyone else away?"

"Stop it!" Ellen stands, spitting fire at her boyfriend. "I know you're upset and angry, we all are, but you can't take it out on Stevie."

"Why not?" He folds his arms and glares at me. "Let's not beat around the bush. Everyone knows why my best friend is lying in this bed." His voice cracks, and he pauses for a few seconds to compose himself. "This is your fault." He waves his finger in my face. "You turned him down, *again*, and he was only driving that piece-of-shit car because you refused the new one he bought you because *he wanted you to be safe*!" He roars the last part, dragging out the words.

"Will, stop this. Please." Ellen reaches for her boyfriend, but he shoves her away. "It's not fair. It was an accident. Stevie didn't want this to happen, and look at her! She's traumatized, and you're only making it worse."

"I should've told him to break up with you when he sought my advice," he continues, tearing another strip from my fragile heart. "I selfishly kept my true thoughts to myself because I didn't want shit to get awkward in my relationship, but he deserved better than you. You were pushing him away and sabotaging the relationship on purpose. Were you going to break up with him? Is that what you were planning after summer break?"

"Okay. That is fucking enough!" Ellen roars at her boyfriend while I sit there in the same numb fugue state. "You are way out of line, Will. Garrick would not want you speaking to Stevie this way or pointing the finger of blame in her direction."

"It doesn't matter what Garrick would want," he chokes out, swinging his gaze to his friend on the bed. "He's incapable of voicing his opinions." Tears stream down his cheeks. "If he doesn't come out of this, I will never forgive you. Never." He drills me with a dark look before storming out of the room, leaving thick tension in his wake.

A shuddering breath escapes Ellen's lips as she slumps into the chair beside me, briefly burying her head in her hands. Tears are stuck to her lashes when she lifts her chin. "He doesn't mean it, babe. He's just really upset. He's been lashing out all week. Don't take any of that to heart because it's not true. Deep down, Will knows that."

"It is true though," I croak, almost choking over the emotion clogging my throat. "Will is right to throw all of that at me and more." I stare into her forlorn eyes. "It *is* my fault. I'm the stupid bitch who refused his sweet, loving, protective gesture, and I'm going to have to live with the guilt of that decision for the rest of my life."

***

SAY IT'S FOREVER - BOOK DESCRIPTION

I was suffocating under an avalanche of guilt and grief until *he* entered my life.

The hot, slightly older guy who looked like a cross between a tatted biker and a billionaire businessman.

Beck understood me, and our situation, in a way no one else could.

As a friend, he held me together and helped to piece back the shredded fragments of my heart.

I didn't mean to fall in love with him—it just happened.

No one understands, least of all me.

Now my heart is split in two, and I don't know what to do.

Is my first love my one true love? Or do I belong with the man who brought me to life?

THE ONE
I WANT
BOOK TWO
Say
IT'S
Forever
USA TODAY & WSJ BESTSELLING AUTHOR
SIOBHAN DAVIS

Say It's Forever

THE ONE I WANT BOOK TWO

USA TODAY & WSJ BESTSELLING AUTHOR

SIOBHAN DAVIS

Chapter One

Stevie

I open the door and almost slam it in the poor delivery guy's face. This can't be good.

"Uh, delivery for Stevie Colson." He thrusts a massive bunch of flowers at me as he struggles to hold on to a large birthday balloon and a black box with a red ribbon tucked under his free arm.

My arms hang uselessly by my sides as I stare at him with mounting agony.

I didn't want to get up today.

I wanted to let this day pass without noting it, let alone celebrating it.

I wanted to wallow in internal tears until the occasion had passed.

But Mom and Nana are determined to stop me from sinking into an even blacker hole. And even more determined I will celebrate my birthday today.

The man is still holding out the bouquet, staring at me like I've got a few screws loose. I'm tempted to tell him he's not far off the mark. Heart-demolishing pain replaces the blood flowing through my veins as I stare at the gifts he carries, instinctively knowing who they're from.

I can't handle this.

This may be the thing that finally sends me over the edge.

It's an effort to remain standing, and I can't force my limbs to move or my vocal cords to work.

"Uh, miss?" His brows knit together in confusion.

"I'll take those." Mom appears, like an angel sent from heaven, smiling as she takes the bouquet, box, and the balloon with the giant twenty-one written on it from the dark-haired guy. "Thanks so much."

Nana materializes in the hallway, and she quietly takes the flowers and the balloon and disappears into the living room.

"I have more," he says, racing back to his van. He returns a few minutes later with one large box and two smaller ones.

Kill me now.

Please.

Mom ushers me to one side so the guy can prop the boxes against the wall in the hall.

He offers me an unsure smile as he stands awkwardly in the doorway. "Happy birthday."

No, it isn't.

"Thanks again," Mom says, waving him off and closing the door before she pulls me into a careful hug.

Warmth from her body seeps into my frozen bones, and I wrap my good arm around her and rest my head on her chest, siphoning what little comfort I can. "He'd want you to celebrate, honey," she whispers, rubbing a soothing hand up and down my spine. "He'd want you to go in there with a smile on your face as you open his gifts."

"I can't." My words are muffled against her chest, and I watch in a kind of a daze as Nana collects each box and carries it into the living room.

"Yes, you can." Nana's confident words filter out from the open door, bouncing off the sage-green walls of our hall. "My Little Poppy is one of the strongest people I know."

It sure doesn't feel like it anymore.

"Come on, sweetheart." Nana comes to my side and curls her small hand around mine. "Let's see what your beautiful young man has sent you."

Garrick is so thoughtful. I doubt there is a man on this planet who comes close to him in that regard or his organizational skills. Although, it's probably more to do with having to get my gifts arranged early around exams.

I let Nana and Mom lead me into the living room and help me onto the couch.

In the six days since I was discharged from the hospital, I've had to rely on them a lot. I can't even do basic things for myself. It'll be five more weeks before the cast is removed from my arm, and I'm already frustrated and impatient at how restricted I am. My ribs will take the same time to heal, so I'm stuck here, trapped in a prison of my own making, slowly going out of my mind with grief and pain and remorse and loneliness.

I miss Garrick so much.

He's become such an integral part of my life that not having him around is already unbearable.

Mom drives me to the hospital every morning on her way to work, and I Uber home. Nana takes me every evening, reading and knitting in the waiting room while I visit with my love. Thankfully, I have managed to avoid Ivy. She only visits in the afternoon when I'm not here.

There is no change in Garrick's condition, and although Hudson says his dad is still hopeful, the risk is higher the longer my boyfriend remains comatose. There is brain activity, which is an encouraging sign, yet he still sleeps.

The colorful flowers take center stage on our glossy black coffee table, and my heart aches as I catalog my favorite flowers, knowing Garrick would have been very specific in his request to ensure I got a bouquet I'd love. He goes to so much trouble to ensure my happiness, and I think I take it for granted sometimes. Presently, I'm making daily promises to myself to be a better girlfriend. I only hope I get the chance to make it up to him. I can't bear to think of him not waking up, so I'm trying not to go there, but it's hard.

Right now, the pain coursing through my body is so powerful I can barely breathe.

"There's a card," Nana says, slipping me a white envelope with my name written on it in Garrick's neat handwriting.

"I feel sick," I whisper, resting my fingers on the paper as I cry buckets inside. On the outside, I'm the same emotionless droid I've been all week. Since those first few early days, when I couldn't open my eyes without crying, I haven't cried a solitary tear. It's as if the well has completely dried up.

Inside, I'm dying a little more each day, and if it wasn't for Mom and Nana, I know I wouldn't be able to get out of bed each morning. But I am trying for them because I see how worried they are. I have already put them through the wringer, and I can't add more to the pile. So, I get up every day, I shower and dress, and I force words from my mouth and plaster fake smiles on my lips. I shovel food that tastes like sandpaper down my throat and wrap my tears up iron tight so they don't have to listen to me vocally falling apart. When the nightmares invade my dreams at night—during the few precious hours of sleep I manage to grab—I scream into my pillow so I don't wake them.

"I can read it to you if you like," Mom offers, yanking me out of my depressive thoughts. Although it's cowardly, I nod and quickly hand the envelope off to her like it's on fire.

Resting my head on Nana's shoulder, I cradle my broken arm against my chest and try to prepare my heart for another onslaught.

Mom clears her throat and squeezes my hand.

"To my beautiful sunshine on her twenty-first birthday. Happy birthday, baby. I'm proud I get to celebrate this special occasion with you as your boyfriend and future husband."

Mom's hand trembles where she clutches the card, and her lower lip wobbles. Her voice is fractured when she next speaks.

"That was probably too much, but you know how I feel about you. You're my entire world. My present and my future all rolled into one. I love getting to make more memories with you."

Mom chokes on a sob, and Nana reaches across me, gently taking the card from her hand. Mom leans back in the couch and slides her arm around my back, sniffling as she carefully pulls me into her side while Nana takes over, reading in a stoic manner.

"These are memories we will look back on over the years with fondness in our hearts. I know I said the car was your birthday gift"

— Garrick actually never said that because I cut him off before he had the chance to properly explain —

"but I have to spoil my girl on her special day. Every girl deserves to look like a princess on her twenty-first, and even though you're beautiful to me every day, no matter what you are dressed in or how you wear

your hair, you deserve to be the belle of the ball tonight."

Mom had rented the function room of a trendy bar in the city for my party. Obviously, we canceled after the accident, but Garrick wouldn't have known that when he was organizing my gift or writing this card.

I have no words to describe the pain eviscerating my insides because no such language exists. I'm a giant ball of pain from the tips of my toes to the top of my head. There is no part of me that doesn't feel tortured and heartsick.

"I hope you like your gifts. They were all my ideas, though Hadley helped me choose the dress, purse, and shoes, and I honestly deserve a medal for enduring that shopping trip! Love you, baby. So fucking much. I can't wait to see you later. Until then, all my love, Garrick."

"God." Mom's body shakes against me as tears wrack her frame. "That boy loves you so much. He's one in a million."

"Garrick is the best of men," Nana agrees. She clutches my pale face in her hands. "Do you want me to open the gifts?"

"No. I can't look at them. Please don't make me." I don't think my heart would survive it.

"Okay, Little Poppy. It's fine. Why don't I take them home with me, and when you're ready to open them, we can do it together?"

"Thanks, Nana." I fall against her chest, loving how well she understands me. She knows I couldn't bear to look at those boxes day in and day out. That it'll be a permanent reminder of everything I'm missing.

Hadley shows up after work—she got a summer job at The Seattle Public Library—and I fake a smile as they present me with a small cake. I dutifully blow out the candles even though my heart is shattered into a million pieces and I'm permanently sobbing inside.

This becomes the blueprint for my life as the months roll by.

JULY

AUGUST

SEPTEMBER

OCTOBER

NOVEMBER

DECEMBER

JANUARY

Chapter Two

Stevie

"Stevie!" I turn around as my name is called, wishing I'd kept walking when I see who it is. Will jogs up to where I am paused on the sidewalk. Men and women in suits rush past me, eager to head home after a busy day.

"Will." I gulp back nerves as I stare at one of Garrick's best friends.

"I wasn't sure if it was you," he says, shoving his hands into the pockets of his dark pants as he casts a quick glance over me. "You look different."

Different is code for shit, and I'm well aware of how much I've changed. "It's been a while," I remind him.

"Eight months too long." Sadness seeps from his pores, and grief clings to him the same way it clings to me. "Can we grab a coffee?"

"I'm heading home to change before going to the hospital, and I'm on a tight schedule."

"I've just come from there," he admits, rubbing a hand across the back of his neck. "It seems like fate I've run into you."

His words might as well be a machete cleaved straight through my heart.

Fate.

I fucking hate that word.

More than ever since the only man I have ever loved has been stolen from me. Garrick is still a prisoner in his own body. His mind trapped who knows where. I wonder all the time if he is aware of anything around him. If he knows where he is and what has happened. If he hears me talking and reading to him. If he hears my footsteps twirling across the tile floor of his private hospital room as I dance to the soundtrack of our romance. If my words of love and regret register with any part of him. If he understands how fate screwed us over. If he now realizes I was right all along about cursed fate.

"Maybe another time." I offer him a fake smile. One I've gotten so good at.

"Please, Stevie." His eyes plead with mine. "I need to apologize, and I'd rather not do it in the middle of downtown during rush hour."

"You don't owe me any apologies, Will."

He steps up closer. "I don't agree. Come on." He jerks his head across the road. "There's a coffee place right there. I promise I won't take up too much of your time."

I reluctantly relent, only for Ellen though, because I know the rift between me and her boyfriend has been difficult for her.

We don't speak until we are sitting in a corner of the coffee shop nursing coffees. I declined his offer of cake, and I could hear the unspoken words hovering in the air as he watched me peel off my coat, revealing my formfitting black pants suit that doesn't disguise the weight I've lost.

You're far too thin.

You need to eat more.

It's not healthy to work all the time, exercise so much, and eat and sleep so little.

You should speak to a therapist.

I've heard it all for months from Mom, Nana, and Hadley.

I've tried telling them this is how I'm coping and they need to get off my case. I know they mean well, but I'm doing the best I can. It's not like I've got an eating disorder or I'm so thin I'm at risk of permanent injury or dying. Most models are thinner than I am, and you don't see them dropping dead.

"How is your job going?" Will asks, blowing on the top of his coffee before he takes a drink.

Small talk.

Super.

"Great. I'm learning a lot." That is true. The company was very understanding after the accident, holding my job open for months until after I had successfully completed my exams and graduated with honors.

The first couple months after the accident were really bad, but when my physical injuries healed, I threw myself into my studies, brushing up on things before I took online exams. As soon as I started at Mimosa Floral Corporate Services in September, I immersed myself in my new role, and it's the only way I'm maintaining my sanity.

"Ellen said you're living in the city with Hadley?"

I nod. Hads goes to school in Seattle, and now she has a paid part-time job at the library, she can afford her share of the rent. "We got a place in the International District, not far from here. It's only a three-minute tram ride to work and fifteen minutes to the hospital, so it's perfect."

"That's good."

God, this conversation is awful. I used to have no trouble talking with Will, but things are so tense between us now. We haven't spoken to or seen one another since that day at the hospital. I haven't seen Ellen since last summer as senior year is crazy busy for her and she's miles away in Oregon. But we talk weekly. However, I had no idea her boyfriend was in Seattle. "How come you're in the city?"

"I had a job interview at one of the big investment banks."

I arch a brow, surprised to hear that. "I thought you guys were job hunting in Portland and Vermont?" Ellen doesn't talk much about her relationship with Will anymore, for obvious reasons, but I know they're serious, and they're looking to stay together after they graduate in May. She said they were looking for work near either of their families, so I'm surprised he's interviewing in Seattle.

"We are. We're just keeping our options open."

A light bulb goes off. "You're considering moving here so you're closer to Garrick."

"Yes."

I gulp back my coffee, not sure how I feel about that. I'm already avoiding Ivy around the hospital. Adding Will to that list will be an additional complication, especially because of Ellen.

The tension is so thick you could cut it with a knife, and I knock back my drink, eager to finish and get out of here.

"I'm so sorry, Stevie." Will's eyes penetrate mine. "The things I said to you that day at the hospital were unforgivable."

I open my mouth to protest, but he shakes his head, cutting me off before a word has left my lips. "Please let me get this out before you say anything."

A lump rises in my throat. "Go on."

"I was hurting and angry, and I said some cruel things which were unfair. Garrick would be so disappointed in me. For blaming you and for disappearing from your life. I should have been there for you, and I wasn't." His eyes rake over me again, and I hate the pity I see in his gaze. "I feel huge guilt and remorse for abandoning you."

"I have Hudson. He checks in with me regularly." I would be lost without Garrick's childhood best friend. I only wish he was here and not at Brown, so we could meet in person, but our weekly phone calls are something I look forward to. He's my only connection to Garrick besides Dawn, Hugh, and the twins. I need them to feel close to my boyfriend at times when it's so hard to look at the man in the bed and remember him how he was. "You have nothing to feel guilty about," I say. "And I hold no ill will toward you."

"We'll agree to disagree."

"You spoke the truth, Will, and I haven't resented you for it for a single minute. You said what others were thinking. What I was thinking." I rub a hand across my chest as if it will ease the permanent tightness there. "I made so many mistakes, and Garrick has paid the price. I hate myself more than anyone else ever could, so don't feel bad about what you said or what you have done. You've always been a good friend to him."

"It hurts me to hear you say that, Stevie, knowing I contributed to that point of view. Ellen was right all along. It was a tragic accident. You know how much Garrick believes in fate."

There's that damned f-word again.

I slam my hand down on the table, rattling our mugs and drawing a few wary glances from neighboring patrons. "Do not tell me Garrick ending up in a coma is fate!"

"It's what he would believe. If he was here, he'd say maybe that wouldn't have been his fate if you'd accepted the car and he wasn't driving the CR-V that day. But fate would have come for him in a different way."

"Stop," I rasp, horrified at what I'm hearing. "If this is your way of trying to make me feel better, it's not working."

"What I'm trying to say is, we don't know why these things happen."

"We do! We know! It's because I wouldn't let him give me such a generous gift. It's because I refused to even test-drive the BMW. Garrick was driving my car that day because of me."

Sympathy splays across his face, and I hate it. "Garrick was driving your car that day because he insisted on being behind the wheel. He made the choice to drive, not you. Have you ever stopped to think about that?"

"Of course, I have." Touching the tattoo on my wrist, I drag my fingers back and forth across the ink.

Will's gaze lowers to the poppy ring on my wedding finger, and tears well in his eyes.

"That was my fault too," I continue. "I should have refused to let him drive. If I'd been behind the wheel, I'd be the one in a coma and he'd be the one living his life."

"It doesn't look like you're truly living."

"Are you done insulting my life and my intelligence?" My cold tone rips through the tense air as I grab my coat from the back of the chair and slip my arms into it. "You have a very warped view of apologies, Will. Is Ellen aware?"

"Don't leave like this." He reaches across the table and takes my hand. "I'm not very good with this stuff, and honestly, I'm ashamed of myself, Stevie. If my words have caused you to blame yourself, I am so fucking sorry. I was wrong. I was really fucking wrong. Please stop blaming yourself. Stop taking it out on yourself. Garrick would hate to see you like this."

I stand abruptly, uncaring my chair falls to the ground with a loud thud. I am beyond enraged. "You don't get to judge me, Will. I am doing the best I can in the worst of situations. My boyfriend has been lying in a hospital bed for over eight months, in a coma, because of *me*." I thump a hand over my heart. "Most days, it's a struggle to get out of bed, but I do it. For my family and for him. Because I know Garrick would want me to live my best life. I am trying really hard, but it's challenging when I'm disgusted with my actions and appalled at the person I am. And it's difficult because I miss him so much."

Pain spears me through the chest as physical longing tears through me. "I miss his protective arms around me and the feel of his lips worshiping mine. I miss his laugh and all the fun we used to have together. I miss his gorgeous eyes and those dimples that used to drive me crazy. I miss the way he always saw so much good in others and in situations. I miss watching him strumming his guitar and listening to his husky voice as he sang to me. I miss him twirling me around the kitchen to The Carpenters."

I stop for a few beats, struggling to swallow over the intense pain attacking me from all sides as I remember the many ways Garrick is the most amazing boyfriend. I somehow manage to force words out past the giant ball clogging my throat. "Garrick was this massive presence in my life, and now he's not there. It's unbearable." My voice cracks. "I exist with a constant pain in my chest and a hollow ache in my heart. So, you don't get to stroll in here after ignoring me all this time and try to dictate how I live my life. You don't get to criticize me or tell me I'm not truly living when you haven't been around to witness the devastation I endure every single day."

I don't realize I'm shouting until I stop to draw a breath and notice the entire coffee shop is silent and every person is listening to every word.

Awesome. That's just awesome.

I slap a ten-dollar bill down on the table with trembling hands. "Now, if you'll excuse me. I'm going to visit my boyfriend."

I'm still shaking twenty minutes later when I approach the hospital doors. I came straight here from the coffee shop, needing to see Garrick immediately after that conversation.

I'm earlier than normal, but there should be no one else here at this time. Ivy comes at midday, and Hugh usually comes in around eight, after he's had dinner with his family and helped to put the boys to bed.

I'm rounding the corner toward the ICU entrance, lost in thought, replaying everything Will and I said to one another, not looking where I'm going when I slam into someone, teetering on my heels and almost losing my balance.

A hand darts out, gripping my upper arm to keep me from falling.

"Oh my god, I'm so sorry," I say, lifting my chin up. "I wasn't—" I stop mid-sentence as I stare at a face I haven't seen in over a year.

Pepper Montgomery looks equally shocked to see me.

We stare at one another in silence for a few moments, both of us frozen, until I realize she's still holding my arm, and I shuck out of her hold and step back. Folding my arms around my waist, I'm instantly on guard. "What are you doing here?" I mean, I know what she's doing here, but I want to hear her say it.

"I visit Garrick every day after work."

Pressure settles on my chest, almost stifling my lungs. "Why?" I ask. Daily visits are for those closest to Garrick, and she's not part of that small pool of people. She has no right to show up here every day. They hadn't even spoken in months at the time of the accident. The whole thing leaves a sour taste in my mouth.

"You know why." She drills me with a sharp look, as if preparing herself for battle. I hate how "together" she looks. Polished and posh in her designer gray skirt suit with green silk blouse and a string of pearls around her neck. Her dark hair is longer now, hitting the tops of her shoulders, and her makeup is on point.

I feel like I was dragged through a bush, in comparison, in my department-store coat, wrinkled pants suit with plain black high heels, and a knock-off Louis Vuitton purse. My hair is scraped back off my minimally made-up face in the austere bun I wear to work. I always wait until I get into Garrick's room before I take out the hair tie and let my long red locks free. I was tempted to hack my hair off at one low point over the Christmas period, but it was Garrick's love of my hair that stalled my hand.

"Oh, there you are, darling. Why...You!" Ivy bitchface comes up alongside Pepper, looping her arm through hers as she glares at me with a familiar expression. "You're too early. Didn't they teach you how to read the time in the slums?"

"Didn't they teach you any manners in public school?" I retort, letting her know I'm aware of her lowly start in life.

"You can't see him." She looks at the flashy watch on her wrist. "Not for another forty minutes."

"Ivy."

"No, Pepper." Ivy cuts across the governor's daughter. "We don't make allowances for scum."

"You are being extremely rude." Pepper narrows her eyes at Ivy. "Garrick would be disgusted if he heard the way you speak to Stevie. What difference does it make if she's early? We are leaving."

"The difference is I won't give that slut anything more than is mandated. She deserves to rot in jail for what she did to my son."

"You're being ridiculous," Pepper says. "The investigation

concluded it was a tragic accident. Stevie had regularly serviced the car, and she wasn't neglectful."

Ivy had insisted on a formal investigation into the accident after one of the drivers caught up in the crash lodged a civil suit against Garrick. Ivy was hopping mad, and so was I. For once, we agreed on something. The insurance paid out, and he was already compensated, so I thought it was disgusting he was trying to extract money from a guy in a coma. The fact he hadn't bothered suing me, as the owner of the vehicle, spoke volumes about his motivation.

He was only going after Garrick because of his wealthy parents. I'm sure he discovered my family has no money, and that's why he didn't bother pursuing me.

I'm sorry he got injured in the accident, but who sues a comatose man?

What a despicable human being he is.

I was glad the court only awarded him a fraction of what he was asking for. When you factor in his legal fees and having to repay the insurance company, he would not have been left with much.

Serves him right for being greedy.

I hate that Hugh had to pay out anything, and it only adds to my guilt.

I know Ivy was hoping the investigation would unearth something she could use against me. Hugh assured me he wouldn't let her sue me or sully my name. In fact, the report concluded Garrick was liable because he'd been the one driving. I hate that any report exists, especially one that tried apportioning blame to my boyfriend.

"I don't care what the report says." Ivy's derisory gaze roams me from head to toe. "I know who's to blame," she scoffs. "I don't know what my son ever saw in you. You look like a ginger replica of Karen Carpenter. One can only hope you'll suffer the same fate."

Pepper and I emit shocked gasps. I cannot believe she just said that. I'm not offended on my behalf—I long since gave up caring what this bitch thinks of me—but on behalf of all women who have struggled with an eating disorder. Karen had a much-publicized battle with anorexia and bulimia, and ultimately, her heart gave out in the end. I didn't think Garrick's mother could sink any lower, but this just proves it.

What a heartless bitch.

I have always known Garrick's mom despises me, but wanting me to die is a whole new level of hatred.

"Ivy! You need to apologize," Pepper says. "That is one of the most hurtful, shocking things I have ever borne witness to."

Ivy rolls her eyes. "You don't have to pretend for *her* benefit. If she hadn't sunk her claws into Garrick and interfered, he'd already be married to you and living his best life. Not stuck in a coma that *she* put him in."

While I know it was an intentional barb, it buries deep.

I can't deny if I hadn't come along, Garrick may have ended up with Pepper.

Looking at her now, I see she's certainly better suited to him.

She fits in his world. I never have.

Exhaustion seeps into my bones, dragging me down, and I'm done.

"I'm going to remind the nurses of your allocated time," Ivy says, spearing me with another venomous look.

"Don't bother," I snap, already turning around. "I'm going."

"Stevie!" Pepper calls out after me, but I ignore her, bypassing the elevator and heading for the stairs.

I fly downstairs with my heart pounding, blood thrumming in my ears, and pain racing through me, hitting everything in its path.

Today has been an emotional day, and I need to take stock and regain my composure.

I'm going to lick my wounds on one of the benches in the little garden area outside and talk myself off a ledge before I turn up at my assigned time. I want to ensure I'm calm enough to sit with my boyfriend and share a censored version of my day.

Little did I know the road is diverging and I am heading down a different path.

Chapter Three

Stevie

Tugging the collar of my coat up around my neck, I lean forward from my seated position on the bench, propping my elbows on my knees and my chin in my hands, with a weary sigh. I don't know how long I've been out here, stewing in my own thoughts, but it's been a while. It's soothing here in the dark, and I have barely felt the cold. The only illumination is from outdoor lights dotted along the stone path and nestled among copious flowerbeds, so it's easy to hide in plain sight.

Darkness is my cocoon. Invisible pitch-black arms welcome me like a ghostly lover, and I fall into the embrace. This little memorial garden has become my special place. I come out here every night, usually after I visit Garrick, to decompress and gather my thoughts before walking home.

Every time after I leave my boyfriend, I'm unbearably sad. Weighed down with guilt, remorse, and longing.

I miss him terribly.

He's still here, but he's not.

Existing in some limbo state.

Like the rest of us.

Even the picturesque surroundings of this gorgeous garden, sheltered in a private cordoned-off section to one side of the hospital, can't pull me out of the dark pit in my mind tonight. My confrontations with Will, Pepper, and Ivy are running on a repetitive loop in my head, and I'm struggling to find any inner peace.

I'm angry at them. At myself. At the world.

"Stupid cunts," I mumble, rubbing my hands together and wishing I had brought gloves. At least the chilly night air might blow some of the anger and melancholy from my brain.

A deep chuckle unexpectedly greets my eardrums, and I whip my head around, my eyes popping wide when I lock gazes with a dark-haired man sitting on the bench beside me. I never even heard or felt him sit down. Though he doesn't look like a stereotypical serial killer in his custom-fit suit under an expensive black wool coat, I'm instantly on my guard.

Narrowing my eyes, I skim over his features. His dark hair is cropped close to his skull, and there's a small hole at the side of his nose, indicating he wears a nose ring sometimes. A few black and silver rings adorn some of his fingers on both hands, and telltale ink peeks over the collar of his white shirt at the nape of his neck. His shirt is unbuttoned at the top, and he's not wearing a tie.

He's older than me. Mid to late twenties if I had to hazard a guess, but he seems even older than his looks, if that makes sense. It's just something about the way he's sitting, permitting my nosy perusal of him in a very dignified manner, and a vibe he exudes from every pore. Like he's carrying the weight of the world on his shoulders, and it's a responsibility he takes seriously.

This man is definitely a bit of an enigma.

He looks like a cross between a billionaire businessman and a member of an MC.

Judgmental much, Stevie?

He holds my gaze, as I blatantly assess him, with no discernible emotion on his face. I watch him assessing me too, and we just stare at one another in silence for a few seconds until he speaks.

"You have no reason to fear me," he says, astutely reading my reaction. "I promise you're safe with me."

"Says every serial killer on the planet."

The smile fades from his handsome face. "I just needed some air. This was the only vacant seat when I came outside."

I glance around the empty garden. "You could take your pick now."

"Yes, I could." Big brown eyes stare earnestly at me, like some form of silent challenge.

I lean against the back of the bench, tucking my hands under my arms, as I stare straight ahead, saying nothing. I don't think this guy has any nefarious plans, but whatever. If I'm wrong and he has sinister motives, it's probably just karma catching up to me.

I'll take whatever punishment comes my way because the universe knows I deserve it.

"If I'm making you uncomfortable, I'll switch benches." He moves to get up.

"It's fine. You can stay." I briefly glance to the side, making eye contact with him. "If you're determined to chop me into itty-bitty pieces, changing benches isn't likely to thwart your plan."

"True." His full lips curl up ever so slightly at the corners.

Silence descends, but it's not awkward.

Loneliness has been a constant companion these past eight months. Even when I'm surrounded by others. But for some reason, sitting on this bench beside this stranger erases some of the isolation.

"I'm getting a coffee before the coffee truck closes for the night," he says, unfurling to his full height. "Would you like something?"

"Coffee sounds good."

He arches a brow.

"Surprise me." I reply to his silent question in a most uncharacteristic way. I'm fussy about my coffee, but we're in Seattle. Home of the best coffee in the entire world, and the vintage silver truck permanently stationed on the hospital grounds serves a decent cup of joe. I'm sure whatever he gets will be fine.

He walks off with a hint of intrigue on his face, and I take a sneaky moment to study him. His long legs eat up the short distance to the coffee truck, and he holds himself almost regally as he scans the menu and places an order. Broad shoulders fit snugly underneath his tight-fitted coat, which highlights a slim physique. Black dress shoes match his suit, tapping quietly off the ground when he returns a few minutes later with two paper cups in his hands.

He reclaims the seat beside me and hands me a cup.

"Thank you." Removing the lid, I lift the cup to my nose and inhale the blended aroma of coffee and buttery, sweet caramel. My tongue darts out, savoring the syrupy froth, and even if I didn't know what it was from that first smell, the taste would confirm it. "You got me a caramel macchiato." I stare at him like he's some kind of magician, or maybe he's psychic. "That's my favorite coffee."

"My sister's too," he says before sipping his drink. The lid is on, so I can't tell what his is. If I had to guess, it's a black coffee. The same kind Garrick drinks. He always joked it was the manliest coffee. Simple and without any embellishments. Just like him.

My heart hurts at the visceral images the memory conjures in my mind. I briefly close my eyes, wrapping my hands firmly around the cup as the tightness in my chest stretches wider.

"Are you okay?" the stranger asks, yanking me back to the moment.

I shoot him one of my fake smiles. "I'm fine," I lie. "Tell me about your sister. She sounds like a kindred spirit."

He examines my face, no doubt seeing the lie, but he doesn't call me on it or pry. "I have two younger sisters. Sarah and Esther. Sarah is the coffee nut. Esther loathes the stuff."

"I'm surprised she wasn't run out of the state."

His lips twitch. "Me too. She only drinks tea. I used to stop by the tearooms in Pike Place Market once a month to stock up on her favorites. Now, she's in Cornell, I ship supplies out every few months."

His face lights up when speaking about his sisters, and warmth spreads across my chest. "You sound like a great big brother."

He shrugs, looking contemplative as he drinks his coffee. "What about you?" he asks after another comfortable quiet interlude. "Any siblings?"

I shake my head. "It's just me and my mom."

Some indecipherable emotion flares momentarily in his eyes as we share a look.

I avert my gaze and drink my coffee. I'm grateful my love for coffee hasn't abated along with my other taste buds. I have found it hard to enjoy food since the accident. Perhaps because so much of my relationship with Garrick was centered around food and wine. I loved cooking for him, but cooking holds zero appeal these days. Now I eat purely to sustain my body, but the only pleasure I derive from putting anything in my mouth is from coffee.

Coffee will forever be one of my great loves.

"Who were the cunts?" he asks after another bout of silence. "I'll confess to being intrigued."

I blink repeatedly until I remember. "No one worth mentioning," I mumble, rubbing a tense spot between my brows. "I just had a bad day." That's not technically true. I had a very productive enjoyable day at work. It was after I left work that everything turned to shit.

He doesn't speak for a few moments. "Sometimes, it helps to talk to a stranger. I've been told I'm a good listener." He traces one slim finger around the rim of his cup. "If you need to vent, you can vent to me."

"Who are you?" I blurt, not meaning to say it out loud. It's more of a general question, not meant literally, but that's how he computes it.

"My name is Greyson though most everyone calls me Beck."

Another déjà vu moment rolls over me, and I work hard to evict the memory from my head. My brain is really doing a number on me today. "Why not Grey?"

"My middle name is Beckett. After Samuel Beckett. He was—"

"An Irish writer," I supply before he can confirm it.

"Yes." He offers me a fleeting smile, and I catch a glimpse of perfect white teeth. "My mom loved his books and his plays. He spent a lot of his life in France, and he wrote in both French and English. Mom grew up in France, and my grandparents still live there. Mom always called me Beckett. When my sisters were little, they could only say Beck, and I guess the name stuck." Creases dent his smooth brow, and he scrubs a hand over his clean-shaven jawline as he stares into space. I didn't miss how he spoke about his mother in the past tense, and I wonder if that's why he is at the hospital.

Although I'm naturally nosy, I'm not going to ask.

He can volunteer the information if he likes, but I would never pry.

When I meet people I know, the first thing they ask me is how Garrick is. I know they mean well, and I love they are keeping him in their thoughts, but it's stressful to repeat the same stale news over and over again. I hate the pitying looks and the platitudes.

It's coming from a good place, but it's soul destroying.

So, I will never put another person in a similar position, because I get it.

Sometimes, you want to speak about them, to help keep the memory alive.

Other times, you just can't talk about it because it hurts far too much.

Beck clears his throat. "What about you? What's your name?"

"I'm Stevie. Everyone just calls me Stevie."

Except for Nana, my love, and his poisonous mother.

In recent times, I have often thought how ironic it is that Garrick calls me his sunshine when I turned out to be his darkness.

And I will eternally be a gold-digging whore-slash-slut to Ivy Allen-Golding-Smith.

At least she won't be adding Walker to her surname. Winston and Ivy broke up last year. I'd love to know if he kicked her bitchy ass to the curb, but Garrick wasn't speaking to his mom or Pepper at the time, so we never got the deets.

"It suits you," Beck says, draining the remains of his coffee.

"Mom named me after Stevie Nicks from—"

"Fleetwood Mac." Now it's his turn to complete my sentence.

I nod, tipping my head back to catch every last drop of my macchiato. When I'm finished, I take his cup and mine and walk over to the trash can to toss them. I glance at my watch, startled to find an hour has passed since my run-in with Pepper and the she-devil.

When I return to the bench, Beck is staring at an expensive-looking silver watch strapped to his wrist.

"Reality calls, huh?" I say, looming over him.

"Unfortunately." His Adam's apple bobs in his throat as he stands, sinking his hands into the pockets of his coat. "Can I walk you inside?" He looks around. "I don't see anyone hovering, but you can never be too sure."

"Okay." Swiping my purse from under the bench, I wrap it around my shoulder and across my body.

We walk amicably side by side, both lost in thought. The closer I get to the hospital entrance, the more stress presses down on my shoulders, cording the muscle into knots. Although I know Pepper and Ivy are long gone, anxiety still flows through my veins. The altercation with them has shaken me more than I'd realized.

Beck and I cross the lobby, heading for the same elevator. Miraculously, it's empty when we step inside, both of us reaching for the same button at the same time. The floor Garrick's new room is on is a private one. All the suites have their own waiting areas, but it's not uncommon to meet other visitors in the hallways, and sometimes people congregate in the communal waiting room for a change of scenery. I regularly bump into the same people in the cafeteria or at one of the espresso stands, the tearooms, or the coffee truck outside.

I have never crossed paths with Beck before, so I'm pretty confident in saying whomever he's visiting must be a new addition to the floor.

Our eyes meet in mutual surprise as the doors close. Beck scrubs a hand along his smooth jawline, standing rigidly still as the elevator begins to rise. I lean against the wall as tension fills the gap between us.

He breaks it first.

"If it's not too intrusive to ask, who are you visiting?" Warm brown eyes pierce mine.

"My boyfriend," I whisper, automatically touching the ink on my wrist. "He's been in a coma for eight months."

Sympathy splays across his face. "That must be very difficult."

"It is." I clear my throat as I watch the numbers go by, bringing us closer and closer to the ward. "I haven't seen you here before."

He wets his lips before speaking. "Brielle...my girlfriend"—his face pulls into a grimace—"just got moved over from the ICU."

I want to ask why she's here, but I don't want him to feel like he has to tell me. He volunteers the information anyway.

"She's in a coma too. Three weeks."

"I empathize. It sucks."

He nods before lowering his eyes and picking at imaginary lint on the sleeve of his coat.

The doors ping as they draw open, and we silently step out into the corridor. We stand in front of the elevator for a few nanoseconds, staring at one another, both of us reluctant to part for reasons that have nothing to do with wanting to remain together. "I'm this way," I say, pointing left, after I pull my big girl panties on.

He jerks his head over his shoulder. "I'm back there."

A pregnant pause ensues. I break it first this time. "Well, it was nice talking with you, Beck, and thanks again for the coffee."

"Any time, Stevie." He runs a hand across the back of his neck. "See you around."

I shoot him a small smile before I turn on my heel and head in the direction of Garrick's room.

Chapter Four

Beck

The door to my office swings open, slamming against the wall with the force of the motion. My father stands in the doorway, and I inwardly sigh. What does he want now? My frazzled assistant looks over his shoulder at me, mouthing "sorry." Lulu—unfortunate name—is far too sensitive to work in the cutthroat environment that is Colbert Aerospace, and I should probably fire her. But her ditzy personality brightens up an otherwise dull day, and I can't bear to let her go. She's been with me from day one—after I finished my MBA and was forced into the family business.

It's been a baptism of fire for both of us, but we're in it together until the bitter end.

"Greyson." Carlton Colbert, my father and the CEO of the second-largest aerospace company in the US, stalks into the room, slamming the door behind him with the same velocity he used for entering. Father always likes to make an entrance, and God forbid he's not the center of attention. He likes to throw his weight around and ensure everyone knows what a powerful man he is.

Pompous asshole.

"Father," I drawl, tapping my pen on top of my desk as I narrow my eyes and contemplate what he wants. I don't rise to greet him on purpose, because I know how much it riles him up.

Lines crinkle at the corner of his brown eyes, and I hate that I see the same eyes staring back at me when I look in the mirror. Sarah and Esther inherited Mom's hazel eyes and dark-blonde hair, while I resemble the man standing in front of me. In physical appearance only. When it comes to our personalities, we are like night and day.

Dad looks good for fifty. He works out regularly and takes care of himself. Scant silvery strands have only begun appearing in his dark-brown hair, and his physique is impressive clothed in a navy Prada suit with a navy-and-silver tie. His six-foot-two-inch frame is a couple inches shorter than my taller, broader body, and I know it bugs him. He likes to be greater than me in every conceivable way. He never wants me to forget my place.

With a scowl, he takes the seat in front of my desk, drilling a hole in my skull as we engage in our usual silent standoff.

I inherited my dad's stubborn streak too. It's the only personality trait we share.

After a few minutes of silence, he clears his throat and eyeballs me. "Are you sure you aren't aware of the circumstances with Brielle?"

"Yes. I already told you," I lie, keeping my poker face firmly planted on my features.

He claws a hand through his thick hair. "This is a mess."

I say nothing, waiting him out, and he doesn't disappoint.

"We need this merger with Cartwright Software Services to go through."

"I'm aware."

After all, it's why he blackmailed me into dating Brielle, the only daughter of David Cartwright, CEO and owner of a tech company that supplies technology used in commercial, military, and space programs.

David and Dad have been business partners for years. The merger was Dad's idea because he's obsessed with making Colbert

Aerospace the largest aerospace employer in the US. With a projected combined worldwide employee headcount of one hundred and ninety thousand, Colbert Cartwright Aerospace and Technological Services would usurp Boeing as the largest employer in this space, but we'd still lag behind them in overall rankings. Something my father, no doubt, plans to rectify in the future.

"We are so close to finalizing the deal, and now this drama with Brielle has thrown a wrench in the works."

"She's in a coma," I say. "It hardly qualifies as drama."

I can't say I'm surprised at his attitude. Dad lives and breathes work. It's all he cares about. Except maybe for Sarah. If he's capable of caring about anything besides his multibillion-dollar business, it would be my twenty-three-year-old sister. She shares the same all-consuming, hardheaded, no-nonsense, rule-the-world attitude he displays.

Sarah is the heir he wishes he had in me.

Unlike him, Sarah is also compassionate and self-deprecating. She's ambitious and champing at the bit to finish her Harvard MBA so she can join the business, but she's way more self-aware than father, and she cares about people. She wants to make her mark through hard work and intelligence, rather than political backstabbing and trampling over the very people who put you where you are.

Sarah will make a great future CEO. We just need to convince the misogynistic fool sitting in front of me. He might care for her more than Esther and me, but that doesn't mean he's willing to let a woman sit at the helm of the company founded by his great-grandfather in 1930.

"Everything about Brielle Cartwright spelled drama," he scoffs, flicking a piece of lint from the sleeve of his jacket.

"Yet you wanted me to marry her."

"Don't be facetious, Greyson." My father is the only one who insists on calling me by my first name. I was named after the founding CEO of this company, and Dad likes to remind me regularly how I sully the name. It's a constant knife plunging into my back. A permanent reminder that I'm an abject failure compared to our ancestor. "You know the nature of the agreement."

Only he could refer to emotional and financial blackmail as an *agreement.*

"Arranged marriages are the best way to ensure a long-lasting business partnership," he continues, telling me something I've heard a hundred times before. He loves the sound of his own voice. "I already told you I didn't care what you did as long as you got her up that aisle and knocked her up a few times. You could fuck half of Seattle after the wedding, and I wouldn't have cared if you were discreet and didn't piss David off."

I told him I never wanted to marry, and I would never disrespect any woman by marrying her and then routinely cheating the way he did when he was married to my mother.

"It's a moot point now," he continues. "She's as good as dead. David needs to stop bowing to that dreadful woman's pathetic whining and pull the plug."

That dreadful woman is Brielle's mom, and her pathetic whining is heartsick grief. I don't blame Pamela for not wanting to turn off life support. She's clinging to hope, and the only asshole who would ever criticize a grieving mother is the asshole I share DNA with.

"Was there a reason for your visit?" I ask in a neutral tone, staring at the man who is a virtual stranger to me.

"This merger needs to happen," Dad snaps as he rises to his feet. "Make sure you are at that hospital every night, crying over that stupid bitch's bedside and comforting her parents. Any chance you get, you remind David of his obligations."

Hell will freeze over before I ever pressure a heartbroken father into signing a business deal. I know what's at stake, and I might not always be able to uphold that conviction, but I'm going to try. What Dad has always failed to realize is, a little humanity can go a long way.

When I don't reply, Dad storms toward the door, stalling with his hand curled around the handle. Looking over his shoulder, he stabs me with a warning look. "You might have gotten a reprieve on the marriage, but this merger needs to go through. If you don't make it happen, your sisters will pay the price."

I'm sitting on the same bench in the memorial garden, at the same time as last night, but there's no sign of the stunning redhead with the mournful green eyes. I have never seen anyone who looks so sad and so lost. Even my similar reflection in the mirror doesn't come close to the depths of misery I spotted in Stevie's eyes. Devastation and grief roll off her in waves of dark despair, and she wears a haunted expression I haven't been able to forget since we met.

She looks the way I feel deep inside.

I'm just more experienced at disguising it.

What happened with Brielle adds more guilt to the festering pile until it feels like I'm drowning under the weight of responsibility and my poor choices.

Swigging from my hip flask, I relish the burn of the expensive Macallan gliding down my throat. I don't make a habit of drinking at random, but my current circumstances warrant it. I can't face that hospital room without some liquid courage.

I'm about to give up on Stevie and force myself inside when she shows up, wearing the same flimsy coat over a navy skirt suit. She has nice legs I notice as she walks toward the garden, head slightly bent, looking lost in thought. Her gorgeous thick hair is in another tight bun on top of her head, and I briefly wonder what it would look like removed from the hair tie. Spotting me, Stevie pauses on the path, for a brief second, before making her way in this direction.

She drops down beside me with a weary sigh, dumping a gym bag on the ground at her feet. Haunted emerald-green eyes turn to mine before lowering to the silver flask curled in my hand. "Can I have some?" she asks, and I wordlessly hand it over, watching her tip it back and drink a healthy mouthful. I expect her to cough, but she handles it with grace.

"Macallan," she murmurs. "Of course." Her lips pull into a tight line as she hands the flask back to me.

"Does scotch offend you or just this particular brand?"

Her eyes lift to mine again. "Garrick, my boyfriend, is a bit of a whisky connoisseur. Macallan is his favorite though he's quite partial to Laphraoig too."

"He has good taste."

My words hang in the air for a few silent beats.

"Yeah," she whispers, looking more lost than ever.

"What happened to him?"

Air whooshes out of her mouth, and pain contorts her face. I regret asking the question, and I'm about to retract it when she answers.

"We were in a car accident. I got off lightly. Only a concussion, a few cuts, bruises, and broken bones. Garrick was driving, and he bore the brunt of the impact."

Fuck. That's rough. And she shouldn't be downplaying her injuries either. I can't imagine how hard that must have been. To wake up in pain and discover your boyfriend was in a coma. I can tell from the way she talks about him that she loves him a lot. "I'm sorry."

"Don't be." Her chin juts up, and her jaw tightens. "The accident is my fault. The only person who deserves your sorrow is Garrick. I deserve nothing but contempt."

I'm shocked speechless for a few tense seconds. "How is it your fault?"

She worries her lower lip between her teeth before releasing it. Her chest rises and falls. I can tell speaking about this is hard for her, but I think she wants to tell me. I think she needs to get this all out. I take another sip of scotch as I wait her out. When her eyes drift to the flask in my hand, I pass it back to her, instinctively knowing she needs some liquid courage.

We pass the flask back and forth a couple of times in companionable silence.

"Garrick bought me a car," she says after I've repocketed my hip flask. I can't show up drunk in Brielle's room, no matter how tempting it is to drown in alcohol.

Stevie stares straight ahead, into the still night air, as she explains. "It was a gorgeous, brand-new, black BMW SUV. We were about to be separated. Garrick still had a year left at UO, but I graduated early, and I was starting a new job in Seattle. He bought it because he wanted me to be safe with all the driving I planned to do. I coveted it the instant he surprised me with it, the day of the accident, but I couldn't let my own petty hang-ups go. I refused to accept it or even test-drive it."

A heavy sigh filters from her lips. "Garrick was only driving my shitty CR-V because I rejected his very generous very thoughtful gift. The brakes failed on my car, and we plowed into traffic head-on. We both knew it wasn't going to end well. The last words he said were he loved me and I was the best thing to ever happen to him."

Her face is worryingly devoid of all emotion except for pain when she turns to face me again. It radiates from her pores like a tangible substance. "I wasn't the best thing to happen to him. I was the worst thing ever. If he'd never met me, he wouldn't be lying in that hospital bed, asleep to the world and the people in it."

The depth of her self-loathing knocks me back, like a punch to the face, and I have an uncharacteristic urge to pull her into my arms and hug the shit out of her. If ever anyone needed a hug, it's Stevie. I hate hearing the desolation in her voice and seeing it painted on her face. Underneath that veil of self-hatred and devastation lies a vibrant woman. I can look beyond the mask she currently presents to the world and see it.

This Stevie isn't Garrick's Stevie.

She's floundering in a world that has let her down.

I shouldn't want to be her savior. I'm incapable of being anyone's savior. But I desperately want to be hers.

Chapter Five
Stevie

"I doubt your boyfriend would agree. In those last moments, all he was thinking about was his love for you," Beck says. "I doubt he regrets a single second of his time with you. I don't think he'd blame you for what happened either."

"You can't say that with any degree of confidence. You don't know him."

"I don't, but I think I might have met him one time." He runs a hand over the top of his short dark hair. "Is Garrick Allen your boyfriend?"

I slowly nod.

"I should have made the connection the second you said his name. My father and I played golf once with Garrick and his dad, Hugh. I can't say I know him very well, but we chatted a bit that day. I remember reading about his accident, and it saddened me. He seemed like a good guy."

"He is. He's the best," I whisper. What are the odds I would bump into someone Garrick once played golf with? The world is such a small place.

"How long were you dating?" he asks, buttoning up his coat. He's wearing another suit underneath it again today, indicating he also came straight from the office.

"Almost a year, but it was an intense year. Garrick is very self-assured, and he knows what he wants from life."

"You." He offers me a sad smile.

"I am a part of it. He also loves music, and he's a talented singer and guitarist. He loves his family, and he's looking forward to working for the family business."

"What have the doctors said of his prognosis?" Beck folds his arms across his waist.

"There is brain activity, which is good, and all his physical injuries have healed, but there was some damage to the nerves in his spine, and if he wakes from his coma, there's a strong possibility he will be paralyzed."

"That sucks."

"Yeah, but I'm sure we'll cope. Right now, I just want him to come back to me. I miss seeing his beautiful eyes. I miss hearing his laugh. I miss his arms around me." I shrug, trying to downplay the utter loneliness that clings to my bones like a second layer of skin. "I just miss him. So damn much. My world is colorless without him in my life."

"What do the doctors say about his coma?" he asks.

It's a diplomatic way of asking if they think he's ever likely to wake up. "The longer he remains in a coma, the less chance there is he'll wake. It's not impossible but rare after so much time has passed." A strangled laugh bursts from my lips, and he looks at me with a dip between his brows. "This is the first time I've been able to admit that out loud." I clasp my hands in my lap, feeling a sudden chill. "I was afraid if I said the words I'd make it real."

"I understand." Sincere warm brown eyes drill into my face.

"Tell me about your girlfriend." I'm ready for a change of subject.

He instantly stiffens, and a muscle clenches in his jaw.

"Unless you don't want to talk about it, which is totally fine. I know how hard it is."

"We weren't like you and Garrick," he says after a few silent beats. "Our relationship wasn't even close to intense love."

I'm intrigued. "How long were you two dating?"

"Twenty months, three days, ten hours, and sixteen minutes."

I blink repeatedly. "That's very specific."

He barks out a harsh laugh. When he turns toward me, I catch a glimpse of all the hurt he works so hard to hide. It's like a brief peek into his soul, and I'm suffocating in the depths of his despondency. I observe Beck composing himself. Tucking his emotions behind that handsome face in well-practiced moves. "Can you keep a secret?" he asks.

"As long as it's not where all the bodies are buried," I deadpan.

This time, his boisterous laugh is radiant, and I'm momentarily captivated at how his entire face just lights up. In this moment, he's not troubled or shouldering the heavy weight of his demons. "I promise there are no dead bodies." His smile gradually disappears. "I can't say the same for skeletons in the closet."

"We all have those."

"I fear I have more than most."

"You won't scare me away. I'm made of strong stuff."

"That's blatantly obvious." He angles his long body on the bench so he's sitting sideways, and his knee brushes against mine. "I'm in awe of you, Stevie. The hand you were dealt was shitty, but you manage it with grace. Most people would cave under the stress and bury their head in the sand. You don't. You get on with things, and you show up here every day, am I right?"

I nod.

"Trust me, you're not the worst thing to happen to Garrick. That's a virtual impossibility. Most girls would have given up by now, yet you are here for him every day. I think you need to cut yourself some slack and give yourself the credit you deserve."

"I can't see past my guilt," I blurt. It's not a lie.

"That is something I can relate to."

"How? Why?" I pull the collar of my coat up as a blast of cold air swirls around my neck.

"I wasn't a very good boyfriend to Brielle, and our relationship wasn't conventional. Our fathers are business partners, conducting an important merger, and, in their infinite wisdom"—sarcasm drips from his tone—"they decided we should date and eventually get married to further enhance the deal and form a permanent lasting bond between our families."

My mouth falls open, and I stare at him in shock. "Sorry, I thought we'd just wandered back in time to the dark ages."

A grimace spreads over his olive-toned skin. "My father didn't give me much choice." His voice is clipped, his words only conveying part of the story.

"I... How does something like that even work?"

He winces. "It doesn't." He sighs heavily. "Like my father would say, we gave it the old college try. But neither of us were feeling it. You can't force something that isn't there. We faked it in public at engagements and when we were with our families, but we led separate lives the rest of the time, just texting every now and then." Pain flits across his face. "I was wrong to keep my distance. I should've been a better friend to her. I'd known Brielle since I was a kid. Our fathers met at Cornell, and they've been best friends ever since. I owed it to Brielle to make more of an effort, but I didn't. If I'd paid more attention to her, I would've been aware of what was going on, and I could have stopped it."

My breath stutters in my lungs. "Stopped what?"

He draws a few deep breaths before continuing. "Brielle overdosed on opioids. On purpose. She's in a coma, with no brain activity, because she wanted to take her own life. She wanted to die."

I clasp a hand over my mouth in horrified shock. Our situations are comparable only in so far as both of our partners are in a coma. That is where the similarity ends. His girlfriend tried to end her life. I thought the guilt I was carrying was the worst, but how bad would it be if Garrick had purposely tried to die? Garrick's in what is considered a "locked in" coma because his brain has him locked inside his body. There is still activity and still hope, albeit slim. There is no hope for Brielle if there is no brain activity. She is already gone.

My heart, already hollowed out and permanently aching, throbs with fresh anguish for Beck.

"She's still on life support?" I ask what seems blatantly obvious.

"Her parents are distraught. Especially her mother. She's refusing to let them switch off the life support machine. She has herself convinced Brielle will wake up. Her husband isn't rocking the boat. He's doing whatever his wife needs even if it's only delaying the inevitable."

"I don't know what to say, Beck. It makes my whining seem so pitiful."

"Don't do that. Don't downplay what you're going through. It's not a competition, Stevie. You're entitled to your guilt just like I'm entitled to mine. No one can tell us what to feel or how to feel it." He runs a hand along the back of his neck. "At least we understand it. No one else truly does." His tongue darts out, wetting his lips. "I couldn't talk to anyone else about this, but I can talk to you."

"I feel the same. I think I was wrong when I said your sister and I were kindred spirits." I pause for a second. "Maybe it's you and I."

"Hey, you," I say in my brightest voice when I enter Garrick's room a short while later. He's alone, like most nights when I arrive. Hugh won't be here for at least an hour, and I welcome the time I get to spend with my boyfriend on my own. Depositing my coat on the chair and my bag on the ground, I lean down and kiss his soft, warm cheek. "I missed you today. I love you so much, babe." I tell him this every day because if there's even a slim chance my words are getting through to him, I never want him to doubt how much I miss and love him.

Dr. Edwards, Hudson's dad, says patients who have come out of comas have spoken about hearing loved one's voices. He actively encourages us to talk to Garrick and to be as normal as possible in our interactions.

It's why I never show up here angry.

Or let my depression show.

Or relay anything negative that's happened in my life in case it causes him stress or worry. None of us know what it's like to be trapped in your head. To be incapable of moving your body. For all we know, he is aware of everything, and he just can't communicate with us.

A part of me hopes he hears everything and it gives him the strength to keep fighting.

Another part of me hopes he hears nothing. That he's not aware of what's going on because the thought of him trapped inside his body, screaming to be set free, is most upsetting. It torments me. Usually at night, when I'm lying in bed, tossing and turning, trying to sleep, but unable to switch my thoughts off.

On weekends, I have resorted to taking a sleeping pill at night. I hate relying on medication, but I can't function if I don't get at least two nights of undisturbed sleep a week.

The door opens quietly, and Helena enters the room. I smile softly at Garrick's physical therapist. Helena works various shifts, alternating between days and nights, so I don't always see her even if she works on Garrick every day. She's only a few years older than me, and she's one of the sweetest people I've ever met. We clicked instantly, and while I wouldn't exactly call us friends, there's a warmth in our relationship that doesn't exist with any of the nursing staff even though I'm on good terms with all of them. "Helena, it's good to see you. It's been a while."

"Good to see you too, Stevie." She pulls me into a brief hug. "I was working days the past two weeks. My sister had a baby, and I've been helping her out at night. Her new son refuses to sleep, and she's exhausted and stressed out trying to get him into a good routine."

"Congratulations, Auntie."

"Thanks." She beams and her pretty face lights up despite her obvious tiredness. "Lennon is the first baby on our side, so it's been wildly exciting. Everyone is tripping over themselves to spend time with him."

"Aw, that's so cute, and I love his name."

"His father is a crazy Beatles fan."

"I figured." I grin and waggle my brows.

"How's our boy?" she asks, glancing down at Garrick as she secures a stray strand of brown hair into her ponytail.

"Beautiful as ever." I sweep my fingers across his handsome face. "It's hard sometimes to see him looking so physically perfect." His physical injuries have healed. The ones we can see, at least, and he looks more like himself. Except he's much paler, and I miss his messy longer hair.

They keep his hair cropped close to his skull. Hudson said it's in case anything happens, and they might need to operate on his brain again. Personally, I think that's bullshit. It would take seconds to shave his head. It's more to do with the nursing staff not having an ordeal every time they need to wash his hair. Cropped hair is way easier to manage. "It's like he's just sleeping. In brief moments when I forget, I expect him to bolt upright, open those eyes, and fix me with one of his dazzling smiles. Then I remember, and the pain digs deeper."

"It's not easy," she agrees, drawing the covers down Garrick's body.

"I'll water the plants and get out of your way." I step away from the bed, letting her do her work.

Taking care of Garrick is more than just hooking him up to machines and drips and feeding him through a tube. Nurses regularly rotate him in the bed to avoid bedsores. A dietician and respiratory care assistant monitor his nutrition and breathing, and Helena conducts daily physical therapy to flex his muscles and stop them from atrophying.

I fill the small plastic watering can at the sink in Garrick's private bathroom before moving around the bedroom and attending to the few plants. I have tried to make this space homey so, when he wakes, he'll see warmth and familiarity. Now that we are away from the main ICU floor, there are less restrictions on what we can and can't do. As well as plants, I bring weekly flowers every Friday, arranging them in colorful floral displays among a few different vases scattered around the space. Framed photos cover one of his bedside tables. His guitar rests in a corner on a stand, and there are more photos pinned to the walls.

A portable Bluetooth speaker plays his favorite music during the day, on low in the background most times. I also bought a scent diffuser because one of the nurses mentioned that scents can trigger memories. I use a variety of different scents, like apples, citrus, and spicy scents reminiscent of his favorite wine and whisky. Strawberry, peach, and vanilla like my shower wash and perfume. I even found some cookie and cupcake scents.

Ivy tried getting rid of some of it, but Hugh laid down the law, and he had the nurses on his side. None of the nursing staff has any time for her, and Harvey Edwards only tolerates her because he's forced to. I heard a few of the nurses bitching about her one night, and I couldn't stop the smile from spreading across my face.

Like now, as I watch Helena with Garrick. She talks quietly to him as she manipulates his muscles, rotating his legs and arms, taking great care of his body. I find a lot of the nurses quite cold. They are never rude or negligent, probably mostly overworked, but they don't show the same tenderness or concerned care that Helena does. She isn't just sweet and kind; she's amazing at her job too.

When I'm finished watering the plants, I sit on the chair by the window, looking out at the pitch-black Seattle skyline. Briefly, I wonder if Beck is still with Brielle or if he's already gone home. Removing my tablet from my bag, I catch up on some work emails while Helena finishes with Garrick.

When she's done, we say our goodbyes, and I settle into the chair by my boyfriend's side, holding his hand in one hand while I open up the book we're reading on my tablet with my free one.

It's the latest Byron Stanley thriller, about a fictional detective named Jake Bennett. Each book is about a new case, but the subplot of his life carries through, progressing from book to book. This one is about a woman who went missing fifteen years ago who is suddenly found. She has no recollection of what happened to her, but Bennett is trying to help her recover lost memories because another woman has been taken in similar circumstances, and they think she can help to locate her.

It's really good, and Garrick would love it. I hope he *is* loving it. Garrick had just discovered this author before the accident, and he wouldn't shut up about how amazing he was.

I was always a romance reader until I decided to purchase Stanley's entire catalog after the accident, and I'm slowly working my way through each one with Garrick. My boyfriend was right. The books are gripping, and Stanley is an excellent author. I now have a newly discovered passion for thrillers, and one of my favorite things to do is read to Garrick.

"Where were we?" I muse out loud, opening the book on my tablet. "Ah, yes. Bennett just received an anonymous tip-off, and he was heading to Maggie's house to ask her about it."

Chapter Six

Beck

"I have something to show you," I tell Stevie one night in early April. We're sitting on our bench, drinking coffee she bought. Stevie insists we take turns paying for drinks, so we alternate nights.

Since that first night, we've settled into a regular routine, meeting here every night before we make our respective hospital visits.

Neither of us ever commented on it or made any commitment.

We just continue to show up here, night after night, and it's an unspoken agreement.

I like talking with Stevie, and I'm opening up to her in a way I rarely do with others. I think I'm that person for her too. I get the sense before the accident Stevie was quite an open book.

She's now one of my closest friends. My best confidant. Someone who makes it easier to face each day. Even if she still doesn't know my most closely guarded secrets. I value her friendship too much to risk losing it if I shared my truths. However, there is one truth I'm dying to share with her. I'd rather show Stevie, and I'm trying to pluck up the courage to ask her to my place.

We don't talk about Brielle or Garrick much anymore. Our

friendship is an escape from reality. Yet we are here for one another, understanding our situations better than anyone else can, and when we need to discuss reality, we do.

It's how I know she's nervous tonight and why.

And how she understands my frustration when we part ways in the hallway in the hospital every night.

Mostly, we talk about our dreams and ambitions, music, movies, books, and a little about work and our families. We exchange stories of our past, places we've been to, places we'd like to go to. Discuss our favorite foods. She tries to convince me to go to yoga, and I attempt to coax her into altitude training.

These conversations have become the highlight of my day and something I look forward to from the moment I wake. It's everything I need to forget the drudgery and pain of my day-to-day life, and I think it's the same for Stevie too.

"Okay, what is it?" she asks, yanking me out of my head. Stevie fidgets with the skirt of her dress, looking anxious and distracted.

"I was hoping we could grab something to eat after our visits tonight, and I can show you some research I found. It's not something I want to discuss out here."

It's brighter now in the evenings, and it doesn't usually get dark until after seven. But that's not the reason. I unearthed a ton of research, and I don't want the pages blowing away. I also don't want to discuss the topic here. Mostly, it's because I think she'll need a distraction after tonight. And maybe, if we start meeting away from this bench, I can broach the subject of cooking something for her at home so I can show her the secret hiding behind the walls of my home office. I think she'll get a thrill out of seeing it, and it's why I haven't said anything to her yet even though I've been tempted when the subject comes up in conversation.

My eyes linger on the wrapped package propped against the side of the bench, and I wonder what gift she bought him.

"I don't think so, Beck." She chews on the corner of her lip. "I won't be the best company later."

"That's why I thought you might need a distraction."

"I'll probably just cry and embarrass you in public. Or not," she mutters, pulling her legs up to her chest. "I still haven't cried. Not since those first few days in the hospital. What does that say about me?"

"Not what you think it says. You're a survivor, Stevie. You do what you must to survive, and no one should ever give you shit about how you do that."

"How do you always know the right thing to say?"

"I do?" I arch a brow. I'm not normally good with the spoken word. Written words are more my thing.

"Yes, you do." A cheeky grin materializes on her face, and I'm glad to see it. She's been very depressed this week, in the run-up to Garrick's twenty-second birthday. Even organizing tonight's birthday party for him hasn't lifted her spirits. "Must be because you're ancient," she quips, and I nudge her playfully in her side.

Her eyes sparkle, and her face glows. I stare at her in a kind of daze for a few seconds. She's wearing makeup tonight, and her hair is hanging in loose waves down her back. Stevie is a beautiful girl, but she's absolutely breathtaking tonight.

"Twenty-seven is not ancient," I say, snapping out of it.

"Almost twenty-eight," she fires back, and I chuckle.

"Math clearly wasn't your best subject at school," I tease. "My birthday isn't until October. Last I checked, six months is not *almost* in any language."

"You're still practically geriatric compared to me."

I roll my eyes. "Age is just a number."

"How cliché." Now it's her turn to roll her eyes.

"All joking aside, Beck," she adds, a few moments later. "You are wise beyond your years."

"I could say the same to you. You're not like most twenty-one-year-olds."

"Nana always says I'm an old soul."

"I agree with her. Talking with you is the best part of my day."

"Mine too," she readily agrees before dropping her feet to the ground and looking away.

"Hey. What's wrong?" I gently touch her arm.

She turns to look at me with renewed pain on her face. "It feels wrong to say that to another man the day of my boyfriend's birthday," she whispers.

My eyes startle in surprise. We have never discussed how our friendship might impact our other relationships, and while I don't share her view, I'm not surprised Stevie has expressed this opinion. I have gotten to know her, and I was expecting this to crop up at some point. "We're friends, Stevie. You and I both know nothing inappropriate has happened between us. If I was a female, that thought wouldn't even cross your mind. You should not feel guilty for our friendship or how it makes you feel. We aren't doing anything wrong."

"That's not how others would see it."

"I honestly don't care what anyone else thinks, but if it matters to you that much, we can stop these meetings. We can end our friendship here." The words kill me to speak. I don't want to stop these garden visits. But I will if it's what she needs. I never want to make her life harder.

She shakes her head, sending waves of glossy red hair cascading over her slender shoulders. "I don't want to stop meeting up. Your friendship has come to mean so much to me, Beck." Sincerity flows through her words and leaks from her expression.

"It means a lot to me, too. I have other friends in my life but no one who sees the real me like you do."

"I know what you mean. I can just be myself with you too."

I nod because it's exactly how I feel. I place my hand carefully on top of hers. "I am here tonight if you need me. But if you need to be alone, that's fine too. I just want you to know I've got your back. Always."

A glassy sheen pricks her eyes, and it's the closest I've seen her come to shedding tears.

"Thank you, Beck. A million times thank you. For being my lifeline. For being a bright spark in a world that's so very dark. I know I can always talk to you, but tonight is something I need to do alone."

"I understand," I say as someone calls out Stevie's name.

We both turn toward the sound of the female voice, and Stevie curses under her breath. "Incoming," she mutters, bending down for the birthday gift and her purse. "I told her not to do this, but she never listens to me."

Watching the tall, thin girl with a shock of wild brown curly hair approach, I instantly know who she is.

Stevie and I stand, and I shove my hands into the pockets of my dress pants.

"There you are." She stops and smiles, her gaze dancing between us.

"Hadley, I presume?"

"She *has* told you about me then. That's a relief. I really didn't want to give you the summary of what we mean to one another in the few short seconds we have before we need to go inside the hospital." The words stream from her mouth in a rush, and she barely pauses to draw a breath.

"Of course, I told Beck about you. You're my childhood best friend, roommate, and perpetual thorn in my side." Stevie leans in and hugs her quickly. "I say that with love. Always with love."

"Ditto, sexy. Look at you." Hadley whirls her hands in front of Stevie. "It's been a while since I've seen you looking anything close to human. This is great progress. I'm proud of you, Opium Poppy."

My brows climb to my hairline as Stevie cringes.

Hadley emits a loud gasp, slapping a hand briefly over her mouth. "Oh my god, Beck. I'm so sorry. That was insensitive."

I have no idea why she'd think that, but I can't get a word in edgewise to tell her it's fine, that I'm not offended, because she keeps talking.

"It's an ongoing joke since we were kids. Nana calls Stevie Little Poppy, and there was this one time a local farmer got caught harvesting poppies for opium, and I tried to convince Nana to change Stevie's nickname, but she wouldn't entertain the idea." She fake huffs. "I thought it was genius, and I like to remind my bestie so she knows how lucky she is to have such an intelligent and entertaining best friend."

"I told you she's a handful," Stevie says. "Count your blessings she doesn't have the time to interrogate you."

"There's always next time." Hadley grins, showcasing a set of perfectly straight white teeth.

"I look forward to it, and it was nice to meet you." I look down at Stevie. "You should go. You don't want to be late."

"Yeah."

I sense the hesitation, and I understand it. "From what you've told me of him, Garrick would be proud you did this. Go up there and celebrate his birthday. When you need to talk, I'll be here."

"Thanks, Beck," she whispers, looking close to tears again. Maybe tonight is the night she gives in to pent-up emotion. If it happens, I hope it's cathartic for her.

Hadley loops her arm through Stevie's. "It was good to meet you too, Beck. You take care." Hadley leads an emotional Stevie away, and I'm glad she has such a great friend.

I reclaim my seat on the bench, letting them leave together. Poor Stevie. Tonight will be rough. It's Garrick's first birthday in a coma and only six weeks until the first anniversary of the accident.

I hurt for her.

Her pain is my pain.

After enough time has passed, I get up and reluctantly make my way toward the hospital entrance. The merger has gone through. On paper at least, but it hasn't been publicly announced yet. There are one or two operational details to finalize. But it's a done deal. So, technically, there is no need for me to visit Brielle every night. Dad told me as much, but it feels wrong to just walk away.

Stevie's devotion to Garrick has rubbed off on me.

I wasn't there for Brielle in life, so I'll be there for her in death.

Unlike Garrick, Brielle isn't alive. Her body may still be breathing, thanks to a ventilator, but her mind is gone. She is only on life support because Mrs. Cartwright still can't accept reality. David is trying to prepare her for the next stage. They can't keep her like this indefinitely. While the hospital has not kicked up a fuss—they are getting paid, and the Cartwrights are big donors—it's not right that she's occupying a bed that someone else might need.

It's not right to delay the inevitable.

Brielle wouldn't have wanted this either.

Brielle is already gone, and Pamela Cartwright will have to accept that truth sometime. I understand why David is taking such a cautious and gentle approach. He's terrified of losing his wife to insanity, and he's already lost too much, so he's let this continue far longer than it should.

Sounds of shouting greet my ears as the elevator doors open on the private floor, and I'm instantly on high alert. When I step outside, a commotion is going on in the hallway close to Garrick's room. Stevie, Hadley, and two older women are standing in front of Ivy Allen-Golding-Smith. Behind her is Hugh Allen and two unfamiliar men in their early twenties. Ivy is screaming and pointing her finger in Stevie's face, and I'm striding toward them without hesitation.

"I'll have you arrested!" Ivy is yelling, spittle flying from her lips as she jabs her finger in Stevie's chest.

"Take your hands off my daughter," a good-looking woman with strawberry-blonde hair says, leveling Ivy with a challenging look.

"Ivy. That's enough," Hugh says, and I don't know how the guy can remain so calm.

"What's going on?" I ask when I reach them. "Stevie, are you okay?"

Ivy's head pivots to me so fast it's a wonder she didn't give herself whiplash. "Greyson?" She blinks several times as she drinks me in from head to toe. "Greyson Beckett Colbert III, is that really you?"

This woman gets on my very last nerve. I cannot stand her. She's a bully and a snob, and I'm not giving her a second of my attention.

Ignoring her, I focus on Stevie. "What's going on?" I ask, peering deep into her tortured eyes. She's pale, shaking like a leaf, and I've never seen her more terrified.

Before Stevie can get a word out, Ivy rounds on her again.

"What's going on?" she screeches as Hugh talks in whispers to one of the hospital directors who has just shown up. "This little bitch is the reason my son is in a coma. He gave her a perfectly good car, which she refused, and it's her fault he was driving that piece of trash that put him in this condition!"

"I said that's enough, Ivy." Hugh's tone is harsher this time as he cuts across his conversation to intervene. "You're making a big deal out of this unnecessarily."

Ivy glares at her ex-husband. "Don't think I've overlooked the part you played in this. You knew about this from the start, and you deliberately kept it hidden from me. You're going to pay for that, Hugh."

"Shut up, Ivy," an unfamiliar woman says, exiting Garrick's room and making a beeline for Hugh. "No one told you because you're a goddamned drama queen, and we all knew you'd overreact. What happened to Garrick is a tragedy, but it was an accident. Stevie is not to blame." The woman threads her fingers in Hugh's, and I'm guessing she must be his current wife. She glances at the troubled faces surrounding her. "This is supposed to be a birthday party for Garrick. The twins are listening to all of this, and it's upsetting them. Garrick is probably hearing this too. Stevie went to a ton of trouble organizing the party, Ivy. Can we just let this go or at least table it until later?"

Ivy harrumphs. Of course, she's not going to let this go. I already know it before she opens her trashy mouth to confirm it. "I'm not letting this go or tabling anything. That little slut isn't getting near my son again. She might have pulled the wool over all your eyes, but she hasn't fooled me. I'm having her removed from the visitor's list. I'll get a goddamned restraining order if I have to. This is her fault. All because she wouldn't accept such a generous gift. My son is far too good for you." She glowers at Stevie.

The older woman to Stevie's left clutches her arm and whispers something in her ear. I'm guessing she must be the infamous Nana.

"Is it any wonder she refused?" A well-built guy with dark hair steps out from behind Hugh, putting his face all up in Ivy's. From the expression on his face, he thinks as much of her as I do. "Stevie was terrified to accept anything from Garrick because you kept throwing shade at her. You were the one accusing her of being a gold digger, to the point where she didn't want to take any gifts from him."

Stevie didn't mention anything about this to me.

"If you want someone to blame," he continues, "how about you blame yourself, you selfish cunt."

"Hudson, I really don't think—"

"No, Hugh. I won't be censored. Everyone lets this bitch get away with murder. I'm not going to stand here and let her hurl baseless accusations at Stevie."

"Baseless?" Ivy screams, throwing her hands around as I spy a couple of security guards approaching from the far end of the hallway. "They are hardly baseless." She jabs her finger in my direction. "She has already moved on to her next victim!" Without warning or expectation, Ivy lunges at Stevie and slaps her across the face. "My son is fighting for his life, and you're already working on his replacement. You make me sick."

Chapter Seven

Stevie

A stinging pain races across my cheek, and Ivy's words cut through me like a knife. She certainly knows how to pinpoint the perfect spot to drive it deep. This is something I was afraid of—other people's perception of my friendship with Beck. Curiosity splays on Dawn's and Hugh's faces, and Will looks downright suspicious. Hudson is the only one who seems indifferent to Ivy's accusation.

Beck steps right up to Garrick's mother. His voice is cold enough to form ice cubes when he speaks. "My girlfriend is in a room at the end of this floor, also in a coma, and I do not appreciate your insinuation. Not that you deserve any explanation, but there is nothing inappropriate in my friendship with Stevie. We understand and support one another in similar situations."

Ivy opens her mouth to speak, but Beck cuts her off with another glacial look. "You may go through men in a constantly rotating line, but Stevie is loyal in her love of your son and utterly devoted to him. It's clear to everyone, but you, that Garrick is the center of her world. If it was up to me, you'd be arrested for assault. And if you think you can threaten Stevie, or try to ban her from seeing Garrick, think again. It would give me enormous pleasure to channel the full weight of the Colbert resources into stopping you."

"Get your hands off me," Ivy shrieks as one of the security guards loosely takes her elbow.

"You need to come with us, ma'am," he replies.

"Like hell I do!" She shrugs off his hand, pointing at me. "If anyone is leaving, it's that gold-digging slut."

Heat crawls up my neck and onto my face. I hate how those words still have the power to upset me. I am usually stronger when faced with this bitch, but this is humiliating, taking place in front of Garrick's loved ones, nursing staff, and medical management, and I'm sure other visitors on the floor have heard this going down.

Now everyone will know the accident was my fault.

Everyone will think I'm a gold digger.

I'm barely holding on to my sanity, and this could send me over the edge.

I'm glad Beck intervened. His words warmed some of the frozen parts inside me. He didn't hesitate to defend and support me, and he can't know exactly how much this means to me.

I'm curious to learn how they know one another. And what it means when he says he'll channel the full extent of the Colbert resources into going after her. Beck doesn't talk about work much, other than to say he loathes it. I know he works in his family business; that he has a degree in IT and business from Cornell and an MBA from Harvard, but that's the extent of my knowledge.

"You need to leave, Ivy," Hugh says, dragging me back into the moment. "You have caused enough trouble for one night."

"I'm not going."

"I'm afraid the hospital will have to insist," the female director says, wearing a "don't mess with me" look as she walks around Ivy to my side. "Would you like me to call the police?"

"Do it," Ivy snarls. "See what I do next."

Beck makes a move toward her, but I stall him with a hand to his arm. I appreciate him helping to fight my battles, but he doesn't need to bring that woman down on himself. This is my burden to bear. Not his.

"I won't press charges, but I don't respond well to threats, Ivy. If you want a fight, I'll give you one." They are brave words because we both know she has powerful resources, important contacts, and a natural evil streak. I wouldn't last more than a couple of rounds in a fight with her.

She barks out a laugh. "I don't need to fight. I already hold the winning trophy."

What the hell does that mean? An icy chill tiptoes up my spine, and an ominous sense of dread washes over me.

Shooting a haughty look at all of us, she straightens her spine and lifts her head. "I'll go. I've already wished my boy happy birthday, and I have no desire to slum it for the rest of the night." She purposely rakes her gaze over me, Mom, and Nana.

"Good riddance," Mom says, adding "cunt" under her breath.

Beck's lips twitch, and Hudson is full-on grinning.

Ivy looks ready to go off again, but the security guards flank her on either side as they prepare to escort her out of the hospital.

"Don't say I didn't warn you, Hugh," she tosses over her shoulder as she walks away. Her eyes bore into mine. "I'll enjoy evicting you permanently from my son's life. He'll thank me when he wakes."

Silence ensues as we watch her being escorted off the floor.

"You should have pressed charges," Hudson says when the elevator doors close taking the Wicked Witch away.

"The last thing I need is my personal business being splashed all over newspapers and society pages. Garrick is estranged from his mom, but I know he wouldn't want me to have her arrested. Nothing good would come from it anyway. It's not like she'd ever be punished. She'd use the governor to have the case thrown out before any report was written."

"I want to know what she's up to," Nana says. "Those threats didn't seem empty to me."

"I agree." Hugh rubs at his temples.

"There is no point worrying about it now," Dawn says. "We'll find out soon enough what she has up her sleeve. For now, I suggest we try to put this behind us and remember why we are here."

"What do you want to do, honey?" Mom turns to me.

"I don't much feel like celebrating," I truthfully admit. "But it's Garrick's birthday, so I'll put a smile on my face and give him his present. I'll stay for the cake cutting, but I'd like to go home then."

"Can I make a suggestion?" Hadley says as Dawn, Will, and Hudson enter Garrick's room, giving us some privacy. Hugh is speaking in hushed tones with the hospital director.

"What suggestion?" I ask, watching Hugh's frown deepen as he converses with the woman.

"Nana, Monica, and Beck should come back to our place after. We can grab takeout, open some wine, and discuss what we're going to do about that bitch."

"I'm in," Beck readily agrees. "If that's okay with you?" he asks, peering into my eyes. "I will visit with Brielle while you're spending time with Garrick. You can text me when you're ready to go."

I don't think about it for long. I was wrong earlier. I do need a distraction, and I need him. If I'm left to my own devices after the shit show this night has turned into, who knows what I might do. "Okay."

Beck takes out his phone as Hugh ends his conversation with the director and slips into Garrick's room. "Add your number," Beck says, placing the phone in my palm.

"Close to You" by The Carpenters trickles through the momentary gap in the door, and my heart stutters in my chest. I don't know if I have the mental fortitude to withstand tonight. Even if I only plan to stay for a little while. It was already going to be difficult enough before Ivy made it worse.

"Hey." Beck's voice softens, and his eyes flood with concern. "Talk to me."

"I'm okay," I lie, and I know he sees through it. "Thank you for what you said. I appreciate it so much." I punch in my digits and hand the phone back to him.

"Yes, thank you." Mom butts in. "You didn't hesitate to defend my daughter, and I'm grateful. I was liable to stab that bitch, so I'm happy you intervened and spared me from spending the rest of my life in prison."

Oh my god.

The Colson family circus is back in town.

"You're welcome." Beck smothers a grin. "I will always support Stevie, and no one deserves jail time over that woman. It would be a travesty."

"Very true. I'm Monica Colson, by the way," she adds, thrusting her arm out. "Stevie's Mom, but you've probably already worked that out."

"I did, and it's nice to meet you, Monica." Beck shakes her hand. "You too, Mrs. Colson," he adds, smiling at Nana.

"Betsy, please." Nana smooths a hand down the front of her wine-colored velvet dress. "I try to forget I was ever married."

I haven't had the chance to properly warn him about my family, but I have a feeling Beck would hold his own.

Hadley opens her mouth to say something, but I cut her dead with a warning look.

"We'll see you in a little bit, Beck." Mom circles her arm around my shoulder as she smiles at my friend. "And thanks again."

"Remember you are strong," Beck whispers in my ear before taking leave of us.

Mom, Nana, and Hadley prop me up as we enter the room, knowing I need the physical and moral support. Dawn and Hugh are dancing, and Will is twirling Helena around to The Carpenters's classic hits. It reminds me of that one Christmas we had together and how we spent hours dancing around the kitchen. Crushing pain presses down on my chest as I contemplate how I probably won't ever get to dance with Garrick like that again.

Life is unfair.

Why did this have to happen to one of the best people I know?

Why did God do this to us?

Hudson is sitting beside Garrick's bed, talking quietly to him, while John and Jacob are stuffing themselves with yummy goodies. I baked Garrick's favorite cookies and cupcakes, and there are store-bought chips, candy, and chocolates. Hugh brought some sparkling wine and nonalcoholic wine for the adults and soda for the boys.

Birthday banners are draped upon the walls and balloons and streamers fill the rest of the space. A frosted red velvet birthday cake rests on a cake stand at the top of the room. I got up early before work today to bake it.

Last year, for Garrick's twenty-first birthday, the cake Dawn had ordered for his official birthday had three different layers. One layer was red velvet, and Garrick fell in love. I had never baked one before, but I found a recipe online, and it was easy enough to follow.

I wish he were able to taste it.

There will be other birthdays, I try to remind myself, but it's getting harder and harder to believe my own words. To believe he will wake. I should not be thinking these thoughts, tonight of all nights, but that stupid bitch has put me in a foul mood, and I'm struggling to snap out of it.

We don't stay too long. Everyone does their best to enter into the birthday spirit, for Garrick's sake, but Ivy ruined the buzz, and the strain is evident in the air. I sit beside Garrick, holding his hand and talking to him. Everyone opens their gifts one at a time, telling him what it is. I unwrap the special edition signed Byron Stanley book and place it in his hand, running his fingers back and forth across the pages. I found this copy in a local bookstore, so it's not personalized, but maybe someday I can find a way to get it inscribed to Garrick.

After, I tuck it back into my purse to safeguard for him. I don't trust Ivy not to burn it in spite.

We light candles on the cake and sing happy birthday to him. I can scarcely push the words out past the knot in my throat, and a few tears well in my eyes. The twins blow out the candles, and we eat cake and toast Garrick.

"Do you want to go, honey?" Mom asks, seeing me wilting.

This is harder than I thought it would be. Garrick should be here, spinning me around the room, blowing out his own candles, stuffing himself full of cake, and unwrapping his own gifts. I'm finding it increasingly difficult to remain upbeat, and it feels like I'm close to losing it.

"Yes. It's time." I tap out a quick text to Beck while we say our goodbyes.

Will is a bit stiff as he gives me a quick hug. "Ellen is sorry she couldn't be here."

"It's fine. I didn't want her skipping her tutorial. Not this close to finals."

"You did good, Stevie," Hudson says, enveloping me in his arms. "You do him proud. He's so lucky he has you. I can only hope one day I meet someone as devoted to me."

"Thanks," I whisper as I break out of our embrace. "And thanks for all the calls. I appreciate you checking in on me. You have kept me going on difficult days."

"It's the same for me, Stevie. I hate being so far away. It's reassuring to know he has you here."

"I'm looking forward to you coming home."

"Me too. Hopefully, I'll find an apartment somewhere close to you."

"That would be great."

Hudson kisses the top of my head. "Do not take a single word that bitch said to heart. Not a single word, you hear me?" He tilts my chin up. "She's rotten to the core."

"I'll try not to."

"I'll find out what she's up to," Hugh promises, appearing at my side. "I'd like to say don't worry, but Ivy can be vindictive."

"Whatever it is, you can count on us for support," Dawn adds, pulling me into an embrace. "Thanks for organizing all of this. You're amazing."

"Dawn is right." Tears glisten in Hugh's eyes as he hooks an arm around his wife's waist. "You are truly amazing, Stevie. I'm not sure many girls would be here after all this time, let alone going to all this trouble."

"Your son changed my life in so many ways. He always took such good care of me. Now it's my turn. I'm not doing anything he wouldn't do for me."

"Thank you all for coming," Hugh says as Nana, Mom, and Hadley flank me. "It means a lot to us and Garrick."

Chapter Eight
Stevie

"This is a nice car," I say as Beck drives his black Audi A7 out of the hospital garage and turns right. It's sleek, comfortable, and luxurious without being over-the-top excessive. I agreed to go with him so he wasn't relying on GPS for directions. Mom, Nana, and Hadley are driving separately to our apartment in Nana's Range Rover.

"It gets me from A to B, and it just about got my father's seal of approval."

"Your dad had to approve your choice of car?" Incredulity underscores my tone. I'm keen to keep the conversation flowing so it distracts me from having a full-blown panic attack. Riding in cars is still traumatic for me.

"He tries to demand approval on every aspect of my life, but I keep him on a tight leash," he says, taking the exit for the I 5 South. "I drove a Volkswagen Passat for a few years. Great car. But apparently not good enough when I started working at the family company. He wanted me to buy a Maserati. It was a ridiculous price, and I refused. We eventually agreed on this one."

Beck has both hands on the wheel as we join the traffic on the highway, and I'm glad to see it. Traffic is flowing freely, as I expected at this hour of night, but I'm still on edge as we merge into the right lane. I grip the sides of my seat tight, digging my nails into the soft leather.

"I'm not big into cars," he admits, shocking the shit out of me.

"Isn't that a male prerequisite?"

His deep chuckle bounces off the tinted windows of his car. "I hate to disappoint you, but I'm not like the typical male."

"That's not a disappointment," I say, glancing at the pristine back seat. "You get major brownie points for individuality and for how clean your car is. I could eat my dinner off the back seat."

"I'm a bit of a neat freak," he admits.

"A man after my own heart," I blurt without thinking. Warmth floods my cheeks. "I didn't mean that literally," I rush to reassure him.

"You never have to explain things to me," Beck says, casting a glance at me. "I see you."

"Keep your eyes on the road!" My high-pitched tone tells him all he needs to know.

Beck stares straight ahead as he purposely slows down—even though he wasn't going fast—and says, "I didn't think to ask if driving is difficult for you. What can I do to make this as comfortable as possible?"

"Just keep your eyes on the road, and don't go too fast."

"I can do that," he softly replies as his fingers grip the wheel tighter.

"I couldn't get in a car for months," I admit after a couple of seconds of tense silence. "Hadley deployed some tough love, and she made me go with her on deliveries one day. I was a basket case, but I survived. So, I sat with her every day for the next few weeks until it became bearable. I still get flashbacks and nightmares, and I'm still petrified every time I get in a car, but it's getting easier."

"Have you driven yourself?"

"No. I haven't worked up the courage yet. My original plan was to save for a car, but I get by fine on public transport."

"When you want to try getting behind the wheel again, let me know, and I'll come with you."

"How do you know I'll ever want to try?"

"Remember, I see you. I know you'll get back on that saddle."

The weight of his statement lingers in the air. "I see you too," I supply after a few silent moments. "Even if you haven't told me everything."

"Are you referring to my name or the fact I know Ivy?"

"Both." I twirl a lock of my hair as I stare at him while he drives. He has a nice side profile.

"My father is Carlton Colbert, and I work for Colbert Aerospace. Under sufferance, as you know. I didn't deliberately conceal my identity or who I worked for. I hope you know that."

"I do," I agree without hesitation. "I don't fully understand it, but I know you are genuine with me."

"I am, Stevie." His fingers tighten on the wheel. "I am more real with you than anyone. Well, besides my sisters. They know the true me. Everyone else gets to see a different side. I like that you didn't know who I was. That you weren't interested in our friendship for what you could get out of me."

"People do that?" The leather squelches as I turn in my seat so I can see more of his face.

He nods. "All the time. It's why I don't have many close friends and I don't do relationships. I learned those lessons early in life. People don't want to know me for me. They want to know me for the money, the connections, the leg up I can give them. It gets exhausting after a while, so I gave up trying to make friends, and I gave up on relationships."

"That is horrible, Beck, and it sounds super lonely even if I understand your motivations are self-protective. I have built plenty of walls around my heart too."

"I liked that you saw me for me. There were no expectations."

"There wouldn't have been if you'd told me from the outset."

"I know that now. But I'm wary when I first meet people. It's a hard habit to break."

"I'll bet." Yet he's been quite open with me. "Turn off here," I say, guiding him off the highway. "It's only about a mile now to our place. You'll be taking a left, then a right, and another right, and then we're there."

"Got it," he says, religiously checking his mirrors as he exits the highway.

"I know you said your father won't let you leave the business, but if you hate your job so much, why do you stay? Why not force his hand?"

He heaves out a sigh. "It's complicated. He's holding shit over me, and until certain things are in place, I must bide my time. It's getting harder and harder to do it though. Every time I step foot in my office, another little part of my soul dies." He looks out the window, up at the hotel sign on the side of the building. "Is this it?" he asks with a slight frown.

"It is." I point at the entrance to the parking garage. "We only have one parking space with the apartment, and Hadley parks her car there, but there's some visitor spots on the first level you can use."

"Is this an actual hotel?"

I shake my head as he drives slowly into the well-lit parking garage. "It's an old, converted hotel. It originally opened its door in nineteen oh nine, and it was renovated a few years ago into separate apartments. There are some businesses on the ground level, and we have a fab communal rooftop and a lounge area on the ground level. It's really cool. Hadley screamed so hard when we got the call to confirm we had this place I thought I'd lost my hearing in one ear."

"I like your best friend. She's good people," he says, following the signs to the visitor parking area.

My heart swells with pride. "She is the best. She's been a rock for me through this whole thing. Hadley won't ever let me fall too far. She's always there to pull me out of the mire. I'll be best friends with her forever."

"I have one friend like that," he says, pulling his car into an empty visitor space and killing the engine. "Lawson Reed and I have been friends since the fifth grade. I don't see him a lot these days, not since his wife gave birth to their first child. They have a cute little daughter, and she keeps him busy. But we talk on the phone every day, and we meet for lunch once a week. Law works around the corner from our building."

"I'm glad you have good people in your life too."

Beck turns to face me. "Before we go up to your place, do you want to talk about what happened at the hospital?"

I bite the inside of my cheek. "Not really. I still need to process it all. This has shaken me." Air rattles from my mouth. "I thought Ivy already knew. Hugh had broached the subject of the BMW with me a couple months after the accident. He'd been storing it in his garage at home, and he asked me what I wanted to do. I told him to give it back to the dealer Garrick bought it from. I couldn't contemplate ever driving it. I couldn't even get in any car at that point without hyperventilating. I assumed if Hugh was aware of the gift he would've told Ivy. I realize now he kept it a secret because he knew how she'd react."

"She's nothing if not predictable," Beck agrees. His features soften as he peers deep into my eyes. "I know it's a stupid question. I usually hate asking it, but are you okay?" Very gently, he touches my cheek. "I would never hit a woman, but I was tempted to hit Ivy after she slapped you."

"It was humiliating." I shield nothing from his intelligent eyes. "God knows how many people heard her mouthing off." Tears stab my eyes, and though they don't fall, it's the most viscerally emotional I've been in months. "I felt so ashamed," I whisper.

"Come here." He opens his arms, and I lean across the console and let him comfort me. "The people who matter know the truth. If anyone else wants to judge, let them. You can't stop it, and it says more about them than you." He runs his hand up and down my spine as I rest my head against his chest.

"Every time I think I'm finally moving past that guilt, something happens to suck me back in." I ease out of his embrace and lock eyes with him. "The things she said to you. The things she accused us of."

"Mean nothing, Stevie." He clasps my face in his hands. "Tell me you know that. No one bought that bullshit, and we know the truth."

I drag my lower lip between my teeth before shrugging, and he astutely reads my reaction.

"Who is Hudson to Garrick?" he inquires.

"His best friend. They've known one another since they were little kids."

"I liked how he defended you. He seems like a good guy. Are you two close?"

I nod. "We talk regularly, and we've helped one another get through this."

"Not so different from our friendship. If it's okay to be friends with Hudson, then why wouldn't it be okay to be friends with me?"

"It seems perfectly logical when you say it like that, but you know how people twist things."

"Let the haters twist shit. Who cares. We help one another, and that's all that matters, right?"

"Right," I say, feeling more confident. "Thank you." My lips kick up at the corners. "I'm going to start calling you YOM."

One brow lifts. "Do I even want to know?"

"Young old man." I giggle. "I'd prefer to call you wise young old man, but I have no clue how to pronounce that abbreviation."

"It's just as well I'm not easily offended." He smirks as he opens his door. "Otherwise, you'd be in big trouble."

"I could take you," I joke, climbing out of the car.

He looks over at me across the top of the car, the lightheartedness replaced with a more serious expression. "I meant what I said at the hospital. If that bitch tries anything, you tell me, and I'll help. We have a whole team of company lawyers, as well as other lawyers who look after our personal business, and we're well connected. I could ruin her with a few well-placed calls."

"I'm tempted to ask you to do it anyway, but that would only be sinking to her level, and I'm better than that bitch."

"Damn straight, you are, but if anything happens or you change your mind, promise I'll be your first call."

I round the back of the car, feeling a little lighter. I could use all the help I can get when it comes to Garrick's mother, so it's not difficult to commit. "I promise."

"I love it," Beck says after I've given him a quick tour of our two-bedroom apartment. "It's got decent natural light and lots of character. My place is similar."

"You're in Capitol Hill, right?" Hadley says, handing him the beer he asked for.

Beck nods. "On Belmont Avenue."

"Not too far from here or the hospital," Mom says, pulling plates out of the cupboard while Nana rummages in the drawer for silverware and paper napkins.

"We ordered Thai," Hads confirms. "Hope that's okay?"

It's a little late to ask now, but Beck is easygoing. "Thai is perfect." He removes his wallet. "What do I owe you?"

"Don't be ridiculous." Nana waves him away. "You're our guest."

"That's very kind. Thank you." Beck puts his wallet away and pops the top on his beer.

"Rest your feet." Mom pulls out a stool at the island for him. "You too, sweetheart." She pulls a second one out for me.

Beck and I sit on adjoining stools, drinking our drinks, while the others set the table. He sips his beer while I'm guzzling my white wine like it's water. At least tomorrow is Saturday, and I don't have to be up early for work.

"Tell us how you know Ivy." Mom leans back against the counter, drinking her wine and staring expectantly at Beck.

"And do you know any hitmen?" Hads asks, propping her elbows on the counter beside me. "'Cause I'd really love to see that bitch with a nice big fucking hole in her skull."

"I don't have any hitmen on speed dial, unfortunately, so I can't help you out there."

"It was worth a try." Hadley pouts. "I work hard not to hate anyone. Hate is such a strong emotion and such a powerful word, so I don't say this lightly. But I really, really hate that woman."

"I love you," I say, yanking my bestie into a fierce hug.

"Love you too, Opium Poppy."

"Little Miss Mischief, do I need to remind you to behave?"

"Never, Nana." Hads breaks our embrace to bundle Nana into her arms. "I'm always on my best behavior."

"That's questionable." Nana pats her arm. "But we love you all the same."

"Back to Ivy," Mom says, redirecting the conversation. "How do you know her, Beck?"

"My family mixes in a lot of the same social and political circles as Ivy. She's often at the same charity events and galas. I got stuck sitting beside her at one event, and I nearly stabbed myself with my dinner knife just to escape her. Since then, any time our paths cross, she makes a point of seeking me out."

"Oh god, please don't tell me she hit on you?" Hadley groans.

Beck turns pale as he shakes his head. "Jeez, don't put that kind of visual in my head. I'm likely to throw up. No, it's not me she wants."

"It's your father," I surmise. His bank balance is more to Ivy's liking though I'm sure she wouldn't be above hitting on the younger, hotter Colbert heir.

Beck nods. "She's wasting her time though. He only likes them young."

"Are your parents divorced?" Hadley is being as nosy as ever.

Beck's Adam's apple bobs in his throat. "No. My mom died when I was ten."

He hasn't confirmed it to me, or mentioned the circumstances, but I suspected as much from the few things he has said about her.

"Oh, Beck." Mom rushes around the island unit to hug him. "I'm so sorry."

Beck is rigidly still in her arms, and I can tell he's uncomfortable.

"Mom. Not everyone is a hugger."

"Sorry, Beck," she says, instantly breaking the embrace. "Occupational hazard if you're involved in this family."

"You don't need to apologize." Beck rubs the back of his neck in a clear tell. "There weren't many hugs to go around in our house after Mom died." He shrugs, like it's no biggie, but it makes my heart hurt harder for him. "My youngest sister, Esther, would love you. She's the only hugger in our family, and she's constantly criticizing Sarah and me for not being more affectionate."

"We'll adopt her," Mom says. "Everyone needs good hugs in their life."

"We'll adopt all three of you," Nana adds as the doorbell chimes, announcing our food has arrived. "Let me know when you're all free to come over for dinner."

Chapter Nine
Stevie

"Beck is a wonderful man," Mom says over the phone the following afternoon. "He's very thoughtful and extremely generous. It's a beautiful gift. My hips won't thank him, but the rest of me does." Beck sent Mom and Nana, and Hadley and me, a hamper of handmade chocolates from a local French chocolate shop to thank us for last night. He even included a handwritten thank-you card, and it was incredibly sweet.

"I'll be sure to pass that along."

"He cares about you."

"Mom." My tone holds considerable caution.

"I'm not implying anything other than he's a very good friend. I'm glad you found one another, and I'm glad I met him now. It has helped to put my mind at ease."

"He's a good guy, and it's awesome to have him in my corner."

We hang up shortly afterward, and I meander into the kitchen to see if Hadley is home from her morning stint at the library. I want to ask if she'll come for a walk with me in the park. Saturdays are busy where we live, but I welcome the hustle and bustle. Sometimes, being left alone with my thoughts is too much, and I welcome noisy distractions.

Normally, I spend Saturday mornings at the hospital, and today is the first Saturday in months I didn't go. To be honest, I'm scared of what I might find when I arrive. Will Ivy have gotten my name removed from the visitor's list? Will the staff look at me differently? Will the other patients' families?

Those fears, combined with a slight hangover, meant I stayed in bed this morning instead of getting up to visit Garrick. Guilt perches on my shoulder, and that negative voice in my ear whispers I'm a coward and I've let him down. I promise myself I'll visit him tonight. That I won't let Ivy scare me away from her son. Garrick needs me, and I will be there for him.

Hadley agrees to a walk, and after we demolish a few chocolates—agreeing we'll burn off the calories at the park—we get changed into training tops, yoga pants, and sneakers, grab our water bottles, and set out in the direction of Daejeon Park. We don't talk much as we navigate the International District, en route to the park, content to absorb the atmosphere of a busy Saturday as we walk past familiar haunts.

A sense of calmness settles in my bones when we reach the park. It's named after Seattle's sister city in Korea, and it has a Korean style pagoda, plenty of open space, landscaped lawns, and several walking paths.

"Spill it, sister," Hadley says after a couple of miles when we've hit a good stride. "I know you have lots weighing on you, and I can practically hear the wheels churning in your mind."

"What if she does it?" I ask, glancing sideways at her as we power walk through the park. "What if Ivy finds a way to ban me from Garrick? What will I do then?"

"You have Hugh and Dawn on your side. They know how much you mean to Garrick. How important you are to his recovery. They'll fight the bitch. And you have Beck. It sounds like he's a powerful ally to have."

"I really don't want to drag Beck into this. He's got enough on his plate."

"I like him," she proclaims, dodging out of the way of a little kid on a kiddie bike. "He cares about you."

I groan. "Did my mom put you up to this?"

She frowns. "Put me up to what?"

"Nothing," I mumble, smiling at an older couple as they walk past us hand in hand.

"What he did today was super sweet." She bites on the corner of her lip.

"Just say it." I swing my arms more vigorously and push my legs to their limits.

"He reminded me of Garrick. It's like something he would do."

A knot forms in my throat. "I know," I whisper. "It's the first thought that entered my mind too, which is wrong on several levels."

"Because we shouldn't compare them. Beck is his own person like Garrick is, and your relationships with both are very different." Hadley verbalizes my thoughts perfectly.

"Yeah, that."

"It's okay to be friends with him," she adds, panting a little. "Can we slow down a bit? Not all of us have supercharged limbs you know."

"Sorry." I deliberately slow my strides. "I'm extra tense today."

"I noticed, and it's understandable. It's natural to feel that way. Your situation is extremely stressful, and you never slack off. It's okay to take time out for you, you know."

Our pace slows even farther as we fall into a more casual walking stride. "I didn't visit him this morning, and I feel so guilty."

"You shouldn't. You're the most dedicated girlfriend on the planet. It's fine if you can't handle it some days. Garrick would never fault you for it. None of us would. You can't be there for him if you aren't taking care of yourself. You need to prioritize *you* more."

We come to an empty bench, and I drop down onto it. We take a breather and drink our water, watching people stroll past us. "What if he never wakes up, Hads?" My voice cracks as I look sideways at my friend. "What will I do? How will I ever get over it?"

"It's a possibility, babe." She places her hand over mine. "I'm glad you are voicing this. It's not giving up on him to discuss all the possible outcomes. You need to be prepared, and I've been worried. You're refusing to think about all the what-ifs. You can't compartmentalize or live in denial forever. You are strong enough to face whatever happens next. There is no one stronger."

"I don't feel strong, Hads. I feel weak and powerless and directionless. My life is in limbo. It feels so selfish to articulate that when Garrick's life is in limbo through no fault of his own."

"You're entitled to your feelings, Stevie. You can't help how you feel, and you have every right to be pissed off and frustrated for *you*. Not everything is about him. It's not selfish to be angry for *you*. You found this amazing guy. You fell in love for the first time. You were planning a future, and then bam! It was all taken out from under you. That's a lot to handle for anyone."

My heart pounds against my rib cage as I admit something out loud for the first time. "I don't know how much longer I can keep doing this. Every day, seeing him like that, it chips away at another piece of my soul, and I'm dying inside. Everyone thinks I'm amazing and loyal, and I want to be those things. I want to be there for Garrick for however long it takes, but I'm struggling. I'm really struggling, and I don't know what to do."

Hadley loops her arm through mine, and I rest my head on her shoulder. "You take it one day at a time, and you stop beating yourself up for being human. If you continue to ignore your needs, you won't be of any help to anyone. You are the best person I know, Stevie Colson. You love that man with your whole heart. It's not your fault you both got dealt this shitty hand, and it's not your fault if some days you just can't be there for him."

She kisses my temple. "It's coming up to one year. I can't imagine the hospital is going to allow the situation to continue indefinitely. I think something is going to happen soon, either way, and you need to prepare yourself," she adds.

I straighten up, tucking my hands between my knees. "I noticed Hugh in an intense conversation with the director last night, and I think you're right. I think something is happening. I have a terrible feeling." I shake all over as if a blast of cold air has just danced over my soul.

"I adore Garrick. You know that," she adds.

"I do." Looking at my friend, I instinctively know I'm not going to like what she says next.

"You have to consider what happens if he remains in a coma indefinitely. If the choice is made to keep him like that. It's already been a year. How long are you going to wait for him? Two years? Five? Ten? More? How long are you going to be able to keep doing this? How long will you let life pass you by while you hope and pray for him to wake? God." She sighs before temporarily burying her head in her hands. "I feel terrible just voicing these things. It feels so disloyal to Garrick."

"Because it is," I calmly reply though I'm not angry at Hadley for putting words to some of the thoughts I've had on occasion. It's actually a bit of a relief to hear it. To know it's normal to think this way.

"Yes," she readily agrees. "But it needs to be said, and I'm not sorry I said it. You need to start seriously considering your options." She stares off into space for a few seconds before swinging her gaze to mine. "What do you think he'd want you to do?"

"He'd want me to fight for him, to fight for us, until all hope was lost. Then he'd want me to live my life even if it meant walking away." It physically pains me to speak those words aloud, but I have thought about what Garrick would expect of me a lot in the time since the accident. I'm pretty confident I know him well enough to know this is what he'd want. He wouldn't want me unhappy and pining for a lost love. "But this conversation is premature. All hope isn't lost, and while there is still the potential for him to wake, I won't abandon him. I don't want to, and I couldn't. I know he wouldn't leave me."

Returning to the apartment, we find a familiar dark-haired man sitting on the floor in front of the door with his long denim-clad legs stretched out in front of him.

"You're early," I say when Beck notices us, quickly scrambling to his feet, holding a large brown envelope in his hand. He had texted me while we were at the park to ask if he could drop by. He has something for me. He did mention it last night, but in all the commotion, I had forgotten.

"I was actually already here when I texted you," he admits, looking a little sheepish. "I didn't want to put you on the spot and make you feel like you had to rush back."

"You've been sitting here the entire time?" I ask as Hadley opens the door to our apartment.

"Nope. I checked out the roof terrace. It's awesome, like you said, and I went for coffee downstairs. I've only been sitting here five minutes."

"Thank you so much for the yummy chocolate," Hadley says, pushing into our apartment.

"Yes, thanks," I add. "It was a really sweet gesture, and you have fans for life in Mom and Nana."

"I'm glad you liked it. It's my favorite chocolate."

"I suspect it's about to become ours too." I stare at him through a new lens. His dark-brown sweater brings out multiple tones in his eyes, and it emphasizes his broad shoulders and well-developed physique. Dark jeans hug muscular thighs and toned legs, and he's wearing navy Vans on his feet. "You look different without the suit," I admit as we traipse after Hadley into the apartment, shutting the door behind us.

"Less YOM?" he quips, and I bark out a laugh.

Hadley looks back at us with slightly wide eyes.

I arch my neck and meet his eyes, grinning. The height difference is more noticeable when I'm not in high heels. "You'll always be a YOM to me, but yeah, you definitely look less ancient dressed like a normal mortal." My eyes drift over him quickly. "Casual looks good on you."

"You too."

I laugh again. "Puh-lease. This isn't casual. This is a hot sweaty mess. I'm going to grab a quick shower, but make yourself at home. Help yourself to whatever."

"Except the chocolate," Hadley calls out from the hallway leading to the bedrooms. "Those babies are ours."

When I return ten minutes later, Hadley has made herself scarce, and Beck is sitting alone at the island unit, nursing a cup of coffee and munching on chocolates.

A laugh bursts from my chest. "She'll kill you—and ask me to help bury your body—if she finds out you dipped into the forbidden chocolate."

Beck shrugs. "I'll buy her more. I'll keep Hadley regularly supplied so she can't ever complain." His boyish grin lights up his face, making him look more youthful.

"That would do the trick," I agree, walking to the coffee pot and pouring myself a cup. "Want a refill?" I ask, lifting the pot.

"Thanks."

After filling him up, I peer at the massive open box of chocolates on the counter, wetting my lips as I decide which one to choose.

"Try the *chocolat irrésistible pêche*," he says in a delectable French accent, trilling the R's on his tongue in a slightly guttural fashion. He chuckles. "You should see the look on your face."

"Do you speak French?" His accent is too polished for someone who only casually knows a few words.

"*Oui, mademoiselle.*" He chuckles again as he hands me an oval-shaped milk chocolate. "Try it. The peaches they use to make it come from my grandparents' farm in the South of France."

"Get out!" My eyes are out on stalks.

"Leona's Chocolaterie originated in Canet-en-Roussillon, the town where my grandparents live. Mom used to take us kids to the farm every summer and my *grand-mére* used to sneak us into the chocolate shop once a week. When the owner's son took over, he expanded the business, and now they export globally, and they have physical stores in ten different countries. I like to brag I have eaten chocolate from the flagship chocolaterie."

"That totally earns bragging rights," I agree before taking a bite of the fruity buttercream chocolate sensation. An explosion of rich flavors melts on my tongue, and I'm in heaven. "This is so good," I murmur as I swallow the last piece.

"Try this one next." Beck hands me an oblong-shaped dark chocolate. "It's an espresso truffle."

I'm in chocolate ecstasy as I let him feed me chocolate after chocolate, glutting myself on the divine creations until it feels like I might burst. "Enough." I shake my head and hold up my hand. "I'll be sick if I eat any more."

He stares at me with a funny expression on his face.

"What?"

"You, ah, have a bit of chocolate at the side of your lip. May I?" He leans forward, and I find myself nodding. His thumb swipes across the right side of my mouth in a couple of slow sweeps before he removes a monogrammed handkerchief from his pocket and dabs at my face.

I swallow thickly while the vein in my neck throbs more insistently as he cleans me up. If I hadn't momentarily lost the ability to speak, I would tease him for his old man's handkerchief.

"There. All done." His voice sounds gruffer, deeper, and his eyes darken to a molten brown.

I clear my throat as I avert my eyes, looking anywhere but at him. "Thank you." My gaze flits to the envelope resting on the counter. "What was it you wanted to show me?"

He stands, grabbing the envelope and handing it to me. "I know you've been extra concerned these past few weeks, wondering what the doctors might say as the one-year anniversary approaches. I hope I haven't overstepped the mark, but I conducted some research I think might help."

"What kind of research?"

"I found examples of people, from all over the world, who were in a coma for years before they woke up. It might give you some perspective and hopefully some peace of mind."

I clutch the envelope to my chest with shaky fingers. "I thought of googling it, but I was too chickenshit. Afraid I'd find the opposite of hope."

"I won't lie. You definitely shouldn't google it. It's rare for people to be in long-term comas and even rarer for them to have a happy ending. But there are exceptions to the norm. If anyone can pull it off, I think Garrick can."

Chapter Ten

Stevie

"And this guy Terry, he was in a bad car accident too," I explain to Garrick as I flick through the pages Beck gave me. I've studied them thoroughly in the days since he handed me his research, and it was exactly what I needed to lift my spirits.

So far, Ivy has made no move, and I'm still permitted to visit my boyfriend. But I'm on edge. We all are. We know she's plotting something, and it can't be good. "He woke after nineteen years, Garrick! Imagine that?" I babble, leaving out the part where he was left a quadriplegic as I'm trying to motivate and encourage my boyfriend.

"Oh, you'll like this next one. It's about a famous jazz pianist named Fred Hersch. Now, he was only in a coma for two months, but he fully recovered, and he even went on to create a concert titled 'My Coma Dreams.'" I reach out and squeeze Garrick's hand. "I hope you are dreaming happy dreams, my love."

I flick over the next case because it's upsetting. Although the police officer came out of a coma after eight years, he sadly died a few days later due to organ failure.

Beck didn't censure his research, and I appreciate it. He wants me to be informed but not naïve to the risks and potential outcomes. He found a lot of cases of survivors waking up after years. Not all of them are happy stories. Some survivors ended up severely paralyzed, and others only lived a short time after waking, succumbing to death due to complications arising from being in a coma so long. However, there are plenty of cases where coma survivors went on to lead long lives too, and those are the ones I'm telling Garrick about.

"Aw, this one is super romantic. Zhao Guihua woke up from a car accident after thirty years! *Thirty. Years!* Holy shit! Her husband stayed by her side all that time, and he was there when she finally opened her eyes. That is true love and devotion." I lean in and kiss his warm cheek. "I love you," I remind him before retaking my seat.

"This one gives me a lot of hope," I continue. "Sarah was knocked down in a hit and run accident, and she was in a coma for twenty years before she woke. Her road to recovery was long and arduous, but she made it. She revealed she was aware of lots of things going on around her while in a coma, and I hope you know we're all here for you. I hope you hear us and you know how much we love and miss you." I raise his hand to my lips and kiss his smooth skin.

"I could go on and on. There are lots of cases of people waking up after a long time in a coma, so it can be done. Keep fighting, Garrick. Don't give up. I need you to come back to me."

Beck also unearthed a case of a man who woke up from a seven-year coma after being given Ambien. I was very excited when I read that and immediately brought the case to Hugh. We discussed it with Harvey Edwards. Unfortunately, they had already given Garrick the drug in the hope it might wake him, but it didn't. Hudson's neurosurgeon dad explained they couldn't administer the drug long-term to Garrick as it can cause breathing difficulties and amnesia.

It was disappointing, but reading about real life cases of coma survivors has lifted my spirits at a time when they were falling to record new lows. I'm reinvigorated and determined not to give up on him or to relinquish hope.

Beck drives me home after our mutual visits are over, like he has been doing every night since last Friday. I'm not sure if it's his way of trying to help me overcome my anxiety, his desire to see me home safely, or a way to prolong our time together. Perhaps it's a combination of all those factors. Either way, I'm grateful.

"I have something to ask you," he says as his car idles at the curb in front of my apartment building.

"Ask away," I tuck my hair behind my ears as I look at him.

"Could I cook dinner for you Saturday night at my place?"

My eyes widen, and air punches from my lungs.

"Not like a date," he rushes to reassure me. "I have something I want to tell you about me. Something no one else knows but my sisters, Law, and Tate." He briefly mentioned Tate before. He's a guy he befriended in Cornell. Some bigshot New York trader, and his only other friend besides his childhood friend.

"Is this about your mom?" I blurt without thinking.

Pain flares in his eyes, and I curse myself for raising the topic. He's closed off when it comes to his mother. I know there is a story behind her passing, and I hope one day he'll share it with me. Until then, I will not force it. I lean across the console and pat his hand. "I'm sorry."

His tongue darts out, wetting his lips. "Don't apologize. Mom is a tough subject for me to discuss. Maybe someday."

He averts his eyes as I thread my fingers through his and squeeze his large hand. "I didn't mean to cause you pain, and I understand. I'm reluctant to talk about my dad." Beck is aware of the backstory, but I only told him recently. "I'm here if you ever want to talk about it." His skin is warm, and his palm is smooth, unlike Garrick's hands with calluses from his guitar playing. The instant that thought lands in my mind I retract my hand, tucking it under my thigh.

"Thanks," he says, wearing a small frown. "It's nothing personal.

If I was going to talk to anyone about it, I'd talk to you, but I've spent years trying to block it out because it hurts so much."

"You don't need to explain, Beck, and it's fine. Honestly."

"What I want to tell you is something entirely different, and it's easier for me to show you. Hence the dinner invitation. I assure you it's innocent. It's just one friend cooking for another. I thought I might wow you with my French cookery skills."

"Okay, now you're just showing off."

He laughs. "I'm actually lying. I can only cook two French dishes. One is *croque monsieur*, which is basically just a grilled ham and cheese, and the other is *boeuf bourguignon* which is a classic beef stew anyone could make with their eyes closed."

"Not anyone. I bet Monica could butcher the shit out of it with her eyes open."

Beck cracks up laughing.

"You think I'm joking, but one day you'll see."

"I love your family." A genuine smile ghosts over his face. "And I'm definitely taking Nana up on her dinner offer. Esther and Sarah will be home over summer break, and I'll pin them to a date."

"Nana will love that. She loves entertaining guests. But back to you. How did you learn to cook? Was it in France?"

He shakes his head. "Nope. Neither my mom nor *grand-mére* taught me any cooking skills. We mostly helped around the farm at times when we weren't trying to drown one another in the pool or racing around the property playing hide and seek. Louis, our family chef, taught me how to cook on the sly. Father would not have approved."

"You seem very inventive when it comes to sneaking stuff past your father."

"I've had to be. Otherwise, my life would be a misery."

"I already dislike your father, and I haven't even met him."

"Say a prayer you never do." A shudder works its way through him. "I don't want you anywhere near that man."

I'm not quite sure what that means, and I don't want to find out.

"Okay, so what time do you want me to come over on Saturday? And should I bring anything?"

"Eight and just bring your beautiful self."

My cell is vibrating on my bedside table when I emerge from my steam-filled bathroom, swaddled in a large fluffy white towel with another smaller one wrapped around my head. Spotting Ellen's laughing face staring at me from the screen, I scoop it up and swipe my finger to answer her call before it stops ringing. "Hey, boo," I say, putting it on speaker and placing it carefully on the pillow while I dry myself. "How are things?"

"Exhausting." Her tired sigh filters through the line. "I have three major assignments to finish in two weeks, and I'm panicking I won't get them all done in time."

"Keep the faith. You'll knock them out. Remember you're on the home stretch now."

"I'm going to collapse in a heap for the entirety of the summer if I make it through finals in one piece."

"You've got this."

"How are things with you?"

"Same ole, same ole." I rub the towel side to side against my back as I dry off.

"I'm sorry I wasn't able to come with Will for Garrick's birthday. He filled me in on what happened. It sounded eventful."

"That's one way of putting it." I drop the towel and pad toward my dresser.

"What has Ivy done?"

"Nothing yet," I say, pulling fresh underwear and pajamas from the drawer. "But I'm on edge waiting to see what she has up her sleeve. I know she's planning something big, and her lack of action makes me anxious." I shimmy my panties up my legs.

"Hugh won't let her keep you from Garrick." She pauses for a second. "And it sounds like Beck has some powerful resources at his disposal."

Tension bleeds into the air, and I stop midway through pulling my sleep pants up my legs. "You're pissed," I surmise, snapping out of it and yanking my pants up to my waist.

"Why didn't you tell me about him?"

"Because of the tone I hear in your voice right now." I pull my silky sleep top down over my head.

"That's not fair, Stevie. I have a right to be angry. I had to hear about Beck from Will. It hurt I knew nothing about him."

"Come on, Ellen. You know why I didn't tell you."

"Because I'd tell Will."

"Exactly."

"If you have nothing to hide, what difference would it have made if I told Will or not?"

"*If* I have nothing to hide?" My voice elevates a few decibels as I yank the towel from my damp hair and roughly drag it across my scalp. "I don't have anything to hide. I didn't tell you because Will has been a total ass to me, Ellen."

"He apologized, Stevie. What more do you want him to do? This has been hard on him too."

"I'm explaining why I didn't tell you about Beck. It's because I knew Will would jump to the wrong conclusions."

"You've got to realize how bad it looks," she replies, and pain lashes against my chest.

I can't believe I'm hearing this from one of my so-called best friends.

"Who is this guy, and how long have you known him?" she prods.

"Didn't Will give you all the details, or did he purposely hold key information back to present me in the worst possible light?" I snap, losing the hold on my tenuous emotions.

"Don't throw accusations at him. That's unfair, and you know it."

No, I don't.

"Beck is a friend. His girlfriend is in a coma, and we've been helping one another deal with it. We've known each other three months, and that's it. The end. Nothing inappropriate has happened at all."

"Yet."

"What?" I splutter, wondering if I'm hearing things.

"It's not a good idea, Stevie. It's the age-old conundrum. Guys and girls can't ever just be friends."

"Ellen, do you even hear yourself?" What the fuck has Will been doing to my bestie? She sounds totally brainwashed. "You are way smarter than to believe every generalization."

"And you're too smart to be this naïve. Will said the guy is good-looking, older, and rich, and he clearly wants in your pants."

I am outraged on Beck's behalf. "Will is a goddamned liar and a judgmental asshole!"

"Watch how you speak about my fiancé," she snaps back.

"Fiancé?" Surprise coats my words. "Since when?"

A pregnant pause ensues for a few beats. "He proposed during spring break, and I said yes."

"Why didn't you tell me?" I'm hurt she'd keep something this big from me.

"You know why."

"No, I don't." I'm genuinely confused.

"Because of Garrick," she quietly says. "You were already going through so much and I knew this would hurt you."

"It wouldn't have hurt me, Ellen." I wonder if she ever really knew me at all. We spent three years together at college, and it's like she has no clue of the person I am. "It would have cheered me up, ordinarily."

"What's that supposed to mean?" she clips out.

"Are you sure about marriage, Ellen? I've seen a different side to Will this past year, and I'm not sure I like this version of him much."

"I've seen a different side to you too, and I'm not sure I like it either," she hisses.

I'm stunned into silence for a few seconds as her words make impact, like a hundred tiny daggers embedding into my flesh. "Wow, I can't believe you just said that. I was in a horrible car accident and my boyfriend is in a coma. I'm sorry if I haven't been full of the joys of spring."

"I know it hasn't been easy. It's why I stuck up for you. Will and I had terrible arguments for months, but I had your back. I can't go out on a limb for you again, Stevie. Will is going to be my husband, and I need to take his side in this. I happen to agree with him this time. This so-called friendship with Beck is a very bad idea, Stevie."

"You cannot be serious?!" I shout, and I'm beyond incensed at this point.

"You're lonely, and he's lonely. You're pretty, and he's hot. He's older and more experienced. You're young, and you have no clue when it comes to relationships. That makes you vulnerable to someone like him."

A red haze coats my eyes as rage consumes me. Who the fuck does she think she is insulting me like this? She has some nerve. "You don't know him! Beck isn't like that, and our friendship is the only reason I can face opening the door to Garrick's room some days. You do not get to cast judgment over something you know nothing about."

I suck in a large breath and continue, totally riled up now. "What if it was you in a coma? How sure are you that Will would visit *you* multiple times a day, day in, day out, for almost a year? And what if Will met a girl whose boyfriend was in a coma? Would he turn her friendship away even though she's the only person who truly understands, just because she's the wrong sex?" I bark.

Silence greets me, and that speaks volumes.

"You don't get to say those things about Beck or me. How dare you throw this shit at me! Does our friendship mean nothing to you anymore, Ellen?"

"Of course, it does. It's because I care, because I'm your friend, I'm telling you this. Someone has to make you see sense before it's too late. What do you think is going to happen, Stevie? You need to walk away now before you make a big mistake. One you can't come back from. No one will forgive you if you cheat on Garrick. You owe it to him to stay by his side until the bitter end, whatever that may look like. You know he'd do that for you. That is the least you can do. Setting yourself up for temptation is not smart."

"Are you done?" I ask in a cold tone.

"I'm not sorry I spoke my mind. It needed to be said. Frankly, I'm alarmed Hadley has let this continue. She should have intervened the minute you met this guy."

"Hadley is my best friend for a reason. Something I won't bother wasting my breath trying to explain to someone whose loyalty is so easily traded. Do me a favor, and lose my number, Ellen. I don't need friends like you."

I hang up before she can reply because I can't listen to another word from her betrayer's lips. Then I bury my head in my pillow and scream.

Chapter Eleven

Beck

The doorbell chimes, and my pulse speeds up as I stir the curry in the pot before racing out of the kitchen, through the wooden archway into the large living room, casting a quick glance around to ensure nothing is out of place, before I skid to a halt in front of the front door. Drawing a large breath, I open the door to Stevie with a smile.

Her answering smile holds a tinge of nerves as she locks gazes with me. "Hey, Beck. I know I'm a little early, but—"

"It's fine. Come in." I step aside to let her enter. My eyes skim over her cute navy and white dress with clear admiration. Navy high heels, edged in a gold trim, complete her pretty yet understated look. Wavy red locks tumble over her shoulders, and I catch a hint of the spicy floral undertones of her perfume as she brushes past me. "You look lovely," I say, adding "Can I take your jacket?" before I close the door.

"Um, sure, and thanks." Setting a box and a bottle of wine down on my hall table, she shucks out of her dark denim jacket and hands it to me along with her purse. "I love your building," she says with a nervous smile, knotting her fingers together in front of her stomach. "The grounds are beautiful, and I like that it's not a high-rise."

"It was a great find," I truthfully admit, hanging up her coat and purse on the wall-mounted coat rack in the hall.

"How long have you lived here?" she inquires, lifting the wine and box from the table.

"I bought it just before I graduated with my MBA. I wanted to have a place to come home to of my own."

"Oh, wow. That's amazing." She holds the wine and the box out to me. "These are for you."

"You didn't have to bring anything, but thank you." I open the box, and my eyes widen at the six cupcakes inside. They look like a work of art. Each one individually decorated with the utmost care. They almost look too good to eat, but I won't be able to resist. My stomach rumbles appreciatively, and saliva pools in my mouth.

"I wasn't sure what flavors you liked so I baked a few different kinds."

My eyes pop wider. "You made these?"

A faint red hue paints her cheeks in a pretty flush as she shrugs. "I like to keep busy. If I have too much time on my hands, I get caught up in my thoughts. After I visited Garrick and went for a walk with Hadley, I came home and baked these all afternoon. This one," she says, pointing to a plain cupcake with white buttercream frosting, "is lemon vanilla. And this one"—she points to a chocolate creation—"is chocolate with a milk chocolate mousse topping." She singles out a red and white cupcake next. "This is red velvet with a cream cheese frosting."

Nibbling on the corner of her lower lip, she looks up at me with so much vulnerability in her eyes it makes my heart ache for her. "I had promised Garrick I'd make him red velvet cupcakes, but I ran out of time. I've been practicing, so when he wakes, I'll have perfected the recipe for him."

Fuck. That's heartbreakingly sweet.

Stevie always talks about Garrick as if him waking is a certainty. I admire her confidence and her tenacity to cling to hope against the odds. I know the research I uncovered boosted her flailing faith, but I hope it didn't inject her with an unhealthy dose.

Nothing is certain, and the longer Garrick remains in a coma, the less likely a positive outlook is.

I have not voiced my concerns, nor will I. It's not my place. I admire her strength and her courage. If she was my girlfriend, I'd be blown away by her dedication and commitment. It feels wrong to say Garrick is a lucky guy when the poor man is lying comatose in a hospital bed, but he is a lucky man to have had Stevie in his life.

Stevie's big green eyes, framed by long thick black lashes, look up at me expectantly, and I realize I've just left her hanging while I've been lost in my thoughts. "It looks delicious. They all do."

"The other three are maple pumpkin with a cinnamon cream cheese frosting, mint chocolate chip, and chocolate strawberry."

"I'm honored you went to so much trouble. Thank you." I lean down and kiss her soft, warm cheek.

The flush on her skin darkens, and she shifts a little on her feet, looking adorably awkward. "Let me pop these in the kitchen, and then I'll give you the grand tour," I say, urging her to follow me into the main living area.

"This is a fantastic room," she rasps, spinning around as she drinks it all in. Her gaze dips to the glossy hardwood floors, roam appreciatively over the large rug resting between the open fireplace and my L-shaped cream couch, and skim over the canvases on the wall and the sleek understated furniture.

Tilting her head back, she admires the wooden beams overhead that match the wooden archway that flows from the living room through an interconnecting space with stone archways leading into the kitchen, another into the dining room, one to my office—the only space locked behind thick double doors—and heading into the hallway that houses the three bedrooms and family bathroom.

"This building was built in the nineteen twenties," I holler, stepping into the kitchen. I put the white wine in the refrigerator and set the box of cupcakes down on the marble countertop before rejoining my guest. "I had all the original features repaired, like the beams and archways, the windows, and you'll notice tons of little decorative features and moldings around the apartment."

"It's really stunning, Beck." Her feet gravitate toward my small dining room where a circular table is covered in a white tablecloth and set for dinner for two.

I didn't light any candles, but I have a bunch of colorful flowers in a vase in the center of the table, and the overhead small chandelier is set to a soft glow.

"Wow, this is a gorgeous room. I love how you've managed to blend new with old and comfort with luxury."

"Thank you. I put a lot of effort into how my home would look even if I did hire an interior designer to bring all my ideas to life."

"You both did an incredible job." She stands in front of the windows. "The view is great."

"It is. Come." I jerk my head to one side. "Let me show you the other rooms, and I have a gorgeous balcony just off my bedroom that offers private views over the landscaped lawns at the rear."

"What's behind there?" she asks as we pass by the closed mahogany doors.

"That's my office. I'll show you my workspace after we eat." I shoot her a nervous smile, hoping she won't be angry when I reveal my big secret.

"This is one of two guest bedrooms," I explain, opening the door to the lavender room. I decorated this one with my youngest sister in mind. "I wanted to have space for my sisters to stay over. It hasn't happened much though. By the time I moved in, Sarah was already at Cornell and Esther was in her senior year of high school. She stayed with me sometimes on weekends, but mostly she preferred to be in Medina. It's where her friends are."

Stevie taps a finger on her chin. "Is that how you know Ivy too? From growing up there?"

I shake my head. "She lives on the other side of Medina and she only moved there maybe ten years ago?" I scratch the back of my head. "I have never bumped into her there, and Dad is particular about who he has over to the house. Someone like her would never have received an invite."

I close the door and open the one to the second guest room. It's painted in pale shades of gray and green. "This is the room Sarah stays in though I can count on one hand the number of times she has stayed over."

"They are both gorgeous rooms. Chic and comfortable. You have great taste, Beck, and I love how neat and tidy everything is."

Her words warm hidden parts of me. "I'm glad you appreciate my strengths. My sisters are so messy, and they don't understand why I get mad when they leave shit all over the place and don't put things back where they belong."

"Tell me about it. I'm constantly picking up after Hadley. She believes life is too short to worry about cleaning and tidying up. She says I'm too anal, but I can't help it. I feel disorganized when everything is all messy."

"I can relate. I feel exactly the same." I close the door to Sarah's room and move to the bathroom. "I have help though. Mary-Beth comes in once a week to clean and do my ironing."

"I'm totally doing that when I can afford it," she agrees, poking her head into the main bathroom.

After that, I guide her into my master bedroom, leaving the door open as I stride toward the double doors that lead to the balcony. Stevie shuffles timidly into the room, her gaze raking over my dark wood king bed with navy silk sheets. The rest of the furniture matches my bed, and the room is decorated in various shades of navy, white, and gray. One side door leads to my walk-in closet and the second to the large en suite bathroom with gray-and-white-marble tiles, dual sinks, a large rainforest shower, and a freestanding claw tub.

I watch her peek into the closet and the bathroom before she joins me on the balcony. "Your room is stunning, and that tub is to die for."

Visions of her long red hair cascading over the edge of the tub as she floats in petal-covered scented water surge to the forefront of my mind. I swallow over the lump in my throat as I punt that visual away before it gets me in trouble.

"One of my favorite things to do in summer is sit out here on the weekends with a book and a glass of wine and just enjoy the serenity," I admit, leaning on the cast-iron railings.

Stevie mirrors my position. "It is peaceful here. It's like you've carved out a little piece of heaven amid all the craziness of city life."

"My dream is to one day own a house by a lake, surrounded by trees and nature and peace and tranquility."

"Sounds dreamy."

Shaking myself out of it, I smile and offer her my arm. "Come on, milady. Your banquet awaits."

We chat casually over a dinner of Thai green curry with rice and noodle accompaniments, and fresh fruit meringue for dessert. She showers me with compliments, and a guy could really get used to this. The wine is flowing as easily as our conversation, and things are just so natural with Stevie. It's like we've known one another for years. There's a comfort and familiarity in her presence I've never felt with any woman before.

I simply adore her.

She's the most incredible woman, and I'm so damned lucky I get to call her my friend.

An inordinate thrill runs through me having Stevie here in my place.

She looks like she belongs.

That thought hinges on crossing a line, and it's borderline dangerous to entertain it, so I don't dwell on it, tossing it from my mind before it grows roots.

Although conversation is lively, I have noticed her drifting away a few times, looking lost in thought. Deep grooves furrow her brow, and

I can tell something is troubling her. "Do you want to talk about it?" I ask when she stares into space again.

"Talk about what?" She blinks profusely.

"Whatever has you so lost in thought."

She swallows audibly, and her hands shake as she raises her wineglass to her lips. I stack the plates and cutlery on the table while she takes a healthy mouthful of white wine, content to wait her out.

"I don't want to put a dampener on tonight. I've been enjoying it, and you went to lots of trouble."

"If something is bothering you, I'd rather you told me. It won't ruin what's already been a great night. Is this about Ellen? Has something else happened?"

She told me Thursday night about her phone call with Ellen, and I was livid on her behalf. I knew I didn't like the look of that other guy last week at the hospital. It seems my instincts weren't wrong. Will is a jackass, and if I ever see him—see either of them—again, they'll be getting a piece of my mind.

She shakes her head, rubbing her fingers back and forth across the ink on her wrist. "It's not that. After you drove me home last night, Mom and Nana showed up. Dawn and Hugh asked us to come over to North Bend to discuss Garrick."

Aw, shit. I hope they're not proposing to shut off his life support. Although I have to imagine it will get to that point one day unless he wakes up soon. "Why don't you go into the living room and take it easy while I clean up here?" I suggest, wanting to move to more comfortable surroundings before we have this conversation.

"I'll help," she insists, and we work together to clean the room and stack the dishwasher. When we're done, I grab a fresh bottle of wine from the fridge and two clean wineglasses, and we head into the living room.

Stevie kicks off her heels and tucks herself into one corner of my couch while I do the same on the other end. "We found out something important about Ivy."

"And?" I ask as I pour wine into our glasses.

"She has durable power of attorney for health care."

Well shit. That can't be good. "How does that compare to regular power of attorney? I'm not familiar with the differences."

"I wasn't either until Hugh explained. He only discovered this a couple weeks ago, and he's been talking to the hospital director and his lawyers to understand what it means and whether there is anything that can be done. It seems it was drawn up when Garrick was sixteen and he went on a European skiing vacation with Ivy and some friends. Hugh wasn't even aware it was in place, and I'm guessing Garrick had forgotten."

I hand her a wineglass, and she gulps back a mouthful before continuing.

"Unfortunately, this type of power of attorney doesn't expire." She traces the Celtic symbol on her wrist with the tip of one finger. "It will hold up unless revoked, which obviously hasn't happened in this case, or until the person regains consciousness and control of their faculties to petition to have it revoked."

"Can Hugh challenge it legally as his father?"

A forlorn expression appears on her pretty face. "He could try, but the lawyers have told him he'd be wasting his money. It's legally watertight."

"Shit."

"Yep." She knocks back more wine, and I get up to fetch a couple of glasses of water.

"Has she played her cards yet?" I hand a glass of water to Stevie before reclaiming my seat.

"Not yet, but now we know this, we know she's planning something that we won't be able to stop." Tears fill her eyes. "She's going to shut me out. I just know it."

Putting my glass down, I scoot down the couch closer to her. Slowly, I take her free hand in mine. "She hasn't done it yet, so try not to worry. At least until we know what we're dealing with. Say the word, and I'll make those calls."

She vigorously shakes her head as a solitary tear leaks out of the corner of one eye. Pain spears me through my heart at the sight of it. "I can't risk doing anything to make this worse." The tear rolls down her cheek and over her chin. "I'm so scared, Beck."

"Come here." I open my arms, grateful when she sinks into my embrace. "I can't tell you not to be, but I can promise I'm here for you. As is Nana, your mom, Hadley, Hugh and Dawn, and Hudson. We'll fight her, Stevie. We'll fight her with everything we've got." I rest my chin on top of her head and hold her close. Her entire body trembles against me, and I feel her pain as acutely as if it was mine. Cradling her in my arms, I squeeze my eyes shut, vowing to do everything in my power to help her.

Stevie has already been through so much.

I won't stand by helplessly and watch her get buried under more shit.

There is one constant she can always count on, and that's me.

Chapter Twelve

Beck

"Okay. I'm dying of curiosity. What's the big secret?" she asks, lifting her head and forcing a smile.

"We don't have to do this today. You're upset."

"I need a distraction, and I told you I won't derail our plans for tonight." A genuine smile ghosts over her full lips. "I feel better after talking to you about it." She briefly squeezes my hand. "You're right. There's no point worrying until I know what I'm facing." She climbs off the couch and drags me to my feet. "Show me what's in your office."

Nerves fire at me from all angles, and she notices.

"Hey." She holds on to my arm. "Don't be nervous. You can show me anything. Tell me anything."

"I know. I'm just not sure how you're going to react. You might get angry, or you could be excited. It could swing either way."

Her brows climb to her hairline. "I am so intrigued. All week, I've been trying to guess what the secret might be, and I'm honestly clueless." She tugs on my arm. "Show me. It's going to be fine."

I hope she's right. "Just know I didn't tell you when you first mentioned it because I was so shocked I didn't know how to say it.

And then it's because I wanted to show you rather than just blurt it out."

"Okay." She looks thoroughly confused, and I don't blame her.

A dry chuckle seeps from my lips. "Did you bring the book?"

She nods. "It's in my purse."

"Good. Good." I scrub a hand across the fine layer of stubble on my jawline. I need to be clean-shaven for work—it's written into the company human resource policy—so the only time I let any facial hair grow is over the weekend.

"You're nervous."

"Fucking petrified."

"I thought nothing fazed you. You always seem so strong and confident."

God, I wish I felt like that on the inside. "Most times, that's all for show. But this is different. What you think matters so much to me."

"Be brave, Colbert. Man up and open the fucking door, dude." She's grinning as she says it, and I silently pray these aren't our last few moments together.

We pad in our bare feet over to the door, and I suck in a deep breath before opening the doors and letting her into my lair.

"What the..." Her eyes are out on stalks as her gaze darts around the room. Wild eyes bounce between me and the fitted bookshelves lining each side of the office, filled with books, neatly organized by title and volume order. The only wall that doesn't have any shelving is the wall surrounding the window. My desk and chair are butted up to the wall, overlooking the view of the gardens outside.

"This is..." Her voice trails off again as she moves over to the free-standing whiteboards lined up in front of the shelving on one side wall.

I point at the pictures of models, celebrities, and actors affixed to one board. "That's where I map out the character bios. I like to pick actual people to represent my characters as I need a visual sometimes to keep me in their heads." I point at the second board. "This is where I plot out the main components of the story, adding and deleting as I write." I tap my finger on the third board. "And this is where I highlight those key elements that follow through from book to book. My assistant types up detailed series notes as well so I don't have to reread each book before I start the next one."

Her wide eyes soak it all in as she clasps a hand over her mouth. "Is this real?" she chokes out, finally finding her voice and spinning around to face me. Her face is flushed, her eyes alight with excitement. "Are you really Byron Stanley?"

"I am." Heat floods my cheeks, and it takes effort not to look away. I'm not good with attention.

"Oh my fucking god, Beck!" She flings herself at me, and I almost lose my balance. I straighten up in time, chuckling as her slender arms go around me. "This is incredible!" Her high-pitched tone is not usual, nor her girlish excitement, but I'm loving seeing this side of her.

"You're not angry?"

"Are you kidding me?" She laughs as she pulls back, spinning around and waving her hands in the air. "This is the best goddamned secret ever. Hadley and I were coming up with theories all week. Like you were a French spy. Or a secret government agent. Hadley threw gay model into the mix. I joked you were a serial killer."

I'll be having words with that little minx Hadley the next time I see her.

Stevie snorts out a laugh, turning around and slapping a hand over her chest. "But this! This is the absolute best. You're a fucking genius, Beck!" She rushes back to my side, resting her small hands on my chest. "Do you have any idea how talented you are?"

Emeralds glitter in her eyes, and her smile is so wide it threatens to split her face. I have never seen her looking so happy and I'm enchanted.

"My mind is seriously blown right now. Your books are amazing. They consume my brain from the first page to the last. I devoured your entire catalog in one month, and then I've been rereading them to Garrick." She squeals. "He'll get such a kick out of this!"

She's practically jumping around the room now, and I'm just staring at her in awe.

"I love Jake Bennett! Like I'm *in love* with him. He's the best book boyfriend, and these aren't even romances. When he saved Maggie after that sick prick came for her again, I just swooned. And I loved that you gave the villain a violent death. I might be sick, but I was cheering Bennett on during that scene. But you almost gave me a heart attack when he got shot. My stomach was in knots, and my heart was in my throat. I was so afraid to turn the page in case you'd killed him off."

"I couldn't do that. He's my most beloved detective, and the series is selling well for me. There is plenty more mileage to go with Bennett, I promise."

"You know what this means?" She throws her arms around me again, and the scent of her perfume swirls in the air, tickling my nostrils and enveloping me in a heady warmth. "I get the inside scoop from now on!" She squeals before stretching up and smacking a kiss on my cheek. "I can help you brainstorm too. Like, if you ever get stuck. Oh, oh!" She claps a couple times, dancing from foot to foot. "Please tell me Bennett and Maggie become a couple in the next book? You were hinting at that in the end, but I need to know. Please. Pretty please." She pins me with doe eyes. "It's been killing me."

"What's it worth to you?" I tease.

"I'd sell my soul to know." She stands before me, looking utterly entranced, giddy with visible happiness, her eyes bright with excitement, her face glowing, and I feel the shift the instant it occurs.

My sisters and my friends were pleased for me when I told them I'd published a book and it was selling well and receiving great reviews. I hadn't breathed a word to a living soul while writing the book, not wanting to set myself up for failure. But when my first book achieved some modicum of success, I finally told the four people closest to me. Sarah was encouraging as was Law. Tate was amused but supportive. Esther was excited for me.

But none of their reactions were anything like this.

Stevie is talking animatedly, waving her hands around and smiling, but her words don't register over the pounding of my heart, racing of my pulse, and the longing emanating from my soul.

My eyes lower to her mouth, and I want to kiss her so badly I can scarcely breathe.

Shock renders me speechless as the thought lands in my brain. I retreat immediately, turning my back on her and striding toward my shelving unit as I scramble to get a grip on myself before I ruin everything.

"Oh god, I'm making a fool of myself and I'm rambling," she says as I emerge from my fugue state. "I just can't believe this."

"I love your excitement," I truthfully admit, plucking the special edition of my first book from the top shelf. "I was worried you'd be angry with me for not telling you. It was so hard keeping it to myself when you were talking about my books," I add, grabbing swag from several boxes as I speak. "But I loved your honesty. Sarah, Esther, and Law have read some of my books, and they said they enjoyed them, but I always wondered if it was the truth." I turn around with my hands full. "I love the raw feedback you gave me. It came straight from the heart, uncensored, because you didn't realize you were speaking with the author."

"Thank fuck I love them and never had a bad word to say. I'd die if I was critical and I'd said hurtful things to your face."

I pull a branded box out, along with two branded bags, dividing the swag up equally. "You couldn't have been more glowing in your praise. You have no idea how happy I went home those days knowing you loved my books." I hand her the box. "This is for you and Garrick."

She examines each item of swag with a humongous smile on her face, oohing and aahing over certain pieces. Her chin lifts abruptly and flames dance in her eyes. "That's why you wanted me to bring Garrick's book!"

I nod. "Go get it, and I'll inscribe it."

While trying to ignore the impulse I just had to kiss another man's girlfriend.

Stevie takes another look around, shaking her head and smiling, like she can't quite believe it, before she literally skips out of the room to retrieve the book.

I take a minute to compose myself, and I can't stop the giant grin that spreads over my lips. My heart swells to bursting point behind my rib cage. If I adored Stevie before, it's nothing compared to how much I adore her now.

Having someone believe in you is an incredible feeling.

Having someone enthusiastically support your passion is mind-blowing.

Having someone so genuinely happy for your achievements is everything.

Chapter Thirteen

Beck

I almost float to my desk with the special edition book in my hand, dropping into my seat and pouring over the inscription page as I write a personal note for Stevie. It doesn't take me long to find the right words.

"I'm still pinching myself," she says, reappearing in the room a minute later. "This is surreal." It shows on her face as she glances around the room again. "You should be so fucking proud, Beck."

"I am." I accept the book from her. "You'll never find me bragging, but I won't shy away from my accomplishments either. I work hard to write the best books I can. And then there's everything that comes with publishing and marketing a book. It's a huge effort, demanding hours upon hours of time, and I have to fit it in around my day job and other commitments."

"When do you find the time to write?" Propping her butt on the edge of my desk, she watches as I personalize the book for Garrick.

"I write every night after I come home from the hospital, often staying up until the early hours of the morning. I don't sleep much anyway." I deliberately downplay that fact. "And I write and work on my publishing business on the weekends, only stopping to get groceries, work out, or occasionally meet up with people. I'm disciplined with my time because it's the only way I can manage it."

"You're so inspirational." She looks at me like I hung the stars in the night sky. "I can't believe my friend is a famous author. Wow. Just wow."

"Hardly famous."

"Successful then."

I shrug. I meant what I said. I am proud of my achievements, but I struggle to accept praise.

"Here." I return Garrick's book to her.

"Thanks so much. He's going to love it."

"This is for you." I hand her the second book. "This is a special collector's edition hardcover copy with foil edges. It was in a subscription book box, but I managed to get a few extra copies. I wrote you a personal note."

She moves to open the book, but I close her hand over it. "Read it at home."

Her lips curve into a smile. "Okay." She holds it close to her chest, hugging it like it's precious treasure. "I will cherish this forever."

I can tell she means it. "If you want more signed copies, now or at any time, just ask." I spin around in my chair, motioning toward the full bookshelves. "As you can see, I have multiple copies of each title."

"I would totally love signed copies, but I'll have to save up for it." She tucks the two books into the box with the swag, taking care not to damage them, before she closes the lid and secures the content.

"You're my friend, Stevie. You don't have to buy them. I want to gift them to you."

"I can't let you do that."

"Why not?" I know she has some hang-ups about money. It's why I don't force anything. But this is different. It's not going to cost me anything to give her these books.

She stares off into space for an indeterminable amount of time before swinging her gaze back around to me. "I'm fiercely independent, and I don't like others paying for things for me. I think you already know that."

I nod, watching the agony spread over her features as she tries to figure it out in her head.

"But that kind of attitude got me into trouble with Garrick, and it's one of my biggest regrets. That I couldn't just be gracious about the gifts he wanted to give me. I swore I was going to work on it, but look how I automatically reacted to you just now?"

"It's hard to change the habits of a lifetime. It's not something you can do overnight, and you're doing it the right way. You are self-aware, and you're stopping to consider it."

"I want the books," she blurts, eyeing my shelves with greed and longing. "I want them all."

I chuckle. "Then you shall have them all."

"Only if you let me pay you back in kind."

I arch one brow on instinct, fighting a laugh when her cheeks inflame.

"Oh my god. I did not mean that how it sounded! I'm not offering sexual favors. I meant like I could bake stuff for you or maybe help with your books or some aspect of your business or something." She buries her red face in her hands, and I can't hold my chuckle back any longer.

"Stevie, it's fine." I pry her hands from her face. "I know you didn't mean it like that, and I have a proposal for you." I purposely use those words, grinning as her eyes widen. "Not that kind of proposal," I chide, tweaking her nose. "Someone has a one-track mind."

"Someone hasn't had sex in over a year!"

We both startle at that admission, and her cheeks are on fire again.

"Holy shit! What is wrong with me tonight? Please pretend I didn't say that."

"Would it help if I said I haven't had sex in over two years?"

Her mouth hangs open. "You haven't?"

I shake my head.

"Why the hell not?"

"I'm pretty much a hermit since I became a writer, but that's not really the reason. I haven't had a relationship since high school, but finding women for one-night stands hasn't been challenging. When Brielle and I started fake dating, it felt wrong to pick up women for casual sex. I would've been discreet. No one would have known, but it didn't feel right."

"Did Brielle show you the same respect?" she wonders, tilting her head to one side.

"I honestly don't know. It's not something we ever discussed. If she was fucking anyone, she didn't tell me."

"You're an enigma, Greyson Beckett Colbert III."

I shrug.

"I mean it," she says. "You're the most intriguing, most noble man I know."

Bitterness snakes through my veins. She'd take that back if she knew the truth.

"I'm far from perfect, trust me." I look around the room at the very essence of my soul laid bare. "What you see here is me at my truest self. I pour my heart and soul into my books. Every word is carefully chosen. If you want to understand the man behind the enigma, you'll uncover the truth between the pages."

"I think I have a pretty good understanding already." Mischief glints in her eyes. "Though I'm going to go home and start rereading your books with a fine-tooth comb. I'm determined to uncover all the hidden meanings."

"Go for it. Let me know what you discover."

"Why are you not doing this full-time?" She folds her arms around her waist and levels me with a serious look. "You hate your job, and you're too damn talented a writer to not be writing books for a career. What is your father holding over you? Because that's what's holding you back, am I right?"

I bob my head. "Yes, it's all connected to him. He doesn't know about any of this, and he never will. It's one of the reasons I write under a pseudonym."

"How did you pick your author name? Does it have some special significance?"

"Stanley is my mother's maiden name. Her family originally came from England before her great-great-grandfather moved to France to start a textiles business. I wanted a connection to my mother because she fostered my love of reading from an early age. As you already know, Samuel Beckett was one of her favorite writers, but it was a bit too close to home to choose that name. Lord Byron was her favorite poet, so I picked his name, and *voilà*, Byron Stanley was born."

"I love that. It's perfect."

"I think so. I hope she's looking down on me and she's proud. She wanted to be a writer, but she ended up becoming a model. Then she met dad, got married young, and..."

Pain rattles through my bones, and I can't say the words out loud.

I never can.

Those gruesome images resurrect in my mind, like they do any time I think about that terrible day.

Gulping back the pain, I subtly take deep breaths, in and out, and forcefully shove the memories from my mind, like I do at night when the horrors invade my dreams, turning them into nightmares.

"She never had a chance to fulfill her dream," I say, trying to resituate myself in the moment.

Sympathy splays across Stevie's face.

I know she realizes there is a story behind my mother's death, and I'm grateful she never asks. One day, I hope to pluck up the courage to tell her.

"Is that why you decided to become a writer?"

"It was a part of it, yes. It's also an escape from those elements of my life I dislike or struggle to connect with. I don't people well. Escaping into a fictional world has saved my sanity more times than I can count. But mostly it's because I wanted to be a detective when I grew up. Father would never permit it, so this was the next best thing."

"Becoming a fictional detective through the pages of your books."

"Yes." I knew Stevie would get it.

"I love your books even more knowing the background now." She looks at me with a myriad of emotions splaying across her face. "This has blown my mind, Beck. I am so in awe of you."

"Thank you. Your reaction has been everything. It's scary admitting it to people, and knowing you support me means the world."

"I have rarely seen you as passionate as you are talking about writing and books. It's clear it's what you're meant to be doing with your life. Can't you find a way to get rid of whatever your father is holding over you now? I know you said previously you had to bide your time, but is there nothing you can do to get out sooner?"

I spin around in my chair, toying with my lips as I reply. "My sisters and I have a considerable trust fund due to us from the Colbert estate. It was set up by our grandfather. Unfortunately, my asshole of a father is the trustee. I got half when I turned twenty-five, and I am due to receive the other half after I have worked for Colbert Aerospace for fifteen years. Dad has the power to alter the terms, and he made me a deal when he approached me about Brielle. He said he'd give it to me if I married her and stayed married to her for at least two years. I honestly couldn't give a fuck about the money. We all got a small inheritance from mom at twenty-one. Between both trust funds and my book income, I have more than enough to be comfortable for the rest of my life. But the way the trust fund works is different for my sisters."

"How?"

"They only get a quarter when they turn twenty-five, and they don't get the rest until they get married." I run a hand over my cropped dark hair. "He has held this over me since I turned twenty-five. My plan had been to resign from the business then, get the fuck out of Seattle, and go somewhere quieter to become a full-time writer. But dad put the screws on me. If I don't stay in the business, he's going to cut my sisters off completely, and the only way they'll get access to their trust funds is if they marry someone of his choosing."

"What the actual fuck?" Her eyes pop wide as her hands fall to the edge of the desk. "Surely, that's not legal?"

"I had it checked, and unfortunately, it is. It's the way the trust fund has always been written in our family. As a trustee, he can alter the terms however he pleases. My uncle is also a trustee, but he won't do anything. Declan is weak, and I suspect Dad is blackmailing him so he never challenges my father on anything. He'll just sign off on any alteration Dad makes."

The usual torment charges through me. "I wish I had enough to support all three of us, so we could break free of him, but the truth is, my sisters are used to a certain lifestyle, and there's no way I could fund it for long. Plus, Sarah wants to work for Colbert Aerospace. It's always been her dream. She's the rightful next heir and CEO. If Dad cuts her off, he will cut her out of the business too. I know my sister. She'll do anything to get back in his good graces, even marrying someone he picks for her. I cannot let that happen. She'd be miserable. Esther too. She's a sensitive soul, and I fear the brute he'd pick for her husband to toughen her up." I sigh heavily.

"So, I'm stuck between a rock and a hard place. I have to stay at least until the girls get the first part of their trust fund." Even then, I don't know if I could walk away. Esther would be fine to take that money and make a life for herself, but Sarah would be devastated if she didn't get to join Colbert Aerospace. I don't know what the solution is to that part of my dilemma, but I'll face one obstacle at a time.

"Which is when?" Stevie asks.

"Two years for Sarah and four for Esther. And that's if he doesn't change the terms again."

"Because of Brielle." Stevie's smart assessment hits the nail on the head.

"What do your sisters think about this?"

I rub the back of my neck. "They don't know. I haven't told them. I don't want them to worry."

"Oh, Beck." She takes my hand. "You've been carrying this secret all these years?"

"Yep. Law and Tate know, but that's it."

"You need to tell them. If you were my brother and our father was using me to blackmail you, I would want to know. Unless you're saying Sarah and Esther would be different?"

"They would want to know," I quietly admit. "But I don't want them to feel guilty or have them decide to call his bluff."

"I think it's a decision you can only make together. Tell them, Beck. You should not shoulder that responsibility alone."

Chapter Fourteen

Stevie

Saturday night dinner at Beck's becomes the norm in the following weeks as the one-year anniversary creeps closer. It's only thirteen days away now, and I'm dreading it. We are all still on edge, waiting for Ivy to make her move. The longer it goes on with no action on her part, the more wary I become. Ellen hasn't made any effort to contact me to offer an apology, which disappoints me, but honestly isn't that surprising. I hope she knows what she's gotten herself into with Will. He's not the good guy he presents himself to be, and I fear she has bitten off more than she can chew.

But that's her problem to handle.

As far as I'm concerned, she's dead to me now.

It saddens me, but I won't be mistreated by someone I called a friend in such a cruel manner. Ellen has made her lonely bed. Now she can languish in it.

Hanging out with Beck is my salvation.

I'm having great fun helping him brainstorm and plot his next novel. I suspect I might be driving him a little bit insane asking a million and one questions about his previous books. I have been rereading them as promised, and I'm annotating the shit out of them and keeping a separate notebook of questions. I find the whole process riveting, and though he might grumble and complain when I start peppering him with questions, I think he secretly loves it. I also butter him up with baked goods, which helps.

We take turns cooking on Saturdays, and I always leave with a goodie bag or two. I think Beck is on a mission to fatten me up. He has started bringing Tupperware containers with curries, soups, stews, stir-fries, and pasta dishes to our garden meetings, claiming he always cooks too much. His food is divine, so I don't complain. He should open his own restaurant or a bookstore-slash-restaurant. He joked we could add flowers and make it a combined business, and we laughed a lot that night, making plans for our fictional business.

When God was dishing out talents, I think he broke the mold with Beck. How can one guy be good at so many things? And be a stellar human too? He's also not bad to look at. Really, it should be outlawed.

I would invite Beck over to our place, but Hadley is seeing a new guy, Mike, and I want to give her privacy. That and listening to the sounds of my bestie getting nailed is too much for me to handle.

I miss sex with Garrick. He was so good at it.

I miss sex.

Period.

My fingers and my little battery-operated friend can only do so much.

It's also the intimacy I miss. That powerful connection you feel when someone knows you inside and out. That feeling you get when you're tangled between the sheets, all sweaty limbs, exploring fingers, and beating hearts with him buried deep inside you, sliding slowly in and out, stroking every heated inch of your body, prolonging the pleasure, and staring so intensely at you it's like he's looking straight into your soul as he makes love to you.

I miss that.

So very much.

And I need to stop thinking about sex and intimacy when I'm here with another man who has come to mean so much to me.

I clear my throat and empty my thoughts of all things sexual. "What did Brielle's dad say tonight?" I ask as I lie tummy down on the rug in his office, fixing dried flowers onto my stencil design.

Beck's creative streak is brushing off on me, and I'm experimenting with different ideas for things I can do with dried flowers. It's such a shame to watch flowers wither and die. Making art with flowers before they perish is one way of preserving them.

I was inspired by Presley Kennedy's framed pictures. She doesn't sell them anymore now she's married to one of the infamous Kennedys. She has family commitments, and she also owns a tattoo business with her brother-in-law, Austen, which keeps her busy. I guess she doesn't have the time anymore, which is a shame, because her pictures are beautiful.

"Earth to Byron Stanley," I quip, and Beck lifts his head from his screen. I know he's finished his wordcount already, or I wouldn't have disturbed him.

Sometimes I come over early on a Saturday when he's still writing. I refuse to interfere with his work, so I always shove him back into his office, insisting he's not to come out until the words are written down. I need the next book like yesterday, I always tease. I potter around, getting dinner ready, listening to music or a podcast on my AirPods, or sprawling on his very cozy couch and reading.

It's remarkable how comfortable I feel here. How it's already like a second home. We even gave one another keys to our places, something the old me would have overanalyzed to death.

"What did you ask?" he inquires.

"What's going on with Brielle?"

"It's finally happening." He fixes me with a sad smile.

"Aw." I push up to my knees and abandon my picture. Brielle's dad, David, has been gently coaxing his wife along this path for months, so we knew it was coming. But knowing, accepting, and handling it are entirely different things. "How are you feeling?"

Beck leans back in his chair, swiveling it around before crossing his long legs at the ankles. "It's an overdue decision and the right one. This way, everyone can try to move on. To properly grieve and heal, but it still sucks."

"Yes, it does."

He stares abjectly into space with a haunted look I haven't seen on his face in some time. On instinct, I get up, cross the space, drop to my knees before him, and stretch up to hug him. Beck's arms go around me instantly, and I rest my head on his chest as we embrace. The steady beat of his heart under my ear is a welcome symphony as is the familiar scent of his cologne.

In some ways, it feels like I've known Beck for years, not just a few months.

It's as concerning a thought as it is comforting.

"Will you come?" he asks after a few minutes of amicable silence.

Easing out of his embrace, I sit back on my heels and peer into his handsome troubled face. Pain shimmers behind the warm chocolaty depths of his big eyes. "To the funeral," he clarifies.

"Of course. If that is what you need."

"I do."

"Then, I'll be there."

Brielle's funeral is well attended, and the church is packed. Not surprising when you consider who her father is. I'm sitting in the second row with a stoic Beck. He hasn't said much, but I think my presence is offering him some peace. He hasn't let go of my hand since we slid into this pew.

I briefly met his sisters outside the church. Sarah, the older and taller of the two women, is twenty-three, and Esther, the younger, petite one, is twenty-one. I land slap bang in the middle of them age-wise. They both look alike with their dark-blonde hair and big hazel eyes, but I don't see a huge resemblance to their older brother. Beck's dad sits in the pew in front of us, offering support to his best friend. I didn't miss the inquisitive look cast over his shoulder in my direction. Neither did Beck. His hand automatically tightened around mine.

At the graveside, I notice a few stares leveled in our direction. Beck is gripping my hand like a lifeline, so there's no way I'm letting go, but the nosy looks from strangers are making me antsy.

The entire thing makes me uncomfortable.

Garrick is on my mind a lot today.

It's impossible not to think about him.

Impossible not to wonder if his funeral will be the next one I attend. The thought has brought tears to my eyes more than once today.

It's hard for me to be here, confronted with what could be my reality soon.

But I didn't want to abandon Beck.

And the truth is, I need to face my fears. This is about as real as it gets.

I travel with Beck and his sisters, in his A7, to the Cartwright house where the wake is taking place. Esther points out the Colbert family home as we drive past, and my eyes almost pop out of their sockets.

It makes Ivy bitchface's Medina home look like someone's guest house.

I can't see the property fully as it's enclosed behind chunky walls and thick gates, but the roof juts out over the boundary wall, indicating it's several stories high. It stretches from left to right for eternity as we drive by, and I'm only now realizing the true extent of Beck's family's wealth and the true extent of the trust fund situation.

Beck hasn't said anything to his sisters yet, and I haven't pushed. It's not my call to make. Seeing this now makes me realize I can't fully empathize with Beck's situation.

Garrick's family is wealthy, but this is on a whole other level.

Beck is not flashy with his wealth at all. His home is tastefully and expensively decorated with the best of everything, but it's still quite a modest home, and I love that he picked something older rather than opting for a penthouse in one of the city's modern apartment blocks.

His home has tons of character, just like its owner.

The Cartwright home is ostentatious and ridiculously large, stretching over three stories and across a plot of acres upon acres of well-maintained land. Inside, the grandiose styling houses expensive furniture and exquisite fittings. I cling to Beck and his sisters like my life depends on it. If I get lost in this place, I'd need GPS to navigate my way out.

"I'm glad Beck has you," Sarah, the elder sister says, when Beck is pulled away by David Cartwright to speak to someone. The massive room is full of people conversing, eating, and drinking. Luxurious silver and gold velvet drapes frame each window, and magnificent chandeliers hang from the high ceiling. High tables with matching long-legged chairs are positioned near the overflowing buffet table, but most people are standing around them rather than sitting. Servers mingle, carrying trays of canapés and wine, and I find it all a bit distasteful. "This will hit Beck harder than he realizes," Sarah adds.

"I agree. No matter how much you think you are prepared, you don't know how you're going to feel in the moment."

"They had a strange relationship," Esther says, snatching two glasses of wine from a passing server. She thanks him and hands a glass to me. "It never seemed like love to me."

I swallow a mouthful of wine to avoid replying.

"It wasn't love," Sarah says. "Beck was settling because it's what Daddy wanted."

"He told you that?" Esther asks, glancing around as she adds, "We should probably cease this conversation. It's not exactly respectful."

"True, and no, no one told me. It's the conclusion I have drawn," Sarah confirms, sipping from her sparkling water. She offered to be the designated driver so Beck could have a few drinks.

"He's different since you came into his life, Stevie." Esther effortlessly switches topics as I watch Beck tug at the collar of his white dress shirt as another couple approaches and engages him in conversation.

"I have noticed the change too," Sarah agrees, smiling at me. "Honestly, I can't remember a time when my brother seemed happier."

"You understand we're just friends, right?" I feel the need to make that clear.

"Beck has explained," Sarah says, her features softening.

"We're sorry to hear about your boyfriend." Esther briefly squeezes my hand. "I can't imagine how difficult it must be."

"Thank you."

"Today must be hard for you," Sarah adds, looking sympathetic as she flips her long blonde hair over her shoulders.

"It is, but I wanted to be here for Beck."

The sisters exchange a knowing look, and I decide that's my cue to intervene in Beck's conversation. He's growing increasingly agitated. "Excuse me a minute." I step aside. "I think your brother needs rescuing."

I walk with confidence I don't feel in the direction of Beck and the people surrounding him, hoping they don't see my hands shaking or my lower lip wobbling. Beck can't see me approaching, because he has his back to me, but his father can. Carlton Colbert's eyes skim over me from head to toe in a way that feels like he's undressing me.

Ugh.

What a creep.

Unease slithers up my spine, and nerves fire at me from all angles.

Holding my chin up high, I clear my throat as I join the group. "Excuse me for the interruption, but I was hoping I could borrow Beck for a moment."

Beck looks at me with blatant gratitude and relief, and my nerves flitter away knowing I've made the right call.

"Who might you be?" a man with a deep voice asks, and I don't need to turn my head to know who articulated the question.

Beck slides his arm around my waist, purposely hauling me in close to his side. Not a single person in this circle misses it, and I grow uncomfortably warm in my skirt suit. "That is none of your business, and we're leaving." Beck practically fires the words at his father, and I inwardly cringe at the look of fury that flares in Mr. Colbert's eyes. It doesn't last long, but I saw it.

"I know you," an unfamiliar woman says, narrowing her eyes at me in instant suspicion. "I saw your picture in the paper last year. You were in that car accident with Garrick Allen." Her gaze drops to where Beck has his arm curled around my waist, and I want the ground to open and swallow me. "Aren't you Garrick's girlfriend?" She arches one manicured brow, and the movement looks weird on her botoxed skin.

"I am Garrick's girlfriend," I say. "I'm here to support Beck because we've both been through similar experiences and become good friends."

"I thought the Allen boy was dead," Carlton Colbert says, picking at an imaginary piece of lint on his suit jacket.

"He's still alive," I say, working hard to keep my tone pleasant. "He's in a coma."

"As good as dead then," the asshole says.

A strangled sound slips from my lips of its own accord.

"Father." Beck's clipped tone contains considerable warning. "That is insensitive, and an apology is in order."

Mr. Colbert drills a derisory look at his son before schooling his features into a neutral line. "I'm just saying what everyone is saying behind closed doors. It's a terrible tragedy, of course, but denying reality is only preventing the inevitable. Look why we're here today? Can you honestly tell me the outcome won't be the same for the Allen kid?"

"He's not a kid," I retort, losing control of my emotions. "He's twenty-two, and you don't know a single thing about his situation.

Last I checked, you weren't a neurosurgeon either. There are several examples of people coming out of yearslong comas from all around the world. Garrick is not dead yet, and it's rude of you to say anything of the sort. As his girlfriend, I am deeply offended by your hurtful comments."

"Says the woman tucked into my son's side." He chuckles, looking around at his cronies, and a few of them join in.

Heat climbs up my throat.

"Anything you'd like to tell us? Or should I just call Ivy Allen-Golding-Smith and have a private chat in her ear?"

Chapter Fifteen

Stevie

"You should just go over there," Hadley says, noticing I'm not paying attention to the movie we're watching. It's been hard to concentrate on anything in the three days since the funeral when there has only been radio silence from Beck. I'm still upset over the horrible things his father said to me, but I'm trying to let it go. He's an asshole. All those people were assholes, and they don't deserve another second of my headspace.

"I can't just show up and barge my way in." Slouching against the corner of our couch, I hug my knees harder to my chest.

"Sure, you can. Beck gave you a key for a reason. You're worried about him, and he's not answering your calls, so go over there. I'll come with you if you like."

I glance at my watch. "It's late. He's probably sleeping or writing."

"It's Saturday night. I doubt he's in bed at ten."

"Maybe I should just let it go." I dig my nails into my thighs. "This friendship is already getting complicated."

"Don't buy into the bullshit those rich pricks threw at you. The people who matter know the truth. Beck is a good friend to you, Stevie. They are judgmental, narrow-minded idiots. Don't let them take him from you. The only way I'm even considering going backpacking with Mike in July is because I know you'll have Beck. I trust him to have your back while I'm gone, and I don't say that lightly."

"Maybe he thinks our friendship is too much trouble. Perhaps that's why he hasn't reached out to me since he dropped me off on Wednesday."

"I don't think that's it at all. He's embarrassed his father was so nasty to you, and he probably thinks you want distance from him."

"He can't think that when I have called every day and left several messages. This is the first Saturday night in weeks we haven't hung out."

There is no reason for Beck to be at the hospital anymore, so I've resumed my solo garden trips. But it's not the same. It no longer offers me the serenity it once did. Now, sitting in the memorial garden alone exacerbates the hollow ache in my chest. It's so freaking lonely without him.

The truth is, I miss him.

It's only been three nights, but I already miss him so much. I have gotten used to sharing my day with him and just shooting the shit.

"Maybe he doesn't need me anymore. Maybe I was just a crutch to help him get through losing Brielle."

"I know you don't really believe that." She swings her legs up onto the couch.

I shrug. I don't know how to feel. Except a little heartsore and a lot sad. I hadn't realized quite how much Beck had brightened up my world until he started ghosting me.

"You're important to him. Don't convince yourself otherwise. I don't think this is about you at all. He just buried Brielle, and he's hurting, babe."

"The funeral was hard on him, and you're probably right. I shouldn't be making this about me. I just want to be there for him, but how can I when he seems to be pushing me away?" I rub at a tense spot between my brows.

"His relationship with Brielle was fake, but she took her own life while she was technically his girlfriend. You said they were friends. I bet he's harboring a ton of guilt. Guilt he was hiding or denying, and now the funeral has brought it all to the surface. He needs you, Stevie. I'd bet my last dollar on it."

I scoot down the couch and grab my friend into a hug. "How did I get so lucky to have you for a best friend?"

"It's cosmic, babe. The stars aligned to bring us together."

"Whatever it is, I'm grateful. Love you."

"Love you too, Stevie." We ease out of our embrace. "Do you want me to come with?"

I shake my head. "I've got this, but thanks for offering." Finals start in nine days, and I know Hadley was only watching a movie to cheer me up. "Go study. I'll text you when I get there."

I set out on foot a few minutes later, keeping alert as I navigate the streets from the International District to Capitol Hill. The brisk night air blows some of the cobwebs from my head. I silently berate myself for being so selfish. For getting so caught up in my own shit I didn't properly consider the impact Brielle's funeral had on Beck. Of course, he's in pain. They might not have been in love like Garrick and me, but she was still his friend. Now, I feel foolish for not visiting sooner.

When I reach his building, I take the elevator to the third floor, frowning when the doors open and loud rock music greets me. It's coming from Beck's apartment, which is strange. I ring the bell and hammer on the door a few times, but it's futile. He can't hear me over the ruckus.

Using my key, I let myself inside, noticing nothing out of place in the hallway. However, panic is instantaneous the second I round the bend and step foot in the living room. Beck is lying on the floor, wearing only gray sweatpants, curled in the fetal position, and not moving.

Rushing to him, I drop to my knees and place a hand over his heart. "Beck, it's me. Stevie. I'm here." His skin is warm and clammy to the touch, but the steady pounding against my palm is reassuring. A groan seeps from his lips as he lowers his knees, and I spot the empty bottle of Macallan his hand is curled around.

Noxious fumes waft in the air when his lips part. His eyes blink open before shuttering again. Rock music blares from his sound system, and I rush to switch it off before dropping down in front of him again. "Beck." I press my hand to his sweat-slickened brow. "Can you hear me?"

"Stevie," he rasps in a hoarse voice, opening his eyes fully. They are bloodshot and red rimmed, and the accompanying shadows under his eyes are testament to lack of sleep. "You're here."

"Yes. I should have come sooner. I've been worried." I gently cup his face. "How long have you been numbing your pain with whisky?"

He shrugs, groaning as he tries to sit up.

"Let me help." Sliding my arm around his back, I help him to sit. Whisky fumes leak from his every pore, and it's obvious he's been drinking for a while to get in this state.

"You shouldn't be here," he slurs before burying his face in my neck. "I'm bad news." His words are muffled against my skin. "I'm not the good guy you think I am."

I have no clue what he means, but now isn't the time to probe him for answers. "I am exactly where I want to be."

He looks up at me with so much vulnerability in his eyes my heart aches for him. "You mean everything to me, Stevie. Everything," he whispers, clasping my face in his palms. His eyes drift to my mouth, and I stop breathing. "You're so good and kind, and I don't want to ruin you." His gaze flickers from my lips to my eyes and back again. "You make it all better." His head falls to my shoulder as his arms go around me. "You make everything better. You're like my personal guardian angel."

Beck clings to me with a desperation I feel soul-deep. I hold him close, running a hand up and down his back, as he shakes and trembles against me. "It's all my fault," he cries a few minutes later. "What happened to Brielle. It's all my fault. I'm the reason she's dead."

"It's not your fault. No one knows why anyone takes their own life. No one understands what triggers them in that moment to make such a drastic choice. If it even is a choice." I rest my cheek on top of his head as I hug him. "You can't take that responsibility on. It's not right and it won't change the outcome."

How easy it is to give advice to others when I suffer under the same weights of guilt and responsibility myself.

"You don't understand." He lifts his head, and we're so close there's barely any space between us. His eyes drop to my mouth again, and butterflies swoop into my belly. I stop breathing. Partly to ward off the alcoholic odors and partly in panic. Beck's entire face is wracked in pain, but his eyes convey other things.

Things I do not want to even think about.

"I…Oh god." Clasping a hand over his mouth, he climbs awkwardly to his feet and dashes from the room.

I give chase, following him into the main bathroom in time to see him empty the contents of his stomach into the toilet. After grabbing a washcloth from a basket on the counter, I dampen it while Beck continues throwing up. Lowering to my knees beside him, I offer silent comfort as I gently place a hand on his shoulder, letting him know I'm here.

Muscles flex and roll in his back as he vomits, and I'm finally getting to see his tattoo. It's an impressive inking of an eagle with its beak touching the lower part of his neck, the large wings covering both shoulders and each side of his upper back, and the main body covering the top third of his spine.

Beck slumps on his side when he eventually stops retching, and I dab his face with the damp washcloth as he moans and clutches his stomach. "Never drinking again," he mumbles, and I hide my smile. How many times have I told myself that?

"Do you think you could get in the shower?" I ask a few minutes later after I've cleaned up the toilet and gotten him to sit against the side of the tub.

"Ugh. Do I have to?" His skin has a greenish tinge to it when he lifts his face to mine.

"You will feel better after a shower, some water, and maybe a little soup? When did you last eat?" I ask, handing him a toothbrush with toothpaste.

"I can't remember." He shrugs as he stands on wobbly feet. "My diet the past few days has largely been a liquid one."

I feel so bad I didn't come over sooner. I turn on the faucet and watch as he brushes his teeth and gargles mouthwash.

"Come on." When he's done, I hook my arm around his back and steer him out of the bathroom and toward his room. "You can shower while I'm fixing you something to eat." My eyes drift to the small tattoo over his heart. It's a cracked heart with the name Colleen and a date inscribed beside it.

"For my mom," he whispers, noticing where my attention has strayed. He stops in the door to his room, hugging the doorway. His eyes glass over, and my heart hurts for him again.

"It's beautiful." I press a kiss to two of my fingers before placing them over the ink.

"She would have loved you," he whispers with a sad smile.

"I wish I could have met her."

"Me too."

After a few beats of silence, when it's clear he's not going to say anything more, I urge him forward, helping him wordlessly into the en suite bathroom.

Making Beck sit on the closed toilet lid, I walk into his impressive shower, with two rainforest heads and a narrow bench that rests alongside the wall underneath the frosted glass window, and turn it on. I hop out before I get drenched, shrieking when I turn around to be greeted with Beck's bare ass. He's bent over, with one hand on the counter to steady himself, while yanking his sweats down his legs.

"Jesus!" I shield my eyes with my hand. "You couldn't have waited until I had left?"

"Shit, sorry," he says, still slurring his words a little.

"Shower and I'll take care of the rest." I hurry out of the room, trying to forget the spectacular visual as I close the door behind me.

I put fresh linen on his bed, with sheets I found in the linen closet, and then I head into the kitchen to make him something light to eat. Pickings are slim, but I forage some vegetable soup and crusty bread that'll work.

When I reappear in his bedroom ten minutes later, Beck is tucked into bed, propped up against the headrest with tons of fluffy pillows behind him, wearing a sheepish grin. I'm glad to see some color in his cheeks. "Sorry about that."

I set the tray down on his lap. "Don't worry about it. It's only an ass."

"How very French of you," he teases, lifting the spoon with a smile.

"How very French of *you*," I retort, also with a smile.

I sit beside him on the bed, watching as he eats his bread and soup. When he finishes, I hand him a glass of water and some pain pills, watching as he dutifully swallows them. "You should sleep. It's late, and you need to sleep off the alcohol."

"I don't want you to go." His eyes bore into mine.

"I'm not going anywhere." I lean down and kiss his brow. "Sleep, Beck. I promise I'll be here when you wake." I can't leave him when he's in this state. I'd only worry he might puke in his sleep.

He lies down on his side, tucking his hands under his cheek as he faces me. I get up and drag the tub chair across the room, setting it by his bed. I sink into it and pull out my phone and my AirPods.

"Stevie," he whispers, his eyes already losing a fighting battle.

"Yeah?"

"Thank you for being here."

"That's what friends are for."

Chapter Sixteen

Stevie

Beck is softly snoring five minutes later with the covers only pulled up to his waist, exposing the top half of his body. I tap out a quick text to Hadley before choosing some music and settling back in the chair.

I can't help inspecting every visible inch of Beck while he sleeps as Halsey's dulcet tones whisper in my ears.

The cropped hairstyle he favors showcases his exquisite face in all its magnificence. He looks so much younger than twenty-seven in sleep. There's a boyish innocence to his face that is hidden during the waking hours. Long lashes fan over high cheekbones, and little puffs of air trickle from his full lips. The hair on his chin and cheeks and above his mouth is denser than usual, but it works for him.

His chest rises and falls in deep slumber, highlighting the definition of his body. His upper torso and his biceps are ripped without being ridiculously muscular. I know he works out and runs daily, but damn, his body is a work of art with an expanse of unblemished olive skin over sculpted muscles in all the right places.

I haven't really noticed it before, but Beck is absolutely beautiful in a totally masculine way.

I force my eyes to look away as the acknowledgment lands in my thoughts. No good can come from thinking those things.

I wake to a gentle shaking sensation, groaning as I move my stiff neck.

"You fell asleep in the chair," Beck says, crouching over me with concern in his eyes. "You looked really uncomfortable. I'm sorry. I didn't even offer you the guest bed."

"It's fine," I say over a yawn. "I knew I could sleep in one of the other rooms, but I didn't want to leave you in case you were sick during the night."

Beck sits on the side of his bed, wearing only light gym shorts. He smooths a hand back and forth across his hair. "I am so sorry for last night, Stevie."

"You have nothing to apologize for." I rub the back of my sore neck.

"I do. I haven't replied to any of your calls or messages. I can't imagine what you were thinking."

"Beck, it's okay."

"It's not. I..." Propping his elbows on his knees, he buries his face in his hands.

I move over and sit beside him on the bed. "You can talk to me. About anything. It works both ways. You have been there for me, and I want to be here for you now. I know you're hurting. I know this is about Brielle, and I want you to know you can tell me anything. I won't judge. I know what it's like to carry so much guilt it feels like you're suffocating."

Tormented brown eyes lift to my green ones. "You're going to think so little of me."

"That is an impossibility."

His tongue darts out, wetting his dry lips, and my eyes track the motion. When I look up, Beck's eyes are glued to my mouth. The tension from last night is back, and that same fluttering feeling erupts in my chest. I shift awkwardly on the bed, avert my eyes, and focus on my lap.

Beck clears his throat after a few seconds. "I left some supplies in the bathroom if you want to take a shower or a bath."

I raise my chin.

"My sisters have toiletries and clothes here. I think Sarah's stuff should fit, so I left a few things out for you. I know she won't mind." He stands, wrapping his arms around his trim waist. "I'm going to walk down to the local bakery and grab us some coffees and croissants if you like?"

"That sounds good." I cough to clear the dryness from my tone.

"Okay." Beck rubs the back of his neck. "I'll leave you to it," he says, making a beeline for his walk-in closet while I hightail it to the bathroom.

When I emerge from his bathroom thirty minutes later, in Sarah's ripped jeans and an off-the-shoulder T-shirt, I feel invigorated after my shower but a little on edge. Something is different between us, or maybe it's nerves because I don't know what he has to tell me, and I hope it doesn't make a liar of me. I make my way toward the door, setting out to find Beck when he calls out to me.

"Out here," he says from the balcony off his bedroom.

I walk out through the French doors and join him. It's a glorious day, and the balcony is bathed in early-morning May sunshine. Beck has the table set with freshly squeezed orange juice, coffee, pastries, and croissants.

"This looks lovely, thanks," I say as I slide onto the chair across from him.

"You're welcome." He hands me my coffee, and I smile as I detect the caramel scents.

"Figured you needed a sugar hit after a shitty night's sleep."

"I actually slept okay," I admit. "At home, I regularly get nightmares, and it's rare I get a full night's sleep without medication."

"I slept good too, which is unusual for me as well."

We dive into our breakfast, not speaking much, but it's not awkward. Amicable silences are part and parcel of our friendship, and I never feel the urge to fill the gaps in our conversation.

"I need to tell you about Brielle," he says when we have finished eating. "If you have time."

"I have time. It's a quicker walk to the hospital from here, and I don't have to leave yet."

His fingers drum on the table, and his jean-clad knee taps up and down.

I reach across the table and squeeze his hand. "Don't be nervous."

"I need you to know the truth. I need to tell someone because it's killing me inside." His voice cracks, and pain gleams in his eyes. "I could tell Tate or Law, but I don't want to. I want to tell you even though I'm terrified you'll want nothing more to do with me."

I scoot my chair in closer. "I'm not going anywhere, Beck." I cup his face, feeling the sincerity in my words despite my previous concern. "Unless you give me the coordinates to the dead bodies, and then I'm out of here." I attempt to lighten the tense atmosphere, but it doesn't raise a smile.

Beck links his fingers in mine, holding tightly on to my hand. "I broke it off with her," he says, staring deep into my eyes. "Five days before she took her own life, I ended things with Brielle. She called me relentlessly in the days that followed, but I ignored her. I was going to check in on her, but then it was too late. She had killed herself, and it was entirely my fault."

Chapter Seventeen

Beck

"Tell me everything," she says, squeezing my hand and maintaining eye contact. "I know there's got to be more to it than that."

"There isn't. I'm a horrible person. The end."

"You're not. Tell me how you came to break it off with her. I thought you said you couldn't because of your father's blackmail?"

"I was miserable, Stevie," I admit, keeping a firm hold of her hand as I stare out over the immaculate grounds of the rear gardens behind us. "I was depressed, and my writing wasn't even helping. I was getting sucked into this dark hole, and I was desperate. It was the day before I was due to go to London on a business trip. Dad stormed into my office with an engagement ring. He told me I was to propose when I returned from England, and I lost it. We had a very heated argument, and I was just done."

Air whistles out of my mouth. She rubs soothing circles on the top of my hand with her thumb, helping to ground me. "I was all fired up, and I went straight to Brielle. I told her I couldn't do it anymore. That it wasn't fair for either of us and our fathers were assholes. She begged me not to do it. Said we could try to make it work. But I told her no."

"I'm confused." Lines appear on her smooth brow. "I thought she wasn't into it either?"

"She wasn't."

"So why wouldn't she just accept it? She was off the hook. You were the one making the decision, not her."

My knee bounces when my foot taps the ground. "I don't know why. I didn't give her a chance to say much. I just told her I was making our breakup official when I returned from London and she was free of me then to properly live her life."

"Do you think she harbored secret feelings for you? Is that why she reacted so strongly?"

I shrug. "I really don't think so. Like I said, we tried at the start, but there was no spark at all. Sex was awkward, and it was clear we just weren't into one another like that."

"Maybe she changed her mind."

"Maybe." I lift our conjoined hands to my mouth and brush my lips across her knuckles. Stevie's cheeks inflame, and I inwardly curse as confusion and panic races across her face. "Sorry." I immediately let go of her hand. Heat creeps up my neck. "I'm not sure why I did that," I lie.

She blinks and waves it off, seeming to shake herself out of it. "Did she leave messages when she called?"

I nod. "She was calling and leaving messages every day, begging me to give us another shot." Pain pierces me in the chest. "I didn't understand it, and I should have called her when the messages became increasingly teary, but I was working twelve-hour days, and with the time difference, it was difficult. I planned to go see her when I returned, but by the time I landed, she was already at the hospital on life support."

I hang my head in shame.

"I understand why you feel it's your fault. I've been in your shoes. But like everyone, including you, has been telling me, you are not responsible for Brielle's actions."

I lift my head, running a hand across the tightness in my chest. "There is no excuse for how I let her down. None. I could have found a gap during my day to call her, and I didn't."

"You were depressed, Beck. If you want to point the finger of blame at someone, point it at your fathers. They forced you into something neither of you wanted."

"It doesn't exonerate me. I was a shitty friend to her in the end. She might still be alive if I hadn't broken up with her. If I had returned any of her calls."

"You don't know that." She leans forward, taking both my hands in hers.

Earnest green eyes pin me in place, and I'm drowning in her beauty and the goodness that radiates from her like a beacon. Stevie has no makeup on, and she's dressed casually, but she's the most beautiful woman I've ever seen.

It is getting harder and harder to deny my feelings when I'm around her.

It seems there's no end to my pitifulness.

Developing feelings for a woman whose heart is already claimed is the definition of stupidity.

Yet I can't help it.

I am drawn to her in a way I have never been drawn to any woman before.

I am powerless to stop it.

"It sounds to me like maybe there was something else going on with her," she muses. "Something that made her change her mind about your relationship."

"Like what?"

"I don't know, and we're probably never going to, but you can't beat yourself up over it forever. The truth is, this might have had nothing to do with you at all, and berating yourself won't bring her back. Just like me blaming myself for not accepting Garrick's gift makes no difference now. It's inconsequential. What has happened cannot be reversed."

"This is why I needed to tell you. You understand in a way no one else does."

"I do, which is why I'm begging you to try to let this go. Drinking yourself into a stupor won't bring Brielle back. All it will do is make you feel worse. I know there's a process you need to go through to purge these thoughts and feelings. You can't bottle them up and pretend they don't exist. I tried that, and it doesn't work. But I'm here for you, and maybe you need to talk to someone."

Releasing my hands, she runs her fingers through her hair. "I'll make you a deal. Mom, Nana, and Hadley have been nagging me for months to go to therapy. I couldn't face it. Still don't know if I can, but I'll go if you will." Her eyes search my face. "Let's go and talk it out with professionals and see if it helps."

"I suppose it can't make things any worse."

Glancing at my watch for the umpteenth time, I fight the urge to call Stevie. Today is the anniversary of the accident, and Stevie wanted to spend it at the hospital with Garrick and their families and friends. I get that, but I'm on edge worrying about her. She's been so low this past week. Both of us have been taking turns singing the blues.

Since the night she found me in a drunken mess, Stevie has come here every day after work. We eat dinner together, and then we either take it easy with a movie and a glass of wine or we work companionably in silence in my office. I write while she crafts dried-flower pictures.

I have never been more at ease with another living soul, and I love having her here more often. I miss her after I walk her back to her place, hating coming back to an empty apartment.

We each found a therapist and have our first appointments next week. I think Stevie is really going to need it. The anniversary has dredged a lot of feelings to the surface, and she needs to confront them. Like I need to confront my feelings about Brielle. It was easier to pretend they weren't there when she was lying in a hospital bed and I had Stevie to distract me. The funeral forced me to face up to it, and I'm struggling to move past my guilt. If I had done things differently, Brielle could be alive. As long as I live, I don't think I'll ever be able to forgive myself for letting her down.

It's funny how we're great at giving one another the perfect advice, yet we're remiss in taking it ourselves.

A loud thump against the front door rouses me from my inner monologue, and I'm up on my feet in a flash. "Beck!" Stevie's anguished cry is muffled through the wood, but her pain is visceral. She falls into my arms when I open the door, clinging to me and crying. Approaching footfalls pound up the stairs as I wrap my arms around Stevie, offering what comfort I can. Hadley appears at the top of the stairs, red-faced and out of breath.

Stevie is sobbing into my neck, and the sounds coming from her mouth are the most agonized sounds I've ever heard. When her legs almost give out, I scoop Stevie into my arms and step back to let her best friend in. Hadley and I exchange a troubled look as she closes my front door.

I carry Stevie into the living room and sit on the couch. She clutches at my shirt, pressing herself as close as possible as she leans her entire body into me.

"Breathe, honey." I rub a soothing hand up and down her back. "Do it for me, nice and slow."

Strangled sounds rip from her mouth, and I don't think she's even hearing me.

"What happened?" I ask Hadley as I cradle Stevie on my lap and do my best to comfort her.

"Ivy bitchface soon-to-be deadface happened." A muscle pulses in Hadley's jaw, and fire spurts from her eyes. "She's moving Garrick to her house, and Stevie is banned from visiting."

"Fuck." I hug Stevie tighter as her wails accelerate. "Can she do that? Is it even safe for him to be moved?"

"Apparently yes, as long as it's done in a controlled manner. Hugh has known this past week about Ivy's plans. He kept it from Stevie as he knew it would upset her. He went to his lawyers to see if he could stop it, but he can't. Ivy has power of attorney, and she's done her homework. The cunt," Hadley adds, and that dangerous gleam is back in her eye.

"She's been gathering a team of experts to take over his care at her home," she continues. "They all gave written reports outlining the conditions for the transfer and how this could be a good thing for Garrick. To be in familiar surroundings with a full-time specialist medical team who is solely devoted to his care."

"Yet she plans to deny his girlfriend access to him?" Disbelief bleeds from my tone. Don't get me wrong. I knew Ivy was scheming to hurt Stevie, but this is completely at odds with this new medical strategy, and it makes no sense.

"From my research," I continue. "I know how important it is for his loved ones to be there for him. Everything Stevie has done for Garrick plays a key part in his recovery. Coma patients have woken up revealing they heard everything going on around them. Many said it was their loved one's voice that tethered them to this world. How the fuck can that stupid bitch claim to love her son when she is cutting out the most important person in his life?" My voice elevates as anger charges through me. I am so pissed on Stevie's behalf. She has been a model girlfriend, devoted to him, and she doesn't deserve to be iced out.

"Because she hates me," Stevie chokes out, sitting back a little on my lap. "She hates me more."

I cradle her tearstained face in my hands. "We'll fight her. We'll visit my lawyer tomorrow and see what can be done. She can't shut you out like this."

"Except she can." Silent tears stream down Stevie's face. "Hugh already asked these questions of his legal team. There is nothing clinically proven that says loved ones aid in coma patient recovery. We have no legal grounds for requesting an order to be granted to permit me to visit him when it's in her home and she has power of attorney. It would just be a waste of your money."

"Hugh proposed that everyone boycott visiting him to force Ivy's hand," Hadley explains from her perch on the arm of my couch.

"But I said no." Stevie accepts the tissues I hand her, blowing her nose and wiping her damp eyes. "I appreciate the gesture, but we can't leave Garrick alone with Ivy and Pepper. He will need familiar voices around him. Especially now Pepper is moving into Ivy's house so she can be around for him more."

I hate seeing the defeat on Stevie's face though I understand it. This is too much for her fragile mind to cope with. Especially today. It's obvious Ivy timed her attack to strike at the most vulnerable moment.

I never thought I'd hate anyone as much as I hate my father, but she's right up there in joint pole position.

"That stupid cunt," Hadley hisses. "Pepper was at the hospital pretending like she wasn't gloating. Garrick has no interest in her. Governor Barbie just looks pathetic with her stupid pearls and her designer clothes and expensive haircut. I have never wanted to cut a bitch as badly as I wanted to tonight. Even Nana was champing at the bit for a go at her."

"There is nothing I can do," Stevie says in a dead voice, resting her head on my shoulder. "I won't ever get to see him again. The bitch won."

Not if I have anything to say about it.

"This sucks, babe," Hadley says. "I hate that woman so much."

"I don't have any fight left in me," Stevie whispers, grabbing a fistful of my damp shirt. "I tried. I tried to be there for him. I've put my life on hold, and it's been for nothing. Garrick is still in a coma. It's been a year, and I need to face facts. He's not ever going to wake up. Maybe she's done me a favor, because this is forcing me to move on whether I want to or not." An errant sob ripples through the air, and I dust kisses into her hair, feeling her pain like a stab wound to the chest.

"I can't tell you what to do, babe," Hadley says, moving to sit beside us. She grips Stevie's hand. "All I can say is no girlfriend could have done more. If Garrick wakes, he'll know that. Everyone will ensure it. He will also know this separation was forced by his mother, not you." She squeezes her hand. "At least you can still get updates. Helena and the nurses will keep you informed too. You know they hate her, and it's only the lure of the money that has enticed them away."

"Who is Helena?" I ask.

"Helena is his physical therapist. She and two of the nurses are going to be moving to his private care team, and Dr. Edwards has an agreement to receive regular reports from the neurosurgeon who is taking over from him, so at least Stevie will know how he's doing."

"It won't be the same," Stevie says in a monotone voice. "I was barely holding on when I got to visit him. I don't think I can do it if I can't see him anymore. This is too hard. My heart can't stand it." She looks up at me with fresh tears in her eyes. "Tell me what to do, Beck, because right now, I'm so lost."

Chapter Eighteen

Beck

"I wish I knew, honey." I brush matted strands of damp hair back off her face. "All you can do is take it one step at a time. One day at a time."

"And it's good you have already decided to go to therapy," Hadley says. "You can't keep this locked up inside any longer, babe. You need to let it all out and start to heal."

"I need to get drunk," Stevie says, climbing off my lap. "I just need to blot this all out." She traipses into the kitchen, leaving me alone with Hadley.

"That won't help," Hadley says.

"Trust me, I know that better than anyone."

"But she needs this."

"Agreed." I rub at the pain in my chest. "I'll take good care of her. She can stay here tonight. I have something to show her that might cheer her up."

"Doubtful, but I appreciate your willingness to try."

Stevie ambles back into the room with a bottle of white wine tucked under her arm and three wineglasses in her hand. Hadley hops up to grab the bottle before it falls. The girls pour the wine into glasses, and Stevie hands me one before climbing back into my lap. I'm not complaining. If she draws comfort from being close to me, I'll gladly oblige.

Hadley watches with shrewd eyes, wisely saying nothing as she kicks her shoes off and curls her feet up on my couch. "Nice place you got here, Beck."

"Thank you. I love living here. I'm a real homebody, and I spend a lot of time in this apartment."

"I love it here too," Stevie says in between guzzling her wine.

I spot an opening and go for it. "I'm glad you do. You know I love having you here." Taking her wineglass, I set it down beside mine on the end table. She pouts, and I chuckle. "You can have it back in a minute. I have something to show you." I stand with her in my arms, reluctantly placing her feet on the floor. I'd happily carry her around all the time if that was an option. I like having her in my arms.

Clutching her hand in mine, I jerk my head in Hadley's direction. "Come look."

We pad out to the bedrooms, and I discreetly wipe my sweaty palm down the front of my jeans. I hope she likes it and that it's not too overwhelming for her.

Before I open the door to the guest bedroom, I turn to face her, softly tipping her chin up with two fingers. "I want you to feel comfortable here. I want you to know you always have a place to stay here. Any night you don't want to go home, this room is yours. No strings attached. No agenda." I smile. "No more sleeping in tub chairs."

She gulps. "Show me."

Without further ado, I open the door to what was once Sarah's bedroom when she slept over, revealing the new interior.

Stevie's eyes go wide and Hadley gasps as they drink it all in.

A distressed white brick wall behind the bed houses a black-and-white framed print with a lone red poppy. Two white and gray bedside tables rest on either side of the bed with small red lamps on top. The bedcover is mainly white with red poppies scattered across the material. The underside is patterned with small red dots. Copious pillows adorn the bed. Some are in plain white or red silk. Others match the covers. Pale gray floorboards rest underfoot, and an enormous fluffy white rug covers most of the space. Poppy drapes frame the window.

"Is that Nana's field?" Stevie asks, spying the eight framed pictures on the wall at the end of the room. She moves toward them.

The photos are stacked side by side, in two rows of four, making one giant picture in squares. In the corner is a large gray leather recliner chair, and I had fitted bookshelves built into the wall. A tall lamp curves over the chair for nighttime reading.

I toyed with the idea of putting a desk in here in place of the large chair, so she could work or make dried-flower pictures, but I want this room to be a place of rest and relaxation. I decided to add a second desk in my study instead, but I won't do that yet. I don't want to overwhelm her, and I can tell this is already a lot to take in.

"It is." I can't keep the smile off my face. "I swore Nana to secrecy when I dropped by last week and took photos. A photographer friend of mind printed and framed them for me."

"They are stunning," Hadley says. "The whole room is." She offers me a warm smile before fixing it on Stevie. "What do you think, babe?"

Stevie audibly gulps as her gaze darts wildly around the room. She tips her head up to look at me. "You did this for me?" Her voice is thick with emotion.

"I did."

"But what about Sarah? Won't she be angry?"

I shake my head. "Sarah hardly ever stays here, and it was never officially her room. I replaced the king bed in the lavender room with two doubles, so if both my sisters are here together, they can just share that room. It's rare they stay over, whereas you are here more often."

"I don't mean to intrude."

I step close to her, lightly placing my hands on her hips. "You aren't intruding. You're my best friend, Stevie. I wanted to do this for you so you feel comfortable to stay over when you want to. I know Hadley has plans to travel during the summer. If you don't want to be alone, you can stay here any night you want. Or not," I add, stepping back and creating space between us when I see the emotions flitting across her face. "There is no pressure. I just wanted to create your own space here. You don't even have to stay. You might like to come in here and read at times when I'm writing."

Slowly, she walks toward me and circles her arms around my waist. "Thank you," she whispers. "This is one of the nicest things anyone has ever done for me."

"You're welcome." I wrap my arms around her back, loving that she's growing more comfortable touching me.

"You're making me look bad, dude," Hadley says, faux glaring at me.

"Shut up," Stevie says, snuggling into my chest.

I could quite happily die in this moment a completely content man.

"You're the motherfucking bestie of besties," Stevie adds, eyeballing her friend. "No one is ever knocking you off the top spot." She peeks up at me. "Sorry, Beck. You're a close second, but Hadley will always be my girl."

"Aw, shucks." Hadley runs over, throwing her arms around us in a group hug. "I think I'm going to cry."

"Please do," Stevie encourages her before we break the embrace. "I can't be the only basket case to fall apart."

"You're allowed to be human," I remind her. "Today's been a really tough day for you. I'd be alarmed if you didn't cry."

"At least I broke my dry-eye spell." Stevie grips my hand. "Sorry for sobbing all over you."

"You never have to apologize for that."

"Come on," she says, tugging on my hand. "I want to drink my body weight in wine and then collapse in my gorgeous new room where I'll hopefully have a dreamless sleep."

Stevie doesn't drink her weight in wine despite her convictions. Hadley left after one glass. I offered her the other guest bedroom, but she politely declined. Her exams start Monday, so she can't afford to have a hangover tomorrow and waste her last precious study day. I put some music on, steering clear of the golden oldies I know remind Stevie of Garrick, and we slowly sip wine as we talk.

"I'm so sad," she admits from her end of the couch. "This day a year ago is when my life, and Garrick's life, irreversibly changed. This date is always going to be hard for me."

"I know, but you'll get through it. No other anniversary will be as hard as this one. The first is always the worst." We don't add how Ivy made a difficult situation even more difficult because it doesn't need to be said.

"Could we listen to The Carpenters?" she asks.

"Of course. Whatever you want."

"'Superstar,' please. It fits how I'm feeling right now."

PLAY ON SPOTIFY

I change the song, putting on the one she requested. I have a lump in my throat listening to the lyrics and the haunting melody. It's so fucking sad. Tears roll down Stevie's face, and I'm struggling not to cry myself. Fuck, this song is too close to home.

Stevie stands, holding her arm out, and I let her pull me up, knowing what she needs before she vocalizes it. I'm surprised she'd want to do this with me, but I don't question it. If this is what she needs, she's got it.

I open my arms, and she melts against me, snaking her arms tightly around my waist and resting her head on my chest. I hold her tight as we sway side to side, slowly moving around my living room to the music. She quietly sobs into my shirt, and a few tears creep out of my eyes. "Put on 'Only Yesterday'," she says when the first song ends, and I oblige.

PLAY ON SPOTIFY

Stevie holds me tighter as the lyrics bounce off the walls, and we dance in the same position, clinging to one another in a way that's super intense. It's impossible not to feel emotional. Her pain is palpable. And it's a struggle not to crush her to me when I want to hold her in my arms for eternity. She molds perfectly to my body, and it feels like she belongs. Nothing has ever felt more right.

I can barely force breaths out my mouth as the lyrics and my thoughts resonate deeply.

This girl.

She. Is. Everything.

Stevie is changing me inside.

Making me feel things I've never felt before.

I'm terrified I'm going to get my heart broken.

Because I can't compete with a guy in a coma.

And I hate that I even want to.

Chapter Nineteen

Stevie

I call in sick to work on Monday, permitting myself one more day to fall apart. I probably should have returned home this morning, but Beck has gone to the office, and I have his place to myself. He told me to make myself at home, so I take a bath in his clawfoot tub, crying an endless stream of tears as The Carpenters play in the background while I sip a glass of wine. I know alcohol isn't the answer and I can't make this a habit, but I'm giving myself today to wallow.

Tomorrow, I'll try to pull myself together.

Hadley drops off a bag with some of my clothes en route to the university to take her first exam. I manage to dry my eyes while she's here. The last thing she needs to worry about the week of finals is her mess of a roommate.

After she leaves, I change into gray sweats and a white tank, pull my hair into a messy bun, and lounge on the recliner in my room. I have my AirPods in, and I'm listening to the playlist Garrick made for me while I scroll through photos of us on my phone through blurry eyes.

If I'd known Saturday morning was the last time I'd see my love, I would have said so much more. I would have told him how much he brightened up my world and how gray it feels without him in it. I would have reminded him he's my everything and told him to keep fighting to come back to me. I would have told him how empty I feel without his love and how much I regret keeping distance between us.

Since the accident, I have questioned everything I thought I knew about my future and what I want from life. I realized too late that Garrick was right. My career goals mean little without him in my life. Why was I so determined to wait until I was thirty to get married and have kids?

You can't plan every aspect of life to the nth degree.

The accident proves that point in the most devastating way.

Life is short, and you need to make the most of it.

I need to make the most of it.

I should have made Garrick my priority.

I should have taken out a student loan and stayed at UO for senior year with my boyfriend and then moved to Seattle with him when we had graduated. Then I could have focused on my career goals with the man I love by my side.

I hate it took this tragedy for me to wake up and understand what is truly important in life.

I enjoy my work, and I give it my all, but I have given no consideration to starting my own business. I'm not sure it's even what I want to do anymore. Nothing matters in the same way. Family and friends are the only things that matter.

Picking up the special edition book Beck gave me, I open it to the first page and reread the inscription through my tears. I haven't stopped reading it since Beck gifted the book to me, and it never fails to warm my frozen heart.

To Stevie,

No one has ever believed in me like you do. No one inspires me as much as you do. Although we met under tragic circumstances, I am so grateful we found one another. Thank you for understanding and sharing my passion. As a writer, I should have the words to properly convey how much it means to me, yet they simply don't exist in the English language.

I adore you.

Love, Beck.

It's even more special that he signed his own name. Placing his trust in me like this is huge. I don't think I would have survived these past couple nights if Beck hadn't helped me through it. I can't even contemplate how much bleaker my life would be without him.

Clutching the book to my chest, I close my eyes and cry as song after song plays in my ears.

That is how Beck finds me when he returns at lunch to check in. Sympathy splays across his face when he lifts me from my chair, cradling me in his arms as he carries us over to the bed.

With great tenderness, he lays me down on the comfy mattress before kicking off his shoes and removing his suit jacket and joining me. He gently pries the book from my hands with a shy smile and places it on the bedside table. Then he pulls me into his arms, and I go willingly, sobbing into his chest as he holds me tight. His large palm runs up and down my back, and he dots kisses into my hair as I fall apart.

It feels horribly mean to cry to him over another man, but he never criticizes or turns me away. He shares my pain, my grief, and my anger at the situation, and he is there for me no matter what I need. He is such a good man. Right up there with Garrick in the gentleman rankings.

I don't know how long we stay like that because I fall asleep. My crying jaunt has exhausted me. When I wake, Beck is still here. His protective arms are wrapped around me, and his lips are pressed to my temple. "Are you hungry?" he whispers, brushing wispy strands of hair off my brow. "You've been asleep for hours."

"I'm sorry," I croak through my scraped throat. "Did you get in trouble with work?"

He shakes his head. "I took the afternoon off. I wanted to be here for you."

Tears well in my eyes. "You are so good to me."

"You're good to me too. You helped keep me together. Now it's my turn."

"What if I never get to see him again?" I ask, peering deep into his eyes. "What if Saturday was the last time I ever saw him and he dies and I never got to tell him again I love him. This is what keeps going round and round in my head all the time. I feel ill." I palm my queasy stomach. "Why does she hate me so much to do this to me?" Sobs rip from my throat, and I bury my face in his shirt.

"This isn't about you, honey," he says in a soothing deep voice. "This is all about her insecurity. She could see how much Garrick loves you, and I bet she feels threatened by it. I'd put money on that being the crux of it. It's not really about Pepper though it would suit her for Garrick to be with the governor's daughter for the political kudos. But I think it's because she knows he would never love her like he loves you. Pepper is the safe predictable choice. You are anything but."

"Do you really think that's what it is?"

Beck nods, shifting to an upright position and taking me with him. "She's still a snob, and no doubt that is part of it, but mostly it's because she feels threatened by you. I'm sure of it." We lie back against the headboard, and he takes my hands in his. "I need to tell you something. I hope you won't feel I have overstepped the mark, but I couldn't sit back and do nothing. I heard you crying the past two nights and it's killing me, Stevie. I want to make this better, but I don't know how."

"You make it better just by being here for me." I smile through my sniffles. "I can't believe we have only known one another four months when it feels like you have been in my life forever."

"I feel the same, sweet girl." Beck presses a lingering kiss to my brow before fixing me with a serious expression. "Which is why I couldn't let Ivy cuntface get away with it."

I tilt my head to one side. "What did you do?"

"I recruited a trusted contact to help, and we spent the morning making calls. The bitch is blacklisted all over town. She's being thrown off charity committees and kicked out of the country club as we speak. Her charity and dinner invites will dry up, and she'll be a social pariah. I even got her personal trainer and her hairdresser to ditch her as clients."

My jaw slackens as I stare at him in amazement. "You did? How?"

"My family name carries a lot of clout in this town. We are influential in a way she is not. Ivy is small fry compared to the Colberts."

"But she has the governor in her pocket. He'll probably find a way to fix everything."

He shakes his head as a devious grin blooms on his face. "Her name is mud, and Paul won't intervene. I made sure of it. Dad recently agreed to fund his future presidential campaign. I reminded the governor I would be succeeding my father as CEO at some point in the near future. He doesn't need to know it's a lie to believe it as it's how things work in family businesses. I made it clear if he made any attempt to help Ivy he could kiss that funding goodbye. He got the message loud and clear. Ivy is on her own."

I stare at him in a bit of a daze, blown away he would go to this much trouble for me.

"Are you mad?" he asks, misinterpreting my shell-shocked expression.

I shake my head. "Not a bit. She had it coming, and she deserves to suffer in a way she understands."

"I called her," he adds, and my eyes pop wide. "I wanted her to know who did this to her and for her to understand you had no knowledge of it. That it was all on me." His Adam's apple bobs in his throat. "I told her I'd retract it all if she permitted you to visit. She told me to go fuck myself. That the only way you'd see her son was if she was dead."

"Maybe she'll get hit by a bus." I swipe at the dampness on my cheeks. I can't believe the lengths Beck has gone to. He has pulled out all the stops to get me in to see Garrick, and I don't know how I can ever repay him. "Wouldn't that be karma?"

"I thought she'd agree to it."

"She probably thinks the governor will handle it."

"Most likely. Perhaps she'll come crawling back then."

"I doubt it. You didn't see how vicious she was on Saturday night. She's not going to back down."

"Perhaps I was wrong to give her an ultimatum. I might have made it worse," he adds, loosening his tie and tossing it to the end of the bed.

I twist around so I can see his face. "She isn't gonna change her mind. Appearances matter to her, but she's stubborn. She hates me, and she's made it her mission to get me away from her son. You didn't make it worse. You did the only thing that might work. If she doesn't go for it, she won't go for anything." I lean over and hug him. "Thank you so much for this. I love how you went to bat for me. You're amazing, Beck. I don't know how I can ever repay you. That you would do something like this means the world to me."

"I had another idea." A smirk plays across his lips.

"Okay." I drag out the word, waiting for him to elaborate.

"Let's make her a villain in my new book. You can help me to plot her character."

A giggle sneaks from between my lips. "Oh, that would be so fun. We'll make her really nasty and ensure she meets a gruesome fate." I rub my hands together as ideas flit through my mind. "Let's do it." I fling my arms around him again. "You're the absolute best, Beck." I peer deep into his warm brown eyes, only now realizing how I'm pressed all up against him with our faces so close our noses are almost touching.

As I pull back to create space between us, the doorbell chimes.

Beck looks at me with a slight frown. "Are you expecting Hadley or anyone else?"

I shake my head. "Nope. Hadley already stopped by, and she texted me after her exam. I told her to go home and study, so I doubt it's her."

Beck is already scrambling off the bed. "Stay here. I'll get it, and then we can order food."

I head to the bathroom to wash my face and clean myself up, grabbing a light cardigan and throwing it on over my tank before I wander out to the living room to see who was at the door.

A somewhat familiar girl with straight jet-black hair is standing in the living room with an ashen Beck. I go immediately to his side, offering moral support as I eyeball the woman warily. Who is she, and what does she want? Her presence seems to have upset Beck, and I don't like it. She returns my probing stare, and we face off for a few seconds. Her purple-blue eyes are striking, and a light bulb goes off in my head. Now I remember where I know her from. "You were at Brielle's funeral."

Sorrow skates over her face. "I was."

Beck threads his fingers in mine. "Jan was Brielle's best friend and roommate."

She looks up at him, knotting and unknotting her fingers as she nibbles on her lower lip. "I'm sorry for just showing up here, but I need to talk to you, Beck. There are things you don't know. Things you need to know and things I need to get off my chest."

Chapter Twenty
Stevie

"How long have you and Beck been together?" Jan asks when Beck is in the kitchen getting coffee.

"We're not together in that way. We're good friends, and we met at the hospital four months ago." I pull my knees up to my chest, wrapping my arms around my legs. "My boyfriend is in a coma."

"Oh no." Sympathy shines from her eyes. "I'm so sorry."

I offer her a weak smile, hoping she drops the subject because I'm too fragile today to entertain any conversation about Garrick. Thankfully, she doesn't pry. "I'm sorry for your loss," I say. "How long had you known Brielle?"

"Six years. We met freshman year of college, and we were thick as thieves from then on. We didn't even discuss moving in together after we graduated. It was a given."

"She valued your friendship a lot." Beck enters the room carrying a tray with coffees and cookies.

"I don't think I was a good enough friend at the end," Jan says, accepting a mug from Beck.

"That's exactly how I feel," he agrees, handing me a coffee.

"It's why I'm here." Jan wraps both hands around her mug as she sips her drink. "I should have come sooner, but I've been wallowing in grief and only thinking of myself. When I saw you at the funeral"—her eyes dart between me and Beck—"I realized I needed to let you know because I recognized the invisible weight on your shoulders. I could tell you were blaming yourself, like I've spent months blaming myself, and I want to put your mind at ease."

"I'm not sure that's possible." Beck sits on the couch beside me. "But I'm interested in what you have to say." His thigh brushes against mine, and I welcome the heat from his body. I've felt a bone-deep chill all day that has nothing to do with the temperature.

"Should I leave the room?" I inquire, my gaze dancing between Beck and Jan. "If this is a private conversation, I can make myself scarce."

"I have no issue speaking in front of you," Jan says.

Beck peers deep into my eyes. "I would like you to stay."

I read everything he's not saying. "Okay."

Relief and gratitude shimmer in his eyes before he turns his attention back to Brielle's friend. "Tell me what you know."

"I know your relationship wasn't real," she says. "I just want to put that out there. Elle and I didn't keep secrets from one another. Well, not until those last few months."

"I suspected as much anyway."

"Did she tell you about Dex?"

Beck shakes his head. "We weren't close in that way."

"She met Dex last summer through a colleague at work. Elle has always been a troubled soul. She was so lost and always trying to find her way. That asshole met her when she was at a real low point. I think he targeted her for her vulnerability." Her striking eyes lock on Beck's. "Were you aware she was addicted to opioids?"

"No. I never suspected. At least not until she OD'd. Then the thought did cross my mind."

I lean a little closer to Beck, for moral support, remaining silent as I drink my coffee.

"That degenerate got her hooked. He deals all kinds of shit, and he became her personal dealer-slash-boyfriend. I hated him on sight. It's the first time we fought seriously over anything. I begged her to get away from him, but she refused. She was having fun at first, and I didn't realize the drugs were anything but recreational. Then she changed, and I confronted her."

She briefly closes her eyes before heaving a sad sigh. "I should've gone to her parents when I realized she was in serious trouble, or I should have come to you. I considered it when she got really out of control, but it felt like such a betrayal. I tried to get her into rehab, but she refused. Then I tried talking to that dickhead. Begged him to walk away from her. His response was to hit on me and laugh in my face when I rejected him."

"He sounds like a real nasty piece of work," I say.

"He's the worst kind of human."

"What did he do?" Beck's jaw pulls tight.

"He knocked her up."

Tension slams into the air, and no one speaks for a few beats.

"I had no idea." Beck slumps on the couch, shock etched upon his handsome face.

"He wanted her to abort it, but she refused." She wets her lips. "That's when she came up with her crazy plan. I'm guessing, from your reaction, she never said anything to you?"

"No, but she was trying to tell me something the last day we spoke." He straightens up and levels her with a solemn look. "I broke up with her and ignored her cries for help. It's my biggest regret."

"I have a lot of regrets too, but months of therapy is teaching me how to let it go. Let's just say I'm a work in progress."

"What was her plan?" I ask, finishing my coffee and putting the empty mug back on the tray.

Jan eyeballs Beck. "She wanted you to marry her and pass the baby off as your own."

Beck spits coffee all over the hardwood floor. "What?" he splutters as I race to the kitchen to grab some towels.

"She didn't want to abort it," Jan says as I return a few seconds later. Tears pool in her eyes. "I hadn't seen Brielle that happy in years. I think that baby might have changed everything for her."

I mop up the floor, and Beck flashes me a grateful smile.

"I didn't let her speak the day I broke up with her, but even if she had, I wouldn't have agreed to her plan. I would have found some other way to help her," Beck says as I walk toward the kitchen to dispose of the wet towels. I don't doubt that at all. If Beck knew Brielle was in trouble, he would have helped her. It's so sad how everything went down.

"I suggested we go overseas. Dex was harassing her about the abortion, and I had a bad feeling. I wanted to get her away from him, but I was too late. He showed up one afternoon with two pricks who worked for him. They had guns, and Dex made it clear if Elle didn't go with him to the appointment he'd arranged he'd kill her and the baby. He threatened me too so she'd go with them without a fight. When she came back later, she was distraught. He'd forced her into an abortion and then kicked her out of the car outside our place, telling her to find herself a new dealer and a new fuck buddy."

"I want his full name," Beck says in an eerily calm voice. "I want everything you have on him."

Jan retrieves an envelope from her purse. "I was hoping you'd say that, so I prepared this in advance. It's all the intel I have."

Beck takes the envelope from her with a terse nod.

"This all went down two days before she took the overdose. That first day, she stayed in bed crying all day. The second day, unbeknown to me, because I'd had to fly to New York for a work conference, she went looking for Dex. Found him balls deep inside a girl she knew from work. He told her to fuck off and if she ever came back he'd put a bullet in her skull." Tears stream down her face. "She went home, drank a bottle of vodka, and swallowed a load of pills. She left me a teary goodbye message. I only listened to it hours later."

Sobs shake her body, and I move to her side, tentatively placing my arm around her shoulders. She doesn't flinch or shuck out of my hold, so I continue to offer silent comfort. "I called her mother, and they went over to our place, arriving the same time as the ambulance. But it was too late."

I hold her as she cries into my shoulder with tears sliding down my face.

I am officially done with this day.

Officially done with heart-wrenching tragedies.

Beck hands us a box of tissues, and sadness permeates the air.

When she composes herself, Jan looks embarrassed. "God, I'm so sorry. I thought I'd done all my crying."

"You don't have to apologize to us," Beck says.

"We get it," I add, gently squeezing her shoulder before I let her go.

"I should have told you this months ago, Beck. I hope you can forgive me." Grabbing her purse, she stands.

Beck rises to his feet the same time I do. "There's nothing to forgive, Jan. Thank you for sharing this with me and for the info."

"Make that bastard pay, Beck. He deserves to rot in hell for what he did to my best friend."

BECK

One week later, Dexter Simpson is headline news as he's arrested in a massive drug bust at his place. A ton of weapons was confiscated as well, and the two dead bodies found in the trunk of his car are the cherry on top of the cake. I hadn't predicted that, but it's the finest evidence of karma at work I've seen.

Jan wanted him to rot in hell, but rotting in a jail cell for the rest of his life will have to do. She sends me a text thanking me, and I tell her to keep in touch. I want to ensure she's doing okay. She was close to Brielle in a way I wasn't, so I can't imagine the depth of her pain.

I head to my front door to let Hadley in when the bell pings. "Hey, Beck," she says, letting her gaze roam the length of me. She whistles under her breath. "You sure make a suit look good. I bet you have all the women in the office creaming their panties and swooning at your feet."

"Yet you still threw gay model into the mix?" I've been meaning to pick a bone with her about that suggestion.

She laughs as she breezes past me. "Just answer me one thing." Hadley flops down on my couch like she owns it. "Have you ever taken it up the ass?"

I blink a couple of times, trying to work out if she's serious or not. Sometimes it's hard to tell with Stevie's best friend. "I'm down for anal if my partner is into it, but I'm a giver not a receiver. I have no issue with men being with other men, but dudes don't do it for me. I'm totally hetero and strictly into women."

"Any women?" She arches a brow, smothering a smirk. "Or do you have a type?" Her eyes gleam with mischief. "Like, say, sexy redheads with a heart of gold?"

I'm so not getting into this. "You're such a shit stirrer."

"The worst." She grins. "And I love the pun."

I roll my eyes as I fight a smile. "It wasn't intentional, trust me, and I'm glad we agree on something."

Mercifully, she lets it go, sitting up straighter. "You said you wanted to talk about a couple of things. I already know they're Stevie related, so hit me with 'em."

"She mentioned last night that you told Mike no to the trip. Why?"

"Why?" Disbelief threads through her tone as she sits forward with her hands clasped on top of her knees. "You know why. Stevie is struggling, and she needs me."

"She has coped better this week than expected, and it'll get easier with the passing of time."

"I know she has, but she's still really fucking upset. As she should be."

"She liked her therapist, and they've agreed on weekly sessions. That will help, and she has me."

The jury is out on the guy I met, but I've decided to stick it out for a few sessions. Despite feeling lighter after Jan's revelations, I'm still harboring guilt. Brielle was going to tell me about Dex, but I didn't give her the chance. I will always regret that, but at least I know breaking things off with her wasn't the reason she took her life.

"I know she has you. You've been amazing with her. I appreciate you looking out for her so much."

"It's not a chore. I care about her. Deeply."

Hadley drills me with a look. "I know."

The unspoken words linger in the air, and I'm grateful she doesn't articulate them.

"Which is why I think you should go on the European trip," I continue. "It's only a month, and I was thinking of asking Stevie to come to France with me in July. My grandparents' estate is idyllic and the perfect place to get away. It's only a few miles from a large town and an amazing beach, yet the farm feels remote. We'll have the best of both worlds, and I think she'll be able to unwind. I also thought I'd try to persuade her to get behind the wheel again. The farm is private, and there'll be no prying eyes. I wanted to ask your opinion before I mentioned it to her."

"It sounds perfect, and you should ask her. But I don't know. I don't like leaving her when she's so upset."

"I promise I'll take the best care of her, and if you and Mike want to come visit, that can be arranged. There is plenty of room."

"Why don't you ask her, and if she agrees to go, I'll tell Mike I'm coming with him."

"Sounds like a plan. I'm going to suggest the trip as a birthday gift on Saturday, which brings me to the next topic."

"I assume she's told you she doesn't want to celebrate it?"

I nod.

"She didn't celebrate her twenty-first last year, and we didn't force it. It was too soon after the accident, but I'm not letting her get away with it this year."

"Do you have something in mind? I was going to suggest we throw a small party here. Invite Nana and Monica, and my sisters will come, and I wanted her to meet my friends."

"That sounds lovely, but can we move the venue? Stevie never goes out, and we need to rectify that. She spends her life here, at our place, work, the park or the gym, and her mom's and nana's places when she goes home. But that's it. She's not living, and now she has extra time on her hands, and I think it's our duty as her besties to rectify that. Starting with her birthday."

"Should we force it if it's not what she wants?"

"Yes." She stands. "A little tough love is required. Leave the details to me. I'll text you a venue and time tomorrow, and invite your friends and your sisters. The more, the merrier. Oh, and we'll be heading to Nana's on Saturday morning, so keep your full day free."

"That suits. Betsy is going to sell some of my books in her store, and I promised I'd make the first delivery this weekend."

"Two birds. One stone." She smacks a loud kiss on my cheek. "Stevie will need us. She has finally decided to open the gifts Garrick gave her last year, and it's going to be emotional."

Chapter Twenty-One

Stevie

"I feel like I'm going to throw up," I admit, rubbing a hand over my flat stomach as I stare at the boxes lining Nana's thick rustic table.

"It's time, Little Poppy." Nana gives me a quick hug.

"You can do this, sweetheart." Mom kisses my brow.

"We're all here to hold you up," Hadley supplies as Beck gives my hand a squeeze.

It's been almost two weeks since I was shut out of Garrick's life, and it still hurts so much, but I'm getting used to my new norm. I have no choice. My therapist is helping a lot as is Beck. He surprised me this morning with a trip to France, and I surprised myself by agreeing without hesitation. It sounds incredible, and I could use a break away from here.

Hugh and Dawn have invited me for dinner tomorrow to celebrate my birthday. Hudson is coming too. They told me to bring Mom, Nana, Beck, and Hadley. My initial instinct was to say no as being at the house in North Bend is hard for me with all the memories. But I have to at least try to move on, and maybe it will help me to feel closer to Garrick.

My biggest fear in being shut out is he will fade from my memory, so I said yes to the invite.

Hadley basically forced me into going out tonight, using blatant emotional blackmail she refuses to apologize for. She told me she'd continue to refuse the trip with Mike if I didn't go out tonight. She's reserved a table at a new restaurant in Seattle that has a bar attached, so we can do cocktails before dinner and stick around for more drinks and dancing later if the mood takes us.

I was against it at first, but now I'm looking forward to it. In a muted enthusiastic way.

"Maybe open this one first," Nana suggests, handing me a white envelope.

I accept it with trembling fingers, sandwiched between Beck and Hadley as I open it. Tears prick my eyes as I remove the airplane tickets for flights that have already flown. I smile over a sob. "It was flights to Ireland for last summer," I confirm, shuffling to the other two tickets at the back. "And tickets to see the Book of Kells and visit Newgrange." On instinct, I rub the ink on the back of my neck and the tattoo on my wrist. I glance up at Beck through glassy eyes. "The Celtic symbols on our tattoos are featured in the Book of Kells and the one on my neck is carved into the walls at Newgrange. We had said we'd visit one day."

"It was a very thoughtful gift."

"It was," I agree, swiping at my tears.

Carefully placing the envelope and tickets down, I open the smaller of the three boxes, revealing a bottle of expensive champagne and a crystal flute with my name and the date of my twenty-first birthday engraved on it. I almost choke on my sobs, and Beck snakes his arm around my shoulders, letting me use him for support.

When I open the remaining boxes to reveal a stunning black and gold designer dress with a strapless top, belted waist, and full skirt and matching shoes and purse, I burst into uncontrollable tears and sob against Beck's shirt.

The poor guy needs a backup shirt whenever I'm around because I always seem to be ruining his with my tears these days.

Nana hands me some tissues, and I finally get a hold of myself, forcing my tears to abate. Today is supposed to be a happy day, and no one needs to see me falling apart again. My family and friends have been so worried about me, and I owe it to them, as well as myself, to not put a dampener on things. I need to try harder and appreciate the trouble everyone has gone to today for me. I'm so lucky to have these people in my life, and I want them to know it.

"Garrick has such good taste," Mom says, trailing her fingers along the gorgeous dress. "This will look stunning on you."

"I don't know if I can wear it." I dab at my damp eyes.

"Course you can." Hadley grips my hand tight in hers. "It would be the greatest way of honoring Garrick. He knew this would look fabulous on you. I say you wear it tonight and we take tons of photos."

The unspoken part of that sentence goes unsaid. I have noticed my family doing that in recent times. No one says "when Garrick wakes" anymore. The anniversary was a turning point in more than one way. It doesn't mean all hope is lost. While he's still breathing and there are signs of brain activity, there is always hope. But it's time to consider the alternative.

That he won't ever wake.

That some tough calls may have to be made, and each passing day brings that decision closer.

"What do you think?" I peer up at Beck.

"I think you should do whatever you're comfortable with, and you will look beautiful no matter what you decide to wear tonight."

I don't miss the look Nana, Hadley, and Mom share, but I choose to ignore it.

Mom treats Hadley and me to manis and pedis while Beck and Nana unload the boxes of books he brought and stack them in the new bookshelves in the coffee shop part of the store. When we return, they have just finished, and we admire their handiwork. The store is packed today, and if Nana hadn't reserved one of the tables for us, we'd be forced to go elsewhere for lunch.

We munch on toasted ciabattas with side salad and cake for dessert. Mom and Nana aren't joining us tonight—they're leaving it to the young ones, according to Nana—so they insisted on a cake with candles. The whole store sings happy birthday to me, and the smile on my face is the first genuine smile I've worn in ages.

Beck blushes when Nana introduces him to the crowded store, and there's a virtual stampede to the bookshelves.

On the ride back to the city, Hadley and I tease Beck nonstop about all the swooning moms and grannies who fawned over him as he signed books. His blush is adorable, and I love how humble he is about his talent and his success. I also love that Nana suggested this to him. It's genius. Coffee, cake, and books seem like a winning combo to me. Several book clubs meet at the store on a weekly basis, so it's a brilliant idea. Beck even suggested he could get some other author friends to supply their books if it takes off.

When we reach the city, Beck drops us off at our place to get ready, agreeing to collect us in two hours so we can all head out together.

BECK

"Oh wow. Look at you! You look gorgeous, Stevie." Esther squeals when Stevie and Hadley slide into the limo alongside me. I would agree with my sister's sentiment, but I've lost the ability to speak. Gorgeous comes nowhere close to covering the vision in front of me. I'm pretty sure my mouth is hanging open and trailing the ground.

Stevie on a normal day is beautiful as fuck.

But tonight?

She is breathtaking in every conceivable way.

The dress is a little big, confirming she still hasn't put back on all the weight she lost, even if she looks less gaunt these past couple of months. The large belt tied securely across her middle mostly hides that fact. A strapless fitted bodice hugs her curves to perfection, showcasing her delicate porcelain skin that has a shimmering glow tonight where it curves over her defined collarbone, slim shoulders, and slender arms. Long toned legs sit prettily in high strappy gold stilettos.

"You look like a princess," I blurt. "You are absolutely stunning." It doesn't come close to describing how she looks, but I'm conscious of our audience.

"Thank you." Her soft smile melts my heart while other parts of my body stiffen.

"Your hair is pretty like that." It's in a half-up, half-down style, softly sculpted around her face, with a few carefully positioned strands hanging loose, and it flows casually down her back in glossy curls.

I have never seen anything more beautiful, and I fall a little deeper in this moment.

"I can't believe you got us a limo," Hadley says, helping herself to the champagne. "This is so cool."

"I hope it's okay," I say, pouring a glass of champagne for Stevie.

"It's more than okay. I have never been in a limo before, so this is amazing. Thank you." Stevie smiles shyly at me as she takes the glass from my hand. Our fingers brush in the exchange and delicious tremors shoot up my arm from that brief touch. It makes me wonder how incredible it would feel if I got to touch her how I want. I instantly shut that train of thought down because it's a fantasy and one unlikely to come true.

"Birthday girls should always travel in style," Sarah agrees, offering her flute to me for a top off.

"I like your thinking." Hadley clinks her glass with Sarah's. "And I love your dress. Red is so your color."

"You all look beautiful, and I'll be the envy of every man when we arrive."

"I really wish Tate wasn't coming," Sarah groans, knocking back more champagne.

"Why?" Hadley leans forward, scenting a story, and I'm curious too.

"I fucked him last year," she says, just casually putting it out there like she's discussing the weather.

It's a miracle I don't drown us all in champagne as I almost choke on my drink.

"And I haven't seen him since. I hope it won't be awkward."

"I'm going to kill him." I grind my teeth to the molars before leveling a glare at my sister. "You too. Why didn't you say anything?"

"Maybe because it's none of your business?" It's no surprise Esther rushes to her sister's defense though Sarah doesn't need the help.

"A lady never kisses and tells, and I'm glad Tate was a gentleman about it. He has gone up in my estimation."

"Why? Was the sex bad?" Hadley asks, eyeballing Sarah.

"On the contrary, it was—"

"I think that's enough tormenting your brother." Stevie cuts across their conversation when she notices the horrified look on my face.

"You can tell me in private," Hadley replies, and Sarah nods.

So much for not kissing and telling.

"Please refrain from starting anything with Tate," Hadley requests, turning to look at me. "This is Stevie's special night and I want nothing ruining it."

"I won't start anything," I agree. "At least not tonight."

Sarah rolls her eyes, muttering something under her breath.

I love Tate like a brother, but he's a manwhore, and I really wish he hadn't gone near my sister. She's a grown woman capable of making her own decisions. I don't have any right to complain, but I'm perfectly entitled to not like it. I plan on making that point to my buddy when I find an opportunity tonight. I really hope his sudden availability to attend Stevie's birthday has nothing to do with my sister, but I suspect it might.

Chapter Twenty-Two

Beck

After we're all seated at our table, introductions are made. Law brought his wife, Jenny, and Hadley's boyfriend, Mike, is here, and Stevie invited Hudson. We're a lively bunch and conversation flows freely during the sumptuous dinner. I intercept a few heated looks exchanged between Sarah and Tate I'm not happy about, but like I said, I can't interfere. It's her life. I just hope she knows what she's getting into if she pursues anything with my stockbroker buddy.

Stevie sits in between me and Hudson, and I catch him checking me out from time to time. I suppose it's natural to be suspicious, but he doesn't send me any outwardly hostile looks. Law and Jenny are on my other side, and I'm thrilled when Jenny and Stevie hit it off, engaging in girly chatter about all kinds of shit.

The servers lower the lights before carrying out a cake and encouraging the whole restaurant to sing happy birthday to the birthday girl. The biggest smile is on Stevie's face as she blows out the candles to raucous applause. I lean in and kiss her cheek. "Happy birthday, Stevie."

"Thank you so much for all this," she says, her eyes bright.

"I can't claim much credit. Hadley organized most of it."

"You have a real problem accepting praise." She tweaks my nose. "You organized the limo and the cake, and she told me you paid for our meal. That's really generous, Beck. Thank you."

"You're welcome. You know I'd do anything for you."

A pretty blush steals over her cheeks. We are straining toward one another with our heads bent together, and I didn't even notice it happening. "I like seeing you happy." At this proximity, her emerald eyes are even more stunning. "And I meant what I said in the car. You look exquisite. Most beautiful woman in the room by a mile." I peer deep into her eyes, unable to resist the urge to touch her. My fingers sweep briefly across her cheek as my eyes lower to her mouth.

Law loudly clears his throat, drilling me with a sharp look when I glance his way.

"I think you're spoiling me because it's my birthday," Stevie says, clearly oblivious as she reclaims my attention.

"Every girl deserves to be spoiled on her birthday, but I tell no lie."

Tears glisten in her eyes and her lip wobbles. "I am happy, but then I feel guilty, sitting here laughing and having fun in an outfit Garrick bought me when he's..."

"He wouldn't want you to be sad," Hudson says, injecting himself into our private conversation and confirming he was eavesdropping.

I shoot him a cutting look. That's not cool.

"I apologize," he says, at least having the decency to look ashamed. "I wasn't eavesdropping. I just heard that last comment, and I couldn't let it go."

I decide to give him the benefit of the doubt, nodding at him to continue.

"Garrick loved you so much, Stevie. Too much to want you to lock yourself away pining. He would want you to live your life to the fullest. The best thing you can do for Garrick is get on with your life." His eyes lift to mine. "It's what he would want for you."

His words do the trick, and Stevie doesn't mention Garrick again.

I'm sure he's still in her thoughts, like always, but it's good for her to be able to set those aside and enjoy herself. God knows she deserves it after the annus horribilis she's just endured.

When dinner is finished, Stevie readily agrees to head into the bar-slash-club. Hadley sneaks a high five with me behind her back as we make our way inside. It's good to see Stevie laughing and looking carefree. Hadley was right. This is exactly what she needed.

"Come dance with me." Stevie grabs my hand and leads me out toward the dance floor. She's giggling and a little giddy from drinking cocktails and champagne.

Beats thump out of several large speakers around the room as we join the busy crowd dancing at the top of the room. Stevie shakes her hips and smiles as we throw some moves on the dance floor. I can't remember the last time I went dancing, but I'm having fun.

"You were holding out on me, Colbert," Stevie shouts in my ear. She prods my chest. "Where did you learn to dance so well?"

"I have two sisters who used me as their guinea pig before every formal." I don't mention the ballroom dancing lessons Father insisted we all take because it's just plain embarrassing. Even if it has been helpful at charity and high-society events.

"Oh, I love this song!" Stevie jumps up and down, and I laugh as I twirl her around to song after song until we've both worked up a sweat. I bow out when the girls surround her, leaving them to it.

I'm at the bar, ordering a scotch on the rocks and a water, when Hudson finds me. "I was hoping we could talk," he says.

"Sure." Turning to face Garrick's best friend, I ask, "Can I get you a drink?"

He shakes his head. "I'm good." He holds up a half-empty bottle of beer.

I pay the bartender before following Hudson to a quieter part of the bar. We set our drinks down on the high table. "What did you want to talk to me about?"

He looks me straight in the eye, exuding quiet confidence. "What are your intentions toward Stevie?"

His question doesn't surprise me. "I appreciate you don't beat around the bush, but I'm not answering that. It's none of your business." I'm not discussing this with him when Stevie isn't aware of the extent of my feelings. I lift my bottle of water to my lips and drink greedily.

"I disagree." He pauses to take a mouthful of beer. "Garrick would want me looking out for her. I have tried my best to do that, but I was in Rhode Island, and I haven't been around to see what's going on."

"She told me you've been a lifeline, and I commend you for your loyalty to your friend. But it doesn't give you the right to pry into Stevie's life. If you need reassurance, I promise you don't need to worry about me. It seems we share the same goal. To take care of her. The last thing I would do is make life difficult for her. I just want her to be happy."

"Happy as in state of mind or happy as in with you?"

"Look, man, I know you mean well, but I'm not doing this with you. Stevie and I are just friends."

"For now." He squares up to me. "She's vulnerable, and I won't see her taken advantage of."

He's starting to get on my nerves, but I know it's coming from a good place, so I try to rein in my anger. "I would never take advantage of her. Whatever I feel or don't feel for her is none of your goddamned business, and you need to back off or we'll have a problem. Stevie loves Garrick with her whole heart. I don't see that changing any time soon, if at all. My role in her life is not to dismiss your friend. I respect her feelings for him. I respect how he loved and cared for her. I met him once, and I liked Garrick. You don't know me, so I get why you have to say this, but I'm not the bad guy in this scenario. I am here for Stevie because I care deeply about her." I knock back my scotch in one go, seriously pissed now. I don't like his insinuation one little bit.

"I'm sorry. I have offended you, and that wasn't my intention." He seems earnest, but I'm all wound up now. "I had to ask. Hadley said you were a good guy, but I needed to verify it for myself. You don't have to say anything, but I saw the way you were looking at one another at the table. It wasn't the way friends look at one another. If something happens with Stevie down the line, I won't stand in your way. I want her to be happy because that's what my buddy would want. If you are her choice, I would support that decision."

"Then what is the point of this conversation?"

"She's not ready."

"I know that better than anyone."

We face off again.

His shoulders relax a little. "But you do want more with her?"

"I refuse to dignify that with an answer. The only person who deserves to know is Stevie, and like you said, we're a million miles away from having that conversation."

The tension leaves his face as he stretches out his arm. "I'm sorry I had to do this, but it was for Stevie. I meant what I just said. If you two get together in the future, you won't get any beef from me. No hard feelings?"

I shake his hand, letting the tension lift from my shoulders. I don't like what he said, but I understand his motivation, and I respect him for it. "No hard feelings. You're a good friend to look out for her, but you don't have anything to fear from me."

"I see that now." He finishes his beer and slaps me on the shoulder. "I'm going to bounce after I say goodnight to the birthday girl."

"Have a good one," I say as I spot Law and Tate approaching.

"What was that about?" Tate asks after Hudson has departed.

Law snorts. "You'd know if you didn't spend the entire meal trading barbs and fuck me looks with Sarah across the table."

I glare at Law. "Spare me the details, please." I rub my temples before turning my glare on Tate. "You should have told me though I understand and appreciate why you didn't. Don't hurt her, or I'll have to kick your ass."

"What did I miss?" Law asks, looking confused as he glances between us.

"We fucked the last time Sarah was in New York."

I thump him in the shoulder, and he's lucky I don't punch him in the face. "She's my sister, asshole!" I hiss. "Don't talk about her like she's one of your usual hookups."

Tate looks instantly chastised. "Sorry, Beck. You're right. I mean no disrespect. Sarah is an incredible woman, and we had a great night."

"You've got big balls, man." Law smirks.

"Or a death wish," I mumble, wishing I hadn't drunk my scotch so quick.

"But back to you," Tate says in a blatant redirection. "What was up with you and Hudson? It looked intense."

"Like I said, if you'd been watching, you wouldn't need to ask any questions," Law replies before I have a chance to. "It's fucking obvious what Hudson wanted to know."

"Which is?" Tate persists.

"How long Beck has been in love with Stevie and what he intends to do about it."

Chapter Twenty-Three

Stevie

The next month flies by as I work late nights to get ahead on tasks before our two-week trip to France. I'm continuing with my therapy and enjoying talking to someone completely neutral about the whole situation. Getting stuff out of my head and off my chest is slowly helping.

Garrick is rarely far from my mind. Hugh and Hudson keep me regularly updated, but there is no change.

Helena called me last week to reassure me about Pepper. Apparently, she works crazy hours and barely manages to squeeze a half-hour visit into her day. I felt like throwing my cell at the wall after I hung up. It incenses me she's allowed to see him and she squanders it. It just proves how flimsy her so-called love is. Work matters more to her than Garrick. Helena said Ivy doesn't spend much time with him either, citing how difficult it is to see her son in that condition as an excuse.

My blood boils that he's trapped in that house with those two bitches, but at least Hugh spends hours with him, and Hudson visits him daily. Knowing Helena and the medical team are taking great care of him helps too.

Nana sold all of Beck's books, and he's now making weekly deliveries to Ravenna. We usually go there on Sundays and stay for dinner. Esther and Sarah came with us one Sunday, and Mom and Nana adore them. There was even discussion of them celebrating Christmas with us this year.

Finally, the first day of our vacation rolls around, and I'm so excited I could pee. Beck collects me from my place, and we drive to SeaTac together.

"No freaking way!" I exclaim when Beck escorts me onto the private jet carrying us to southern France.

A light chuckle shakes his shoulders as I stare in awe at the plush surroundings of the mid-sized private plane. It has walnut walls and gray leather recliner chairs, and there's even a dining area and couch with a TV. Dumping my bag on a seat, I explore the three rooms at the back. One is an opulent bathroom with a toilet and sink. The second is a full bathroom with a rainforest shower, and the third room is a bedroom with a large bed and wall-mounted TV.

"Does it pass inspection?" Beck teases, extending his head through the bedroom door, as I pinch myself.

"This is unreal." I lift my eyes to his. "This cannot be my life."

He saunters into the room with a smile. "Were you not expecting this?"

I shake my head, and waves of red hair spill over my shoulders. "I just assumed we'd be flying commercial. When Garrick and I flew to Cyprus, he booked us first class seats, which was a huge treat, but this is something else entirely."

Beck places his hands gently on my shoulders. "You are a breath of fresh air in a world consumed with materialism." He kisses the top of my head. "Never change, Stevie."

Warmth floods my face, and it's a mix of pride at his compliment and embarrassment at not realizing the obvious. Beck's family business is aerospace. Facepalm. Of course, we'd be flying in a Colbert airplane. I'm guessing Beck's family always flies in a private jet.

The flight is almost twelve hours long with a stopover in Iceland to refuel. Beck does a little writing while I critique the first half of the book he's already written. I get an enormous thrill getting to read his early drafts. I love seeing how the book takes shape through each revision, and I've given him some ideas he's incorporated in the story too. After, we enjoy a gourmet dinner and sip champagne cocktails while watching a movie, side by side, on the couch.

A girl could really get used to this lifestyle.

Beck suggests we get some sleep as it will help us acclimate to the time difference, which is a whopping nine hours. We are due to land at ten a.m. local time, so if we don't sleep now, it will be virtually impossible to stay awake when we get to the farm. After a brief argument over who will take the bedroom, we sleep in there together on top of the bed, in our clothes, and covered by a light sheet.

A car is waiting when we land to ferry us the short journey to Canet-en-Roussillon. Poking my head out the window, I admire the stunning scenery as glorious sunshine beats down on my face. Despite minimal sleep, I'm wide-awake and as excited as a kid on Christmas morning. Beck asks the driver to take a longer route so we can check out the beach and the harbor before heading out of the town to the farm.

Anxiety makes an unwelcome appearance when we drive through rustic wooden gates and enter his grandparents' farm. Beck told them all about me, and they're expecting us, but I'm nervous to meet them.

The air seems still here, almost magical. It feels like we're miles away from civilization and the thriving town we just drove through. Invisible arms envelop me in a welcoming hug as we bump along dusty roads, surrounded by fields and acres and acres of prime farmland.

"Look on this side," Beck says, taking my arm and hauling me toward him on the back seat.

A gasp leaves my lips as we pass by fields filled with different fruit trees. "It's so pretty! Is this a dairy farm too? I saw a field of cows back there."

Beck ruffles my hair and smiles. "It is and that was livestock you saw. It's a combined dairy and fruit farm, and they have some vineyards too. Most modern farmers have to diversify to survive, but my grandparents are lucky because they were able to buy the farm outright when they sold the family textile business, so at least they don't have a big mortgage hanging over their heads."

"What kinds of fruit do they grow?" I inquire, almost sitting in Beck's lap as I lean forward to stick my head out his open window. "Besides peaches," I add, remembering his story about the chocolate shop. A delicious sweet lingering smell swirls in the air, and my tummy rumbles, suggesting it wasn't a good idea to skip breakfast on the plane. Excitement had my stomach in knots, and I didn't think it was wise to eat.

"They grow nectarines and apricots too." His arm slides around my waist, holding me in place as I continue to stare at the never-ending row of trees as we drive by. "Wait until you taste them. They are out of this world and like nothing you've eaten before."

"I can't wait," I admit as we round a bend, bypassing a succession of warehouses and barns. Up ahead, the road veers to the left, but we stop in front of a set of closed high wooden gates, shielding whatever lies beyond.

Beck turns me around by my waist, positioning me on the seat right beside him as he points to the left. "That road leads to a petting farm open to the public. It's super popular with tourists, and there is also a shop where they can buy fruit, milk, yogurt, cheese, cream, and freshly baked breads and pastries. The farm is famous for its jams, and there's a wide variety to choose from."

"Oh my god, I'm already starving, and you're only making it worse!"

Beck laughs. "Trust me, *grand-mére* will have a heavenly breakfast prepared for us. The French seem to have mastered the art of abundant eating and drinking that isn't to excess. You will go home with a greater appreciation of food."

"Have I thanked you for taking me here?" I grin as strands of my hair float around my face.

"Only about a hundred times." His entire face lights up as he smiles, and I'm momentarily dazzled. I love seeing him like this. Dressed casually in shorts and a T-shirt, wearing a ball-cap and shades, and just seeming so much freer. It's like this giant ball of stress lifted from his whole persona the second we set foot on French soil.

"You love it here," I surmise as the wooden gates open electronically to grant us entry.

"I truly do." A nostalgic expression appears on his face. "Some of the best times of my life were summers spent here." A veil of sadness flows over his features.

"Is it hard here sometimes because of your mom?" I quietly ask, reaching out to take his hand.

"Yes and no. I feel closest to her here. Sometimes it's a comfort. Other times it's the opposite."

"Will you tell me if you feel down when we're here? I want to help."

"Of course." He squeezes my hand as we drive toward a large farmhouse up ahead. It's two stories comprised of wood and stone with copious small windows all over the structure.

"This is the private part of the farm, and the public has no access. This is my grandparents' house. We used to stay in the main house as kids, but we were each gifted a cottage on the grounds, and we'll be staying at mine. It has two bedrooms," he adds, and I'm not sure what expression he saw on my face. "It's about a half mile in that direction." He points beyond the house. "It's not far to walk to the lake from my place, and this side is private." His lips twitch as he says, "I usually go skinny-dipping late at night."

"Is that a challenge, *Monsieur* Colbert?" I waggle my brows as the car slows down and approaches the house. "Because I'll have you know, it wouldn't be the first time this girl went skinny-dipping."

"Is that right?" He arches a brow as his smile expands.

"It is." I clutch his hand harder as we draw up in front of the house where a smiling gray-haired couple awaits us.

"I think you'll fit seamlessly into French culture." He holds my hand tight before leaning in to kiss my cheek. "Don't worry. I already know they're going to love you."

Thirty minutes later, it feels like I'm already a part of the furniture. Beck's *grand-mére* and *grand-pére* are very welcoming, and they instantly settle my nerves, kissing me on both cheeks and telling me to call them Margot and Alain. Margot's English is very good, but Alain's is a little rusty; however, we manage to converse just fine.

I stuff myself full of the most mouthwatering fruit and creamy yogurt I've ever tasted, followed by melt-in-the mouth pain au chocolate and real French croissants that bear little resemblance to the ones available back home.

Margot gives me a tour of their gorgeous traditional farmhouse, complete with a review of old photo albums from when Beck was a kid. We drink delicious coffee on the patio that overlooks a large outdoor pool and stunning gardens. Margot and I have a full-blown conversation about flowers, and I promise to help her weed some flowerbeds before we leave for the US. She has arthritis in her knees and her hands, so the garden has gotten a little overgrown.

The second Margot took the family photo albums out, Beck hightailed it with my laughter following him. Alain and he are taking our bags to his cottage. I took my sneakers out before he absconded, along with some sunscreen, so we can explore the property on foot before heading there. I'm dying to see everything and glad jetlag hasn't kicked in yet.

"We're so pleased to have you here, *ma chère*," Margot says, kissing me on both cheeks, when Beck has returned and it's time to leave. This is a working farm, and Margot and Alain have things to do.

"Thank you for having me. You have a beautiful home and a beautiful farm, and I can't wait to explore it and the town."

"You are welcome any time." Her soft smile is warm, and it feels like a gentle hug.

"It's so good to see you." She envelops Beck in an embrace before kissing him too. "You look happy, and it pleases me." She casts another motherly smile in my direction before smooshing his cheeks. "Tell your sisters I expect a visit before the end of the summer."

"I'll make sure of it even if I have to drag them here myself."

"Have fun, you two!" She waves us off, and we set out in the direction of the shop and petting farm.

"Just roll me over," I plead, groaning as I rub a hand across my full belly. "If I keep this up the entire vacay, you'll be rolling me onto the plane too."

He chuckles. "I told you the food is good." He points things out to me as we walk, waving at farm hands out in the fields as we pass by.

"So good. I have a feeling I'll want to relocate to France before we leave."

"I have thought of moving here often," he says, pressing a button to open the large double gates when we arrive at them.

"I can already see why it would be a writer's paradise. It's like an entirely different world. The smells and the scenery and the peace and quiet is idyllic."

"If I can extricate myself from Colbert Cartwright, I will definitely be spending some time here. Not year-round, but I can see myself living here part of the year."

We walk through the gates and swing a right. I bat an insect away from my face as we stride toward the public area in the near distance. "Have you given any more thought to speaking to Sarah and Esther about your father's blackmail?"

"It's been on my mind, yeah," he admits.

"I won't nag you, it's your decision, but I hate you can't pursue your dreams because of your dickhead dad."

Laughter spills from his lips. "I might start using that."

"You should. If the name fits and all that jazz."

He slows to a stop outside the shop, loosely linking his fingers in mine. "One part of me is scared of getting everything I want." Sun glints off his shades, almost blinding me behind the lenses of my own glasses. "What if I've built it up to be this great something and it's not? What if my writing career fades? What will I do then?"

I step closer and place my hand on his arm. "It's only natural to have fears, but like a wise man once told me, it's one step at a time, one day at a time."

His lips kick up at the corners.

"It's a good motto and one I'm trying to live by," I say. "The first step is getting free of those shackles, and then everything else will slide into place."

Chapter Twenty-Four

Stevie

My heart is pounding against my rib cage so fast it feels like it's gonna burst through my body and escape. Wiping sweaty palms down the front of my jean shorts, I attempt to summon courage from some long forgotten place as I survey the old Land Rover like it's a pit of writhing snakes Beck is asking me to step into. "I don't think I can do it."

"You are stronger than you realize." Beck's confident expression contradicts the tremors shaking my body from my head to my toes. He stands poised between the open door and the driver's seat, watching various emotions flit over my sun-kissed skin.

We have been here one week already, and I wish I could slow down time. It's been action-packed, and we've visited the town, the beach, the harbor, and the mountains and explored the main parts of the farm. One afternoon was spent gorging ourselves on the decadent chocolate from Leona's flagship chocolate shop, and another was spent with Margot in her garden while Beck helped Alain repair some broken fences.

We either go out for dinner in the town, eat with his grandparents at the farmhouse, or we take turns cooking at Beck's gorgeous stone cottage. Traditionally, lunch is the biggest meal of the day in France, but I can't eat a lot of food in the middle of the day, especially when it's so hot, so we generally reserve our main meal for nighttime.

"Why don't you try sitting behind the wheel?" he suggests, pushing off the car and walking toward me. "You don't have to drive. Just get behind the wheel and see how you feel? Then we can hang out by the pool all afternoon relaxing."

"I'm being a pussy, aren't I?" I murmur, still eyeing the car like it's personally affronted me.

"Not a bit." He brushes wispy strands of hair from my face, tucking them back into my messy topknot.

I've been wearing it up most of the day to keep it out of my way, and it's cooler like this.

"What you are experiencing is natural," he says. "You suffered something hugely traumatic. If you're not ready, we'll leave this. I just thought it might be good to try where there is no one around and you have privacy."

"It is better than attempting to drive in traffic with some asshole honking his horn if I stall in the middle of the road," I admit, chewing on the inside of my cheek. "And my therapist has been encouraging me to try."

"You are much more relaxed in my passenger seat." He reminds me of the progress I have made.

"I am," I agree. "Thanks to you." I don't freak out getting into anybody's car these days, but it's vastly different than driving myself. Which kind of doesn't make sense. I wasn't driving at the time of the accident. It should be easier to be the one in control rather than the one in the passenger seat, but it's the opposite way around. When I mentioned this to my therapist, she said the brain is a complex organ and there is nothing right or wrong about my reaction. It is what it is, and people react differently to all kinds of things. All I need to concentrate on is how it impacts me. It's been fourteen months since the car crash that changed my life, and it's time I overcame this.

I have to try sometime, and Beck is right. This is the perfect place to get back in the saddle. I lift my head and thrust my shoulders back. "I'm going to do it."

Pride races across his face as I stride to the car and climb into the driver's seat. My hands are shaking as I place them on the wheel and slowly inhale and exhale. Beck throws the bag with our towels and sunscreen in the back seat and hops up beside me. "Take your time. There is no rush. Let yourself get used to the feeling of being in the driver's seat."

Reaching forward, I turn the key, and my pulse beats faster with the deep rumble of the engine. I gulp over the lump in my throat as my feet hit the pedals, and I put the car in gear.

"Take it nice and slow," Beck advises as I let the handbrake down, and the SUV lurches forward.

Butterflies are playing havoc with my chest, and acid churns in my stomach as I drive along the bumpy road that leads toward the main house. Nausea swims up my throat, but I persevere.

"Well done," Beck quietly says as I drive.

"It's not like I'm rocketing into outer space," I tease, loosening my neck from side to side as I keep my eyes trained on the empty road. "I'm only driving."

"It's a big deal, and you're amazing. I'm in awe of you."

I can tell he means that, and tears prick my eyes. "I couldn't do this without your support. I couldn't do any of it without you," I say, accelerating a little.

It's the truth, and sometimes it scares me how much I've come to depend on Beck always being there for me.

What happens when he meets the love of his life and I get pushed out?

What happens if Garrick wakes? Will he understand my friendship or feel threatened by it?

Pain spears me through the heart at the thought of not having Beck in my life. But I'm trying to live in the present. To not trade in what-ifs, so I force those thoughts from my mind and just focus on getting to the farmhouse in one piece.

Beck grabs me into a bear hug when I successfully park at the side of the house and kill the engine. I'm shaking all over, but I have the biggest smile on my face. "I did it."

"I'm so proud of you, honey." He clasps my face in his hands and presses a prolonged kiss to my brow.

My flesh tingles where his lips touch my skin, and I'm overheating.

His eyes drop to my mouth and linger. It's not the first time I've noticed him fixated on my mouth, and it stirs confusion inside me.

Sometimes, when he looks at me, it's as if he's diving deep into my soul and connecting with me on a transcendent level, willing me to want more.

It's intense in a way I don't want to explore.

Tension charges the air, crackling in the small space between us, and my chest heaves as I consider, for one horrifying moment, that he might be thinking about kissing me.

The euphoria on his face fades as he abruptly wrenches his hands away and turns around. "Come on," he says in a gruffer voice than usual while curling his hand around the door handle. "Let's hit the pool." He climbs out without looking at me, and I can't shake the feeling I've done something wrong.

Beck is quiet as we dry out on sun loungers after a quick dip in the pool. Margot left us a jug of homemade lemonade, but I think we need something stronger. I excuse myself to use the bathroom, and after attending to business, I hunt Margot down and ask if she has the ingredients for bellinis. Considering they grow peaches and produce sparkling wine, I'm guessing she has supplies somewhere in the house.

Margot leads me to a large refrigerator in the basement, sharing her secret stash with me. Inside are jars of homemade delicacies, hidden among bottles of chilled wine. We take a jar of peach puree and a bottle of sparkling wine upstairs, and we make bellinis together.

The French aren't big on snacking, but I baked chocolate chip cookies this morning, and I brought a small box with me from the cottage. I wanted to do something to thank Beck's grandparents for their hospitality, so I've taken to baking every day. Stealing two cookies from the box, I head back out to the pool with my peace offerings.

"Look what I have," I say in my brightest voice, setting the small tray down on the tile-top table between our loungers. I brought a couple bottles of water out too.

"Good thinking," Beck says, offering me a smile that looks semi-forced as he gets up and adjusts the height of his lounger into a more upright position.

I do the same with mine before handing him a bellini and shoving the plate with the cookies in his direction. Then I lie back on my lounger—checking that my black bikini is intact and I'm not flashing the goods—and help myself to the other bellini. "Fuck, this is so good." I moan appreciatively as the fruity bubbly liquid glides down my parched throat. I tip my head back, basking under the cloudless sky, enjoying the heat bathing my skin.

"It hits the spot," Beck agrees. The usual warmth is missing from his tone, and I need to know what I did to alter his mood.

Sitting up, I swing my legs to one side, remove my sunglasses and look at him. "Did I do something wrong?" I just put it out there. "I feel like I've hurt you, but I don't know what I did."

His Adam's apple bobs in his throat as he pitches his gaze in my direction, purposely keeping his attention fixed on my face. "You haven't done anything wrong. I'm just feeling a little down today."

My heart hurts looking at the sadness clouding his handsome face. "What can I do to help?"

"I don't think there is anything you can do." His eyes drop down to my body for a fleeting second before he yanks them back up to my face. "Except maybe keep these coming," he adds, holding his glass aloft.

"That I can do," I promise, feeling a little off center myself.

After demolishing our bellinis and cookies, we dive into the pool and float side by side on inflatables while we sunbathe and keep cool.

"What is your favorite book of yours?" I ask, turning my head to face him.

I'm lying on my stomach, working on my pasty back, while Beck is lying on his back with his eyes closed, tanning his already ridiculously tanned body.

Beck has Mediterranean blood flowing through his veins and the olive-toned skin to match. He tans effortlessly as evidenced by his current rich-bronze-colored flesh. Meanwhile, I'm slapping sunscreen on every hour to avoid burning, and my skin barely looks any different from how it was when I arrived. Not counting the smattering of freckles that have shown up on my cheeks and across the bridge of my nose or the inconvenient patch of sunburn on the tips of my ears and the back of one calf.

"I imagine that's like asking a mother to pick a favorite child," he replies, opening his eyes and smiling as he turns his head in my direction.

"That's a valid point," I agree, trying not to stare at his broad shoulders, toned chest, and rock-hard abs. "What about a book that's been extra special to write?"

"That's easier to answer," he admits, dragging his hand slowly through the water. "*To Catch a Killer* is special because it was my first book." A slight shiver works its way through him. "Though I couldn't bear to reread it and see all my rookie mistakes."

I gently splash him. "Blasphemy. That is one of my favorite books of yours." He narrows his eyes in fake annoyance, and I giggle. "Go on, tell me another one."

"*The Return* is special because I really felt the connection between Maggie and Bennett, and he shows a vulnerability we haven't seen before. The scenes at the end were different for me to write, and I liked challenging myself."

We sip our waters as I quiz him back and forth for ages about different aspects of his books, pleased when he visibly relaxes. "You should see your face when you talk about your books. You exude passion when talking about writing and your characters. Your whole face lights up, and your body becomes animated. You were born to do this."

"I think so." If it wasn't sunny and we weren't already sweaty and flushed, I'm guessing his cheeks would be red. Beck doesn't accept praise easily, and it's one of his most endearing traits. "I used to think everyone heard voices in their head," he admits. "I didn't think I was anything special until I mentioned it to Esther, and she stared at me like I'd been possessed by some demonic spirit."

I giggle as Margot steps out onto the patio carrying two full glasses in her hands.

"I thought you might like some more," she says, wincing as she bends over at the side of the pool.

"I'll get those," Beck says, sliding off his inflatable into the pool.

With graceful strokes, he swims to the edge and effortlessly hauls his powerful body up and out of the pool. Muscles bunch in his arms and roll in his back with the motion, and I'm momentarily tongue-tied.

He could be a fitness model.

Or a catwalk model.

You know, if the writing gig doesn't work out.

Water sluices off his tanned muscular back, rolling down under the waistband of his blue designer swim shorts, and it's like a slow-motion scene from a movie.

"You should take it easier," he chastises Margot, giving her an affectionate kiss on the cheek. "You work too hard, and you need to relax more."

"I don't like to be idle. You know this. Consequence of living on a farm." She hands him two new bellinis, and I briefly consider getting out to kiss her, but I'm far too comfortable and way too lazy to move.

I blow her a kiss. "Thanks, Margot. You're the best."

"Anything for my grandson and his pretty friend." She points at me. "Your back looks a little red. You might need more sunscreen."

Of course, I do.

I sigh, bemoaning the need to get up.

"Stay put," Beck says as Margot heads back into the house. "I'll grab the bottle."

Trailing my fingers through the water, I watch him grab the sunscreen and walk around the pool in my direction. "Come here, lazybones." He is grinning as he sets the drinks down and sits at the edge of the pool with his feet dangling in the water. I am glad his mood seems to have lifted.

Using my hands, I "swim" over to him on my inflatable.

"Put your legs over each side and turn around so I can reach your back," he instructs, popping the cap on the sunscreen and pouring a generous amount into his palm.

I manage to do what he says and stay afloat, which is a miracle.

I'm sitting on the inflatable with my back to Beck and my feet bobbing in the water as I wait for him to apply the cream to my skin. For some reason, my mouth is extra dry, and my heart is galloping like a racehorse on Derby Day.

Beck clears his throat. "Do you, ah, want me to untie your top?"

Heat flares in my cheeks. "Um, no. It's fine. You can just work around it. I don't mind if you get lotion on it. It will come out in the laundry."

"Okay." His voice sounds deeper with an undercurrent of something I can't name, and it's doing strange things to my insides. Butterflies skate around my tummy, and I feel a little on edge.

A yelp rips from my mouth when his large palms land unexpectedly on my shoulders.

"Sorry." His voice sounds clipped as he tears his hands away. "I tried to warm it up with my hands."

It's not cold, but I don't correct him. "It's fine."

Weird tension lingers in the air, and my chest heaves as I gulp back nerves.

"Shall I continue?"

I jerk my head, incapable of speaking.

This time, he is very careful when he places his hands on my shoulders. "Is this okay?"

I nod again, wondering if I might pass out from sunstroke because it feels like I'm burning up from the inside out.

His magic hands and deft fingers are thorough as he works the sunscreen into my flesh. I'm barely breathing as I close my eyes and try to ignore the tremors tiptoeing over my skin from his touch. Reaching the bikini string, he is careful to hold it out a little from my body with one hand while he uses his other hand to rub the milky-looking lotion into the skin above and below the band.

It's a miracle I don't expire from lack of oxygen to my lungs or take a nosedive into the pool as he continues applying sunscreen to my back. His fingers brush my sides, and as they creep lower and lower, heading toward the top of my bikini bottoms, I'm a freaking inferno, so hot it feels like I'm ready to spontaneously combust.

When his fingers reach the waistband of my bottoms, I can't stand it a second longer. Emitting a little shriek, I swivel around on the inflatable, hoping he thinks my red face and splotchy neck is the result of sunburn and not an acute overreaction to feeling a man's hands on me for the first time in a long time.

That's all it is.

My neglected body is thirsty for touch.

It's not as if I'm attracted to my best friend.

Because that would be a travesty.

"I can do the rest," I croak, averting my eyes as I hold out my hand for some cream.

He says nothing as he squirts a little into my palm. Even though I'm not looking at him, I feel the intensity of his stare as I hastily rub sunscreen along my lower back. Honestly, at this point, I'll gladly accept painful sunburn over the alternative. "All done." I fix a cheery smile on my face as I summon bravery and look up at him. "Thanks for your help."

"You're welcome." His eyes drift to my mouth and lower, and I'm hoping he doesn't notice the hard points of my nipples poking through the bikini fabric. I don't want to have to explain how it's just a natural reaction because I haven't had sex or felt a man's touch in so long. I wouldn't want to make him feel he's not attractive when he's one of the most attractive men I've ever known.

"Here." He hands me a bellini, and when I lean forward to take it, there is no mistaking the heated look in his eyes as his gaze dips to my cleavage or the growing bulge behind his swim shorts.

I almost drop the glass in the water when I spot the obvious evidence of his arousal. Fire blazes in my cheeks when I realize I'm ogling him, and I jerk my head up, catching him staring at my mouth with abject longing.

Oh fuck.

I wasn't wrong earlier.

I know what I see in his eyes.

He wants to kiss me.

He's staring at my mouth like he wants to devour me.

And I don't know what the hell to do about it.

Chapter Twenty-Five

Beck

"What did you want to talk to me about?" Law asks as we share lunch in a private room of the men's club I'm a member of. Ordinarily, I hate coming here. I wouldn't even be a member if father hadn't signed me up to his good-old-boys club. It's full of leering misogynistic perverts who think their shit doesn't smell. I made a reservation because it's the only lunch place that guarantees privacy, and I don't want anyone privy to this conversation.

"I need your advice," I say, finishing my lunch and pushing the plate away.

Law finishes his food and takes a drink of water as he eyeballs me like he wishes he could drill into my head.

It doesn't take a magician to work out what's on my mind.

The same woman who has been on my mind from the minute I met her.

He puts his glass down and clears his throat. "Has something else happened with Stevie?"

I shake my head as I cross an ankle over my knee. "No, we're both still pretending like nothing happened that day in France."

It's been two months since our vacation, and I still overanalyze every aspect of that day. My hurt at the horrified expression on her face when she realized I wanted to kiss her in the car. The awkward aftermath of "poolgate" as I inwardly refer to it. She was aroused. I know she knows I noticed. Like she noticed the boner I tried so hard to avoid. But it was impossible.

The entire vacation was a test of self-control. Stevie looking like a beautiful enchantress in a succession of gorgeous summer dresses and like Peitho, the Greek goddess who personified seduction, in those skimpy bikinis. If I didn't know her personality and how she's pretty much oblivious to my obsession with her, I'd think she wore them on purpose to exact the worst form of torture on me.

Neither of us brought up the subject of the lake that second week. I certainly didn't have the restraint for skinny-dipping, and after her reaction that day at the pool, I know she would not have risked putting us in another intimate situation.

Still, I don't regret a single second of the vacation even if things were a little strained between us for a while. It got Stevie driving again, and I only had one nightmare the entire vacation. My new therapist is helping, and so is Stevie. She just makes everything better.

My grandparents adore her, and I swear *Grand-mére* is already planning our wedding in her head. At least, that's what Sarah and Esther said when they visited the farm at the end of August. Esther said *Grand-mére* talked nonstop about how lovely Stevie is, how much happier I seem, and how perfect we look together.

"Beck." Law snaps me out of my inner monologue. "You were miles away."

"Sorry, I tend to do that when I'm thinking of the vacation, and no, nothing else has happened. That's my problem."

"You know we love Stevie. Hell, Jenny would probably divorce me and marry her if she could, but are you sure she is who you want?"

We enjoyed barbecues and casual brunches at Law and Jenny's a few times over the summer, and the girls have become firm friends. I spoke to Law after we returned from France, and I poured my heart out to my childhood best friend, so he already knows how I feel. "She is. Stevie is all I see."

"I just worry you're setting yourself up for major heartache. What happens if Garrick wakes? Do you think he'll want her spending time with you? And how would you cope with her falling back into his arms?"

Pinpricks stab my heart like a thousand knives embedding in the organ. "It would kill me, and I'm long beyond worrying about heartache. I can't help how I feel, Law. It's not like I wanted to fall in love with a girl who is already in love with another man."

"It's an impossible situation."

"It is." I pull at the restrictive tie around my neck, loosening it and the top button of my shirt, because it suddenly feels like I can't breathe. "I can't do anything about my feelings. I can't say anything for fear I'll scare her away and lose her forever. Having her in my life as a close friend is better than not having her in my life at all. And even if I wasn't afraid of that, how could I ever make a move on her when her boyfriend is lying in a coma? It'd be the very definition of selfish to try to steal a girl from a guy who can't fight to hold on to her."

"I feel for you, man. I really do. It's a shit situation." He leans back in his chair, drumming his fingers on the arm while he looks off into space.

"What do I do, Law? It feels like I'm slowly dying inside. Being around her and not touching her, not getting to be with her the way I want to, is the ultimate torture. I have to talk myself off a ledge every time I'm with her, and the devil on my shoulder is taunting me to just grab her and kiss her and see where the chips fall."

"That would be one way of forcing the issue," he says, scrubbing a hand across his jaw. "Or you accept she's not available right now, and you remain friends until the timing is right. In the meantime, you date other women." He sits upright, leaning his elbows on the table.

"Or just go out and get laid regularly to ease the stress of the situation." He shrugs, and a hint of a grin lands on his lips. "Who knows, maybe you'll make her jealous and it'll force her hand? You could even stage a scene and have her show up when you're on a date with another woman. If that wouldn't make her confront her feelings, I don't know what would."

Red-hot rage surges up my throat, and I dig my fingers into the arms of my chair as I glare at my buddy. "That's your advice? I tell you I'm completely in love with Stevie and pining for her, and you suggest I date other women? Fuck other women? And torment her by making sure she not only knows it but stage it so she sees? Did I get that right?" I stand abruptly, knocking my chair to the ground.

"When you say it like that, it does sound bad." Law at least has the decency to look ashamed.

"What the hell is wrong with you?" I snap, snatching a few bills from my wallet and tossing them on the table. "This isn't high school or college, and we're not teenagers anymore. Or at least I'm not." My hands ball into fists at my side. "I would never hurt Stevie by playing games. And why the fuck would I date or fuck any other woman when the thought of it makes me want to puke?"

I yank my tie off completely and shove it in my pocket as I glare at my best friend. For once in his life, he looks defenseless. "Imagine I had given you this advice when you thought you'd lost Jenny to her ex during senior year of college. Could you have dated and fucked other women when you were so fucking in love with her and terrified you would never get to keep her?"

He stands, shoving his hands in his pockets, looking remorseful, but it does little to quell the storm raging inside me. "Beck, I—"

"Forget it, Law. I'll know better next time than to come to you for help." With those parting words, I storm out of the room and hightail it out of the club.

I still haven't calmed down by the time I return to the office. Sight of the building I have grown to hate does little to ease my temper. Lulu takes one look at the expression on my face when I get out of the elevator and cowers behind her desk, leaving me to stew in this mess alone.

I am pacing the floor of my office, dragging my hand back and forth across my head, for once wishing I had longer hair so I could pull on it, when the door opens without invitation, and Sarah swans into the room.

My sister chose to do year two of her MBA online so she could join the business early.

I want to run screaming from this place, and she's champing at the bit to get her feet under the table.

Dad didn't object as long as she pulls her weight and doesn't fall behind with the Harvard program. He insisted all three of us attended Cornell as undergraduates and Harvard for our postgraduate studies. Her office is right beside mine, and it's been fun spending more time together. I have missed her these past few years.

Sarah takes one look at my agitated state and frowns, kicking the door shut with her foot and advancing toward my desk holding a bottle of Macallan and two glasses. "Sit your ass down, big brother. You're making my head spin with all that pacing."

"I think I'm going insane," I mumble, still wearing a path in the carpet.

"Love *is* insanity," she says, setting the bottle and glasses down on my desk and walking toward me. "It gets the best of all of us at some point in our lives, or so I've been told." She pulls at my wrists, tugging my hands down by my side. "Beck, stop." She clasps my face in her hands. "You're going to give yourself an ulcer." Sarah wraps me in an awkward hug, and she must be really worried about me because we don't do this. She runs a hand up and down my back as I just kind of fall against her, wallowing in self-pity.

At some point, my anger transformed to depression and frustration and a feeling of utter helplessness.

"Please tell me you feel better because this feels so unnatural."

A chuckle breaks through my melancholy as I break our uncomfortable embrace. "Thank god you gave up the idea of studying psychology," I tease.

She rolls her eyes. "You don't need to be a hugger to be a psychologist."

"No, but you need to be able to offer comfort, and that was pathetic even if I appreciate the gesture."

"I got you to stop pacing, didn't I?" She waggles her brows. "I'm counting that as a win." She loops her arm in mine and drags me over to my desk, pushing me down in my chair. Sarah rounds the desk and glides elegantly into the chair across from me. "Here. Drink this," she says, pouring a generous measure of whisky into the glass and handing it to me.

I knock it back in one go, and the familiar burning sensation in my throat is oddly soothing. Sarah refills my glass before pouring herself a small measure. She leans back and surveys me. "You look like shit. Are you sleeping?"

"Fitfully," I admit, sipping my drink at a more leisurely pace this time. I swivel on my chair, glancing out of the high-rise at the bustling street below.

"Nightmares or?" She lets it hang in the air.

"You know why."

She wets her lips. "Law called me. He feels terrible."

"As he should." I take a healthy mouthful of whisky. "He'd make a worse therapist than you."

"He didn't go into detail, but I know it's about Stevie, so talk to me. Maybe you just need a female perspective."

"I don't know what to do, Sarah." I haven't said anything to either of my sisters about this. "I love her as more than a friend."

"You say that as if we don't know." Her features soften. "The only person who doesn't know you love Stevie is Stevie."

"Well, shit." I scrub my hands down my face. "So much for hiding my feelings."

"I'm not sure it's possible when you're madly in love with someone like you are with her."

"It hurts so much," I quietly admit. "The thought she might never be mine." Frustration pervades every cell in my body. "It's been eight months since she entered my life, yet it feels like forever. I think I fell in love with her that very first night, and not getting to be with her the way I want is soul-crushing. It is literally killing me inside."

"That might be a slight exaggeration." Sarah tries to lighten the mood. "It's the writer in you."

"It's the *man* in me," I protest, sighing as I lift the glass to my lips. I take a drink and swirl the whisky around my mouth before swallowing. "Why put the perfect woman in my path and make it so I can't have her?"

"Who says you can't?" She arches a brow before sipping her drink.

"You know why. She's in love with Garrick, and only a prick would try to steal his girl."

"You're the last person to steal anything from anyone, and I might have called you a prick when I was a rebellious teen, because you were always trying to clip my wings, but it's the furthest from the truth." She reaches across the table and takes my hand. I'm startled to see tears glistening in her eyes. "You're the best man I know, Beck. The absolute best, and I want this for you so badly. I want you to be happy, and she's your happy place."

"So, what do I do?"

"You *wait*." She squeezes my hand. "You continue doing what you have been doing. Quietly loving her from the sidelines, and you wait for her to realize she's in love with you too."

Chapter Twenty-Six

Stevie

"You're amazing." Beck pulls me into his arms, hugging me tight. "When you said you wanted to throw a release party to celebrate my new book, I thought you meant a small get-together with close family and friends, not all this." Breaking our embrace, he throws his arms out as his gaze skims the large room. Nana has been instrumental in ensuring the success of tonight, not least because she gave me the use of the store to host it. We've been advertising it online and locally for weeks. The place is jam-packed with well-wishers and loyal readers, and we've already sold out of every signed copy.

"You deserve it all. You are so talented and so hardworking, and I want you to acknowledge your achievements. To celebrate each book because each one deserves all the accolades and applause."

"You might be biased." He shoots me a lopsided grin.

"I totally am." I twirl around, purposely skimming the room. "But so is everyone else here tonight because we all think you're wonderful." I'm glad he patched things up with Law. I don't know what their argument was about, but they didn't speak for a couple of weeks until Jenny organized a dinner and forced them to kiss and makeup.

"I think you're the wonderful one, and I don't know how I can ever repay you for organizing this. It means so much, Stevie." He threads his fingers in mine. "Thank you."

"You're welcome." Heat blooms in my cheeks when I see the way he's looking at me. "I wanted to do something nice for you to demonstrate how grateful I am for everything you do for me."

"You thank me just by breathing, Stevie."

A frisson of electricity crackles in the air, like often nowadays. Something altered in our relationship during our vacation in France. Things haven't been the same since we returned, and we're both pussyfooting around the elephant in the room.

I cannot go there.

It feels like too much of a betrayal for those kinds of thoughts to even be lurking in the back of my mind, let alone to admit them. So, I'll happily drown in denial and cling to our friendship because I cannot lose Beck.

It would destroy me.

I think he feels the same way and that's why he hasn't broached the subject.

I didn't tell Hadley or my therapist what happened that day at the pool because I know they'd make me confront my reaction and my hidden feelings, and I can't do it.

Every so often, Beck says something or does something that hints at his feelings for me, and it sends equal jolts of joy and pain to every nerve ending in my body.

So we exist in this weird space, where we coexist happily and peacefully as best friends, still doing everything together, where rarely a day goes by when we don't see one another, while ignoring the deeper undercurrents that are never far from the surface.

All it would take is one crack, and they'd burst free.

I live in fear of that day and pray it never comes.

Beck's gaze lowers to my hands, where my fingers are frantically rubbing the poppy ring on my left hand, and he quickly pulls his other hand out of mine and looks away.

It hurts.

Every time I hurt him, I hurt me too.

Which is why we must stop doing this. We need to keep it friendly and easy-breezy, and then no one gets hurt.

"You say the sweetest things, Beck." I finally acknowledge his words. "I'm so glad you're one of my best friends." I stretch up and kiss his cheek, pretending I don't smell the familiar minty spicy smell emanating from his warm skin. "Now, go mingle with your adoring public. We're having the speeches and cutting the cake in twenty minutes, and then the party can begin in earnest." I hired a local DJ to spin the tunes and a bartender to serve drinks. We're staying at Mom's tonight so neither of us has to drive.

"Aye, aye, boss lady." He salutes me with a smile fixed on his face as he wanders off to talk to more readers.

I watch him get submerged in a crowd of older women, smiling to myself as they stare at him with dreamy eyes and shower him with attention.

Beck thinks he owes me, but I owe him so much more.

I am driving again thanks to him. I have put back on most of the weight I lost, and I credit him with reigniting my love of food. My passion for flowers and planning my own business is back, inspired by his writing career and how happy fulfilling his dreams makes him. Thanks to therapy—something I only agreed to because of Beck—I am sleeping better and working through my issues and residual guilt from the accident.

For the rest of my life, I could do numerous things for Beck, and it still wouldn't bring me close to repaying him for everything he has done for me.

"Hey, Stevie." Hudson approaches with a glass of white wine from the bottles Hugh donated for the party. "You look like you need this."

I whip it out of his hand, and he chuckles. "Thanks. I'm parched." I drink a few mouthfuls, feeling some of the stress ease as the crisp peach-flavored wine glides down my throat. Any time I smell peaches now, I'm reminded of the farm in France, and it always brings a smile to my face.

"I like seeing you happy," Hudson admits. "I like seeing color in your cheeks again and some of that old Stevie swagger returning."

"I'm not sure happy is the right word," I truthfully admit. "I'm as happy as I can be knowing Garrick is still in a coma." I glance at the ink on my wrist with a painful pang in my chest. "I haven't seen him in five months, and I hate I have to rely on memories and photos to picture his gorgeous face."

"I wish we'd been able to do something about Ivy. It's disgusting how you were cut out of his life."

I shrug. "There's a special place in hell reserved for people like Ivy and Pepper. I fully believe that."

"He'd be happy you're moving forward, Stevie. It's all any of us can do now."

All that's left unsaid lingers in the air like a bad smell. It's been seventeen months since the accident. Seventeen months since Garrick last opened his eyes, and the inevitability of his future seems more and more determined with every passing day.

"It's so unfair this happened to him," I say. "He had his whole life mapped out. He barely got to experience it."

"I know. Out of everything, that's what gets to me the most at times. He was struck down before he hit his prime. He had so much more living to do."

Mom frantically waves at me from the top of the room. I knock back the rest of my wine and hand the empty glass to Hudson. "I've got to go. It's time for the speeches and to cut the cake."

"I saw it and couldn't believe you baked that yourself."

Pride puffs out my chest. "It's my first time baking a novelty cake, but I wanted to go all out for Beck. Keeping it a secret was hard, but he was totally surprised and delighted when I showed it to him earlier."

I baked a two-tier cake with one chocolate layer and one red velvet layer. Covered in white fondant icing, it has blue piping around the edges, and I molded all the objects on top from icing. It was painstaking work to craft a man sitting at a desk, an ink and a quill, and several books with the titles of Beck's books on the front. It took hours and hours of practice, but I'm really pleased with the result. The look on his face made all the effort worthwhile.

Hudson scrutinizes my face, and I raise my fingers to my skin, suddenly self-conscious. "What? Do I have something on my face?"

"No, you're as pretty as a picture." He clears his throat, looking a little awkward. "I want to say something. You don't need to reply. I just want to put this out there, and it's up to you what you do with it."

My brow puckers. "Okay." He's acting a bit weird.

"It's okay to love him, Stevie. I'm not saying you do or don't, but if Beck is the reason you wear a smile on your face again, and if you have feelings for him, there is nothing wrong with it. It's not wrong to love him. It's not wrong to move on."

"Oh my god." My heart leaps to my throat as I clamp a hand over my mouth and stare at the screen in shock.

"What's wrong?" Beck is instantly on his feet, walking over to where I'm seated at my desk. He surprised me with my own desk and chair in his office a few weeks after he revealed the poppy bedroom, saying he wanted me to have a proper place to work on my artwork. He is always so considerate.

"Look." I angle my screen so he can see. "The DNA site found a new match."

"Holy shit." He crouches down beside me, blinking furiously as he quickly reads the report. Beck laces his fingers in mine and smiles. "You have an uncle."

"I do." Tears stream down my face. "And he wants to meet." I click out of the report and open up the message inbox, showing him the message that greeted me when I logged in. It was sent a week ago, and I missed the email notification. I don't check the system that often, having given up on ever finding anything. "I'm going to find out about my dad. I'm finally going to know."

"I feel ill," Mom says as Beck kills the engine of the rental in front of the small restaurant facing the beach at Siesta Key in Florida where we have agreed to meet my dad's family.

"I know the feeling," I murmur as knots churn in my gut.

"It's natural to feel nervous. This is a big deal." Beck unfurls my knotted fingers, rubbing at the tension he finds there. "Just take a few minutes to compose yourselves. You have both waited over twenty-two years to find out what happened to Liam; you can wait a few minutes longer."

In the two weeks since I read the message from Sean—my father's brother—we have been trading emails back and forth. Beck was beside me when I had my first call with my uncle, and he held me together when Sean revealed the sad truth. Beck came with me to tell Mom, and she broke down in tears when I told her Liam was dead.

I don't know the circumstances yet. It's one of the reasons we flew on the Colbert private jet to Florida, but Sean was forthright in telling me over the phone that my father wasn't alive. He didn't want to mislead me. All I know is his family wasn't aware he had a daughter, and they were totally shocked by the DNA findings.

"Come on, missy." Mom squeezes my shoulders from the back seat. "The Colson women are made of tough stuff. We don't cower in cars. We came for the truth; now let's go get it." It's sad Nana couldn't come with us, but she came down with some bug, and she wasn't feeling up to traveling.

Beck opens Mom's door before helping me out of the car. I almost face-plant on the ground, but Beck catches me and steadies me.

"Shit." I laugh, and it comes out sounding high-pitched and borderline hysterical. "I think I've lost the use of my legs."

"I've got you." Beck slides his arm around my shoulders. "Just hold on to me." I drape one arm around his waist as we follow Mom into the restaurant.

She gasps before holding a trembling hand to her mouth as a tall man with a lean muscular build advances toward us with obvious emotion on his face.

Beck holds me a little tighter as I stare at my uncle with a lump in my throat. He has auburn hair, like me, except his is much darker. Navy-blue eyes glistening with tears latch on to Mom and then me.

"My god," he whispers, "you look so much like him."

"You look like him too," Mom chokes out. "His image has long since faded in my memory, but watching you walk toward us was like seeing a ghost."

Sean's gaze bounces between Mom and me. "Forgive my bad manners. I'm Sean." He thrusts out his hand, shaking Mom's hand first, then mine, and then Beck's.

"I'm Beck. We spoke on the phone."

"I remember." Sean nods respectfully. "Thanks for bringing Stevie and Monica. This is a big day for our family."

"This feels surreal," Mom says.

"I know." Sean smiles, shuffling awkwardly on his feet. "Mom and Anne are waiting back here." He jerks his head toward the corner. "Come and I'll make introductions."

I clutch Beck like a lifeline as we follow my uncle to a private booth in a corner of the restaurant facing out onto the white sandy beach. It's not as hot or humid in Florida in November as in the height of the summer, but it's still warm enough to see sunbathers on the beach and plenty of activity in the turquoise sea.

"Here we are," Sean says when we reach the table where an older petite woman with reddish-blonde hair and green eyes sits beside a taller younger woman with dark auburn hair and the same blue eyes as Sean.

"Mom, Anne, this is Stevie, Stevie's mom, Monica, and Stevie's boyfriend, Beck."

I'm not surprised he jumped to the obvious conclusion, and I don't bother correcting him. I'm too freaking nervous to concentrate on anything but the people in front of me. People who are now part of my family.

After awkward hugs and a strange start, we all loosen up over iced lattes and cake. Mom tells them how she came to meet Liam and the efforts she made to contact him after she discovered she was pregnant. Beck keeps his arm wrapped around my shoulders as he sits alongside me in the booth, and I'm grateful for his physical and emotional support.

"The Navy didn't pass any letters on to him," Sean says, leaning back in the booth. "My brother would not have abandoned you."

"My Liam lived for family," Susan says. "He would have done right by both of you had he known."

I can't believe I have a second grandmother. I was already blessed with the one I have, and I can tell I'm going to be blessed to have Susan in my life too. She's softly spoken with a warm smile, and she has talked so reverently about her three children. Anne is the oldest, followed by Liam, and Sean is the baby of the family. Though it sounds funny saying that when I know he's forty.

"I got that sense from him," Mom says with a sad smile. "He talked about his family, and I could tell you were all close."

"What happened to him?" I ask.

"He died a year after you were born. He was traveling by helicopter to land, from the ship he was stationed at, when they ran into engine trouble and crashed into the sea," Sean explains in a haunted voice.

"They never recovered the bodies," Anne confirms. "We didn't even have his body to bury."

"It still breaks my heart," Susan says. "It broke my Arthur's heart too. He died with a smile knowing our son was waiting for him in heaven." Sean had previously explained how his father, my grandfather, had died seven years ago from lung cancer.

"Looking at you is like looking at Liam," Susan says. Tears glisten in her eyes. "We thought he was lost to us forever, and then we discover a miracle." She reaches across the table for my hand. "A piece of my son lives on in you. We're so glad we found you, and we only wish it hadn't taken so long."

"Better late than never, Mom," Anne says.

Susan squeezes my hand before withdrawing her own. "Absolutely. We already love you, Stevie, and we hope we can become a part of your life." She smiles at Mom. "Both your lives."

"I would like that," I choke out. Mom and I already discussed potential outcomes of today's visit, and I know she will agree.

"Wonderful." Susan swipes tears of joy from her eyes. "We look forward to getting to know you." She retrieves a heavy photo album from under the seat. "I pulled out all the photos I had of Liam after Sean told us about you. I got duplicates taken, and I made this for you. I thought you might like to have it." She hands it to me.

Tears pool in my eyes as I accept the gift. "This is very thoughtful. Thank you." Beck hands me a monogrammed handkerchief. I swear he only stocks up on them for me. I peer into his eyes, comforted by his presence. "Thanks."

He kisses my cheek.

"Why don't we go back to the house?" Sean suggests. "It will be more comfortable there, and we can go through photos, and I can show you his room and the places we hung out as kids?"

"If you aren't in a rush, that would be lovely," Susan adds, looking hopeful.

I glance at Beck, not sure if he'd agreed a time with the pilot for the return journey.

"Take as much time as you need," he says, answering my unspoken question. "The plane is on standby."

I look at Mom.

"It's your call, sweetheart, but I am happy to find out more about

Liam." This has been a big shock to Mom. I hadn't even told her I'd submitted DNA on the site, so it's been a lot to take in. But I think she's relieved. Obviously, it's really sad my dad died, but knowing he didn't purposely abandon us has given Mom the closure that has evaded her for years.

"That sounds perfect," I say, smiling at my uncle, my aunt, and my grandmother. "Show us the way."

Chapter Twenty-Seven

Beck

"I can't thank you enough," Jan says, pulling me into a bear hug. "It's perfect and Brielle would've gotten a kick out of it," she adds with tears in her eyes.

"Don't thank me." I shuck out of our embrace. "The idea for the memorial garden was all Stevie's." I smile at the beautiful redhead pressed into my side trying to siphon some of my body heat. It's freaking cold this time of night in mid-November, yet we all felt it was most appropriate to open the memorial garden in Brielle's name with a candlelight vigil and a prayer service.

"You got the approval from the hospital," Stevie confirms, "and you worked as hard as Jan, Hadley, Mike, Hudson, and I did planting the flowers and trees."

"I'm grateful to everyone." She hugs Stevie. "Especially you two. It's such a sweet, considerate gesture."

"This garden gave me a lot of comfort at a time when I badly needed it." Stevie looks up at me with a sad smile. "Extending it and adding another couple of benches means more people will draw strength from it now, and we have a permanent way of remembering Brielle."

"It's helped me too," Jan says. "Getting to do this for my best friend helps me to overcome the residual guilt I still feel."

"I can relate," I admit even if I have come a long way thanks to therapy and Stevie. I no longer harbor the self-loathing and remorse I did, but a part of me will always feel guilty I didn't give Brielle more of my time at the end. But I have accepted it wasn't my fault. It's a tragedy, like what happened to Garrick is a tragedy, albeit in a different way.

Stevie doesn't mention him as much these days. I don't doubt he's still on her mind, but talking about him hurts her. There is no change in his condition, and she's still iced out. While she continues to wear his ring and the locket he gave her, she doesn't continually touch them or reach for them at times of stress like she used to.

It's supremely selfish of me to hope it means she's ready to let him go, but I do. I'm patiently waiting on the sidelines, being the best friend I can, while I give her time to process all the changes in her life.

We spend most of our spare time together, and she stays over at my apartment every weekend. Mondays, Tuesdays, and Thursdays are usually spent at her place at the end of our working days. After dinner, we generally go for a run or a walk or head to the gym before I go home to squeeze some writing in. It's always difficult to drag myself away from her because I never want to leave. Wednesdays, we catch a movie at the theater. Mike and Hadley, or Law and Jenny, sometimes join us. Fridays, we go out for dinner alone or catch up with our friends, and Saturdays are spent at my apartment, where I write and Stevie works on her dried-flower pictures or her future business plans. We generally stay in on Saturday nights, unless there is a special occasion, and we cook or get takeout before snuggling on the couch to watch a movie. Lazy Sunday mornings with a breakfast of pastries and coffee are the norm before we head to Ravenna for dinner with her mom and nana.

I love it.

I wake every morning with a spring in my step and the image of her beautiful face on my mind.

There's no doubt she is my person.

The other half of my heart and soul.

It already feels like we're a couple in most of the ways that count. All that's missing is the intimacy I crave, but I can be patient. I will wait for eternity, if I must, because she is worth it.

"I'm going to head home because I'm freezing my butt off out here," Jan says. "Keep in touch," she adds as she backs up, waving, and we promise we will.

After the last stragglers have left, Stevie and I sit side by side on the new bench bearing a plaque with Brielle's name.

"We did a good thing," she says, shivering as a gust of wind whistles by, lifting strands of her gorgeous hair.

"We did," I agree, sliding my arm around her shoulders and pulling her into my warmth. "It feels good to do something like this. In my new life, I'm going to make more time to do charitable things."

Stevie picks her head up and stares inquisitively into my eyes. "Your new life? And what charitable things?"

I tweak her nose, chuckling as she swats my hand away and mock scowls. "I'm not sure what charitable endeavors I'll get involved in, just that I want to give back more. As for my new life." I pause to draw a breath. "I'm ready to talk to my sisters and cut ties with my father."

Twisting around, she flings her arms around my neck, and the biggest smile breaks out across her face. "Really? You're really going to do it?"

I nod. "I'm twenty-eight now, and I've wasted enough of my life doing things that don't fill me with passion."

My birthday was a couple weeks ago, and I'd selfishly wanted to celebrate it just with Stevie. Of course, she wouldn't let me do that, so we had dinner and drinks in a new steakhouse a few blocks from my place, and then everyone came back to my apartment to cut the cake

Stevie baked. It was another delicious masterpiece and almost a shame to eat it. We were dancing, singing, and drinking until five a.m., and I had the mother of all hangovers the next day. But it was worth it to spend time with all my favorite people.

"I'm proud of you." She kisses my cheek and tightens her fingers around my neck.

I try to avoid consciously thinking about how good it feels when she's close like this, touching me, skin to skin, and beaming at me like I'm her favorite person in the entire world. My body reacts automatically, whether my brain goes there or not, and it's getting harder and harder—pun intended—to hide the almost permanent boner I seem to sport in her company. I'm sure she has noticed, but she never mentions it, and I don't mention how I've caught her looking at my mouth or staring at my body when we work out or if we happen to bump into one another when I'm just out of the shower and wearing nothing more than a towel.

I don't think she realizes how much she touches me these days. It's never inappropriate, but she will often reach for my hand before I reach for hers, or cup my face, or brush my arm, and she always seeks my comfort when we're snuggling on the couch watching TV.

All of it gives me quiet confidence she's coming around to the idea of us as a couple. I can't broach the subject. If we go there, Stevie has to start the ball rolling, but I'm hopeful we are getting closer to that place.

When contemplating all of this, I realized my melancholy wasn't just emanating from my predicament with Stevie but also from the futility of the professional life I'm leading. Working for my father is slowly chipping away at my self-worth and my newly found happiness, and I need to stop the bleed now. I can't control what happens with Stevie—she will set the pace—but I *can* control what happens with my father.

"Thank you. Your encouragement gives me the strength to do this."

"I can't take any credit. I'm just glad you are putting yourself first."

"Enough is enough," I say, internally crying when she removes her hands from my neck, already missing her touch. "It's time to lay all the cards on the table."

Chapter Twenty-Eight

Beck

"I'm going out for a walk and meeting Hadley for lunch," Stevie says, bending down to kiss my cheek. "I'll be gone for ages, so take your time."

"You don't have to make yourself scarce," I remind her. "There is nothing I plan to say to my sisters you can't hear."

"I know, but this is something you should discuss with your sisters alone. It's a family matter."

I want to say she'll be family one day, but that's an extremely premature thought.

"Okay." I stand and wrap my arms around her. "Be safe."

She rolls her eyes. "It's only a walk, and lunch, in the middle of the day. I'm sure I'll survive."

I follow her out to the hall, watching as she puts on her coat and grabs her bag. "I worry about you when I'm not there to protect you."

She cups my cheeks. "You're so sweet."

It's so difficult not to grab the back of her head and pull her mouth to mine, but somehow, I resist.

A knock on the door ends the moment anyway. We break apart, and Stevie opens the door to my sisters. Esther and Stevie hug it out while Sarah looks on in amused confusion. With one last goodbye, Stevie is gone, and I'm closing the door after her and ushering my sisters inside.

"Wow." Sarah stands in front of the new framed picture on the wall behind the couch. "Stevie is getting so good."

"She's very talented." Pride suffuses my tone as I stand alongside my sisters, admiring Stevie's latest work of art. I have four original Stevie Colson masterpieces around my house now, and I smile every time I look at them, instantly thinking of the amazing woman who created them. Law and Tate would give me such shit if they were privy to my thoughts.

"Is that your eagle?" Esther asks, tilting her head to one side as she inspects the exquisite dried-flower rendering of the ink on my back.

"It is." Stevie took a picture of it to use as her inspiration.

Sarah's head whips to mine. "How would Stevie know about it?" Her mouth curves at the corners and her eyes scrunch up. "Has something happened with you two?"

"I wish." Shoving my hands deep in the pockets of my jeans, I sigh. "I'm still firmly in the friend zone."

"Aw." Disappointment crests over Sarah's face, and I love how much my sisters want this for me.

"Just give it time." Esther pats my arm. "We all see the way she looks at you. She'll find her way onto the same page."

"How long do you think Garrick's family will let him remain in a coma before they force the issue?" Sarah asks, sinking onto my couch.

I shrug. "I don't know if they'll force the issue at all. They have the resources to keep him on life support forever." I drop onto the recliner chair, running a hand over the top of my head.

"I would hate to be in that position." Esther sits beside Sarah. "I hope nothing ever happens to the two of you. Imagine having to even contemplate such a thing? I don't think I could ever willingly decide to turn off life support."

"If there is no brain activity, like in Brielle's case, it would be cruel to everyone to not do it," I say. "Garrick's situation is difficult because there is evidence of brain activity, but the longer he is on life support, the more risk there is to his lungs, his heart, and his brain."

Sarah tucks her hair behind her ears. "You mean if he wakes there's a greater chance he could be in a vegetative state?"

I nod.

"God, that would be awful. For him and his loved ones," Esther says with tears in her eyes. "It's an impossible situation. I feel so bad for him and his family. For Stevie too."

"It sucks for everyone involved." Sarah looks pointedly at me.

"It does, but I didn't ask you to come here today to talk about Garrick. We need to talk about Dad and how he's blackmailing me into working for the business."

"Finally," Sarah says, clasping her hands in her lap.

"What do you mean *finally*?" Esther asks, looking thoroughly confused as her gaze bounces between her older siblings.

"You wouldn't have noticed because you're younger and you're not at the office, but Beck is fucking miserable working for Dad."

"You knew?" Shock filters through my words.

"I have eyes. I know you hate your job, but I know nothing about blackmail. What has the asshole done?"

I fill them in on how Dad's been holding their trust funds and their futures over my head as a way of forcing me to do his bidding.

"That fucking bastard," Esther seethes, clenching her hands into fists. "How dare he use me to make you do something against your will." She leans forward, resting her hands on her knees. "I hate that you've been dealing with this for years. Why didn't you say anything?"

Sarah snorts. "That part is obvious." Her features soften. "Beck has a savior complex, and he's always been overly protective of us."

Emotion floods Esther's eyes. "Because of Mom."

"What happened to Mom was not your fault, Beck." Sarah drills me with a look. "You couldn't have saved her. You were only a kid, and you've punished yourself enough."

"Does Stevie know?" Esther asks, and I shake my head.

"She has enough on her plate without me adding to it." Ironically, I was planning on telling her, and then she found her father's family, and she's happier than I've ever seen her, and I don't want to bring up my depressing story and have her worrying about me.

"Tell her," Sarah says. "You have carried it with you long enough."

"Therapy is helping, and I will tell her when the time is right."

"I don't think I've ever properly thanked you," Esther says. "I was so little when Mom died, and I barely remember her."

"I hate that for you," I croak.

"Me too," she whispers, and sadness seeps from her pores. "But I remember you stepping into that parental role and ensuring I wanted for nothing. It wasn't Nanny Claudia who raised me. It was you." Tears pool in her eyes. "You were always so protective, so patient, so kind."

"You're the best big brother," Sarah agrees. "You couldn't have done more for us."

"It ends now." Esther straightens up and steely determination glints in her eyes. "Father has preyed on your vulnerability for the last time."

"He knows how protective you are of us, and he played you perfectly," Sarah says.

"He will probably cut you both off to spite me." I rub at the tight pain spreading across my chest. "But I'll make sure you're looked after. With full-time dedication to my writing, I'm sure I can make enough to support us, and we have our inheritances from Mom, and I got my full trust fund. We can make it work."

Sarah turns to look at Esther. "Will you tell him, or shall I?"

Esther glues her gaze to mine. "We're grown women, Beck. It is not your place to support us, and I will not take a single penny from you."

"Nor I," Sarah says, tossing waves of dark-blonde hair over her shoulders. "And it won't be necessary. By the time I'm finished with Father, he'll be kneeling at all of our feet."

A look of glee appears on Esther's face, and she rubs her hands together. "You have a plan. I knew you would! What are you going to do?"

"*We*"—Sarah enunciates the word as her gaze skitters between us —"are going to teach that manipulative dick a valuable life lesson."

"How?" Anxiety churns in my gut at the thought of Dad calling our bluff, changing the terms of my sisters' trust funds, and cutting them off. It's always been my biggest fear.

"Think of this logically, Beck. If you'd done that at the start, you would never have let Dad manipulate you. He won't ostracize his three children as that would leave him without any heir. Think of how it would look. He won't risk that."

"I wouldn't be so sure. He's a stubborn old goat."

"I know exactly how to play him. I wish I had pried more and done this sooner. I knew things weren't right between you and Brielle. I can't believe he forced you into a relationship and he was trying to force you into marriage. It's insane!" Sarah's voice pitches higher than I've ever heard it. "This isn't just about extricating you from the business. This is about making a point. So, this is what I propose. You go into the office on Monday and resign. Then we'll come in and back you up. If he threatens you or us, I'll resign too. I'll tell him I'm going to work for Boeing."

The widest grin materializes on my face. "That's genius. He'll be apoplectic." Worry filters into my veins, dampening my initial euphoric rush. "What if he calls your bluff?"

Sarah smirks as she takes out her cell. "That's the beauty of this plan. I will have a job offer from Boeing to rub in his face."

"You will?" My eyes pop wide.

She taps out a text and tosses her phone aside. "I was at Harvard with the son of the Boeing chairman. He has a bit of a crush on me."

Esther snorts out a laugh. "It's more than a crush Mark has on you."

Sarah shrugs, grinning as her phone pings already with a reply. "It will never amount to anything, but he doesn't need to know that. I'm glad I kept him on my side," she says, swiping her finger across the screen, "because now I have a Boeing offer to throw in Daddy's face."

"Excellent." Esther raises her hand and they high-five like they're back in school.

"So, are we in agreement?" Sarah asks, eyeballing both of us. "We're doing this on Monday?"

"Are you sure?" I ask. "This could blow up in our faces."

"It won't," Sarah assures me. "We also have Cartwright to throw into the mix if Dad tries to reject me as his successor. The only other alternative is Brewster Cartwright, and Dad won't let that happen. He didn't build that clause into the merger contract for nothing. He needs a successor, and he'll have to accept it's me or risk losing control of the business that's been in his family for almost a hundred years."

"We're more than sure," Esther adds. "You have done so much for us, Beck. It's time to let us do this for you so you can become a full-time writer and live your dream."

Chapter Twenty-Nine

Stevie

"Thanks for spending the day with us," Mom says, pulling Esther in for another hug. She managed to trick Sarah into a hug earlier when Beck's sisters arrived at Nana's house for Christmas dinner, but she knows not to push her luck. Nana already retired to bed and said her goodbyes earlier. She kept falling asleep on the couch. I think the fire was making her drowsy.

"You don't have to leave," I remind them for the umpteenth time. "Nana has two spare bedrooms, and Beck and I are already staying at Mom's, so you aren't inconveniencing us."

"You've very kind," Esther says, giving me one final hug. "But we promised Father we'd drop by on our way home, and we've ruffled his feathers enough lately."

Beck's sisters rallied around him like I knew they would. Together, they tackled their father, forcing him to acquiesce to their will. Beck's final day at the office was Thursday, and Sarah is now the official heir apparent. The Boeing offer was the ace up their sleeve, and Carlton Colbert folded on the spot when faced with the prospect of losing the only child who actually wants to succeed him in the family business. Beck negotiated for the girls to receive half their trust fund now, and the moneys were wired into their account last night.

His father can't hold anything over him anymore and he is free to live his life how he pleases.

I am so happy for him. It's like the biggest weight has been lifted from his shoulders, and I've never seen him more excited. He's getting his home office remodeled after Christmas and taking a part of the dining room into the office space so it's bigger now he will be spending more time in there.

"Tell him I wish him a Merry Christmas," Beck says, kissing his sisters on their cheeks.

Carlton might have capitulated to his children and released Beck, but it doesn't mean he's a happy camper. He is frothing at the mouth and extremely angry at being outmaneuvered. He is refusing to speak to Beck. It's laughable he thinks it's some kind of punishment when it feels like a special reward. Beck isn't close to his father, and I don't think he cares much except that it upsets Esther.

"You should be able to tell him yourself," Esther grumbles.

"He will come around," Mom says purely to reassure the girls. She knows, as well as we do, that men like Carlton Colbert are as stubborn as a red wine stain.

"Take a walk with me?" Beck asks after his sisters have left. "I thought we could exchange gifts in the poppy field?" I didn't want to give my gift to him with everyone around, and he was the same, so we have been putting it off all day.

"Let me help Mom with the cleanup first."

"Shoo." Mom practically shoves me at Beck. "You and Nana did all the cooking, and Beck already cleared most of the table. I can load the dishwasher by myself."

Bundling up in coats, scarves, and heavy boots, we step outside and walk in the direction of the poppy field. I'm carrying the bag with his gift in one hand, and my free hand is curled around Beck's. Although it's cold, I barely feel it wrapped up in cozy layers and the warmth of Beck's hand in mine. I don't know when I got so comfortable with him because it's happened gradually. Holding hands with him is as natural as breathing to me now. The thought causes a little stabby pain to attack my heart as I think of Garrick.

He's been on my mind today. Hugh and Dawn invited us for Christmas, but I didn't want to go. I didn't want to be sad again this year, and going to North Bend would have made me sad because all I'd be thinking about is that one Christmas I had with my boyfriend.

It's been seven months since Garrick left the hospital and nineteen months since the accident, and it's getting harder and harder to hold on to what we had. It feels like a distant memory now. Whomever coined the saying "out of sight, out of mind" wasn't entirely right. Yes, I don't think about him as much, and it's harder to picture him in my mind now I no longer see him, but I won't ever forget him.

"Are you okay?" Beck asks, staring at me with concerned eyes.

We are almost at the poppy field, and I have barely noticed the walk. "Yes." I squeeze his hand. "It's been a good day."

"It's been amazing and the best Christmas I've enjoyed since my mom died."

"I'm glad. Christmas should be a happy time."

"Every day with you is a happy time." His eyes fill with unbridled emotion, and I don't look away like I usually do.

"You make me happy too," I quietly admit.

Beck stops at the entrance to the field and pulls me into his arms. Resting my head on his chest, I close my eyes and just breathe him in.

The only sound is the gentle sway of the trees in the breeze and the faint yapping of a dog in the background. Bright colors shine from the string of Christmas lights draped around the fences bordering the field, and the twinkling glow of the stars overhead is the only illumination in an otherwise pitch-black night. An earthy, slightly nutty smell tickles my nostrils as I stand enveloped in Beck's body heat, savoring the tranquility of our environment and the moment.

"Sometimes, Nana's farm reminds me of France," Beck says in a gruff voice before pressing a lingering kiss to my hair.

"You took the words right out of my mouth."

"We could be the only two people in the world right now."

"Two people and a dog," I quip as the distant sound of barking persists.

"That would make a great book title."

I ease back and grin at him. "If you didn't write gritty thrillers with tons of blood and gore."

He tweaks my nose. "Maybe I'll write a biography someday and I'll document this moment."

"Go for it. You can put a picture of us on the cover in front of the poppy field and show a restless dog hiding between the flowers."

"This is why I keep you around," he teases, grasping my hand and leading me toward our bench. "You're full of good ideas."

"You're going to need me now, Mr. Full-time Author. In case you ever run out of ideas."

"I don't think that's likely." He taps his temple as we stride through the field. It's mowed at this time of year, and the poppies won't bloom until late February. "I have enough story ideas to last me a lifetime." He pulls me down on the bench beside him.

Nana had it built over the summer. She said she wanted to give me a safe, quiet place to come if I ever needed to think, and I know she was trying to replicate the bench in the hospital garden, understanding how precious it was to me. Most Sundays, Beck and I come here after we've eaten dinner.

"But I'll always need you, Stevie." Beck pulls me back into the moment as he brushes a few wandering strands of hair out of my eyes. "Don't ever doubt that."

Electricity sparks in the tiny gap between us, and instead of shying away from it, I embrace it and how it makes me feel. On this Christmas night, I need to feel alive, and Beck makes me feel more alive than anyone or anything. I'm done denying how important he is to me. "I need you too." My voice rings out clear and confident. "Don't ever doubt how important you are to me because I care about you deeply."

"Ditto, beautiful." We stare at one another with so much unspoken sentiment hovering in the space between us.

"Open your gifts," I say in a raspy voice, grabbing the bag and handing it to him.

I chew on the corner of my mouth as I watch him open his presents. Moonlight bathes him in an ethereal glow, highlighting his masculine beauty. Beck truly is the full package with his olive skin, dark hair, strong nose, full lips, and chiseled high cheekbones. But it's his eyes—his gorgeous, big, warm brown eyes, framed by thick black lashes—that mesmerize me.

If eyes really are the window to the soul, Beck's soul is beautiful.

Utterly beautiful.

Like every part of him.

I watch him uncover his gifts with a new appreciation. Deep down, I know it's not new. It's always been there, but I've been too afraid to acknowledge it.

I don't think I can bury my head in the sand any longer.

The thought terrifies me, but I'm not being fair to any of us pretending like I don't have strong feelings for him.

Feelings that are more than friendly.

I expect to be struck down for thinking such a thing, but it doesn't happen.

"This is incredible, Stevie," he says, holding up the rectangular frame I made him from dried flowers.

"It's a door sign," I explain in case it's not clear.

Taking out his phone, he turns on the flashlight and shines it across the picture. "Do not disturb. Genius at work," he reads. His eyes flare with warmth as he stares at me. "I love it. It will look perfect on my new office door."

I'm glad it's dark out so he can't detect the flush staining my cheeks. It's hard to buy something for a man who has everything he needs. A man who isn't flashy despite his wealth.

"Open the other gift," I say, retrieving the smaller box from the bag and giving it to him.

"Stevie, this is too much," he says in a tone full of awe as he removes the silver and blue ballpoint Montblanc pen from the box.

"Shush. It's not," I say even though it cost me almost seven hundred bucks. To me, it was worth every penny because Beck's presence in my life is priceless. I swivel it in his fingers. "Look, I had it personalized." They only allow you to use thirteen letters, so it simply says 'For Beck,' but I'm hoping it's the thought that counts. I considered inscribing his pen name instead, but this seemed more personal. More intimate.

His gorgeous eyes pin me in place as he leans in close. So many emotions flit across his face as he maintains eye contact while brushing his lips against my cheek, blazing a trail in every place he touches. "This is the perfect gift, Stevie." He pulls back a little, but our faces are still super close, and our knees are touching. "I love it. I love it so much." It looks like he wants to say more, but he's purposely holding himself back.

"Every writer deserves a special pen." It's a miracle I get the words out, because with the way he's looking at me now, I'm liable to melt into a puddle at his feet. He's looking at me like, like...he loves me.

Butterflies dance in my chest as adrenaline kicks in, and my pulse throbs in my neck. Beck's eyes drift to my mouth, and I stop breathing for a second. He breaks the connection first, and I release the breath I was holding. My heart is racing behind my rib cage, my palms feel sweaty, and my tummy is in delicious knots.

I know what I'm feeling, and I'm scared. But I'm more scared of not feeling this ever again.

Beck slides a long rectangular gift, wrapped in festive packaging, from his back pocket and hands it to me. "This is for you. I hope you like it."

I tear eagerly at the wrapping, scrunching the paper into a ball and stuffing it in my coat pocket before opening the box. A gasp leaves my mouth as I lift the stunning silver charm bracelet from inside. "This is beautiful, Beck." Emotion pricks the backs of my eyes as I look between him and the bracelet.

"I left room so you could add more charms in the future," he explains as I examine the objects.

There is a book, a poppy, a picture frame, a little group of people, a barn, a bar of chocolate, a peach, and…a guitar. Tears swim in my eyes. How can this man be so wonderful? I know he has strong feelings for me, yet he never wants me to forget Garrick.

"Let me put it on," he says, taking my right wrist in his hands.

"Not there," I whisper. "On this one." I tap my left wrist where the tattoo I got with Garrick is inked on my skin.

I want to wear Beck's bracelet on the same wrist.

This way, I get to keep both of them close.

Beck peers deep into my eyes, and my chest heaves as he tries to extract my thoughts with a penetrating gaze. After a few silent beats, he nods, putting my right wrist down and lifting my left one. His thumb sweeps reverently over the Celtic shield knot, and my heart swells to bursting point. He is so careful as he secures the bracelet around my wrist, and my skin is on fire from his worshiping touch.

I'm awash with want and need.

Every part of me is fully alive for the first time in a long time, and I couldn't stop this even if I wanted to.

Which I don't.

The remaining barriers around my heart crumple, and I can't claim to fully know what I'm doing, but I know what I want in this moment, and I'm done holding back. Nothing that feels this good and so right can be bad or wrong.

I deserve to be happy, and Beck is my happy place.

I refuse to feel anything but love and desire in this moment.

"Beck," I whisper in a voice strangled with potent emotion,

pulling him closer to me until our noses are touching and our breaths are mingling.

"Yes, honey," he whispers back, his hungry gaze dipping to my mouth with powerful longing.

It seems we are both done shielding the truth from one another.

"Kiss me. Please."

Chapter Thirty
Stevie

Beck moves his hand to my neck and gently tugs me closer, ending the small gap between us. The second his soft lips meet mine, I lose myself to our kiss. He takes full control, slanting his mouth over mine in firm sweeping strokes that are equally tender and commanding. His hands cup my face as his tongue laps at my lips requesting entry. I gasp into his mouth as his kiss hardens, and his tongue pushes inside, stroking my tongue and licking the roof of my mouth.

Stars float behind my closed eyelids as he devours my mouth with skill. Things heat up as our tongues clash for supremacy, stroking and dancing, while his lips press passionately against mine in an increasing frenzy. I'm grabbing his shoulders, his neck, his face, greedy to touch every part of him.

Mutual moans pass between our mouths, and every cell and nerve ending in my body is electrified. I squirm on the bench as a persistent throbbing takes up residence between my legs. I ache so badly for him. It's been so long since I felt a hard cock pushing inside me, and I'm ready to jump in his lap and impale myself on his dick when reality comes crashing down on me.

Garrick's smiling face resurrects in my mind, and I yank my lips from Beck's and stumble off the bench, falling sideways onto the trimmed ground in my haste to retreat from my actions.

"I've got you." Beck helps me to my feet. Gently gripping my forearms, he bends his head until we are eye to eye. "Talk to me, honey. What just happened?"

Tears stream silently down my cheeks. "I just cheated on Garrick," I sob.

Pain rips across Beck's face until he hides it. "You weren't ready," he says in a dead voice. "I'm sorry, Stevie. I should have checked."

"No." I shake my head as I shuck out of his hold, wrapping my arms around my waist. "Don't apologize. This isn't on you. It's on me."

"I...fuck." He averts his gaze and hangs his head for a few tense seconds while I quietly cry and try to unscramble the jumble in my head and my heart. "Do you regret it?" he asks, lifting his head. I hate the pain and sadness I see on his face, knowing I put it there.

"I don't know," I truthfully answer.

His Adam's apple bobs in his throat, and I feel like the worst person on the planet. I don't want to hurt him any more than I have, and he deserves honesty.

Well, he deserves so much more, but he deserves that for starters.

"Beck, it was amazing. Kissing you felt like..." My voice cracks, and my sobs filter into the air. He makes no move to comfort me, and I don't blame him. "Kissing you felt like home," I say when I can get the words out. "I wanted it. I have wanted it for some time, but I was lying to myself. I still want it. I want that and more, but I'm so confused." A hiccup filters into the eerie night air. "I'm so freaking confused, scared, and I feel so guilty."

"Come here," he says. "Please."

Slowly, I walk to him, and my arms drop listlessly to my sides.

He envelops me in a protective embrace, and I sob against his chest. "I'm sorry," I croak, holding on to him as I lift my tearstained face up to his. "This is so unfair to you."

"This isn't about me. I'll be fine." His thumbs swipe at the dampness pooling on my cheeks. "I'm worried about you."

That only makes me cry harder. He is such a good man. So incredible. "You deserve better than me," I sob. "I'm a mess, and you deserve the world."

"Look at me, honey." He clasps my face in his hands. "You are everything I deserve. Everything I need and want, but it's not as simple as want or need. If it was, we would have been together like this months ago."

"I do want you, Beck, but I don't know how to do this or if I can. How can I do this to Garrick?"

"I'm not the best person to speak to about this because I'm selfish when it comes to you, and you need someone impartial. Have you spoken to Ramona or Hadley?"

I shake my head. Ramona, my therapist, has tried to coax me into talking about Beck, but I have routinely shut her down. Hadley has made the odd passing remark, but she hasn't probed. I know my bestie. She is nosy and not above exercising a tough-love approach, but even Hads hasn't broached this subject because she's waiting for me to do it.

"The last thing I want to do is give you space, because I need you like I need oxygen, but you need some time away from me to think about what you want." He tips my face up. "I won't pressure you, but I'm not going to lie. I want to be with you as more than a friend. I have strong feelings for you, Stevie, and I've been waiting to see if you shared them."

"I do," I admit in a whisper. "But that doesn't mean anything will come of it. I still have a boyfriend." I shuck out of his arms, feeling like a whore thinking about my boyfriend while seeking solace from a man I just kissed. A man who has been there for me through so much, and this is how I repay him?

I am so disgusted with myself right now. How could I do this to Garrick? To Beck? To myself? Because I'm torn in two now and it's agony.

"God, I'm the worst kind of human. What woman cheats on her comatose boyfriend? Right now, I am everything Ivy has accused me of being."

"Nope." Beck vehemently shakes his head. "I will not let you think that about yourself. You are not in any way how that woman tries to depict you."

"I just kissed a man who isn't my boyfriend! That makes me a cheater. All that's missing is the gold-digging part."

Beck opens and closes his mouth before hanging his head and rubbing the back of his neck.

I'm hurting him again.

I couldn't hate myself any more than I do right now.

"I need to go." I knot and unknot my hands. "I'm sorry to do this, but I think it'd be best if you went home tonight."

The saddest expression washes over his face as he nods. Horrible tension descends while he wraps up his gifts and then hands me the bracelet box. He does something on his cell, and then we walk back to the house in silence, and my heart is shattering all over again.

Guilt wars with longing inside me, and I'm consumed with terror at the thought I may have just lost my best friend.

Why did I think it was a good idea to kiss Beck?

Now I have ruined Christmas, hurt both of us, and changed everything.

When we reach Nana's house, an Uber is waiting for him. A lump rises in my throat, and I'm on the verge of tears again. Beck stows his gifts in the back seat and says something to the driver before walking over to me.

"Listen to me, Stevie." He takes my cold hands in his. "You are not to beat yourself up over this. I won't tell you you've done nothing wrong, even though it's what I believe, because you need to draw that conclusion yourself." He peers deep into my eyes as tears roll down my face. "I'm here for you, and I'm going nowhere. Do you understand?"

I stare numbly at him through blurry eyes.

"Stevie, honey." He squeezes my hands. "If we have to go back to being friends, we'll do that. Losing you from my life is not an option. Okay?"

I think I nod.

"I'll give you space. Take whatever time you need. When you're ready, call or text me." He presses his lips to my brow, and it's a miracle my legs are still holding me up. "Take care, honey, and I'll see you soon."

I'm reluctant to let him go, clinging to him, until I realize how unfair I am being when he's trying to do the right thing.

"I'm sorry," I say, finally letting him go.

"Don't be." He offers me one sad smile before sliding in the back seat of the Uber.

We stare at one another as the driver reverses and then pulls out onto the road.

I don't know how long I stand outside staring into the empty darkness, sobbing and hating myself, feeling like I've just made the worst mistake of my life in letting him go, before Mom finds me and drags me inside.

I collapse into her arms, inconsolable and in horrific pain as it feels like my heart is being torn violently from my chest.

Mom holds me for hours as I cry on her shoulder. She doesn't attempt to make me talk; she just cradles me while I fall apart and then helps me into bed. We decide to stay at Nana's tonight because I'm in no fit state to walk to Mom's and she refuses to leave me.

The following morning, I wake to find Nana perched on the corner of my bed, looking pale and wearing a troubled expression. "I made tea," she says as I drag my weary ass up and lean against the headboard.

"Where's Mom?" I ask in a scratchy tone.

"She went to tidy up the house before the Ryans arrive later." I'd forgotten my dad's family is arriving today from Florida. They are staying at a hotel in Seattle for a couple days.

"I should help." I throw the covers off my legs.

"Your mom has it handled, Little Poppy. Stay where you are." Nana gets up and pours tea into two cups from her fancy teapot and hands one to me with slightly shaking hands.

"Are you okay, Nana?"

"I'm fine." She brushes off my concern as she sets her cup down on the bedside table. "Scoot over."

I move over, and she climbs onto the bed alongside me. "I didn't make anything to eat. I figured you wouldn't be able to stomach it." She pats my hand. "Any time I've been heartsick, I've lost my appetite."

"Yeah. I think I'm the same." I couldn't eat after the accident because my stomach was in knots worrying about Garrick, and my stomach has been in knots since my betrayal.

"Let it out, sweetheart." Nana kisses my temple. "Tell your old Nana what's troubling you."

"I kissed Beck," I say before sipping the hot sweet tea.

"We thought something must have finally happened."

I perk my head up. "Finally?"

Her wrinkled features soften with pure unadulterated love. "That boy is so in love with you." Only Nana could call a twenty-eight-year-old man a boy, but we're all kids to her. She sweeps tangled strands of hair behind my ears. "And you're so in love with him."

"I am," I admit as a single tear leaks out of my eyes. I thought I must have permanently emptied my tear ducts last night, but I guess I was wrong.

"This is a good thing, Little Poppy. You should be happy you've found love again."

"I still love Garrick." I sniffle. "Kissing Beck, wanting to do more than kiss Beck, feels like the worst betrayal."

"Garrick isn't here, sweetheart, but Beck is, and your heart will never lead you astray."

"It feels wrong to do this to Garrick, but it feels so right with Beck. I'm so confused, and I don't know what to do."

"You are not the first girl to love two boys at one time, and no one can tell you what to do. Only you can decide what is best for you. We loved Garrick. He was wonderful to you, but Beck is a wonderful man too, and you're different with him. I don't envy you your decision, but it's time to make one."

"How, Nana?" I lift my face to hers. "How do I make this decision? It's impossible."

"Trust your heart to guide you, Little Poppy. It will lead you along the right path."

Chapter Thirty-One

Stevie

"Honey, I'm home!" Hadley calls out just before the front door to our apartment slams shut with a bang. "Stevie? Are you home?"

"In here," I call out through my open bedroom door.

"It smells like ass in here," Hadley proclaims, sauntering through the door of my messy bedroom. It looks like a bomb went off, but I can't find it in me to care.

"Missed you too." My attempt at humor falls flat.

Hadley has been gone for ten days. She spent the holidays with Mike and his family at their home in Vermont, and then they were skiing in some resort in Ontario, Canada.

She bounces on the bed, wrinkling her nose as she crawls up beside me. "Please tell me you haven't spent every day since Christmas Day in bed. I knew I should have cut my trip short and come home."

Beck called Hadley because she phoned me a couple nights after Christmas to see how I was doing. "I would have never spoken to you again if you did that. I'm not your child, Hads. I'm not your responsibility."

"You're my best friend. The loyalty feels the same. If you hurt, I hurt." She lies on her side, propping her head up with one hand. "I knew you'd feel like this when you realized the truth."

"Did everyone know but me?" I ask, tugging the comforter up under my chin. "And why didn't you say anything?" It's a rhetorical question, but I'd still like to hear her admit it.

"It was tempting. Oh, so fucking tempting. But you needed to do this by yourself. You would not have admitted it if I'd said it to you, and it was important you reached this point alone."

"I was in denial for a reason."

"I know, babe." She hugs me to her, and I let her comfort me. After a few minutes of amicable silence, she pulls back a little. "I love you, Stevie, but even I have my limits. When did you last shower?"

"I showered while I hung out with my new family. It was hard putting on a brave face, but they'd come all this way to see me, so I did it. But it took every ounce of strength from my body, so after they went back to Florida, I crawled under these covers and I have only come out to pee and make coffee or grab some water."

"I know you're hurting, but this isn't the way. You cannot abuse your body again. I won't let you."

"I have no appetite, Hads. I'm a fucking mess." A sob rips from my throat. "I have to go back to work tomorrow, but how do I do that when I can't stop freaking crying all the time? And I have this awful pain in my chest. It won't go away. I think my heart might physically be broken or maybe it's just ripped in two." Tears stream down my face. "I'm a horrible person."

"No, you're not." She links her fingers in mine. "What I said on the phone still stands. You are not a horrible person. It's physically and emotionally impossible."

"I see his face every morning when I wake, and he's the last thing on my mind at night. Beck," I clarify. "Beck is all I see. It used to be Garrick, and now I've replaced him with Beck, and what kind of person does that to a man in a coma? And I'm not just talking about now. When I was in France, I barely thought about

Garrick at all because I was too busy having fun with another man."

"You listen to me, Stevie Colson, and you listen good." Hadley wears her "don't mess with me" face. "You didn't plan this. You have been incredibly loyal to Garrick, and you didn't set out to fall in love with another man, but you did. It just happened, and you shouldn't beat yourself up for feeling what you do. It's only natural. You can't fight your heart if he is who you want. You two are so flipping good together, and it would be a travesty if nothing came of it."

Sympathy splays across her face as she brushes the dampness from my cheeks. "Think of it like this. Beck has been in your life almost a year. It's the same amount of time you were with Garrick. Garrick has been gone from your life for almost two years. You and Garrick have been separated longer than the length of your relationship. Garrick would not want you to waste your life in bed crying over something you couldn't control. He'd say it was fate you met Beck, and he'd be happy someone is loving you the way he can't. It's not wrong to want to be happy, and it's not wrong to love Beck. He's amazing, Stevie. Garrick was too, but he's not here. Beck is, and I would hate to see you throw away a love like this out of guilt or remorse or fear."

"What would everyone think? It would look so bad if I started dating Beck."

"Babe, most people already think you are. People are not blind. It's impossible not to see the love radiating between you when you are together."

"Great, that's just great." I bury my head in my pillow, thinking of how awful Dawn and Hugh must think I am.

"Who gives a fuck what anyone thinks?" Hadley says, taking a brush and combing my knotty hair. "This is your life, Stevie. You only get one shot at it, and things can change in the blink of an eye. You know this better than anyone."

I tip my face up and haul my back against the headboard when she's finished trying to tame the wild mess on top of my head. "I know life is short and you need to make the most of it. I learned that lesson the hard way, but how can I do this to Garrick?" I lean my head on her shoulder.

"This will sound cold, but it's not my intent. Garrick doesn't know any different, babe, and he's probably never going to. We don't know if he's aware of anything around him or not. If he is, you're no longer part of his world, through no fault of your own. Garrick may have already said goodbye to you in his mind. I'm not saying you should discount him. I'm not saying that at all. I know you need to process everything, but you need to prioritize yourself, and you need to consider Beck."

"Of course, I'm considering him. He's on my mind constantly. I miss him so badly. It feels like I'm missing a limb, and it's killing me to be apart from him."

Beck is staying true to his word and giving me space. He only broke it one time. I received a text at midnight on New Year's Eve wishing me a happy new year and letting me know he loves me and misses me. I was supposed to be ringing in the new year with him at Jenny and Law's party, and it made me sad I wasn't there. I replied telling him I loved and missed him too, and that was the end of our conversation.

"Poor Beck. He's been in love with you for so long. He has the patience of a saint to wait for you to acknowledge your feelings. But for him, it's always been about you. He has proven it, repeatedly, how he places your needs before his own, and I couldn't love him any more for it."

"How did I get here, Hads?" I wrap my arm around her. "How did it get to the point where I love two guys? I'm never throwing shade at Mom again."

"Life is strange, but it is what it is." She forces me to sit up. "It would be worse to not love anyone. You need to face up to it and stop wallowing in a pity party for one. My best friend is made of inner steel, and she can face any challenge put in her path. So, get your stinky ass out of bed, Opium Poppy, and into the shower. I'm going to clean your room, change your sheets, and call for takeout. Then you're going to get your stuff ready for work tomorrow, and you're going to call Ramona for an emergency appointment. You need to get your head sorted and put both of you out of your misery."

"How is work?" Ramona asks on Friday evening after I have settled on her blue velvet couch for my appointment.

"It's been difficult this week. I'm distracted and making mistakes."

"I'm sorry to hear that. Why are you distracted?"

I fill her in on everything that has happened, pouring my heart out, explaining how guilty I feel for cheating on Garrick and for harboring such strong feelings for Beck. "Then I feel guilty for feeling guilty for loving Beck when he is so deserving of my love. He has been a rock for me, and now the fog has lifted from my mind, I am not surprised I fell for him. Only that I didn't see it for so long." I frantically twirl a lock of my hair around my finger. "On and on it goes. All of this playing on a repetitive loop in my mind, and it feels like I'm going insane. I'm only eating because Hadley is forcing me to, and I get up and go to work because I don't want to let my employer down, but I'm just going through the motions. I'm getting no enjoyment from life anymore. Wallowing in self-pity is like my full-time occupation these days."

"There is a lot to unpack there," Ramona says, passing me a box of tissues with a soft smile.

"I didn't even realize I was crying," I admit, mopping my tears with a tissue. "I'm crying at the drop of a hat again. It feels like I'm regressing."

"I'm glad you came to see me. It's important you don't undo all the great progress you've made. This is the second stage of your grieving process, and you can't fully move forward with your life without dissecting these feelings. Overcoming your guilt over the accident was the first part, but your work isn't done."

"What do you mean?"

"This is the part where you fully grieve for Garrick and your past relationship and move on to a new future with Beck."

My jaw slackens at the casual way she puts it out there.

"I'm not surprised by this latest development. It was clear to me from the way you spoke about him and the way your eyes always light up when you're discussing Beck that you'd fallen in love with him. I was trying to encourage you to talk about it, but you weren't ready. I knew you would reach this point yourself. We need to break it down, but ultimately, it boils down to happiness, and it's not selfish to be happy."

"I cheated on Garrick, and I don't deserve to be happy."

"But did you?"

"What?" I knot my hands on my lap, staring at her in confusion. "I don't know what you're inferring. Garrick is my boyfriend. I'm his girlfriend, and I shouldn't have kissed another man. I shouldn't love another man. It's the ultimate betrayal."

"Can you consider yourself to still be in a relationship if you haven't talked to the person in nineteen months or seen them for seven months? I know there are extenuating circumstances, but I don't know if you have a title any longer. Are you going to remain his girlfriend forever? Live in limbo indefinitely? At what point will it ever feel right to not call yourself that? Can you put a time frame on it? On love?"

"But we didn't break up," I splutter, trying to make sense of the mess in my head. Ramona has raised valid points, but it's not like there's a rule book for this situation. "We were very much together at the time of the accident."

"The accident and your relationship are in the past. Have you ever considered what might have happened if there was no accident and you had moved to Seattle while Garrick stayed at UO? Would you have stayed together? Or would you have broken up?"

"I can't answer that, and I don't see how it helps."

"You're a very different person now, Stevie. A different woman than the woman who first came to my office. Your experiences have shaped and matured you. Would this Stevie be happy in a relationship with Garrick if he woke?"

"Again, that's irrelevant."

"But is it?"

She's starting to piss me off. "He's not awake, so how does talking about it make any difference?"

"You need to consider all angles before you decide how to proceed with your relationship with Beck."

"I don't have a *relationship* with Beck. We're friends."

"Friends who love one another as more than friends. You can label it however you want, Stevie, but you can't ignore the truth. You don't have a relationship with Garrick now. You have a relationship with Beck. Garrick hasn't been the man in your life for some time. Beck is."

I leave therapy with more questions than answers, and I'm in a foul mood. My first instinct is to call Beck and ask if he wants to get drunk, but I can't do that to him. I can't contact him until I know what I want and I'm no clearer on a decision. Hadley is working at the library until eight tonight, so I guess I'm flying solo.

I stop at a bar a few blocks from home, order a whisky, and settle into a booth to drown my sorrows. Thoughts are rotating through my head nonstop, and I need alcohol to blot it out. Deep down, I know what I want and what I'm going to do, but accepting that decision is not easy. I can't reconcile it within myself because it feels like the worst betrayal, but I can't keep doing this either because I'll go crazy.

My phone vibrates across the table, and I snatch it up, swiping to accept Mom's call.

"Stevie." Sobs filter down the line, and I'm instantly on high alert.

"Mom? What is it? What's wrong?"

"It's Nana."

My heart stops beating for a split second.

"She's gone, honey."

"What?" I splutter. I don't trust my ears because that can't be true.

"Nana collapsed in the shop, and they couldn't resuscitate her. When the ambulance arrived, they pronounced her dead."

My phone clatters onto the table as heart-wrenching sobs wrack my body. I'm shaking, and I feel so cold. This can't be real. It must be a nightmare. I only spoke to her a few days ago. She made me tea and consoled me the day after Christmas. She told me to follow my heart. Nana always knows the right thing to say, and she wouldn't leave me. Not when I need her so badly. I can barely swallow over the lump wedged in my throat and the pressure sitting on my chest as more anguished cries rip from my mouth.

The ruckus I'm making draws a concerned bartender to the table. He says something to me, but I don't hear the words. I can't hear anything, see anything, or think anything over the intense pressure sitting on my chest.

Nana can't be gone.

She's too young and too vibrant to no longer exist. She's not even seventy. We were going to throw her a big party in May because she wouldn't celebrate her last two birthdays due to the anniversary of the crash.

And now she's gone?

"No," I wail, clutching my stomach as the bartender talks on my phone. "No!"

She can't be gone. I can't lose her too. I won't survive the crushing pain again.

Chapter Thirty-Two

Beck

"Thanks, man. I've got it from here," I say to the bartender when I reach the bar and find Stevie sobbing in a booth and rocking back and forth with her arms clasped around her waist. "Does she owe anything?" I ask, removing my wallet.

He shakes his head. "It's on the house."

"Thanks." I tip my head at him before sliding into the booth beside the love of my life. These past two weeks have been hell without Stevie, but I know she needs time to process her emotions. I was so fucking sad that first night, but I snapped out of it. I'm choosing to see it as a positive sign. Stevie acknowledged her feelings for me, and that's huge. She told me she loved me in her text, and I know she wouldn't lie to me. She has strong feelings for me, and they're not going away, so I just need to be more patient. I know she'll come back to me after she has properly grieved for Garrick.

This belief is the only way I've gotten out of bed every day because my world is so dull without her in it.

Stevie lifts her tearstained face to mine. "Beck?" she whispers as tears roll down her face.

"It's me, Stevie. I'm here. Your mom called me. She was worried."

"Nana's gone," she sobs, flinging her arms around my neck and clinging to me.

Pain infiltrates my heart, comingling with relief at having her back in my arms. "I'm so sorry, honey. I know how close you two were."

"It's like losing my mother," she sobs, fisting my shirt and holding on to me like she's worried I might leave. "I can't believe it. She can't be dead. She was so fit and young for her age. It doesn't make sense."

"I know." I smooth a hand up and down her hair. "It's unfair." I dot kisses on top of her head. "So unfair."

"I need to be with Mom."

"I'll drive you."

"Beck." She clutches my shirt tight and peers at me with blatant vulnerability. "Don't leave me. Please."

"I told you I'm going nowhere, and I meant it. I won't leave your side unless you ask me to."

Her shoulders relax a little, but pain remains etched on her face.

I help her out of the booth and slide my arm around her shoulders. Sympathetic faces watch us leave, and I hold Stevie closer when I feel her trembling alongside me. It's not a far walk to my car, but she doesn't speak as we head toward it. Stevie is wearing a dazed expression on her face, and no doubt her head is spinning. I was only ten when my mom died, and I remember how confused and upset I felt in those initial days.

Stevie is going to need me in the coming days, and I'm glad I'm my own boss now, and I can be here for her for however long she needs.

When we reach my A7, I open the passenger door and help my heartbroken girl inside. Then I climb behind my wheel and head out in busy traffic for Ravenna. I crank the heating up and put some classical music on as we drive. Reaching across the console, I take her hand, relieved when she curls her fingers in mine and accepts my comfort.

There are a bunch of cars parked at Nana's house when we

arrive, and Stevie starts shaking in earnest. Getting out, I race around the hood, open her door, and help her out. I bundle her in my arms, and she lets me hug her. "I've got you, okay?" I say a few minutes later, tucking a piece of her hair behind one ear. "Lean on me however you need to."

Her eyes are red rimmed but dry as she looks up at me. Her palm cradles my cheek. "I love you."

It seems wrong to feel happy when Betsy is gone and I'm grieving her loss, but I can't help the euphoric surge that wells inside me at her words. I have waited so long to hear them. I brush my lips softly against hers. "I love you too, and I'm here for you. Whatever you need."

Tears stab her eyes. "You are always so good to me."

"It's what you do for the person you love most in this world."

"You're my person, Beck." She eases out of my embrace, swipes at the moisture under her eyes, and links her hand in mine. "Thank you for always being here for me."

The funeral takes place three days later. The autopsy revealed Betsy was riddled with cancer, but it was her heart that gave out in the end. Nana hadn't confided in anyone that her cancer had returned. Not Monica or Stevie or any of her friends. She had been ill with colds and bugs, but no one realized it was so serious.

Stevie's emotions are all over the place, veering from sadness to anger to guilt. She feels abandoned, and I can relate. Though I don't remember a lot from when Mom died, because I was so young, I remember the sense of abandonment I felt. It's unfair Stevie has to lose another person close to her, and it's times like this when I question if there is a god.

Stevie is drained after the funeral, so we head back to my place. She's been staying with me since I picked her up from the bar on Friday. Hadley brought over a bag with some of her things, and she stayed a couple nights too. If it was up to me, Stevie would permanently move in, but I can't get too ahead of myself. Nana's funeral doesn't mean things are resolved between Stevie and me, and now isn't the time to get into it. So, I'm being the friend she needs and supporting her the best way I can.

"Why don't I run you a bath?" I suggest when we enter my apartment. "Then I can order takeout, or I'll cook us something if you prefer?"

"A bath sounds nice, but I'm not sure I have much of an appetite," she admits, shucking out of her coat.

I hang it up on a hook and set her purse down on the hall table. "Let me order some stuff, and you can see if anything tempts your taste buds." I press a kiss to her cheek. "You need to take care of yourself."

"I know. I'm just so tired of feeling like this lately."

"You're mourning, and you'll come through it."

Stevie leans her head on my chest and places her hands on my hips. "I'm not just mourning Nana."

"I know." She's letting Garrick go too, so it's a double hit. I close my eyes and savor the feel of her in my arms. It never gets old. "There is no rush. I'm going nowhere. You take all the time you need."

Taking her hand, I lead her to my en suite. Stevie sits on the edge of the tub as I fill it. "I know what I want, Beck." Stevie tucks her long wavy hair behind her ears. "I want a future with you. I have known that deep down for some time, and I'm not afraid to confirm it, but I'm so fucking scared. The people I love tend to get taken from me, and I can't lose you too."

Tears pool in her eyes, and I pull her down to the floor with me, positioning her on my lap. "That's a risk we all take when we choose to share our lives with others. You've been dealt two hard blows in a row, so I understand why you feel like this. It's why you need to continue speaking to Ramona and working through everything. There is no timeline. I love you, and I will wait for you for as long as you need. Do not rush this process on my account."

She kisses me sweetly before pulling away. "You are the very best man I know, Beck. I feel so blessed to have met you."

I lift her wrist, the one with the tattoo she got with Garrick and my charm bracelet, and I kiss her soft skin. "No woman has ever held my heart the way you do. I offer up thanks every day that you came into my life."

After adding some oil to the water, I leave her with the bath filling to pour her a glass of wine.

When I return to the bathroom, I almost drop the wineglass as I enter through the open door and find her naked in the tub. Perfect porcelain skin coasts over exquisite womanly curves as she soaks in the oil-scented water, and abject longing crashes into me. Her long red hair cascades over the edge of the tub in a replica of the fantasy I've often had about her. My dick instantly thickens, and I adjust my hard-on through my dress pants to disguise the evidence of my arousal. Shielding my eyes, I cautiously approach the tub. "You should've closed the door, and I would have known to knock." I hand her the wineglass.

"I'm not ashamed of my nudity." The water sloshes as she sits upright against the back of the tub, and I get an up-close view of her magnificent tits. Her heavy breasts are full and perfectly shaped, and her unblemished creamy skin is topped with small pert pink nipples.

"Fuck." I adjust my raging hard-on and look away before I'm tempted to drop to my knees and suck one of those taut pink buds into my mouth.

"I miss sex," she blurts. "My fingers and my vibrator are no substitute for the real deal."

"Stevie." I groan, feeling a bead of precum leak in my boxers. "If you're trying to torture me, you're doing a good job."

A smile crests over her lips as she leans against the side of the bath with her arms stretched over the edge, concealing her impressive rack, but now I've got a front row view of her toned back and shapely ass. She is really trying to kill me here. Stevie holds her wineglass in one hand while piercing me with a sultry look that causes my dick to throb behind my zipper.

Fuck my life.

"That is the last thing I would do. Maybe I want you to join me." She licks her lips. "Maybe I want to feel your cock inside me."

"Maybe?"

"Okay, there is no maybe about it. I want you to fuck me, Beck."

I close my eyes briefly, hating myself for what I'm about to say. I sink to my knees and kiss her briefly. "As much as I'd love that, it's not happening tonight." I sweep my fingers across her face. "I want you so badly, but not like this, honey. You've just lost someone important to you, and you haven't finished mourning Garrick. When we make love, I want it to be for the right reasons and for you to be guilt free. I need it to just be us in that moment and for you to be clear about what you want."

"I am clear now. In a warped way, losing Nana"—her voice cracks and pain spreads across her face before she composes herself—"has helped me to confront my feelings. Life is too fucking short. I don't need any more reminders of that, and I'm done feeling guilt and pain and remorse. You brought me back to life, Beck, and I want to start living life to the max. With you."

She trails her fingers softly through my hair. "Garrick was my first love, and I will never forget him, but he's no longer a part of my life. He hasn't been for a long time. What we had is gone. You're my here and now. You're my future. I'm sure of it. I love you, and I know you love me, and I want us to properly be together as a couple. Nana told me to follow my heart, and my heart leads to you."

Taking the glass from her, I set it down on the tile floor and hold her face in my hands. I look deep into her emerald eyes and see nothing but love shining back at me. I claim her lips in a passionate kiss full of pent-up longing. Water sloshes over the edge of the tub as we kiss, splashing my pants and the floor, but I couldn't give a shit. My fingers twine in all that glorious red hair, and she's attacking my mouth with the same ferocity I feel, her lust a mirror image of my own. I drink from her lush lips over and over again until it feels like my cock is about to explode.

"Beck," she whimpers into my mouth. "I'm so horny."

I stand and hold out my hand. Stevie rises and she looks like a goddess of fire and lust with all that lustrous red hair and water sluicing over her gorgeous tits, down along her flat stomach, over the curve of her hips, her tempting bare pussy, and dropping between her toned thighs.

I help her out of the bath and wrap her in a fluffy towel before scooping her into my arms and carrying her to my bedroom. Laying her down gently on the bed, all bundled up in the towel, I crawl over her. "I'm not making love to you tonight." I peer directly into her eyes so she can see the truth laid bare for her. "I need you to be sure, Stevie. I don't doubt you meant what you said in the bathroom, but you've been through a lot these past few days, and you need to reflect on it."

I brush my nose against her. "When I take you, there will be no going back. I already know I'm going to be insatiable for you, and I need you to be sure. I need you to be mine before we take that step. Please say you understand. I don't want you thinking I don't want you when it's taking every ounce of self-control to hold myself back. All I want is to bury myself deep inside you and never come out, but it's important we do this right."

"I want to be angry at you, but I can't. I know you're doing this for us, but I'm so turned on right now. Could you just put the tip in me?" Her eyes flare with desire. "I bet I'd come just like that."

A deep chuckle rises from my chest before I swoop down and claim her lips in a searing-hot kiss. When we break for air, I stare adoringly at her, wishing I didn't have a conscience and I could devour her the way I want to.

But we haven't come this far to make that leap too soon.

She needs to be sure.

For her and for me, and this is emotion and lust speaking. "I said I won't make love to you, but that doesn't mean I'll leave you suffering." Slowly, I unwrap the towel from her naked body, and my cock pulses against my thigh. "I would never leave you in pain," I add, brushing my fingers across one hardened nipple. "I want to touch you and taste you, if that's okay?"

A giggle bursts from her lips. "Beck, you're too funny. I'm seconds away from grabbing your head, thrusting it between my legs, and rubbing my pussy all over your face." She grips my chin hard. "Of course, it's okay." She kisses me hard on the lips. "It's more than okay." A mischievous grin lights up her face. "Now get to work."

Chapter Thirty-Three

Stevie

"I love you," Beck whispers over my lips before kissing me deeply.

My fingers curl around his neck, and I pull him down flush on top of me, feeling the outline of his impressive erection against my thigh through his pants. My hands gravitate to his ass, grabbing handfuls of his cheeks, as his lips trail a scorching-hot path from my lips to my jawline and along my ear. "You're wearing too many clothes," I pant, spreading my legs to accommodate him.

"This is about you," he whispers in my ear before tugging on my lobe with his teeth.

"I need to feel your skin against mine." Although I'm tempted to seduce him into fucking me, I know Beck is right and we should wait. This is about me needing to feel his silky-smooth skin under my hands as he worships my body.

Beck rises to his knees and begins unbuttoning his shirt. His dexterous fingers work the buttons in an unhurried manner while his eyes devour me from my head to my toes. I'm on fire everywhere, tingling in every place his gaze lands. The noticeable bulge pressing against his zipper causes saliva to pool in my mouth. I'm drenched between my legs, and I can't stop the whimper from escaping my mouth any more than I can halt the automatic grinding of my pelvis as my body throbs with need.

Beck's pupils darken as he continues popping those buttons and feasting on my naked flesh. "You are so fucking perfect, Stevie. Like the physical manifestation of my every fantasy. Look at you." He reaches the last button and tosses his shirt away. His eyes burn with lust as he sweeps his fingers over the curve of my hips, across my flat stomach, and under my breasts, purposely avoiding the apex of my thighs where I'm desperate to feel his touch. "You're beautiful, honey. Inside and out."

"I could say the same to you." My greedy gaze rakes over his broad shoulders, defined pecs, chiseled abs, and tapered hips with potent longing. "You're gorgeous, Beck."

He leans down and kisses me. "Not as gorgeous as you," he adds, moving his lips from my mouth to my ear. His tongue teases my lobe before he sucks that sensitive spot along my neck, and I arch my back, thrusting my breasts up.

Beck glides his lips down my neck and along my collarbone. A throaty whimper flees my mouth when he licks the space between my tits while he fondles both with his hands. I gasp when his mouth closes around one hard nipple, and he sucks and tweaks it between his lips. I touch his chest, exploring the firm contours of his body, with my eyes closed, as he lavishes attention on my tits while I roam his hard warm flesh.

"Beck, please," I moan, dry humping the air as my hips grind and my pussy clenches and unclenches with need. I dig my nails into his shoulders and bite down on my lower lip.

"Be patient, my love," he purrs before pecking my lips. He kisses his way down my ribs and across my stomach, licking and sucking the skin over my hips, before he finally makes his way to my pussy. "So pretty," he says from his position between my legs, parting my folds and staring at me before he glides one finger inside me.

A strangled sound rips from my throat, and I arch off the bed as he slowly pumps one finger in and out.

"Watch me," he commands, and I blink my eyes open and stare at him between my thighs.

Spreading my legs farther apart, he maintains eye contact as he withdraws his finger and sucks it into his mouth. His eyes are ablaze with heat, and I think I could come just watching him taste me. "So sweet." He licks every last drop of my essence before lowering his face right to my pussy. "And I need more," he adds before plunging his tongue into my channel without warning.

"Aggh." My hips tilt and my chest heaves as he drives his tongue in and out of my pussy while his fingers toy with my clit.

Grabbing my ass, he lifts me a little higher, and his tongue hits deeper, sending delicious tremors shooting from my core. He eats me out, keeping his eyes locked on mine, and it's the hottest moment of my life. My climax is building fast, and I squeeze his head with my thighs as I rotate my pussy, shoving it into his face, desperate to get off.

Beck lowers my ass back to the bed and replaces his mouth with his fingers. He looks up at me, and the sight of my juices coating his lips elevates my arousal to a new level. "I'm going to come," I pant as the crescendo builds and builds when he roughly thrusts three fingers inside me.

"Come for me, honey. Come all over my face." He whips his fingers out and replaces it with his skillful tongue as he pinches my clit, and I erupt like a volcano. My pussy tightens around his tongue, my back arches, my hips lift, and my thighs clench as the most earth-shattering orgasm lays siege to my body, dousing every part of me in the most blissful tremors.

Beck watches me with rapt attention, and I blush a little when I eventually come down from my high. He crawls up beside me, curling me against his hard body. "That was so sexy, and I adore you." He kisses me softly, once, twice, three times. "Was it okay?"

A laugh bursts from my lips as I slide my arms around his neck and press my hot flesh against his bare chest. "It was incredible. Don't go all shy on me now. You know you were good."

"I wanted to make it perfect for you."

"It was." I kiss his beautiful lips as my fingers roam the curves and indents of his muscular stomach, before my hand slides down the gap between us. I grip him through his pants, and my core pulses with fresh need as I feel how long, thick, and hard he is.

Beck gently clasps my wrist, pulling my hand away. "Not today, honey."

"Why not?" I gulp over the lump in my throat.

"I want it, but you've been through a lot today. You're emotional and—"

"I know what I want, Beck. I want to taste you. I want to give you pleasure too." I sit up, feeling on the verge of tears.

He curses under his breath, adjusting himself in his pants before he pulls himself up against the headboard. He lifts me up into his lap so I'm facing him. "Feel what you do to me. I'm like this all the time around you, Stevie. I've learned to live with it."

"You don't have to live with it anymore," I say, planting my hands on his chest. "I want to take care of you."

"And you shall. Just not now." He sweeps his lips against mine. "Do you trust me, Stevie?"

"You know I do."

"Then trust me with this." He cups my face. "I love you so very much, and we'll have the rest of our lives to do this. Tonight, just let me take care of you. Please."

It's hard to stay sulky when he says all the right things and looks at me with so much adoration it's almost surreal. "Okay." I lean down, resting my head against his chest and he holds me against him as we snuggle on the bed.

"I'm going to order takeout and grab a quick shower. Do you need me to get you anything now?"

I shake my head. "I'm good."

He's still sporting the tent in his pants when he climbs out of the bed to grab his phone and order food. I crawl out of his bed naked and head into my room to change into some sleep shorts and a top. When I return, his en suite door is closed, and the sounds of running water tickle my eardrums. Sliding under the covers, I wonder if he's rubbing one out in the shower.

When Beck emerges a while later, he's wearing cotton pajama pants, a plain white tee, and a soft smile when he sees me propped up in his bed, watching TV.

"Did you jerk off in the shower?" I ask, noticing his erection is gone.

"I did." He sits on the edge of the bed beside me. "Does that bother you?"

"Yes," I truthfully admit. "I wanted to suck your cock."

He closes his eyes briefly, and his dick visibly jerks. "You make it so hard to be good, and I mean that intentionally."

My lips curve as I slink into his lap. "I like that you're the good guy. I know I need to say my final goodbyes to Garrick. I understand you are doing this for me, for us, but that doesn't mean I'm not sulking about it."

His face shines with love as he circles his arms around my waist. "We have waited this long; it won't kill us to wait a little bit longer."

"You're amazing, Beck, and I love you very much." I kiss him, but before it can turn into more, the doorbell chimes.

I pad into the kitchen to grab plates and silverware while Beck goes to the door to collect our takeout. We enjoy amicable silence as we eat, and I surprise myself by eating a full bellyful of delicious Chinese food. After, we climb into Beck's bed and watch a movie. I'm tucked under his arm, feeling loved and protected, and it helps to offset the heartfelt pain searing my insides at the loss of my beloved grandmother.

I wake the next morning, still in Beck's bed, facing the wall, with his warm body spooning me from behind. The hard length of his morning wood is strategically positioned against my ass to inject an instant shot of liquid lust straight to my core. Beck's large warm palm is resting on my bare lower stomach, just above the waistband of my shorts, underneath my tank top.

I take a moment to savor his protective comfort before easing carefully out of his bed and heading to the bathroom. I attend to business and borrow his toothbrush to brush my teeth while cringing at my scary reflection in the mirror. I didn't wash my hair last night, but it was damp getting out of the bath, and it's a tangled mess.

Beck's eyes light up when I enter the bedroom, and my heart ping-pongs around my chest. "Morning, honey," he says, in a sleep-drenched tone. "Did you sleep okay?"

"I did." I walk to his side and bend down to hug him. "Thank you for taking such good care of me. Not just last night but in the days since Nana passed." I perch my butt on the edge of the bed.

"I love taking care of you. It's what I was put on this earth to do." His tender smile oozes sincerity.

"You look beautiful when you wake." It's true. His eyes are glistening, his skin is flushed, and there's a sexy layer of stubble on his chin and cheeks.

"Ditto, honey."

I snort out a laugh. "Don't lie. I saw myself in the mirror."

He pulls me down onto the bed, cradling me in his arms. "You always look beautiful to me."

"You're biased."

"I don't think I am." He kisses the tip of my nose. "Stay here. I'll be right back."

He climbs out of bed, yawning as he strides toward the bathroom. At some point during the night, Beck removed his shirt, and I admire the ink on his back and the way his muscles undulate as he walks.

Returning a few minutes later, he slides back under the sheets. "Come here." He reels me in tight to his chest. "I've decided my day doesn't start until I've kissed you."

"You won't hear any complaints from me."

My hands snake around his shoulders as he angles his head and slants his mouth against mine. His minty breath comingles with mine as we kiss leisurely. Thoughts empty from my mind as we make out, gently exploring the contours of one another's bodies as our lips and tongues dance a slow passionate tango. When his hard length presses against my leg, a shudder works its way through me. I move my lips to his ear. "Please let me taste you. I want to make you feel good."

I prop up on one elbow as he scrutinizes my face.

"No regrets about last night?"

I shake my head. "None. You were right. I still have stuff to process, but it's only a formality now, Beck. I am all in. I agree we need to wait to have sex, but I need to taste you, baby. Please."

His fingers tangle in my hair. "You don't have to beg, but only if you let me reciprocate."

A slow smile spreads over my mouth. "Now, you're talking my language."

A deep chuckle shakes his shoulders as Beck pulls us up against the headboard. I lift my arms, and he pulls my top up and discards it. He kisses my lips before kissing my breasts, sucking each nipple into his mouth and moaning around the hard tips. Snagging his erection through his thin cotton pants, I stroke him slowly through the material.

We quickly get naked and lie down on the bed sideways with my face at his crotch and his head between my thighs. I ogle his gorgeous cock as I pump my hand up and down his hard shaft. He's long and thick, and his crown is a little angled, perfect to hit the right spot inside me. But that's not in the cards now, and I'm okay with it.

Beck parts my folds and draws a long line with his tongue up and down my slit. My mouth closes over his aching cock, and I slide my lips up and down his erection, licking, sucking, and tasting. With one hand, I cup his balls and fondle them while his tongue plunges inside me and his fingers rub my clit.

We devour one another in record time, coming seconds after one another. I keep my lips locked on his warm cock, relishing the splashes of cum as it coats the back of my mouth and slides down my throat.

After, we lie naked, wrapped in one another's arms, sated and content for now. The steady beating of his heart against my ear is beautiful, and I could stay here like this forever. My fingers roam his bare skin, mapping every curve and dent. I trail a line up and down his spine and trace my fingers over the eagle tattoo on his back. "Does your tattoo have special significance?" I ask as he presses feather-soft kisses along the column of my neck. I was tempted to ask when I was creating his dried-flower drawing, but he didn't volunteer the information, and I chose not to pry.

"Yes. My mom inspired this one too."

We prop up on our pillows on one elbow and face one another on our sides.

"In what way?" He hasn't opened up to me about his mother yet, and I want to know. If we're going to do this, there can be no secrets between us.

"Getting an eagle tattoo is quite popular with men because it's a symbol of American patriotism. That's not why I did it. Eagles can soar to great heights and hunt with great precision, and those two things resonated strongly with me at eighteen when I was choosing what to get inked on my back." He brushes hair off my face. "I want to soar to dizzy heights in my career, and I always want to protect those I love. To hunt the predators who might prey on them."

I wasn't expecting him to say that. "How does that relate to your mom?"

"She was murdered when I was ten, and I saw the whole thing."

Chapter Thirty-Four

Stevie

"Oh my god." I clasp a hand over my horrified mouth for a second. "That is awful. What happened?"

Beck winds his finger around a lock of my hair. "I haven't spoken about the events of that day for a long time. Dad sent me to a kiddie shrink after Mom died, but I couldn't talk to him about it, and Dad gave up after that. It's only since I started going to therapy last year that I've confronted my feelings. I had locked them up inside and thrown away the key. I refused to face up to them until recently."

"That is a lot to carry on your shoulders."

"It is, and I have you to thank for helping me to process it. If you hadn't made that deal with me, I might still be in the same dark place." He threads his fingers in mine. "I owe you so much. I wanted to tell you about Mom, but it's been hard to talk about."

"We don't have to discuss it now if it's still difficult."

"It will always be difficult to talk about, but I want you to know. I don't want to have any secrets from you."

"I was just thinking the same thing."

We move as one, and our lips meet in a tender sensual kiss.

"You're the other half of my soul, Stevie." Beck presses a lingering kiss to my brow. "I'm not surprised we're always so in tune with one another."

I press a kiss over his heart, right where the tattoo in memory of his mother is inked. "Tell me about her. What was she like?"

"She was the best mom, and she loved us so much. Things weren't perfect when she was alive. Dad's always been an ass, but she made up for it. Mom was only nineteen when she met Dad and still so innocent, or so *Grand-mère* says. She was working as a model in New York, and she met Carlton at some party. He swept her off her feet, and when she got pregnant with me, he proposed, and they got married two months later. My grandparents begged her not to do it. Afraid she was moving too fast. They didn't like Dad. He was a snob, and they feared for their only daughter. By all accounts, things were okay the first few years of their marriage. Mom gave up her career to raise us, and she seemed happy. Then Dad started cheating. He didn't like how she took us to France every summer, leaving him alone, and that's how he paid her back." A muscle tics in his jaw. "I overheard them arguing one time, shortly before she died. He told her it was her fault for not giving him enough attention."

"Of course, he'd try to blame her for his betrayal. Your father is an asshole."

"He's self-centered and obsessed with power and wealth. I will never relate to him. Thank god, I'm more like my mother. I might have inherited his looks, but my personality is more like my mother's." He rubs circles on the back of my hand as he talks.

"You aren't anything like your father," I agree.

"Mom was going to leave him. She went to an attorney, and they were working through the details of what to request before serving him with divorce papers when she was murdered." Pain flits across his face, and he closes his eyes.

I hug him, holding him tightly as his body trembles.

"My sisters were at ballet that day, and Dad was still at work," he explains, easing back to look at me. "Our housekeeper had just gone home for the day, but Benjamin, our live-in butler, was at the door when three armed men arrived. They entered our property from a neighboring property and stole across the grounds. Mom shoved me into her closet when she heard a commotion and gunshots at the front door. I was so scared, and I wanted her to hide too, but she made me promise not to make a sound. I watched it all go down." His Adam's apple bobs in his throat, and he's trembling all over.

I rub my hands up and down his arms while I wait for him to continue.

"They wanted the contents of the safe. My parents had cash and jewels worth over a million stowed in the safe of their bedroom. Mom wasn't stupid. She gave them the code, thinking they'd leave if they got what they came for. But they shot her. They didn't want to leave any witnesses. If they'd found me, they would have murdered me too." Beck stares off into space, lost in the horrors of the past.

I continue rubbing his arms, my heart aching for the little boy who lost his innocence in such a brutal way.

"I wanted to help her, but I was too scared. I couldn't move. I was barely breathing. I pissed my pants, and I sat there for ages after the men left, terrified to come out in case they were hiding around the corner waiting to shoot me too. I watched the pool of blood grow larger underneath my mother." He squeezes his eyes shut again before opening them and staring at me. "That image haunts me. I had nightmares for years. Barely slept more than four or five hours a night for years until you came into my life and made everything better."

"Do you still get nightmares?" I recall him having them a few times when I've been around, but he never wanted to talk about it when I asked him the next day.

"Only on rare occasions. Confronting that day and my pent-up feelings has helped me to move past it. I will never forget it or how helpless I felt. For years, I blamed myself for not doing anything to help my mom."

"You were only a kid. Like you said, if you'd come out, they would have killed you too. Your mom wanted to protect you. Her death would have been in vain if you had died too." I hug him again, needing him close because all this talk of him dying has terrified me.

"I know that now, but for a long time, I felt like a failure. It's why I'm so protective of Sarah and Esther. I failed Mom, but I never want to fail my sisters."

"It all makes more sense now. Why you wanted to be a detective and why you let your father blackmail you." I hold his face in my hands. "You're an amazing big brother, and you've been amazing with me too. No one could do more for their loved ones than you. I hope you realize that now." I dot kisses on his face before releasing him.

"I do. I don't think these protective instincts will ever go away, but I have a handle on them now."

"Did they ever catch the guys?" I inquire.

He nods. "The cops didn't get anywhere, so Dad hired some private detectives, and they found the murderers." A muscle clenches in his jaw, and his shoulders bunch with tension. "One of the guys was interning at the law firm Mom's attorney worked at. He was copying files and identifying wealthy clients to steal from. It was him and his two buddies who murdered Mom and Benjamin. The defense at the trial argued for life imprisonment with no parole, but Dad was out for blood, and he wanted the death penalty. Not sure if he greased any palms, but the judge passed the sentence, and all three were executed."

"I thought they did away with the death penalty in Washington in 1975?"

"Not for aggravated murder, which this was deemed to be because the murders took place at the same time as another crime, and they were used to conceal that crime."

"I'm glad the bastards are dead."

He bobs his head. "I think it's the only time Dad and I agreed on anything. I remember the weeks before they were caught. I was terrified they'd come back for me or my sisters. Dad must've been scared too because he installed a high-end security system and employed a full-time team of bodyguards."

"That is a horrible way to lose your mother. I'm so sorry, Beck." I squeeze him in a bear hug.

He kisses the top of my head. "I would like to take you to Mom's grave. To formally introduce you."

"I'd like that, and we can visit my father's grave in the military graveyard too. So I can meet him and formally introduce you."

"Are we really doing this?"

"We are." Confidence imbues my tone, and I'm speaking from the heart. "I'd like a little time to say a proper goodbye to Garrick, and there are a few things I need to do, but yes, I want this with you. I love you, and I want us to be a proper couple."

"I want that more than anything because you mean everything to me, Stevie. You're my entire world."

I don't see Beck at all the rest of the week and into the next, but we stay in constant contact by text. I make a point of telling him I love him every day because I don't want him to doubt my feelings. He's working on a tight deadline, so it suits anyway. I cook up some meals, along with some cookies and cupcakes, and get a courier to deliver them to him. Beck tends to not eat when he's close to his deadline, because he writes around the clock, so I want to ensure he's getting some sustenance.

Mom and I clear Nana's house with Hadley's help. Lots of tears flow and a few bottles of wine are consumed, but we get through it. Nana would want us to be strong and to not wallow. My emotions seesaw from one day to the next, and I know it's going to take time to come to terms with the fact I won't ever see her again. I miss her so much. Some days, the grief is so intense I can barely function. But I keep myself busy. I have a few extra sessions with Ramona, and I plan a visit with Dawn and Hugh, and Hudson, for the weekend.

On Friday night, Hadley cancels her weekly date with Mike to stay home with me as I box up Garrick's things. "Drink this." Hadley hands me a whisky. "There's no way we're doing this sober."

"Thanks." I take the drink and knock back a healthy mouthful. "I didn't realize I had accumulated so many mementos." I remove old game, movie, and concert tickets from the bulletin board in my room and stash them carefully in a storage box along with some of Garrick's T-shirts, one of his UO sweaters, our boudoir photographs, and all the memorabilia from our trip to Cyprus.

"You fit a lot into a year." Hadley looks sad as she unpins photos from the bulletin board and adds them to the box.

"This hurts," I admit, doing a sweep of my room for anything I might have missed.

"It's hurting me, so I can only imagine how you're feeling."

"It's painful, but it's right. I am moving on. Garrick will always have a special place in my heart, but Beck owns it now. It's not fair to him to cling to any part of my past relationship."

"I'm proud of you, Stevie." Hadley bundles me into a bear hug. "What you have endured is not easy, but you've done it with grace and humility."

"I have tried my best."

"No one could argue you haven't."

I pick up the framed picture of Garrick and me by my bed with a heavy heart. It was taken at one of his gigs at The End Zone. His arms are wrapped around me from behind, and I'm staring up at him. We're both smiling, and it's clear to see we're in love. I've always adored this picture, and it gave me strength in those early days when I didn't think I'd survive the aftermath of the accident and the severe emotional trauma I was suffocating under.

Tears roll down my cheeks unbidden, and I sob. Hadley holds me close as I hug the picture to my chest and expunge the last of my grief. When my sobs finally subside, Hadley passes me some tissues, and I scrub my hands down my face before mopping up my tears.

I trail my finger along his handsome profile in the picture. "Goodbye, my love. I will never forget you." I kiss his face through the glass, almost choking over another sob as I carefully set the picture down on the top of the box.

Hadley pops the lid on and carries it into my closet, sliding it on the bottom shelf where I made space for it.

"Anything else?" she inquires when she comes out.

I hold up my phone as I get off the bed. "I need to archive the photos and videos on my phone, but I need more whisky for that."

Sitting side by side on the couch, we demolish a few more glasses of whisky, both of us crying as we scroll through my photos, song lists, and videos. Most of my videos are from Garrick's gigs. I can't watch after the first few because it hurts too much to hear his husky voice and see the love in his eyes when he looks out over the crowd at me. Watching him in his element, with his talent on showcase, makes the anger rush to the surface again. How could God do this to someone so amazing? Life isn't fair.

I send everything to a folder in the cloud and then wipe them from my phone. Unclasping the locket from around my neck, I set it on the coffee table and then stare at the poppy ring on my hand for ages before I pluck up the courage to remove it. Hadley holds me as I sob, coming with me to my closet and helping me add the jewelry to the stash of Garrick mementos.

More tears stream from my eyes as I put the lid back on the box and close that chapter of my life.

Chapter Thirty-Five

Stevie

The following day, I go to visit Hugh and Dawn. Mom told me I didn't need to do this, but I want to. They have always been so kind to me, and I'd hate for them to hear this from anyone but me.

"Come in, sweetie," Dawn says when she opens the door. "Let me look at you." She gives me a quick once-over. "You look beautiful, Stevie." She pulls me into a warm embrace. "We're still so shocked about Nana."

"I don't think it's sunk in with me yet," I truthfully admit.

"Grief is hard." She squeezes my shoulders before releasing me "Hugh is in the sunroom waiting for us."

I follow her to the large room at the side of the house with the stunning views over the lake and the mountains in the distance. Hugh stands and gives me a hug before we all take seats. "The view from this room is breathtaking," I say, accepting a mug of coffee from Garrick's father.

"I find solace here," Hugh says, circling his arm around his wife's shoulder on the wicker couch. His dark hair is threaded with more gray strands, and the lines around his eyes are more pronounced. What happened with Garrick has taken a toll on him.

"How are the twins?" I ask because I haven't seen them in months. They didn't come to the funeral with Hugh and Dawn.

"They are doing as well as can be expected," Hugh says.

"They miss their big brother," Dawn adds with a sad smile.

"I know. It's hard to believe it's been so long."

"In some ways, it feels much longer," Hugh says, "but in other ways, it only feels like a few months."

There isn't much I can say to that because it doesn't feel like a few months to me. It feels like an eternity since I last saw Garrick, but I don't want to admit that and upset them, so I say nothing.

"What did you want to talk to us about?" Dawn asks after a few awkward moments.

"I need to tell you something, and it's not easy." I wet my dry lips and knot my tense fingers.

"You can tell us anything, sweetie. Anything." Dawn reassures me with her words, and I draw a brave breath, mentally going over the little speech I've prepared.

"I love Garrick. He was the best boyfriend, and I will always cherish the time we had together, but it's been hard for me to hold on these past eight months when I've been denied access to him." Nerves fire at me, and nausea swims up my throat as they both give me their full attention.

Fuck. Why did I feel the need to do this again?

I clear my throat and press on. "I didn't plan to fall in love again, and I didn't set out to find anyone else, but Beck came into my life at the perfect moment. He's been a rock for me. He was, is"—I stumble a little, and I'm sweating profusely under my clothes even though it's not hot—"my best friend, but lately I've realized he's become so much more." I squirm on the seat as they look at one another. "What I'm trying to say, really badly, is I love Beck, and he loves me, and we want to be a couple. I'm not here to ask your blessing or anything," I babble, ad-libbing now, "but I wanted you to know we're together.

And it wasn't premeditated. A part of me will always love Garrick, but I need to move on."

Dawn reaches forward and takes my hands. "It's okay, sweetie. We suspected as much, and we don't harbor any ill feelings toward you. You can't remain stationary in your life even though Garrick is."

"My son would want you to be happy, Stevie. This much I know to be true," Hugh adds with pain in his eyes. "My ex-wife hasn't made it easy for you, and I can't say I'm surprised you found comfort in the arms of another man. You should not feel guilty for it either. We know you have a good heart and you loved our son. The truth is, Garrick isn't here, but Beck is."

"He seems like a lovely young man," Dawn says.

"He is, and he's been very considerate of Garrick and my feelings for him all along. I don't want you to think he planned this either."

"I think I'm a pretty good judge of character," Dawn says, "and I know he didn't set out to woo you."

"Thank you for telling us," Hugh says.

"We wish you both all the best," Dawn adds.

"And you're always welcome here, Stevie." Hugh reaches out to hug me. "You're like a daughter to us."

Tears leak out of my eyes. "You are such good people. It's no wonder Garrick is so amazing."

They exchange another look. "We have something we need to tell you as well," Hugh says as the doorbell rings.

"That will be Hudson," Dawn says with a smile.

Dawn returns with Hudson a few minutes later. After he says his hellos, he sits down beside me, kissing me on the cheek and squeezing my hand.

"There's no easy way to broach this subject," Dawn says after everyone has coffee. No one has touched the sumptuous cookies or cake, and I have a feeling I might regurgitate anything I've eaten in a few minutes, so I resist temptation. There's a distinct tension in the air that is unnerving. "So, we're just going to be blunt."

"Garrick has been in a coma for twenty months with no change,"

Hugh begins. Dawn places a reassuring hand on his thigh. "He's been on a ventilator the entire time, and the longer he remains on one, the more risk there is to his brain, his heart, his lungs, and other organs. He can't remain on it indefinitely."

"We know you found cases where people were on life support for years and they came out of it and recovered," Dawn says.

"But they are rare miracles," Hugh continues. "And in some of those cases, the individuals died a few days later from organ failure, or they were in a vegetative state and never regained any quality of life." A sob rises up his throat, and pain grips my heart.

My hands shake, and Hudson pulls me in close, wrapping his arm around me. We trade a pained look, both of us sensing where this is going.

"I don't want to keep my son alive by artificial means if he comes out of it impaired. What life is that? It's one thing to consider he may be paralyzed from the waist down but quite another to consider him in a vegetative state. I don't want that for Garrick. That is no life."

"What are you proposing?" Hudson asks, getting to the heart of the matter.

"We want to take Garrick off the ventilator," Dawn confirms, clutching her husband's hand.

"That doesn't necessarily mean he'd die though, right?" I ask, remembering some of the research I've read.

"Right." Hugh rubs his temples. "He could breathe by himself, and maybe that might trigger him to wake up."

"There is no medical connection between those two things and no guarantee that would happen. He will either breathe by himself or he will pass away," Dawn says.

"At least this way, we're letting it happen naturally," Hugh says. "We're leaving my son in God's hands, and he'll do what is best."

Garrick would call that leaving it to fate.

I want to call bullshit, but I won't chastise anyone for their faith. We might have a difference of opinion, but they are entitled to their beliefs. I just don't share them.

"What about Ivy?" I ask because I can't see her agreeing.

"We haven't discussed it with her yet," Hugh says.

"But we expect her to throw a hissy fit and kick us out," Dawn adds, taking a sip of her coffee.

It prompts me to take a sip of mine before it goes cold.

"Then what?" Hudson asks.

"Then we petition the court to turn off the ventilator," Hugh says.

"What about her power of attorney? Doesn't she get the final say?"

"This is a unique situation, and Hugh still has rights as his father," Dawn says.

"There is some precedent, so all isn't lost. It all depends on getting a sympathetic judge."

"How long would this take to happen if you go legal?" Hudson asks.

"We could probably get a hearing in a few months, but it could drag on for years," Hugh confirms.

Air whooshes out of my mouth as I grip my mug. "I can't imagine how difficult it must've been to make this decision, but, for what it's worth, I think you're right."

"Me too." Hudson removes his arm from my back and rubs his face. "I love Garrick like a brother, but I hate seeing him like this. None of us have a crystal ball. How long do we leave him like this before saying enough is enough? He could be in a coma for thirty years and never wake up. We just don't know."

"We agree." Dawn's face is a mask of sorrow.

"If there were any encouraging signs, I'd be in favor of waiting, but there has been no change for almost two years. I love Garrick so much." Tears spill down Hugh's cheeks again. "I'm so proud to be his father, but I can't do this to him. To all of us. It's hurting the twins. It's hurting me and Dawn. It's hurting you and his other friends. If we do this and he breathes by himself, it'll give us some sign that we should hold on. If he doesn't, then he will be at peace."

"I'm sorry you have to make this kind of decision," I say, getting up and going over to hug Garrick's dad. "You are very brave, and there isn't anyone who doubts how much you love him."

"If I can do anything to help," Hudson says, "you only have to ask."

"I know I'm not his girlfriend anymore," I say, straightening up, "but I would like to be kept informed, and if there is anything I can do to help, I'll do it."

"Thank you both for all you've done for him," Hugh says, patting my arm. "I promise we will keep you updated as this progresses."

"Now that we're both here, do you want to talk today?" Hudson asks when we step outside the Allen house.

"I don't have plans this afternoon, so I'm good to talk now." Originally, I had planned to talk to Hudson tomorrow, figuring one difficult conversation at a time was the best way to go. But I might as well get it over and done with now and save myself another trip to North Bend tomorrow.

"What about hiking the usual trail?" he asks, frowning as he looks at my ballet pumps.

"I have boots in the trunk of my car, and I'm down for a hike." Hiking was one of Garrick's and my favorite things to do when we were here or at the winery in Woodinville. We even went camping with Hudson one time.

Hudson grabs some waters from his truck while I retrieve my boots and my jacket from the back of the Land Rover. Nana left it to me along with a little money, a few pieces of jewelry, and the house. She left Mom the rest of the property, including the business, as well as the remainder of her jewelry.

Mom has already handed in her notice to the architectural firm, and she's going to run the business with the help of Nana's oldest friend. She asked me to consider joining her, but it's not something I'm ready for yet.

We set out in quiet companionship along the familiar route, both of us locked in thought. I'm sad for Garrick. Though I don't want to see him in limbo, this is still a hard pill to swallow. After an hour, we reach Garrick's favorite spot, halfway up the mountain, and we sit side by side at the edge of the cliff face with our feet dangling below. It's cold but not too windy. In the distance, ice-capped peaks rise toward the dull sky. Down below us, the navy-blue lake stretches for miles like a giant puddle, surrounded by dense forest and occasional residential pockets.

"I hoped it wouldn't come to this." Hudson passes me a bottle of water. "My heart is breaking even if I know it's the right thing to do."

"Poor Hugh and Dawn. It's a terrible decision to have to make." I uncap my water and drink some.

"Ivy is going to go nuclear. She'll force Hugh to go to court when I'm sure he'd rather keep it private." He tips water into his mouth.

"She's a horrible human, and I've no doubt she'll make it difficult. She'll drag this out as long as possible."

"My buddy had so many great plans. It sucks he ended up here."

"Yes, it does," I say in a quiet voice, dropping my chin and picking at the label on my water.

"If you want to talk to me about Beck, I will understand."

I jerk my chin up, eyes popping wide as I examine his face. "Did Hadley say something to you?"

"I haven't spoken to Hadley in months." A muscle pops in his jaw as he picks up a stone and sends it careening into the air.

"I had hoped you two might reconnect after you graduated. You seemed so good together."

He takes a swig from his bottle. "I did too, but shit happened, and then she met Mike." He peers into my eyes. "It seems serious with him."

Compassion washes through me. "It is." I like Mike. He's a great guy. Very laid-back and easygoing, and he embraces all that is quirky about my best friend. But I'm not sure he's who I'd pick for her. I can't help wondering if what happened with Garrick and me has influenced the choices Hadley has made. I asked her outright, and she swears it hasn't. At least not consciously. Subconsciously is an entirely different matter.

"Well, good for her. Hadley is wonderful, and she deserves to be happy."

"You do too." I nudge him in the side. "Met anyone special?"

"Nope." He finishes his water and recaps the bottle. "I'm not exactly looking though. Between work, family, and visiting Garrick, I don't really have time for a special someone in my life."

"I might have agreed at one time but not anymore. When you find the right person, you don't make time for them; it just happens naturally because you can't bear to be apart from them for long."

"Like you and Beck."

"Yes." I take another drink of my water as I look out at the glorious scenery laid out before us. "I didn't see it happening. It was a natural gradual thing."

"It's okay to love him, Stevie. It's more than okay."

I whip my head to his. "You can't really mean that? Garrick is your best friend."

"I do mean it, Stevie. You're my friend too, and I like seeing you happy. You were miserable for so long, and life is too short to be unhappy."

"I didn't plan for it to happen. It just did."

"I know. No one was more devoted to Garrick than you. Don't feel guilty for finding happiness elsewhere."

"I think I'll always feel some guilt because saying goodbye to Garrick so I can give my heart to Beck is difficult—even if I love Beck so freaking much."

He taps my knee, drawing my focus to him. "I'm going to say something that probably goes against the bro code, but I feel like Garrick would be okay with me saying it."

"Go on." I chew on the inside of my mouth.

"Garrick loved you, Stevie. You know that. Like I know you loved him. The thing is, Garrick also loved being in relationships. From the time he was fourteen, he was almost permanently in a relationship. He fell in and out of love a lot. Not like how it was with you," he rushes to reassure me. "That was the real deal, but Garrick needed to be in a relationship to feel fulfilled."

He pauses to let that sink in. "I think it was all tied up with his parents and their divorce. Anyway, the point I'm making is, I don't know if you two would have lasted doing the long-distance thing. You may have broken up already, and the second point I want to make is, I don't think Garrick would have harbored as much guilt if the roles were reversed. If you were in a coma, he would have been devoted to you the same way you were to him that first year. But after being iced out, if he'd met his Beck, I don't think he'd have agonized as much over starting a new relationship. I'm not saying he didn't love you, Stevie, but I think, if Garrick was in the same position, he'd have moved on quicker. I think he'd have been with Beck a long time before you even acknowledged you had feelings for him."

"Jeez." I stare at him a little speechless.

"You think I'm a terrible friend."

"No. I think you're an amazing friend, Hudson, and an amazing person." And I wish you were with Hadley because I believe she's missing out on her special someone by not choosing you. I don't articulate that part because it would only hurt him.

"Go be with Beck with a free conscience, Stevie." He stands, extending his hand and pulling me to my feet. "Go be happy, free of remorse and guilt, because you deserve it."

Chapter Thirty-Six

Beck

My phone flashes with a text Saturday night as I'm lounging on the couch attempting to watch a movie. I know Stevie was going to talk to Hugh and Dawn today, and I've been on edge waiting to hear from her. So, I snatch my cell up and read the one-word message.

INCOMING.

I hop up as my front door swings open, and my fiery goddess saunters into the living room with a glorious smile on her face. "Hey, babe," she says, grinning as I slam to a halt and drink her in.

It's only been twelve days since I last saw her, but honestly, it feels like twelve years.

Her hair is styled and hanging in glossy waves down her back, and she wears a light dusting of makeup. Long legs covered in sheer black stockings are propped up by skyscraper black heels. Stevie's lush curves are hidden behind a black belted trench coat.

"You are a sight for sore eyes, honey." Rosy cheeks, lush pink lips, and sparkling emerald eyes light up her entire face, and my heart swells with love.

Putting the bottle of champagne and box down on top of the sideboard, she licks her lips as her gaze drags over me. "So are you. I have missed you, and I'm so hungry."

Weird change of subject, but whatever. "I have leftover pasta I can heat up for you."

"I'm not talking about food," she says, unlatching her belt and opening her coat. "I'm hungry for my man."

My eyes are out on stalks as the coat pools at her feet, revealing the surprise underneath. My dick hardens in a nanosecond as my gaze roams over the black lace bra, matching thong, and garter.

"Fuck. Me," I rasp over a dry throat as she moves toward me like a gazelle.

"That's the idea," she purrs, placing her hand on my T-shirt. Her eyes are alight with love and lust as she peers into my face. "I'm ready, Beck. I'm all yours." Her features soften. "I have said my goodbye to Garrick, and I've spoken with Hugh and Dawn and Hudson."

"How was it?"

"I couldn't have asked for better." Her eyes shine with unshed tears. "They all give us their blessing. Not that we needed it."

I take her free hand in mine. "We didn't, but I know they're important to you and what they think matters." Garrick's dad and stepmom are good people. I rub my fingers over her hand, and my heart stutters in my chest. Lifting our conjoined hands, I spot the difference immediately. "You're not wearing your ring."

"It was time to remove it. My locket too," she says in a clear voice, and her eyes are free of tears. She fingers the charm bracelet I gave her and touches the ink on her wrist. "I won't wear another man's gifts when I'm with you because that would not be fair, but I'm hoping you're okay with the tattoo. It was my idea to get them, and I paid for it. Yes, it's something we did together, but it was as much about friendship as love. If it bothers you, I will get it removed or transformed into something else."

"It doesn't bother me." I lift her left wrist to my mouth and press my lips to the ink. "I'm confident in our love and happy for you to do whatever makes you comfortable."

"Thank you, my love." She presses her lips to mine, and I envelop her in my arms, holding her flush against my body as my cock leaks precum behind my sweats. Stevie breaks our kiss before it develops. "I want to say one final thing, and then it's behind us." Reaching up, she palms one cheek. "I love you, Greyson Beckett Colbert III. You have my heart now and forever. I have never been surer of anything. You are my person, my love, my life, my future. I want everything with you."

My heart is beating so fast I swear it's about to take flight. "You are all that and more to me, honey."

"I'm giving you everything, Beck, but a small piece of my heart will always belong to Garrick. I can't lie, and I need you to know that before we go any further." The look of vulnerability on her face as she admits her truth guts me. I can't imagine how difficult this has been for her because I've only ever seen her. If I had loved Brielle the way Stevie loved Garrick, I know it would have been agony making a decision. That she has chosen me speaks volumes, and only a prick would resent her holding some residual love for the man who was her first love.

"You wouldn't be you, Stevie, if you didn't feel this way." I thread my fingers in her hair. "Garrick helped to shape the woman you are today. He was your first love. He showed you what it is like to be in a loving relationship. I will forever be grateful to him, and I could never hold it against you if you always feel some love in your heart for him."

"I love you more." She says it with conviction, and I feel like fist pumping the air.

We are finally in the same place, and we get to move forward as a couple in the way I have dreamed about.

"I know, and I love you too. I have never loved any woman the way I love you."

"Are we done talking now?" A mischievous glint appears in her eyes as her hand lowers to my crotch, and she squeezes my aching shaft. "Because I have other things I plan to do with my mouth."

"Oh yeah?" I flash her a lascivious smile as I move to pick her up.

"Nuh-uh." Stevie pushes me back, and I almost stumble. "This is my show." She wiggles her finger at the couch. "Sit on the couch, sexy."

Grabbing the back of her head, I slam my lips to hers, ravishing her mouth as I use my free hand to squeeze her bare ass cheeks.

"Beck," she moans into my mouth. "Stop being such a naughty boy and get on the couch."

Pulling her in flush against my body, I rub my hard dick against her lace-covered crotch. "What will you do to me if I misbehave?" I rasp in her ear before grazing my teeth up and down her neck.

"I'll bite your dick," she says, and I burst out laughing.

"No, you won't, honey. You want it too much to hurt it."

"Babe, please. I want to suck your dick. You said you wouldn't make me beg."

"Maybe I've changed my mind," I tease.

She slithers to her knees and peeks up at me with big doe eyes. "Please, baby. Can I suck your dick?" She flashes her long lashes while I loom over her in shocked silence. Her palms glide up my thighs, and my cock is weeping in anticipation. "I promise to suck every gorgeous hard inch until I feel you hitting the back of my throat, and I'll drink every drop of your cum like a good little girl."

Fuck me. I think I've died and gone to heaven.

I love this new side of Stevie.

"Get up," I growl in a voice thick with lust, helping her to her feet. I pull off my clothes in record time and stalk to the couch. Sitting down, I spread my thighs and stroke my cock, watching her eyes turn black with lust as she walks toward me. "Get on your knees and suck my dick like the good girl you are."

She licks her lips and sinks elegantly to the floor, pressing her nose to my balls and inhaling deeply. I almost come on the spot. Her tongue darts out, and she licks and sucks my balls while her fingers toy with my puckered hole.

A string of expletives leaves my mouth. If she keeps this up, I'll explode before my dick has even met her hot mouth.

"Does my bad boy like that?" she asks, rimming my hole with the tip of her finger.

"Fuck, yes." Reaching down, I curl her hair around my fist and force her head back. "But I need those fuck-me lips wrapped around my dick right now, honey."

"Your wish is my command." Wasting no time, she lowers her mouth over my shaft, drinking my dick down and peering at me with big beautiful green eyes and a wanton expression that has me panting. Stevie hollows her cheeks and relaxes her throat as I ease further into her mouth. Her fingers grip my cock at the base, and she pulls the skin taut as she slurps up and down my length. I'm struggling to hold my release back, but I want to because this is too fucking good. When she moves one hand into her panties and starts rubbing herself, I almost lose my load.

"That's it, honey. Suck my dick and rub that pretty clit. I want you to squirt all over your hand as I fill your greedy throat with my cum."

Her eyes flare with heat as I tighten my hold on her hair and take control, ramming in and out of her mouth as potent need fires at me from all angles. "Rub faster, honey. I'm about to fill your tummy with my seed."

Tears leak from her eyes and saliva dribbles from her lips as I fuck her mouth like a maniac. I watch for any signs she's uncomfortable, but from the way she's rocking her hips and jerking her hand, I can tell she's loving this as much as me.

"Pinch your clit, baby, and come now!" I roar as my balls lock up, tingles shoot up my spine, and I spurt into her mouth. I hold her face steady as my cock pulses in her mouth, spewing cum down her throat. Stevie moans and writhes, and her eyes flicker under the intensity of her own climax.

The second we're done, I pop out of her mouth and lift her onto my lap, holding her close as I smooth a hand up and down her hair. "Are you okay?"

"Fucking hell, Beck." Awe glistens on her face. "What just happened? I didn't know you had that in you."

"Oh, honey. Is that a challenge?" I tease, swiping some tissues and helping to clean up her face.

"I don't know," she says, beaming. "Is it?"

"I think you have a bad girl alter ego." I slip my hands into the front of her thong. "And you're dripping."

She maneuvers herself on my lap. "You make me so horny, and I'm already hungry for more."

"Good." I throw her over my shoulder as I stand, slapping her ass as I all but race toward my bedroom. "I warned you I was insatiable, and you're about to discover exactly how much."

Chapter Thirty-Seven

Beck

Carefully, I spread my gorgeous woman out on my bed and crawl over her, pumping my dick in my fist a few times. "I want to make love to you our first time," I say, leaning down to kiss her swollen lips. "Then I'm going to fuck you six ways to Sunday."

"Tomorrow *is* Sunday," she says, giggling.

"I love you so fucking much, Stevie. You've made me the happiest man today."

"Come show me then." She palms one tit through her bra and tweaks her nipple.

I make quick work shedding her bra and panties until we're both naked and gazing at one another with excitement. "Do I need a condom?" I ask, running my fingers all over her beautiful body.

"Not unless you want to wear one. I'm clean, and I'm on the pill."

"I'm clean, and I've never gone bareback before."

"I like being your first." She reaches for my dick.

"First and last," I say before claiming her mouth in a hungry kiss.

"Beck, you say the sweetest things," she says when we break our lip-lock.

"It's the truth."

"For me too," she adds. "Now stop talking and make love to me."

I spend a few moments sucking, licking, and teasing every inch of her body even though it's not needed because she's already so turned on. I drive my fingers slowly in and out of her slick pussy, loving the sounds she's making. Her stunning red hair is like a halo around her head, streaming across the pillow like dancing flames. Flawless pale skin and sumptuous curves complete the package, and I don't know how I got this lucky.

She is truly magnificent.

And all *mine.*

Gathering her juices on my fingers, I move them lower, tracing the edge of her puckered hole. "Has any cock been here?" I ask, slipping the tip of my pinky into her ass.

Her pussy clenches as I gently probe her other hole.

"No," she pants. "But I'm down to try."

My cock leaks precum at her words and the vision that just popped into my head of claiming her tight virgin hole. "We'll need to work up to it," I say, pulling my pinky out.

"Beck, please. I need you."

"I've got you, honey." I position myself at her entrance, lining my cock up with her pussy. Holding myself there, I lean down and kiss her. "I love you so much."

"I love you too." She grabs my face and kisses me passionately as my tip breaches her hole. She gasps into my mouth, and we break our kiss to look down, both of us watching as I slowly inch inside her.

Watching my dick sink into her is one of the most erotic moments of my life.

Her tight warm walls are hugging me as I fill her up, and a sense of utter contentment floods my chest.

When I'm all the way in, I hold myself still, propping up on my elbows so I don't crush her, and stare into her eyes. I know this is her first time since Garrick, and I want to ensure she's okay. "Are you good?" I ask, peering deep into her eyes.

"Yes," she chokes out. "You feel so good, Beck. I feel you everywhere."

"This is what it's like when you're with your soul mate," I say, slowly dragging myself out and then pushing back in. "Nothing has ever felt more incredible."

"Oh god, I know." She drags her nails up and down my back as I pick up my pace and gently rock in and out of her.

"Keep your eyes on me," I say. "I want to experience every second of this with you."

Her legs wrap around my waist as I grind my pelvis and rotate my hips, sinking deeper.

Our hands and mouths are everywhere, lips touching, fingers caressing sweat-slickened skin, and mouths suctioning on nipples. I drive into her, over and over, setting a casual pace to make it last.

I flip her over onto all fours and plunge back in, my balls slapping against her as I pound into her at a more frantic pace. My fingers toy with her clit and tweak her nipples as I fuck her from behind. Then I move us down onto the bed, on our sides, wrap my arms around her from behind, and slide slowly in and out of her. I like this position because I have easy access to all of her body, and I caress her silky skin as my dick pumps in and out of her tight pussy.

Stevie moves slightly so she's looking up at me, and I drink from her lush lips as I pivot my hips and shove in and out of her pussy. Her tits jiggle as I make love to her mouth and her cunt. My hands roam her stunning curves, cupping her breasts and pinching her nipples, as a familiar tingle starts at the base of my spine.

"I'm close, honey."

"Me too," she pants, grabbing my head and pulling my mouth back to hers.

Her tongue pushes between my lips as I fuck her, and my fingers slide to her swollen clit.

"Tell me when, honey." I purposely hold myself back until she's ready.

"Now, Beck. Now please, baby," she cries, and I press down hard on her clit with my thumb and shove my cock in deeper, lifting her leg up and curling my hips so I hit the right spot.

Stevie screams out my name as she comes, and I grunt and moan as I deposit my seed deep inside her, feeling a sense of manly pride as I fill her up. She writhes around my fingers and my cock, whimpering blissful sounds as we ride the crest of the wave together.

When we are both sated, I turn her around and hug her close to me, dotting kisses all over her face and whispering I love you over and over again.

Never in a million years did I think sex could be like this.

Now I have found the other half of my heart and soul, I am never letting her go.

"What time is it?" Stevie asks, lifting her head with a groan the following morning.

"Eleven, sleepyhead."

"Still too early," she mumbles, brushing knotty strands of hair back from her face.

"I have your favorite coffee." I lower the takeout cup to her nose letting the caramel scents tickle her nostrils.

"Have I told you how much I love you?" she says, pulling herself upright with a low moan.

Concern surges through my veins, warring with lust at the sight of her full tits and hard nipples. "Are you okay? Was I too rough last night?" After we made love, I fucked her four more times, only stopping when we both physically couldn't move. I woke an hour ago, and I was tempted to surprise her with my tongue on her cunt, but I figured she'd be sore. So, I somehow dragged myself out of our warm bed and walked to the bakery to pick up pastries and coffees.

"Nope." She leans in to kiss me, aiming for my cheek, but I angle my head and meld our mouths. "Morning breath," she mumbles, softly shoving me away. "Hold that thought." Stevie climbs naked out of the bed, and I greedily track her every step, sporting an instant boner.

She returns a few minutes later and kisses me hard on the lips with fresh minty breath. Pulling back, she snags her coffee and sits against the headboard, patting the space beside her.

"Do you have plans today?" she asks in between sipping her caramel macchiato.

"Nothing concrete."

"I want to visit Nana's grave, and I thought maybe we could visit your mom's too, if you like?"

"I would like that."

"Mom's expecting us for dinner later, if that's okay? She wants to keep the tradition going."

"That's cool too."

She beams at me. "Great."

After breakfast, we shower together, which turns into sex and the need for another shower. Then we visit the graveyard together and head to Ravenna for dinner with Monica.

Over the next three months, we slip into an easy routine. Stevie spends most nights here with me, sleeping in my bed instead of her room, only going home to catch up with Hadley. We are basically living together although we haven't discussed it or made it official. I'm happy to just go with the flow as long as I get to have her in my life and in my bed.

Sex is incredible, and we can't keep our hands off one another. All our friends tease us about it, but they're just jealous.

Although we make time for date nights—catching a movie, or going out for dinner, or meeting our friends for drinks—we are both homebodies, preferring to stay in.

I have never felt more at ease with anyone.

Stevie and I just fit.

When I'm on a deadline, she does her own thing, without complaint, knowing I have to work nonstop until my manuscript is ready to send to my editor. She drops in with coffee, water, and snacks and even brings my meals into the office when she knows I'm in the zone and won't stop to eat at the table.

Other times, we work side by side in the office, and she helps me with research and plotting, and she's even managing my online street team now.

"Babe?" Stevie calls out on Friday night. "Where are you?"

"In the office," I shout, casting a glance at the clock on the wall. I was so lost in a scene I didn't realize it was late. We're meeting Jenny and Law and Mike and Hadley for dinner at a Mexican restaurant tonight.

Stevie waltzes in carrying a bouquet of flowers, and I arch a brow. "Secret admirer?" I tease. "Point him out to me so I can eliminate the competition."

Setting them down on her desk, she practically skips over to me. I make an oomph sound when she plops unceremoniously onto my lap. My arms go around her on autopilot as I brush my nose against hers. She beams at me, and her smile is so wide it threatens to split her face in two.

"Good news?" I inquire, dipping my fingers under the top of her blouse to caress the soft swell of her breasts.

"I got a promotion."

A shit-eating grin appears on my mouth. "That's my girl." I peck her lips. "Congratulations, honey. Now we have something to celebrate tonight."

"Is it wrong to want to stay at my job and not set up my own business?" she asks, her brow puckering a little.

"Not at all. You're in the driver's seat, and you're still young. There is plenty of time to set up a business in the future." Personally, I think Stevie will end up joining her mom and running the family business in Ravenna in the future.

"Sometimes, the old me rears her head, and I internally beat myself up over letting go of my goals."

"Your life changed. It's only natural your goals did too."

"True." She looks pensive as she stares into space.

"You're one of the smartest, most focused people I know, Stevie. If you want to set up your own business in the future, you'll do it, and you'll have my help."

"I'm so lucky I have you," she says, smiling as she purposely grinds her ass on my growing dick.

"Want to see just how lucky?" I waggle my brows, and she giggles.

"Yes, please, sir." She mock salutes me before I set her feet on the ground and spin her around, bending her over my desk.

Pushing her skirt up to her waist, I pry her legs apart before kneeling on the ground and pressing my nose to her lace-covered pussy. Bunching her panties into a thin strip, I use it to work her over good before dragging the lace down her legs and worshiping her with my tongue and my fingers. Rising to my feet, I lower the zipper on my jeans and shove them and my boxers to my ankles.

Stevie turns her head to the side on the desk, pinning me with a devilish look. "You writing a novel back there or what?"

My hand comes down on her bare ass in a firm slap. Her eyes roll back in her head as she grinds her hips against the wood, and I know she's gagging for my cock the same way I'm gagging for her cunt.

"Well, what are you waiting for Mr. Hotshot Author?"

I give her what she wants, cracking my palm on her reddening ass cheeks again, and precum leaks from my cock at the sight of her lust dampening the tops of her thighs. I position my dick at her entrance and ram into her in one powerful thrust. Then I proceed to fuck the shit out of her on top of my desk until we climax together, both vocal in our releases as her pussy milks every last drop from my cock.

"Please tell me you're late because you were having wild monkey sex," Hadley says when we finally arrive at the restaurant twenty minutes late.

"We were having wild monkey sex," Stevie confirms with a grin before giving everyone hugs and kisses.

"Well done, stud." Hadley smirks at me while Law looks on in bewildered amusement. Mike looks practically horizontal in his chair, but that's nothing new. If the guy was any more laid-back, he'd fall over. Jenny grins. She's a firm member of the Hadley fan club. It's hard not to like Hadley. She's quirky and amazing and the most loyal friend. Because of the way my relationship evolved with Stevie, Hadley has become one of my best friends too, and we regularly text and talk.

We settle down for dinner, chatting casually until Law brings up a topic I really wish he hadn't.

"I saw an article in the New York Times about the Allen court case," my buddy says, bringing all conversation to a halt around the table.

"Darling," Jenny says, subtly digging her nails into her husband's thigh under the table. "I don't think now is an appropriate time to discuss it."

"Don't worry on my account." Stevie links her fingers in mine on top of the table. "Beck knows Hugh and Hudson have been keeping me updated. Ivy isn't playing ball, so Hugh had no choice but to take things legal."

"It's sad it's come to this. It should've been settled in private," Hadley says.

"I agree. Garrick would hate this, but it's not like Ivy left Hugh with any choice."

"Will you attend court for the hearing?" Jenny asks, shooting a cursory glance in my direction.

"I've told Stevie she should go if she wants."

"I don't want to," Stevie confirms what she's already told me in private. "It wouldn't be appropriate. I'm not with Garrick anymore, and while I care what happens to him, I don't want to be in that courtroom. Hudson will update me."

We order some cocktails, and the conversation gets back on track.

My phone pings with a text, and I read Hadley's message, excusing myself from the table to join her in the hallway leading to the bathrooms.

She practically jumps on me when I open the door. "Show me, show me, show me!" She jumps up and down like a five-year-old on a sugar high.

"Jesus, woman. Control yourself."

"I've been bursting to ask you all night."

Pulling out my phone, I scroll through the photos and show Hadley the picture of the engagement ring I purchased last night. "What do you think?" I ask. "Will she like it?"

Hadley gasps, and tears prick her eyes. "Oh, Beck. It's stunning, and it's perfect for her. Not too flashy even though it's exquisite."

I hadn't planned on buying Stevie an engagement ring yet, but I know I want to propose to her sometime in the future. I was walking past a jewelry store last night and saw this emerald and diamond ring in the window, and I knew it was perfect. "It reminds me of her eyes, and I was instantly drawn to it."

"It's so pretty. I love the diamonds around the emerald and the finer ones on the platinum band. She will love it. You did good, Beck. Real good."

Her praise means a lot. "Thanks."

"When are you going to pop the question?" she asks. "Her birthday is only six weeks away. You could do it then."

I shake my head as I repocket my phone. "It's too soon. I'd have popped the question the day she told me she was mine, but I don't want to freak her out. Besides, her birthday is only two weeks after the accident and Nana's birthday, and she's probably going to be sad. I don't want our engagement to be associated with a sad time."

"You're right, of course. I'm just excited to see my best friend get engaged."

"If she says yes."

Hadley rolls her eyes. "You're so ridiculous. Of course, she'll say yes. She is head over heels, tits over ass, crazy in love with you."

The door to the hallway opens, crashing noisily against the wall and we both jump.

Law stands in the doorway wearing a troubled expression. "You need to come quick. Stevie needs you."

We race out of the hallway back toward our table. Stevie is pale and shaking, and her eyes are glassy.

"Honey, what's wrong?" I crouch beside the table, and my eyes inspect every inch of her for damage, but she's physically unhurt. "Stevie, baby, talk to me." I take her trembling hands and rub them, hoping to get some warmth back into her skin because she feels ice cold.

"It's Garrick," she chokes out, pinning me with shell-shocked eyes. "He's awake. He has come out of his coma."

Chapter Thirty-Eight

Stevie

It's been six days since Hudson called me with the news Garrick woke from his coma, and I have barely slept. I got a doctor's note and called in sick to work because there's no way I can function right now. All manner of emotions is tormenting me. I'm trying to contain them, because it's not fair to Beck, but this is a complete shock, and I'm all over the place.

I don't know how to feel.

What to think or what to do.

Everyone else has visited him, but I'm still banned.

I need to see Garrick with my own eyes. I won't believe he's awake until I see him in the flesh. Then, I need to find a way to explain I'm in love with another man and no longer his girlfriend. I am dreading that conversation, but I can't shy away from it. It would be unfair to Garrick to mislead him, and we both deserve closure.

I was tempted to show up in Medina and try to barge my way in, but I don't want to make a scene and risk a commotion that might harm Garrick's recovery, so I have to wait and trust that Hugh and Hudson will come through for me.

From what Hudson has said, Garrick is confused and sleeping a lot, and when he's awake, he's nonverbal and agitated.

"I made lunch," Beck says, holding on to the top of the archway between the living room and the interconnecting space that links the rest of the rooms in his apartment. His shirt rides up a little, showcasing a tempting glimpse of toned olive skin.

"I'm not hungry."

"Honey, you need to eat." Beck strides toward me, lifting me up and sitting down on the couch with me in his lap. His reassuring arms band around my waist as I lean into him, resting my head on his shoulder. "I'm worried about you."

"I'm sorry. I know this is hard for you."

"It's no picnic, but you're my priority, and you need to eat, Stevie. You'll make yourself ill. I made that vegetable soup you like, and I have some of that bread you love from the bakery. At least try a little bit."

"You are so good to me." Tears stab my retinas as I lift my head and brush my lips against my boyfriend's. "I hate that you're worrying about me, and I hate that I'm turning into a basket case again. I don't want to feel like this, if it helps."

"You can't control how you feel, and it's only natural. It's a big shock, and I'm sure it's dredged a lot of emotions to the surface."

I've been talking with Hadley, trying to make sense of the jumble of emotions in my head, because I cannot torture Beck any more than I am. "It has." I clasp his face in my hands. "But I love you, and that's not going to change."

"I'm scared I'm going to lose you," he admits.

"You won't."

He doesn't look convinced, but I don't know how to reassure him. I can't ignore what's happened, and I can't ignore Garrick. He went into a coma with life a certain way, and he's woken to a vastly altered one. I can't forget I'm the reason he was in a coma in the first place, and I can't abandon him now he's awake.

Beck takes my hand, leading me into the dining room, and we eat our lunch in strained silence. My ex waking is the elephant in the room. I won't lie and say it's not already impacting my relationship with my boyfriend because it is.

It's a mess, and I'm a constant ball of anxiety.

At least if I could get in to see him, it might help make things clearer.

The doorbell chimes, and Beck sets his soupspoon down. "Are you expecting anyone?"

I shake my head.

"I'll get it." He leans down to kiss my cheek. "Eat." He points at my plate, and I stuff a piece of crusty white bread into my mouth to appease him. Food has lost all taste for me, but if it'll help to reassure my boyfriend, I will force myself to eat.

Muffled voices greet my ears, and I shovel the remaining soup down my throat and get up to investigate.

"Oh, hey, Hudson," I say when I spot Garrick's best friend standing in the hallway engaged in a hushed conversation with Beck. All the blood drains from my face as I remember something Hugh said that day in the sunroom, about coma patients dying from organ failure a few days after waking up. "Oh my god." I stagger against the wall, and the tears are automatic.

"Honey, breathe." Beck is by my side in a flash, pulling me into his arms. "Garrick is alive. Hudson dropped by to update us."

My chest heaves, and a strangled sound leaves my mouth as I struggle to breathe after almost giving myself a coronary.

Hudson shoots Beck a concerned look.

"I'm okay," I rasp, clinging to my boyfriend. "Sorry." My gaze is sheepish as it dances between the two men. "I just assumed the worst."

"It's all right, Stevie. It's been a stressful time for everyone."

"Come inside, and let's talk," Beck says, scooping me into his arms and carrying me back to the couch. Hudson trails us inside, taking a seat on the chair in front of the fire.

I lean my head on Beck's chest and hug him close as Hudson

clears his throat. "Garrick is still agitated and confused, but every day, he's awake for longer than the previous day, and his memories are returning in spurts. The doctors have confirmed he is paralyzed from the waist down, and he has a lot to do to return his body to physical strength, but the early signs are encouraging. They don't think he's suffered any permanent brain damage, which is the best news."

"They can tell now even though he's not speaking?"

"They've done a bunch of tests. His vocal cords have been sleeping, and it will take him a little time to recover his full speech, but they are hopeful now he's said a few words." Hudson's tongue darts out, wetting his lips, and he looks uncomfortable as he glances at Beck.

"Tell us," Beck quietly says, wrapping his arms tighter around me.

"He said Stevie," Hudson admits. "That's the only word he has said, but he's repeated it over and over."

An emotional tsunami batters me from all sides at his admission. Tears instantly leak from my eyes, and I'm choking on the lump in my throat and struggling to breathe over the boulder pressing down on my chest. Beck turns rigid underneath me, and I can't fall apart in his arms over another man again.

I cannot do it to the man who is my rock.

This man who is my everything.

So, I dip my head and force my emotions aside, stamping them out and only lifting my chin when I feel I'm more in control. "How am I going to tell him, Hudson?" I whisper. "It's going to devastate him."

Beck recovers himself, rubbing his hands up and down my arm. "You haven't done anything wrong, Stevie. You need to remind yourself of that."

It's easier said than done. And it was way easier to believe it when Garrick was in a coma. Now that he's not? I feel like a cheating bitch all over again.

"Unfortunately, that ship has sailed," Hudson says with a grimace, and I swear my heart stops beating.

"What?" I splutter, horror threaded through my tone. I had already discussed the topic with Hudson, Hugh, and Dawn, and it was collectively felt it was better to wait until Garrick was more stable before telling him about me and Beck. Beck wasn't happy when I broached the subject, but he understands, and he agreed, albeit reluctantly.

As long as I live, I will never be worthy of this amazing man.

Ivy was always the wildcard, but I still can't believe she's done this.

"That conniving bitch," Beck hisses, drawing the same conclusion I have.

"Yep. So much for caring about her son." Hudson's jaw tightens. "She threw a hissy fit when Garrick was calling for Stevie. Instead of thinking about her son, and doing what is best for him, she only thought about herself and her stupid vendetta." He looks at me. "She wants to keep you iced out, so she told him you stopped seeing him eleven months ago and you were living with another man. She also insinuated you tried to ruin her."

I close my eyes as my heart tears into little strips.

"How can she be so reckless?" Beck asks. "She could set back his recovery."

"He had a seizure," Hudson confirms, and I whip my eyes open. "He's okay," he rushes to reassure me, "but she induced a seizure with her cruel words. The neurosurgeon was furious, and he ripped her a new asshole. He made it clear, in no uncertain terms, that he would join with Hugh and go to court to confirm Garrick was no longer safe living under her roof if she pulled anything like that again."

"I hope that shut the bitch up," I say in a shaky voice, snuggling against Beck and clinging to his muscular arms.

"It did. She knows she's treading on eggshells now. She knows Garrick will find out what she did to you and how she has cut Hugh and Dawn out in recent months, only granting them access again because Hugh threatened to request an emergency meeting with the judge to demand visitation rights to his son. Ivy can't afford the bad publicity, so she was forced to relent, and now she's forced to relent in your case."

"What do you mean?"

Hudson rubs the back of his neck, glancing awkwardly at Beck again. "I'm sorry, man. I know this is rough for you," he says before turning his attention to me. "Garrick is asking for you repeatedly, Stevie. His doctors want you to visit him ASAP because they're worried he's going to have another seizure if he doesn't see you."

I look at my boyfriend, swallowing anxiously over the golf-ball-sized lump clogging my throat.

Beck caresses my cheek. "I'm not your keeper, Stevie. It's your choice." His voice hints at the emotion he's trying so hard to hide.

"I love you." I kiss him hard on the lips. "I love *you*." I peer deep into his eyes. "I know this is an awful situation, but I'm still yours. No matter what happens, I'm yours."

"For how long?" he asks with tears in his eyes.

Pain eviscerates me on the inside when I see the agony etched upon my boyfriend's face.

"I'm sorry," he adds, wiping his eyes and sitting up straighter. He clears his throat. "I'm being selfish."

"Fuck, no." Hudson shakes his head. "You're not. It's only human to feel conflicted. If this was my girlfriend, I'm not sure I could be as generous as you."

"Trust me, the thoughts in my head right now are less than generous, and I feel like a prick for them," Beck says.

"One final thing," Hudson says, rubbing the back of his neck. "I want you to know I have spoken to Garrick about this. Dr. Mann felt it would be a good idea to talk to him about some of the stuff he missed and to clarify what Ivy said. He knows you were there every single day until his mom iced you out, Stevie. I told him how devoted you were. I didn't say too much about Beck. I thought you'd want to explain yourself. But he knows you're with him and that it's serious."

His eyes probe mine. "I hope you're not angry, but I thought it best to somewhat prepare him."

"I understand, and it's better in a way."

"Are you sure you should visit him? If Garrick knows, maybe it's best to let it go," Beck supplies. There is no malice in his tone, and I know his suggestion is coming from a place of love for me.

"I don't want to hurt you, but I can't ignore him, Beck. I can't let Garrick suffer any more than he has. If he is asking for me, I need to go see him." I have no choice now Ivy cuntface has spilled the beans. I'm pissed about the seizure, but in a way, she's probably done me a favor. "I will explain I can only be there for him as a friend now."

Tension bleeds into the air until Beck breaks it. "Okay. Go and visit him." He attempts a smile, but it's impossible not to see the worry behind his eyes. "I'll be here for you when you get home."

Chapter Thirty-Nine

Stevie

"Will she be here?" I ask Hudson as we park in front of Ivy's house, and he kills the engine.

"No. The doctors insisted she make herself scarce. You won't see her."

"What about Pepper?" I ask, trying to stop the full-body tremors coursing through me and quell the nausea crawling up my throat. I'm regretting the soup and bread earlier. I'm liable to vomit it back up any second now.

"She packed her bags the second day Garrick was chanting your name. When she visited him, he barely acknowledged her. I think she knows the game is up. Garrick will never love her, and she's a fool for ever believing he would."

"At least Garrick has been spared that drama."

"Are you ready?" Hudson asks, eyeing my shaking form with concern.

"No, but I don't think I will ever be." I pierce him with a stare. "How does he look?"

"Not like himself, but every day, there is a little more color in his cheeks and a bit more awareness in his eyes. Garrick is a fighter." A wide smile crosses his mouth. "My best buddy battled a coma and won. He'll get through this next fight."

Hudson reaches across the console and hugs me. "We have to remember the important thing here. He's alive, Stevie. He's alive, and he's going to be okay. It sucks he'll be in a wheelchair for the rest of his life, but otherwise, he's expected to recover. He can go on to live a full life." He kisses my brow. "I know this is awkward for you and very upsetting. I feel for Beck, and I don't know what I would do in his shoes or yours. No one can force you to be here, Stevie. You don't owe anyone anything."

"That is simply not true, Hudson. It's amazing he's alive. I'm elated he's come out of it, and like I said to Beck, I can't abandon Garrick. It would be supremely selfish and heartless, and I can't do it. But I can't pretend I'm not in love with another man either. Of course, there is still love in my heart for Garrick, but I love Beck. I have made a life with Beck. My future is with Beck."

If I don't fuck it all up.

I slam my head against the headrest and close my eyes. Round and round it goes in a loop in my brain, like it has the past six days.

"It's an impossible situation, and I need someone to tell me what I'm supposed to do," I say, opening my eyes and realizing I'm rubbing the tattoo on my wrist.

"There is no rule book, and I think we'll probably have to let Garrick guide us."

I run my fingers back and forth against the Celtic shield knot on my skin. "I promised to look out for him, to always protect him, the day we got these tats, and my heart won't let me forget that promise. I cannot be with him as his girlfriend, but if he needs me as his friend, I won't abandon him."

"How do you think Beck will cope with that?" Hudson asks in a soft tone.

"I don't know." Tears cloud my vision as I turn to Garrick's friend. My friend. "How can I ask him to do this while I support another man?" Tears turn to full-blown sobs. "I don't want to lose Beck, but I fear I might."

"Beck loves you, and he's been understanding about Garrick in the past. Try not to worry and trust it will be all right."

"I wish I could." I swipe at my tears as Hudson passes me a tissue. "God, I sound so selfish. Garrick is inside waiting to see me, and I'm out here throwing a pity party for one." I force a smile as I open my purse and pull out a compact. "I'm just going to focus on one step at a time, and right now, what's most important, like you said, is he's alive and he has a future. That is all I prayed for, for months after the accident, and now it's come true."

"Some miracles do happen," he says, smiling as he watches me patch up my makeup.

"They do." I lift my chin and steady my nerves. "Let's go see him."

"Stevie!" Helena—Garrick's physical therapist—rushes toward me in the hallway, pulling me into a hug. "I'm so glad you're here." Tears glisten in her eyes. "Isn't this amazing?"

"Yes. It truly is."

"He is so anxious to see you." She releases me before hugging Hudson. "He's said a few more words today, and Dr. Mann is very happy with his progress. All his vitals look good, and it's looking really positive."

"Awesome." Hudson kisses Helena on the cheek.

"He'll be so happy to see you," Helena says, squeezing my arm.

"I hope so." I slant her a weak grin. I'm not sure what kind of reaction I will get now he knows I'm in a relationship with another man.

We say our goodbyes, and Hudson loops his arm in mine and leads me through the ground floor of Ivy's house to the wing where Garrick's bedroom is.

I'm on edge as we walk through rooms, glancing all around, waiting for the witch to jump out with a knife and stab me through the heart.

"Wait!" I say as Hudson curls his hand around the door handle to Garrick's room. "I need to know something before we go in. When you told him about me being in a serious relationship with Beck, how did he react?"

Hudson's Adam's apple jumps in his throat, and anguish splays across his face. "He cried."

I grip my chest because it feels like I'm having a heart attack. I press my brow to the wall and take deep breaths as I blink my eyes shut and force my tears back down. I can't begin to imagine how much that must have hurt Garrick. He woke asking for me, believing I was still his, and he had to hear it from others that I betrayed him and I'm now in love with another man. The sense of helplessness I feel is overwhelming. I'm back to hating myself with a vengeance. I hate I have hurt Garrick and that I'm hurting Beck too.

Hudson rubs my back. "I'm sorry, Stevie. My heart is breaking for all of you."

"Yeah, me too." I push off the wall and remember what I came here to do. This isn't about me, and I need to stop being so selfish. I need to be strong for Garrick, and I need to pull myself the fuck together.

"One other thing, we only want you visiting when Hugh or I am here. We don't trust Ivy not to pull some stunt, and neither of us want you hurt."

"Thanks, I appreciate it, but let's not get ahead of ourselves. Garrick may not want anything more to do with me."

A part of me hopes for that outcome. It would be easier if he took the decision out of my hands. I hang my head in shame as the thought resurrects in my mind. I'm a horrible person for thinking it.

"I don't think so, but I don't know what's going through his mind. When he's better able to communicate, I'll talk with him. I'm here for both of you," he confirms, taking my hand. "I'll do what I can to make this work."

"Thank you so much, Hudson. For everything."

"You're my friend, Stevie, and I like Beck too."

Thrusting my shoulders back, I draw a brave breath and level him with a look. "I'm ready to see him now."

Hudson enters the room with me, holding my hand tight when he feels me trembling. It's a miracle I can put one foot in front of the other.

The room is large and airy with a vaulted ceiling and gorgeous views over the gardens and the lake at the rear of the property. Behind us is a seated area with couches, a TV, and a fireplace. In front is the bedroom part of the room. Lighting is low as Hudson confirmed Garrick has been getting headaches. An unfamiliar nurse lifts her head and smiles from a desk in the top corner of the room. She's seated behind it, quietly typing on a tablet because her patient is asleep.

A fluttery feeling swoops into my chest as knots form in my tummy. Hudson guides me to the bed as blood thrums in my ears and my heart begins racing. I drag my lower lip between my teeth and clutch Hudson's arm tighter as I take my first look at Garrick in almost a year. It's been nineteen days since he turned twenty-three, and it's only twenty-seven days until the second anniversary of the accident.

Tears flood my eyes as I stop at his bed and drink him in. He's thinner and paler than I remember him being in the hospital, but that's probably just my faulty memory. While his hair is thicker, it's not the messy chin-length hair he was sporting when we were dating. Nor is it the cropped look he wore while in the hospital. His hair is how I imagine Ivy wants him to wear it, slicked back at the front and tighter at the sides. I bet he hates it and can't wait to grow it out again.

He looks so frail lying propped up on copious pillows on the elevated bed, and it brings it all back to me. A bunch of machines surrounds his bed, and he has tubes in both hands. It's also a reminder of how precarious his situation is. Although the doctors are pleased with his progress, anything could go wrong. It's still early days, and he's not out of the woods. That thought sends shards of pain digging into my heart, and I reach for his hand, softly placing mine on top of his. Warm skin meets my palm, and his fingers twitch.

His eyes pop open, instantly gravitating toward me.

"Hey, man," Hudson says in a quiet voice. "Look who came to see you."

Garrick's eyes instantly fill with tears as he stares at me, and there he is. The familiar amber flecks in his beautiful eyes ignite so many happy memories, and I can't trap my emotions anymore. They strain for freedom, laboring against the walls I shoved them behind, until they break free, and I burst out crying. My anguished cries bounce off the walls of the quiet room as Garrick pushes the button on a fob curled around his other hand, and the bed elevates.

His fingers thread between mine as Hudson hugs me from behind, offering silent support.

"Stevie," Garrick croaks in a hoarse voice. The bed stops moving when he's more upright, sitting against the mountain of pillows. "Love...you."

I cry harder, sniffling and almost choking on the strangled sounds emerging from my throat, before I force myself to get a grip. I'm upsetting him further. Garrick needs me, and I won't let him down. I have to remain strong for him. He's the one lying in a hospital bed. "I love you too," I say over a sob, and it's not a lie. There will always be love in my heart for this man.

He tries to lift his arms, but he can't manage the effort involved. I know what he wants. Shucking out of Hudson's embrace, I bend down and hug my ex. I'm extra careful not to suffocate him or squeeze him too hard, just lightly resting my upper half against his and slightly touching his cheek. His clean-shaven skin is unusual for Garrick, but I'm sure it's something else he'll rectify.

I close my eyes as I hug him. I can't believe it. It feels surreal. For so long, I wished he would wake. I never imagined when he would that things would be so different between us.

A clinical smell emanates from his skin, but he smells like himself too. Garrick used citrusy shower gel and he always wore spicy cologne, but his skin naturally emitted a vanilla scent that always reminded me of him.

"Do you need anything, Garrick?" the nurse asks from the other side of the bed, and I ease back, kissing his cheek before I straighten up.

Garrick squeezes my hand with more strength than I would have thought him capable of.

"No." He swallows heavily. "Just Stevie." The words are thick and slightly garbled but clear enough to make out what he's saying.

The nurse smiles at him and then me. "He hasn't stopped asking for you."

Hudson pulls a chair up behind me. "Rest your feet," he says, helping me into the seat. Garrick doesn't let go of my hand. "I'm going to sit down there," Hudson says, pointing at the end of the room. "And give you two some privacy." He kisses the top of my hair. "Holler if you need me."

I look up at him. "Thanks, Hudson."

"Hold it together, man," he teases Garrick, leaning down to hug him.

My nerves jangle, as Hudson walks off and the nurse goes back to her corner, which is ridiculous. I used to be able to tell Garrick anything, but now it feels like we're strangers.

"Hey." A blush warms my cheeks as I softly smile at him.

"Beautiful," he says, smiling at me through tears.

"I missed you so much," I truthfully admit. "And I'm so sorry, Garrick. If I had just accepted your gift, the accident wouldn't have happened."

Some of the light leaves his eyes, and I regret mentioning it. But I'm nervous, and I'm not quite sure what to say. I glance around the room, spotting none of the pictures or things I had bought him for his hospital room. I'm not surprised. Ivy probably cackled while setting them on fire.

Bitch.

"I visited you every day. Usually before work and after work. I read to you and played your favorite music, and I prayed so hard for you to wake, and now you have."

"Remember," he says, his eyes dancing all over my face.

My eyes pop wide. "You heard me?"

He nods and winces.

"Try not to move your head, sweetie," the nurse calls out.

"I'm sorry you're in pain, but I'm so glad you are awake."

Tears fill his eyes, and his mouth opens and closes a few times. I press a kiss to his knuckles as I wait him out.

"Beck," he rasps, and my stomach drops to my toes.

The smile fades from my face. I really don't want to have this conversation now. It's too soon and Garrick's too fragile, but I can't lie to him either. "Yes, I'm with Beck now," I quietly say. "I didn't mean for it to happen, but it did. But I'm still here for you, Garrick. I'm still your friend, and I still love you. That's not going to change."

He closes his eyes, and I feel something irreparable crack inside me.

"Hurts," he says when he opens his eyes, and tears roll down his face.

"I'm sorry," I whisper as tears leak from my eyes. "I waited for you, and then I was shut out, and it hurt so much. Beck was my friend for almost a year before anything else happened. He helped keep me together when I was missing you so badly and hurting a lot."

"Mine," he says, holding my hand tighter. "Mine," he repeats as fire replaces the moisture in his eyes.

Fuck my life.

"I'm here for you." I don't think pointing out I'm not his anymore will help his recovery, so all I can do is fudge my reply.

"Need you." His familiar eyes bore into mine.

"I'm going nowhere," I say, praying I haven't just lied to him.

Chapter Forty

Stevie

"Sorry, I'm late," Hadley says, out of breath as she plops into the chair across from me in the restaurant. "This lady wanted to check out a book our system said was on the shelves, but the book fairies must have stolen it because I spent a whole freaking hour trying to find it before I had to call it quits. Then I realized it was lunch and I hadn't left yet."

"It's fine," I say, stirring the coffee in my mug. It's my second helping and a much-needed injection of caffeine. "I've just been sitting here drowning in dark thoughts while I wait for you."

"Fill me in." She hangs her jacket on the back of the chair.

The waitress arrives, and we order salads and smoothies, waiting until she's gone to talk.

"My life is falling apart, and I seem powerless to stop it."

"Has Garrick asked to see you again?"

I shake my head. "Not yet, but Hudson said he doesn't want me to see him like that again, so he's working hard with his speech therapist these past two weeks to recover his communication skills."

"And Beck? How are things with him?"

"Terrible." Tears flood my eyes, and I angrily swipe at them. "It feels like I've regressed two years, and I'm crying at the drop of a hat again. It's pathetic. I'm pathetic."

"You're not. You're under a huge amount of stress, and you've got to cut yourself some slack."

"I'm going to lose him," I admit before gulping back hot coffee. I purposely asked for a black coffee because it tastes as bitter as my soul feels these days.

"No defeatist attitude, Opium Poppy. Beck loves you. It's natural he's sullen, but he won't leave you."

"You didn't see him when I told him what Garrick said." Beck looked like he was going to throw up when I told him how Garrick called me his.

"Maybe you shouldn't have told him everything."

"I'm not going to lie to him, Hads. I might as well kiss my relationship goodbye if I start concealing things." I exhale heavily, grateful for a reprieve when the waitress appears with our lunch.

I pick at my salad, forcing a few mouthfuls down my throat, purely to keep Hadley off my case.

"We haven't had sex since Garrick woke," I blurt, needing to get it off my chest.

Hadley puts her fork down and stares at me with her serious face. "Why not?"

My lower lip wobbles. "I want to. I crave Beck's touch. I miss it so much, but every time he initiates anything, I flinch." Tears roll down my cheeks, and I don't even care that people are staring at me. "It feels like I'm betraying Garrick all over again, and I'm hurting Beck. The look on his face every time kills me. I'm a horrible girlfriend, and I deserve to lose him." I sob, pushing my salad away and burying my head in my hands.

"Can we have the check?" I hear Hadley ask a few seconds later while I cry. I can't plug my tear ducts even though I know I'm embarrassing myself in public.

My bestie takes charge, calling both our jobs and clearing our afternoons. Then she calls Mom—telling her we're on our way—and

Beck—explaining I'm staying in Ravenna tonight. She recommends he goes out with Law to let off some steam.

I'm aware of all this going on around me, but I'm not an active participant.

Mom is waiting for us at her house when we arrive. She takes one look at me and grabs me into a motherly hug, and I fall apart, clinging to the familiarity of her embrace and her soothing words.

After a few hours, when I've finally stopped crying and I'm somewhat coherent, I cuddle on the couch with Mom as Hadley calls for takeout. When she returns, she hands me a tumbler of whisky. "You need it."

"Thanks." I take a sip, and the familiar burn helps to ground me. "I'm sorry for falling apart."

"It's no surprise," Mom says, sweeping my hair over my shoulders. "This is all too much, and I should have intervened sooner, but I didn't want to interfere in your relationship or tell you what to do."

"I don't know what to do, Mom. That's the problem. No matter what action I take, what decision I make, I'm hurting one of them."

Mom gently clasps my face, forcing my gaze to hers. "Who do you love, Stevie?"

"I love Beck, but I still have love in my heart for Garrick too."

"Who is your soul mate?" Hadley asks. "Who do you see a future with?"

"Beck," I say without hesitation. "It's Beck."

"Then I think you need to walk away from Garrick, sweetheart," Mom says.

"I can't. I can't be selfish. I'm the reason he's in this condition, and if he needs me, I'm not abandoning him." I knock back a mouthful of whisky, hoping we have a full bottle because I need to drown out everything going through my head. Lack of sleep, food, and the agonizing, conflicting thoughts circling round and round in my head are driving me insane. It feels like I'm losing my mind, and I need to blot it all out.

"Even if you lose Beck?" Mom asks. I've already had this conversation with my therapist, and it didn't help.

"I don't want to lose him, but how do I abandon a man who's in a wheelchair because of me?" My gaze bounces between them. "How do I abandon a man who looks me in the eyes and says he needs me, and loves me, and I'm still his?" Air gushes out of my mouth. "I cannot be that heartless. I cannot walk away and leave him to deal with the aftermath of the accident I caused."

Mom and Hadley exchange troubled looks.

"Yes, I know. I'm regressing and letting guilt consume me again. You don't need to say it. Ramona already did."

"Sweetie, I'm really worried about you." Mom strokes a hand up and down my back. "Why don't you and Beck go away for a weekend somewhere and try to destress? It sounds like you both need it."

"He's working on a deadline, and I'm not exactly his favorite person right now."

"That's impossible," Mom says. "That man would step in front of a bullet for you."

"Well, he shouldn't," I snap, rubbing a tense spot between my brows. "He should throw me at it, and problem solved." I knock back the rest of the whisky and hold out my glass to Hadley. "Refill, please?"

"I'm calling Ramona," Mom says.

"Don't. She can't help me. No one can."

Mom ignores me, and my therapist shows up an hour later after I have forced some shrimp and fried rice down my throat. I'm feeling all kinds of special Ramona paid a house visit. I'm guessing Mom told her I was suicidal or something, but I didn't mean what I said. I'm just exhausted, depressed, stressed, confused, and scared, and I've reached my breaking point.

Garrick waking up is an amazing miraculous thing, and I wouldn't change it for anything. I am so happy he'll get to live a full life, albeit in a different way than he imagined. At least he's no longer lost in an abyss. He's finally able to move forward. It sucks he's in a wheelchair, but he hasn't suffered any permanent brain damage, and that's huge. It's what I have always wanted for him.

But I am in my own personal version of hell, and there is no way of breaking out of it without hurting one of the men I love.

I cannot reconcile that within myself, and I cannot force the situation.

It's impossible.

I don't know what to do, and I feel selfish for being so obsessed with my predicament instead of worrying about Garrick's recovery and the long road he faces.

Mom goes to the pharmacy to fill the prescription Ramona organized for sleeping pills and antidepression medication.

I pop my pills and sleep soundly, in my childhood bed, for the first time in weeks.

When I wake, Beck is sitting in a chair by my bed, snoring softly with a blanket over his lap. I take a few minutes to study him, noting the bruising shadows under his eyes and the extra thickness on his chin and cheeks. Beck rarely sports the clean-shaven look he wore to the office anymore, favoring a trimmed light layer of facial hair, which makes him appear even more manly. He keeps his hair cropped, and I love it because he has the most gorgeous, most expressive eyes, and I never want them hidden.

His signature rings adorn his fingers, and I admire his elegant hands and talented fingers. These hands have explored every part of me. Beck's magical hands have enticed so much pleasure from my body, and I miss his touch.

He is so beautiful, and there is something so vulnerable about him in sleep. It hurts my heart knowing that frown he wears, even in slumber, is caused by me. Everything was perfect between us until Garrick woke, and now everything has turned to shit.

I climb out of the bed, intending to use the bathroom, but I can't resist leaning over my boyfriend to softly peck his lips. Beck's arms band around me, and he pulls me down on top of him. "Now my day can start," he says in a deep sleep-laden voice, and my tear ducts swing into action. From that first time we slept together, Beck has said this every morning. That his day won't start until after he's kissed me. It's so sweet, but it's breaking my heart right now.

"I love you," I whisper. I say it every day, but I fear he no longer believes me.

"I know you do," he says as his eyes pop open. They are bloodshot and red rimmed, and more guilt lumps onto the pile I'm keeping on my shoulders. "Like I love you."

"I'm scared of losing you."

"I fear the same thing."

A lump rises in my throat. "Let me go pee, and then we'll talk. Stay here."

When I return, Beck is on his side in my small bed, and the first genuine smile in ages ghosts over my mouth. I get in beside him, snuggling into his warmth as his arms wrap around me. "You scared everyone last night, honey." He brushes hair out of my eyes and fixes me with his concerned gaze. "You've got to take better care of yourself and let me do more for you."

"I can't ask more of you. You do so much already, and I don't want to burden you with all the shit in my head. It's not fair when half of it is about another man."

"I knew what I was getting into when we met, and I can handle it."

"You shouldn't have to. I have cried on your shoulder over Garrick more times than I can count. I hate myself for being back here and for putting you through this."

"Stop." He tilts my chin up with one finger. "Stop taking on this extra stress. Let me carry some of it."

"How do we do this, Beck? I don't know how to navigate it, and I'm already failing so bad."

"We take it one step at a time. One day at a time. And we do it together."

Tears spill out of my eyes. "I am not worthy of you, and you're a god among men. Or maybe an angel."

"I prefer god." His lips twitch.

I snort out a laugh.

"Stop pushing me away." The hint of a smile is gone, replaced with pain.

"I'm not doing it purposely."

"I know. You have a self-destruct button you're pressing without even realizing it."

"How do I stop pressing it?"

"Let me love you. Let me protect you. Let me help you through this."

"I'll try," I say, palming his cheek. "You're too good for me."

"I'm perfect for you, and you're perfect for me." He kisses me passionately, stroking the sides of my body through my tank top. His lips glide to my neck, and he sucks softly on the sensitive skin just under my ear, eliciting a rake of shivers all over my flesh. "Let me make love to you," he whispers, nudging my earlobe with his nose. "We have the house to ourselves. Let me remind you of how good we are together." He crawls over me, propping himself up on his elbows. "Let me make you feel good. Let me show you my love."

I cry through tears as I reach up and kiss him. "I love you. Make love to me, Beck."

There is no flinching this time, only heartfelt emotion as he carefully strips me out of my clothes before getting rid of his own. When he slowly pushes inside me, maintaining eye contact as he thrusts in and out, I cling to his powerful body, reacquainting myself with all the dips and curves of his physique as he worships me with tender loving care. Adoring kisses and feather-soft caresses are shared as we reconnect, and he's never made such sweet love to me before.

It's everything I didn't know I needed.

When we come together, collapsing in a tangled heap of sweaty limbs, I feel like everything will be all right as long as we don't lose sight of one another.

Chapter Forty-One

Stevie

Garrick asks to see me again, almost one month after our first reunion meeting, on the day of the second anniversary of the accident. I'm presuming he knows the significance of the date and asking to see me today is on purpose. Beck was nervous about the meeting, but he'd never stop me. It was my call, and I didn't see how I could decline given the occasion.

Things are better with Beck since my meltdown and our subsequent lovemaking at Mom's. I have spoken with Ramona several more times, and the medication is helping. I am making an effort to eat, hydrate, and exercise. I go walking every day with Hadley or work out with Beck at the gym. I don't flinch when my boyfriend touches me, and we're making love every day, both of us keen to maintain the intimacy and fight for our relationship. The only times I truly feel like myself are when I'm wrapped in Beck's protective arms or when he's driving his cock inside me and staring deep into my eyes like he's staring straight into my soul.

Garrick is always hovering in the air like a thundercloud. It feels wrong to call him that. Like he's some dark menace, but I can't deny he is a very real threat to my relationship.

Hudson said Garrick's speech is much better now, so I'm hoping today we might be able to have a proper conversation. At least if I'm not in a limbo state and Garrick understands we can only be friends, it should eradicate the strain in my relationship and reduce the stress I'm feeling.

Hudson is waiting outside Ivy's house when I arrive. "Hey." His smile looks strained.

"What's wrong?" I hold the confectionary box against my chest as I frown.

"Have you spoken to Hugh or Dawn this week?"

"No. Why? What's happened?"

"Garrick has banned them from coming to visit."

My eyes almost bug out of my head. "What? Why?"

"Ivy told him about the court case, showed him the legal submissions, and he's pissed."

"Would someone please put a bullet in that woman," I snap, deliberately stating it out loud.

"Maybe we should pitch in for a hitman. Think, with his contacts, Beck might know someone?" he jokes.

"Have you talked with Garrick about this?"

"I have, but I can't talk sense into him. I was hoping maybe you could try?"

"Of course. He needs his father and his stepmom."

"He needs to get out of here."

"Yes, I agree." The familiarity of the house in North Bend and being surrounded by the natural environment he loves would surely aid his recovery. Plus, he'd get the right kind of emotional support. Something Ivy is ill-equipped to provide her son.

"I'm hanging around, but I'll be outside in the hallway. Garrick wants to speak to you in private."

"I'm assuming he knows what day it is?"

"Yes." He drags a hand through his hair. "Fair warning, his mood swings are all over the place. He might lash out, but don't take it personally. He's been grumpy with everyone."

"Thanks for the heads-up." I heft my purse higher on my shoulder and step inside the house with Hudson at my side.

The nurse exits the room when I enter, nodding before she leaves. Garrick is in a wheelchair, facing the window, with his back to me. He must have heard me come in, but he doesn't turn around. Trepidation tiptoes up my spine as I walk toward him. Acid churns in my gut, and nausea swims up my throat.

"Hey, Garrick," I say, hating the audible tremble in my voice.

Slowly, he spins around, taking his time eyeing me from head to toe. I'm glad to see him looking healthier. He appears to have put on some weight, his hair has grown out a little, and there is more color in his cheeks.

"You look pretty," he says in a voice that sounds more like him than the last time we talked. He grips his chair a little tighter, and I'm glad to see some slight muscle definition in his arms. Helena's and Garrick's hard work is starting to pay off. "Is that for my benefit or *his*?" He hisses the last word, and I visibly flinch.

"Please don't do this."

"Do what?" he asks, wheeling past me and heading toward the couch. "Hudson grabbed some coffees for us. I got you your favorite."

The rapid change in our conversation and his tone is already giving me whiplash, but I go with the flow. "That was thoughtful, thanks."

"Come sit beside me, baby." He pats a spot at the end of the couch beside his chair.

I gulp over the messy ball of emotion in my throat as I take a seat beside him, setting the box on the coffee table alongside our drinks.

"What's in the box?" Garrick asks, dazzling me with a smile, as if he hadn't just been rude.

I decide to let it go. It's not his fault if his mood swings are erratic.

"I baked you red velvet cupcakes."

His eyes light up. "You promised me you would."

"You remember?"

Turning his head from the box, he drills me with an intense look.

His eyes are more green than brown today and missing those amber flecks I used to adore. "I remember everything about *you*, Stevie, but the rest of my memories are sporadic. What do you think that means?" He flashes me a confident smile, and it takes me back in time.

But I'm not answering that. "Do the doctors think you'll get the rest of your memories back in time?"

"They don't know." The smile disappears off his face.

"Would you like to sample a cupcake?"

"Yes." His features soften. "Thank you for baking them."

"You're welcome." It didn't go down well with Beck. He didn't say anything, but he didn't have to. The look he gave me when I told him what I was doing this morning said it all. I made double the batch and left half for Beck, but I don't think it appeased him.

His jealousy is new and not something I'm used to dealing with. Especially when it comes to Garrick. But everything is different now he's alive.

I give Garrick a cupcake and place his coffee in the cupholder attached to his chair.

"So, tell me what's been going on in your life? Hudson says you still work at that company in the city."

I relax into the couch, hoping his initial grumpiness is over. I give him the CliffsNotes version of my life in the past two years, purposely steering clear of mentioning Beck. Which causes the guilt on my shoulders to extend, but there is no sense in riling Garrick up. I need to ease him into the discussion about my boyfriend.

"Wow. I have missed so much. I'm happy you found your dad's family but sad to hear about Nana."

"Thanks. I'm still struggling to accept it. Sometimes I think I hear her voice in my head, and I get a sharp pain in my chest when I realize I'm only imagining it."

He places his hand on mine. "I'm sorry I wasn't there for you."

I squirm on my seat, stuffing the last of my cupcake into my mouth so I don't have to answer.

"Want more coffee?" Garrick asks.

"I'm good."

"It's no trouble. One of the nurses will make us some," he says, pulling a cell phone out of the pocket attached to the side of his chair. "Mom has a top-of-the-line coffee machine in the kitchen. It won't be a macchiato, but it's decent. Only the best for Ivy." He rolls his eyes, and I force a fake smile. His brow puckers as he deliberates over the keypad on his phone.

"Want me to do that?"

He shakes his head. "My medical team want me to use it as much as possible so I regain dexterity in my hands, but it's hard. Sometimes I don't remember how to spell a word, or I get a pain in my fingers when typing."

"I imagine it would be worse if Helena hadn't been working on you while you were, ugh...in a coma."

His head picks up. "You can say it. *Coma*." He drags out the word. "It won't change the fact it happened by not saying it." His tone is a little snippy, but I ignore it. "Yeah, Helena's been great. She pushes me hard, but it's what I want. I need to regain muscle and strength."

"It looks like it's working." I cast another glance at his broader arms.

"Liking what you see, baby?" He waggles his brows.

Thankfully, the door opens, so I get out of having to answer.

The nurse comes in carrying a tray with two coffees. Garrick makes her take a cupcake for her and one for Hudson before she leaves.

"So, I'm guessing you know what day today is?" I tentatively ask as I sip my fresh coffee.

Garrick snorts. "Yeah. It's not like I'm ever going to forget the day my life turned to shit."

He says it with such venom, in a way that is not characteristic of the guy I knew, that I almost choke on my coffee.

Garrick pats my back until I've regained composure, but his hand lingers, making me uncomfortable. "This hair," he murmurs, threading his fingers through the soft strands, and I regret not putting it up. It wasn't a conscious decision to leave it down. It's how I normally wear it these days, but I forgot how much Garrick loves my hair. His eyes flare with heat when he lifts his gaze from my hair to my face. "Remember how I used to wrap it around my hand when I was fucking you from behind?"

Two red dots sprout on my cheeks, and he grins, reaching out to touch me. "And this blush. So pretty. It still gets me every time."

I jerk away from his touch and remove his hand from my hair. "This isn't appropriate anymore," I quietly say, hating the pain I see flashing in his eyes.

"Oh, that's right," he says, snatching his coffee from the holder and drinking from it. "I forgot that while I was in a coma, fighting for my life, you were out fucking some other guy." His hand shakes, and I can only watch in horror as the cup falls from his fingers, spilling hot coffee all over his legs.

"Oh fuck." I hop up, frantically looking around the large room for a towel or a cloth or something to mop up the hot liquid. "Let me call someone."

"Why?" He looks at his sodden jeans and the coffee spilling down his legs and onto the floor before lifting sad eyes to me. "There's no panic. It's not like I can feel anything."

Tears threaten as my chest tightens, and I'm speechless for a moment until I get a grip. "Your skin can still burn even through jeans. You need to call the nurse."

I step outside, while the nurse attends to Garrick, sitting on the bench in the hall with Hudson with a heavy heart and pain rattling around my skull.

"How bad is it?" he asks, a few minutes later, and I know he's not talking about the hot coffee debacle.

"Bad." I swallow thickly. "He seems normal, happy one minute, and then it's like a switch flips, and he's angry."

"Yeah. He's experiencing the full gamut of emotions."

"Is it any wonder after what you've put him through," Ivy says, materializing at the end of the hallway.

I ignore her. I don't have the energy to battle the bitch today, and I won't argue with his mother and upset Garrick any more than he is. Hudson glares at her over my shoulder, and she thankfully disappears back to whatever dark hole she crawled out from.

"She'd love to ban me too, but Garrick won't entertain it." He sips his coffee. "Here's hoping I don't piss him off one day. My biggest fear is he gets isolated in this house with that cunt."

"I haven't gotten an opportunity to talk about Hugh or Dawn, and I'm not sure it's wise to touch the subject when he's so volatile."

"I know what you mean, but they're devastated. Hugh drove John and Jacob over to see him a few days ago, and it killed him not being able to come inside. He doesn't want the twins to know or give them any reason to be angry with Garrick, so he told them he had a cold and couldn't be around Garrick in case he got an infection. There's only so long excuses like that will hold up."

I think of all the times Hugh has gone to bat for me, and it's a no-brainer. "I'll talk to him," I say as the door opens and the nurse pops out.

"He's all cleaned up and asking for you," she says, patting my shoulder. "I know his mood swings are tough, but it won't last forever. Most coma patients are not themselves for a while. He's dealing with a lot more than just the physical effects of the accident."

"I know. It's a lot to wake up to." I keep those sentiments in mind when I reenter the room.

Relief is evident on his face when he sees me. "I was worried you'd left."

"I wouldn't leave without saying goodbye."

"You did already," he retorts, and if it didn't hurt so much, I'd be impressed at how quickly he came back at me. "Shit. I'm sorry." He holds out his hand. "Forgive me, sunshine. I know that wasn't your doing."

"You don't need to apologize. None of this is your fault." I sit back down beside him and take his offered hand.

"It's so fucking hard." His voice cracks, and anguish paints his face as he eyeballs me, shielding nothing. His fingers thread through mine. "It's like I went for a big sleep and woke up two years later, and everything is different. I've lost the girl I love. I'm stuck in a wheelchair for the rest of my life, and my father, the man I have always looked up to..." He sobs. "He gave up on me. He was willing to pull the plug and watch me die."

"Garrick, no." I take both his hands in mine and lean closer. "Your father did it because he loves you. He was worried about the long-term risks of you being on life support, and he was hopeful you might breathe by yourself and it might trigger you to wake." I smile through harrowing emotion and squeeze his hands. "But it wasn't needed because you woke up all by yourself."

"Imagine he had convinced Mom to agree? Imagine he had shut off the ventilator before that happened and I died? He would have killed me, Stevie, and I can't forgive him for it."

"Could you not try? Your dad visited you every single day. He was by your side as much as he could be. He loves you, and he was devastated. He hated seeing you in that condition, and he only had your best interests at heart."

"That's not how it seems to me."

I switch tack. "Everything happened the way it did for a reason. It was fate, right?"

His lips pull into a sneer. "Fate is bullshit. You were right all along."

"I might be willing to concede I was wrong because you waking up is a miracle, Garrick. It's so rare, but you did it. If that isn't fate at work, I don't know what is."

"This is why I need you," he whispers with tears running down his face. "I cannot do this without you, Stevie. It's so daunting. Everything I have to do to try to get my life back on track scares the shit out of me."

"I'm here for you, Garrick. I promise."

"What about your boyfriend?" His face contorts into a nasty grimace I have never seen on his face before.

"Beck is still my boyfriend, and that's not going to change." He tries to wrench his hand away, but I don't let him. "Listen to me, please. It doesn't mean we can't be friends. We were friends first." I rub my fingers over the ink on his wrist and then on my own. "The day we got these, we said we'd always love and protect one another, and I haven't forgotten."

Tears well in his eyes as he fingers the charm bracelet on my wrist. "Did he buy you this?"

I had considered removing it before I came, but I never take it off, and it would be a betrayal to Beck to do so even if he were never to know. "Yes." I show him the guitar charm. "This one is for you. Beck has always been considerate of my feelings for you."

"Before or after he stole you from me?"

"It wasn't like that." I unlink our hands and tuck mine between my knees.

"It looks like that from where I'm sitting." His cold tone matches his expression.

"I never set out to fall in love with anyone else, but it happened. I can't lie about my feelings, Garrick. I could never be that dishonest with you. I am so sorry I'm not here as your girlfriend anymore. I understand if you don't want to see me again. I never want to cause you pain, and I do love you, a part of me always will, but I love you as a friend. It can't be more."

"You owe me, Stevie."

His words send a chill down my spine.

"If you'd just test-driven the BMW that day, I wouldn't be sitting here in a fucking wheelchair." He grips my hand. "Please, baby. Please don't abandon me. I'll lose the will to live without you. I don't want to go on if you're not in my life."

Pain lashes me everywhere as if I've just been flayed alive. "Garrick, I—"

"Just don't leave me, Stevie." Desperation is written all over his face. "I'm begging you. I'll take you as a friend if that's all you can offer me. Just don't leave. I cannot do this without you."

Chapter Forty-Two

Beck

"You look like shit," Law says when he answers his front door to me.

"Matches how I feel on the inside," I reply, brushing past him into the hallway of the home he shares with his wife and daughter. They are away this weekend, visiting Jenny's parents, so Law has the house to himself. I thrust a six-pack of beer at my buddy's chest.

"No Macallan?" He arches a brow as he shoves the door closed with his bare foot.

"I'd be liable to drink the entire bottle, and my liver wouldn't thank me." I head toward the large family kitchen.

"I'm out on the deck," Law says, stopping in the kitchen to deposit my beers in the fridge, while I head out through the open double doors onto their wide deck.

I flop onto a chair around their circular table, admiring the colorful flowerbeds and shrubs Stevie helped Jenny to plant. "Garden looks good, man," I say when Law appears carrying two beers and a large bag of chips.

"The girls did an awesome job." He hands me a cold beer.

"They did." I swallow a healthy mouthful of beer as my buddy sits beside me.

"I'm here if you want to off-load," he says after a few minutes of companionable silence.

"I'm losing her, Law." Pain claws at my throat as I articulate my biggest fear.

"I thought things seemed strained between you at her birthday dinner."

"They are. We're having sex. Lots of it, but I think she's using it to paper over the cracks that are appearing."

"It's a shit situation, Beck, and I was afraid of this."

"We agreed to be honest with one another, and we're both trying. She tells me everything, and I tell her how it makes me feel. But it means we are arguing all the time because I don't agree with how she's letting him manipulate her, and she thinks I'm being selfish and unfair. My relationship is falling apart because of him, and I hate it."

I swig more of my beer, and it tastes extra bitter gliding down my throat. I throw my feet up on an empty chair. "For the past month, she has visited him every day because he guilts her into it. He calls and texts at inconvenient times and expects her to just drop everything for him." I rip through the label on my bottle and grind my teeth to my molars. "He gave her an expensive locket for her birthday. Probably because he noticed she isn't wearing the other one he bought her." I drain the rest of my beer and barely resist the urge to fling my bottle at the wall.

I glance sideways at my buddy. "He fucking inscribed it with a romantic message, and he's insisting she wears it every time she visits."

"And Stevie is just going along with this?" Disbelief is transparent on Law's face.

"She's afraid to do anything that might set him off. Emotional turmoil and mood swings are common side effects from brain trauma, so she's treading on eggshells. Hudson came to see me, to tell me he's watching out for her and to explain that Garrick is not acting like himself. I appreciated the gesture, but how the fuck am I supposed to deal with this? I'm a mess. I can't even find sanctuary in my writing. I sit at my desk and stare at a blank screen for hours on end. I don't sleep well because I'm constantly worrying about her. I'm the one holding my girlfriend at night while she internalizes a ton of guilt and pain, and I don't know what to do about it."

"You have more patience than me, man."

"My patience is threadbare at this point." I eyeball my friend. "Do you think God will strike me down for visualizing punching a man in a wheelchair? Because I dream about knocking Garrick the fuck out at least once a day."

"You need more beer." Law hops up, returning with a fresh beer for me.

I immediately lift it to my lips and drink greedily.

"Maybe you should go and talk to him. Man to man."

"I have considered it," I admit in between gulps. "But after he threw a hissy fit when he discovered I was Byron Stanley and he ripped the inscription from the book Stevie had been saving for him, I decided it was probably wise to steer clear of the guy."

"Shit. That must have upset her."

A muscle pops in my jaw as I recall that day last week. "He threw the book across the room and screamed at her."

"Now I'm having visions of punching him."

"She was a mess when she came home. Sobbing against my shoulder for hours. I begged her to walk away, but she says she can't."

"I know it's already been established I'm shit at offering advice, but can I tell you what I think I'd do if I was in your shoes?"

"Go for it. I'm at a loss what to do. All I know is if we keep going like this we're not going to have anything left to salvage of our relationship."

"I say *think* because no one knows how they will react until faced with a situation, but if it was me and Jenny, I would walk away."

I open my mouth to tell him he should get a Razzie for worst advice in the history of the planet, but he holds up one palm, stalling me, so I clamp my lips shut.

"You said it yourself; if it continues like this, your relationship will be ruined. But she's not going to walk away, and I understand that, dude. I can see it from her perspective as well as yours. Stevie has a big heart, and she feels things deeply. As long as Garrick is saying he needs her, she's not going to abandon him, and I'm not sure she should. That could hammer the final nail in the coffin of your relationship anyway."

"What are you saying?" I tip more beer into my mouth.

Law sits up straighter and leans his elbows on the table as he looks at me. "Stevie loves you, man. I don't think that will change. I don't think she loves Garrick or that she ever loved him like she loves you, but who knows?" He shrugs. "I gave up trying to figure out the female brain a long time ago."

"You're right," I say. "You're so shit at this."

He shoves his middle finger up. "Let me finish. I think you need to walk away to save your relationship. If she's going to fall in love with Garrick again, it will happen whether you want it to or not. You can't stop these things. Just like if she's always going to love you, you walking away won't change that. Except this way, you protect yourself. It's impacting your health and your work and maybe, just maybe, the best thing you can do for the woman you love is to give her space to figure out what she wants by herself."

As much shit as I gave Law on Friday, I haven't been able to stop thinking about what he said. The thought of walking away from Stevie kills me, but what if my buddy is right? What if setting her free is the best way to ensure she comes back to me? I don't know. I just know I can't take much more of this.

On Thursday afternoon, I return to the apartment after a trip to the grocery store to find Stevie curled up in a ball in the living room, on the floor, crying her eyes out.

I dump the grocery bags in the hall and rush to her side, dropping to my knees beside her quivering form. "Honey, I'm here. What happened?"

Anguished howls tear from her throat, and it's the kind of sound that destroys my battered heart. I have never heard such heartfelt pain.

"Beck," she gasps, letting me lift her into my arms. Choking sobs echo in the room as she clings to me and cries. Her pain is visceral, and it's killing me inside. I rock her in my arms, holding her tight and pressing kisses into her hair as she purges her grief.

After a while, the sobs subside, and I carry her to the couch. Silently, I pass her some tissues, watching as she blows her nose and rubs at her red-rimmed eyes. Maybe I should take a picture of her like this and show the asshole what he's doing to her because I don't need her to say anything to know he is behind this latest meltdown.

"What did he do?" I ask when she has fully calmed down. I brush damp strands of hair behind her ears.

"You're going to be so angry," she whispers, and my heart stutters in my chest.

"What did he do?" I ask again in a much harsher tone.

"He kissed me."

Her words light a fuse inside me, and all I see is red. How fucking dare he touch her against her will! Fuck punching the prick. I'll fucking put him back in a coma where he should have stayed.

I don't even feel bad for thinking something so hideous.

I'm that angry.

Her lower lip wobbles. "I didn't consent or kiss him back. He surprised me, and then he was upset when I broke away from him and told him he couldn't do that."

"Enough is enough," I say through clenched teeth. "You're not visiting him again. You call him and tell him you can't be friends."

"What?" Her eyes probe mine. "You can't be serious?"

I bark out a bitter laugh. "Do I look like I'm fucking joking, Stevie?"

She scrambles off my lap. "What he did is terrible and very wrong, but he didn't really mean it."

Another bitter laugh rumbles from my chest. "Don't be naïve, Stevie. Of course, he meant it." I stand and pace the floor. "Everything he has done this past month shows his friendship pact is a load of bull. He's trying to win you back. It's obvious to everyone but you!"

"Don't you dare raise your voice to me, Beck." She rises to her feet, leveling me with a sharp look. "And you can't make demands of me."

"Why the hell not?" I roar, losing the tenuous hold on my control. "He makes them all the damn time, and you drop everything to comply."

"You know why!"

"He is emotionally blackmailing you, Stevie, and I'm not okay with it. I cannot stand by and watch this happen anymore. I cannot be the one to pick up the pieces when you fall apart because he's said something cruel or lashed out at you again."

"He's not like that all the time, and he can't help it."

"Of course, you'd defend him. He can do or say what he wants, and you will always forgive him. I can't fucking win." I drag my nails through my hair as a wave of defeat crashes into me. "I can't do this anymore, Stevie. I can't share you with him. It's killing me and destroying our relationship."

Panic flares in her eyes. "What exactly are you saying, Beck?"

The words linger at the back of my throat, and I stop for a second to consider if it's right to let them loose, deciding it is. I think Law was right after all, and this is the only way. "You need to choose. It's him or me."

She stumbles, tipping back onto the couch with tears in her eyes. "What? No! Please, Beck. Don't make me do this."

"I don't have a choice anymore, Stevie, and I'm doing this for you." All the anger and fight has left me. I walk to the couch, sitting at the opposite end to my girlfriend. "This is the best way I can protect myself, and you, and our relationship. If we continue like this, we'll ruin everything." Tears stream down her face, and I hate seeing them, knowing I'm the reason for them this time. My arms twitch with a craving to comfort her, but I don't act on the feeling. I'm enabling this behavior, and the best thing I can do for Stevie is to force the issue. Otherwise, this will continue, and she can't see it, but Garrick is fucking with her head and her sanity. I can't hold her together any longer. Not when I'm losing it too.

"Please don't do this, Beck. I'm begging you."

"It's for your own good, Stevie."

"I can't abandon him," she whispers. "What if he dies?"

"It's been over two months, and the prognosis is good. I'm sure he'll be fine."

"You don't know that. If I abandon him, it could set his recovery back, or he might do something rash. How could I live with myself if I walked away and something happened to him?"

"What about me?" I snap. "What about what this is doing to me, or don't I matter at all now your first love is back?"

Shock splays across her face, quickly transforming into anger. "I can't believe you just said that. I have been brutally honest with you, Beck, because you asked me to tell you everything. I am doing the best I can! I am trying to make time for both of you, and it's like being pulled in two vastly different directions, and it's fucking killing me!"

"Do you love me?" I calmly ask.

"You know I do! I love you more than I can say, and I don't want to lose you."

"I'm sorry to do this, honey. I really am, but I need you to do this for us. I need you to choose *me*."

She scoots down beside me and takes my hands, pinning me with pleading eyes. "Please, Beck, don't make me do this. I love you, and I know this has been difficult for you. Just give me a few more months until he's stronger, and then I'll walk away."

Sadness washes over me. "That won't happen, and we both know it. In a few months, there will be some other excuse, and I can't live like this watching you drop everything for him. It hurts me, Stevie." I wrench my hand back and thump a fist over my heart. "It hurts so much."

"I'm sorry." She buries her face in her hands, and that urge to comfort her rides me hard, but I fight it.

A strange numb feeling flows through my veins, and I don't even sound like myself when I speak. "I'm doing this for both of us. This is destroying you. I can't watch you go through this anymore. Tell him you can't see him again, and let's go to France for a couple of months."

"I've got a job," she feebly protests.

"A job you're going to get fired from if you keep taking time off and calling in sick every time he says he needs you."

Look at today. She's home at a time when she should be at the office. I hate she is throwing everything away for him, and I hate him for doing this to her.

It's not like I don't have some sympathy for him, despite my earlier angry words. I do. I can't imagine what it was like to wake from a coma and find out the girl you still loved was now in love with someone else. That is rough. But the way he's treating her and trying to sabotage her relationship is not cool, and I've lost a lot of respect for Garrick Allen. Even if it is as Stevie claims and he can't help his emotional outbursts and uncharacteristic actions. He still knows what he is doing. He knows he is not treating her right.

"I owe him," she quietly says.

"You don't fucking owe him anything. You have sacrificed enough for him, Stevie. No one could have done more for him, but it's time to prioritize yourself and to prioritize us. It's time to walk away from him."

"I can't," she sobs.

"I'll give you a week to think about it." My voice sounds so cold, but I can't help how I'm feeling. "It's probably best if you went back to your place."

"Beck, don't do this."

"I love you, Stevie, but I can't continue like this any longer. I'm sorry."

I'm tempted to sink into a bottle of Macallan and not resurface for a week, but I've got to get a grip. It's been four days since I issued Stevie an ultimatum, and I am already missing her so much. She's left me a ton of teary messages and sent heartfelt texts, and I've nearly buckled so many times, but then we'll just end up back in the same awful place. I have spells where I regret what I said and I pick up the phone to tell her I didn't mean it and to come home, but I never go through with it. Deep down, I know I've done the right thing even if it doesn't feel like it. Even if she doesn't understand, and some days, I don't either.

Hadley shows up on day five.

"You've lost your mind," she says, pacing the floor of my living room. "It's the only conclusion that makes sense."

"It feels like it some days," I truthfully admit, leaning against the wall with my hands in the pockets of my shorts.

"Don't do it. Don't go through with it." She stops in front of me. "This isn't you. I know you didn't mean it."

"I did. I do," I say even if I've had my doubts. "We can't continue like this." I rub at my sore temples. "My heart is broken, Hadley. She's slipping through my fingers, and I'll lose her anyway unless something changes."

"I'm not disagreeing, but this isn't the right way."

"I can't compete with him. He has this hold over her, and nothing I say will break it. I think I've always known it would come to this if he woke up. How do I compete with a guy in a wheelchair? A guy who is facing a long road to recovery? Stevie's savior complex will never let her walk away from him."

"It might seem like that now, but it won't be forever."

"He's not going to stop until he wins her back."

"She doesn't love him anymore."

"I wonder how long it'll take her to fall back in love with him once I'm out of the picture."

Hadley narrows her eyes and jabs her finger in my chest. "That is low, Beck, and way out of line. This is the wrong course of action, and you're making a big mistake. She won't betray you with him. I know my best friend, and she won't. You're her ride or die, Beck. You're the one she loves."

"Then she needs to pick me. If I mean that much to her, she needs to put me, put *us*, first."

"She isn't thinking clearly right now, Beck. She's all messed up and drowning in guilt all over again. I know it's unfair to you, but would you not reconsider and give it a little more time?"

"Prioritizing my mental health and that of the woman I love is what's important right now. I am doing this for Stevie and for the sake of our relationship."

She releases a shuddering breath. "She is trying to do the right thing. She wants to help Garrick get back on his feet, and then she'll walk away. By then, he'll realize he can't win back someone who has already moved on."

"I cannot share her any longer, Hadley. I cannot do *nothing* while she systematically unravels herself and our relationship one brick at a time."

"She'll fall to pieces without you. Her heart is already so fragile, and this will send her over the edge. Please don't do this."

Her words dig the knife in deeper, but she just doesn't get it. "I have to. It's the only way we stand any chance of a future together."

She plants her hands on her hips and glares at me. "So, you're just going to walk away without a fight?"

"This *is* me fighting, goddamn it!" I bark, pushing off the wall. "I will never stop fighting for her! She's my ride or die too, and it will always be her for me. If Stevie won't make the call, I'll make it for her.

She's tearing herself apart trying to please both of us, and one of us has to be man enough to walk away."

Stevie calls me after a week of tearful calls and messages, begging me to reconsider. When I tell her I can't, she says she can't choose. Hurt crashes into me. I suspected it would come to this, but hearing her tell me she can't prioritize us devastates me. I haven't felt this much pain since my mom died. I tell Stevie I will always love her, but I cannot do this anymore, and then I hang up.

I walk around my apartment with a sharp pain in my heart and a tightness in my chest, packing up all her stuff. When the courier arrives to collect the box, I hand it to the guy without a word. Then I crawl into bed and cry.

Chapter Forty-Three

Stevie

"I know something that'll cheer you up," Garrick says when we come back to his room after a stroll outside. Apart from that one run-in with Ivy, I haven't seen her at all, thankfully. I'm still working on Garrick, trying to convince him to forgive his dad and move to North Bend. Helena and Hudson are working on him too, and I'm confident between the three of us we will get him to change his mind. Sooner rather than later, I hope.

It's been two weeks since Beck sent me a box of my belongings and broke things off with me. I thought my heart was shattered before, but it's nothing compared to how I feel now. I am a walking zombie, and all that's left of the organ in my chest is bloody, mangled shreds. I cry myself to sleep every night, constantly second-guessing myself and wondering if I did the right thing. But how can I walk away from Garrick? I can't abandon him. I just can't. So I have no choice but to let Beck go even though it has crushed me.

"I've been practicing," Garrick says, lifting his guitar onto his lap, and my stomach lurches to my toes.

Which is really fucking mean because it's incredible he's able to do this only three months after coming out of a coma. I sit on a chair, already knowing this is going to destroy me. An ominous sense of dread washes over me as he tunes the guitar, flashes me one of his trademark smiles, dimples and all, and gets ready to play. His hair has grown long again, and he looks more like the Garrick I remember.

Nostalgia floods the room as he plucks the strings. Sadness and pain are my constant companions these days, and never more so than now. It's almost like returning to the past, seeing Garrick looking like himself, happy with a guitar on his lap as he serenades me.

He's a bit out of sync at the start, but he quickly finds his rhythm.

All the color drains from my face when he starts singing "Only Yesterday." Oh god. I think I'm going to be sick. Visions of the night I cried in Beck's arms as we danced to The Carpenters surges to the forefront of my mind, and a sob pushes out of my mouth. That night, I asked Beck to play this song for him. I wanted the words to comfort him. To let Beck know how much he had done for me. How much he had given me to live for, and it's too painful to listen to Garrick play this now for me, conveying a very different message with the same words.

"Stop! Please." Tears roll down my face as I hop up from my chair and wrap my arms around my waist.

"Baby, what's wrong?" Garrick wheels toward me with concern in his eyes and his guitar on his lap.

"I can't listen to that song." I brush the tears away, hating how much I'm still crying. I'm like one of those weak heroines you read about in books who cries at the drop of a hat. "It makes me really sad." I don't want to admit why because he's liable to fly off the handle. His erratic mood swings give me whiplash on good days, but anything Beck related brings out a cruel irrational side of his personality, so I try to avoid mentioning my ex.

"Shit." Garrick takes my wrist, rubbing the tattoo we share. "I didn't stop to think. I know you played those songs for me all the time. I didn't think how sad they would have made you."

I don't correct him.

A familiar scowl appears on his face, and I'm instantly on high alert. Garrick fingers my charm bracelet. "Why are you still wearing this?" he asks in a voice devoid of any warmth.

I snatch my hand back, fearful he'll break it because he's got an evil glint in his eyes I've grown accustomed to.

"Answer me!" he snaps, glaring at me. "Why are you still wearing his bracelet when you refuse to wear the poppy ring I gave you?"

"I wear your locket," I remind him, lifting it from my neck to confirm it.

"Then you can put my ring back on." He arches his neck to look up at me.

"I can't. It's from the past when we were together. That's not our relationship these days. I wear this locket because you gave it to me as a friend."

"Baby, you know I'm going to win you back. We started out as friends before, and it developed into more. It's going to happen again. I'm glad he's gone so we can get back on track, but you've got to lose the bracelet, Stevie. It hurts me to see it on your wrist. It's contaminating our tattoo."

I didn't plan on telling Garrick Beck and I had broken up because I knew it'd fill him with false hope. But Ivy discovered the truth, and she told him. I didn't believe it at first because surely it suited her that I had a boyfriend and was relegating her son to the friend zone? However, it seems she tried to put a self-serving spin on it. She claimed Beck had seen me for the conniving gold-digging slut I am and he'd kicked me to the curb. She told Garrick he needed to do the same. It backfired massively because it's only made Garrick more determined to win me back. And made the entire situation more stressful for me.

Even though I risk starting World War Three, I can't let that go without a response. I steel my spine and draw a brave breath. "I'm wearing it because I love him."

"He left you!" he shouts.

"Because I was hurting him. Not because we don't love one another."

"He doesn't love you like I do! I would never leave you. Never!"

"Garrick, I don't want to hurt you, but you need to forget about us as a couple. I don't love you like that anymore. I can only be your friend. I—"

I don't get any more words out before he loses it. I jump back when Garrick emits a gnarled rage-filled shout as he lifts his guitar and slams it on top of the coffee table, smashing it repeatedly until it's broken into smithereens. "Look what you made me do!" he shouts as the door swings open, and Hudson dashes into the room with one of the nurses. "This is all your fault! Just like me being stuck in this fucking chair is your fault because you never make the right decisions!" He starts beating his chest and grabbing handfuls of his hair before he purposely throws himself out of his chair, landing face-first in the broken remnants of his most treasured guitar.

I'm too shocked and scared to cry as Hudson lifts me away from the mess while Garrick screams obscenities at me as the nurse calls for more help.

"Jesus Christ. What happened?" Hudson asks, dragging me from the room as Garrick's rage subsides and he starts crying. Two more nurses and the doctor rush past us into the room.

"I think Beck was right," I say in a bit of a daze. "I think I'm doing more harm than good."

"It was just a bad day," Hudson says. "Ivy was in his ear this morning spewing more venom. She got him all riled up."

"Look at him, Hudson." I remove his arms from around me when we reach the doorway, turning to watch the medical team help Garrick up. Blood is seeping from cuts on his face, and his shoulders are shaking as tears roll over his cheeks. "Look at what he did to himself."

"We need to get him out of here."

"Stevie!" Garrick cries, thrashing against the team as they lift him toward his bed. "I'm sorry! Don't leave me. Please."

These kinds of sentiments ordinarily work but not today. I'm drained, and I can't be here a second longer. "I need to go." Sympathy splays on Hudson's face. "Will you stay with him?"

"Of course." He presses a kiss to my brow. "Go. Take some time out. I'll look after him."

When I get back to the city, I go for a walk, and my feet take me to Capitol Hill and Beck's apartment. I didn't set out to come here, but now that I am here, I don't know whether to turn around and go home or show up at his door.

I guess I'm supremely selfish these days because I can't force myself to leave, and a few minutes later, I'm standing at Beck's door with my heart pounding and butterflies skating across my chest. I rest my palm on the door and close my eyes, trawling through the memory bank in my head, remembering all our happy times. I love Beck so much. I miss him so much. And I think I made a terrible mistake.

No, I don't just think it. I *know* it.

Beck needed me too, and I failed him. I was a horrible girlfriend to him in the end, and I won't ever forgive myself for letting him down.

I rap on the door three times, wishing I hadn't mailed my key to him in a moment of anger. I have no clue what I'm going to say to him, but I've got to make this right. I cannot live without him. He's my entire world, and I'm self destructing without him.

He doesn't come to the door, so I continue knocking until my knuckles are red and stinging. The elevator pings behind me, and I swing around, hope and expectation swirling through my veins as the doors glide open. My chest deflates when a portly middle-aged man with a bushy gray mustache steps out into the hallway. "Hey, Mr. Hynes."

"Why, hello there, young Stevie." He smiles before looking over my head at Beck's door.

"I was looking for Beck, but he doesn't seem to be home." I hide my red knuckles behind my back so he doesn't see the evidence of my desperation.

"He didn't tell you?" His expression softens into pity.

"Tell me what?" Blood rushes to my head, and knots form in my stomach.

"He's gone, my dear. Overseas, I believe."

"It's July. He always visits his grandparents in France in July," I say in a relieved tone. However, it's short-lived.

Mr. Hynes shakes his head. "I don't think he's in France. I met him the day he moved out and he had a lot of luggage. He said he wasn't sure when he'd be back or if he'd be back at all."

I clutch the wall so my legs don't go out from under me. It takes every ounce of acting ability to keep from bursting into tears in front of Beck's elderly neighbor. "Oh, I see. Well, he must've forgotten to tell me. I could have saved myself a wasted journey." A brittle high-pitched laugh flees my mouth, and I inwardly cringe. "I'm going to head home now. You have a great rest of the day, Mr. Hynes."

"You too, honey. Take care."

I make the journey home on autopilot, not even aware of my surroundings because I spend the fifteen-minute walk repeatedly calling Beck's number only to be greeted with a disconnected tone.

When I get to our apartment, I'm grateful Hadley is out with Mike tonight so she can't bear witness to my breakdown. I crawl under the covers in my clothes, shivering even though it's the middle of summer and our apartment is like a furnace, because I'm chilled to the bone, and heartsick doesn't even come close to describing how I feel.

Beck either changed his number or he blocked mine.

Either way, the message is clear.

He has moved out and left me no way to contact him.

It really is over between us.

He is gone, and he doesn't want me to find him.

Chapter Forty-Four

Stevie

The rest of the summer passes in a blur. I'm barely functioning, and I count it a win if I can get up in the morning. I wish I could speak with Ramona daily because she helps to keep me somewhat sane. But I won't be attending any more therapy sessions for a while. At least, not until I get a new job.

With nothing better to do, I drive over to Medina to see Garrick. I don't usually drop by in the mornings, so he's not expecting me. The unfamiliar sound of Garrick's laughter filters into the hallway when I arrive, and I frown. I haven't heard him laugh like that since before the accident. His door is partway open when I reach it, and I peek through the gap, watching him and Helena cracking up laughing.

"What's so funny?" I ask as I step into the room.

"Lena was just telling me about this guy she went on a date with last weekend, and it's too fucking funny." Garrick cracks up again, his face awash with pure joy.

"If I wasn't rushing to my next appointment, I'd give you the uncensored version." She winks at me as she hefts a large backpack onto her shoulder. "Trust me when I say never go out on a date with any guy named Boris Yatizi. If you see him on a dating app swipe past real quick!"

"Stevie doesn't need to worry about dating apps," Garrick says, instantly losing his good humor. "The only dates she'll be going on are with me."

I force a strained smile. It's been months of this bullshit, and I'm at the end of my tether. "Garrick, don't start this crap again. I'm really not in the mood today."

"I've got to go," Helena says, clearly detecting the tension between us. She strides speedily toward the door. "Keep up the exercises, Rick!" she calls out over her shoulder. "Take care, Stevie," she adds, waving at me before she disappears.

"Rick and Lena?" I say, quirking a brow. "You two seem cozy."

"Jealous?" He grins, wheeling toward me.

"Of course not. You should date Helena. She's awesome."

"I don't want to fucking date Helena," he snaps. "You know I only want you. How long are you going to keep up this friends charade?"

"For fuck's sake, Garrick." I throw my hands in the air. "How many times do I have to tell you it's not a charade?"

"You're so grumpy these days, Stevie. You really need to lighten up. Or get laid." He drills me with a look, and his lips curve at the corners. "I could help with that." He grabs his dick through his jeans. "I've been talking to Dr. Mann about sex, and it's encouraging. There's no reason why I can't get an erection with the right stimulation, and while I can't control my cock to direct it inside you, you can ride me." His eyes darken with lust. "Maybe that's what we need to get things back on track."

I'm sure my mouth is trailing the ground. He cannot seriously be suggesting this? Has nothing I've said these past months sunk in at all?

"Or we can just be friends with benefits for now." He starts unzipping his jeans as he blatantly stares at my chest. "I bet if I just imagine sucking your tits I'll get hard. Or I can replay one of our memories in my mind. We were so hot together. Remember that time—"

"Stop, Garrick. Please."

"Why? You're single. I'm single, and I really want to have sex, Stevie. You're miserable as fuck, and you know this will cheer you up."

I work hard to be sensitive. "Garrick, having sex again has got to be a big deal for you. You should wait for the right woman."

"You are the right woman!" he yells. He wheels toward me, and I jump back before he tramples my toes. "Don't try and sugarcoat this when we both know what it is."

"Friends with benefits would be a bad idea, Garrick." And there's no way I would ever entertain the idea. I'm in love with Beck. The thought of being with any other man makes me ill. The only man I want is Beck. "I'm thinking of you," I say, which isn't a lie. It's just not the full truth.

"You're such a hypocrite! You don't want to fuck the cripple! At least be fucking honest about it!"

"No, Garrick. No." I bend down so I'm looking directly into his angry hurt face. "That is not it at all. You're still a beautiful, sexy, desirable man, Garrick. Any woman would be lucky to be with you."

"Not any woman," he snaps, but it lacks bite.

"I think this was a mistake, Garrick. I only seem to make you angry, and you make me sad. I'm not sure we're good for one another at all."

Panic flares in his eyes, and he grabs my hands. "I'm sorry, Stevie. I'm so sorry. It was inappropriate and selfish when you've made your feelings clear. I just love you so much, but I know I need to get over it. But please don't abandon me. You're all I've got. I can't lose you."

"I'm not all you've got, Garrick. You have other people who love you. Like your father and Dawn and the twins. Like Hudson and Helena, and I hear Will and Ellen paid you a visit."

"I'll move back to North Bend," he blurts. "It's this house. Mom has been a bitch to you, and I know it must be hard coming here. I'll move back home, and everything will be easier then."

"I think you should move back home, but don't do it for the wrong reasons."

"Don't leave me, Stevie. Please." It's hard to deny Garrick anything when he looks at me with those big hazel eyes and so much longing on his face.

I lean in and hug him. His arms go around me, and he holds me close.

Some days, I wish I did feel the same way about him because it would make these visits easier. This isn't the first day he's accused me of not being with him because he's in a wheelchair, and that guts me the most. I don't see the chair when I look at him. I see the man. If I still loved him, I would be with him as his lover and his life partner, chair or no chair. I would never walk away from him because he's paralyzed. I am not that kind of woman.

I am not with Garrick now because I don't love him in that way anymore. I would never admit it to his face because it would be cruel to do so, but the love I shared with Garrick pales in comparison to the love I shared with Beck. Now I know what it's like to love and be loved like that, I cannot go back. I cannot force myself to feel things for Garrick I no longer feel.

It would be easier for everyone, in a way, if I did, but I don't.

I can't spell it out like that to him because I could never be that selfish or hurtful.

I ruffle his hair before pulling away. He tries to cling to me, but I don't let him even though it tears strips off my heart to not give him the things he clearly craves. "I do love you, Garrick. I wish it was in the way you want, but I won't lie to you. I care about you so much. Your happiness means everything to me, but you can't rely on me for it."

"I wish I had a time machine," he says in a sad voice. "I wish I could rewind time and go back and do everything differently."

"We can't look back, Garrick. Only forward."

"I'm trying." He squeezes my hand.

"You're doing amazing, and you have to remember how far you've come."

He nods, and we are quiet for a bit. "How come you're here?" he asks as if just realizing it's early for me to visit.

"I got fired," I admit, flopping onto the couch.

"Your boss is a bitch."

"She's really not. I would have fired me a long time ago."

I have been distracted and absent for months. My boss has been more than patient and fair. It's why I didn't even attempt to protest earlier when she told me to pack up my stuff. I should be upset, but I can't find it in myself to care, which is a common theme with me these days. Life is dull and bleak and lonely without Beck. I hope, wherever he is, he's doing better than me. At least one of us deserves to be happy.

"I think we should focus on the positives."

I arch a brow. "Such as?"

"You have more time to spend with me." His dimples make an appearance, and I can't help but smile.

"Not really, but it's a nice thought. I'll have to start job hunting immediately."

"Whatever for?" His brow scrunches, and I crank out a laugh.

"For money, Garrick. I have rent to pay and utility bills." And a therapist I need to keep on speed dial.

"You're being ridiculous. I have enough money to support us." He takes my hand and lifts it to his lips. "I've got you covered, babe."

I sigh, wondering what else I can do to get through to him because he can't keep deluding himself. We aren't a couple anymore, and we won't ever be again. I just wish I knew how to get that message across because he's not listening to me, and I can't do this for much longer.

Chapter Forty-Five

Stevie

Something resembling pleasure tugs the corners of my lips as I pass the sign for North Bend. I'm reluctant to call it happiness because I've forgotten what that feels like. I'm glad Garrick is at his father's place now, and I hope it will help improve his mood. The past month, while we waited for arrangements to be made to relocate Garrick and get the power of attorney overruled, have been stressful to say the least. Thankfully, he hasn't brought up sex or the whole friends with benefits suggestion again, but he's not happy I'm job hunting, and he continues referring to things as if we're still a couple.

I broke into my savings account to go see Ramona. Mom and Hadley have been pushing me to start breaking away from Garrick, and they think this is the perfect opportunity because he's in a supportive environment now, and his dad and Dawn will take good care of him.

Ramona agrees. She's worried because my moods are still dark, I'm not sleeping great, and my weight has dropped again. I'm just finding it hard to care about much these days. It's been over four months since I last saw Beck, and I miss him so much. I'm only a shell of the person I used to be without the other half of my heart and soul. I miss the life we shared, and I wish I could go back and pick him.

There. I said it.

The queen of selfishness is back in the house.

I was a fool, and I lost the best thing to ever happen to me. Beck was right to give me an ultimatum, and I should have chosen him. I wanted to, but that doesn't count. I'm sure he feels like I abandoned him when he needed me, but it wasn't the truth. I just didn't see, at the time, how I could walk away from Garrick, but I should have.

It would have been best for everyone.

Hadley wants me to fight for him, but how do you fight for someone who no longer wants you? Beck didn't fight for me. He let me go, and that speaks volumes.

Ramona wants me to go back on antidepressants, but I don't want to. I was on them for six weeks for depression and anxiety; however, I'm convinced they exacerbated my anxiety and contributed to my insomnia, and I'm reluctant to try them again. Perhaps the brand didn't agree with me or I'm allergic or something because Ramona says it's rare any of her clients complain of such side effects with SSRIs. But I know how I felt on them, and it wasn't good, so I have zero desire to start taking them again. I know antidepressants help a lot of people, and I'm not knocking anyone who takes them. You do you, blah, blah. But they're not the solution for me.

Now, I veer between bouts of insomnia and nights where I sleep for ten or twelve hours without interruption. There is no norm, and I never know what kind of night I'm in for when I climb into bed. I keep sleeping pills for the bad nights when I can't switch my brain off and my thoughts linger on Beck. Those nights, I cry into my pillow with a constant pain in my heart. I'm loath to take the pills too regularly in case I become dependent. Life is plenty shit right now without being addicted to medication.

I park the Land Rover and hop out, hugging John and Jacob as they fly past and climb into their dad's truck. Hugh waves as he drives off with the twins, and I head to the front door where Dawn waits for me. "Hey, sweetie." She pulls me into a bear hug. "Come on in. How is the job hunting going?"

"Not great, but I've decided to take Mom up on her offer. I'm going to become her partner and manage the store and the farm. She's open to my new business ideas, and it'll give me something to focus on. I'm also going to move into Nana's house and start remodeling it." This is the plan Ramona and I came up with. I need to keep busy, and this way, I can also focus on properly healing because Mom and I are going to split shifts so neither of us are working full weeks. That way, she'll have time to travel to Florida to meet Sean, and I'll have time for therapy and self-love.

I wonder what my dad would think about Mom dating his younger brother. Of course, Liam isn't here to pass judgment, but I'd like to think he's happy for them. It's only early days, but I have a good feeling about this relationship. I really like Sean. I like all my dad's family though I haven't had a ton of time to spend with them.

"That's wonderful, Stevie. You need to take better care of you. I know your mom's worried about you." At one time, Mom and Dawn were close, but they've drifted apart since the accident. Mom said it was hard spending time with Dawn because she felt guilty her daughter emerged from the accident while Dawn's stepson was in a coma. And then I was with Beck, and it might have gotten awkward. They still talk occasionally, but it's not often and usually about me. Case in point.

"I'm trying. It's been hard."

"I know." She hugs me again before pulling back. "Look, I need to warn you he's not in the best of spirits."

What's new.

I immediately chastise myself for my uncharitable thought.

Sometimes it's hard to stick to the conviction Garrick still isn't himself because he doesn't seem to get as angry or lash out as much at Hudson, and he is all smiles for Helena. Ramona asked me if I think he's punishing me for the accident, and the more I think about it, the more I think he is. I don't think it's a conscious thing. Garrick was never cruel. He was always so kind and thoughtful, so I don't think he's doing it on purpose. And honestly, I don't blame him.

It's why I think it's best if I start gradually breaking away. This moment was always inevitable. He needs to live his life independently of me, and I can't fully heal until I break ties. These past few months have proven we can't be friends. It's making both of us miserable. I just need to convince Garrick this is the right move, and that won't be easy.

"Sorry, I got sidetracked," I say when I come out of my head and realize Dawn has been talking to me. "You said he's not in the best of moods. Did something happen?"

"It looks like his bed got damaged during the move. He was uncomfortable last night, but instead of pressing the button for the night nurse, he tried to fix it himself, and he ended up falling out of the bed and hitting his head off the side of his bedside table. He's been checked out, and there's no serious damage, apart from a goose egg on his brow, a gash on his cheek, and a bruised ego."

"He wants to be independent, and he hates relying on others to do so much for him."

"It's been a big adjustment, but we're amazed at his progress."

They haven't seen him in months, so I'm sure they've noticed big changes.

"He's doing so well," she continues, "and he needs to give himself more credit and be a little more patient."

"Hopefully, now he's home, it'll be easier."

"We will do everything in our power to ensure it."

Dawn walks me to the remodeled dining room on the ground floor which is now a luxurious suite for Garrick. It faces over the lake and mountains at the rear and it's a stunning view to wake up to.

"Let me know if you need anything," Dawn says before shutting the door and leaving me with Garrick.

He is sitting in his wheelchair staring out at the window.

"Hey," I say, dumping my purse on a table and walking toward him. "I bet it feels good to be home."

"Does it?" He lifts his head to look up at me.

"Look at that gorgeous view."

"It's torture," he says, swiveling in his chair and giving me a good look at his injured face. It's as Dawn said. He has a Band-Aid over a gash on his cheek and large bump on his brow.

"Torture?" I frown, purposely not commenting on his fall because he'll probably just shout at me.

He waves agitated hands in front of the window. "It's not like I'll ever go hiking or camping again. It's a reminder of everything I've lost. I should have stayed in Medina."

I want to tell him he's wrong. That there are ways he'll be able to enjoy a lot of the things he used to enjoy again, and he's much better off here. But I don't bother pushing it. When he's in a pissy mood, there is no convincing his stubborn mind of anything. "Maybe I should go and come back at a better time," I suggest.

"Or maybe you should just suck my dick," he snaps, glaring at me as my heart sinks. "Oh wait. You don't want to touch it, do you?" He grabs my wrist. "Well, tough luck, baby. I need cheering up. I need to blow a load, and you fucking owe me."

I yank my hand back and stumble away from him. "I'm not doing this again with you, Garrick. We already discussed it."

"You owe me, you selfish bitch!" he yells, and I clamp a hand over my mouth as he lowers his zipper and pulls his cock out. "Get on your knees, Stevie, and suck me off."

Tears well in my eyes. "Stop this, Garrick. This isn't you."

"News flash, sweetheart," he yells. "I'll never be me again! You made damn sure of that when you refused to accept the BMW. My life is ruined, and it's all because of you! Fuck you, Stevie! You don't get to walk away unscathed. You fucking did this to me, and the least you can do is suck my fucking dick!"

"That's enough," Hudson says, charging into the room. Shock splays across his face when he sees Garrick sitting there with his cock in hand and venom bleeding from his eyes.

"Stevie, sweetheart." Hudson clasps my face, but I can barely see him through my tears. "Go out to Dawn, and leave me to talk to Garrick for a few minutes."

"Just fuck off," Garrick snaps. "Unless you're going to suck my cock, you're no good to me."

"Shut your fucking face, Garrick," Hudson bellows. "Or I'll shut it for you."

"Hit guys in wheelchairs a lot, buddy?" Garrick retorts.

"There's a first time for everything, and the chair has nothing to do with it. Someone needs to knock some sense into you, and it's going to be me."

Hudson holds me close as he takes me out of the room and into the kitchen where Dawn is waiting with tears in her eyes and open arms. I fall into her embrace, and we both cry for a little bit.

"I'm so ashamed you heard that," I admit as we nurse hot sweet tea around the kitchen table while Hudson attempts to calm Garrick down.

"You have nothing to be ashamed of, sweetie. Garrick is an entirely different matter."

"He can't help it."

"Yes, he can." Dawn splits a cookie in two and passes half to me. "How long has he been speaking to you like that?"

I shrug, not wanting to rat him out.

"I want the truth."

"He's like Jekyll and Hyde with me," I explain, dunking the cookie in my tea before taking a bite. Dawn waits me out. "There are times when he's the Garrick I remember, and we chat about everything and anything, and it's normal. It feels like we're true friends again. Then there are the times when he's a person I don't know. He wasn't like that before the accident. He gets angry quickly, and he has a tendency to blame me for everything, and it's okay because it is my fault."

"No, no, no, Stevie." She shakes her head as tears pool in her eyes. "It is not your fault, sweet girl. I would not be surprised if Ivy has been filling him with nonsense about the accident."

"She hates me, and we all know she never has anything good to say about me. But why would Garrick listen to her?"

"Anyone with a traumatic brain injury can easily have confabulation. We spoke with Dr. Mann about this last week. It's an unintentional recollection of false memories including elaborations or embellishments that can range from subtle to delusional. Ivy could easily have planted false memories during his recovery. Ivy is jealous. She resents how much Garrick loves you, and she will never stop trying to sabotage things between you. I wish we could have gotten him out of there sooner."

"I seem to only find more reasons to hate that woman."

"Tell me about it. If you knew the things she put Hugh through when they were married." Her jaw tightens, and fire blazes in her eyes.

"I'm glad he got away from her and he found you."

"He's the love of my life," she says with a dreamy smile.

We are both lost in thought for a few minutes.

"My therapist thinks Garrick is punishing me because he needs someone to blame for the accident, and I'm the obvious choice."

"That makes sense, but it doesn't make it right, and I won't allow it. Whatever is the reason for it, it ends now. Garrick is not going to treat you or anyone else in such a hurtful manner. I'm cognizant of everything he is going through, but he meets with his psychologist twice a week, and he shouldn't be acting like this still."

"Maybe it's a me thing."

"Or it's an Ivy thing. I suggested to Hugh we should replace some of the staff, and I think I'll be putting his psychologist at the top of that list."

I shrug as I sip my tea and finish my cookie. I barely tasted it.

"I'm going to say something I think you need to hear from me. No one could have sacrificed more for our son than you. You have done your best for Garrick, and we are so grateful. I hate seeing what it's done to you, and it's time you prioritized yourself, Stevie."

"What exactly are you saying?"

"It's time to let Garrick go, Stevie. He might not realize it, but he needs to let you go too."

I nod slowly. "I know. I wish I could be who he needs me to be, but I can't." A sob rips from my throat. "I'm too broken to help him."

"Oh, Stevie." She gets up and pulls me into a hug. "You're made of strong stuff, girl. You're going to be okay, and Garrick will be too."

"I love you, Dawn. I just want you to know that."

"We love you too, sweetheart." She kisses the top of my head. "There is no point in prolonging this. I think it's time to cut all ties and finally move forward with your life. You've been waiting long enough to do it."

Chapter Forty-Six

Garrick

“I have bitten my tongue for too long, and I can’t hold this back any longer, man,” Hudson says, sitting beside me at the window after I have somewhat calmed down.

We’re sipping Dawn’s homemade lemonade and looking out over a view I used to love. Now, it makes me sad. It’s a visual reminder of how different my life is, and I don’t know if I will ever get used to my new reality. It hurts. It has fucking devastated me.

“I have tried not to interfere. I know you’re going through so much shit, but the way you’re treating the girl you claim to love is so wrong.”

“I know.” The weight of my agreement hangs in the heavy air. “I always feel like shit after I lose it with her, but I can’t help the sudden spurts of hot anger that consume me without warning. Stevie seems to trigger that reaction the most.”

“She doesn’t deserve this, Gar.” He pierces me with a solemn look. “You need to let her go. You’re both miserable, and you’re dragging each other down.”

“I can’t let her go. I love her too much. I need her to be mine again, and everything will be all right.”

He clasps a hand on my shoulder and shakes his head. "That is never going to happen, and you cannot rely on anyone else for your own happiness. That's a lesson Stevie needs to learn too. I don't say this to hurt you, but you need to accept the truth. She's in love with another man, Gar. She's in love with Beck, and before you blow up and tell me he's not here, he walked away *for her*. He saw how this was tearing her apart, and he left to make it easier. It doesn't mean he's given up on her because he hasn't."

"I can't lose her too." My voice cracks. "I've lost everything else, and if I lose Stevie, what do I have to live for?"

"Dude, you have everything to live for! You have your whole life ahead of you. You can still do the things you planned. You can succeed your dad in the business, and in time, you'll find the right woman, get married, and have the family you dreamed of. Everything is possible. I know it sucks to be in this chair, but your life isn't over, Gar. It's only beginning. I know it's easier for me to say it. You're depressed, and it's a massive adjustment, but you're alive, and you're getting stronger every day. You have so much living left to do. You've been given a second chance, and you shouldn't waste it."

Tears well in his eyes. "We thought we lost you. We thought we'd never get to see you again, and then a miracle happened. You need to embrace it, man. You need to embrace life and look at everything you still have and not what you have lost. You still have the things that matter. You have your brothers, your dad, and Dawn, and you have me." Hudson thumps a hand over his heart. "I spoke to your dad this morning, and I dropped by to tell you I'm moving in. I'll be here for you every day. You need to do the heavy lifting, but I'm going to be with you every step of the way. I promise."

Emotion swells in my chest as I pull him into a hug. "Thanks, man. I love you."

"I love you too." He grips my head in his hands. "Which is why this needs to be said. Cut Stevie loose, Gar." We ease out of our embrace. "If you truly love her, you will let her go. That girl has endured a world of pain, and I hate seeing her robbed of her hard-won happiness. Be the bigger man. Be the man I know you to be. That man would want Stevie to be happy even if it was with another guy. That Garrick would never hurt the woman he loves or repay her loyalty with cruelty." He places his hand on my chest. "That Garrick is still you. He's still in there fighting to break free. We both know it. So, prove it. Set Stevie free."

I break down, sobbing into my hands as my shoulders shake and sharp pain stabs me through the heart. The thought of never seeing Stevie again hurts so badly, but Hudson is right. I have to let her go. I hate myself for hurting her, but I can't seem to stop it. We're both miserable, and we're holding one another back.

Hudson holds me as I cry, and I try not to think of myself as a pussy. Mature men cry, and this sob fest has been long overdue. I need it to purge the vision I have of my future with her.

From the time I met her, Stevie is all I have seen.

She pulled me out of that coma.

It was her face and her voice that tethered me to this world.

It's surreal thinking about the time I spent in a coma. It's all a bit of a jumble in my head, but I remember feeling like I was floating on a cloud. Light was everywhere. I remember wanting to move and not being able to. I had an acute sense of smell. Favorite foods and scents brought memories to mind. I heard music. Familiar songs. And familiar voices. I heard Stevie reading to me. I didn't recall the words or the stories after, but her voice lingered more than most.

My loved ones' faces floated around me like a revolving slideshow, but it was Stevie's face that appeared the most. Even after her voice had gone, it was her face that stuck with me. My entire being screamed to reach out to her, and I believe it was that frustration that kept me holding on. It ultimately dragged me back to the land of the living.

She saved me, and now it's time for me to do the same for her.

I don't know how I'm going to let her go, but I must.

It's been so hard not being able to touch her and kiss her. Not being able to sink into her comfort in the way I would like. She's here, but she's not. I have been selfish and cruel, and she didn't deserve it.

This is not how I saw our fairy tale ending, but it's the only ending that makes sense.

I shuck out of our embrace, swiping at my damp eyes as I try to summon the strength I'll need to do this.

"It's time to move on, and I'm not sorry we had this talk," Hudson says. "At some point, when you're thinking more clearly, you're going to want to kick my ass for letting it go on so long. You're going to hate yourself for the way you treated her, but you need to forgive yourself because you're still recovering, and it wasn't entirely your fault."

I grab some tissues from the box on the coffee table and dab my eyes. "This is going to be one of the hardest things I've ever done."

"I know, but you can do this. It's the right thing."

"I want to speak with Beck," I say, trying not to snarl his name, but it's challenging. I have an irritational level of anger when it comes to the man who stole my girl.

Hudson's eyes pop wide. "Why?"

"I need to look him in the eye and see for myself that I can leave Stevie in his care and trust him to love her the way I would have."

"He's a good guy, Gar, and he loves her good. I can vouch for him."

"I trust you, man, but I want to meet him. I need that reassurance so I can let her go and not worry about her."

"I'm not sure it's wise." He drags a hand through his hair.

"You can be in the room if it makes you feel better. I'm not planning on punching the asshole though I'll probably want to."

"Okay." He nods. "I'll organize something."

I stare out the window, wondering how I'm going to do this. And whether I can say what I need to and remain calm.

"Do you want me to get Stevie?" Hudson asks.

"Give me a few minutes alone, and then send her in."

My best buddy stands. "You're doing the right thing, and I'm proud of you."

I snort out a harsh laugh. "I doubt there is much to be proud of, but I'm going to rectify that."

Hudson gives me one last hug. "There's my buddy. Good to have you back, man."

Stevie

"Hey," I whisper as I enter the room for what I know is going to be the last time.

"Hey, beautiful." His red-rimmed eyes shine with honest emotion, conveying so much without words. "Come sit with me."

I walk quietly to the window and sit beside him, memorizing the stunning view I have always loved.

He takes my hand, giving it a gentle squeeze. "I'm so sorry, Stevie."

"Me too."

"I never meant to hurt you."

"Nor I you."

"I was selfish and cruel and reckless with your feelings, and I won't ever forgive myself for it."

"Forgive yourself," I say without hesitation. "There's been enough hurt, guilt, and blame." I lean in and kiss his cheek with tears in my eyes. "I already forgive you."

"You shouldn't."

"I love you and care deeply about you. That won't ever change. A part of my heart will always belong to you." Removing the jewelry he bought me, I place it on the coffee table, and it makes it final.

This is the last time we will ever see one another.

As much as this needs to happen, it's sad it has come to this.

"But you love him more." Pain underscores his words, and I hate I'm the cause of it.

My inclination is to refuse to answer or deflect, but we're not tiptoeing around one another anymore. "I do."

Agony flares in his eyes, and it hurts, but I'm not sorry I was truthful.

"I will always love you," he says as we stare at one another through blurry eyes. "It's because I love you I am letting you go. We need to let what we had stay in the past and move forward along different paths. We're very different people now."

"We are," I acknowledge with a nod. "And it's neither of our faults we have ended up here."

"I thought we would grow old and gray together," he says with a sad smile.

I'm not sure I did, but it's hard to remember exactly what I was feeling at the time. "Things happen for a reason. Some lucky woman is out there waiting for you to find her. I hope she doesn't have to wait too long."

He brings our conjoined hands to his mouth and brushes his lips across my knuckles. "I want you to be happy, and he's your happy place. I see it now."

He is, and I hope it's not too late to reclaim what we had.

"I won't ever forget you," I say over a sob. "And I will always cherish the time we shared. Be happy." I swipe at the tears streaming down my face. "It's all I want for you. Don't ever stop fighting for that happiness because you deserve it."

I don't protest or pull away when he leans forward and kisses me softly and briefly on the lips.

It's the only goodbye we can handle.

I hug him for the last time, and then I get up and walk out the door and out of his life.

Chapter Forty-Seven

Stevie

After breaking all ties with Garrick, I was hugely tempted to rush to the Colbert building in the city and beg Sarah to give me Beck's address, but I managed restraint. I was a mess those first couple of weeks and in no fit state to rock up to Beck's door and beg him for forgiveness. I owed it to both of us to get myself together.

It's going to take serious groveling to win back my man, but I'm determined to fight with everything I have to reclaim our relationship and the love I recklessly pushed aside. I take a few months to self-heal, and when January rolls around—the beginning of a new year and a fresh start—I'm feeling more like myself, so I show up at Colbert Cartwright Aerospace and Technological Services and ask to meet their current president of marketing. I half expect to be frog-marched out the door like a criminal, so I'm relieved when Sarah agrees to meet with me, and I'm escorted to her offices by an assistant.

My relief is premature.

Sarah's frosty expression stares at me from behind her desk as I enter her office. Thrusting my shoulders back and lifting my chin, I force my nerves to one side and give her a big smile as I walk toward her. "Sarah. It's been a while. You look great, and it seems everything is going well here for you. I'm happy for you."

"Can we cut the chitchat. I'm a busy woman," she says, not getting up and not inviting me to sit either.

Okay, so it's going to be like this. I can't say I blame her.

"I know you probably hate me, but I need to see Beck. I was hoping you could tell me if he's in France or else pass on his address?"

I didn't think it was possible, but her expression turns even more glacial. Her eyes narrow as she stands, placing her palms flat on the desk. "You need to leave my brother alone. Haven't you done enough damage?"

Hurt flays me on the inside at her words. "It wasn't intentional, and I hate myself for it."

"Not as much as I do," she snaps.

"That's...fair." I rub at the tight pain in my chest. "I would probably feel the same if it was my brother. I made a mistake, Sarah, but I never stopped loving him. I love him so much, and I miss him like crazy. Beck is the love of my life, and I just want an opportunity to make it right."

"You're too late." She purses her lips. "It's been months. He's moved on."

The meaning behind her words is clear, and the arrow hits true. Pain stabs me straight through the heart like someone just plunged a sword in it. "What?" I whisper, fighting the rush of emotion those words induce.

"Did you really expect him to wait for you after how you treated him? You ditched him for your ex."

"I didn't. It wasn't like that. I—"

She presses a button on her desk phone. "Ms. Colson is leaving, Simone. Please escort her to the lobby and out of the building."

"Sarah, please." I rush around the desk, stopping right in front of her. "I'm begging you. Just tell me where he is. I owe him an apology at the very minimum."

"Stay away from Beck, Stevie. If you love him like you claim to, you'll leave him alone. He is better off without you."

A year passes by, and it seems to go equally slow and fast. I keep myself busy to distract my aching heart. I join a weekly yoga class, and I volunteer at a local youth center one night a week. I'm eating the healthiest I've ever eaten and taking a host of supplements to boost my immune system. My anxiety and depression are a thing of the past, and I'm sleeping well again at night without the need for any medication.

I attend therapy regularly, and I'm working through my issues in a healthy manner. I had a lot to unpack from the past few years. I undid a lot of progression during that period I tried to support Garrick, and I can see things more clearly now. That relationship was toxic and unhealthy for me. I let Garrick manipulate me, and I didn't prioritize myself or Beck or our relationship. I'm trying not to have regrets. I meant what I told Garrick that last day we spoke. I have forgiven him, and I'm working now on fully forgiving myself. To focus on moving forward and not looking back to past mistakes, but I will always regret losing the best thing to ever happen to me.

I haven't spoken to Garrick, Hudson, Hugh, or Dawn since that day in North Bend. I knew saying goodbye to Garrick meant saying goodbye to them too. There is no way it would have worked otherwise. I miss Hudson a lot. He was a good friend to me for a while, but Garrick needs him, and I'm glad they have one another.

Two weeks ago, there was a big event held at the Allen Winery in Woodinville to raise funds for a new charity the Allen family has set up to support coma patients and their families. There were pictures online. Pictures of Garrick, looking handsome in a tux, with Helena sitting in his lap on his wheelchair. They were laughing and staring at one another with obvious adoration. They looked happy, and I felt nothing but joy in my heart.

The article accompanying the pictures confirmed they are dating, and I couldn't have picked a better woman for him. Helena is one of the sweetest, kindest people I ever met, but she takes no prisoners either. She is exactly what Garrick needs, and I'm crossing everything it works out for them.

I just want him to be happy.

Mom and I work well together, and the business is going from strength to strength. We just opened a corporate division, which I am managing, while Mom oversees the shop and the farm.

In my downtime, I completely remodeled Nana's house, modernizing it and adding an extension to the back and one side. It's now a large four-bedroom home with a wraparound deck and a large private garden at the rear. I bordered it with tall weather-treated fencing, so I have complete privacy. One of my favorite things to do is work in my garden. I spent all last summer creating my own personal haven in my backyard, complete with a gazebo, a love swing, and a small pond with a stone water feature in the middle. A gate at the end of the garden leads to a private access path to the poppy field, and I still spend a lot of my time there.

Most nights, I sit on the bench, reliving precious nights spent with Beck.

He might have moved on, but my heart hasn't gotten the memo. I still pine for him and miss him so much. I don't know if I'll ever get over losing him. He was my everything, and he's still the best man I know.

I was at a bar with some of our staff last month, and this guy asked to buy me a drink. I sat with him for a while but turned him down when he asked me out to dinner. No one can replace Beck, and I don't even want to try. I have zero interest in dating or being with any other man.

Beck is the only one I want.

Which is problematic when he's no longer mine.

Hadley is convinced Sarah lied. She tried talking to her but couldn't get past the lobby at the Colbert building. Then she called

Esther at college and left a bunch of messages, but Beck's youngest sister didn't return any of them. I'm not surprised they've closed ranks. Those three have always been protective of their siblings. However, my bestie is persistent, and she refused to give up. So, she reached out to Beck via the Byron Stanley social media pages, but that was a dead end too.

It seems Beck has hired an agency to manage his advertising, his inbox, and his social media, and there is no way of reaching him directly. Beck always hated that side of the business, preferring to concentrate on writing, and he values his privacy, so it doesn't surprise me he has outsourced everything else. She asked them to pass on her messages, but we've had no contact from him. Hadley is convinced they didn't pass anything on, but I'm beginning to think Sarah was telling the truth and Beck has moved on and put me firmly in the past. I wouldn't blame him after the way I treated him at the end.

Hadley's next suggestion was to fly to France and just show up at the farm, but I'm not doing that if Beck is shacked up with some other woman. I think that might kill me stone dead.

I forced Hadley to pinky swear she'd give up then before she was arrested for harassment or stalking

Anyway, she's busy now she's gotten a new swanky job at a top legal firm. She was earning peanuts at the Seattle Public Library, and she has tripled her salary working as an information officer gathering research and data analysis and writing reports for a bunch of snooty lawyers and attorneys. She's been at her new job for almost eight months, and she loves it. The firm is a gossip lovers' haven, so she's in her element.

After I moved back to Ravenna, Mike took over the lease with her, but they broke up three months ago when he proposed and Hads realized he wasn't the man she wanted to spend forever with.

So, that's how we find ourselves footloose and fancy-free on Friday night. I join her and some colleagues for one drink after work, ignoring the advances from several dashing men in suits to drag

Hadley outside after an hour, before our night gets hijacked. We buy a couple bottles of wine and head toward Hadley's new apartment where I'm spending the night. We're going to order takeout and catch up over the latest season of *The Crown* on Netflix.

"Hold up!" Hadley shrieks, slamming to a halt on the sidewalk in front of a bookstore. "What the actual fuck!?"

"What is it?" I inquire, peeking around her. My heart jackhammers behind my rib cage when I spot the window and what has clearly caught her attention. We walk closer, in tandem, with matching slack jaws and wide eyes.

"Oh my god, Stevie." Hadley clutches her chest as she stares between me and the big display behind the window promoting a *New York Times* bestselling new release.

I place my palm on the glass, blinking repeatedly, sure I must be seeing things. But nope. The book in the window is an autobiographical novel titled *Auburn Sunrise* by Beckett Colbert.

Chapter Forty-Eight

Stevie

"He has poppies on the cover, and he wrote it in his real name." Hadley sounds all choked up as she points out the obvious.

I'm glad she's articulated it as I have currently lost the ability to speak, and I'm barely keeping myself upright.

Her eyes narrow, and her nose scrunches as she reads one of the large signs propped beside the book. "It details Colbert's romance with the only woman who has ever, and will ever, own his heart." She grips my arm as she scans the rest of the text. "It's an enthralling, sweeping, heartfelt love letter to the woman he loves and a tour de force masterpiece that will warm even the most frozen hearts." Hadley is fit to burst as she looks at me. "That's from a top critic. Oh my god, Stevie." She starts jumping up and down, garnering strange looks from people walking by. "It's about you. I told you! I told you! I knew he wouldn't give up on you."

"Come on." She drags me inside the store. "Fuck *The Crown*. We're buying copies of Beck's book and going home to read it from cover to cover."

"Babe, you're shaking like crazy, and I'm starting to worry you've lost the power of speech," Hadley says as we're perched on top of her bed, propped up against the headboard, cushioned by numerous pillows.

"Don't worry, you're talking enough for the two of us," I tease. Hadley babbled nonstop the entire way home. A journey I barely remember walking because my heart was pounding so hard against my rib cage and my head is mush. I can't believe this. I'm astounded and in complete shock.

Hadley playfully shoves me in the ribs. "He wrote you a book, Stevie. Not just a poem. A whole freaking *book*!" She hops up and starts jumping on the bed. I look at her with part amusement and part fear. Has my bestie finally lost her mind? "He loves you. He loves you. He loves you," she croons, and I swat her with a pillow.

"Get down here, you goofball. We don't know anything until we read his words. For all we know, this is a love letter to some other woman."

"Stop being silly." She flops down on the bed, jostling the mattress. "You don't really believe that, do you?"

"No, but I'm scared to hope. This is everything I have dreamed of every day of the nineteen months we've been apart."

"Keep the faith, babe." She snuggles into my side and hands me a wineglass before tugging on a lock of my hair. "He even named the book after you. Beck hasn't written this book for anyone but you. I don't need to read a word to know that." A dreamy look coasts over her face. "He's so romantic, and this is amazing." She clinks her glass against mine. "To love and romantic men."

My lips curl at the corners. "To love and Beck. Both are synonymous for me."

Wordlessly, she hands me a book, and I stare at the cover as I sip my wine, tracing my shaking finger over each letter of his name and the pretty poppies.

"It's time." Hadley takes my wineglass and sets it down on the bedside table nearest me. "Enough Dutch courage. We need to be sober to soak up every word." She opens her book and gasps. Her chin lifts, and she spears me with more glassy eyes.

We are not going to be able to get through this without it becoming a total blubber fest. I don't need a crystal ball to confirm it.

"He dedicated it to you." She puts her hand over her heart as she reads the inscription out loud.

For Stevie with all my love.

You are my muse, my best friend, my soul mate, and the reason I get out of bed each day. You are the only woman who will ever own my heart, for now and all time.

P.S. I briefly considered naming this Two People and a Dog, but it's not very romantic, and we're the only people who would get it. My sun rises and sets with you, my auburn-haired love, and there was no more perfect title.

Tears prick my eyes as I turn the page of my book and read the same words. Oh, Beck. My pulse is racing like crazy, and I'm equal parts excited and terrified to read this, but here goes nothing.

We read side by side, but Hadley is ahead because she's dying to get to the end. I forbid her from skipping to the last page even though I'm sorely tempted. I want to read it from cover to cover, page to page, and no shortcuts are allowed. I want to absorb every single word my love put to paper and imprint them on my heart.

It starts the first night we met at the hospital in the memorial garden. His thoughts about Brielle are peppered through those early sections, and it gives me greater insight into what he was thinking and feeling at that time.

"Gosh, Stevie, he loved you from the moment he met you. The way he speaks about you is beautiful. So freaking beautiful." Hadley sniffs, and I pass her the tissue box. We've been exchanging it back and forth as needed.

I knew he had romantic feelings for me way before I realized it, but I didn't grasp how strong they were until now.

His pain is palpable during the period where we were transitioning from friends to lovers, and I cry as he describes his longing and fear as I struggled to deal with my changing feelings and the guilt I felt at betraying Garrick.

It brings it all back, and I have to take a break.

Hadley can't drag her eyes from the book, so I leave her reading while I top off my wine and catch a breather on the small balcony outside her living room. It's nearly midnight, but the streets are still busy as people enjoy their Friday night with friends and loved ones.

Leaning against the railing, I stare out at the city streets I love with new appreciation. Seattle will always have a special place in my heart, for many reasons, but mostly because it's where I fell in love with the man who is my everything. My heart is currently doing cartwheels, and it's swollen to bursting point. I wish Beck was here so I could throw myself at him and return all his professions of love.

I have never felt worthy of Beck, and it might be easy to say it's so true now, but it's not. We are worthy of one another because we love each other with the same deep intensity and conviction.

I head back to the bedroom, pick up the book, and continue reading.

"Ho. Lee. Shit. Babe." Hadley bolts upright, stabbing me with wide eyes. "I know you're behind me, but I have to read this part out loud. He spoke to Garrick! Beck and Garrick met."

"What?!" My eyes almost bug out of my head. "When?"

"It was after that last day in North Bend. Garrick initiated the meeting, and Hudson was there." Her eyes narrow to slits. "That little shit could have told us."

"Never mind that. What happened?"

"He doesn't say much about it, just that Garrick wanted to make sure Beck was going to love you right." Her eyes soften. "That was sweet. And protective though unnecessary."

"That sounds like Garrick." I smile because it's further proof we did the right thing walking away. I think we were pulling a dark side to the surface within one another, and we needed to sever all ties to reclaim the light.

She wraps her arm around me. "You need to brace yourself for this part. I'm going to read it as Beck wrote it." She clears her throat, and I snuggle into her side, listening attentively as she reads the passage.

I left the meeting feeling lighter and more hopeful than I had in months. I knew I should have headed straight to the airport and gone home, but I couldn't resist temptation. I had given Stevie an ultimatum for good reason. To protect our love and safeguard our relationship, but it was also to give her time to heal. I knew she wouldn't be in a good place. I knew I needed to leave her alone until she was ready to come back to me, but I've never been good at staying away from her. It's why I left Seattle and cut off all communication. I purposely changed my number, adopting Hadley's tough-love method, so we wouldn't be tempted to keep in regular contact.

"Well, fuck." Hadley looks a little sheepish as she looks at me. "That's taking tough love to extremes. Who does he think I am? A freaking masochist? I would never do something that severe."

"Keep reading," I encourage, desperate to find out what he did.

If there was an emergency, Stevie could always reach me through my sisters or Hudson. I didn't want to leave her isolated without any way of contacting me if she needed to.

. . .

"What the actual fuck?" Hadley almost spills her drink as she glowers at the page. "Hudson had Beck's number, and he didn't think to share it with you?"

"It was probably some stupid bro code arrangement. Now, stop with the commentary and read the rest!"

I had gone to such lengths because we needed to go cold turkey, so acting rash was not wise, but I couldn't help myself. I was missing her so much, and I knew she was in pain. Our connection is intense. I often sensed her presence in a room before I saw her, and I was very attuned to her feelings. Like a form of twin telepathy. Stevie's heart had taken another hammering this week, and I needed to see her.

I didn't expect it to be so easy, but perhaps Nana was aligning the stars from heaven.

A sob breaks free of my throat, and Hadley rubs my arm as she continues reading.

It was early evening in mid-October and dark. The shop was closed. The farm was locked up. And Nana's house was under the cloak of night. I knew where I'd find her. In her poppy field. On our bench. Slivers of moonlight cast her lonely shadow in scant illumination, and my heart broke anew as I watched her huddled in a ball, crying. It took every ounce of my self-control not to go to her. It felt cruel not to comfort her. The pain in my chest was so extreme I worried I might be having a coronary. She was lost, heartbroken, and miserable. I wanted to swoop in like her knight in shining armor and save the day.

But I knew I couldn't.

This was one battle Stevie had to fight alone.

She needed time to fully heal. And she needed to do that without Garrick and without me.

Stevie has always been one of the strongest people I know, but she had lost a lot of her inner belief, and I couldn't be selfish. I couldn't run back to her without giving her the opportunity to do this herself. She needed it to believe in herself again. And I needed her to do it so when she came back to me it would be forever.

Walking away that night was one of the toughest things I have ever done. Right up there with sticking to the ultimatum I'd given her. I hated myself as I turned my back on her and headed to the airport. I cried as the plane took off. It felt cruel and cowardly to leave her alone.

But I had faith.

I have always had faith in her and in us.

So, I returned home and continued waiting.

Hadley has to stop because she's crying too hard, and so am I.

"It's so weird," I say, sniffling as I pass the tissue box to Hadley. "But I felt him there that night."

"It's not weird." Hadley mops at her eyes. "You two are true soul mates. It's no wonder you were both sensing one another. I hope one day I find someone like Beck." She blows her nose and shoves my book at me. "Now, hurry and catch up. We need to reach the end so we can get to your new beginning."

We read until the early hours, switching wine for herbal tea as it gets late, and when I turn the last page, I'm filled with elation and more energy than I should have.

"There's a special acknowledgment for you," Hadley says, drinking the last of her peppermint tea before she reads it aloud.

Stevie, if you are reading this, I want you to know I'm waiting at our cottage. There is no rush. I will wait for you for eternity if I have to because there is no one else for me. I love you, honey. When you are ready, come home.

. . .

I hop off the bed and grab my purse, rummaging in it for my cell.

"What are you going to do?" Hadley asks, kneeling on the bed.

"What do you think?" I toss her a grin over my shoulder. "I'm booking myself a seat on the next flight to Perpignan. It's time to get my man."

Chapter Forty-Nine

Beck

I return from my early morning run and check my emails before planning to take a shower. I have another bunch of offers from foreign publishers, via my agent, and an updated sales report showing healthy US and UK sales.

I wonder if Stevie has seen the book yet. If she's read it.

I miss her so much, and I'm praying she comes back to me sooner than later. I didn't think our separation would be this long. I've been tempted to text her so many times, but I promised myself I'd give her all the space she needs. This will have been for nothing if she doesn't come back to me in her own time, when she is ready. I trust in our love, and I know she will come to me when the time is right.

I grab a quick shower, and my mind wanders to my red-haired beauty like it does every day. Stevie is never far from my mind at any time of the day or night. She's the sweetest addiction. I hope she is doing better and looking after herself, and I hope she is happy. Her happiness means everything to me. It's why I made the ultimate sacrifice. Why I have put all my faith in our love. Someday, we will be reunited, and then we will never be separated again.

I dry off and throw on a pair of sweats just as someone knocks on my door. I'm not expecting anyone. It's only six thirty a.m. so it must be *Grand-mère*, looking for my help with something. Throwing the wet towel into the laundry basket on my way out of my bedroom, I stall for a moment as all the fine hairs rise on the back of my neck. A familiar prickling sensation ghosts over my skin, and I know.

She's here.

My baby has come back to me.

My heart gallops around my chest like a racehorse on a track as I sprint to the front door and fling it open.

And there she is. Looking like a fiery goddess with a golden sunshine halo outlining her beautiful form. My eyes drink her in, cataloging her glossy waves, perfect curves, slightly parted lips, and the emotion in her shiny eyes. So much emotion it looks like she's drowning. I'm feeling everything she's feeling, and I can't drag my eyes away from her. We stare at one another, exchanging so many words with emotional looks and a familiar simmering energy crackling in the air. She looks so fucking beautiful, and I'm done wasting another single second.

She obviously feels the same way because we move as one, drawn together like magnets. Stevie throws herself at me, and I lift her up, relishing the feel of her pressed against me and her familiar scent tickling my nostrils. Our mouths melt together in a passionate kiss I feel everywhere. Stevie's legs wrap around my waist, and my arms band against her lower back as I move us into the hall and slam the door behind me.

Our kissing is desperate, greedy, fumbling, and frantic as we stumble our way along the hall, groping and clinging to one another. Something smashes as we crash into the table, but I barely hear the shattering noise. My entire being is consumed with the woman I love, and Stevie is all that matters. My erection pulses behind my sweats, thrashing against the soft damp spot behind her leggings, and I'm devouring her mouth like a crazy man who's been lost in a desert for years and just discovered an oasis.

"Beck," Stevie moans against my lips as I carry her into my bedroom. "I love you."

I lay her down on my bed and crawl over her, tenderly wiping the tears from her eyes. "I love you too. I've been waiting for you to show up."

"I missed you so much." More tears leak from her eyes as I caress her gorgeous face.

"I know." I lean down and brush my lips against hers. "It's been agony, but you're home now."

Her face lights up in the most glorious smile. "I am." Her palm covers my heart. "You're my home, Beck. It's not a place; it's wherever you are." Her eyes lower to my chest, and she gasps when she notices the new tattoo over my heart. To the side of the cracked heart representing my mother is a gloriously full one with vines of pretty poppies winding around it and Stevie's name alongside it.

I place my hand over hers on my chest. "You're my beating heart, Stevie."

"I haven't been with anyone else. It's only ever been you."

"I haven't been with anyone either. You are my only love, Stevie. My forever love. My future wife and mother of my children."

Tears glisten in her eyes as she smiles. "Love me, Beck."

"Always," I promise before I claim her lips again.

I peel the clothes off her body until she's lying underneath me, gloriously naked, watching as I kick my sweats away and climb back over her. We kiss more leisurely this time, but that frantic need for one another still simmers in our veins.

I want to take my time and savor every inch of her. I've been waiting a long time to be with her like this again.

My lips trail a scorching path along her body, stopping to ravish her tits and suck her taut nipples. Stevie writhes and moans, and those sounds are music to my ears. My fingers sweep across her ribs and down over her flat stomach until I reach the apex of her thighs and part them.

I lie between her legs and part her folds, blowing gently across her pussy lips while I drink my fill. Her clit is already swollen with need, her pussy glistening with her arousal. I swipe a finger up and down her slit before sliding it easily inside. Her warm walls hug one finger and then another and another as I pump them lazily in and out of her. Stevie's breathing turns heavy, and she grinds her hips as I replace my fingers and tongue fuck her how I've been imagining it every day we've been apart. I shove my tongue in and out of her while I rotate my finger on that glistening nub, and she falls apart in exquisite waves while riding my face.

I move up and over her body, positioning myself at her entrance as I peer into her beautiful face. Fiery strands of hair float around her head like bright rays of reddish sunshine. My heart is consumed with love for her, and I have never felt more content. "I love you," I remind her as I inch inside her nice and slow.

"You're my world." Tears crest in her eyes again. "I never want to be separated again, Beck." She gasps as I push all the way in.

I lean down and claim her lips in a searing-hot kiss. "We will never spend a day apart again."

"I'm making it a rule," She pants as I pick up my pace, driving in and out of her in worshiping strokes. "We always go to bed together every night."

"Deal, honey." Taking her legs, I fling them over my shoulders and toy with her clit as I thrust in and out of her, taking my sweet ass time. My hands roam over her beautiful curves as I make love to her, and my heart is bursting with love and happiness.

I bend down, needing to taste her lips again, and her legs drop to my waist and curl around my back. She clings to me, tracing her hands up and down my back as we kiss and I pump in and out of her, and it's everything I remember and more.

This. I want this every single day for the rest of my life.

I pull back into a sitting position with Stevie in my lap. Her legs straddle me, and she bounces up and down on my cock as I thrust up inside her. My arms hold her firmly at the back, and we stare at one another as we make love slowly and deeply, feeling every thrust and hearing every steady beat of our hearts.

I have never felt closer to another soul.

We take our time on purpose, slowing down to enjoy being together again. I drive in deep, and she pushes down hard, perfectly in sync, like two pieces made to fit perfectly together. We continue staring at one another, and it's an intense, magical, erotic moment I want to experience repeatedly.

My fingers explore her back and roam over the globes of her ass as my lips worship her mouth and her tits. Burying my head in her chest, I lick and suck her all over, teasing the hard peaks of her nipples gently between my teeth. Our pace picks up as we head toward the end line, still in no hurry to finish, but we can't delay our release indefinitely.

Besides, we have the rest of our lives to make love, and fuck, to our hearts' content.

When I feel her getting close, I set her down flat on her back and increase my speed, rutting in and out of her at a more frenetic pace. Stevie grabs my ass, pulling me in closer and deeper as she whimpers and writhes and meets me thrust for thrust.

We shatter into blissful bursts of energy at the same time, moaning against swollen lips as my hips jerk, and I shoot my load deep inside her.

I didn't ask if she's on birth control, but I don't care if she's not. While I'm in no rush to see her belly swollen with my baby—I only just got her back, and I need time alone with her—I wouldn't be unhappy if we just made a new life.

When we're done, I get up and grab a wet washcloth from the bathroom and return to clean her up. Then we slip under the covers, facing one another with our arms wrapped around each other in an intimate embrace. I stare at her pretty flushed face, her stunning green eyes, and lips that are puffy from my kisses, and my heart is so full it might push through my chest.

"Marry me," I say.

"Yes," she replies instantly without hesitation.

Our lips meet in a deep intense kiss, and I hold her to me, so happy I could burst.

"Today," I rasp when we finally come up for air.

She giggles. "That might be a little difficult to arrange. Mom would kill me if I got married without her, and let's not even mention Hadley."

I peck her lips. "I've spent too long without you, and I can't wait to make you my wife." I sit us up and reach into the drawer of my bedside table for the small black box.

Her eyes pop wide as I turn back around to her.

"This wasn't exactly a very romantic proposal," I say.

"I just need you." She leans in and kisses me sweetly. When she pulls back, she's grinning widely. "And I don't know what you're talking about. You wrote me a *novel*, Beck. The most beautiful, heart-warming, romantic love letter. No proposal could ever beat that."

"I'm glad you liked it," I say, popping the lid on the box.

Stevie gasps when she spots the emerald and diamond engagement ring nestled inside. I had purposely left mention of the ring out of the book because a guy has to keep some secrets.

"How did you? Where did you..."

I chuckle as I watch her struggle to form words. "I bought this a couple of months before we broke up. I saw it in a store window, and it reminded me of your eyes."

"Oh, Beck." Her lip wobbles and her hand trembles as I slide the ring onto her finger. It's a perfect fit. "It's beautiful. I love it," she adds, holding it out in front of her and admiring how it glistens on her hand.

"Just like you." I can't describe the pride I feel seeing my ring on her finger.

"I'm so happy, Beck." She crawls into my lap. "You make me so incredibly happy, and I can't wait to spend the rest of my life with you."

Epilogue One

Stevie

"Knock, knock." The door creeps open, and a familiar face pops into view. "Could we talk for a minute?" Sarah asks, hovering uncertainly in the doorway.

"I'll give you some privacy," Mom says, inspecting my hair before she stands. "I'll work on your makeup when I return."

I kiss her cheek. "Thanks, Mom."

Mom gives Sarah's arm a reassuring squeeze as she passes by. The door snicks shut with a loud click.

I'm getting ready in the main farmhouse while Beck is getting dressed with Law, his best man, at our cottage. We ignored tradition last night and spent it together. We made our own vows a month ago, when we reunited, and they're as real to us as the vows we're about to make in a marquee in *Grand-mère's* gorgeous back garden in front of our families and a small handful of friends. Beck has been helping Margot maintain the grounds and run the farm now his *grand-père* is no longer with us.

Alain died of colon cancer six months ago. I'm sad I wasn't here for Margot and Beck, but I'm here now, and I'll be by my soon-to-be husband's side every day until I draw my last breath. Beck will never go through anything alone ever again.

"I owe you a huge apology." Sarah looks awkward as hell.

If I was a meaner person, I'd make her sweat for a while, but I'm letting bygones be bygones and only looking forward from now on. "I have already forgiven you," I say, folding my white silk robe around my body as I turn on my chair to face her. I pat the chair beside me that Mom just vacated. "Have a seat."

She sits stiffly and eyeballs me. "I was a giant bitch the day you came to my office. I am really truly sorry, Stevie."

I can tell from her tone and her genuine expression she means it. "You were protecting your brother. I get it."

"I interfered, and you spent longer apart than you should. I left you with no way to contact him, which is unforgivable. Beck is disgusted with me, and I'm ashamed for lying to you even if I thought I was doing the right thing."

"Like I told Beck, you did us a favor. I wasn't fully healed yet. I hadn't taken enough time to work through all my issues. If I'd gone back to Beck then, it might have been too soon."

"He doesn't see it like that." Creases appear in her otherwise smooth brow.

"I can't tell Beck what to do, but I asked him to forgive you. Your heart was in the right place. Beck and I are together now, and that's all that matters. I only want to look forward. I never want to look back."

"You are a wonderful, kind, forgiving person, Stevie. It's no wonder my brother is crazy in love with you."

"I'm crazy in love with him too," I say with the biggest grin on my face.

"I'm so happy you're getting married and we're gaining another sister." She leans in for a hug, and I almost fall off my chair in shock.

Her lips twitch. "This is the best way I can show you how sorry I am."

After a brief hug, I let her go. She's been tortured enough. "As far as I'm concerned, this is water under the bridge now. We're going to be family in a few hours, and I already love you and Esther like sisters."

"She's waiting outside to see you, or should I say waddling."

"I can't believe I'm going to be an aunt soon. Beck is super excited for the baby." Esther surprised everyone by dropping out of the Harvard MBA program and returning to Seattle with a fiancé and a bun in the oven. Carlton Colbert was not happy, but screw him. It's nothing new.

He still doesn't speak to Beck. He's less than impressed with his writing career, and he can't understand why he gave up the family business for it. Any other father would be proud of Beck's achievements, but not that horrible man. We didn't invite him today. No one wants him here, and I don't think he would have come anyway.

"We're all excited," Sarah says, smoothing a hand down the front of her pretty white, purple, and pink dress as she stands. "Esther feels bad she never returned any of your or Hadley's calls. You should know I bullied her into ignoring you. She wanted to call you back."

"Like I said, water under the bridge."

"You have a beautiful soul, Stevie. Thank you for forgiving me and being so gracious about it."

"Ready?" my uncle Sean asks as the pianist we hired for the wedding ceremony plays the opening notes of the bridal chorus. We're conducting the marriage part in the marquee in the garden and then moving inside for the wedding dinner and dancing. It's only February in the South of France, and while it's not cold, it's not warm enough to stay outside all day and night.

"Yep. Let's get this show on the road." I tip my head at Hadley, and she sets off up the makeshift aisle toward the altar where Beck is waiting for me with Law at his side. The celebrant is an old family friend, which is lucky, as I doubt we would've found any other minister to do this at such short notice.

"You look stunning, Stevie," Sean says, sweeping his eyes over my simple lace dress.

The fitted bodice is strapless, and the skirt flows in wispy layers to my calves. Hadley bought me stunning white and silver Jimmy Choo sandals. Mom did my hair and makeup. My red tresses are silky smooth and hanging in soft waves down my back. At the front, a plaited band wraps around my head, and a few artfully styled strands frame my face. A short lace veil is pinned under the plaited part of my hair at the back. In keeping with my usual look, my makeup is subtle with peach lips and soft browns on my eyes.

"Thank you for asking me to give you away," he adds. "It's a great honor to represent my brother."

"Thank you for being here," I say as we walk slowly up the aisle. "It means a lot to me that you, Susan, and Anne and her family are here to help us celebrate."

I smile as I walk past our mutual friends. Beck's agent, assistant Lulu, some other bookish colleagues, and author friends are in attendance along with Law and Jenny and their daughter. They left their newborn son at home with Jenny's parents. Tate is here too, standing alongside Sarah, Margot, and Esther and Rob.

Some friends from my yoga class and a few of our employees I'm closest to are here on my side along with Nana's two oldest friends. I hope Nana is looking down and cheering us on. She loved Beck, and I know she'd be happy for me. The sapphire bracelet I'm wearing was Nana's because I wanted to have something of hers with me today. The gorgeous diamond necklace around my neck is a wedding gift from my generous fiancé, and I feel like a million dollars.

Sarah chartered a private jet to fly everyone here at enormous expense, but she insisted it was her wedding gift to us, and Beck wouldn't let me decline it. It's her way of trying to make amends.

I feel Beck's heated stare on me before I twist my head, and we lock eyes. He looks totally fuckable in a sharp navy suit with a crisp white shirt. It's unbuttoned on top, and he chose to go without a tie. His usual rings don't adorn his fingers today because he's decided not to wear them anymore. He wants the only ring on his finger to be the platinum wedding band we chose together, and I fully agree.

I want every bitch to know he's mine!

He stares at me with his big seductive brown eyes, fringed by the longest eyelashes, and I drown in his gaze. Beck has always had the most beautiful, most expressive eyes, but the look in them now takes my breath away. So much emotion stares back at me, and my chest heaves. The way this man loves is incredible. I am the luckiest woman in the world today because I get to claim him as mine forever.

He's wearing the biggest smile on his face as his gaze rakes over me like a sensual caress. My skin tingles all over, and though I love this dress and feel like a princess in it, I'm already counting down the hours until I can take it off so my husband can ravish me. Beck's pupils darken, and I suspect his mind has gone to the same place mine has.

When we reach the top of the aisle, the music cuts off, and the celebrant smiles. Sean places my hand in Beck's. "Look after our girl. She's precious."

"Why do you think I'm marrying her?"

Sean grins before taking his seat beside Mom, and my smile expands as they automatically link hands. I would not be surprised if theirs is the next wedding in the family.

"You are so beautiful you steal all the air from my lungs," Beck says, peering adoringly into my eyes.

"You look handsome," I admit as he takes both my hands in his. "And sexy as fuck," I add, channeling my inner Hadley.

Beck presses his mouth to my ear. "I have so many dirty plans for you later."

A delicious shiver ghosts over me. "I can't wait."

The celebrant clears his throat, and we get down to business.

Thirty minutes later, he pronounces us husband and wife, and Beck kisses his bride.

Beck and I accept heartfelt congratulations as we mingle with our guests, drinking champagne and eating canapés. Margot and Susan are already firm friends, and both groups of friends are mixing well.

We head inside when dinner is served. We hired a local catering company, and the food is sumptuous. After the requisite speeches and toasts, we step out into the middle of the room for our first dance. We chose a traditional French song that was played at Margot's wedding to Alain.

Beck sways me around the dance floor, holding me tight as he peers deep into my eyes. We're both sporting massive grins and matching heart eyes. "This is the best day of my life," he says before twirling me around and reeling me back into his chest.

"Mine too." I cup one side of his handsome face. "I love you so much. I can't believe you're my husband. It feels like a fairy tale."

"Believe it, Mrs. Colbert, because you're all mine."

The crowd whoops and hollers as Beck dips me down low and kisses me passionately. His lips make silent promises that are verbally repeated when he whispers all the naughty things he plans to do to me in my ear.

An hour later, unable to keep our hands off one another any longer, we sneak outside to a hidden corner of the garden, and Beck fucks me from behind, with my dress shoved up to my waist, while our unsuspecting guests dance, laugh, and drink wine.

Epilogue Two

Stevie – Ten Years Later

"Livvie! Slow down!" Beck calls out after our precocious daughter as she races off into the garden with one of her classmates.

"She is too used to running free on the farm," I remind my husband, leaning into him as he wraps his arm around my shoulders. "You'll never tame our free spirit."

"Nor would I want to." He pecks my lips before his proud grin follows our daughter around the large garden.

Beck is an amazing father and husband, and I pinch myself all the time that he's mine and we share this incredible life. I fall more in love with him every day. We are living our dreams together, and life really doesn't get any better than this.

A woman approaches with a smile, casting a glance at the boisterous kids playing tag on the grass. "If they're this excitable now, I dread to see them after the sugar high." She extends her hand. "I'm Kylie. Reyna is my daughter."

"Oh, of course." I recognize her now from the school gates. Beck mostly drops Olivia off at school and picks her up as his schedule is more flexible than mine when we're back in Ravenna. "It's lovely to meet you, and thanks for the invite. Olivia has been very excited all week."

"It's nice to meet you." Beck extends his hand toward our hostess. "I'm Beck, and this is my wife, Stevie."

Kylie's smile is welcoming as she shakes both our hands. "I know who you are, and thanks for coming."

Beck and I exchange a knowing look. That kind of comment and reaction is normal when we're in Seattle. Beck has a flourishing literary career, writing in his own name and as Byron Stanley, and he started a secret pen name recently. He's a bit of a local celebrity here. We both prefer France where no one gives a fuck he's a famous writer. They just treat him as one of their own.

"This is for you," I say, handing over the bag with a bottle of wine, a bouquet of flowers from the shop, and a box of cupcakes for the kids.

Personally, I think she's nuts hosting a birthday party for her six-year-old daughter on the Fourth of July and inviting the entire class. But that's probably my pregnancy hormones speaking.

I smooth a hand over my bump. Our son is due in three weeks, and that's the only reason we didn't head home to France after the school term ended last week. Beck was too nervous flying long distance when I'm heavily pregnant, so we agreed to stay in Seattle this summer. It will be the first time in years we've been back in Ravenna for the entire summer.

Olivia is looking forward to spending time with her nana and our extended family. Mom married Sean the year after Beck and I got married, and two years later, the rest of Sean's family relocated to Seattle.

"This is so kind. Thank you very much." Kylie eyes the contents with a little chuckle. "We certainly won't run out of alcohol. My brother-in-law owns a winery, and he supplied all the wines today." She looks over my shoulder. "Oh, there he is." She looks sheepishly at me as Beck slowly turns us around and stiffens.

Now her reaction makes sense.

We come face-to-face with our past as Helena and Garrick Allen make their way toward us. Garrick is wheeling his chair one-handed while cradling a tiny baby in his arms.

"I'll leave you to catch up in private," Kylie says, confirming she knows who we are for very different reasons than my husband's celebrity status.

"This feels like an ambush," Beck says, tightening his arm around my shoulders. "We should leave."

"Let's hear what they have to say," I murmur as I plaster a smile on my face.

Garrick wheels to a stop in front of us, and Helena comes up beside him, placing her hand on his shoulder. The four of us stare at one another for a few awkward moments. Garrick's eyes gravitate to my round stomach as I gaze at the adorable little boy with a mop of jet-black hair snuggling his father.

The baby lets out a little cry, which breaks up the tension.

Garrick lifts him to his shoulder and pats his back, instantly soothing him.

"You're a natural," I say, smiling.

"Rick is amazing with him," Helena confirms, beaming at her husband.

I saw the announcement of their wedding online a year or two after Beck and I tied the knot, but other than that, I have not kept up with things going on in his life.

"How old is he?" Beck asks.

"Six weeks," Garrick confirms, nestling the boy in the crook of his arm now he's settled again.

"Congratulations," I say.

"Thank you." Helena presses a kiss to the top of the baby's head. "He's our little treasure."

"When are you due?" Garrick asks, staring at my stomach for a second.

"Three weeks." I rub a hand over my belly as the baby kicks.

"Olivia must be very excited," Helena says.

"She is. She's been begging us for a sibling the past couple of years," Beck admits. He's being polite, but I hear the concern in his tone.

"Our little guy will have to get used to being an only child," Helena says, rubbing Garrick's arm.

"We had a difficult time getting to this point," Garrick explains.

"Well, then he is a little treasure," I say.

"Not to be rude," Beck says. "But it's clear you knew we would be here today, and I'm guessing there's a reason for it?"

"I hope you're not upset," Helena says. "My sister mentioned Olivia was in Reyna's class this year, and Rick was hoping he might have an opportunity to speak with you, Stevie."

"Why?" Beck asks.

"I owe Stevie a massive apology, and it needs to be said face-to-face," Garrick says, eyeballing Beck. "I assure you I mean your wife no harm." Garrick's hazel eyes latch on to my face. "I have wanted to reach out for years to apologize, but I didn't want to just contact you out of the blue."

Helena tucks errant strands of her long brown hair behind one ear and wets her lips. "We thought it might be better for it to happen naturally. When we heard you were coming today, it seemed like a good idea. But I can tell you feel ambushed, and we really should have considered that."

"Advance warning might have been nice," Beck diplomatically says.

"We should have asked Kylie to mention we'd be here and to ask you if we could speak privately," Garrick agrees. "If I'm making you uncomfortable, we can leave."

"That won't be necessary. It's your niece's birthday party," I say, looking up at Beck, and we trade silent words. I already knew what he'd say, but he's always extra protective when I'm pregnant. I return my focus to Garrick. "We can talk."

"Thank you, Stevie." Helena smiles warmly at me before

extending her hand to Beck. "I know you know who I am, but we haven't formally met. I'm Helena."

Beck shakes her hand. "Beck. It's nice to meet you."

Garrick wears an amused grin that takes me back in time.

"What do you say we go check on the kids, Beck?" Helena says. "I need to wish that niece of mine a happy birthday, and I'd love to meet your daughter."

"Of course." Beck kisses me quickly, checking I'm okay with his eyes. "Can I get you something to drink before I go, honey?"

"Actually, a water would be good." It's hot, and I'm already sweating under my white maternity summer dress. Wearing high wedges probably wasn't my smartest idea either.

"Garrick, can I get you anything?" Beck asks.

"I'll take a water too."

Beck moves into the house to grab drinks while I stand with my ex and his wife.

Helena moves to take the baby from Garrick, but he shakes his head. "Leave him, he's sleeping."

"He's getting too attached to sleeping in your arms," Helena says.

"When Olivia was born, the only place she would sleep was on Beck's bare chest. It was hell trying to get her into a crib, but we managed. I think those early weeks are precious and important for bonding with your child."

"That's what I keep telling my wife." Garrick pecks her lips.

"I tend to freak a little," Helena says. "Even though I have tons of nieces and nephews, it's different with your own child."

"It definitely is," I agree as Beck returns with two bottles of water, handing one to me and one to Garrick.

"Okay, we'll let you two talk," Helena says, looking expectantly at Beck.

Beck sends Garrick a warning look, and my husband kisses my cheek before walking off into the garden with Helena.

"Protective, isn't he?" Garrick says with a chuckle.

"Very, especially when I'm pregnant. I think pregnancy brings out Neanderthal vibes in every man."

"I wouldn't know," Garrick says with an easy smile. "We got pregnant via IVF and a surrogate."

"That was insensitive of me."

"Not at all. How could you know?" He jerks his head toward a small table and two chairs tucked into the corner of a quiet part of the garden. "Could we talk over there? Kylie's a great sister-in-law but far too invested in this conversation, and I'd rather not have prying ears."

"Sure." I walk alongside him as we take a stone path to the area in question.

When we are settled with drinks in hand and a softly snoozing baby, I turn to face him. "What did you want to talk to me about?"

"Well, first, I just wanted to check you're doing okay. It seems obvious because you look great, and you seem content, but are you happy?"

"Very. Beck is an amazing husband and father, and we're fortunate to live a good life."

"Do you still run the business with your mom?"

I nod. "Yes, but only part-time. For the first few years after we got married, Beck and I traveled the world. We're lucky with Beck's job that he can work anywhere. I'm actively involved in his business too. I do his accounts and some of his marketing."

"Wow, that must have been amazing." He drags his hand through his dark hair, which he still wears the same way.

"It was. I even got to visit Ireland, and I saw Newgrange and the Book of Kells." My eyes lower to the ink on his wrist.

"We visited too," Garrick confirms, his gaze moving to my wrist. "You still have the tattoo."

"As do you."

He rubs his fingers back and forth across it. "I would have removed it or inked over it if it had upset Lena, but she was fine with me keeping it."

I can't help grinning. "Beck was the same. I considered replacing it, but it didn't feel right. It's a protective shield, and I was nearly afraid to get rid of it in case I brought the ghost of dead Celts down upon me."

Garrick laughs quietly, looking down at his sleeping son, ensuring he hasn't woken him. "You didn't strike me as the superstitious kind."

"I'm not usually." I run my fingers across the tattoo. "Beck is confident in my love. He didn't need me to change it to reassure him."

"That is exactly what my wife said." He grins before taking a drink.

"We married amazing people."

"We did."

"Are *you* happy, Garrick?" I ask, rubbing a hand over my belly.

"Very. I'm the CEO of Allen Wineries, and when dad retires from the lumberyard in a few years, I'll have additional responsibility there. Lena only works part-time as a physical therapist, and she'll probably give it up altogether now we have this little guy."

"It's nice to be able to do that if it's what you want."

"Yes, it is."

"How are the twins? Are they at college or working in the business?"

"They're both starting senior year at UW next month. John is a great golfer, and he's hoping to make a career doing something golf related, and Jacob wants to travel after he graduates. I'm not sure either of them will join the business, but the door is always open."

"What about your mom?" I ask, taking a sip of my water.

The smile slips off his face. "We don't have any contact with her. She didn't approve of Helena, and she refused to come to our wedding. I haven't spoken to her in years."

"I'd say I'm sorry, but it'd be a lie. You're better off with her out of your life."

"My wife agrees with you."

My lips twitch. "Is it true what was reported in the papers last year? That she fell prey to some con man boy toy who stole everything and left her broke?"

"Yes, it seems so. She had to sell the house and downsize, and all her so-called-friends deserted her. Can you believe she had the nerve to call my father and ask him for money?"

"I can, and I hope he didn't give her any!" Hugh was always a big softie.

"Not a chance. Dawn wears the pants in that marriage."

We quietly laugh.

"I'm sorry you have such a shitty mom, but your dad and Dawn more than make up for her failings. Tell them I said hi."

"I will. They were always fond of you." He presses a kiss to his sleeping son's head.

"What's his name?" I ask.

"Max."

"Cute name for a cute little boy. He looks so much like you."

Garrick's shit-eating grin brings his dimples out, and I remember a time when I used to go gaga for them. "Helena says he's my mini-me. She's not happy he doesn't have any of her features."

"He's young, and his looks could change. Or he might have her personality."

"Let's hope so. My wife is one of the sweetest, kindest people on the planet."

"I always liked Helena. I was really happy for you when I read about your engagement."

"I met Beck one time," he says, eyeballing me.

"I discovered that when I read my husband's book." I didn't ever ask Beck what happened during that meeting, and his account in the book was brief. When Beck and I reunited, we left Garrick firmly in the past.

"I read it too," he says, surprising me. "It helped me to understand your relationship and how it had come to be, and it opened my eyes to how much you suffered."

I smile softly at him. "It was a long time ago, and we're all in a much better place now."

"We are, and everything happened for a reason. We ended up with the right people."

"We did."

"I love my wife more than I can express, but there will always be a small part of my heart that belongs to you. I'm not telling you anything Lena doesn't already know. She knows what I want to say to you today, and she has actively encouraged me to find a way to talk to you."

"When I first got together with Beck, I told him a part of me would always love you, and he has never begrudged it." I run my fingers over the tattoo. "It's why he has no issue with the tattoo. He knows how infinite my love is for him."

"I think everyone harbors a little love for their first loves."

I'm not sure that's true in every case, but it's a nice sentiment. I swig from my water. "If you are feeling any residual guilt, Garrick, let it go. If that's what this is about, and you need closure, take it. I didn't blame you for anything back then, and I don't blame you now."

"I said terrible things to you, Stevie, and I'm so, so sorry. It was inexcusable. I was cruel, and I took my anger out on you, and you didn't deserve any of it. I manipulated you and broke up your relationship, and I cringe when I think of the things I said to you that last day. It was unforgivable. Honestly, I don't know how you can even bear to look at me."

"It's in the past, Garrick, but I do appreciate the apology."

"I didn't know everything you did for me until I read Beck's book, and I was so ashamed of my behavior. No one could have done more for me." His Adam's apple jumps in his throat as he looks me directly in the eye. His features soften. "Thank you, Stevie. Thank you for loving me like that. Thank you for sacrificing your own happiness to be there for me. You were the one who saved me. I held on for you, and I can't ever repay you."

"You continue to live a full and happy life, Garrick. That's how you repay me."

"I just need to say one final thing, and then we'd better rejoin the party. It won't be long before someone sends out a search party." He looks deep into my eyes. "The accident was never your fault. I know I accused you of it, but it's not how I feel. These things just happen. No one knows why. I can't complain about how my life has turned out. I'm in a good place. If any part of you still feels blame, please let it go."

"I have let it go, Garrick. Years of therapy helped me to deal with all the guilt and blame I felt." I pat his hand. "You don't need to worry about me. I'm good. I'm happy. I'm loved."

"That is all I could ask for you."

"I hope this has given you the closure you seek," I say, capping my bottle and standing.

"It has."

"Good."

We move slowly side by side toward the bounce house where all the kids are now congregated. I spot our spouses chatting with a couple of other parents.

"Did you hear about Will and Ellen?" he says, switching his son to his other arm so he can push his wheelchair with his less tired arm.

"No. I haven't spoken to Ellen in years."

"I didn't have anything to do with Will after Hudson told me how he treated you when I was in a coma. I just thought you might have seen the articles online."

"What articles?" I uncap my bottle and drain the rest of my water.

"Will has been named in Judge Whelan's divorce petition. He was having an affair with his wife and a bunch of other women, it seems. He might face criminal charges because some confidential paperwork went missing from the judge's house, and they're trying to prove Will stole it and sold it for money. Keeping a harem of women happy must have been costly."

"I'd like to say I'm shocked, but I saw a very different side to Will after the accident. I tried to warn Ellen, but she wouldn't listen. She had chosen her side. Still, I'm sorry this happened to her."

"Yeah, me too. She's humiliated and might be left to raise their four kids alone if he ends up in prison."

"Poor Ellen. I hope she has a support network."

"By the way, Hudson says hello. He was hoping to be here today, but he got called into work."

"Hudson was a great friend to me during that time. Hadley and I missed him a lot."

"How is Little Miss Mischief?" he asks as we come up to our respective spouses.

"Still as mischievous as ever."

Beck moves to my side and circles his arm around my back. "All good, honey?" He inspects my face for any sign of distress.

"All good, my love." I stretch up and kiss him. "Garrick and I had a good talk, and we were just catching up on mutual friends."

"Is Hadley married?" Garrick asks, cradling his son in one arm and his wife in the other. Helena is sitting on his lap with her arm around the back of his chair.

"No."

"She's been engaged three times," Beck confirms, rubbing his free hand over my belly when he spots movement under my dress. Our boy is very demonstrative, and he likes to kick his legs around in a very visible manner.

"They are never the right guys," I explain.

"Hudson is single again," Garrick says, waggling his brows. "I seem to remember those two being hot and heavy for one another."

"They were," I agree. "I think if the accident and everything hadn't happened things might have worked out differently between them."

"Maybe we should do something about that," Helena says, grinning at her husband.

"You took the words right out of my mouth," Garrick says, turning to look at us. "What do you think?"

"Hudson's good people," Beck says. "But I'm not sure we should interfere."

"Maybe we should talk to them, see if they'd be interested in a date," I muse, leaning against my husband.

"Hadley is sick of meeting jerks on those dating apps," Beck says. "She might go for it."

"Hudson is the same," Helena says. "He's met a few crazies."

"*Maman*!" Olivia screeches, racing toward me like she's on skates. "Did you see? I jumped off the roof of the bounce house and did a tumble midair."

"Do you want to give me heart failure?" Beck asks, scooping our wild daughter up into his arms and throwing her in the air. Olivia squeals, sporting the biggest grin.

"And he wonders where she gets it from," I tease, rolling my eyes.

"She has your hair." Garrick smiles at my daughter as her father throws her into the air again.

"That's all she has of me. She has Beck's face shape, his lips, and his brown eyes."

"Personality wise, she's all Stevie," Beck supplies, finally putting our daughter on the ground. "Come and say hi to Garrick and Helena."

"Hi." Olivia waves before leaning in to inspect baby Max.

"He's so cute." Livvie examines every part of him she can see.

"Thank you," Helena says.

"My mom's going to have my brother in a few weeks. I hope he's as cute as your baby."

"Well, if he's anything like his big sister, I'm sure he will be," Garrick says, and my daughter blushes.

"I'm going back to play," she announces a second later before tearing off.

"She's gorgeous, Stevie. She'll have all the boys beating down your door in no time."

"Not if I have anything to say about it," Beck says, looking ready to murder some teenage boy already.

We spend another couple of hours sitting around a table with Garrick and Helena while the party is in full swing, and there is none of that earlier awkwardness. It turns into a really nice day. Garrick confirms he has read all of the Jake Bennett novels, and he pleads with Beck not to retire him in the next book. Helena and I swap keto recipes and trade romance recommendations. It feels normal, nice, and when the party ends, we part ways as firm friends.

Later that night, I'm lying naked beside my husband in bed, feeling blissfully content. Beck is spooning me, and we've just finished making love. I can only do it on my side with him entering me from behind these days. I'm certainly not as horny as I was in the early months of my pregnancy, but I love having sex with my husband. It helps me to always feel close to him.

With great effort, I push up and turn over so I'm facing my husband.

"If you'd asked, I would have swapped sides with you."

"You're sweet." I kiss his lips as he rubs circles on my swollen belly with his fingers. "Are you okay after today?"

"Surprisingly, yes."

"It wasn't weird for you?"

"A little at first, but it ended up being a good day, and I think maybe we all needed to clear the air. We're going to be spending more time in Seattle with the kids going to school here, so we'd probably have bumped into them at some point."

When I got pregnant with Olivia, we stopped our travels and returned to France where we lived most of the time, returning to Seattle for extended trips a few times a year. We decided we wanted her to attend school in the US and for her to be closer to our families, so now we split our time between both places, tending to return to France only during school breaks.

"True."

"Garrick seems happy, and Helena is lovely."

"She is, and they are happy. Everything happened the way it was meant to." I touch the ink on my wrist. "We haven't spoken about this in ages. Be honest. Does it bother you that I still have it?"

"Not a bit. We all have pasts, and because of what happened,

Garrick will always be a big part of yours." Beck lifts my wrist to his lips and kisses the tattoo. "I'm not threatened by a tattoo or the man you share it with because I get to share my *life* with you." He leans down and reverently kisses my bump. "I have gotten to wake beside you every day for the past ten years, and I'll get to wake beside you every day for the rest of our lives. Garrick might own a tiny piece of your past, but I own everything else. Only an immature, jealous idiot would demand his wife get rid of this tattoo."

Tears well in my eyes as love swells in my heart. This man amazes me every single day.

"I'm not an idiot," Beck continues, lovingly caressing my face. "Because I'm married to you, and you're the sweetest, sexiest, smartest, most compassionate woman on the planet."

"Babe, you're going to make me cry."

"I love you," he says.

"I love you too."

"I realized something today." Beck kisses the tip of my nose before threading his fingers in my hair.

"What?"

"If you'd never met Garrick, you might never have met me. And if the accident hadn't happened, Helena might never have met Garrick."

I think about it for a few seconds and Beck is right. "I have never thought of it like that."

"Neither had I until we were sitting around chatting today." He presses a lingering kiss to my lips. "Fate works in mysterious ways."

At one time, I would have groaned at the mention of fate.

At a different time, I would have hissed that fate had screwed me over.

But not now.

How can I deny fate was at work when it got me to this point and I lead such an amazing life?

As I lean in to kiss my gorgeous husband, I can't help but agree. "We're proof that it does."

To download the bonus scene where Garrick and Beck meet, please type this link into your browser: https://bit.ly/TOIWBonusGBBB

Want another emotional angsty romance with all the feels? Check out *Inseparable, When Forever Changes, Still Falling for You, Always Meant to Be,* or *Say I'm the One*. All these titles are available in audio, ebook, and paperback format now.

Angsty Emotional New Adult Romance

I'm head over heels in love with my best friend. Although, I can't pinpoint exactly when Reeve Lancaster became my entire world.

Was it when we were little kids, practically brought up together, after Reeve's mom died during childbirth and his dad subsequently fell apart? Or when I doodled his name in my school journal at age ten? Maybe it was when we became boyfriend and girlfriend at fourteen or when we shed our virginity at sixteen, pledging our forever?

I was there as his star ascended—like I'd always known it would—and there wasn't a prouder person on the planet. As the only child of Hollywood's golden couple, I've lived my life in the spotlight enough to know it wasn't what I wanted for my future. But I sacrificed my own desires, because Reeve's happiness meant everything to me.

Until he crushed my heart into itty-bitty pieces, forcing me to fly halfway around the world just to escape the gut-wrenching pain.

The opportunity to study at Trinity College Dublin came at the perfect moment, and I jumped at the chance without hesitation. If I'd known fate was meddling in my life, perhaps I would have chosen differently, but my future was cemented the instant I laid eyes on *him*.

Dillon O'Donoghue was Reeve's polar opposite in every way, and perhaps, that's why I felt drawn to him. He was the dark to my light. The thorn in my side, irritating me with his cold disdain, wild recklessness, and a burning rage hidden deep inside him that spoke to a silent part within me. Yet Dillon showed me what it was like to truly live, opening my eyes to endless possibilities.

What happened next was inevitable, and I only have myself to blame. He warned me, and I knew my reprieve was temporary, because there is only so far I can run.

Especially when fate hasn't finished messing with me yet.

Available now in ebook, paperback, alternate paperback, and audiobook.

CLAIM YOUR FREE EBOOK – ONLY AVAILABLE TO NEWSLETTER SUBSCRIBERS!

The boy who broke my heart is now the man who wants to mend it.

Jared was my everything until an ocean separated us and he abandoned me when I needed him most.

He forgot the promises he made.

Forgot the love he swore was eternal.

It was over before it began.

Now, he's a hot commodity, universally adored, and I'm the woman no one wants.

Pining for a boy who no longer exists is pathetic. Years pass, men come and go, but I cannot move on.

I didn't believe my fractured heart and broken soul could endure any more pain. Until Jared rocks up to the art gallery where I work, with his fiancée in tow, and I'm drowning again.

Seeing him brings everything to the surface, so I flee. Placing distance between us again, I'm determined to put him behind me once and for all.

Then he reappears at my door, begging me for another chance.

I know I should turn him away.

Try telling that to my heart.

This angsty, new adult romance is a FREE full-length ebook, exclusively available to newsletter subscribers.

Type this link into your browser to claim your free copy:

https://bit.ly/TITMHFBB

OR

Scan this code to claim your free copy:

Acknowledgments

Thank you for reading ***The One I Want Duet.*** If you have read some of my other books, you will know I like to write about challenging and sensitive topics because I like to think about the "what ifs." What if I was in a car accident with my boyfriend and he ended up in a coma and I totally believed it was my fault? What if his nasty, spiteful mother cut me out of his life and I was scared, lost, and consumed with guilt? What if I met a guy at one of my lowest moments, and he helped piece me back together? What if I developed feelings for him? What if we acted on those feelings? What if my boyfriend woke up from his coma and I was no longer his?

Those thoughts prompted me to pen this romance. That was the only idea I had when I started writing this book. I had plotted out the locations and characters, but I never know how a story is going to develop until I write it, and this time was no different. It never fails to blow my mind that my stories develop from a tiny nugget of an idea. It truly is the most magical process, and I am so blessed to get to do this for a living.

I hope you enjoyed reading this duet as much as I enjoyed writing it. I try to ground all my stories in reality, but I had to take a lot of creative license with Garrick's coma, especially his recovery and rehabilitation, which would not be so swift in real life. I purposely glossed over the harsher realities, because this is a romance and I felt this was the best way to treat this delicate subject. The case studies Stevie read to Garrick at his bedside, that Beck had researched and compiled, are actual real case studies of people who came out of comas after long periods of time. Thank you to my critique and research partner, Jennifer Gibson of The Critical Touch, for all her help with this book. You know I couldn't do it without you!

Birthing a new book takes a mini-army and I want to thank everyone who helped: Kelly Hartigan, Imogen Wells, Shannon Passmore, Daisy Zorman, Ciara Turley, Trevor Davis, Hollianne Sullivan, Keeley Witham, Zsuzsanna Gerhardt, Sarah Ferguson and her team at Literally Yours PR, Michelle Lancaster, Sarah Puckett and her team at Pink Flamingo Productions, Narrators Silas Hart and Alexander Neal. A special shout-out to my review teams, my street team, and Siobhan's Squad on Facebook. You ladies give of your time to support me and my work, and I am very grateful. On bad days, your encouragement and enthusiasm lift me up.

Thank you to all my author friends–you know who you are–for always being there for me. I was writing this book while undergoing tests for a serious medical condition, and the outpouring of love from my friends and readers in our community was incredible.

A massive thank you to my husband, Trevor, for all he does to support me. From day one, he has only ever encouraged me. Now, he works alongside me and keeps the household running while I type away like a crazy person in my writing cave. My two sons are incredibly supportive too and they never complain when I'm pulling long hours or consumed in a fictional world. Love you guys to the moon and back.

I love to hear from my readers. Email me anytime – siobhan@siobhandavis.com

About the Author

Siobhan Davis is a *USA Today, Wall Street Journal*, and Amazon Top 5 bestselling romance author. **Siobhan** writes emotionally intense stories with swoon-worthy romance, complex characters, and tons of unexpected plot twists and turns that will have you flipping the pages beyond bedtime! She has sold over 2 million books, and her titles are translated into several languages.

Prior to becoming a full-time writer, Siobhan forged a successful corporate career in human resource management.

She lives in the Garden County of Ireland with her husband and two sons.

You can connect with Siobhan in the following ways:

Website: www.siobhandavis.com
Facebook: AuthorSiobhanDavis
Instagram: @siobhandavisauthor
Tiktok: @siobhandavisauthor
Email: siobhan@siobhandavis.com

Books By Siobhan Davis

NEW ADULT ROMANCE

The One I Want Duet
Kennedy Boys Series
Rydeville Elite Series
All of Me Series
Forever Love Duet

NEW ADULT ROMANCE STAND-ALONES

Inseparable
Incognito
Still Falling for You
Holding on to Forever
Always Meant to Be
Tell It to My Heart

REVERSE HAREM

Sainthood Series
Dirty Crazy Bad Duet
Surviving Amber Springs (stand-alone)
Alinthia Series ^

DARK MAFIA ROMANCE

Mazzone Mafia Series
Vengeance of a Mafia Queen (*stand-alone*)
*The Accardi Twins**

YA SCI-FI & PARANORMAL ROMANCE

Saven Series
True Calling Series ^

---

*Coming 2024
^Currently unpublished but will be republished in due course.

www.siobhandavis.com

Printed in Poland
by Amazon Fulfillment
Poland Sp. z o.o., Wrocław

36190706R00430